Library of America, a nonprofit organization,
champions our nation's cultural heritage
by publishing America's greatest writing in
authoritative new editions and providing resources
for readers to explore this rich, living legacy.

BERNARD MALAMUD

Bernard Malamud

NOVELS AND STORIES OF THE 1970s & 80s

The Tenants
Dubin's Lives
God's Grace
Stories & Other Writings

Philip Davis, *editor*

THE LIBRARY OF AMERICA

BERNARD MALAMUD:
NOVELS AND STORIES OF THE 1970s & 80s

Published in the United States by Library of America.
Visit our website at www.loa.org.

This paper exceeds the requirements of
ANSI/NISO Z39.48–1992 (Permanence of Paper).

Distributed to the trade in the United States
by Penguin Random House Inc.
and in Canada by Penguin Random House Canada Ltd.

Library of Congress Control Number: 2022938546
ISBN 978-1-59853-745-1

First Printing
The Library of America—367

Manufactured in the United States of America

Bernard Malamud:
Novels and Stories of the 1970s & 80s
is published with support from

ARLENE HEYMAN

with love and admiration and
"with harps and even with cymbals."

Mit harfen und mit zimbeln schön.
—From Johann Sebastian Bach, Cantata No. 140
(See *Dubin's Lives*, page 494.6 and note)

Contents

THE TENANTS

For Janna

"Alive and with his eyes open he calls us his murderers."

ANTIPHON
Tetralogies

"I got to make it, I got to find the end . . ."
BESSIE SMITH

LESSER CATCHING SIGHT OF HIMSELF in his lonely glass wakes to finish his book. He smelled the living earth in the dead of winter. In the distance mournful blasts of a vessel departing the harbor. Ah, if I could go where it's going. He wrestles to sleep again but can't, unease like a horse dragging him by both bound legs out of bed. I've got to get up to write, otherwise there's no peace in me. In this regard I have no choice. "My God, the years." He flings aside the blanket and standing unsteadily by the loose-legged chair that holds his clothes slowly draws on his cold pants. Today's another day.

Lesser dresses unwillingly, disappointing surprise, because he had gone to bed in a fire of desire to write in the morning. His thoughts were sweet, impatient for tomorrow. He goes to sleep in anticipation and wakes resistant, mourning. For what? Whom? What useless dreams intervene? Though he remembers none although his sleep is stuffed with dreams, Lesser reveries one touched with fear: Here's this stranger I meet on the stairs.

"Who you looking for, brother?"

"Who you callin brother, mother?"

Exit intruder. Yesterday's prowler or already today's? Levenspiel in disguise? A thug he's hired to burn or blow up the joint?

It's my hyperactive imagination working against the grain. Lesser makes things hard for himself for certain reasons. That's a long tale but right now it means he doesn't know how to end his book. Nor why the ending, this time, is so hard to come by if you've invented every step that leads to it, though some crumble when you look hard at them. Still, it's bound to come, it always has. Maybe it's some kind of eschatological dodge? Like an end is more than I can stand? Each book I write nudges me that much closer to death?

As soon as he ends one he begins another.

Now that the imagination is imagining Lesser imagines it done, the long labor concluded at last. Relief, calm, mornings in bed for a month. Dawn on the sea, rose lighting the restless waves touching an island waking, breathing the fresh breath of its trees, flowers, bayberry bushes, seashells. Ah, the once more sensuous smells of land surrounded by the womanly sea. Birds rise from the shore, wheel, fly above the ragged, mast-like palms into the lucent sky. Gulls mewling, sudden storms of blackbirds shrilling over the violet water. Ah, this live earth, this sceptered isle on a silver sea, this Thirty-first Street and Third Avenue. This forsaken house. This happy unhappy Lesser having to write.

On this cold winter morning when the rusty radiator knocked like a hearty guest but gave off feeble warmth, yesterday's snow standing seven stiff inches on the white street, through which indigenous soot seeped, Harry Lesser, a serious man, strapped his timepiece on his wrist—time also lived on his back—and ran down six dirty flights of the all-but-abandoned, year 1900, faded bulky brick tenement he lived and wrote in. Thirty-five families had evacuated it in the nine months after demolition notices had been mailed but not Lesser, he hung on. Crossing Third against the light, feeling in the street's slush that he had left his rubbers under the sink, Harry, in wet sneakers, popped into a grocery store for his bread, milk, and half dozen apples. As he trotted home he glanced peripherally left and right, then cagily back to see whether his landlord or one of his legal henchmen was hanging around in somebody's wet doorway or crouched behind a snow-roofed car, laying for Lesser. A wasted thought because what could they do but once more try to persuade, and in this matter he is not persuasible. Levenspiel wants him out of the building so he can demolish it and put up another but Levenspiel he holds by the balls. The building was rent-controlled, and from the District Rent Office—they knew him well—Harry had learned he was a statutory tenant with certain useful rights. The others had accepted the landlord's payoff but Lesser stayed on and would for a time so he could finish his book where it was born. Not sentiment, he lived on habit; it saves time. Letting go of Levenspiel's frozen nuts he raced home in the snow.

Home is where my book is.

In front of the decaying brown-painted tenement, once a decent house, Lesser's pleasure dome, he gave it spirit—stood a single dented ash can containing mostly his crap, thousands of torn-up screaming words and rotting apple cores, coffee grinds, and broken eggshells, a literary rubbish can, the garbage of language become the language of garbage. Emptied twice weekly without request; he was grateful. Along the street in front of the house ran a pedestrian pathway through the unshoveled snow. No super for months, gone like a ghost. The heat was automatically controlled, on the sparse side for the lone inhabitant on the top floor, for the last three and a half months Robinson Crusoe up there, the thermostat set in the cellar's bowels by Levenspiel himself. If it pooped out, and it pooped often—the furnace had celebrated its fiftieth birthday—you called the complaint number of Rent and Housing Maintenance, who bedeviled Himself; and in a few hours, if not more, it reluctantly came back on, thanks to the janitor in the pockmarked imitation-Reformation gray job across the street who poked around when Levenspiel begged him on the telephone. Just enough heat to be cold. You saw your inspired breath. Harry had a heater in his study to keep his fingers fluent in the dead of winter, not bad although noisy and costs for electricity. Things could be worse and had been, but he was still a writer writing. Rewriting. That was his forte, he had lots to change—true, too, in his life. Next building on the left had long ago evaporated into a parking lot, its pop art remains, the small-roomed skeletal scars and rabid colors testifying former colorless existence, hieroglyphed on Levenspiel's brick wall; and there was a rumor around that the skinny house on the right, ten thin stories from the 1880's (Mark Twain lived there?) with a wrought-iron-banistered stoop and abandoned Italian cellar restaurant, was touched for next. Beyond that an old red-brick public school, three stories high, vintage of 1903, the curled numerals set like a cameo high on the window-smashed façade, also marked for disappearance. In New York who needs an atom bomb? If you walked away from a place they tore it down.

In the grimy vestibule Harry obsessively paused at the mailboxes, several maimed, hammered in, some torn out; he set down his grocery bag, his right eye twitching in anticipation of a letter from a publisher he couldn't possibly get until he had completed and sent out his long-suffering manuscript. Reverie: "We have read your new novel and consider it a work of unusual merit. We are honored to publish it." Praise for the book, not for holding out.

Lesser had held out, thirty-six, unmarried yet, a professional writer. The idea is to stay a writer. At twenty-four and twenty-seven I published my first and second novels, the first good, the next bad, the good a critical success that couldn't outsell its small advance, the bad by good fortune bought by the movies and kept me modestly at work—enough to live on. Not very much is enough if you've got your mind on finishing a book. My deepest desire is to make my third my best. I want to be thought of as a going concern, not a freak who had published a good first novel and shot his wad.

He fished an envelope out of the slot of his mailbox with both pinkies. If he didn't some curious passer-by would. Lesser knew the handwriting, therefore source and contents: Irving Levenspiel, BBA, CCNY, class of '41, an unfortunate man in form and substance. One supplicatory sentence on thin paper: "Lesser, take a minute to consider reality and so please have mercy." With a nervous laugh the writer tore up the letter. Those he kept were from the rare women who appeared in his life, spring flowers gone in summer; and those from his literary agent, a gray-haired gent who almost never wrote any more. What was there to write about? Nine and a half years on one book is long enough to be forgotten. Once in a while a quasi-humorous inquiry, beginning: "Are you there?", the last three years ago.

I don't know where's there but here I am writing.

He ran with his milk, bread, fruit, up six flights, chewing a cold apple. The small green automatic elevator, built for four, had expired not long ago. The attorney at the rent office had said the landlord must keep up essential services till Lesser moved out or they would order a reduction of his rent, but since he was screwing Levenspiel by staying on, keeping him from tearing down his building, out of mercy Lesser did not complain. So much for mercy. Anyway, climbing stairs was good exercise for somebody who rarely took any. Kept a slim man in shape.

The stairs stank a mixed stench, dirt, the dirtiest, urine, vomit, emptiness. He raced up six shadowy flights, lit where he had replaced dead or dying bulbs, they died like flies; and on his floor, breathing short, pushed open the noisy fire door, into a dim, gray-walled, plaster-patched—holes with slaths showing—old-fashioned broad hallway. There were six flats on the floor, three on each side, deserted except for Lesser's habitat on the left as one came into the hall; like turkey carcasses after a festive Thanksgiving, the knobs and locks even, picked off most of the doors by uninvited guests: bums, wet-pants drunks, faceless junkies—strangers in to escape the cold, the snow, and climbed this high up because the sixth floor lies above the fifth. Poor man's Everest, even the maimed aspire, a zoo of homeless selves. Seeking? Not glory but a bedless bed for the small weak hours; who in the morning smashed in a window or two in payment for the night's unrepose—thereafter the wind and rain roamed the unrented flat until somebody boarded the broken glass—ransacking what they could: light fixtures, loose nails, mirrors, closet doors lifted off hinges or left leaning on one; and pissed and shat on the floor instead of the toilet, where it was available. Even some of the bowls were gone, or where unsnatched, their seats removed; for what purpose—hats? firewood? pop art pieces?—in contempt of man's fate? And in the morning stumbled out, escaped into the street before this one or that was by chance unearthed by Levenspiel, up for a long-nosed snoop or pleading visit to his uncooperative writer-tenant, and threatened severely with arrest for unlawful entry and trespass. They disappeared. A smell remains.

On the roof was once an attractive small garden where the writer liked to sit after a day's work, breathing, he hoped, as he watched the soiled sky—the moving clouds, and thought of Wm. Wordsworth. Occasionally a patch of blue escaped from somewhere. Gone garden, all gone, disassembled, kidnapped, stolen—the potted flowering plants, window boxes of pansies and geraniums, wicker chairs, even the white six-inch picket fence a civilized tenant had imaginatively put up for those like him who enjoyed a moment's repose this high up in the country. Mr. Holzheimer, a German-born gentleman, originally from Karlsruhe, among those requested to move in the recent past, his six-room apartment next door to Lesser's three, desecrated now, the bedroom walls defaced, torn by graffiti, bespattered with beer, wine, varnish, nameless stains, blots, a crayon cartoon of A. Hitler wearing two sets of sexual organs, malefemale; in a second bedroom a jungle sprouted—huge mysterious trees, white-trunked rising from thick folds, crowding four walls and into the third bedroom, dense ferny underbrush, grasses sharp as razor blades, giant hairy thistles, dwarf palms with saw-toothed rotting leaves, dry thick-corded vines entangling thorny gigantic cactus exuding pus; eye-blinding orchidaceous flowers—plum, red, gold—eating alive a bewildered goat as a gorilla with hand-held penis erectus, and two interested snakes, look on. Deadly jungle. And he, Herr Holzheimer, so gentle, clean, orderly a man. I hope he comes back to haunt the bastards, for a change clean whammying unclean. Lesser tried to scare off the nightcrawlers on his floor—God knows what masked balls go on below—by playing loud his hi-fi at night; and he left every light burning when he went out of an evening. He felt, when he thought of it, a fear of the booming emptiness of the building where whole families had lived and vanished, and strangers came not to stay, but to not stay, a sad fate for an old house.

A sense of desolation numbed him—something lost in the past—the past?—as he entered his apartment, stoutly protected by two patent locks plus a strong snap-lock enclosing heavy circular bolts. Only when inside his safe-and-sane three rooms Lesser felt himself close off the world and relax. Here is where he forgot all he had to forget to work. He forgot amid books packed thick along living room walls of pine shelves he had laboriously built and varnished years ago, mss. of two published novels and one in progress nearing its end, stored in a large carton in the closet; hi-fi equipment, records in stacks and holders on bottom bookcase shelves, other necessary stuff elsewhere in closets, bureau drawers, and medicine chest. His bedroom-study was a large uncluttered room: daybed, narrow dresser, old armchair at the window, floor lamp, short desk plus straight-back chair—all this the evidence and order of life in use. He would not think how much of life he made no attempt to use. That was outside and he was in.

Harry, in his small kitchen, refrigerated the milk container and considered a bit of breakfast but gagged at the thought. He had never been one for more than a cup of coffee; had got bread, fruit for later. Really to give himself time to think how the writing might go. The irresistible thing—the thought he wasn't yet at work gave him the shakes—was to get at once to his desk, anchor, gyroscope, magic mt.: it sits there but moves. Long voyage in a small room. There's a longtime book to finish. Coffee he could cook up when he had a pageful of words on paper. You can't eat language but it eases thirst.

He entered his three-windowed study, raised the cracked green shades without looking into the street and arranged himself at his desk. From the top drawer he removed a portion of manuscript. Harry felt a momentary sense of loss, regret at having given his life to writing, followed by a surge of affection for the imaginative self as he read yesterday's page and a half and found it solid, sound, going well. The book redeemed him. Another two or three months ought to finish it. Then a quick last rewrite of the enterprise—call it third-and-a-quarter draft—in about three months, possibly four, and he'd have it made, novel accomplished. Triumph after just ten years. The weight of a decade lay on his head but neither cracked nor crushed—the poor head. Harry felt an impulse to inspect his face in the bathroom mirror, tired gray eyes, often bloodshot, utilitarian lips, wry, thinning, he thought, as the years went by, interested nose, observer too; but successfully resisted. A face is a face: it changes as it faces. The words he writes on paper change it. He was no longer the young man, twenty-seven, who had started this book, nor had any desire to be. Time past is time earned unless the book was badly conceived, constructed, an unknown lemon; then it's dead time. Perish the thought.

Lesser, as he wrote, was sometimes a thundering locomotive, all cars attached except caboose, cracking along the clicking tracks into a country whose topography he suspected but did not know till he got there. Lesser explorer. Lesser and Clark overland to Manifest Destiny. Or maybe Mississippi steamboat with booming, splashing paddlewheel, heartrending foghorn, and other marvelous inventions. Not a bad metaphor, boat. Lesser in short-masted bark with a puff of wind in its sail on the Galilean Lake, trying to spy out on the apostolic shore what it's all about. Lesser sculling on the Hudson, seeking Hendrik, listening to the booming bowls in the metaphysical hills; or rowing to music on the sweet-flowing Thames: he loved the moving English water. Better still, the artist as broad swirling river, flowing freely amid islands of experience, some dense green, luxuriant, treeful; others barren, soft sand with wet footprints; the flow embracing multifarious isles and islets, in flood tide spreading over each and all beyond both muddy riverbanks of life and death.

"Whereof my bowels shall sound like a harp"—Isaiah.

Without looking up at the windows at his side the writer imagined the wintry day beyond, crystal bright, lit cold beauty; glad of its existence but without desire to be in or of it, breathe its stinging glow into his half-retired lungs, live it. This sort of pull and push he had long ago quelled in the self else he would never have seriously written. He itched with desire, as he wrote, to open the nearby closet and stare at his box of accumulated manuscripts. He also half masted an erection—creativity going on. Harry scribbled with a growing sense of pleasure as the words flowed fruitfully down the page. Already he tasted the satisfaction of a good morning's work done. In the afternoon he would type what he now wrote with his fountain pen in longhand. Who was it who had said he thought with his right hand? After work he would make his bed, shower warm and cold—hot was out of the question, and afterwards listen to some of his records with a drink in his paw. Tonight an unexpected party, possibly a lay with a little luck; with more a bit of human love in a mad world. You got to use words but you got to use more than words. Lesser knew the doorbell was ringing and went on writing. It rang insistently.

It rings forever.

Levenspiel ringing.

The writer sits at his desk and talks through two rooms. He knows the words and music, they've sung it together many times before, begun with assertions of mutual regard. Each proclaims consideration of the other. Lesser promises to get out as soon as he can so the landlord can knock over his building. Levenspiel, a thick-chested man whose voice lives in his belly, swears he wants the other to write the best book he can; he respects serious writers.

Goatskin siren, stop piping to my heart.

Then to business: The landlord is just back from a funeral of a close relative in Queens and thought he'd stop by to say hello. Have a little mercy, Lesser, move out so I can break up this rotten house that weighs like a hunch on my back.

Lesser argues he can't leave in the middle of a book. If he did, in his present state of mind it would take him six months to overcome distraction and get back to work, not to mention the chill he'd have facing material he'd lost the feel of. You have no idea how it changes when you're away from it. I'm afraid what will happen if my conception shifts only a little bit. You don't know what you're asking, Mr. Levenspiel.

We'll find you a nice apartment somewhere in the neighborhood where you'll be more comfortable than in this bad-smelling place. So if you stopped writing a week or two it wouldn't be the end of the world. Suppose you got sick and had to go for a while to the hospital? You're as pale as a dead fish, Lesser. You need more action, more variety out of your poor life. I don't understand how you can stay in this lousy flat every day. Think it over and listen to reason, for your own benefit.

I'm listening. I've worked hard, Levenspiel. It's my sacrifice more than yours. I'll finish soon if you have patience. My last book, for reasons I won't go into, was a bomb. I have to redeem myself in my own eyes with nothing less than a first-rate piece of work. I've practically got it done, but the last section, I confess, is resisting a little. In fact it's beginning to crock me out of my skull. Once I hit it right—it's a matter of stating the truth in unimpeachable form, the book will be off my chest and your back. I'll breathe easy and move out overnight. You have my word on that, now go away, for Jesus' sake, you're eating up writing time.

The landlord's voice grows gentler though his big fist rhythmically pounds the locked door.

Hab rachmones, Lesser, I have my own ambition to realize. I've got fifteen years on you, if not more, and I'm practically naked as the day I was born. Don't be fooled that I own a piece of property. You know already about my sick wife and knocked-up daughter, age sixteen. Also I religiously go one afternoon every week to see my crazy mother in Jackson Heights. All the time I'm with her she stares at the window. Who she thinks she sees I don't know but it's not me. She used to weigh ninety pounds, a skinny lady, now she's two-twenty and growing fatter. I sit there with tears. We stay together a couple of hours without words and then I leave. My father was a worry-wart immigrant with a terrible temper who couldn't do anything right, not to mention make a living. He wiped his feet all over my youth, a bastard, thank God he's dead. What's more, everybody—*everybody*—wants financial assistance. Now I have an opportunity, even with my limited capital—I can get a Metropolitan Life loan—to set up a modern six-story apartment building, five floors of big-room flats over a line of nice stores, and make myself a comfortable life if that's still possible in the world of today. Every other goddamn tenant has left out of here for a $400 settlement. You I offer $1,000 cash and you look at me as if I have a social disease. What's more, you bitch to the District Rent Office and tie me up in red tape with what not—with examiner trials, rehearings, and court appeals that'll take my lousy lawyer another year and a half to untangle it all. Outside of your $72 monthly rent, which doesn't a half pay for the oil I use on you, I have no income coming in from here. So if you're really a man, Lesser, a reasonable being, how can you deny me my simple request?

What about your tenement in Harlem?

I don't know where you find out such things, Lesser, maybe it's because you're a writer. That building I inherited from a crippled uncle, let him stay forever in his grave. It's a terrible trouble to me for reasons you know well of. I'm not speaking racially. All I'm saying is it loses me money under the present conditions. If this keeps up I'll have to abandon it. It's a disgusting state of affairs nowadays. Rent control, if you aren't afraid to listen to the truth, is an immoral situation. The innocent landlord gets shafted. What it amounts to is you're taking my legal property away from me against the Constitution.

You have an easy out, Levenspiel. Add to your projected plans for the new house you intend to build twenty percent more apartments than you're tearing down, and according to the regulations you can give me an immediate boot into the street.

A long sigh inducing heavy breathing.

I can't afford that, Lesser. It means another whole floor and possibly two. You have no idea what building costs are nowadays, twice what you estimate, and till you got the house standing, three times what you figured. I admit I had that idea before, but Novikov, my high-rise partner died, and when I thought about another partner, or to try to borrow more cash, I thought no, I will build it according to my dream. I know the kind of place I want. It's got to be comfortable to my nature. I want a smaller type house. Also I'd rather deal with five-six storekeepers than twenty-percent more tenants. It's not my nature to go after people for rent. I'm more sensitive than you give me credit, Lesser. If you were a less egotistical type you would realize it, believe me.

Lesser searches his mind. I'll tell you what I'm willing to do that might be helpful. I'll sweep the halls and stairs of the building once a week. Just leave me the janitor's broom. I don't write on Sundays.

Why not, if you're so anxious to finish your book so you can't even take off a day to move?

An old habit, the spirit rebels.

What do I care about the feshtinkineh halls here? All I want is to be able to pull this sonofabitchy building down.

The writer speaks from the depths of his being:

"It's just this last section I have left, Levenspiel. I've been working on it the better part of a year and it's still not right. Something essential is missing that it takes time to find. But I'm closing in—I can feel it in my blood. I'm proceeding within a mystery to its revelation. By that I mean whatever is bothering me is on the verge of consciousness. Mine and the book's. Form sometimes offers so many possibilities it takes a while before you can determine which it's insisting on. If I don't write this novel exactly as I should—if, God forbid, I were to force or fake it, then it's a dud after nine and a half long years of labor and so am I. After that folly what good can I expect from myself? What would I see when I look in the mirror but some deformed fourassed worm? And what's my future after that with the last of my movie money gone?—redemption in another book I'll maybe finish when I'm forty-six and starving to death?"

"What's a make-believe novel, Lesser, against all my woes and miseries that I have explained to you?"

"This isn't just any novel we're talking about. It has the potential of being a minor masterpiece. It exemplifies my best ideas as an artist as well as what life has gradually taught me. When you read it, Levenspiel, even you will love me. It will help you understand and endure your life as the writing of it has helped me sustain mine."

"For Christ's sake, what are you writing, the Holy Bible?"

"Who can say? Who really knows? But not while you're making that fucking racket. How can I think if my mind hurts already from the sound of your voice? My pen is dead in its tracks. Why don't you go somewhere and let me work in peace?"

"Art my ass, in this world it's heart that counts. Wait, you'll get yours one of these days, Lesser. Mark my words."

His booming fist echoes in the hall.

Lesser had given up writing and gone to read in the toilet. After the noise had departed he once more urged forth the pen, but it no longer flowed though he filled it twice. He willed but could not effect. The locomotive, coated with ice, stood like a petrified mastodon on the steel-frozen tracks. The steamboat had sprung a leak and slowly sank until clamped on all sides by the Mississippi thickened into green ice full of dead catfish staring in various directions.

Though agonized, best pretend you have stopped writing of your own accord. The day's work is done; you are relaxing in the can. It says in this book, "I should not think of devoting less than twenty years to an Epic Poem"—Coleridge. Lesser shuts his eyes and reads through the last pages of his ms. He tests his fate: He lives to write, writes to live.

The writer stands on the roof in the midst of winter. Around Manhattan flows a stream of white water. Maybe it is snowing. A tug hoots on the East River. Levenspiel, resembling mysterious stranger if not heart of darkness, starts this tiny fire in a pile of wood shavings in the cellar. Up goes the place in roaring flames. The furnace explodes not once but twice, celebrating both generations of its existence. The building shudders but

Harry, at his desk and writing well, figures it's construction in the neighborhood and carries on as the whining fire and boiling shadows rush up the smelly stairs. Within the walls lit cockroaches fly up, each minutely screaming. Nobody says no, so the fire surges its inevitable way upwards and with a convulsive roar flings open Lesser's door.

END OF NOVEL

A WET DOG WITH A BLEEDING EYE hopped up six flights the next morning, and clawed and yelped at Lesser's door. Although it made piteous noises, Harry grabbed the mutt, alternately whimpering and snarling, by a frayed rope collar around the neck, and by offering a bony bit of stale bread every so often, succeeded in enticing him down the stairs and out of the house. It should be so easy with Levenspiel.

As he trudged up the stairs, Lesser heard muted cries, distant wailing—was there a funeral parlor on the premises? He had heard sounds of the sort before, unspecific, floating. Hard to say where or what—seemed to unpeel from city noise—unearthed?—and sing in a strange tongue. That's if you owned a certain kind of ear, not always a blessing. Hunting a real enough source of whatever it was he heard, Lesser stopped at the fifth floor and listened in the hall, his ear pressed against a knobless apartment door for telltale interior noises, possibly crowbar wrenching at a screaming wall? the landlord sneaking in a secret blow? Not bloody likely so long as the last legal tenant hadn't been formally notified—you couldn't tear down a fifth floor without displacing a sixth, even if it managed to stay afloat a while; still a palpable fear. He feared for the house and what was worse sometimes feared the house. The flat, as Lesser listened, resounded of mournful winds, Aeolus' bag. Why do wailing winds, nothing human, give off human sounds? He pushed the door and entered listening: pure deep silence. Harry wandered from room to room, the empty former kitchen minus stolen sink, a cracked washtub remaining; the living room a rectangular circle of naked hairy men disporting themselves on three walls; both bedless bedrooms despoiled; the bathtub filthy with residues of piss. Silence flowered into primal noise, utter deep silence: graveyard music.

He felt in the house, legacy of Levenspiel's visit? stronger than ever before, a presence other than himself. Nothing new but who now? Private Eye snooping for one cause or another?—you never know all the regulations of eviction. Anonymous caller drifting up from floor to floor without plan or purpose except a concealed dagger? Home is where, if you get there, you won't be murdered; if you are it isn't home. The world is full of invisible people stalking people they don't know. More homeless strangers around than ever before. God since the dawn of man should have made it his business to call out names: Jacob meet Ishmael. "I am not my brother's brother." Who says? Back in his study he wrote hurriedly, as though he had heard the end of the world falling in the pit of time and hoped to get his last word written before then.

One early morning when the writer, with his paper bag of bread and milk, was letting himself into his triple-locked door, he could have sworn he heard the sound of typing coming from one of the flats fronting the hall, and for an odd minute played with the thought he had left himself hard at work somewhere around while he was out getting his groceries. Lesser turned, facing the dimly lit hall.

The empty hall was empty.

Straining, he listened, and though he listened not to hear, heard the dulled clack of surely a typewriter. He felt, despite his familiarity with the sound, as though he were hearing it for the first time in his life, sensation not unmixed with competitive envy. He had been too long on one book—here was somebody writing another? Lesser felt a loss of body heat and was about to be prickly necked but gave it an afterthought: typing was typing, a typewriter, at least when in use, no lethal weapon. Still came the discomforting after-afterthought: who was the unknown typist?

Entering his flat, Harry stowed away his groceries and returned to listen in the hall. He walked stealthily past one shut door and one missing. He dipped his head into the dark open room. Nothing he could truly hear. Scouting the other side of the hall, he paused longer before each door to the end of the floor, tightly attentive to whence the continuous clicking. Again crossing the hall he located it finally next door to his, in Holzheimer's flat, astonished to have wandered far to find it close.

He was wishing Holzheimer were here to keep him company in this unpeopled place. Of course the old man was gone; and besides he couldn't type. The door was ajar. Lesser, head bent, listened. Plak plak plakity plak. Had Levenspiel set up a spy office here, CIA sub-headquarters for tuning in on Harry Lesser engaged in writing a subversive novel? Every letter he typed on paper, neatly bugged, flashed on a screen in the Attorney General's office, Department of Justice, Washington, D.C.? To end the suspense he gave the open door an adventurous thrust and it squeakily swung in. He was set to run but nobody emerged; he had to enter.

In Holzheimer's former kitchen, facing the wintry windows, sat a black man at a wooden kitchen table, typing, his back to Lesser. Though the room was perceptibly cold—the radiators and steam pipes removed, pipe openings sealed to prevent flooding, he wore overalls cross-strapped over a green hand-knit sweater rubbed through at the white-shirted elbows. The black seemed at first a large man, but it turned out that his typewriter was large, and he, though broad-shouldered, heavy-armed, and strongly built, was of medium height. His head was bent over an old L. C. Smith, vintage of pre-World War I, resembling a miniature fortress.

The man, head bowed in concentration, oblivious of Lesser, typed energetically with two thick fingers. Harry, though impatient to be at his work, waited, experiencing at least two emotions: embarrassment for intruding; anger at the black intruder. What does he think he's doing in this house? Why has he come?—where from?—and how will I get rid of him? Who's got the time? He thought of phoning Levenspiel, but maybe he had booked the act. Having waited this long for acknowledgment of his presence—it was not in him to interrupt a man writing—also for a few basic facts of information, he waited longer. The black must have known someone was standing there because the open door created a draft and once Lesser sneezed; but he did not turn to look at him or whoever. He typed in serious concentration, each word slowly thought out, then hacked onto paper with piston-like jabs of his stubby, big-knuckled fingers. The room shook with his noise. This endured for five full minutes as Lesser fumed. When the typist turned his head, a goateed man, darkly black-skinned, there seemed in his large liquid eyes poised in suspension as he stared at the writer a detachment so pure it menaced; at the same time a suggestion of fright Lesser felt reflected Lesser's. His head was large, lips moderately thick, sensuous, nose wings extended. His eyes, in concentration, swelled; but he was youthful and not bad-looking, as though he considered himself not a bad-looking man and that helped. Despite the chill he seemed to be sweating.

"Man," he complained, "can't you see me writing on my book?"

Harry apologetically admitted he had. "I'm a writer myself."

That brought forth neither lightning nor thunder, nor small degree of admiration. The black stared at Lesser as though he hadn't heard, and the writer thought he might even be a little deaf until the man reacted: breathed in relief—knew now he wasn't dealing with the landlord? Had been bluffing? A smile seemed possible but did not come to pass.

On the table at the black writer's left lay a pile of well-worn, somewhat soiled, manuscript from which it seemed to Harry an unpleasant odor rose. He noticed then the man had his orange work shoes off and was sitting there writing in white wool tennis socks. Even now he wiggled his toes. Hard to say whether the sulphurous smell came from the manuscript or the feet on the floor. Maybe it's me, Lesser thought, smell of fear? Anyway, something malodorous.

Then to make his point, the point of it all—the reason he had waited to speak to the black and give notice—Lesser said, "I live here alone in this building, alone on the floor. I'm trying to finish a book."

The stranger responded to the news, rolling his eyes in thought.

"Baby, it's a hard and lonely life." His voice was low, resonant, raspy. As though relating a decision decisively arrived at, he then remarked, "I'll be working around here daily as of now on and according to the way circumstances go."

"You mean Levenspiel's letting you?" Lesser felt on the verge of frantic. He saw in the man's presence on the floor a serious threat, perhaps latest variation of the landlord's tactics of harassment.

"Which cat is that?"

"The owner of these premises, hard-luck guy. Haven't you met him—I mean wasn't it his suggestion that you work here?"

The black casually denied it. "I got no interest in any Jew landlord. Just come on this place while hunting around and entered quickly. I found this table in the cellar and the chair in a room down under here, but the light is better up high so I moved them up. I been looking for a private place to do my writing."

"What sort of writing if you don't mind me asking?"

"Now that's a personal question and what I am writing is my own business."

"Of course. All I meant, out of curiosity, was are you writing fiction or something else?"

"It might be fiction but ain't nonetheless real."

"Nobody said it wasn't."

The black said his chick was an Off-Broadway actress. "Mornings when she ain't out working, which is whenever she ain't rehearsing, the apartment's too tight for the both of us. She hangs around mixing up in my thoughts and I can't get my ass to my work. I'm not saying I don't appreciate her company, especially when my meat's frying, but not when I have something I got to write."

Lesser nodded; he knew the story.

He told the stranger Levenspiel had been trying to force him out so he could wreck the building.

"But I'm rent-controlled so he's stuck with me for a while. Harry Lesser's my name."

"Willie Spearmint."

No handshake though Harry was willing, in fact had stuck out his white paw. There it remained—extended. He was, in embarrassment, tempted to play for comedy: Charlie Chaplin, with his moth-eaten mustache, examining his sensitive mitt to see if it was a hand and not a fish held forth in greeting before he told it to come back home; but in the end Lesser withdrew it, no criticism of anyone intended or implied. Who said anybody had to shake somebody else's hand? That wasn't in the Fourteenth Amendment. He was tempted then to explain that he had, as a boy, for years lived at the edge of a teeming black neighborhood in South Chicago, had had a friend there; but in the end skipped it. Who cares?

Lesser felt ashamed he had bothered Willie Spearmint. If a man typed—a civilized act—let him type where he would. Mind your business.

"Sorry I interrupted you. Better be getting back to my own work now—on my third novel."

No response from Willie other than the absent-minded descent of a nod.

"It was a surprise to find somebody else up here typing away. I had got used to being the only man on the island."

Though tempted not to—he bit his tongue for time was of the essence, he was late getting to work—Lesser heard himself say, "Well, pardon again, I hate interruptions myself. Still, knock on my door if you have to, should you need something—eraser, pencil, whatever. I'm in the flat on your left and generally free in the late afternoon after the day's work, the later the better."

Willie Spearmint, obviously a dedicated man, stretched both green-sleeved arms aloft, wiggling his stubby fingers with ease and contentment so that Lesser envied him, then bent over the large black machine and, focusing on the words, went on plakity plak as before. If Lesser was still present he didn't seem to know it.

Harry reflected in his study how much he had liked, all things considered, being alone on the top floor. I think of myself as a lonely guy, which is to say I am the right man for the work I do, which is to say, in these circumstances. I may hate going up six dark flights wondering who am I going to meet next, man or beast—but otherwise I've enjoyed this big empty house. Lots of room for the imagination to run around in. Fine place to work when Levenspiel is somewhere collecting his rents, or otherwise keeping busy. The truth of it is I could do without Willie Spearmint.

Shortly after noon—after a nearby siren yelped for a few seconds to remind one, if he had forgotten, of the perilous state of the world—Willie kicked on Lesser's door with the heel of his shoe, holding in both arms, in fact weighed down by it, his massive typewriter. Lesser, for a surprised second, couldn't imagine why he had come, was startled by the sight of him. Willie wore a blue-and-purple sack-like woolen African tunic over his overalls. His hair wasn't Afro-styled, as Lesser had thought, but combed straight as though against the grain, with a part on the left side, and raised in back like a floor plank that had sprung up. The stringy goatee flowering under his chin lengthened his face and seemed to emphasize the protrusive quality of his eyes, more white than brown. Standing, he was about five ten, taller than Lesser had imagined.

"Could I park this gadget here till the morning? I would hate to have it stolen out of my office. I been hiding it in the closet but that ain't hiding, if you dig."

Lesser, after hesitation, dug. "Are you through for the day?"

"What's it to you?"

"Nothing, I only thought—"

"I go on from eight to twelve or thereabouts," said the black, "full four hours' work and then goof off—visit friends and such. Writing down words is like hitting paper with a one-ton hammer. How long do you stay on it?"

Lesser told him about six hours a day, sometimes more.

Willie uneasily said nothing.

Harry asked about his manuscript. "Wouldn't you like to leave that too? Needless to say I'd respect its privacy."

"No siree, man. That stays with papa. I have my briefcase for that."

A bulky zippered briefcase was squeezed under his left arm.

Lesser understood how he felt. The safety of your manuscript was a constant worry. He kept a copy of his in a metal box in a nearby bank.

"About what time will you be coming for the machine?"

"Make it like eight or around that if it's no skin off you. If I miss a day don't fret on it."

This man's making me a daily chore. But on consideration Lesser said, "I'm up then except on Sundays."

"Sundays I ball my sweet bitch."

"Well, I envy you that."

"No need to, man, there's meat all around."

"The women I meet generally want to get married."

"Stay away from that type," advised Willie.

He lugged his typewriter into Lesser's flat and after surveying the living room laid it with a grunt under a small round table near the window, with a potted geranium in a saucer on it.

"It'll be handy here."

The writer offered no objection.

"Man, oh man." Willie gazed around in envious pleasure at the shelves crammed with books, books on their backs, magazines, some small objects of art. He inspected Lesser's hi-fi, then slowly shuffled through a stack of records, reading aloud titles and artists, mocking some of the names he couldn't pronounce. A Bessie Smith surprised him.

"What's this girl to you?"

"She's real, she talks to me."

"Talking ain't telling."

Lesser wouldn't argue.

"Are you an expert of black experience?" Willie slyly asked.

"I am an expert of writing."

"I hate all that shit when whites tell you about black."

Willie roamed into Lesser's study. He sat at his desk, fingered his typewriter, tested the daybed mattress, opened the closet, peered in, shut the door. He stood at the wall examining some small prints the writer had collected.

Lesser explained about his movie money. "I made forty thousand dollars on a film sale about eight years ago and took it all in deferred payments. Less my agent's commission and living on roughly four thousand a year, I've done fine until now."

"Man, if I had that amount of bread I'd be king of Shit Mountain. What are you going to do after it's gone?"

"It's almost gone. But I expect to finish my book by summer, or maybe before if my luck holds out. The advance on it should carry me into the next book another two or three years. That'll be a shorter one than this."

"Takes you that long, I mean like three years?"

"Longer, I'm a slow writer."

"Raise up your speed."

Willie took a last look around. "This is a roomy pad. Why don't we party here some night real soon? Not this week but maybe next. I'm full up this."

Lesser was willing. Though he didn't say so, he hoped Willie would bring along a lady friend or two. He had never slept with a black girl.

Willie Spearmint usually knocked on Harry Lesser's door at a quarter to eight. The end-of-year weather was bad and now, as he wrote, the black kept his orange shoes on and wore a thick blood-red woolen hat against the cold. He pulled it down over his ears and kept his tunic on. Harry offered to have an old heater fixed he would then lend to him, but Willie said that once he got going with the writing it warmed him to his toes.

Not so Lesser. Some days he typed with a scarf around his neck and his overcoat spread on his knees. His feet froze even with the heater going.

If it had been sleeting or heavily snowing, Willie's goatee, when he appeared at the door in the early morning, was laced with ice or snow. He beat his wet hat against Lesser's door to knock off the slush. Sometimes he looked unsettled, sullen to a degree the weather couldn't account for. And except for picking up his machine and returning it at noon, he had little to say to Harry and requested not even a glass of water during the day although the faucets had been removed and sealed off in Holzheimer's kitchen. Fortunately the toilet in Mr. Agnello's flat diagonally across the hall flushed once in a while so he relieved himself there when he had to.

One drizzly morning, Harry, stuck for a transition between scenes, was standing at the window trying to draw up an idea out of the street, the city, the human race, when he saw Levenspiel drive up in front of the pockmarked gray house across the street and park his Oldsmobile at the curb. The landlord gazed up at the window just as the writer was drawing down the shade. Lesser went at once to Willie's place and knocked on the door. No response, so he turned the knob and, calling out his own name, entered.

Willie was sucking the point of a yellow pencil stub over a difficult spot in his manuscript. He gazed at Lesser in anger at the interruption.

Lesser said the landlord was on his way up.

The black glared at him in haughty coldness.

"Fuck his ass."

"Fine," Lesser said uncomfortably, "but I thought I'd let you know." He apologized for barging in. "I wasn't sure you'd heard my knock."

Willie's expression as he contemplated the page he was working on slowly altered. He seemed uncertain, concerned if not worried.

"How will that dude know I'm here if I sit still and don't move the air? He don't go around peeking in every apartment, does he?"

Lesser didn't think so. "Usually he comes up to nudgy me while I'm writing, but he might just walk into your place when you weren't expecting it. That's his type. My advice is you ought to duck down to the floor below and wait till he's gone. Take your manuscript with you and I'll hide the typewriter. I'll let you know the minute he leaves."

They quickly carried out the operation, Willie going down to the fifth floor with his briefcase, hastily stuffed, and Lesser hid the L. C. Smith in his bathtub. Not that Levenspiel would get his intrusive foot in the door, but one never knew. Every six months, just to be a nuisance, he insisted on his prerogative to inspect the flat.

The landlord several minutes later pressed Lesser's bell, then knocked sternly on the door. The writer pictured him coming up the stairs, breathing noisily, holding the banister all the way. Levenspiel rolled a little as he walked. Better he saved himself the long trek; he looked like a heart attack type.

"Open up a minute, why the hell don't you?" Levenspiel called, "so I can talk to you man to man."

"I'm hard at work," Lesser answered from the living room, scanning a newspaper as he waited for the landlord to go. "Nothing new to report. The writing moves, there's progress."

A moment of listening silence. When he spoke, Levenspiel's rumble was throaty, low, closer to the self, as though he had gone for a walk in the park, thought things over, and was trying for better effect.

"You remember," he said, "I told you about my daughter, Lesser?"

Lesser remembered. "The knocked-up girl?"

"That's right. So she took her pennies out of the savings account that she started at age six and bought herself an abortion according to the new law. God knows what kind of a doctor she got, I've heard stories. Anyway, she didn't consult me for advice. The upshot was they penetrated the uterus with a curette and a hemorrhage started. My wife is frantic about blood poisoning. I'm on my way to the hospital to see my baby in intensive care."

"I'm sorry, Levenspiel."

"I just thought I'd tell you. You can't tell everybody such things, but I thought maybe to a writer."

"Accept my sympathy."

"I accept," said the landlord, "so much as you can spare."

"So what else is new?" he said after an unused minute.

"Nothing."

"Nothing at all?"

"Nothing."

"No change in your attitude to the human race?"

"It still salutes."

Levenspiel left in silence.

Lesser tried to wrestle the incident out of his mind. Clever bastard, he knows I feel guilt. Another dollop on my head and I'll go through the floor down to the cellar. That's his plan, I bet.

Willie, watching from a window below, had seen the landlord leave the house and had hastened up. He tapped on Lesser's door and lifted the typewriter out of the tub.

"Fartn Jew slumlord."

"Willie," said Lesser, "if it's news to you I'm Jewish myself."

"All I'm saying is an economic fact."

"I'm telling you a personal one."

"Thanks anyway for swinging with me, baby. Lots of appreciation."

"My pleasure."

The black smiled, beautiful teeth, a rare gesture.

"Let's have that party we were planning on, this Friday night. I'll bring my bitch and tell a few friends."

Willie's friends who climbed up the six frozen flights to Lesser's flat during a blizzard on the first Friday of the new year, a dusting of snow on their heads, included his "bitch," Irene Bell, to Lesser's somewhat surprise—that she was Willie's taste, he had expected a less striking type—a white girl verging on beautiful. She hadn't quite made it; he couldn't guess why, as though beauty were more of an obligation than she cared to assume. She had glanced at Lesser's small mirror on the wall—her eyes wavered—and turned away in annoyance as she removed her voluminous cape. She wore on her face a depleted smile, sour at the edges, and troubled eyes. Some sadness. Lesser stared at her. Willie, when he got around to introducing her to him, said she was his white chick, not giving her name. At that she walked away. The writer figured they had quarreled on their way over.

The other two people were a black couple: Mary Kettlesmith, a hardassed attractive girl with an animated open face and fine figure. She wore a natural of small silken ringlets, and a plain white mini with purple tights. She talked easily, touching Lesser's arm with ten fingers when Willie introduced them. He touched hers and felt various hungers. Sam Clemence, her eyeglassed Afro'd boyfriend, was a quiet type on his way to stoned. Harry had not much impression of him one way or another. He himself was not in rare shape. He had expected fourteen people but because of the weather there were only five; he felt forlorn, a fool for not having invited a woman for himself.

Willie, as though unable to bear parting with it, wore his writing sweater, decorated with a string of Arabian glass beads as large as walnuts. Otherwise he was dolled up in hip-hugging yellow pants and two-tone brown-and-black shoes, wet from the snow. His goatee and hair had been combed and creamed, and he seemed to be engaged in enjoying himself. He moved lightly, strutting, finger-popping. Though he pretended no great wit, what he said made them laugh and his gestures were witty. Now and then he glanced at Irene sitting by the window, sometimes blankly, as if trying to remember something he had forgotten. Or heard voices? Here was something new of the stranger levitated out of the street up to the floor where Lesser for months had lived alone, housemate now, fellow writer, maybe future friend. His lonely girl, possibly waiting for a good word, looked on from a detached distance. If Willie noticed he seemed not much affected; he kidded with those close by. Lesser thought how easily he shucks off the writing self, whereas he, in his active mind, rarely stopped writing. He determined tonight to take pleasure.

Though pretending not to, Lesser looked Willie's Off-Broadway actress over carefully. He pretended, not she; Irene sat as though to say she was no more than he saw, had no statement to make about herself. She was about twenty-five, her long dyed blond hair drawn thickly over her left shoulder, where it lay across her bosom like an emblem—the mystery why it all but wounded the host. Two women walk into my house and in a minute flat I'm standing on my hands. He greeted an old self.

Come out of momentary seclusion and whatever mood, the actress pulled off damp boots and, drink in hand, explored the apartment, slightly pigeon-toed in large narrow feet suiting a tallish girl. Where she had been Lesser breathed in gardenia scent. He was partial to flowers. She wore a buttoned short skirt and a flushed pink blouse, her milkwhite breasts visible when she bent to rub away a cigarette ash stain on her knee. She sat on his hassock with legs parted. Lesser looked all the way up. Irene rose as though she had sat on an egg; she said something to Mary, who laughed into cupped hands.

Lesser escaped to his study.

My God, why are all my desires visible?

After a while he returned to music going on; his guests were dancing, Mary, gorgeously, with Sam; Irene with Willie; Lesser suspected she had sought him out, not vice versa. They danced to some rock records Willie had brought along in a paper bag, a boogaloo of rolling shoulders and butts. And though they danced as if in truth conjoined, Willie's mocking heavy eyes concentrating, Irene gyrating around him with muted smile set on pale face, as if the face weren't dancing, and with nobody but each other, the writer sensed they moved partly as though to hold off contact although talking intently all the time. Trying to assess degree of mutual discontent—or was he kidding himself, was this apparent resistance to the other a mode of attachment, an emotion ambivalently stronger than pure anything else? Lesser twice attempted to slip in between them but neither of the dancers would have it. Yet at one point Irene slapped Willie; he slapped her harder; she wept for a minute and they went on dancing.

Lesser cut in on Sam and Mary. Sam momentarily held tight but Mary eluded him and stepped up to Harry. The black girl danced with him as though going on in a dance previously begun. Her eyes were shut, her movements sexy. Lesser stopped to watch her twist. Mary, opening her eyes, laughed, held forth both arms; he came forward doing his little thing as she shook exotically. Her steps were quick, graceful, magical; she danced the leaves to Lesser's tree. He loosened up, swung himself around, Mary encouraging him. As they boogalooed in the center of the room—Sam pissing out of a window at the blizzard—Mary whispered to Lesser that she lived no more than two blocks away. After considering the intent of her information, in his study later, he made a play for her, when the rock was loud, Sam in half a stupor, and Willie and Irene still engaged in their curious courtship ritual.

Aroused by Mary, Lesser kissed her and slipped his fingers into her brassière; she, breathing heavily, kissed wetly in return but showed not much inclination when he tried to lead her to the daybed. She seemed to weigh something in herself, then with a sigh squeezed his hands and put them away.

Her eyes bright, she stood with pelvis thrust forward, neck arched. Her breasts were small, body slender, legs slim and beautifully formed. Harry, erected, hoping his desire would inspire hers, lifted her mini over her purple tights.

Mary forcefully shoved him away. "Split, honky, you smell."

Lesser felt desire ebb out of him.

"I didn't mean to offend you."

After a tense minute she softened, then quickly kissed him. "Now don't take on personally. I have to set my mind up for sex, that's how I am. Just be like nice and I'll be nice to you. Okay now?"

Harry offered her an artificial violet from a pitcherful on the windowsill. Mary took the flower, looked for where to pin it on her dress, then dropped it into her purse on the daybed.

He apologized once more.

"Don't hold it against yourself, Harry. I like you fine."

"Then what's this smell you mentioned?"

"Like you smell white is all I mean."

"How does white smell?"

"No smell at all."

"So I won't worry."

"Don't," she said. "Life is too short, okay now?"

Sam glared into the room, and Mary, taking her purse, went to him. Lesser warned himself not to let his poor party turn into a bad scene.

Harry requests to borrow a strawberry-papered joint from Willie.

Willie offers to share his. They sit crosslegs on the small kitchen floor, shoulder to shoulder, passing a rumpled wet cigarette back and forth.

This here is part Lebanon hashish. Don't smell it, boy, suck it in your gut.

Lesser holds the sweet-burning smoke down till the room turns radiant and grand. Arches soar, the rose window flushes deep rose. Bells bong in a drowned chapel.

Now this cathedral is a floating island smelling of forest and flowers after summer rain. The roots of a thousand trees trail in the yellow water. We're alone on this floating island, Willie, full of evergreens and wild purple roses. We're moving with the current. Bells toll in the deep woods. People on both shores of the river are waving as we sail by. They wave red white and black flags. We have to bow, Willie. I'm bowing on this side. They're cheering and I'm bowing. You better bow, too.

Thanks, folks, my next will be my best.

Who are those cats, brothers or ofays?

Black cats with white hats and white ones with black hats. They're hip hip hooraying because we're good writers. We confess the selves we pretend to know. We tell them who they are and why. We make them feel what they never knew they could. They cry at our tears and laugh to hear us laugh, or vice versa, it makes no difference.

What's your book about, Lesser?

Love, I guess.

Willie titters, rowing calmly, steadily, his muscles flashing as the water ripples.

It's about this guy who writes because he has never really told the truth and is dying to. What's yours about, Willie?

Me.

How's it coming?

On four feet, man, in a gallop. How's yours?

On one. Clop.

I'm gon win the fuckn Noble Prize. They gon gimme a million bucks of cash.

After me, Willie. I've worked since the ice age and tomorrow is another day.

Willie rows coolly, sighting ahead in the swift shifting current of the broadening river, watching out for snags and sandbars and the hulks of wrecked ships.

What's more I'm writing my best book. I want all the good

people on both shores waving their little paper flags, all those grays and blacks, to admit Harry Lesser is King David with his six-string harp, except the notes are words and the psalms fiction. He is writing a small masterpiece though not too small. How small are the psalms?

Lesser gives three clops for Harry Lesser.

Pile it on, man. Pile on the shit. Pile on the coal and let's see the smoke. Pile on the bread. You can have the noise they makin but I gon shovel up the bread.

It's only money, Willie. What of remembrance in future time, a small immortality? Consider the human condition and how soon gone.

I want green power. I want money to stuff up my black ass and white bitch's cunt. I want to fuck her with money.

Think of this sacred cathedral we're in, Willie, with lilting bonging iron bell. I mean this flower-massed, rose-clustered, floating island. I guess what I mean is what about art?

Don't talk flippy. I worry about it gives me cramps in my motherfuckn liver. Don't say that dirty word.

Art is the glory and only a shmuck thinks otherwise.

Lesser, don't bug me with that Jewword. Don't work your roots on me. I know what you talkin about, don't think I don't. I know you tryin to steal my manhood. I don't go for that circumcise shmuck stuff. The Jews got to keep us bloods stayin weak so you can take everything for yourself. Jewgirls are the best whores and are tryin to cut the bloods down by makin us go get circumcise, and the Jewdoctors do the job because they are afraid if they don't we gon take over the whole goddamn country and wipe you out. That's what they afraid. I had a friend of mine once and he got circumcise for his Jewbitch and now he ain't no good in his sex any more, a true fag because he lost his pullin power. He is no good in a woman without his pullin power. He sit in his room afraid of his prick. None of that crap on me, Lesser, you Jewbastard, we tired of you fuckn us over.

If you're an artist you can't be a nigger, Willie.

WILLIE

Nigger, nigger, never die
Shinin face and bulgin eye.

LESSER
Nigger, nigger, shining bright
In the forest of the night.

Willie rows until his eyes are white stones. He rows as he sleeps. The shores of the river fade in the dark. The cheers are silent stars. The floral island disappears in mist. A galaxy moves like a jeweled wheel in the night sky.

I'm gon drop a atom bomb on the next white prick I see.

Lesser wrestles clouds of mosquitoes.

Lesser, lonely at his sad little party, gets to talk to Willie's girl. She had been wandering through living room and study, perhaps to evade him. There was no peace in her eyes or big feet. When he had been about to cut into her dance with Willie he heard him say, "Irene, I can't lay up with you tonight. You know how hard that part I am now writing on my book has got. I need my strength and juice on my work tomorrow. Wait till Sunday."

"I hate your shitty book," Irene had said.

The heat had gone off and the apartment was cold. Irene lay under her long cape on Lesser's sofa, and when the writer tentatively got under it with her she let him, saying nothing. The gardenia scent rose from her body touched with a faint odor of sweat. Sam and Mary, Afro to Afro, were asleep in the study on the daybed with the electric heater on. Willie, a joint in his mouth, was still rowing on the kitchen floor.

Irene wore on her blond head a chaplet of wax violets she had woven from a bunch one of the women of Lesser's past had left in a small cracked pitcher on a window in his study. They were faded but brought out the bluish green of her eyes. Lesser had noticed she bit her nails to the quick, plucked her brows clean and badly smeared on brown penciled ones. One was too long, one too short. This gave her face a clownish touch. He was sure her discontent was with herself.

"What's the true color of your hair?"

"Black," she mocked, in a low voice. "And my name is Belinsky, not Bell. And Willie has been my lover for two years. What else do you want to know? I know why you're lying here. You heard him say he wouldn't sleep with me tonight. I saw you listening."

"I wouldn't mind offering my creative juice."

"Fuck off, I'm Willie's girl."

It was a bleak night. Lesser heard himself apologizing again.

"It's not because of what I heard Willie say. When you came into the house tonight I felt this sense of something I'd lost in the past."

"What past?"

"As though I hadn't been where I should've been once when you wanted someone."

"I got the one I wanted."

Lesser wondered how the writing would go in the morning. Probably badly.

"What's your book about?" Irene asked.

"Love," he said, his breath rising.

"What do you know about love?"

Lesser wouldn't say.

She fell asleep with a sour smile.

Willie appeared in the room.

"Like cool it, man," he said to Lesser on the sofa. "None of that apeshit on me."

When Willie and his friends left the apartment the blizzard had spent itself. The black, his eyes still glassy, slapped Lesser on the back.

"We groove on art, dad. You and I are gonna be real tight."

They embraced like brothers.

A few hours later when Willie came in for his typewriter he spoke not a word to Lesser though his lips worked nervously. His expression was tense. He seemed like a man staring at two thoughts, neither of which he could stand.

Lesser at first was afraid Irene had told him he had tried to make her after overhearing Willie's remark to her. Or had Mary Kettlesmith described his acrobatics with her miniskirt?

But Willie had nothing to say, and alarmed at the thought of an argument that might upset the morning he was balancing like a ball on his nose, the writer offered strict silence in return. He was more than a little hung up, stupid from lack of sleep, worried about his work.

Willie, with a grunt, lifted his machine and stepped into the hall. Lesser shut the door in relief and was immediately writing. He worked steadily into a very good day; this sometimes happened when he was worried little sleep would lock the gears of concentration. At half past twelve the black had not appeared. At seven that night, washing his two supper dishes, the writer found himself wondering if—wishing?—Willie had for some reason cut out of here, located himself a new place to work. Maybe an abandoned apartment house all to himself? Lesser could do without his daily don't-do-me-any-favors visits although he was willing to help a fellow writer out. Writers helped writers. Up to a point: *his* writing came first.

At 9 P.M., Lesser reading in his rocker, Willie kicked the door, hugging his machine as though he were pregnant with it. After setting it under the table, the black after a minute of fixed thought, said: "Lesser, I have to pull your coat about a certain matter."

The writer apologized in advance for his behavior last night.

"It was the hashish I'd say. It doesn't agree with me. I'd better stay away from the stuff."

Willie flicked his nail along the part in his hair. After a while he scratched both pink palms with hard brown nails and blew into his stubby-fingered fist. He shuffled one foot, then the other.

Lesser was uncomfortable. Has he been seeing old Stepin Fetchit films, or is something the matter with him?

Willie spoke brusquely. "I thought I would leave my manuscript of my book here tonight."

"Ah, it's welcome," Harry said, relieved if that was all. "Don't worry about anybody reading it. You have my word on that."

Willie drew a restless heavy breath. "Man, I'm *asking* you to read it."

He bent as though afflicted by a spasm but at once straightened up.

"Like I have a belly ache about my work." Sweat gleamed on his brow. He touched dry lips with his pink tongue. It seemed to Lesser he had never seen his eyeballs so large before, inflated, white, scared.

"Belly ache?"

"On my writing. I am revising some of it again but every

time I read it I do something very new, like I never got it right in the first place. The picture keeps shifting on me, you know what I mean? Yesterday I thought I laid down some good pages but when I was reflecting about them in my chick's apartment the whole scene I wrote blew up in my mind like a brick shithouse. Man, that wipes you out. I didn't feel like coming to your party. I wanted to go on back to my work and stay on it till I got the wrong stuff out and the right stuff in but Irene told me to renew myself with some relaxation and fun. Today I sat in my office all day reading on my book and I have this fuckn feeling I rode off the main track in some places but I don't exactly know where that starts or why it does. Anything I read now looks blurred up, as if I am wearing my grandpappy's eyeglasses, and throws me off my balance. I feel like I am somewhere else than I ought to be. What do you think I have to do now, Lesser?"

The writer, conscious Willie was seriously asking for advice, answered cautiously.

"If you get the right distance it's easier to regain perspective. Sometimes I pick up an earlier chapter and retype it, at the same time making notes about the one that doesn't satisfy me. That's one way of quickening insight, there are others."

"I tried all that crap," Willie said impatiently. "Lesser," he went on, trying to restrain the emotion in his voice, "I could save on lots of worry and trouble if you could put your eye on what went wrong."

"You want me to read your manuscript?"

Willie, averting his stiffened eyes, nodded. "Nobody else I know has got two novels published."

Harry reluctantly agreed. "I will if you really want me to."

What more could a man say?

"Would I ask you if I didn't want you to?" The black threw him a look of hatred as he left the room.

Harry slowly read the funky manuscript of the touchy man, almost two hundred oversize thick pages. He read at first against the will, two sentences for every one. He read of two minds—curious; resistant. He had promised Willie but after this nothing more. No further involvements with his dissatisfactions, sentiments, labor.

The wind in the street complained as he read holding a handkerchief to his nose to keep off fumes. He hadn't heard so pure and sustained a keening outside his window in the almost ten years he had lived in the house, the wind like a live ghost haunting itself. A door slammed in the distance and slammed again, Lesser jumping twice as he read. He heard whispering voices in the hall. Willie, wandering, talking to himself? Levenspiel muttering? Explorers from a ship offshore? Or the lower depths? Going to the door, he put his eye to the keyhole. Nothing he could make out but gloomy hall. Lesser unbolted the door and went in his sneakers to Willie's office, expecting momentarily to hear his smoking plak plak, though the formidable typewriter visibly sat under the table by the window as he read. Not a serious inside sound of any sort. Maybe a rat scuttled down a toilet hole. Nothing really happening but imagination working overtime, the writer's bag. You worked with it, you had to live with this hyperactive genie. Yet he listened obsessively as though he might lose some small bite of experience if he didn't; then tapped with his fingernails on the door, turned the tense knob and entered. Pure black night, no moon or stars. Who could see a black in all this black?

"Willie?" Harry whispered.

He snapped on the one-hundred-watt bulb Willie had screwed into the socket one rainy day. The bare kitchen, lit in a glare, stared from afar. Willie's table and cracked chair—lonely, distant minus the writer writing, two hunks of wood; but if one wrote on them, a dignified desk and chair, serious business going on, the fabrication of fiction.

Lesser returned to his rooms and went on reading. The manuscript literally gave forth a gassy odor. Stench of toil?—accrued Willie Spearmint sweat plus something mildewed or smelling so? Perhaps odor of decay abetted by the chemistry of very cheap green paper—pulpy sulphurous stuff, typed on, erased often with burning, rubber-stinking eraser, typed over, et cetera? Or maybe the foul blow to the nose derived from the festering lives the words created, or their vengeful human farts?

Willie's book had once been entitled *A Nigger Ain't Shit*, crossed out for *Missing Life*, by Bill Spear, ingenious pseudonym, part surname, part tribal hunting weapon, plus overtone of Shakespear, also Willie. A third title had been very lightly penciled in. Examining it closely with his better-visioned eye, Lesser made out *Black Writer*—followed by a question mark. Anyway, the manuscript, which Lesser read slowly, making notes, in the course of three nights—Willie liked to keep the pages stacked before him on his desk as he continued to work long hours on whatever he was now writing or rewriting, at least he typed—was in two main parts, apparently a Life and Work, six chapters of the first, totaling one hundred forty-eight pages, followed by fifty of short stories concerning Harlem types living their black experience, a not bad approach to an autobiography, though Willie had never called it that. He hadn't talked much about his book. Lesser had thought of it as a novel possibly because he was writing one himself.

The book, although for various reasons not a finished piece of work, was absorbing to read, Willie's human history: from "Downsouth Boy" to "Black Writer"; via progression "Upsouth," "Harlem Nights," "Prison Education." The short last chapter was entitled, "I Write for Black Freedom." The book was mainly naturalistic confessional, Willie's adventures simply narrated, the style varying from Standard English to black lingo, both the writing and psychology more sophisticated than Lesser would have guessed. "I" grows up in redneck Mississippi in pure black poverty. He is knocked around by kith and kin more than whites, but it seems to him his first major insight into his life is how much he hates *them* for maiming the blacks who maim him, in particular his miserable meager mother and white-ass-kissing stepfather. One day, Willie, age thirteen, stepping out of the path of an approaching Charlie wearing a straw boater, shuts his eyes tight so The Man won't see in them the image of Black Boy crushing under his heel the white's bloody balls. "My hate of him was so pure it warmed me the rest of my life."

To escape the primal cemetery, Eden where nothing black grows green, he hops a freight to Detroit. "Where I spend the most of my days cleaning out white shitstalls for the Ford Company." And on the side breaks into clothes lockers to steal loose cash; at which, in spite of some tight squeaks, he is never caught. He finally has to face up to the self-hatred living in him like a sick dog in a cellar. This comes like a kick to his head after he beats half to her death his black bitch for no reason he is sure of. He accuses her of sleeping with a white man though she swears, and he in his heart believes, she hadn't. What he had done to his broken-faced seventeen-year-old girl becomes terrified awareness of something frightening in his nature. The panic of his guilt causes him to split. "I thought if I looked in a mirror it would show I had turned white." But the depression that afflicts him is because he is black.

Willie grooves through the Harlem scene in skin-tight satin pants and fast buckskin shoes, from jazz to jail in easy stages, through numbers, hustling, pimping two white whores. "All you got to know is a white chick loves a black prick." He pushes hard stuff, and while sick for dope—nose running, cramps, nausea—attempts housebreaking and burglary at which he is caught by two big white pigs he fights in terror with his bare fists. "On my first solo gig I was bagged out of my own stupidity, beaten shitless, and dumped in jail." He is tried, convicted, and sent to prison for a five calendar stretch. His new discovery is "How low your misery can go. All day I walk on myself and the shit sticks to my shoes." He hurts in terrible ways. But the hurt hurts less once you begin to hear the blues deep down in you. He listens and hears. "Willie Spearmint sing this song."

Time is slow and sickening but by some crazy mix of pain, luck, and what he still has left of his will, serving time serves him. "Stopping your running you have the time to think. I think clearer about myself, who I am, and if I will ever be more than the lowest." "If they didn't put me away then I would've murdered somebody for sure." To take his mind off the soul-destroying prison, to teach himself what he had to know to survive, to put himself together better than he was, Willie begins to read in the prison library. "Once I got started on that I never stopped. I read one book after the other, slow at first, then quicker once I get to know more words." At first he read fiction more than anything else. He read some Dickens, Dreiser, James Farrell, Hemingway, Richard Wright, Ellison, Baldwin and others. "And I read hundreds of short stories from the word go right up to modern times, both black and white." "And while I am reading I have this important, exciting and also frightening playback in me *that I can write.*" "It isn't hard to do when you have just finished reading one story you have liked to make it go on further. Or change the ending. Or write something like it." He wonders if he can write stories that have happened to him. "And the next thing I know my head is so crammed full of them I can't separate one from the other." Willie laughs, shouts, and dances in his cell. He begs for paper and pencil, gets them, and sits down at his table. He writes about the real funk of life. He writes in tears. "I cry for my goddamn mother, and everybody black I write about, including myself." He loves the words he puts on paper; out of them black people are born. He loves who they are, their voices and their wit. Willie gets high when he writes, this pleasure is the sweetest. As the sentences fill up the pages and the people and their actions come alive, his heart fills with pride. "From then on I am not afraid of the fucking prison because I am out of it as much as I am in. I am in my imagination. I swear to myself I will be the best writer, the best Soul Writer." He writes dozens of stories. "The more I write on the terrible and violent things of my life, the more I feel easier on myself. The only thing I am afraid of, I don't want to get too soft in my nature."

Willie also mentioned reading some of the revolutionary writers because he wanted to know more what the whole scene was about. He read in Marx, Lenin, Trotsky, Mao. He read every book he could about black men: books on Africa, slavery, black customs and culture. He kept notes in a looseleaf notebook, but when he tried to write about issues usually it came out little stories about black people. In the main he wrote fiction. As Willie came to a broader understanding of his people's history and the injustice of their suffering, he felt for them a deep, sweet, overpowering love. For the whites he kept his hatred. Maybe not in his mind every minute of the day but he kept it in principle. When he was sprung out of prison, he left with five folders full of writing he had pledged to the cause of Black Freedom.

This was the end of the autobiographical section; then came the short stories. None of Willie's protagonists fared as well as he. No one of them found a way to save himself.

Bugsy is shot thirty-eight times in Catshit Alley by two white pigs who had cornered him there after a mugging. He had shot back with his razor, flung it once.

Ellery is cooked to death in Sing Sing. He had tried to convince the judge, "Judge, you got the wrong black man. Black is an easy color to recognize if you lookin for a nigger. I swear to you out of the bottom of my heart I did not kill a white man on that dark night. I am not the one you think I am."

Daniel chokes his father to death for spitting in his mother's face. After, he asks his mama to forgive him and she says she might but the Lord won't. "I don't know why I do it, why I kill him all the way," Daniel says. "I guess I hate him more than I hate you."

In a weird story called "No Heart," this unnamed black man has a hunger to murder a white and taste a piece of his heart. It is simply a strong thirst or hunger. He tricks a drunken white down into a tenement cellar and kills him. He cuts into the dead man but can't find the heart. He cuts into his stomach, bowel, and scrotum, and is still cutting when the story ends.

In the last piece Harry (Harry?) is painted white by three brothers after they had considered stomping on him, or maybe tar and feathers, for what he did. He had betrayed a numbers runner, his friend Ephraim, to the pigs. Ephraim had taken his true bitch away from him. The runner's friends trap Harry in his room and force him to strip off his clothes. They pour three cans of white lead paint all over him as he kneels on the floor, the paint so thick on his head only his eyes are black. He escapes into the hall and runs up the roof stairs as they pursue him. The last they see of him is Harry leaping off the roof into the street below, a white nigger lighting up the night.

Five stories, five deaths—four blacks, one white. The violence shows the depth of Willie's unspent rage. Maybe his tears had scorched the paper and stunk up the pages? On rereading the book Lesser, though he sniffs now and then, smells no smell at all.

Lesser is moved by Willie's writing. For two reasons: the affecting subject of the work, and the final sad feeling that he has not yet mastered his craft. My God, what he's lived through. What can I say to a man who's suffered so much personal pain, so much injustice, who clearly finds in his writing his hope and salvation, who defines himself through it? He comes in the end, as in the old slave narratives, to freedom, through his sense of writing as power—it flies up and carries him with it—but mainly in his belief that he can, in writing, help his people overthrow racism and economic inequality. That his freedom will help earn theirs. The Life he writes, whatever he calls it, moves, pains, inspires, even though it's been written before, and better, by Richard Wright, Claude Brown, Malcolm X, and in his way, Eldridge Cleaver. Their self discoveries have helped Willie's. Many black men live the same appalling American adventure, but it takes a unique writer to tell it uniquely, as literature. To make black more than color or culture, and outrage larger than protest or ideology. Willie has good ideas for stories but doesn't always build them well; in the end they fall short of effective form. Lesser sees irrelevancy, repetition, underdeveloped material; there are mistakes of arrangement and proportion, ultimately of focus. There's more to do than he does. On the other hand, he seems to be sensitive to good writing and that may account for his suspicions concerning his own. He writes with feeling, no doubt with pleasure, yet senses he ought to be dissatisfied. He may not even know that his writing shows impatience with the craft of writing. I think he wants me to point this out to him. Should I do it—say what I think, or less?—soft-pedal maybe, encourage, try to even the odds, given what he's gone through? I wouldn't want to hurt a sensitive man. Yet if I don't tell him what I think is true how can I help him improve his work?

And if Lesser suppresses truth Lesser is a fake. If he's that, how can *he* go on writing?

When he returned the manuscript to Willie the morning after he had finished his second reading of it, Lesser said he was ready to discuss his work whenever it suited Willie's convenience. He wanted now to get it off his chest but wouldn't press. Willie, dead-pan, except for an absent smile that grazed his lips, as though he had not heard what Lesser had said but having seen his moving lips was more or less acknowledging somebody had spoken, accepted his briefcase without a word. He didn't so much as glance at it or look at Harry. On Lesser's afterthought Willie seemed wounded, hurt before the fact?—by me? unless the writer was misreading. Maybe he had a toothache, or hemorrhoids—some personal problem?

Whatever that was, his silence translated into annoyance more than wound; perhaps with himself, as though he might be regretting having asked Lesser to read his book and say what he thought might be wrong with it. But in a minute the black's lips parted, he gazed into Lesser's doubtful eyes with his own heavy eyes softened, as though forgiving him for whatever he had or hadn't done, and said sonorously, "I thank you for reading it." That's all. And left so cleanly, although hauling the iron load of typewriter and weight of his book in his arms, it seemed to Lesser as though he had willed his disappearance in a prestidigitated poof. Talented man Willie Spearmint.

That same noon, in a relaxed mood—he had somewhere got a cigar—Willie remarked, "I can't stay on to talk to you now, Lesser. My bitch is itching. We partying tonight in our place and have to buy some bottles and stuff, but I'll be around in a day or two to consummate that little mutual matter."

"Suit yourself, Willie. Whenever you say. At your convenience." Mixed in was envy for not having been invited to the party at Irene's.

He's afraid, Lesser thought. Shits green. So do I, to admit the truth. It's bad enough to criticize a man's living flesh, as whose book isn't. But with color added? It's a black life, understandably touchy stuff. Lesser dreaded a little what he had let himself in for. He had felt forewarned he would have to pay for doing Willie a favor. The nature of certain things, the weight of color.

Maybe I could make it easier all around by writing him a note? On paper there's no personal confrontation—who needs it?

As he took time to write it the next morning—it was only eleven but Willie was on his mind and he was getting little done—the black knocked, not kicked at the door.

Lesser rose, nervous but relieved, eager to dump the burden that Willie had laid like a paving block on his head.

Willie, eyes downcast—obviously he'd had trouble working, because he was already putting the typewriter away under the table—as he straightened up seemed to tighten, as though no move but the next was possible and he had no love for it. He stood staring for a while out the window. Lesser looked too. He saw nothing.

Willie kept staring, then seemed to give up, as though

whatever he was looking for wasn't there, if he were looking. What was there—or what there was, was in this room. In the room, whatever he was he wasn't exactly. But after a while he was with Lesser, in his study, sitting like an ebony statue in the straight-back chair, and nobody, his presence stated, was his Pygmalion. He had sculpted himself.

The writer, sitting forward on his daybed, rubs dry white palms together.

"Drink?"

"Let's cut out the preliminary crap and get down to where we are at."

Lesser defensively reminds Willie he hadn't asked to read his book. "You asked me to. If you think you made a mistake and are going to be stiffassed and uptight by what I say, maybe we ought to call it off before we start? I'm obliged to you for letting me see your manuscript."

"I *am* uptight, man, because it's my nature as well as my personal privilege, but let's talk anyway, dig?"

Lesser asserts he is not out to arouse anyone's antagonism. "I've got my own nature to consider. It likes to live in peace."

"My antagonism is also my privilege and don't go giving yourself too much credit for certain circumstances, like me asking you for a favor."

"All I'm saying is if we can't have a reasonable talk, let's forget it. I've been on my book for years and finally want to get it done. For that I need peace and quiet. That's why I like it up here—no serious disturbances, I can work. Levenspiel stalks me but I can stand it. Still, I wouldn't want anybody else on my tail or in my hair, with or without cause."

"Instead of preaching all those words, Lesser, why don't you get off your white ass and say your true piece? I ain't asking you to fatmouth me, just as I am not interested in getting into any argument with you."

"I heartily agree."

Lesser considers reading the part of the letter he had composed but drops that thought and says what he feels he has to as Willie, pretending patience, calm, nothing much to worry about, interlocks stubby fingers on his green-sweatered chest, then gives up immobility and strokes his little woolly beard.

Lesser says: "To start with, there's no question you're a writer, Willie. Both parts of your book, the autobiography and the five stories are strong and moving. Whatever the writing lacks there's obviously a talent at work."

Willie laughs mildly derisively. "Oh, come on, dad, who you telling that to? It don't mean anything much when you know your book is in trouble. Come on down to the cold-shit truth of it."

Lesser says the truth of it is the book is good but could be better.

"I told you that myself," says Willie. "Didn't I say I wasn't satisfied? Now go on to what I really asked you, like *where* I steered off the track."

"I was going to say if you aren't satisfied with the writing, Willie, then I guess you have reason not to be. I would say that the form of the whole is not sufficient. There's a flawed quality, what you call blurred, that gives the shifting effect that bothers you."

"Where does it *start*, man?"

"Right from the beginning of the autobiography. Not that you don't work hard but there has to be more emphasis on technique, form, though I know it's not stylish to say that. You've got to build more carefully."

Willie rises, groaning, as though somebody would nail him to the chair if he didn't.

"I want to show you how full of crud you are, Lesser, in what you just said. First off, you dead wrong in the way you classified my work. The part you call autobiography is pure made-up fiction that I invent as I go along. Man, I am makin it up. The I guy who is narratin it ain't me. That cat is straight out of my imagination all along, pure and simple, comin and goin. Myself, I was born on 129th Street in Harlem and moved to Bedford-Stuyvesant with my mama when I was six years old, and which I ain't been south of except to swim at Coney Island. I have never been in Mississippi and would not put my foot in that shithole. I never in my whole life ate chitterlins because my mama and me couldn't stand the smell of them, and I think I would throw up if I did. I never worked in Detroit, Michigan, though my true daddy did for three years in a job cleanin toilets. But on the other hand, four of the short stories happen to be dead true. They happened to brothers I knew all my life just exactly like I tell it, and everything I say really happened and that's the only real autobiography there is and there is no other, period and end of period."

Lesser admits surprise.

"The book has the tone of autobiography, but even if it's pure fiction the point is that something's not coming off right or you wouldn't have asked me to read it."

Willie calmly and thoroughly scratches his balls.

"I'm not soundin on you, Lesser, but how can you be so whiteass sure of what you sayin if my book turns out to be two different things than you thought?"

"In any case we both agree it needs more work."

"Work," Willie mimics him, his moist eyes rolling. "I've worked my ass to the flat bone. I've worked past misery, man. This is my fourth draft, how many more do I have to do?"

His low voice rose high.

"Maybe try one more."

"Fuck you on that."

Lesser is angry with himself for having got into this hassle, having known it would end as one.

"Willie," he says irritably, "I've got to get on with my own book."

Willie's bulky body sags, ebony turned tar.

"Don't put your whammy on me, Lesser, you. Don't give me that grief. Don't hit me on my self-confidence."

Lesser asks Willie to grant him good will. "I know how you feel, I put myself in your place."

In cold and haughty anger the black replies. "No ofay motherfucker can put himself in *my* place. This is a *black* book we talkin about that you don't understand at all. White fiction ain't the same as *black*. It *can't* be."

"You can't turn black experience into literature just by writing it down."

"Black ain't white and never can be. It is once and for only black. It ain't universal if that's what you are hintin up to. What I feel you feel different. You can't write about black because you don't have the least idea what we are or how we feel. Our feelin chemistry is different than yours. Dig that? It *has* to be so. I'm writin the soul writin of black people cryin out we are still slaves in this fuckn country and we ain't gonna stay slaves any longer. How can you understand it, Lesser, if your brain is white?"

"So is your brain white. But if the experience is about being human and moves me then you've made it my experience. You created it for me. You can deny universality, Willie, but you can't abolish it."

"Bein human is shit. It don't give you any privileges, it never gave us any."

"If we're talking about art, form demands its rights, or there's no order and maybe no meaning. What else there isn't I think you know."

"Art can kiss my juicy ass. You want to know what's really art? *I* am art. Willie Spearmint, *black man*. My form is *myself*."

They faced each other, their eyes reflecting their images, Willie fuming, Lesser cursing himself for having lost the morning.

"What a blackass fool I was to let you read my book."

Lesser desperately makes a final suggestion. "Why don't you send your manuscript to a publisher and get somebody else's opinion if you're not satisfied with mine?"

"Because I tried ten of those rat-brained Jews and they all turned it down for a lot of horseshit reasons, because they are *afraid* of what the book says."

The black, his eyes tumid, beats his head against Lesser's wall, as the writer, not without pleasure, looks on.

LESSER BEACHES HIS BATTERED RAFT.

A woman appears on the dunes.
Mirage, he mutters; but it's the real thing.
He leaves no footsteps following hers.
"If she be black and thereto have a wit,
She'll find a white that shall her blackness fit."

WILLIE SHAKESPEAR

Though he can't speak her language, nor clearly remember her face although he has invented it, they comprehend each other at a glance and are at once locked in four arms.

The lovers lie in the hot hungry grass, canaries flitting through the feathery palms above. Just as he is having it as he always hoped to with a black gal, a white hand touches his shoulder and he wakes against the will on this snowy cold morning in Manhattan, trying to remember if it was as good as they say.

Lesser hungers to sleep again and does for a change after awaking. Fog lifts on the beach. The sea at the shore is green—purple beyond, the salt air warm, ocean-fresh. In the distance clouds of islands float on the swelling sea.

He finds her in the dunes, dancing to herself, her nude blackness dancing in the dance.

As he runs to her a crow, cawing, with a rush of wings swoops down between her legs and flies off with a puff of black wool.

Holding her plucked member she curses the bird.

She curses Lesser.

Willie raps on the door.

"Lesser, I need my fuckn machine. I got to get on to my work."

Willie, bleary, taut, suppressing rage, hauled out his typewriter the morning after their unhappy talk and did not return come siren, come noon. He didn't show up that day or the next, Thursday. Lesser vaguely worried but did not seek him out.

Had he let a fellow writer down? Said it wrong? Could he have put it more tactfully? He had told Willie what he thought he must but wondered if he mightn't have said it more subtly, in a way that eased frustration and avoided anger. He might have encouraged him more actively, kept from hassling with him, gong to gong, though that wasn't easy when you were dealing with a man whose writing wore his own thin skin, not to mention color.

After work Lesser went into the hall to Willie's office, listened at the door, heard nothing, peeked in. The table and chair were there but no sign of Willie Spearmint or his L. C. Smith. Harry wondered had he left the building for good. He searched through the flat, opening closets, and discovered the typewriter on the floor in the corner of the one in the bedroom. There it lay, vulnerable, unguarded. The writer figured Willie must still be upset, pissed off, else he would never have left it unprotected. He worried: Suppose some bum found it and dragged it off to a pawnshop? Unlike himself, who could get by with a pen, Willie, except for penciling in corrections, typed from first to last sentence. He said he thought better, typing. Lesser considered carting the machine into his place but wasn't sure Willie would appreciate that. When he comes back should I say he still ought to store it with me, or is he now and forever unwilling to accept the smallest favor from a white?

Should he forget it?

Over the weekend he forgot. Not totally. The thought of Willie's typewriter at times weighed in his head; but on the whole he forgot.

Monday morning he was in the thick of his long last chapter, stalking an idea that had appeared like a crack in night pouring out daylight, Lesser trying with twelve busy hands to trap the light—anyway, an exciting idea aborning that lit him like a seven-flamed candle. At just that minute Willie ponderously kicked the door. Boom, kick, boom. Lesser groaned as he ran to open it. Willie entered, hauling in his machine, and without explanation set it down under the table.

Welcome, Willie, I worried.

He was keeping his fingers in the flowering light, trying to seize, hold it, while at the same time foreseeing what it might illuminate in time's every direction; and memorize all this as he dealt with Willie.

Looking fully recovered except for a purple bruise on his brow, the black laughed.

"Call me Bill, Lesser, man. My writing name is my real one from now on I decided—Bill Spear."

Bill it was then, Lesser laughing self-consciously.

"I want to say something going back to our rap that other day."

Exuding damp, the writer gave birth to several excuses why he couldn't just then listen, but could not bring himself to utter them.

He cracked his knuckles.

"Won't take but a minute. All I want to tell you, Lesser, is I went to the library where my chick's house is near and took out your books. I borrowed them both out. The second one gives off a bad smell"—he held his broad-winged nose as Lesser felt himself blush—"but that first one you wrote, man, I got to tell you it's a cool piece of work. After reading it, Irene said I was talking to myself. I tell you the Jesus truth, Lesser, I didn't expect it to be that good, not from the square dude you are."

Thanks anyway, Bill.

"Although I got some real reservations and one particular one."

Such as what?

"The black sister in that book, you don't touch her exactly right."

Lesser said she was a minor character he hadn't too much to say about.

"Like she ain't really black," Willie said, "not that chick, though I like her attitude. She has a whole lot of nature going for her and I wouldn't mind laying some pipe in her pants."

Wouldn't she be real if she got that kind of response from him?

"She's not like anybody real I know, leastways nobody black. In some of the ways she does things she might be white under that black paint you laid down on her."

Was it the white in the black that aroused him? No matter, Willie had liked the book.

Lesser glanced behind him as though expecting something he had left cooking to boil over and evaporate: He goes back to his desk, looks at the pages he had written that morning: not a visible word.

Willie looked too but went on talking, chop chop. A deep crease had appeared on his brow. He sighed, biffed one hand with the other, studied the scene outside the window, then turned to Lesser.

"Also I will admit it got me thinking. What I am thinking about after reading your book—both of them—is I understand a little different now some of those ideas you were preaching about form and that jazz, and which way it gives proportion to the writing. I also realize some things I could have done better in my book, and why I wasn't sure what was giving me the feeling of words and ideas shifting and moving after I thought I got them nailed down tight. In other words, Lesser, I am revising some of my thoughts and ideas about writing, though not all the way, don't get me wrong about that. But like I am thinking things through more than I did before on some of them."

Bravo, Willie—I mean Bill.

"What's the matter, man, don't you feel right?"

Lesser felt not too bad, he said.

"Got a belly cramp?"

No. Just something on his mind.

"What I said about revising some of my ideas don't mean I'm changing how I feel on black writing in comparison to white. Art is O.K. when it helps you to say what you got to, but I don't want to turn into a halfass white writer or an ass-kissing Neegro who imitates ofays because he is ashamed or afraid to be black. I write black because I am black and what I got to say means something different to black people than it does to whites, if you dig. We *think* different than you do, Lesser. We *do* and we *are*, and we *write* different. If some white prick tears a piece of black skin off your ass every day, when somebody says, 'Sit down,' it's gonna mean two different things to me and you, and that's why black fiction *has got* to be different than white. The words make it different because the experience does. You know that, man. Also we are the rising people of the future, and if the whites try to hold us down it ain't no secret we might have to cut your throats. You have had your day and now we are gonna have *ours.* That's what I got to write about but I want to write it in black art, in the best way I can. In other words, Lesser, I want to know what you know and *add on to that* what I know *because* I am black. And if that means I have to learn something from whitey to do it better as a black man, then I will *for that purpose only.*"

Bill blew his breath into one large fist, then the other. There were two creases on his brow.

He said he had decided to put aside the book Lesser had read—he would work on it again later—and start something new with an idea that had been flapping around in the back of his mind since he was a kid trying to understand what his skin color had to do with why his life was so weird and crazy.

"It's about this black kid and his mama and how they burn off and work against each other till they kill themselves off, but not before—when this guy is a man—he goes out and gets him his revenge on the whites, maybe in some kind of riot, maybe in some personal way, because whitey is the real cause of his main troubles. Maybe he shoots twenty ofays before the pigs get to him. The point I am making, Lesser, in case you not with it, is I think this is the main way the blacks have to head along—to kill whites till those who are alive vomit with pain at the thought of what wrongs they have done us, and better not try to do any more. Now all I want you to do for me, Lesser, and I wouldn't be asking if we both wasn't writers, is not to spend any time criticizing the subject of any stuff I might show you, but to tell me the best way how I can write the same thing, with the same ideas, better. Only about the form of it, in other words, dig?"

Lesser, dreaming of new light in his book, beheld in his dark thoughts Bill Spear, potential executioner, requesting him to midwife his bloody fable.

He said he wondered whether that was such a good idea, considering how their talk had gone the other day. Subject and form were inseparable. Suppose he said something that was ultimately critical of an idea or two, would he have to worry he might have his throat cut?

Having said this he wished he hadn't. Not being able to get to work had set Lesser on edge.

"Baby," said Bill, in a sudden rage, "don't fuss your skull. If you don't want to read what I show you, fuck your bloody ass."

He slammed the door.

Lesser, momentarily relieved, returned to his desk to write a long note to himself about a new approach to his final chapter; but when he sat down he got up and followed the black back to his office.

He apologized for his impatience. It had caused him to express himself badly, Willie—I mean Bill. I think we can get along all right if your purpose is to improve the artistic quality of your work. Nobody says I have to love your ideas.

"I know your type, Lesser."

Lesser explained he had been nervous about the loss of his writing time. On the other hand I want to help if I can because I respect your ambition to be the best writer you can be, I really do.

Bill quieted down.

"Now all I am asking you to do, Lesser, is after I get a few chapters going along, to look at them and say *no more* than I am or I am not on the right track form-wise. You just say it and I'll be the one who makes up his own mind if you right. I don't plan to hang on to your tail for a free ride, you can bet your ass."

Lesser agreed to do his best if Bill was patient.

"And if you have a little bitsy of extra time," Bill said, wiping both palms on the apron of his overalls, "I want to catch up on some grammar—about noun clauses and such as that, even if nobody I know has much use for them. But I figure it won't hurt me to know about them though I don't want to do anything that will fuck up my own style. Like I like the way you write, Lesser, there's no crap in it, but I don't want to write like you."

Lesser said he would lend Bill a grammar. He could read it through and if he came across anything that interested him, they could talk it over after the day's work.

"Right on."

They shook hands.

"I like to bullshit with you, Lesser, you don't put on. We swinging real fine."

Lesser saw himself swinging.

He hurried at last back to his work. His inspired idea, possibly for an ending, whatever it might be, lay buried in an unmarked grave.

After Willie Spearmint became Bill Spear he added hours to his working hours. He no longer trudged into Lesser's flat at noon to put away his writing machine but appeared conveniently later, at three or half past three; and sometimes he sat late at his kitchen table, staring at the darkened sky. Lesser figured he was at work on his new book but did not know for sure because Bill said nothing and he would not ask him.

As for grammar, they talked once or twice about noun clauses, gerunds and gerundives, but the subject bored Bill. He said it killed the life out of language and never referred to it again. Instead, he studied his paperback dictionary, making lists of words in a notebook and memorizing their meanings.

After he knocked on Lesser's door in the afternoon, sometimes he stayed for a drink and they played records. The black responded to sound. As he listened his body spread an inch and his face took on an expression of repose and innocence. His protrusive eyes were shut and his lips tasted the music. But when Lesser put on his Bessie Smith, Bill, stretched out on the sofa, listened restlessly, squirming as though bitten by bugs.

"Lesser," he said in a slow burn, "why don't you give that record away or break it up or eat it? You don't even know how to listen to it."

To avoid argument Harry said nothing. He removed the record from the turntable and replaced it with one of Lotte Lehmann singing Schubert lieder, which Bill, his stubby fingers locked on his chest, heard contentedly.

"Nice cat that Schubert," he said when the songs were sung. Then he rose, stretched his arms, wiggling his fingers, and yawned. He looked sadly at his face in Lesser's mirror and left.

"Jesus, man," he said the next afternoon, "how do you keep yourself working so fuckn long every day?"

"Same six hours daily," the writer replied. "I've done it for years."

"I thought it was more like ten. Yessir, looking at you I thought he's at it at least ten. Myself, I work close to seven now and hardly have time to wipe my ass. The worst about it is I don't want to do anything else but sit there and write. It's getting me scared."

Lesser said he wouldn't advise him to work his hours. A writer had to discover his own rhythm.

"Don't nobody have to tell me about rhythm."

"You might be more comfortable on your old schedule, quitting at noon."

"I don't appreciate you talking about quitting at the same time as I got my mind fixed on getting started."

His moist eyes reflected the windows.

"All I mean is my way of working isn't necessarily yours."

"What I like to know," Bill said, "is what do you get out of your life besides your writing? Like what do you do with your nature, man? Like with your meat tool? You got no girl, who do you fuck other than your hand?"

Lesser said he made out now and then. "Sometimes there are sweet surprises."

"I ain't talking about surprises. I am talking about life. What do you do for fun besides chess and push-ups?"

Less than he ought, Lesser admitted. He hoped for better once his book was done.

"With a decent advance I could maybe live in London or Paris for a year. But first I've got to do the kind of job I have to as an artist—I mean realize the potential of my book."

"You talk and you act like some priest or fuckn rabbi. Why do you take writing so serious?"

"Don't you?"

"Man, the way you go about it drags me to the ground." Bill began to shout. "You've bitched up and whammied all my pleasure that I used to enjoy out of my writing."

That night he moved a lumpy, urine-stained mattress into his office flat so that he could sleep over if he worked very late.

Here's Lesser enjoying Harlem.

He had asked Willie to go along to a restaurant for a soul-food meal of barbecued ribs, collard and kale, and sweet-potato pie; but the black said it was impossible, LIKE IMPOSSIBLE, so Lesser descended by parachute into Soul City by himself.

He sees himself walking on Eighth above 135th, drifting uptown alone on the wide dark sea, though the place is alive with many bright-sailed small craft and colored birds, brothers and sisters of all shades and shapes. Anyway, he is walking amiably along, not even thinking of writing, in love with the sights and sounds of this exotic small city on a warm and sunny day, waiting for somebody, blood or chick, young or old, to say as people once did in the not-so-long-ago-past, "Peace, brother, peace to you"; but nobody does, although this red-dress fat lady with an open-eyed dead plucked chicken in her string shopping bag laughs raucously when Lesser, lifting his straw skimmer, wishes her peace and prosperity for this and the coming year. The other passers-by either ignore him or cut The Man with scornful jibes:

Show-off cracker.

Ofay spy.

Goldberg hisself.

A stranger is a man who is called a stranger. Lesser, pleading innocence, makes hasty plans for departure.

It's then that Mary Kettlesmith, in an orange knitted mini way up her perfectly proportioned naked thighs, waltzes by in the company of Sam Clemence, a Mephistophelean type in yarmulke and yellow dashiki, who though he listens with head close to all the words they say has few of his own to offer.

Are you sportin tonight? Mary asks Lesser in a friendly way.

All the time, it relaxes me for writing. Too much work, too long, gets you uptight.

Black cunt, I mean?

Not that I would mind, Harry says.

Lemme see the color of your green.

Sam nods in grave agreement.

Money? Lesser turns pale. I was hoping to be invited out of friendship and affection.

Sam flips open his eight-inch mother-of-pearl switchblade, as Lesser, at his desk on Thirty-first near Third, brushes the reverie aside and returns to moving along his lonely sentences.

Although it was less than an hour after Bill had picked up his typewriter for another long day's banging that Harry heard—and felt—a kick on his door one dreary February morning, the writer cursing fate, opened it expecting to see Bill's black head, but the big foot in the door and the cold eyes confronting Lesser's were unmistakably the pale-faced Levenspiel's.

"Who's the gorilla in Holzheimer's old flat? Friend of yours?"

"Which gorilla do you have in mind?"

"Don't play hard to get, Lesser," the landlord rumbled. "I found a typewriter there on the table in the kitchen. Also an apple less a few bites, and there's a piss-smelling mattress in the bedroom. Where's he hiding?"

Lesser opened the door wide.

Levenspiel, resting his meaty hand on the door frame, hesitated.

"I'll take your word but tell me who is this sonofabitch?"

"He comes and goes. Nobody I really know."

"He's some kind of a writer. I read a couple of the paper balls he rolls up and throws on the floor. One begins about a small boy in Harlem. Who is he, a colored?"

"I wouldn't know."

Levenspiel made a face.

"He's trespassing on private property, whoever he is. Tell him I'll throw him out on his ass."

Lesser said the landlord was trespassing on his writing time.

Levenspiel, still holding his foot athwart the threshold, softened his voice.

"So how's the work coming along?"

"On and off, too many interruptions."

"Would you consider $1,500 if I made you the offer, Lesser? Take it, it's pure gold."

Lesser said he would keep it in mind. Levenspiel, with a sigh, withdrew his foot.

"I won't repeat my troubles to you."

"Don't bother."

"You can imagine what I endure with three sick women around my neck, you're a writer, Lesser. You can appreciate the nasty little tricks of life, so yoishe, anyway, for Christ's sake. I can't go on like this forever. I'm not such a bad person. I beg you, yoishe."

"I'm writing as fast as I can. You push, you distort."

"So that's your final word?"

"Final once removed. What's final I seek but can't find. Maybe it's a blessing, I wish I knew."

Levenspiel then said sternly, "Tell your nigger friend I'm coming back with a cop."

"You tell him." Lesser shut the door.

He awaited the booming fist. Instead he heard the fire door slam. Stepping out in the hall, he listened, the heavy door held open a crack, until the landlord's flat footsteps had faded down the stairwell.

He looked into Bill's office. To his relief the L. C. Smith, a wordless sheet of pulpy, egg-yolk-yellow paper in its carriage, sat monumentally on the table. No doubt the weight of it had kept Levenspiel from hauling it down five flights, but he would surely send somebody up to grab it.

Harry carried the machine to his flat and laid it gently in the bathtub. He returned to search for a manuscript but there was none. Gathering up Bill's ream of new paper, his box of clips, pencil stubs and eraser, he also quickly stuffed some balls of paper, like overgrown bright yellow flowers on the floor, into his pants pockets.

Lesser returned to his study and picked up his fountain pen.

Bill knocked on the door, his face gray.

"I went out to find me a typewriter ribbon. Who took my stuff, you, Lesser?"

"Yes. Levenspiel found your setup and went out to get a cop."

"What the fuck for? What harm am I doing him?"

"Trespassing."

"In this smelly joint?"

"He had one writer to get rid of, now he's got two. There's a further indignity—you don't pay rent."

"Jew slumlord bastard."

"Shit with the Jew stuff, Willie."

"Bill is the name of my name, Lester," the black said, his eyeballs reddening.

"O.K., Bill, but cut out the Jew stuff."

Bill stared out the window. He turned to Lesser, his brow creased.

"What would you do if you was me?"

"Stay here," Lesser suggested. "Levenspiel's car is still parked across the street. Since you've got your typewriter here, why don't you go on with your work while I go on with mine? Use the kitchen table. I'll shut the door between us."

"I'm worrying about my desk and chair in my office. I don't

want any trouble just now because the writing is beginning to roll along more lively. I would've had a great day's work if my typewriter ribbon hadn't got torn."

The fire door slammed. There were voices in the hall.

Lesser advised Bill to hide in the bathroom.

Bill, his throat cords taut, answered, "Not me, I ain't hiding anywheres."

Lesser whispered he had wanted to move the table and chair into another apartment but figured Levenspiel would hunt down the furniture if it had disappeared out of the room.

"I also thought of lugging it up to the roof."

"I appreciate your thoughts, Lesser."

"We're writers, Bill."

The black nodded.

A recognizable nightstick rat-tatted on the door.

"Open it up in the name of the law."

Bill slipped into Lesser's study.

The writer opened the door. "The bell still functions," he reminded Levenspiel. He asked the cop to state his business.

"Our business is legal," the landlord said. "We broke up your friend's furniture in the apartment where he was trespassing, but I know you are in possession of his typewriter that I already saw, Lesser."

"I hope you're proud of yourself."

"What are my rights, though they are rare for a landlord in this bastard city, are my rights. I doubt that I owe you any personal apologies, Lesser. Right now I'm about to search every goddamn apartment in the house and if I don't locate your black friend anywhere, then he's hiding here."

"Bring a search warrant if you want to get in."

"Damn right we will," said the young cop.

A half hour later, as Bill lay on the sofa with his hands clasped under his head, from his study window the writer watched Levenspiel drive off in his Oldsmobile. The cop remained across the street for an impatient ten minutes, then looked at his watch, threw a glance up at Lesser's window where he stood peeking behind the drawn green window shade, yawned, and sauntered off.

Bill and Lesser hurried to his office. When he beheld his smashed table and chair—they had pulled the legs off the table and broken up the chair—and his slashed mattress, Bill, jaw and lips tight, trembling, ultimately wiped his eye with his hand. Lesser, respecting his privacy, returned to his desk but was too disturbed to work.

Later he asked Bill what his plans were.

"I have no fuckn plans," he said bitterly. "My chick and I had a pissass flap and I ain't planning to go back there, leastways not just now."

"Work in my kitchen tomorrow," Lesser offered, overcoming indigenous reluctance. "Or if it makes you feel claustrophobic we can put the table in the living room."

"If you insist on it," said Bill.

Lesser slept badly that night. A guest forever is all I need. What is this strange curse on my book that I can't get the right conditions to finish it?

But in the morning he had made up his mind: do something about getting Bill another place to work. They ate breakfast. Bill, though disconsolate, devoured three eggs, a can of sardines, two cups of coffee with rolls, as Lesser downed a dish of oatmeal and a cup of black coffee. The writer suggested they search around in some of the second-hand furniture stores on Third Avenue and pick up a few necessary pieces for Bill.

"There's no bread in my pants, man. That's one of the things Irene and I were arguing about. Her new show is postponed and one of her nags on me, though her old man walks on bread, is to worry about when it's not coming in, and she keeps bugging me to get a gig. I told her, 'Sister, I have to start my new book off and I don't give a living shit who is slaving but it won't be me except on my writing.' I said if she was short on confidence in me I will find me another bitch."

"Forget about money. I still have a few bucks in my bank account."

"That's fine and dandy of you, Lesser, but could we take the chance of putting another table and chair in just after this bust? Suppose those birdturds come back here today?"

Lesser agreed. "Let's wait a day or two and meanwhile you work here and I'll work at my desk."

"Right on."

Two difficult days later, neither Levenspiel nor the cop having returned to the hunt, they bought Bill an unfinished maple table, a cane-bottom, solid black chair, a folding cot, and a tasseled, old-fashioned floor lamp with a marble base. Lesser tried to persuade him to move down a floor or two but he objected because there was no view lower down.

"What view is there up here?"

"I like to look at the roofs, man."

He was, however, willing to move across the hall into Mr. Agnello's former flat that had the toilet that sometimes flushed.

They carried the new furniture up the stairs during the evening, with the assistance of Sam Clemence and a friend of his, Jacob 32, a modest gent, Bill said, though Lesser was not comfortable in his presence. Jacob 32, who had uneasy eyes and a pencil-line mustache, was not comfortable in Lesser's presence.

They swept and mopped up the rooms with Lesser's broom and wet mop. The writer also gave Bill a worn afghan for his cot.

The next afternoon they found a typed notice pasted on Holzheimer's door: NO TRESPASSING OR ILLEGAL ENTRY UNDER PENALTY OF ARREST! IRVING LEVENSPIEL, OWNER!

The landlord fortunately had not looked into Agnello's apartment. But after that, Bill, worrying about his new possessions, agreed to move down to a not-bad back flat on the fourth floor, the opposite corner from Lesser's. He and the writer hauled down the furniture. Bill wrote busily every day, including Sundays, but after another week he and Irene made up and he returned to her apartment, though only for weekends.

"Like I concentrate better when I don't see her during the week," Bill told Harry. "I got my first chapter in the breeze at last. If you see cunt you want cunt though she is pissing a lot lately so it ain't that much of a problem."

"Pissing?"

"She's got cystitis and you can't ball them then or the germs might penetrate in you and then you have to piss all day."

"Really?"

"That's what I hear. Irene has this on and off. It started when she was a little chick. She has that and some other hangups I got to be patient with, but that's the nature of her nature."

"What sort of hangups?"

"She was a fucked-up nigger-struck chick when I took her on. She had nothing she believed in herself. I straightened her out in the main ways because I gave her an example, that I believed in my blackness."

"What does she believe in now?"

"Me more than herself, and sometimes she believes in God, which I don't."

He said nothing more about her.

"I'm writing hard," he told Lesser. He wore wire-framed, blue-tinted granny glasses and had grown a bushy mustache to go with his goatee.

Bill had nailed up pictures of W.E.B. Du Bois, Malcolm X, and Blind Lemon Jefferson on the wall of his new kitchen-office. It wasn't a bad place to work, Lesser thought, though it looked a little barren and wasn't so well daylit as the upstairs place. A wash of shadow hung in the light.

Although Lesser feared it would not be long before Levenspiel chanced on Bill's new furniture, he left a bottle with six red-and-white carnations in it on a shelf in his new office.

"Luck with your new book," he wrote in large letters on a sheet of typing paper. Partly he left the flowers in relief to have Bill out of his flat. Lesser felt he hadn't worked in an age.

Bill, perhaps embarrassed by the carnations, said nothing in the way of thanks for anything, except once he remarked there might be a diddle of black in Lesser's blood.

In the Babylonian past a black slave socks it to a white bitch from the Land of Israel?

Bill insisted on showing the writer the first chapter of the novel he had recently begun. Lesser asked him not to just yet, but Bill said it would help him know if he had started off right. He said this was a brand-new book although there were some scenes from the other novel, brought from Mississippi to Harlem, where most of the action would take place. Bill asked Lesser to read the chapter in his presence. He sat in Harry's armchair, wiping his glasses and looking at a newspaper on his knees as the writer, chain-smoking, read on the sofa. Once Harry glanced up and saw Bill sweating profusely. He read quickly, thinking he would lie if he didn't like the chapter.

But he didn't have to. The novel, tentatively called *Book of a Black*, began in Herbert Smith's childhood. He was about five in the opening scene, and nine at the end of the chapter; but in truth he was an old man.

In the opening scene, one day the boy drifted out of his neighborhood into a white neighborhood and couldn't find his way home. Nobody spoke to him except an old white woman who saw him through her ground-floor window, sitting on the curb.

"Who are you, little boy? What's your name?"

The boy wouldn't say.

In the afternoon this old-smelling white woman came out of the house and took the boy by the hand to the police station.

"Here's a boy that's lost," she said.

He wouldn't answer the white pigs when they asked him questions. Finally they sent in a black cop to find out where he belonged.

"Can't you talk, boy?"

The boy nodded.

"Then talk and tell me where do you live at."

The boy wouldn't answer.

The black cop got him a glass of milk to drink, then lifted the boy into his car and drove into Harlem. They walked from street to street, the policeman asking people sitting on the stoops if they knew this kid. No one did. Finally a fat black woman, fanning herself though the day was cool, said she did. She led them two blocks up the street to the tenement where she said the boy lived.

"Do you live in this here house?" asked the cop.

"He sure do," said the fat woman.

The boy said nothing.

"You sure are a terror," said the cop. "If you was mine I would blast you ass."

In a flat on the top floor of the house they found the mother drunk in bed. She was naked but did not pull up the blanket.

"Is this you boy?"

She turned her head and wept.

"I asked you to tell me is this you boy?"

She nodded and wept.

The cop left the boy there and went downstairs.

The woman wept.

The boy smeared a slice of stale bread with some rancid lard and went down to the street to eat it.

In the last scene of the chapter the mother has a visitor who drops in every other night.

. . . He was an ofay who liked to pretend to talk nigger talk. It made him feel good to do it though it was fake black talk. He did not come from the South, he came from Scranton, Pa. He came to my mama because she charged one dollar and it wasn't before long that he used to get it for free. And also my mama did all the things he wanted her to do. Sometimes he left us a loaf of sandwich bread on the table or a can of pears, or string beans, or mushy canned fruit. I remember he left a can of tomato paste that my mama smeared on the bread and gave it to me to eat. Sometimes he also gave her two packs of Lucky Strikes. My mama was about twenty-seven years then and I was nine years old. On the street they called this guy "Rubber Dick." He was a tall stringy Charlie with long legs and a big prick. He liked to take it out and show it to me and scare me off. I hated him and had thoughts to kill him off with my zip gun but was afraid to. I told my mother to warn him to stay out of the house but she said she didn't mind having him for company.

"Is he comin here tonight?" I asked her.

"Well, he jus might."

"I hope he dies before he gets here. I hope I kill him if he comes in this here room."

"I gon wash your mouth with soap if you say that word again."

"I got nothin to be shame of."

"He treats me real fine. Las week he buy me a pair of pretty shoes."

I know he didn't buy her no shoes.

I left the house but when I came back to eat some supper, he was there, smoking a Lucky Strike cigarette.

"Wheah at is Elsie?" he asked me in nigger talk and I said I didn't know.

He looked at me in a way that was supposed to witch me and he sat on the bed with a shit smile on his mouth.

"I gon wait for her."

He told me to come over to him on the bed, he wouldn't hurt me.

I was scared so nauseous I thought if I moved one teensy bit I would crap in my pants. I wanted my mother to come back fast. If she came back I would not mind what they did to each other.

"Come heah, boy, and unzip mah pants."

I told him I didn't want to.

"Heah's a nice tin cints piece you kin have."

I didn't move at all.

"Heah's a quotah mo. Now unzip mah pants and the money is yo's. Bof the dime and the quotah."

"Don't take it out, please," I asked him.

"Not till you show me kin you open yo mouf wide an covah yo teef wif yo lips like this."

He showed me how to cover my teeth.

"I will do it if you stop talking nigger talk to me."

He said honey he would, and also I was a smart boy and he loved me very much.

He was talking like a whitey again.

Lesser said it was a strong chapter and praised the writing.

"How is the form of it?"

"It's well formed and written." He said no more than that, as they had agreed.

"Damn right, man. It's strong black writing."

"It's well written and touches the heart. That's as much as I'll say now."

Bill said that in the next chapter he wanted to get deep into the boy's black consciousness, already a fire of desire and destruction.

He lived that day in a potless triumphant high.

That night both writers, over water glasses filled with red wine, talked about being writers and what a good and great thing it was.

Lesser read aloud a passage he had written in a notebook: "I am convinced more and more day by day that fine writing is next to fine doing the top thing in the world."

"Who said that?"

"John Keats, the poet."

"Fine dude."

"And here's something from Coleridge: 'Nothing can permanently please which does not contain in itself the reason why it is so and not otherwise.'"

"Copy that down for me, man."

Depressed, one useless morning, dispossessed of confidence in himself as writer, as he sometimes was, Lesser, shortly before noon at the Museum of Modern Art, stood before a painting of a woman done by a former friend of his, a painter who had died young.

Although he had sat at his desk for hours, that day for the first time in more than a year Lesser had been unable to write a single sentence. It was as though the book had asked him to say more than he knew; he could not meet its merciless demands. Each word weighed like a rock. If you've been writing a book for ten years time adds time to each word; they weigh like rocks—the weight of waiting for the end, to become the book. Though he struggled to go on, every thought, every decision, was impossible. Lesser felt depression settle on his head like a sick crow. When he couldn't write he doubted the self; this expressed itself in reservations about the quality of his talent—was it really talent, not an illusion he had dreamed up to keep himself writing? And when he doubted the self he couldn't write. Sitting at his desk in the bright morning light, scanning yesterday's pages, he had felt about to throw up: language, form, his plan and purpose. He felt sick to death of the endless, uncompleted, beastly book, the discipline of writing, the overdedicated, ultimately limited, writer's life. It needn't be so but was for Lesser. What have I done to myself? So much I no longer see or feel except in language. Life once removed. So against the will he had taken the morning off and gone for a walk in the February sun. Lesser tried to put his thoughts out of mind as he walked. He named his unhappiness "depression," and let it go at that; for though he presently resisted everything concerned with writing he could not forget he wanted more than anything else to write a fine book.

It was a warmish cold day of snow melting, and he drifted aimlessly uptown, pretending not to be thinking of his work, whereas in desperate truth he was scribbling away in the head—it came to not much. Though the writer was not crippled he walked with a limp. He saw with a limp, nothing quite meets his gloomy gaze or fastens there. He is missing something—that begins in an end. He thinks of settlement, compromise, a less than perfect conclusion—how many will know the difference? But when he sneaks around his malaise and sees himself once more at his desk, writing, he can't imagine he will settle for less than a sufficient ending, the one that must be if the book is to be as good as it must. Anyway, Lesser, after a dozen blocks, admits that whatever presently afflicts him is not an incurable disease. A man is entitled to be momentarily fed up. All he has to do to scare the puking bird off his skull, dispel the despondency that keeps him from working, is go back to his desk and sit down with his pen in his hand; asking not what the writing will or won't give him. So it's not the whole of life but who holds the whole of life in his two hands? Art is an essence, not of everything. Tomorrow is a new day; finish the book and the day after comes bearing gifts. If he began once more to work, settled, calm, *at it*, the mysterious ending, whatever it was or might be, would come of itself as he worked. My God, here it is on paper. He could not conceive how else it would come. No angel flies into his room with a scroll revealing the mystery baked into a loaf of bread, or hidden in a mezuzah. One day he would write a word, then another, and the next is the end.

But the longer Lesser walked the winter streets, the less he felt like returning home and at last gave up the struggle and decided to take a holiday. Big laugh if holiday comes by default. You couldn't do—for whatever confused reason—what you wanted most to do, ought this minute to be doing, for in essence the job was almost done—hadn't he invented every step that led to an end? Hadn't he written two or three endings, a combination of endings? You had only to choose the right one and put it down once and for all; perhaps it needed one final insight. Then you could, after the book was *there*, reconsider your life and decide how much of the future you wanted to invest in writing—something less than past investment of time and toil. He was tired of loneliness, had thoughts of marriage, a home. There was the rest of one's life to live, uncertain but possible, if you got to it. Harry promised himself to take at least a year off after finishing this book before beginning another. And the next would go three years in the writing, not seven, not longer. Ah, well, that's the future, what do you do with a holiday? Since it has been months that he had stepped into a gallery and prowled amid pictures, Lesser, on Fifty-third Street, walked west to the Museum of Modern Art, and after wandering through the permanent collection not really looking—he found it hard to be attentive—stopped in the last room, before his former friend's abstract and fragmented "Woman."

Lazar Kohn, an inscrutable type, had been a friend of Lesser's for a short time in their early twenties. He had become successful too soon for the continuance of their friendship—while the future writer was hating himself for not having yet begun. After a while Kohn stopped seeing him; Lesser, he said, spoiled his pleasure in his triumph. When Lesser's first novel appeared, Kohn was abroad; when his second was published, Kohn was dead. His motorcycle had crashed, one rainy night, into a huge moving van on Hudson Street. His work, it was said, had been going badly.

There was his green-and-orange picture: a woman trying to complete herself through her own will, as willed by the painter. Otherwise she was an appearance of a face and body trying to make it through a forest of binding brush strokes.

The portrait of the woman—Lesser had once met the model at a party but nothing had come of it—had never been completed. Kohn had worked on it for years and then given up. Lesser had learned this from the model, Kohn's one-time mistress. Kohn, in defeat, after all his labor, doubt, despair he was not making it, nor ever would, had turned the unfinished canvas to the wall; she had eluded him. You work as you always have but with this picture for no reason you can give or guess, except that it means so much to you to do it as it should be done, you can't this time make it. She isn't what I hoped she might be. Whoever she is I don't know and want no further part of. Let time fuck her, I can't. But friends who had seen the portrait in Kohn's studio, in various aspects and colors, said the painter had "made it" despite himself, whether he thought so or no; it was accomplished as art whether or not accomplished as subject, or as originally conceived. Whatever he put his hand to was Lazar Kohn and Kohn was a distinguished painter. His friends persuaded him to release the picture to his gallery for sale. The museum had bought it and hung it in its permanent collection.

The picture deepened Lesser's dejection. Why had it been abandoned? Who knows?—like Lesser, Kohn had had his hangups. Maybe he had wanted to say more than he could at that time, something that wasn't then in him to say? He might have said it after the motorcycle accident, if he had survived. Or had he been unable to separate the woman from who she really was: she had as self got the better of his art? He could not invent beyond her? She was simply the uncompleted woman of an incomplete man because it was that kind of world, life, art? I can't give you more than I have given you—make you more than you are—because I haven't presently got it to give and don't want anyone to know, least of all myself. Or perhaps it was the painter's purpose to complete by abandoning, because abandonment or its image was presently a mode of completion? Peace to Valéry. In painting, Lesser thought, you could finish off, total up, whether done or undone, because in the end (the end?) you hung a canvas object on the wall and there was no sign saying, "Abandoned, come back tomorrow for more." If it hung it was done, no matter what the painter thought.

Thinking of his own work, regretting that he had never been able to talk with Kohn about it, Lesser reflected that if he could not complete his novel; in the end something essential missing—the ending—some act or appearance or even promise of resolution, hence the form unachieved; then it was no completed work of art, did not deserve to be a book—he would destroy it himself. Nobody would read it except those who already had—besides himself perhaps some bum who had fished a few pages of a prior draft out of the garbage can in front of the house, curious to know what the words said. Lesser then vowed, as he often had, that he would never abandon this novel, never, for whatever reason; nor would anybody good or bad, Levenspiel, Bill Spear, for instance, or any woman, black or white, persuade him to give it up; or call the job done before he had completed it. He had no choice but to bring his book to its inevitable and perfected end.

Who says no?

As Lesser leaves the last gallery, wondering what would happen if he went home and picked up his pen, a blue-hatted black woman in the lobby drops a mirror out of her cloth handbag and it shatters on the floor. A girl in a voluminous silk-lined black cape coming out of the ladies' room quickly walks away from it. Lesser, stooping, hands the black woman a large triangular sliver of glass. In it he sees himself, unshaven, gloomy, gaunt; it comes from not writing. The black woman spits on the fragment of mirror Lesser has given her. He backs off. Lesser hurries after the girl in the cape into the street. He had often thought of her, sometimes while writing.

"Shalom," he says in the street.

She looks at him oddly, coldly. "Why do you say that?"

He fumbles, says he isn't sure. "I never use the word."

Irene, a moody type, walks in noisy boots along the slushy sidewalk, going towards Sixth Avenue, Lesser walking along with her, surprised to be though he invents surprises of this sort easily enough in his fiction. She moves with a loose-limbed, slightly pigeon-toed stride, wearing a knitted green wool hat from which her hair pours down her back. Her intricate earrings clink faintly. Lesser is thinking of her as she looked at his party—her short thick skirt and pink blouse, her plump white breasts; of looking up her legs to the conjoining thighs. He remembers her dance with Bill he hadn't been able to break into.

She's a black man's girl, they're a special breed. I'm on my way home.

"How about coffee?" Irene asks.

He says fine.

They sit at a counter. She holds the hot cup with both hands to warm her nail-bitten fingers. Her eyes are evenly green and blue. Her black hair, in daylight, is golden blond.

Lesser, as they drink their coffee, waits as though expecting a confession but she makes none.

He tries to breathe in her perfume but the scent is hidden. Behind the ears? Under her long cape? In her sweaty armpits? Between breasts or legs? He has made the grand tour but hasn't sniffed flowers. No gardenia, no garden.

"Don't you have a girl?"

He asks why she asks.

"You had nobody for yourself at your party."

"The last girl I had was about a year ago. I had one the summer before that. They get impatient waiting for me to finish my book."

"Willie says it's taking forever."

"I'm a slow writer. It's my nature."

She smiles sourly.

"Let's get out of here," Lesser says.

They walk up Sixth to the park, dirty with melting snow, the pale dead grass on hard ground visible in dark circles under trees. They stand by the low stone wall on Fifty-ninth, overlooking the snowy meadow. The park is of diminished reality to Lesser, tight, small, remote. The book he is writing is unbearably real in his thoughts. What am I doing so far away from it? What am I doing here on a working day in the middle of winter?

"When do you laugh?" she says. "You're so deadly serious. It's your fucking book."

"I laugh when I write," Lesser says. "I haven't written a word today. I ought to be writing now."

"Why aren't you?"

Lesser sees himself leaving her at the wall. He crosses Fifth and heads for Third. Halfway to Madison he stops, experiencing a sense of loss. What a fool I am, he thinks. He walks back to where he has left Irene. He thinks she won't be there but she is. She's standing at the wall in a long cape, like a bird about to fly off.

"Why is it taking so long?"

He says he doesn't want to talk about it.

"Is it still that book about love?"

"That's the book," he says.

"I read your first novel. Willie got it out of the library and gave it to me after he finished it. It's very good, better than I thought it would be. The girl reminds me of myself when I was her age. I don't like her. Did you have anyone real in mind?"

Lesser says no.

They sit on a bench.

"You're all such self-conscious characters," Irene says. "When Willie's hung up on his writing he's awful to live with. He fights all the minutes of the day. It's hard to take."

Again the small smile as she inspects her pigeon toes.

"It was bad enough for him but you've made it worse. He was awfully hurt by your criticism of his book."

"I didn't want to hurt him."

"He said you didn't think much of it."

"I like the stories better than the Life. They're a lot more original."

"It isn't just autobiography. Willie came from Georgia to Harlem with his mother and kid sister when he was sixteen."

"I thought it was Mississippi."

"He changes his birthplace every time he talks about it. I think he hates to remember it."

"There's a lot he hates to remember. Did he serve a stretch in prison?"

"Two years. But a lot of the book is made up. Willie's an imaginative guy. He enjoys being imaginative. You should hear him when he gets talking about himself. That's the tone I'd like to see in his book. Do you like what he's writing now?"

"So far," says Lesser.

"Do you think he is a good writer—I mean will he be?"

"He is though not consistently. If he stays with it seriously he ought to be good."

"How seriously? Like you have to break your balls to be a writer?"

"There's no halfass way to be a good writer."

"There's nothing halfass about Willie."

Lesser asks her how she and Willie stand as of now.

She strikes a match, then finds she has no cigarette.

"What do you mean?"

"You seem to be together but you seem to be apart."

"That's a good description of us."

"It's none of my business," Lesser says.

"If you say that it means you think it is."

He says he wishes it were.

"I'm not objecting to your question. I'm wondering how to answer it."

"Don't if you don't want to."

"Willie and I met about three years ago—that was about a year and a half after I'd quit college to try being an actress. Not that I was that much of one but the idea of it had become an obsession. My God, what a batty girl I was, and I weighed a good twenty-five more pounds than I do now. I'm not bad in my performances but I can't go down low enough when I have to, or up as high as I would like to. What I'm saying is I wanted to act mainly so that I could skip being myself. A lot of this came out in my analysis. I wasn't very self-knowing."

"You look like an actress but you don't playact."

"I used to an awful lot. Anyway, what it amounted to is acting as a means of getting away from myself. I was a fucked-up kid, I drew men like flies and slept around till I began to wake up frightened."

It seems to Lesser he had left his room that morning to hear her talk about herself.

"I had a very rough time for over a year—but never mind that. I met Willie and we began to see each other. The blackness of him scared and excited me. I asked him to live with me. I was beginning to be in love with him and I also wanted to know if I could be faithful to one guy. Anyway he moved into my apartment. He wasn't writing as steadily as he is now—for a while he was hung up on whether it was going to be revolution or soul, and I don't really think he's resolved that. He used to write only when he felt he had to. At first we got along badly, then we got kinder to each other and began to have a better time all around. Certain things eased up in me. They stopped being so important—like acting, because I began to have a realer understanding of myself and I don't want to be a halfass anything. And I told you I'm in analysis, which I couldn't bring myself to do before I met Willie."

"Do you love him?"

Irene's eyes are suddenly hungry. "Why do you want to know?"

"Because we're sitting here."

She flips the matchstick into the snow.

"Outside of his love for black people I don't really think he loves anything but his work. Otherwise I think we'd've been married by now. Willie was always conscious of his color but it's more so now. The more he writes the blacker he becomes. We talk an awful lot about race and color. A white chick is no longer such a hot thing for a black man, especially the activists. Willie won't let me hold his hand in public any more. Just when I thought there was a chance we might get married he began to say, 'I'll tell you the truth, Irene, my writing doesn't come on right with me living with a white chick.' I said to him, 'Willie, do what you want to, I have only so much energy.' He moved out of the apartment for a while, then one night he called me up and moved back in. Now it's just a weekend deal till he really gets into his book, he says."

Lesser says nothing. What she has told him has set off an excitement. He feels in himself a flow of language, a surge of words towards an epiphany.

"What about you?" she says. "I told you about me."

He rises craving to write.

"Do you want to walk any more?" Irene asks. Her eyes are vague, unsure. She opens her purse and roots around for something she can't find, maybe a mirror. Lesser thinks of Lazar Kohn's "Woman."

"One thing about loving a black man," Irene says, "there are times you feel black yourself."

In that case find yourself another.

The writer says he has his work to get back to.

February had stepped aside to let a whiff of leaf and flower into present time. Tomorrow will again be winter; in the meantime this puff of promised spring tormented Lesser.

The writer, alone, this end-of-February night, heading downtown on the east side of Lexington for no other reason than that he had walked uptown on the other side last night, heard laughter across the street and recognized, amid the stream of people passing by, Bill Spear with Irene Bell. They were at the head of a small parade within the Friday night crowd moving along on the sidewalk; behind them was Sam Clemence and behind him four other blacks walking in pairs: a small neatly dressed brown man wearing a big-brimmed black velours hat, with a heavy, light-skinned, fur-coated woman holding his arm; then two iron-bearded black men in long cloth coats, one carrying a flute case, the other a bongo drum he tapped as he walked. The man with the bongo had a broken nose taped with adhesive.

Lesser, recognizing four of the seven and hearing their laughter, felt longing invade his gut and began to follow them. As he watched Irene with Bill, both enjoying themselves, his feeling turned unpleasant, desire in corrosive emptiness, intensified by shame for feeling as he felt. Could I be jealous of them? How can that be if I have nothing to be jealous of and am not, so far as I know, a jealous type? Recalling that he had experienced a similar seizure on first seeing Irene at his party, something more than hunger touched with regret that he hadn't got to her before Willie had, Lesser felt a disquietude so strange he had to stop a minute to brace himself against a lamppost.

From across the street near a florist shop Bill spied him and whooped, "Lesser, man, for Christ's sake, cross on over here. I got some soul people with me."

Lesser, struggling to settle his confused state, waved, and stepped into the street, bucking the light in heavy traffic as the blacks and Irene watched with interest to see if he would make it. Eventually he did, hiding his uneasy excitement, trying not to reveal himself to Irene, who was distantly observing him with eyes wondering why he had appeared, if not who was he.

If you swim the Hellespont where there is none, what are you trying to tell yourself? Or anybody else?

"We are partying at Mary's pad," Bill said. "How do you like to come along?"

Lesser said he wouldn't mind.

"Join the train."

Harry glanced at Irene as though for her sanction but she was already walking on.

"What for this ofay type?" Sam asked Bill, loud enough for Lesser to hear.

"He is a fuckn good writer in one of his books and you were there when he laid down his bread for my furniture that's in my office now."

"Join the train," he called.

None of the pairs made room for one more abreast and Lesser preferred not to walk with Sam, so he tailed the line to Mary's. He had met only one of the four people in the rear, the man with the light-skinned woman, Jacob 32, who nodded gravely with both eyes shut. The others ignored him but Lesser was glad to be with them, even as caboose to their train. The jealousy that had invaded him had vanished and he enjoyed the promise of spring in the February night.

Mary lived in a psychedelically painted loft with a girlfriend who was an illustrator. She said she was happy to see Lesser. Who was happy to see him Lesser was happy to see.

"I thought you might come around sometime," Mary said, "seeing we live so close by. My phone is in the book."

He said he had thought of it. "I thought of it the other night, then I remembered that smell that bothered you last time."

"Oh I was zonked that night," she laughed, touching Lesser's arm. "You shouldn't have held back or felt shy."

"Are you zonked now?"

"I'm staying off grass. When I'm high on it I get low."

As she spoke she watched his eyes. "Are you partial on Irene? You been eye-eating her."

"She's Bill's girl."

"Your eyes stay soft on her."

"It's her mini, I like those long legs."

"Mine are better shaped."

Lesser agreed. "You're a good-looking woman, Mary." In a moment of loneliness and daring, he said to her, "If you liked me I could give you back affection."

Mary, her neck arched, blinked both eyes and walked away.

I write it right but say it wrong, Lesser thought. I write it right because I revise so often. What I say is unrevised and often wrong. Then he thought, I write about love because I know so little about it.

There were about twenty souls at the party, the writer and Irene the only whites. White souls? Four of the brothers sat barefoot on the floor, improvising black sound with a heart-rending beat. Above them rocked a fifth musician with his bull fiddle. Everybody else was dancing, rocking. As he listened to the music the writer felt a yearning, longing for life. The brother with the taped nose beat his bongo with eyes shut. His twin, flowers woven into his stiff beard, played his flute high and sweet. One man plucked the strings of a twelve-string guitar, listening privately to each sound. A brother wearing a gold blouse and red fez beat a rhythmic spoon on an empty bottle. The standing brother, rapping his fingers on his booming bass fiddle, hugged and swayed with it. Each of them whipped up an island of sound around himself. They played to each other, saying their music was beautiful and so were they. Over them hung an umbrella of sweet smoke, and Lesser felt high.

Feeling high, he asked Irene to dance but she was engaged

with Sam, who said he didn't appreciate being cut in on. Irene shrugged in mock frustration but said nothing. Lesser thought of the jealousy he had felt before. A short aberration, he thought, directed nowhere in particular, just pro-desire. Bill, in yellow cords, purple silk shirt, short brown boots and a flowered headband, circled Mary, boogalooing. Irene, in an orange mini, was dancing barefoot, her narrow feet honest, her face flushed. She abandoned Sam as Bill left Mary. They bopped in unison like contrasting birds, each dancing in his casual, habitual orbit as though forever. Bill smiled benignly at his bitch and Irene gazed at him with sad affection. They looked like married folk.

Mary danced with Sam, who shimmied high and shimmied low. Sam moved like a stork with palsy, Mary, both arms aloft, danced with hot eyes. At last she left Sam to dance with Harry.

"Listen now," Mary said as they stepped and twisted, "I got the door key to a friend's apartment across the hall. As soon as people get a little more high I will go on in there and you come in if you have the mood to. Only give me ten more minutes of time so nobody sees us going out of here one right after the other, or Sam might feel bad."

"All right," Lesser said. "But don't get zonked before you go in."

"Okay now. I'll do like you say, honey."

Harry ducked, swung his arms, stepped to the beat of the music as Mary Kettlesmith, in a short slender white-green-and purple striped dress danced exotically around him.

She soon slipped out of the loft, Lesser's anticipation rising, his throat dry. Bill, he saw, looked bleary—tonight he was drinking. Irene was in and out of the bathroom, still with cystitis?

The writer, after a quarter of an hour, stepped into the barren outer hall and entered the one-room apartment across from Mary's loft, his heartbeat shaking his frame. Mary lay waiting in bed, covered with a rose blanket. A canary flitted on a bar in a cage by the window.

"Do you mind me getting undressed first? The room is cold and I thought it would be warmer waiting in bed."

Lesser lifted the blanket for a look at her.

"My God, you're lovely."

"Tell me what you like."

"Your breasts and belly. The black of you." He passed his hand over her velvet skin.

"Haven't you had a black woman ever?"

"No."

"Don't make too much out of it. Come on in bed now, honey," she said.

When he had undressed and got under the covers with her, Mary said, "Lesser, I want to tell you something. My doctor says I am built a little small. You have to go easy not to hurt me at first."

He said he'd be gentle.

"If you would."

They embraced. Her fingers moved over his face, then down his side and between his legs. He touched her breasts, soft belly, and felt the wet between her thighs.

Mary put out the lamp.

"Don't," said Lesser.

She laughed and put it on.

Sweating lightly, moaning to herself, after a while Mary said, "You better come on and come, I don't think I will make it, Harry."

"Is it some smell of me?"

"No smell at all."

"Try. I'll hold a while."

For a time she tried with him. Then Mary said with a sigh, "I'm not going to make it at all. You better come on now."

"Did you drink much tonight?"

"Only one scotch and part of another. I didn't take a thing after you said not to."

"I'd like it better if you came too."

"So would I but you better go on alone. I will help you if you tell me what you want me to do."

"Just stay with me," said Lesser.

He came with pleasure, cupping her buttocks. Mary kissed him affectionately. "Lay on me for a while, it keeps me warm." She entwined both arms around him.

Lesser lay on her half asleep. "This is good, Mary."

"I'm sorry I didn't come along with you."

"Don't worry about it."

"Just I like you and would like to come along."

"Next time," Lesser said.

Later, after she had gone to the bathroom, she hung a string of green and violet beads around his neck.

"What's this for?"

"For our luck," said Mary. "Okay now?"

They lay in bed, passing a cigarette back and forth.

He asked her whether she had ever come with anybody.

"I huff and puff with Sam to make him feel good but I don't really think I have."

He said she would.

"I almost did with you."

"How long haven't you?"

"I don't want to think about that."

"Do you have any idea why you don't?"

"Unless it was because I was raped when I was little, which happened to me on the cellar stairs after he dragged me down there."

"Jesus—who?"

"This redhead nigger neighbor boy from upstairs. His daddy was white and beat the shit out of his black mother. My mama said it got the boy so frustrated he hated everybody and wanted to hurt them. He finally got sent away."

"Tell me, Lesser," said Mary after a while, "do your girls come all of the time?"

"Most of the time."

"Do they come more than once?"

"One used to."

"The bed is not my most favorite place," she said.

"Are you crying, Mary?" Lesser asked.

"No, sir, I am not."

"It sounds as though you were."

"That's not me. Usually it's Sam out in the hall, kneeling by the keyhole and crying," Mary said.

"A Salaam Aleikum," Jacob 32 said to Lesser when he returned to Mary's loft. Mary had gone back first. Jacob was a narrow-eyed man in a dark blue suit. His gaze locked with Lesser's, but he spoke gently, as though he had been asked to.

"If you think you white you wrong," said Jacob. "You really black. The whites are black. The blacks are the true white."

"I think I know what you mean."

"No, you don't. You see us wrong and you see yourself wrong. If you saw me right you would see me white in the manner which I see you black. You think I am black because your inside eyes are closed to the true vision of the world."

Lesser said no more.

"This is a eye-to-eye confrontation of the force of evil versus a vessel of good," said Jacob 32, "and it ain't up to me to reveal to you which is the which."

Mary had locked herself in her bathroom and Lesser was left alone with a crowd of silent blacks. He guessed that Sam had told them and nobody cared for the news. Irene was standing at a dark window in the loft, looking out, her face haunted in the glass. Lesser saw himself in it, staring at her.

We're both scared but what is she scared of?

Bill Spear, his mouth slack, heavy eyes glazed, drunk but steady on his feet, summoned Lesser from across the room. Beside him stood Sam Clemence, thick-calved in striped bell-bottoms, aloof but mourning. A cluster of blacks with inexpressive faces was massed around them.

"Lesser, move your paleface ass on over here."

Now I take my lumps, he thought. Maybe for not satisfying Mary. Maybe that's the name of the game. The stranger who fails is a dead duck. It's an ancient entrapment and I shouldn't have played. I'm too young to be the sacrifice in a stomp-in. He was alarmed by the thought of broken fingers and bloody eyes.

Bill's flushed eyes were sullen. Of the blacks he was the blackest present.

"Chum," he said, tapping his stubby finger against Lesser's noisy chest, "we have a game we got we call the dozens. Like the brothers play it no ofay has that gift or the wit, and also since whitey ain't worth but half a black I'm gon play you the half-dozens. Now it's a game of nothin but naked words. I'm gon do mine on you and you do yours on me, and the one who bleeds, or flips, or cries mama, he's the loser and we shit on him. Do you dig?"

"What's the point of it?"

"The point is the point."

"I thought we were friends, Bill?"

"You got no friends here," Sam told Lesser.

"Suppose I don't play?"

"If you gon fuck black you gon face black," said the light-skinned woman, Jacob's friend.

"Off the shmuck," said the flute player with flowers in his beard.

Several of the brothers nodded. Lesser felt his testicles tighten.

"I'll begin like easy so you can join the fun," Bill said in his resonant raspy voice. "I ain't gon work on your mama and sister which is the way we do it, but come right to the tough-shit funk of it, special for you:

"Lesser, don't think you so hot,
You got the look of a shit-pot."

Some of the blacks snickered as the bull fiddler bowed a high chord.

"Now raise me on that."

Lesser stood mute.

"If you don't we might have to play a different kind of a game."

"Poker?" the writer bluffed, truly frightened.

"Man, have you lost your nuts down the can?"

The blacks laughed.

Lesser figured it was a game so long as he played it.

"Willie, your mouth is a place of excrement."

To his surprise he roused a titter of amusement.

The bull fiddler fiddled a low note.

Bill blinked in scorn, his tumid eyes momentarily refusing to focus.

"Lesser," he said, when he had got a new fix on him, "I see you runnin a bad trip. And I see that you a mammyrammer blowhard fart that has no respect for hisself."

"What good is a contest of imprecation? All it does is arouse bad feeling."

He roused raucous guffaws.

"Listen to that soft bullshit," Sam said huffily.

"Now you leave this honky to me," said Bill. "He is my guest."

More laughs.

Irene came over, her cape and hat on, leather purse hanging from her shoulder. Her long hair seemed longer.

Lesser thought if he hadn't gone to bed with Mary he might now be outside somewhere with Irene.

"Willie, can we go home now?" she said, not looking at Lesser. "I'm tired."

"Go on home."

"Couldn't you come with me?"

"Go fuck yourself."

"If I could what would you do for kicks?"

The sisters let out little shrieks of laughter and some of the brothers laughed. The bull fiddler slapped his knee. Irene retreated to the window.

"Lesser," said Bill, testily impatient, "I called you a mammyrammer blowhard fart. Don't that tempt you to return me an answer?"

"If you have to do this, why don't you write it? I thought you were a writer." Lesser's voice was hoarse, his underpants damp.

"Don't tell me what to write, chum," Bill said, raising his head haughtily. "I don't need no bleached-out Charlie to tell *me* what to write."

"Amen," said Jacob 32.

Lesser's fear incited anger. "If you have some kind of complaint about me why don't you say it directly? Why pretend to play this stupid game? If what you want to say is none of your business in the first place, then let Sam say it."

"I told you not to let this redneck shiteater come along here," Sam complained.

Jacob 32 nodded.

"What is the answer to the words I have laid down to you?" Bill said, irritated. "How much more of a motherfuckn coward you gon be?"

"I could call you filthy prick," Lesser offered.

He saw Irene, across the room, make a gesture of silence.

"I withdraw that."

"You can't withdraw nothin," Bill said, moving his glowing face close to Lesser's. "That's the fuckn rules of it. Now isn't the reason why you want to withdraw it because it really don't say what you wanted to call me? Wasn't you plannin to say filthy nigger prick, without havin the courage to get it out? Tell the truth, man."

"I'll tell the truth—I thought of it because I know you want to hear it."

"Fine and okay," said Bill. "But now I'm gon call you a fartn shiteater faggot whore kike apeshit thievin Jew." He spaced each word slowly and ended with a hard beat.

The blacks murmured approval. The bongo player tapped out a little tune. Sam wiped a happy tear from under his eyeglasses.

"I get the message," said Lesser, "and concede the game. That's my last word."

There was a hush. The room smelled of sweat. He thought he would be struck on the head, but nobody moved. Those who continued to look on were bored. The man in the red fez yawned. The bull fiddler packed away his instrument. People drifted away. Bill seemed satisfied and Jacob 32 enjoyed a cigar.

Lesser pulled his hat and coat off a hook on the wall and headed for the door. Irene, as he went by, threw him an embittered look.

Three brothers sprang to the door to block Lesser's exit but Bill whistled shrilly and waved them aside.

"Let the white spook exit out."

The spook, whiter than ever, humiliated to the soles of his shoes but still in one piece, left the loft as Mary burst out of the bathroom and embraced Irene.

Down the block Lesser waited across from a broken street light, hoping Irene would walk out after him, but when she came out she was with Willie. They headed the other way. Throughout the night Lesser dreamed of her. He dreamed she had come to his room and they sat without touching because she was married to Willie. When he woke in the dark, thinking of her, from the weight on his heart he knew he was in love.

Bill, with a low snuffle, came in after work the next afternoon. He sat in Lesser's ragged armchair, thick hands clasped between stubby knees, gazing at the floor. He looked as though he had shrunk an inch, lost weight. His overalls hung droopy over his newly washed bulky green sweater. He adjusted his wire-trimmed glasses and smoothed the bushy ends of his Mongolian mustache.

"I sure got nothing done today, not even one lousy sentence left over to keep. Man, I have a hangover bigger than an elephant ass."

Lesser, sitting motionless, did not speak.

Bill said: "I want you to know, Lesser, that was how I saved your skin last night."

"Saved whose skin?"

"Sam wanted the brothers to beat up on you and crack your nuts for putting the meat to his bitch, but I got you in the game so they could see you get your shame that way and not want your real red blood."

Lesser said he was, in that case, grateful.

"You sure as shit don't look it."

"Take my word."

"I just wanted you to know how I did it."

Lesser afterwards thought it would be better not to know. Not to be concerned with gratitude or ingratitude. To love Willie's girl in peace and with joy.

Sheltered in a doorway late one afternoon, Lesser watches it snow. A black head looms out of the snow, stares at him fixedly and disappears like a moon entering a cloud bank. The black head is in Lesser's. He has been tormenting himself all day about Bill: He has little, why should I make it less? Less if he loves her, more if he doesn't—I wish I knew.

He waits in the doorway above a five-step stoop across the street from where Irene lives, in a red-brick apartment house on West Eleventh. He had gone that morning into the vestibule to look at the name on the mail box: IRENE BELL—WILLIE SPEARMINT. Harry sees a letter in Irene's box, one he has written often but not on paper. He imagines Willie reading it by matchlight.

The letter speaks of Lesser's love. Willie reads it and sets it afire with a match. Maybe he would if he were there, if the letter were there. But Willie's in his room on the fourth floor of Levenspiel's deserted house, hard at work on his new book. Lesser, since the morning after Mary's party last week, has not been able to concentrate on his writing. He walks back and forth in his room, but when he sits down at his desk he does nothing desperately and gets up.

He hadn't tried to write that morning. He had left the house early. He had walked to Fifth Avenue, caught the bus there, then cut over to Sixth. He had rung her bell. Lesser had missed Irene, gone off to a rehearsal. He had gone back home, tried to write, returned after a day of not writing. He had told himself not to go. Stay the hell away. Wait it out. This wasn't the time to be in love. Willie was a complicated guy. Lesser felt he wouldn't want a white man to be in love with Irene.

But he had left the house again to see her.

It's night. It's snowing. After a while he sees the snow. He watches it fall into the street, cover the sidewalks, window ledges, the cornices of the houses across the street. Lesser has been waiting for hours. He has to tell her he loves her or he may never write again.

A church bell faintly bongs the quarters, making the wait longer. Lesser adds up each quarter of an hour. He always knows what time it is. It is past six. At last a tallish girl in boots and cape, wearing a green wool hat dusted with snow over her blond but truly black hair, comes around the corner. Lesser watches her in the snowy light of the street lamp. He crosses the street and calls her name.

Irene looks at him as though she doesn't know him. Then she looks as though she reluctantly does.

Lesser says it's Lesser. Who else can it be?

She wants to know why he had said shalom that day, meeting her outside the museum.

"I meant don't be a stranger."

"Be white? Be Jewish?"

"Be close is better."

"What are you doing here?"

"It's a simple thing," Lesser says. "I came to tell you I love you. I figured you'd want to know. I've wanted to tell you the last couple of days but I've also not wanted to. I think you know why."

She seems not greatly surprised although her eyes are apprehensive, then moved. It's hard to tell; she is after all a stranger.

"I thought you were interested in Mary?"

"I won't say I wasn't. I slept with her for want of you. I felt jealous of you and Bill when I saw you on Lexington Avenue."

She gazes into Lesser's eyes. "Are you in love with me because I'm Willie's Jewish white girl? I mean does that have something to do with it?"

"Maybe. I wouldn't say so."

"Do you want to save me from a miserable life with a black man, an ex-criminal?"

"My love professes no more than love. Do you love him or don't you?"

"I've already told you. We talk about breaking up but neither of us makes a move. He still pits his black book against his white bitch. I see him weekends but we don't really enjoy each other. I don't know what to do. I want him to do it first."

"I love you, Irene, I want you."

"What kind of want?"

"A long want."

"Say it plainly, I'm not very subtle."

"I'd want to marry you after I finish my book."

She is moved, her hungry eyes searching his, yet smiles sourly. "You're both alike."

"I've got to write but I've got to more than write."

Irene listens, then takes his hand. They kiss with cold lips.

"These boots leak. My feet are wet. Let's go upstairs."

They enter the building. Irene removes her boots and dries her feet with a black towel as Lesser watches.

"Take off your coat," she says.

In the bedroom stands a double bed, a picture of a black Jesus hanging on the wall above the headboard.

"Why a black Jesus?" Lesser asks.

"Willie won't let me hang any pictures of whites. I won't hang flower pictures—I like real flowers."

"But why Jesus?"

"Rather than Rap Brown. Is there a black Moses? I believe in God."

Through the windows it is snowing heavily.

They embrace, her hands moving up his back.

"I'm afraid of what we're doing though I want to do it."

"Willie?"

"Also myself."

"I love you, you are lovely."

"I don't feel lovely. I feel off-base, off-key, dissatisfied. I'm also afraid to get involved with another writer."

"You said you were more confident about your life now."

"That comes and goes."

"You're beautiful, Irene."

"I don't feel it."

"Feel it in me."

In bed she feels it. They kiss, grope, bite, tear at each other. He licks the floral scent of her flesh. She digs her nails into his shoulders. He is aroused by their passion.

She comes as though astonished, touched by lightning, whips both legs over his back. He spurts into her.

Afterwards Irene asks, "Do I smell black to you?"

"I smell your sex. Do you feel black?"

"I feel satisfied. I still feel some guilt but I feel satisfied."

"I want you to let the blond hair grow out. Let it grow black."

"I've started already."

As they lie together, Lesser on his back, Irene resting on her side, her face pressed to his, he watches the blowing snow tinkling against the windows and thinks of Bill Spear alone in the vast empty house, writing at his kitchen table. The snow swirls in a white haze around his head.

It's a free country.

LISTEN, LESSER, I JUST WROTE DOWN THIS SONG:

I got this redhot with mustard on it
    I'm gonna eat my meat,
I got this hamburg with onion on it
    I'm gonna eat my meat,
I got this spare rib with BarBQ sauce
    I'm gonna eat my meat,
I got you in bed with nothin on you
    You gonna eat my meat.

Who's it about, Willie?
Bill, Lester, call me Bill.
Bill—excuse me.
Just me and my gal Sal. How do you like it now, gentlemen?

Clouds pile high over the island,
  Thunder crack them nuts,
  Lightnin run out on catfeet,
  The rain pour,
  Wind fly,
  Coconut trees bend low,
  Waves crashin rocks on the shore,
  Dead gulls gonna lay on the beach in the mornin,
  Rotten fish slop in the sea,
  Storm wake up Lesser,
  He hang onto his bed,
  Know it pitch black without tryin no light,
  He try his light,
  It pitch black,
  He run down them shadow-flyin stairs,
  Light Lucifer matches,
  Go in the cellar with a #30 fuse plug,
  When the lights turn on,
  This unknown dude layin on the cement floor,
  One leg sawed off to his knee,
  He layin in front the hot furnace,

His pants leg bloody,
Puddle of wet blood on the floor,
Lesser shriek out,
Can't see no bleedin leg layin round,
He run upstairs to tell Willie,
What he done did see,
He gnawin this white bone,
What that you eatin, Mr. Bones?
Don't shit me, Lesser,
I know your real voice,
What are you eating, Bill?
Breast of chicken,
White meat part,
Honest to God?
Looks like a big bone,
It's pig's foot, boy,
Kosher meat, wanna bite?

Irene moans. Lesser wakes out of unsound sleep and snaps on the bed lamp.

Lying in bed with her one night under the picture of the black Jesus, Lesser wanted to know when they would tell Bill.

"What do you want to tell him?"

"You know what. Either you tell him or I do, or we tell him together."

"Couldn't it wait for a while?" Irene lay with her head in a mass of darkening hair on her pillow. She looked very lovely and it troubled Lesser that she had become apprehensive at his question, her eyes gone somber.

"Couldn't we let it die naturally?"

"It weighs on my mind."

"I'd like it better if Willie tells himself—when he tells *me* it's over. But if it actually comes to having to tell him, I'd want to do it myself."

"The sooner the better or he'll be knocking on your door on Friday."

"Would that bother you so much?"

"Wouldn't it bother you if he expected to get into bed with you? You're not his bitch any more."

"Fuck you if you use that word. It's his word, not yours."

"Whoseever word," Lesser said. "I'm not sharing you with him or anybody. Either you're committed to me or you're not."

"I'm committed to you, though I'm not all the way uncommitted to Willie."

"You wouldn't expect to go on sleeping with him while you're sleeping with me?"

"The sex part isn't what worries me right now," Irene said.

"What does?"

"For instance Willie was here yesterday."

"He was?"

"For a shower. He showered, changed his underwear and left. I was gone before he got out of the bathroom. That's how much sex there was. I sense he wants to leave me though I'll be frank and say that if he stopped writing for any amount of time he might want me again. Not that I'd be available of course. I have other fish to fry."

"Like me?"

"You know what I mean."

She reached for a comb, sat up and swept several long strokes through her hair.

"You'll have to trust me, Harry."

"I trust you."

"Sex isn't the important thing."

"What is?"

"The important thing is what happens to Willie after he leaves here. He hasn't got two nickels to rub together. How's he going to live and write? I worry about that. Willie's struggle to be a writer—from being in prison to actually writing the kinds of things he is, his stories and novel, is one of the most affecting things I know about anybody's life. It moves me an awful lot. He has to go on."

"He will."

"That's what I'm worried about. It's true he doesn't pay rent in that creepy building you're in, but he's got very little to live on—a tiny Black Writing Project grant he got in Harlem that pays him a little bread a week. He and I agreed I would help him till he got some kind of advance cash on his book, but what it's really amounted to is I've been supporting him most of the time since he moved in with me. I wouldn't want him to go back to numbers, or pushing, or anything like that."

"That's the past," Lesser said. "You're dealing with a committed writer now."

"Suppose he has to look for work, when will he find time to write? He writes slowly and needs a lot of free time. He's slower than ever since he met you."

"I don't make his choices for him."

He told Irene he had worked part-time in a factory when he was on his first novel.

"I still had plenty of time to write."

"Any factory would probably pay him half of what they paid you and expect him to do twice the amount of work."

"I worked my ass off."

"Willie'd tell them to shove it."

"Not if his writing comes first."

"I know we're not," Irene went on, "but I have this awful feeling as though you and I are a couple of Charlies giving a nigger a boot in the ass."

"I don't feel that way," Harry said. "All this amounts to is two people—you and Willie—finally agreeing to end an affair. If you aren't betraying him as a man you aren't betraying his color. Forget the Charlie bit."

Irene nodded. "I know it's crazy, but he's been hurt so often because he's black. You've read his writing. I can't help being sensitive about it. It's one of the reasons I feel afraid to tell him about you and me, though I know he has to know."

"That's assuming he'll be hurt. You also said he mightn't be."

"I just don't know for sure. Willie's such an unpredictable man."

"So am I," said Lesser.

The telephone rang: it was Bill.

Irene put her finger to her lips. Lying beside her in the black's former place in her bed, Lesser listened to his voice on the phone.

"I won't be coming around to say howdo this Friday, Irene," Bill said tonelessly. "I was thinking I would but my chapter is down on me right now and I got to stay with it till it lets up and I got the right action moving along."

"What's the right action?"

"If I knew I wouldn't be talking about it."

Irene said she was sorry.

At the same time she gave Lesser's fingers a squeeze.

Willie was saying he'd be around in a week or two. "I can think of a whole lot of things I like to do to you then."

"Don't depend on it," she said quietly.

After a short silence he said, "Now don't think I have stopped feeling affection for you, baby."

Afterwards Irene, her eyes uneasy, said to Lesser, "I guess we'd better tell him, but I want to be the one that does."

"The sooner the better or it might get sticky. I wouldn't want it to mess up my mood for writing."

"Oh, the hell with your mood for writing," Irene said.

She seemed about to cry but when she had shaken that off was again affectionate to Lesser, cradled his head on her breast.

Though Lesser had worried being in love with Irene—Willie in the wings—might complicate his life and slow down his work, it did not. Finishing his book after ten years of labor had of course to be his first concern. But mostly what happened was that he was often high on reverie and felt renewed energy for work. When passing under a leafless maple tree he thinks of Irene and a blessing descends. Then he notices its branches swollen with buds and has this livened hunger to write. Lesser was rid of oppressive loneliness and every dirty trace of jealousy; he felt a fluent breadth to his emotions, a sense of open sea beyond, though he didn't kid himself about objective freedom in the world he lived in. Still, one was, in a sense, as free as he felt, therefore he had never been freer. Because of Irene he lived now with a feeling of more variously possessible possibilities, an optimism that boiled up imagination. Love's doing. It helped him write freely and well after having had to press for a while. And when you were writing well that was your future.

They met almost daily now, yet as though in secret, for although Bill was staying away he still had his key to her apartment and might at any time pop in. If he found them together it might go well, it might go badly. Lesser hoped it would not go badly. Irene and he met in the late afternoons, walked in West Village streets and parks, hunting signs of spring; they stopped at bars and ate in restaurants she knew. They talked of their lives from childhood and often embraced. She was not, Harry thought, truly in love with him yet, but was closer to it today than she had been yesterday. He felt she trusted him, though still not sure of herself. Lesser waited, it wasn't a bad thing to be doing while you were pushing ahead with your book. During evening rehearsals, or performances once the show had opened, he waited for her in a bar near her house. He wanted to see her act but Irene asked him not to come. Once he sneaked into the theatre and watched her in Ibsen for an act. She was better than she said; he'd thought so. She fought her way into a part and that helped the emotion. Her voice in the theatre surprised him; it was lower, stronger than he had thought. Sometimes Lesser waited for her at the movies and afterwards they went to her place to make love. Irene insisted on going up first, then buzzed the buzzer and he, releasing his breath, came up.

The writer saw little of Bill, very little, thank God, considering circumstances. The black, locked in struggle with his difficult chapter, barely surfaced. All day he typed and at night kept his smoking machine by his mattress as he slept. Sometimes when he had to go somewhere, he left the L. C. Smith with Lesser and was then in and out, hardly stopping to say a word. His face was strained, almost stricken, his tumid eyes clouded. He could barely bring himself to nod to Lesser's hello. The writer felt especially bad to be sleeping with his girl—to be in love with her—and keeping it from him whose present pain he so well understood. As though Bill's travail made him all the more victim; for this reason all the more necessary to tell him the truth, whereas, logically, considering the trouble he was having with his writing, maybe it was best to keep the news from him until he was in better shape to hear it—bad news or good.

"Still, once you tell him I'll feel a hell of a lot better," Lesser said to Irene. But she was convinced Willie would almost momentarily appear in the flat to say, "Thanks, Irene, it was real sweet but now I got plans that don't include any white chick, which I am sure you understand why." He had been in again to take a shower and had left a little note of greeting: "Hi, sugar, I took a ten-spot out of your loose change. I will be seeing you soon but not that soon as long as this crucial chapter is still acting up so bad. Chow."

After another week of not seeing him—they were into early April at last—though one of her eyes at times tended towards despondent, Irene was on the whole more relaxed; she was more easily affectionate with Lesser out of bed, as though she had proved her point: her affair with Willie Spearmint—since there was no affair where there was no Willie—had run its course and was dead on both feet; nor had there been any serious stress, rending of garments, nasty recriminations. It was best to have handled it as she had insisted, and if Willie felt like blaming anyone he had himself to blame first.

Lesser once asked her whether she missed the mood, the pitch of black life—as much as she had had of it with Willie. "Some," she said. "But I've personally gone through that bit. I see Mary once in a while"—she gazed into Lesser's impassive eyes—"but I don't really miss those who weren't my friends, though I think of some of them on and off. I liked Sam, you have to get to know him. Willie used to take me to Harlem when we first began to go together and that was like a perpetual carnival or trip all its own. But after one of the brothers had talked to him privately—I think it was Jacob—he stopped inviting me and used to go by himself. He even began to say he wasn't sure that I ever really did understand soul. That hurt me a lot and was one of the things that made me begin to have doubts."

Her hair grew in like a black cap on her blond head. Irene folded up and put away on the closet shelf the two thick black bath towels that were always adrift in the bathroom, and she took down, wrapped in brown paper, and hid, the picture of the black Jesus. Her nails had grown in; she plucked her brows thick and shaped them neatly, sometimes they looked like broken wings; she had redeemed her face, and perhaps something inside her, for she seemed kinder to herself. One day she told Lesser she had made up her mind to quit acting. "I'm not a natural. This present play is my last, I've decided. I want to really change my life. I've had enough of certain kinds of experience."

He asked what other kind.

"Well, you know most of it, and besides that, psychoanalysis.

I bore myself silly at the trivia I give out. My analyst doesn't even try to hide his yawns." She said she was convinced there was little left to say. "I feel attached to him and a little afraid to be all on my own, but I really feel that it's winding towards the end." She then suggested they might want to move to some other city; she was fed up with New York. She hoped to find a job that really interested her, or maybe go back to school for a while.

"Would you consider moving to San Francisco, Harry?"

"Sure, when I'm done."

In another couple of months or even less, he thought, he would have fashioned the true, inevitable end of his novel; it was working itself out—really moving lately. Then a quick intense last correction of only such pages as needed it and done.

"Should we think in terms of three or four, or maybe five months at the latest?"

"Why not?" said Lesser.

Irene said she would write Willie a note, asking him to pick up a couple of cartons of his things she'd packed up.

"You could slip it under his door maybe? And once he gets it, then we'll have to have that talk we have to have."

"Write it and I'll slip it under his door," Lesser said.

When they were in the street, later, Irene kept glancing back as though expecting someone to catch up with them, who would say would Lesser kindly split and leave him with his bitch; but if Willie was around he was nowhere in sight.

One morning after knocking on Lesser's door, Bill, not really looking at him, thrust into his hand a sheaf of yellow papers, about forty. A few were cleanly retyped but most were soiled and smeared, lines and paragraphs crossed out, with smudged interlinear rewriting, scribbling also in the margins in pencil and purple pen.

Bill's face was drawn, eyes fatigued, introspectively bleak until he focused them into strained attention through his granny glasses. His goatee and bushy mustache were badly cut, frazzled, and he looked as though he were afloat in his overalls. He swore he had lost twenty pounds.

"How's every little thing, Lesser? I keep on knocking on your fuckn door every night but nobody opens up. Are you hiding on me or really balling it now you got started again? You young bloods have got it all over us alter cockers."

He winked with weary slyness, his face burnished dry. Lesser felt a quickened heartbeat, suspecting Bill had nosed out his affair with Irene but after a minute figuring he was wrong, he hadn't. She had not yet written her letter. Lesser was still concerned that they hadn't once and for all told him. Jesus, I ought to myself, even now, this minute; then he thought, it's her picnic really. But since he had built up a relationship of sorts with Bill, circumscribed but civilized, he wished, for as long as they lived in the house he could be openly in love with Irene yet on decent terms with her ex-lover, because they were both writers living and working in the same place and faced with the same problems—differing in degree because they differed in experience.

"I've had to get out more often lately," Lesser explained, glancing at Bill's chapter in his unwilling hand. "My writing was sitting in a hole for a while. Now it's out and so am I."

Bill, listening greedily, nodded.

"You have got past your rough swampy place?"

"That's right."

Lesser sweated in holding back what he felt was the reason for his renewed good work.

The black sighed.

"Mine has been smelling up my room for a lot more time than I like to count up. This chapter that you holding in your hand, for weeks I was plowing in a garbage dump, turning up old shoes and broken scissors that other people had dumped and discarded. I was writing like Richard Wright and trying to sound like James Baldwin and that made me write things that didn't belong to me. Then when I finally raised up some of my own ideas they played dead. Also lots of people who jived around in my mind just laid down and died when I wrote them in language. Man, I don't appreciate the fright it throws on your gut when your writing won't go where you are pointing to. Or you are on your knees *begging* it. Not only does that raise up doubts if you really have a true book there; but even though you know you are well-hung and your LBJ salutes when it sniffs ass, you have these rat-face doubts are you still a man. That's no good advantage to your morale. When I open my eye in the morning and see that big typewriter machine staring at me like a motherfuckn eagle, I am afraid to sit in a chair in front of it, like the keys are teeth raised to take a bite out of my personal meat."

" 'None but the brave deserve the fair,' " Lesser said.

"Come again?"

"It's a poem."

"Black or white?"

"John Dryden, an Englishman."

"Right on, I will read it. Anyway, why I came up here is I like you to see how this new chapter chalks up. It's on that kid you read about last time, Herbert Smith, how he grows up on his street in upper Harlem and finds he has got nothing to look forward to but more shit and stress for the rest of his unnatural life. The mother in it was giving me cramps up my ass when I tried to kill her off. I couldn't get her to die right but I wrote it like twenty more times and now maybe she's expiring the way she ought to be. After that comes some other stuff I have my doubts on because it's the first time I used that technique and don't know if I handled it right. That's what's been giving me my most trouble."

Lesser finally agreed to read it, because Bill didn't know he was in love with his girl.

Maybe his reluctance showed because Bill then said in a tense voice, "If somebody doesn't read this real fast and tell me how it's going I'll blow my mind. I was thinking of telling Irene to read it but I've been staying away from her while I was writing about my—about this kid Herbert's mama, so I could write it pure. And besides that, Irene has this shitfuckn habit of saying what I show her is good even when it ain't that good."

"How do you think it is yourself?"

"If I really knew I wouldn't ask you, I honest-to-God wouldn't. When I look at it now the words look unfriendly to me. Could you read it today, Lesser, and then we can rap it over for about a half hour?"

Lesser said he thought most every good book was written in uncertainty.

"On that—up to where the book gets real terrible to write. That's where I have to get off that trolley car."

Lesser, still in conflict, said he would read the chapter after he had finished his day's work and would then go down to talk to Bill.

"It will be a real relief to me to get this part finished off," Bill said. "I been a hermit with lead balls for more than a month and looking to pass some time with my chick. Man, she pestifies me but what a sweet lay."

Lesser did not testify.

"She's a dissatisfied chick both with herself and you if you let her, and nothing much you tell her sets her right in her self-confidence so she stops analyzing and complaining about herself, excepting what you put to her in the sack."

"Do you love her?"

"Man, that's my business."

Lesser asked no more.

"If I get to see her now depends on this chapter that you got in your hand. If you say I have it right or I'm halfways home, which I think I am, I'll goof off this weekend in her pad. But if you think it's—uh—it needs more work, and I agree with you on that, then I will lay in my office and bang on it some more. Well, read it anyway and let me know."

Lesser poured himself half a water glassful of whiskey and gloomily began reading Willie's work.

Since the first chapter was good there was no reason why this shouldn't be, but Lesser resisted reading it. He considered hurrying downstairs and returning it to Bill, asking out for one reason or another, because in truth he wondered if he could judge it objectively. If I say it's good, off he trots to Irene's. Which wouldn't in itself be bad, because she would then and there have to face up to telling him what she had been unable to say before. Either she told him or they were all involved in a tougher situation than Lesser had allowed himself to imagine.

With increasing uneasiness he read the forty pages, plowing through every interlinear and marginal revision; then in a wet sweat rereading every page. In the end he groaned noiselessly and afterwards was unhappy. Though the opening pages were harshly effective, the chapter as a whole, although worked and reworked, was an involuntary graveyard.

It began with Herbert's mother attempting one night to

stab the boy with a bread knife. He was awakened by her smell. When he escaped down the booming steps she stumbled into the toilet and swallowed a mouthful of lye before throwing herself out of the bedroom window, screaming in pain, rage, futility.—So the chapter opened strongly with four horrifying pages of human misery, but the remaining thirty-six, to put straight the effect of her life and death in her son's mind, went badly off. Bill took on a sort of stream-of-consciousness and heavily overworked association. He stuffed the pipes. His rhetoric, though dealing with a boy's self-hatred and his blazing fantasies of sex and violence, became florid, false, contradicting the simplicity and tensile spareness of his sensibility. Here and there appeared insights, islands of reflection, that were original, authentic, moving, but even these he had rewritten so often that the language became a compound of ashes and glue. Part of Bill's trouble was that he was trying to foreshadow a revolutionary mentality, and it didn't always fit. Partly he was attempting in his fiction to shed an incubus—his former life. This was not necessarily bad in itself but could be bad if he insisted, and he was insisting. As a result nobody in this long section came halfway to life. At best the boy was a zombie, incapable, except fitfully, of a recognizable human emotion. His remembered mother, of past and future presence, floated around enclosed in a shallow grave with a breath-stained green glass lid. Death had leaked beyond its domain.

My God, if I say that he'll hate my guts. Why do I keep getting myself into this kind of mess with him? Who's hiring Willie Spearmint to be my dybbuk?

Lesser considered lying. After inventing and discarding several strategies, then deciding to rely on what he had had to drink and another for the road to help him improvise a better one, he ran in his stocking feet down the stairs to Bill's flat to tell him what he truly thought about the chapter before his courage gave out.

He needn't be false or evasive. They had agreed that if Bill should ask him to read any more of his work, Lesser would limit himself to matters of form and would try to suggest better ways of doing what had to be done better. And Bill, on his part, had promised to listen patiently.

He did. Lesser did: fine opening even if not entirely satisfactory chapter. More ambitious than the first, good in itself but no need of this stream-of-consciousness bit—at least not so much of it: it poured forth like lava, heavied up, gave a rock-like quality to the subjective section; which could perhaps be done better in twenty pages, possibly fewer. Lighten, ease up, cut, rework; do this and this, try this, drop maybe this and that, and you may have it more effectively in the next draft. Lesser talked coolly at first, though inwardly questioning his credentials—what made him such an authority on the art of fiction—fifteen years of writing, adding up to one good book, one bad, one unfinished? And in the last analysis could a writer tell another how to write his book? Theoretically possible, but in effect useful? useless? doubtful?—who really knows? Yet, having gone this far, he droned on, both of them sitting crosslegged on the floor, Lesser holding his stocking feet as he talked, his body swaying back and forth in pure sincerity. Bill listening patiently, studying him, nodding gravely, sagely, his swollen eyes, despite a will to objectivity, becoming pinkly glazed, his body tightening; Lesser noting this as he talked on, worrying secretly, growing dry-mouthed as he finished up with a nervous smile. He felt then as though he had just assisted in the act of tossing himself off a cliff. One thing he knew for sure: he had made a serious mistake. I should never have got into giving literary advice to the man. I should have told him about Irene and me. That's what it's all about. What a jackass I am.

Then, as though backtracking, he said, "Bill, I truly don't think I ought to fool around any more with your book. At this stage whatever you think you're doing right you ought to go on doing. As for what you doubt, maybe you ought to wait till you have a complete first draft before you decide what to change. Once you know everybody's past you'll know how to handle their future."

Bill was still nodding, his eyes shut. He opened them to say, still quietly, "I know every bit of their fuckn future. What I still like to know, outside of what you have said on the stream-of-consciousness, which I don't have to use *your way* but have to use *my way*, is have I got the boy and his mama right as far as I have gone? Are they for real, man? Don't shit me on that."

"Up as far as the mother's death," Lesser said, "but not beyond that, in his consciousness."

Rising with a weird cry, Bill flung the chapter at the wall. It hit with a crack, the yellow pages flying over the floor.

"Lesser, you tryin to fuck up my mind and confuse me. I read all about that formalism jazz in the library and it's bullshit. You tryin to kill off my natural writin by pretendin you are interested in the fuckn form of it though the truth of it is you afraid of what I am goin to write in my book, which is that the blacks have to murder you white MF's for cripplin our lives." He then cried out, "Oh, what a hypocrite shitass I am to ask a Jew ofay for advice how to express *my* soul work. Just in readin it you spoil what it says. I ought to be hung on a hook till some kind brother cuts off my white balls."

Lesser, having witnessed this or something similar before, hurried from the room.

Ten minutes later he pulled a hamburger in a frying pan off the flame and shut the gas. Lacing on his shoes he trotted down the stairs back to Bill's.

The black was sitting naked at his table, his head bent over his manuscript. He had on his glasses yet read as though blind. His bulky body, reflecting the ceiling light, looked like a monument cut out of rock.

Lesser, in astonishment, asked himself: self-mortification or cooling off the heated self? Maybe he compares his flesh to his black creation on paper? Or is he mysteriously asserting the power of his blackness?

"Bill," he said with emotion, "there's more to it than I told you."

"I'm quittin my writin," the black said, looking up gently. "It's no fault of you, Lesser, so don't worry yourself about it. I have decided it's no gig for a man and rots your body bones. It eats my heart. I know what I *got* to do so why don't I do it? I got to move my broke ass to get to the true action. I got to help my sufferin black brothers."

"Art is action, don't give it up, Bill."

"Action is my action."

"Forget what I said and write the way you have to."

"I got to move on."

Bill glanced at the door, then at a window, as though trying to determine his future direction.

"What more have you got to say that you didn't tell me?"

"This," said Lesser, as though he had been everywhere and there was only one place left to go. "Irene and I are in love and we're talking about getting married when I've got my book done. We thought you wouldn't care one way or the other because you had more or less broken off with her. You said so to both of us. I wish I'd told you this before."

Bill, as he reflected, began to believe. A sad and terrifying groan, a sustained tormented lament as though erupting from a crack in the earth, rose from his bowels.

"She's my true bitch. I taught her all she knows. She couldn't even fuck before I taught her."

He rose and hit his head against the wall until his broken glasses fell to the floor. His head bounced with crack and thud until the pictures on the wall were bloodied. Lesser, in anguished horror, grabbed Bill's arms to make him stop. The black twisted out of his grasp, caught him in a headlock and with a grunt slammed his head into the wall. Lesser went down on his knees, clutching his head in blinding pain. Blood flowed into his eyes. Bill, grabbing him under the arms, lifted him, and dragged him to the window.

Lesser, coming to, grasped both sides of the window frame, pushing back with terrified force, as the black, his veins bulging, shoved forward with savage strength. The window broke and a jagged section of glass, after a day or a week, crashed on the cement of the alley below. Lesser saw himself hurtling down, his brains dashed all over. What a sorry fate for a writer. What a mad sorry fate for his book. In the sky above the desolate rooftops the moon poured a shroud of light into the oppressive clouds surrounding it. Below, a distant red light gleamed in the thick dark. The moon slowly turned black. All the night of the universe concentrated itself into a painful cube in Lesser's head.

Crying out, he jammed his heel down on Willie's bare foot. The black gasped, momentarily loosening his grip. Lesser twisted out of his sweaty armlock and they grappled, wrestled around the room, overturning the table, the typewriter crashing to the floor. The lamp fell, light rising eerily from below. They circled each other like lit shadows. Willie's eyes blazed, his breath rang like struck metal. They grunted as they fought, uttering animal noises, Willie limping, Lesser struggling to maneuver himself to the door. They caught each other again, the black pulling, Lesser shoving him off. They broke, grabbed, and were once more locked together, head to bloodied head.

"You trick me, Jewprick, got me writin so deep you stole my bitch away."

"Let's stop and talk or we're dead men."

"What's wrong is I forgot to go on hatin you, whiteshit. Now I hate you till your death."

Neither let go, Lesser trying to force Willie away from the window, as the black, with his tense bulk, legs set back to avoid Lesser's shoe, again inched him towards the broken glass.

The door shot open: Levenspiel staring in gross disbelief.

He waved both arms. "You dirty sons of bitches, I'll get a court order."

They jumped apart. Willie, scooping up some clothes, ducked around the overturned table and behind the astonished landlord vanished from the room.

Lesser sat on the floor wiping his face with his shirttail, then lay on his back, his chest heaving, breathing through his mouth.

Levenspiel, holding his hairy hand to his heart, looked down at Lesser's blood-smeared face and spoke to him as to a sick relative. "My God, Lesser, look what you have done to yourself. You're your worst enemy, bringing a naked nigger into this house. If you don't take my advice and move out you'll wake up one morning playing a banjo in your grave."

Lesser twice telephoned Irene as he washed. No one answered. He combed his hair over the wound on his head, changed his bloodstained shirt and hurried in a cab to her house.

When he arrived Willie had been and was gone. She was still agonized. He had come without shoes, had pulled a pair of sneakers out of one of the cartons Irene had packed, laced them on, washed, soaped his bloody bulging forehead. They had talked bitterly. He was bruised, breathless, enraged, his eyes violent. He had left her with a black eye and swollen mouth. She wept profusely, resentfully when Lesser appeared. Irene went into the bathroom to cry, flushed the bowl and came out crying. She was barefoot, had on a black brassière and half-slip, her hair piled on her head, clasped in a wooden barrette. Her mouth was crooked, her left eye black, both eyes wet and reddened from crying. Her earrings clinked crazily as she moved.

"I begged you to let me tell him," she sobbed angrily. "Why the hell didn't you at least say you were going to?"

"There was no chance, it came up suddenly."

"Shit, there was no chance. It's your goddamn pride. You had to be the one to tell him. It's your profession to tell everybody everything. You couldn't wait."

"I waited," said Lesser. "I wait. I waited too damn long for you to tell him. You're crazy if you think he was about to leave you. It would have gone on like this for years. I had to do something."

"I know Willie. I know he wasn't happy with me any more. I know him."

"Who are you concerned about, him or me?"

"I told you I love you. I'm concerned about Willie."

"He tried to shove me out of his fucking window."

She wrung her hands.

"Levenspiel broke it up."

They held each other.

Lesser said he had read Willie's chapter and it wasn't working out. "I told him that and yet I felt I hadn't told him anything. I had to go down and say how else I was involved in his life. That's when he flipped. I'm sorry he hit you."

"He called me filthy names," Irene said. "He said he couldn't stand the sight of me. That I had hurt his blackness. He belted me in the eye and left. Then he came back for his cartons, slapped me across the mouth and left again. I locked myself in the bathroom. This is the third black eye he's given me."

Crying again, Irene went into the toilet and the bowl flushed.

"Willie doesn't like things taken out of his hands, especially by whites. He cursed you and said we had betrayed and degraded him. I told him that what had happened between him and me wasn't all my fault. Then he said he was giving up his writing. I felt terrible. That was when he hit me. This all turned out exactly the opposite of what I was hoping. I hoped he would still feel affection for me when we broke up. I wanted him to remember whatever happy times we'd had, not to leave hating me."

"Don't cry," said Lesser.

"I wish you had let me tell him."

"I wish you had."

"Are you sure you're right about his chapter? Is it that bad?"

"If I'm not I'm wrong about a lot of other things. It's a first draft, so what if he has to make changes?"

"I don't know what he'll do if he gives up writing. It makes me sick to think of it."

Lesser didn't know either.

"I just can't believe it," Irene said. "It isn't natural. The thought must frighten him. I'm frightened and I'm also frightened for you."

"Why for me?"

"I wouldn't want you to be hurt by anyone, Harry."

"Nobody'll hurt me." He hoped nobody would.

"Couldn't you stay with me for a while?—I mean live here?"

"I have my work to get on with. All my things, books, notes, manuscripts are at home. I'm close to the end of the book."

"Harry," Irene said insistently, "Harry, they could easily get at you in that creepy empty tenement. Willie's friends are very loyal to him. They could hide in the hall or on the stairs and wait until you came out. They couldn't do that here. The elevator man watches. If he saw any strangers hanging around he'd call the cops."

"Anybody who's out to get me can get me, elevator man or no elevator man," Lesser said gloomily. "They could jump me in the street at night. They could drop a brick on my head from the next-door roof—"

"All right, stop. Then how are you going to live in the same building with Willie?"

"I don't think he'll stay there now that the landlord has found his place again. But if he does and he thinks things over he'll know I felt good will to him. If we meet I hope we can get to talking like civilized beings. If we can't we're in trouble."

"Harry," said Irene, "let's get married and move either to a different neighborhood or some other city."

"That's what we'll do," said Lesser. "As soon as the book is out of the way."

Irene was crying again.

Suppose he were to marry her and leave the house, abandoning it to Willie? But if he moved out Willie would have little use of it. Once Lesser had gone the wreckers would descend like vultures on a corpse.

Lesser hopped off the Third Avenue bus and hurried along Thirty-first, hugging the curb so he could watch the roofs ahead and duck if a hunk of iron came flying at him.

At the door he hesitated, momentarily afraid to go up the badly lit stairs. A million stairs, five hundred dreary floors, Lesser living at the top. He had visions of a pack of rats, or wild dogs; or a horde of blacks descending as he tries to go up. His head is riddled with bullets; his brains are eaten by carnivorous birds. There are other fearful thoughts. Enough or I'll soon be afraid to breathe. He went up two steps at a time. Lesser pushed open the fire door on the fourth floor, listened intently, holding his breath. He heard waves softly hitting the beaches, shut the door with a relieved laugh and trotted quickly up to his floor.

At his door the wound on his head pained as though struck a hammer blow. He felt death had seized him by the hair. I can't believe it, I have nothing worth stealing. But his snap lock lay on the floor sawed in two. The door had been jimmied open. Crying out angrily, flailing both arms against evil, Lesser stepped into his flat and switched on the light. With a groan of lamentation he ran from room to room, searched his study closet blindly, stumbled into the living room and frantically hunted through masses of old manuscript pages, poured over piles of torn books and broken records. In the bathroom, after looking into the tub and letting out a prolonged tormented sad cry, the writer, on the edge of insane, fainted.

Here's this tiny accursed island.

The war canoe touches the wet shore and the three missionaries, tucking in striped paddles and holding up the skirts of their robes, hop onto the sand and beach the long bark.

The drowsy air is stirred by whispering voices, insects buzzing, muted strings, a flute in the lonely forest, woman singing or sobbing somewhere.

The Headman Minister, in voluminous black robe with leopard epaulets and hood, and the two missionaries in white robes, wearing black masks, wander from room to room of the long hut, uncovering hidden stores. They find the wrecked man's everything: Dutch cheese, dried meat, rice, nails, carpenter's saw, jug of rum, cornbread, compasses, ink and paper.

Sitting in a triangular circle they feast on his dried goat's flesh and drink his spirits. Though not present he knows what's going on. It's that kind of day.

The Headman Minister shatters the empty crock on the ground and rises to his feet.

Bout time we start our mission. Go on and hammer up those records, Sam.

Right on, but is it civilized to break all that music?

Black or white civilized? What orientation do you have reference to?

Just plain human?

He fucked your black woman right in front of your human eye, didn't he? Was that real nice of him to do that crime?

Sam smashes up the records with a rusty heavy hammer.

Except save that Bessie Smith, a Leadbelly he has, and that old Charlie Parker I lent him.

Right on, says the Headman. Now what about you pullin down those bamboo shelves of his books, Willie? And then we will gut the pages out of them.

Willie doesn't move.

The Headman Himself, grabbing the bamboo poles, wrenches down five cracking shelves of water-stained, leather-bound volumes saved from the sea. The books fall with a crash. He kicks them with his leather boots as the printed pages fly all over the hut.

He pulls open the stuck cabinet door. A chestful of yellowed manuscripts rests on folded canvas, formerly sails.

I brought some sulfur matches. Make a warm fire.

He toasts both gloved hands.

Warm day anyway, Sam says, sweating.

Those are old books of his he wrote long ago, says Willie. Both been published.

Then it makes no nevermind if we burn them.

The Headman drags out the chest of manuscripts, lifts the box onto his bent knee, turns it upside down and pours out the papers, shaking out the bottom pages, over the torn broken books.

Make a mighty warm fire.

Willie mops his dry brow. Hot day outside.

Where's this one he's writin now?

Willie points with pale finger.

The Headman scoops up the pile of closely written vellum manuscript pages from the three-board desk in the lattice-roofed outer room. He searches through drawers and cabinets until he finds the copy of it too, lettered out neatly on yellow foolscap.

You ought to burn up both of these yourself, Willie, on account of this cat stole your white bitch and pissed up your black book. Deprived you of your normal sex life and lifelong occupation according to the choice you made. Must feel like you been castrated, don't it? You got to take an eye for a ball it says in the Good Book.

Willie privately burns the vellum manuscript and its foolscap copy in a barrel in the outhouse, his eyes tearing from the thick smoke—some heartburn. The hot ashes stink of human flesh.

He dips his fingers into the cinders and smears a charcoal message on the wall.

REVOLUTION IS THE REAL ART. NONE OF THAT FORM SHIT. I AM THE RIGHT FORM.

He signs it NEVER YOUR FRIEND. And pukes in the smoking ashes.

After a night of grief echoing through the years of his life, Lesser searched Willie's office for *his* manuscript, though that wouldn't be the same thing, not a true revenge, because he had abandoned his novel; but the briefcase with the manuscript in it, or any part of the manuscript, was not there. Neither was the typewriter. The writer ran to a hardware store on Third Avenue and bought a small ax. In rage and mourning he hacked up the table and chair he had bought for the black. With brutal force he chopped at his tasseled lamp as it bled sparks, and slashed his stinking mattress to shreds. Lesser spent hours hunting from floor to floor, flat to flat, cellar to roof, for Willie Spearmint, who was nowhere around. The assassin had fled.

Lesser wandered the rainy streets, adrift without his book to write. Harry Lesser's lost labor, lost time, aching void. Nights he lay nauseated in piss-smelling hallways, sick, grieving, the self to whom such things happen a running sore. Endlessly he cursed himself for having brought home the carbon of the final draft of the book. Each week, for years, he had placed a copy of the week's work in a safety-deposit box in a bank on Second Avenue. The box also contained a copy of the first draft of the novel Lesser had been rewriting with such unutterably high expectations. Nearing the end of his last draft he had removed the carbon of it from the box to have on hand when he wrote the last word and was ready to note final corrections on both copies, one for the publishers, one for himself. Now they were ashes. He saw himself buried in ashes.

Mourning died slowly. It never fully dies for something truly loved. He read an ink-stained wet letter he found in a puddle. In it a man wept for love of a woman who had died. How can Lesser go on after the loss of his manuscript? It isn't all, he tells himself, but doesn't believe it. It isn't all, it isn't all. The book is not the writer, the writer writes the book. It is only a book, it is not my life. I will rewrite it, I am the writer. As spring flared with leaves and flowers, Lesser having cleaned up his room and restored whatever he could, began, against the will, to rewrite once again, working from a photocopy of his first draft, typing two carbons of each new page, both of which he deposited daily in the bank box. This slowed him but after a while he didn't mind. What had happened to him had happened to others. Carlyle had had to rewrite his whole *French Revolution*, the manuscript accidentally burned in J. S. Mill's fireplace. T. E. Lawrence rewrote *The Seven Pillars of Wisdom* after leaving his manuscript on a train. Lesser pictures him running after the train. It had happened countless times before. Harry figured this time it would take less than a year to rewrite the book—because he still remembered much he had reworked. He wrote down major changes to remember. He also had a thick ledger of notes for each chapter the destroyer had missed. Willie, if he could do nothing else, or more, had long ago disappeared. His empty flat resounded silence. Alas that he had ever come to this house. Irene, Lesser rarely saw just now; she said she understood. Tears came to her eyes; she had turned her back and sobbed, her hair grown black six inches down her head, the blond strands fading. Levenspiel, despite his threats, did not bother Lesser much. He had his troubles; for one, his crazy mother had cancer and was dying. He had sent the writer a special-delivery letter offering him $7,000, four thousand of it supplied by the wreckers, impatient to be at work dismembering the building. The letter had read in part, "Considering the circumstances I could get a court order to have you legally ejected for immorality and trying to burn my house, but why don't you accept my sincere offer instead and leave quietly? Be a man." Lesser carefully considered the offer before ripping it up. He listed the advantages and the disadvantages on a sheet of paper and tore that up too. True, there would be little to eat in the course of a year but he ate little anyway.

He sits at his desk in his daylit spacious study, more spacious than ever, typing as fast as he can. He hopes this time to do a better job than he had done in the previous draft Willie Spearmint had so heartlessly burned.

LESSER WRITES.

The skinny ten-floor house next door is being gutted, torn down floor by floor. The wreckage chutes into the green truck-size container in the street. The huge iron ball the crane heaves at the collapsing walls, and the noise of streams of falling bricks and broken wooden beams deafen the writer. Though he keeps his windows tightly shut his flat is foul with plaster dust; he sneezes in clusters all day. Sometimes his floor trembles, seems to move; he envisions the building cracking apart, collapsing in a dusty roar. Lesser and his unfinished book go shrieking into the exploding debris. He wouldn't put it past Levenspiel to blow up the joint with a long stick of dynamite and blame it on the times.

Lesser writes extra hours at night. He sleeps poorly, one eye on tomorrow morning when it's time to write. His heavy heartbeat shakes the bed. He dreams of drowning. When he can't sleep he gets up, snaps on his desk lamp and writes.

Autumn is dark, rainy, chilly. It scuds towards an early winter. His electric heater has pooped out and is being repaired. He writes in his overcoat, woolen scarf, cap. He warms his fingers inside the coat, under his arms, then goes on writing. Levenspiel provides a mockery of heat. Lesser complains to the housing authorities but the landlord resists cleverly: "The furnace is age fifty-one. What kind of performance does he expect out of this old wreck? I had it repaired two hundred times. Should I maybe install a brand new one for one lousy uncooperative tenant?"

"Let him move out and collect $9,000 cash."

The bribe has increased but this is where Lesser's book was conceived more than a decade ago, died a premature (temporary) death, and seeks rebirth. Lesser is a man of habit, order, steady disciplined work. Habit and order fill the pages one by one. Inspiration is habit, order; ideas growing, formulated, formed. He is determined to finish his book where it was begun, created its history, still lives.

A wonderful thing about writing is that you can revise, change images, ideas, write the same book better than before.

Some of it already reads better than before, though not all; and Lesser is worried about the very end. He feels he hasn't conceived it as it should be. But he will, he will. There's no reason I shouldn't except that some endings are more elusive than others. As though, with them, you are secretly dealing with death although your purpose is to comprehend life, living. Some endings demand you trick the Sphinx.

Maybe I ought to write the end now and carry on up from where I left off, rise to the mountain from the plain? I might then feel secure. If I got the ending down right, as it must be, I could collect Levenspiel's bribe, move off this brick glacier and write the rest in comfort, maybe at Irene's?

Lesser has his doubts.

Sometimes the writing goes really badly. It is painful when images meant to marry repel each other, when reflections, ideas, won't coalesce. When he forgets what he meant to write and hasn't written. When he forgets words or words forget him. He types *w*ither for *e*ither all the time, Lesser sometimes feels despair's shovel digging. He writes against cliffs of resistance. Fear, they say, of completing the book? Once it's done what's there to finish? Fear of the ultimate confession? Why? if I can start another book after this. Confess once more. What's the distant dark mountain in my mind when I write? It won't fade from inscape, sink, evanesce; or volatilize into light. It won't become diaphanous, radiance, fire, Moses himself climbing down the burning rock, Ten lit Commandments tucked under his arm. The writer wants his pen to turn stone into sunlight, language into fire. It's an extraordinary thing to want by a man his size and shape, given all he hasn't got. Lesser lives on his nerve.

Irene said she understood, really.

She had at first been dreadfully upset, hurt at the way things were going. She had hoped her life would go more evenly, predictably, than before. "Though what Willie did to you was an outside act and I oughtn't to blame myself for it, I suppose. I mean blaming myself for not telling him we were thinking of getting married before you did. But I do feel guilty at what happened to your book. I feel awful." She was for a while moody, depressed, waked at four in the morning and for hours lay awake contemplating her life, before she fell asleep and slept late. She said she understood only too well how Harry had felt at the destruction of his manuscript, and why he was now so driven in working out this new draft of his book. She had known beforehand his nature; Willie had told her he was married to his book. She said she loved him and would try to wait with patience.

Lesser was grateful to her. Since he worked nights now he saw her weekends only. Saturday afternoon he would pack his shaving kit and a change of underwear, and move in with Irene until Sunday night. After supper Sunday he walked crosstown to Third Avenue and took the bus back to his street. As a rule she did not complain when he left. It was like life with Willie recently, she said with an ironic laugh. But one Sunday when he was tossing his shaving things into his kit, Irene said in sudden irritation, "Really, Harry, all you do is sit on your ass writing. When you come here you sit on your ass reading."

"Not when we're in bed."

"That's the order of things. You write and read and you leave time to get laid, then you head back home. What sort of life is that for me? Why don't you fuck your book and save time all around?"

"The only way to get a book done is to stay with it. Why I read your detective stories is to turn off my writing thoughts, though just holding a book in my hand is enough to turn them back on. It's no fault of intention."

"I'm not saying the way you are is a fault. In fact I'm not sure what I'm saying, I feel that mixed up." She sighed, stroking his face with the back of her hand, "I understand, Harry, honestly. I'm sorry I'm impatient."

They embraced tightly. He said he would call tomorrow. She nodded, her eyes dry.

On the bus it seemed to Lesser that his book was a smaller thing in his mind than when he had thought of it last. But when he arrived home and flipped through the good pages he had written last week, it regained its size and promise.

Lesser sat at his desk and wrote Irene a love letter. Remembering the time of his first love for her, he tried to say honestly that although his feeling now was less intense—life flows, changes, the regularity of sex reducing desire, his book eternally in mind—in truth he loved her and wanted her love. After he posted this letter he remembered he had written much the same one last week.

Irene looked lovelier than ever. She wore tight brown boots with gold buckled straps around the calves. Or red suède boots laced with black laces; and moved with pigeon-toed grace. She wore short thick expensive skirts, embroidered blouses, and hats that looked like exotic woolen flowers. She had snipped off five inches of her blondest hair; it hung now to just below the shoulders. Her eyebrows were more thinly plucked, her pink nails long and smooth, with elongated crescents. She wore complex structures of dangling earrings she liked to look at in the mirror. She had given up her gardenia scent, then tried one new kind after another. Lesser loved to watch her dress. She dressed slowly, a cigarette held loosely in her mouth as she selected things to wear. She concentrated on dressing as she dressed. He wondered if Willie, passing her on the street, would recognize her at first glance.

Irene asked Lesser how long it would take him to finish finally and he said six months though he thought closer to ten. He didn't tell her he sometimes feared the book would fall apart before the end, a fear he hadn't had with either of his other novels. Irene said in that case she might stay on with her Off-Broadway group if they did another play, she wasn't sure. She also thought she would go on with her analysis. She had been about to terminate it but since their plans were unsettled she thought she might continue for another six months, though she felt she knew most of the important things about herself. "For one, I'm not career-oriented; I'd rather be married and have a family. Does that disappoint you in me, considering how many women are going the opposite way nowadays?"

Lesser said it didn't.

"I figure one fucking creative person in the family is enough," Irene said. She laughed self-mockingly. "What a bourgeois shit I've become."

Lesser said if a family was what she wanted, she deserved to have one.

"It's what I want but who deserves anything? Is marriage what *you* really want, Harry?"

He said it was and didn't say more. He did not add, after he had finished his book.

After Willie was gone, Irene told Lesser, she had considered moving out of her apartment, thinking he might sometime return. She felt she could not face him again after what he had done to Lesser's manuscripts. Willie hadn't given back her door key, so when she decided not to move she had had her lock changed. But he stayed away and it sometimes troubled her that she had changed the lock, as though that held some symbolic meaning she wasn't sure of, concerning herself. She was sorry she did not know where he was now and sometimes worried whether he had enough to eat. She would have liked to talk to Willie as a friend, to find out what he was thinking and doing. He had always generated excitement around him when he wasn't writing, or at least was not as worried about his work as he later became. Though in the end he had loved his black book more than he had her, Irene thought of him with warmth and affection.

"Naturally I'm attracted by characters like both of you," she said to Lesser, "men more deeply involved in their work than with me, maybe because that's the way I really want it. That's in my mind although I'm not sure and my analyst won't comment one way or another. Maybe it's because I can't do certain things I admire and want to be close to men who can. I just happen to like guys with imagination, though they can be awfully self-concerned bastards and make life more complicated than it should be."

As she spoke, her expression was restless, her eyes vague, her attempted smile neither smile nor not smile.

When Lesser's funds began to go seriously low he limited his spending to necessities, except for movie tickets and an occasional meal out for Irene and him. But Irene, who had observed he was parting more reluctantly with a buck, insisted on lending him a few dollars when he was short of cash. Lesser accepted, provided she would let him pay her back when he got the advance on his book. He considered, as he had more than once, asking his agent to get him an advance on the basis of the first draft of his novel but decided not to; he preferred to show only finished work. He could show the section he had already completed but did not like to submit part of a novel;

they might get a wrong idea what the rest of it would be like. He couldn't really tell them what it would be like until he had finished.

Irene reminded him that if he accepted the nine thousand dollars from Levenspiel he'd have it made.

"We could get married, Harry, and move to a big apartment with a quiet, well-lit study for you. What difference does it make if you write some other place than this morgue you live in? I'd keep on working and your writing would go on with lots less distraction all around."

Lesser said he had thought of that but the writing was going better now and he didn't want to interrupt the flow of it by having to pack all his things, move into a new apartment, unpack his and her stuff, and have to get used to a new place to work, as well as to a new way of life in marriage. All this would have to wait a little longer.

"I thought you were wanting more from your life than just writing," Irene said. "You said that the night we first slept together. You said you wanted your writing to be only half your life."

"I do and thanks to you I'm less uptight and not lonely. But the book, for the time being, has first priority."

"Now and forever, till death do you part. And if not this book, then the next."

Lesser, searching in one of Irene's bureau drawers for a small pair of scissors to trim the hairs in his nostrils, came across an old snapshot. It was Willie laughing at an egg in his hand, not bad looking without his stringy goatee and bushy mustache despite the eyeball prominence of his eyes. The laugh did it.

"I treated him like a man."

"Harry," said Irene, one late-November night as they sat at her table eating sandwiches and potato salad bought at the corner delicatessen, "tell me what your book is really about. All I know is it's supposed to be about love."

Without revealing much of the plot, Lesser said his book was called *The Promised End*, title and epigraph from *Lear*. He said it was about a writer, a black-bearded, prematurely old thirty-five-year-old man who is often afflicted by the thought that he has wasted more of his life than he was entitled to, or essence thereof. His name, in the first draft, was Lazar Cohen. Night after night he wakes in sweaty fright of himself, stricken by anxiety because he finds it hard to give love. His present girl hasn't discovered that yet but she will. He has always been concerned with love, and has often felt it for one or another person but not generously, fluently, nor has he been able to sustain it long. It's the old giving business, he can and he can't, not good enough, too many unknown reservations, the self occluded. Love up to a point is no love at all. His life betrays his imagination.

Anyway, this writer sets out to write a novel about someone he conceives to be not he yet himself. He thinks he can teach himself to love in a manner befitting an old ideal. He has resisted this idea for years; it's a chancy business and may not pay off. Still, if during the course of three books he had written himself into more courage, why not love? He will learn through some miracle of transformation as he writes, betrayal as well as bounty, perhaps a kind of suffering. What it may come to in the end, despite the writer's doubts, is that he invents this character in his book who will in a sense love for him; and in a sense love him; which is perhaps to say, since words rise and fall in all directions, that Lesser's writer in his book, in creating love as best he can, if he brings it off in imagination will extend self and spirit; and so with good fortune may love his real girl as he would like to love her, and whoever else in a mad world is human. Around this tragic theme the story turns. The epigraph from *Lear* is, "Who is it who can tell me who I am?" Thus Lesser writes his book and his book writes Lesser. That's what's taking so long.

Irene said it was a wonderful idea and she was sure the book would be wonderful too.

"This is an important letter, Lesser, read it over more than once. I have found out I am a sick man, my doctor gave me warning. I have steady biting pains around my heart. Though I gave up cigars it didn't help. My family is seriously worried. Lesser, you have caused me grievous and unnecessary personal worry and misery. But I am a mensch. $10,000 is my absolute top offer. Give it your serious personal consideration. I'm giving you ample notice that I have received in the mail a bid from Tishman & Co. to take over this property for high-rise construction, and I am considering selling out to them. They'll get rid of you in one way or another, leave it to them. Don't think their lawyers are like my shtunk who couldn't get you thrown out for what you did to me. They have the means to deal with the City or send in tanks. You will get hurt more than you imagine. Save yourself the pain.

"But if I sell to them you get nothing—horseshit—and I lose out to capital instead of producing it. Think about this with due deliberation and care, not to mention whatever you have left in the way of consideration for other people's troubles. No other offer will be forthcoming. Take my word, I am finished with you. This is the end."

The building next door had become a huge hole strewn with pale broken bricks and shards of plaster giving off an acrid smell after rain. It seemed to Harry that the house, supported by air on four sides, swayed in a high wind. Cockroaches left without lodgings streamed into Levenspiel's wretched tenement to stay with relatives; also some hefty rats the writer met hopping up the stairs, sniffing as they traveled. Lesser stuffed his food into the refrigerator, canned goods and all; he often ate cold meals not to create cooking odors, also save time. The plumbing, if not actively sabotaged, deteriorated further. Kitchen and bathroom taps gave forth slender streams of rusty orange water he washed with and drank like wine. For two numbing days the hot water turned cold and stayed like ice as Lesser yelled on the phone in a public booth at the Rent and Housing Maintenance people. They advised be patient, the landlord was ailing yet had promised to do his best. The writer cooked up pots of hot water to shave with and wash his few dirty dishes. For a week the toilet wouldn't flush. After trying a few filthy ones in the house, which also wouldn't flush, he had to pay a dime a shot to use the subway urinal until a plumber at last appeared.

One night he was awakened by sirens in both ears, a fire in the apartment house across the street. Crouching in his underwear at the window, Lesser saw a glow in a fourth-floor room but no flames. Lights went on here and there in the building. The street throbbed with engines pumping, squirming hoses, men running. What was burning was quickly extinguished but left Lesser actively fearing his fear: a fire would leap alive in the house and finish off what was left of his literary and other remains. He saw himself fleeing naked down the fire escape, holding to his heart his new manuscript. Sometimes as he wrote he would picture the heavy-breathing landlord touching a match to a rubbish pile in the cellar to see what came of it. One nervous night Lesser descended to the basement to have a look around. He searched through the cobwebbed bins and janitor's paper-strewn hollow former flat. Though he found nothing to speak of he came up tensed. The useless side of my imagination. Lesser muttered against himself for having had his phone removed, stupid time to be saving money. Reluctantly he ascended the stairs. Truly I hate this place. The next morning he wrote badly and had doubtful thoughts of love and marriage.

He had this crawly feeling he had been watched in the cellar. One-eyed man? One-legged? Nasty thoughts. I'd best control myself, one can make trouble for himself. If anyone was there it was some poor bastard who had crept in out of the night. Maybe Levenspiel had hired a nemesis to stretch his nerves. Against the will Lesser began to search out whoever it might be. If bum or strayed hippie he would call a cop and have the cat ejected. Awful thing to do to somebody without shelter but he had to fend off distraction. Lesser considered having the door lock fixed, to control immigration from the outer city, paying for the job himself. He could have the cylinder changed and send a duplicate key to his nibs, who could then not claim in court that he had been boycotted out of his building; but Levenspiel in his present state of mind might have the lock jimmied off to spite him. A loss of ten or so dollars he could not afford after the big locksmith's bill for his flat: three strong new ones plus an alarm box.

Holding the short-handled ax in his moist hand, more as warning than weapon, the writer started at the ground floor and searched each dismal flat. As he rose from floor to floor he found no one present, nothing new. In Willie's old rooms, where Lesser had looked forever out of a broken window, he was astonished to find scattered over the warped kitchen floor the remains of the furniture he had bought for the black and had, in fury and misery of loss, hacked to bits. Lesser arranged the wood into a pyramidal pile. Instinctively he once more searched the closets for some sign of the manuscript of blessed memory. Not a single page resurrected but he couldn't help looking. Much that was difficult to reconstruct in the present rewriting, sometimes impossible, he had written well in the destroyed draft—words, transitions, whole scenes he could no longer recall, squeeze his brain as he would. On the fifth floor, except for some sticks of human excrement which looked a year old, and on the sixth, he found additional nothing. No signs of life to speak of. Putting possible presence out of mind he returned to his work. It occurred to him that he ought to have searched the cellar again. For what—winter?

It is winter.

The wind wails. Lesser listens and warns it to fuck off. Cold waves lash the barren shore. On the leaden sea something's adrift he can't explain. Still suspects Levenspiel's around on one crutch, or maybe his lawyer? Is it a new prowler, smoke rising from his tracks? If I were superstitious I'd be in bad shape. He remembers, as he writes, the disjunct past, fleeting images. Death of his mother in a street accident when he was a kid. She had gone out for a bottle of Grade A milk and had not come back. Death of his older brother in the war before this war. He had disappeared, "missing in action," no sign of him ever. No last word. Still waiting in some Asian jungle for a train? Useless deaths. Life so fragile, fleeting. One thing about writing a book you keep death in place; idea is to keep on writing. An aged father he hasn't seen in years. About time I wrote him again. Once I finish up I'll fly to Chicago for a visit. He thinks, too, of Holzheimer and some of the other tenants who had lived and died in the house before Levenspiel decreed Exodus. Lesser feels an excess of unnatural fears: daily fears that the day's addition to his ms. will be stolen, snatched in the street before he can get it into the bank box; that this miserable building will fall like a wounded hippopotamus spewing forth his lost pages; or the writer will be mugged on the subway stairs and lie there unable to crawl home. There's his abandoned book on his desk being read by the room. The next day—Levenspiel swears Lesser has moved to San Francisco—the wreckers descend, with crowbars rip out the tenement's intestines, heart (where he wrote), and kick in its shell. End of book, era, civilization? Man's hasty fate?

He swears he hears stealthy footsteps in the hall, takes a bread knife out of the kitchen table drawer, foolishly flings open the door and sees no one. Was it somebody real? Negative presence as though on film? The white figure of a black man haunting the halls? He goes to Irene's doctor and is told he is suffering from a deficiency of vitamin B. He is injected at intervals, feels healthier, and writes faster.

One morning as the writer, standing in the January snow, is emptying his wastebasket into the dented rubbish can in front of the building, he discovers a barrelful of crumpled typewritten yellow balls of paper. Lesser, horror-struck, drops the lid with a clang on the can.

Willie's back, I knew in my bones.

Setting down his basketful of torn strips of white paper in the soft snow, Lesser in heavy cap and overcoat, holding his frosty breath, again lifted the lid and rooted around in the mass of rolled balls in the can, unfolding some, reading quickly. Willie's typewriter, sure enough; it typed these stiff inelegant letters. One after another Lesser plucked out and unfolded twenty of surely two hundred paper balls, and carefully arranged the crumpled sheets as well as he could. Some pages were missing, but Willie rewrote so often it was not hard to make sense of what he was saying. There were notes for stories, outlines short and long, pages of fiction barely begun, letters of exhortation to the self, pages from his old novel, pages from a new one about a sadistic pimp and his whore. Judging from the amount of work in the can alone, Willie had been in the house for a couple of weeks, if not longer. Where? Maybe he had been moving from one flat to another. He knew I was looking for him, was he looking for me?

Afterwards, not knowing why exactly, but thinking in terms of better know than not know, once more he listened from flat to flat, not necessarily to confront Willie but at least learn where he was. Lesser had to keep things in order, make plans if necessary. Maybe telephone Levenspiel and have the intruder bounced to protect their property? Still—so long as he writes he's not dangerous, or so it would seem. On the second and third floors, Lesser, moving stealthily from door to door, heard no one. On the third, softly pushing open the fire door, listening with held breath to detect, absorb every source of sensation on the floor, oppressed, he heard at last a faint typing in a rhythm he recognized.

It's Willie come back, all right. Lesser located the flat and stood, on edge, at the door. He considered abandoning the building but where would he go? Through the mess of moving now? Why should he, his novel unfinished? The book was progressing fantastically at the moment. Excellent day yesterday, eight typed pages—rare for Lesser. He sensed a breakthrough—either total recall of some of the key scenes he had been unable to reassemble, or glorious recombination of events to achieve, hopefully, a better effect than before. The right end too. Besides who's the legal paying tenant?

Why had Willie returned? Is it revenge he wants? *More* revenge? Lesser shivered in his coat. He concluded he had returned to write; he was a writer. It said so in the desperate notes he addressed to himself that Lesser had found in the can: "I have got to write better. Better and better. Black but better. Nothing but black. Now or never." He had come back to the house because he had no money for rent anywhere else. Maybe he had returned in order to finish the book begun here? A man liked to stay in place when he was writing a book. You did not want to change around when you were so deep into something.

Lesser worked later that night, later most nights thereafter. Sometimes he stopped to listen, wondering if Willie had stolen up the stairs and laid his envious ear against the door to hear the writer jive-typing away.

He read what the other discarded in the garbage. Lesser emptied his wastebasket in the cans across the street so that Willie wouldn't see his work.

For a while Willie was rewriting the disastrous last chapter of his novel about Herbert Smith and his mother. The boy is fifteen and on hard stuff, stealing steadily to support his habit. The mother is a lush, smelly, wasted, unable to stay sober for an hour a day. Once in a while he comes to her room to cook up a fix; or sleep on the floor as she snores on her urine-wet mattress. The suicide is omitted. She dies unattended, of malnutrition, as

Herbert jerks off in the hall toilet. When his mother is buried in her pauper's grave nobody's there to pretend to mourn. The next day the boy appears at her raw graveside and tries to work up an emotion. He tries to imagine her feelings about her life but soon gives up on it. Sick for a fix, he leaves, but on looking back from the fence, sees a white Jesus standing by her black grave. The boy runs back to shoo the fatass dude away.

This part of the chapter was excellent but that was as far as Willie had gone. Maybe he hadn't faced up to the rest. Maybe he couldn't.

He had written several drafts of a weird, disturbing story entitled "Goldberg exits Harlem." A Jew slumlord in a fur-collar coat, come to collect his bloodmoney rents, is attacked in a dark hall by three old men and a Jamaican woman. The Jew struggles and cries out but they stab him until blood spurts from his nose, then drag his fat body down the stairs to the cellar.

"Let's cut a piece off of him and taste what it taste like," says the old man.

"He tastes Jewtaste, that don't taste like nothin good," says the Jamaican woman.

They remove Goldberg's stabbed clothes and leave his body in the cellar.

Then they go to a synagogue late at night, put on yarmulkes and make Yid noises, praying.

In an alternate ending the synagogue is taken over and turned into a mosque. The blacks dance hasidically.

Willie had written the story at least four times but it hadn't worked out the way he wanted. After another week he was still trying.

He then wrote some experimental pages, one entitled "Manifested Destiny." This went

> black, white, black, white, black, white, black, white,
> (go to bottom of page)
> black, whit, black, whit, black, whit, black, whit, black
> (go to bottom of page)
> black, whi, black, whi, black, whi, black, whi, black,
> (go to bottom of page)

black, wh, black, wh, black, wh, black, wh, black, wh,
(go to bottom of page)
black, w, black, w, black, w, black, w, black, w, black,
(go to bottom of page)
black black black black black black black black black
black black black black black black black black black
(make two pages)
BLACKBLACKBLACKBLACKBLACKBLACKBLACK
BLACKBLACKBLACKBLACKBLACKBLACKBLACK
BLACKBLACKBLACKBLACKBLACKBLACKBLACK
BLACKBLACKBLACKBLACKBLACKBLACKBLACK
(make five pages of this)
BLACKNESSBLACKNESSBLACKNESSBLACKNESS
BLACKNESSBLACKNESSBLACKNESSBLACKNESS
BLACKNESSBLACKNESSBLACKNESSBLACKNESS
BLACKNESSBLACKNESSBLACKNESSBLACKNESS
BLACKNESSBLACKNESSBLACKNESSBLACKNESS
BLACKNESSBLACKNESSBLACKNESSBLACKNESS
BLACKNESSBLACKNESSBLACKNESSBLACKNESS
BLACKNESSBLACKNESSBLACKNESSBLACKNESS
BLACKNESSBLACKNESSBLACKNESSBLACKNESS
(This is the rest of the book).

There were some short poems related to "Manifested Destiny":

White has no glow
No light for white;
Black is true glow
Is lit from in.

I love you
Black Woman,
Touch me
To Love,
Make me
ALL BLACK

Lesser found three variations of a love poem to Irene. He had no idea whether these or "I love you/Black Woman" had been written first.

4.

Irene
Lost Queen
I miss
To be between
Your
Jelly Roll

5.

My bitch was born white
No fault o mine
I am black night
No fault o mine
This chick I used to fuck
Now I fuck my luck
No fault o mine

6.

Irene
White Bitch
You ditch
Black Knight
Willie fuck
His luck
Howdo
Sadeye Blues

Lesser gave up poking around in the can in the snow.

Here's this double wedding going on, that's settled in his mind.

The old tribal chief, the marriage guardian, holding the dying goat, four quivering legs in two big hands, grunts as he lets the thick blood pour from its cuntlike wound over the threshold of his long hut. That fixes it with the spirits. Blood won't make it kosher but the white bride, dark, Jewish, beautiful, isn't really orthodox. Anyway, it's a broad threshold and a lot of red blood.

On this cool tropical summer's morning the white-haired, black-eyed skinny chief, wearing a goatskin cap with an eagle feather on his toothless head, had neatly slit the throat of the noisy he-goat for his son's daughter—the ill-starred gent who went off to America against the advice of the oracle of the Hills and Caves. He died in his blood, stabbed in chest, stomach and kidney in a Boston crap game.

"Feh," says a voice in the rear.

"Sha," says his son.

Both brides had been merrily delivered to the wedding hut by a procession of kinsmen, neighbors, and a few curious strangers. The girls of the clan, oiled and ornamented, had chanted poems along the dusty forest path, to the music of gongs, small drums, and an iron flute played by a cripple, as the sweaty youths, holding long spears, leaped and yelped as they danced, their man-meat swinging like grapes in bunches in their loincloths.

In the direction of the horned daylight moon a slender river moves to the sea in an arc from the restless ocean. The young men stack their spears against the thatched roofs of the huts surrounding the grassless courtyard. The fowl go crazy in the crowd and peck at people's feet. An old man kicks at a rooster. A dry inland wind blows in the ripe stench of cow dung.

"Feh."

"Sha."

A small brown man with scrofulous face and hands, skin like curdled milk, the chief's interpreter for the wedding, who had once in the dim past worked as a librarian's assistant in Whitechapel, says the smell is a good sign. The omen is of plenty.

"Plenty of what?" Willie asks.

"The cow which do not eat do not make excretions."

Kinsmen and wedding guests crowd into the windowless homestead, hazy with smoke from the grass fire. The notables of the tribe in soft caps and brightly colored robes sit on their carved wooden stools. Some of the elder tribesmen roll out goatskin mats and seat themselves crosslegged, puffing pipes and talking cows. They sneeze on snuff. The older wives, wearing ivory ornaments and beads, give high-pitched directions to the younger women as they prepare the chicken and yams and pour out calabashes of beer. Against the musty sides of the long hut the young men and girls lay laughing plans for later in the grass. It's a good time for almost all. The visitors from the distant country, relatives and friends of the white bride and bridegroom, of varying moods and dispositions, eye each other and wait.

The marriage guardian, his indigo toga knotted over his bony left shoulder, sits with the interpreter, their backs to the wall, as the nervous rabbi in grizzled beard and black fedora, stares in amazement at the assemblage. One bridal couple is seated before the toothless chief, the other stands with the rabbi mopping his dry brow with a gnarled handkerchief. Lesser and Mary, wearing less than most, are sitting on a leopard skin. He rubs his arms briskly, gooseflesh despite the fire on the platform that illuminates the long hut. Willie, dressed to kill, sports a black velvet hat and embroidered yellow tunic over his newly washed overalls. Irene, immaculately groomed, her thick black hair drawn in a bun over her left ear, has wound a flowered scarf around her head. She wears long golden earrings and carries a bouquet of white irises and daisies. The rabbi under the silk wedding canopy, held up by split triangular poles of quartered eucalyptus exuding an aromatic sap, is ill at ease but ready for business. He's a middle-aged Litvak, a stocky man in mud-spotted trousers that drip over dried muddy heels. His smoker's nails are soiled yellow, his beard is in disorder, his expression dazed. With furrowed brows he reads the marriage contract over and over, then nearsightedly reads it again.

The chief speaks in a guttural voice to the scum-skinned man at his side and the interpreter's words rise high-pitched to Lesser and his bride. She seems calm but he sees her hard heartbeat under her breast.

"He say. 'When our black daughter marry the white mens we do not rejoice but this is less so bad than if our sons marry so, for then a white woman will turn a man's face from the village and his kinsmen.'

"He say. 'My daughter's father, my own son, he is among the deads. So he ask me to speak with his voice, and so he give her to this white man to marry her. This be of her wish. The bride price, you bring ten cows, do be paid and we make acceptance. I have told this to the wedding gods and say to the shades of my ancestors that she be married before the people of the tribe, not with shame or hiding. The cows are not sick, they are fat, you did not cheat us.' "

The old chief, holding Lesser's image in both black eyes, nods.

"'Our daughter will live with you and cook your food and rake your garden if you plant it for her. And she will born a manchild to carry on your lineages so your name and presence will remain here on this earth after you die. She will please your heart and you must treat her with kindness.'"

The bridegroom, in a smoked raffia skirt from waist to knees over his jockey shorts, promises he will. He is wearing the string of green and violet beads Mary Kettlesmith once gave him, a blood-red goatskin cap, and now holds upright a tall rusty spear.

His bride, holding in her hand a purple feather, says she will be kind. Her silken hair is trimmed with small blue flowers and her legs have been rubbed with camwood. A red necklace, hung in three coils, descends between her succulent breasts. Under a short maternity skirt her stomach is in flower.

"You are married now," the interpreter says, "yet so by our customs the wedding is not done till when the first child be borned."

"It's a long wedding," says Lesser.

"You had your choice," says Mary.

Who has choice? What am I doing so far from my book I have to finish? Why am I giving spades to fortune? What you don't know who will tell you?

The chief speaks again:

"'I am old man of many weathers and you be young. You know more book but I be wiser. I have lived my long life and know what did happen. Well, I have had six wives and twenty-nine childrens. I have oftentimes sat with death and do know the pain of many losses. Listen to my words.'"

Lesser, afraid not to, listens hard.

"He say. 'When the evil spirit try to climb in your eye keep it shut till he fall asleep.' He say. 'Do not push your spear in the belly of them which is not your enemy. If somebody do bad it do not die. It live in the hut, the yard, and the village. The ceremony of reconciliation is useless. Men say the words of peace but they do not forgive the other. He say if you be sure to remember his words.'"

"Tell him I understand."

"He say you will understand tomorrow."

The old chief's eyes fasten more tightly on Lesser's. He listens harder.

"He say. 'The darkness is so great it give horns to the dog.' He say. 'The mouse which thinks he is the elephant will break his back.' "

"I get it."

"He say tomorrow."

"Anyway I'm listening."

"He say to you. 'Eat the fruit where you do find it. The tiger which tear his gut do not digest his food.' He say to you. 'Enjoy your life for the shades paddle the years in swift boats, they carry the dark. Pass on my wisdom.' "

"I will. I'm writing a book."

"He say he do not wish his words to be in your book."

Lesser stands mute.

The chief rises. " 'Go well, you and your bride.' "

Released from his gaze, the bridegroom rises relieved.

The interpreter yawns.

The chief drinks from a gourd of palm wine.

A youth drums a hand drum.

The writer, enjoying life, shuffles into a barefoot dance with his spear. The tribesmen clap in rhythm. Lesser's raffia skirt rustles, his ankle bands clink as he thrusts his spear this way and that to drive off any lingering unclean spirits. He grunts as he lunges.

When the dance is done his poor father, A. Lesser, once a healthy tailor, now skin and bones, an irritable old man in a tubular aluminum wheelchair, says to his sweating son:

"You should be ashamed to dance like a shvartzer, without any clothes on."

"It's a ceremonial dance, papa."

"It's my own fault because I didn't give you a Jewish education."

The old man weeps.

The groom speaks to his pregnant bride. "Mary, I'm short of love in my nature, don't ask me why, but I'll try to give you your due."

"What's in it for you, Harry?"

"I guess the kind of person you are. The rest I'll know later."

"Okay now."

They kiss.

"Okay," says the scrofulous interpreter.

The rabbi intones a prayer in Hebrew.

The tribal talk subsides.

Irene and Willie, under the white silk canopy, sip imported Mogen David from their glass goblet. The bridegroom's parents, white bones in black graves, can't make it back to the old country today; but Sam Clemence, a witness from Harlem U.S.A., despite a bad case of the runs and that he suffers intense feelings of personal loss, stands up for his friend Willie.

Irene's father, mother, and younger sister, a genuine blonde, are bunched together at the side of the canopy. The father, David B. Belinsky, a man with florid face and uneasy feet, in black homburg and silk suit, striped shirt and big tie, manufactures buttons. He smiles stricken. The tall mother sits home all day; she wears a plain white dress, orthopedic shoes, and a blue cloche hat that hides her eyes. Half her nose is visible. The saddened sister is the wife of a successful insurance broker, home minding the business and three small children.

Though the old chief's long hut is not a ship they all look seasick.

The bridegroom, after twice thoroughly searching his pockets, says he guesses he has forgotten to bring the wedding ring. All stare in astonishment. The father breathes momentarily easily but the rabbi says it is permitted to give the bride a coin instead, so Willie passes her a warm dime out of his pants pocket which Irene holds tightly in her palm during the ceremony.

The second time round—the first he listened intently to the words, Willie slowly recites after the rabbi, "Hare at mekudeshet li betabaat zu, kedat moshe veyisrael."

"What am I saying?" he asks Irene.

"I told you: 'Behold thou art betrothed to me with this ring in accordance with the Law of Moses and Israel.' "

Willie wets his dry lips. "That just for the wedding?"

"For as long as you like. You said we'd get married if we had the wedding here."

He nods and they kiss.

The guests shout, "Ya."

The rabbi recites the seven benedictions.

Willie, with two bangs of his boot, crushes the wine goblet.

"Mazel Tov," says Lesser.

The musicians pat and thud their drums, lightly, gayly. A bamboo flute sings.

"Now you are man and wife," says the rabbi. "I feel like crying, but why should I cry if the Lord says, 'Rejoice!'

"Willie and Irene, listen to me. Oh, what a hard thing is marriage in the best of circumstances. On top of this what if one is black and the other white? All I am saying is the world is imperfect. But this is your choice and I wish you health and happiness and the best of circumstances for you and your children. My rabbinical colleagues will criticize me strongly for performing this ceremony, I know this, but I asked myself would God let me do it, so I did it.

"Willie and Irene, to enjoy the pleasures of the body you don't need a college education; but to live together in love is not so easy. Besides love that which preserves marriage is that which preserves life; this is mutual trust, insight into each other, generosity, and also character, so that you will do what is not easy to do when you must do it. What else can I tell you, my children? Either you understand or you don't.

"I also ask you to remember that a wedding is a covenant. You agree to love each other and sustain your marriage. I wish to remind you of Abraham's covenant with God, and through him, ours. If we stay covenanted to God it is easier to stay covenanted each to the other."

"I will," says Irene.

"Ain't no god been in my house or ever was," Willie says. "Like what color is he?"

"The color of light," says the rabbi. "Without light who sees color?"

"Except black."

"Someday God will bring together Ishmael and Israel to live as one people. It won't be the first miracle."

Willie laughs, cries, then stands mute.

"Let's dance," says Irene.

The guests, including the notables, rise, lift their feet, and dance. Some of the youths try to imitate the newly married couples shaking their hips and shoulders but give it up and break into a stomp, shake, and whirl. The women serve a feast of chicken with sesame and tomatoes, roasted yams, and palm wine. Some of the girls, wearing flowers in their hair, dance in a circle. The black youths whoop and shout as they whirl around them.

Those who feel like crying, cry. A wedding is a wedding.

Irene asks Lesser, as they dance a last dance together, "How do you account for this, Harry?"

"It's something I imagined, like an act of love, the end of my book, if I dared."

"You're not so smart," says Irene.

THE END

Lesser lifted the lid of the garbage can and a hot ordurous blast thickened his nostrils. He stepped back as though struck in the face. "A dead rat," he muttered, but all he could see was a mass of crumpled blue paper balls—Willie had run out of yellow. Holding his nose he approached the can. Standing away from it, he unfolded and put together several pages from at least three pieces of writing Willie was currently working on:

In this story, on a hot summer evening as supper smells of cabbage and spare ribs linger in the shimmering air outside the tenements on 141st Street near the river, four black men station themselves on four soft-tar rooftops along the street—two on either side: they stand in an uneven quadrangle. The people on the stoops fold up their chairs and quickly move inside. A blue Chrysler drives up and stops at the curb. The brothers on the roof open fire from four directions at the uniformed black cop getting out of his new car. Two of the bullets strike him in the belly, one near the spine, and one in the right buttock. The cop spins around waving his arms as though trying to swim out of an undertow but is dead as he sits on the bloody sidewalk, staring without sight at a pigeon coop on a deserted rooftop. The story is called "Four Deaths of a Pig."

Lesser found a protest Blues song Willie had knocked off apparently in one draft, "Goldberg's Last Days," also called "The Goldberg Blues":

Goldberg, and Mrs. Goldberg, goodbye goodbye
All your life you been cheatin us poor black
Now we gon take that gold pack off your back.
Goldberg, and Mrs. Goldberg, goodbye goodbye
Your day is gone past
You better run fast.
Goldberg, and Mrs. Goldberg, goodbye goodbye
Comin a big U.S. Pogrom
Well, I'm gonna sing and hum.

He had signed it "Blind Willie Shakespear."

Related to this was a piece called "The First Pogrom in the U.S. of A." In it a group of ghetto guerrillas in black leather jackets and caps decide it will help the cause of the Revolution to show that a pogrom can happen in the U.S. of A. So they barricade both ends of a business block, 127th Street between Lenox Avenue and Seventh, by parking hijacked trucks perpendicularly across both ends of the street. Working quickly from lists prepared in advance, they drag out of a laundromat, shoe store, pawnbroker's shop, and several other kinds of establishments owned by them on both sides of the street, every Zionist they can find, male, female, and in-between. There is none of that Hitler shit of smashing store windows, forcing Zionists to scrub sidewalks, or rubbing their faces in dog crap. Working quickly in small squads, the guerrillas round up and line up a dozen wailing, hand-wringing Zionists, Goldberg among them, in front of his Liquor Emporium, and shoot them dead with pistols. The guerrillas are gone before the sirens of the pigs can be heard.

Willie had rewritten the pogrom twelve times, Lesser gave up searching for more of it. In one draft, some of the black clerks try to protect their former bosses but are warned off by shots fired in the air. One of them who persists is killed along with the Zionists. As a warning to Uncle Toms he is shot in the face.

There was a penciled note at the bottom of the last page of the story, in Willie's handwriting. "It isn't that I hate the Jews. But if I do any, it's not because I invented it myself but I was born in the good old U.S. of A. and there's a lot of that going on that gets under your skin. And it's also from knowing the Jews, which I do. The way to black freedom is against them."

Fog seeped into the building, filling each empty floor, each freezing room, with deadwater smell. A beach stank at low tide. A flock of gulls, wind-driven in a storm, had bloodied the cliff and lay rotting at the foot of it. The hall lights, except on Lesser's floor, were out, bulbs smashed, stolen, screwed out of their sockets. The dirty stairs were lit at descending intervals by bulbs shedding watery light. Lesser replaced the burned-out ones but they did not last long. They shone like lamps on an ocean front on a wet night. No one replaced the dead bulbs on Willie's floor.

One night Lesser, hearing footsteps as he trod down the stairs, glanced into the stairwell. In the dim light he caught sight of a black man with a thick full beard, wearing a spiky Afro like a dangerous plant on his head. Or helmet of Achilles. He looked for a moment like an iron statue moving down the stairs. Lesser's heart misgave him and he stopped in his tracks. When he gazed with eyes carefully focused the man was gone. Frightened imagination? Optical illusion? Could it have been Willie? Lesser hadn't got a good view of his face but was certain the black had held in his hand a glittering instrument. Razor? Knife? Civil War saber? Against what atavistic foe? Not me: if it was Willie he's had his revenge—more than revenge—destroyed my best creation. Reversing direction, Lesser hurried up to his room, hastily unlocked three locks with three keys, checked his dusty manuscript as a matter of course, then searched for something to protect himself with if he had to. He opened the closet door, the ax hung on its hook. He laid it on his desk by the typewriter.

Agitated, hungering to know was it Willie or was another black living in the house—a gang of them?—he crept stealthily down to Willie's floor. His door was open, a shaft of shadowed yellow light falling into the pitch-dark hallway. Who's he expecting? Elijah? Inspiration? Pok pok pok. Son of a bitch, what's he writing now? Boy murdering his mother? Or who dies in what pogrom?

Willie, in six-inch Afro, his bulky green sweater pulled on over patched overalls—Ecce Homo!—his thick back to the door, sat on an apple box, furiously typing on the L. C. Smith atop an upended egg crate.

Hey Bill, Lesser thought in the hallway, moved by the sight of a man writing, how's it going?

You couldn't say that aloud to someone who had deliberately destroyed the almost completed manuscript of your most promising novel, product of ten years' labor. You understood his history and possibly yours, but you could say nothing to him.

Lesser said nothing.

He tiptoes away.

Maybe Willie ascends to his locked door and listens to him at work. This is no rat listening to food, this is a man, a writer himself, best at stories, Bill Spear. What's he listening for? To find out if I have survived? He listens for the end of my book. To hear it. To learn that I have, despite certain misfortunes, impediments, real tragedy, finally achieved it. He wants to believe I have—has to—so he can go on with his pockitying. Finish a book of his own—whatever. He lacks belief in his work and listens to mine for the promised end. If Lesser can make it, then so can he.

But what he listens for I am unable to construct. If his ear is sensitive he hears degrees of failure. Maybe he listens with evil ear, fingers crossed, to hinder me doing what he can't? He could be witching my nail cuttings or crooked hairs caught in a broken comb he found in the garbage can. He wills I crack, fall apart, wither. He listens for, imagines, craves to create, my ultimate irreversible failure.

One winter's night they meet on the frigid stairs. Darkness seeps up from the lower floors. It's Willie all right, though he looks taller, thinner, his face knobby, his kinky hair standing on end. It's Lesser, growing a limp Leninesque goatee crawling with fright. Willie's going up, Lesser, ready to spring if he is sprung at, on his way down. They stare at the other, listening to him breathe, their discrete white breaths rising in the cold. Willie's swollen eyes are the color of black paint, his sensual lips hidden by thick mustache and finely woven beard. His stubby, heavy-jointed fingers ball into huge fists.

Lesser, raising his coat collar, intends to squeeze by the

black in silence, sees them, mutually repelled, drawing aside to let each other pass.

Instead, suppressing hatred, he makes a breathy effort:

"I forgive you, Willie, for what you did to me."

"I forgive you for forgivin me."

"For burning my book—"

"For stealin my bitch I love—"

"She made her free choice. I made mine. I treated you like any other man."

"No Jew can treat me like a man—male or female. You think you are the Chosen People. Well, you are wrong on that. *We* are the Chosen People from as of now on. You gonna find that out soon enough, you gonna lose your fuckn pride."

"For God's sake, Willie, we're writers. Let's talk to one another like men who write."

"I dig a different drum than you do, Lesser. None of that fuckn form for me. You hurt my inside confidence with that word. On account of you I can't write the way I used to any more."

Eyes glowing, he rushes headlong down the stairs.

Lesser goes up and tries to write.

Nothing comes of it. A faint unpleasant odor rises from the paper.

Lesser is afraid of the house, really afraid. Familiar things are touched with strangeness. Green mould on a pencil. A broken pitcher, standing, breaks apart. A dry flower falls to the floor. The floor tilts. A cup he drinks from he cannot recognize. A door opens and bangs, opens and bangs. He tries half the morning to find it and can't. Levenspiel banging? As though the house has grown larger, leavened a couple of useless floors, made more empty rooms. The wind, weird sad sea music, lives in them, moving through the walls as through trees in the woods. It sings above his head. He listens as he writes. Lesser writes "the wind is gone" but hears it still. He is afraid to leave his room, though sick of it, lest he never return. He goes out rarely, once a week for a bag of groceries. Sometimes when he dozes over his work he gets up to trot in the hall for exercise. Otherwise he writes.

Rereading the words he sees scenes he hasn't written, or

thinks he hasn't. Like when Willie plants a lit match in a box of oily rags in the cellar and a roaring tree of fire bursts into bloom, its flaming crown rising through each melting floor. Lesser to save his manuscript—it's been weeks since he has deposited his new pages in the bank box—rushes to the fire escape. The window is blocked by thickly interwoven branches of crackling flames, heavy flaming fruit. Lesser flees to the roof. Around him long spark-filled plumes of smoke, horns of glowing ashes, ascend to the reddened sky. Masses of burning houses in a forest of fires. From close by, like the sound of waves breaking, rise a muted roaring, screaming, sobbing. Who cries there? Who dies there? Riot? Pogrom? Civil War? Where can I run with my paper manuscript?

Lesser writes. He is writing this book about love. It's his need and he must. All he has to do is imagine it to its unforeseen end as he puts the words down on paper. Irene has left for San Francisco. She wrote him a note goodbye, enclosing no address. "No book is as important as me," she wrote. With or without her he has to finish, create love in language and see where it takes him, yes or no. That's the secret, you follow the words. Maybe this man in the book will learn where it's at and so will Lesser. Although if you have to make a journey to track love down maybe you're lost to begin with. No journey will help. Yet better look for something than just not have it. The looking is the having, some say. He'll know for sure when he finishes the book. What a shame, he had written it so well in the draft Willie burned. It seems to him he understood it better than he does now despite the double thought, double labor expended. It was a good book to its about-to-be-end. He remembers almost everything in it but can't get it down again as he had it there. How can one write the same thing twice? It's like trying to force your way back into yesterday. All he would have had to do was reach out a hand, the words flow out of it. I had only to write the last scene and spring the final insight. It would have come, completed the fiction, freed it from me, freed me. Freedom favors love. I'd've married Irene and gone to San Francisco. It wouldn't have been a bad life with her. She respects my work. We might have made it together.

He sees himself sitting in his room forever trying to finish his book as it should be done. If only Willie hadn't destroyed both copies of the manuscript. If only one had survived. He sees it clearly, every word in place. Mourning his lost manuscript Lesser rose from his desk, in misery, enraged. Snatching up the ax, he ran down the stairs, two at a time. He pushed open the fire door and strode silently up the hall. Hearing Willie typing, Lesser, alternately moved and nauseated, stole into a flat across the hall. He hid there, in states of anticipation and gloom, until the black left for coffee, or maybe he had run out of blue paper. Lesser entered his room, read the sheet in the carriage—nothing memorable—ripped it out. Then blow by blow, his eyes exuding damp, he hacked up Willie's typewriter. His blows made a clanging music. He chopped the machine till it was mangled junk. It bled black ink. The ax survived with jagged broken blade. Though Lesser shivered feverishly, he felt for a while an extraordinary relief. He did not care for what he had done; it sickened him deeply, but for a while he thought the writing might go well thereafter.

Lesser, unable to sleep nights, from his window on the sixth floor watches Willie, at dawn, poking into the garbage cans across the street. He had day by day been putting together Lesser's torn strips of white paper to see how his book was coming. For weeks there has been nothing in the can, but Willie still searches. Spring is coming. There is nothing in Levenspiel's deep-dented can either, no crumpled balls of blue paper written by hand. The cans are emptied twice a week, wordless.

The landlord, ill, pale, bad-breathed, began to cover up the door frames on the first floor with sheets of tin. With long nails he hammered them down. A month after finishing the first floor he began to nail the tin over the second-floor door frames. Good, thought Lesser, I'll soon be rid of Willie Spearmint. Either he'll be fenced in, unable to get out; or fenced out, unable to get in. Once he stops haunting this house I'll get my work done.

The writer was nauseated by not writing. He was nauseated when he wrote, by the words, by the thought of them.

Each morning, nevertheless, I held the fountain pen in

my hand and moved it along the paper. It made lines but no words. A great sadness came on me.

They trailed each other in the halls. Each knew where the other was although the terrain had changed. The trees in Holzheimer's room had moved off the walls onto the dank floors in the flat. Taking root, they thickened there and spread into the hall and down the stairs, growing profusely amid huge ferns, saw-toothed cactus taller than men, putrefying omnivorous plants.

One night Willie and Lesser met in a grassy clearing in the bush. The night was moonless above the moss-dripping, rope-entwined trees. Neither of them could see the other but sensed where he stood. Each heard himself scarcely breathing.

"Bloodsuckin Jew Niggerhater."

"Anti-Semitic Ape."

Their metal glinted in hidden light, perhaps starlight filtering greenly through dense trees. Willie's eyeglass frames momentarily gleamed. They aimed at each other accurate blows. Lesser felt his jagged ax sink through bone and brain as the groaning black's razor-sharp saber, in a single boiling stabbing slash, cut the white's balls from the rest of him.

Each, thought the writer, feels the anguish of the other.

THE END

Mercy, the both of you, for Christ's sake, Levenspiel cries. Hab rachmones, I beg you. Mercy on me. Mercy mercy

DUBIN'S LIVES

Max and Bertha,
my father and mother

And for
Anna Fidelman

"*What demon possessed me that I behaved so well?*"
THOREAU

"*Give me continence and chastity, but not yet.*"
AUGUSTINE

One

THEY SOMETIMES met on country roads when there were flowers or snow. Greenfeld wandered on various roads. In winter, bundled up against the weather, Dubin, a five-foot-eleven grizzled man with thin legs, walked on ice and snow, holding a peeled birch limb. Greenfeld remembered him tramping along exhaling white breaths. Sometimes when one was going longitude and the other latitude they waved to each other across windswept snowy fields. He recalled Dubin's half-hidden face on freezing days when it was too cold to talk. Or they joked in passing. Had he heard the one about the rabbi, who when his sexton prayed aloud, "Dear God, I am nothing, You are everything," remarked, "Look who says he's nothing!" Dubin hoarsely laughed. Once, looking not at all well, he said, "This has to be the center of the universe, my friend." "Where?" "This road as we meet." He stamped his boot as he spoke. Once in passing he said, "Ach, it's a balancing act," then called back, "a lonely business." A minute later: "In essence I mean to say." There were times Dubin handed him a note he read later and perhaps filed. Once the flutist read the slip of paper on the road and tore it up. "What are you doing?" the other shouted. "This I've seen before." Afterward he asked, "Why don't you keep yourself a journal?" "Not for me," the biographer replied. "None of this living for the gods."

They embraced after not meeting for months. Nor was Dubin afraid to kiss a man he felt affection for. Sometimes they wrote when either was abroad—a card might bring a letter, but otherwise now saw little of each other. Their wives weren't friends though they spoke at length when they met. There had been a time when both men drank together on winter nights, and though the talk satisfied, neither was able to work steadily or well the next morning. Eventually they stopped visiting one another and were the lonelier for it. Dubin, as time went by, found it hard to bear the other's growing quietude, and Greenfeld did not that much care for confession. Dubin could stand still, look you in the eye, and say some intimate things. Greenfeld liked not to know all.

Although it isn't yet end of summer, William Dubin in a moment of his walk into the country—rural into pastoral—beats his arms across chest and shoulders as though he had unexpectedly encountered cold, clouds have darkened, a snowstorm threatens. He had, in a way, been thinking of winter.

The biographer had left the house in late-afternoon warm sunshine and had casually walked himself, despite nature's beauty, into a small gloom. He imagined it had come from sensing change in the season, one day to the next. August was a masked month: it looked like summer and conspired with fall; like February it would attempt to hide what it was about. Dubin had uncovered bright-green shoots under dead leaves in February. In the woods today he had spied a flare of red in a broad maple. A sense of short season: Northeast cheat. The days had secretly cast off ballast and were drifting toward autumn. Cold air descended to the roots of trees. The leaves, if you touched, were drying. The noise of bees sucking pale flowers, of crickets rasping, seemed distant. Butterflies, flitting amid trees, flaunted their glad rags a moment before generating and expiring. Dubin felt change and could not bear it. He forbade his mind to run to tomorrow. Let winter stay in its white hole.

Beating his chest he flails at time. Time dances on. "Now I am ice, now I am sorrel." He shakes his useless fist.

Dubin, the biographer, a genial angular middle-aged type with a bulge of disciplined belly—thus far and no farther—and a grizzled head of hair, his head perhaps a half-size small for his height, walked briskly toward a dark-green covered bridge about a mile up the dirt road. His arms and legs were long; deep chest; shoulders, when he straightened himself, upright. He had gray-blue eyes, a slender long nose, relaxed mouth; he smiled now, touched by a pleasant thought. The mild existential gloom he had experienced in the woods had evaporated; he felt serene, doing his walk. Dubin had a way of breaking into a run when something intensive rose to think of. He was running—marvelous gait for a man of fifty-six. For a minute he shadow-boxed on the road, desisting when a woman in a passing car laughed aloud. He trotted on, enjoying the sweep of space in every direction. He loved the free pleasures of perspective. Fifty yards from the road, a narrow stream, turbulent and muddy after a heavy morning shower, wound through the pasture. To the east rose masses of green trees climbing New York hills; beyond were the looming low Vermont mountains in misty receding planes. Dubin remembered once, in approaching Capri in search of D. H. Lawrence, the hills like a big-breasted woman on her back, raising her head to kiss the sky.

Remembering his work, he unconsciously slowed to a brisk walk. He'd had thoughts while shaving that he ought to try developing a few notes for an autobiographical memoir—type a page or two to see if they came to life with texture, heft. Or do it the way Montaigne did—you start an essay and thus begin an examination of your life. "Reader, I am myself the subject of my book; you would be unreasonable to spend your leisure on so frivolous and vain a matter." His smile turned into snicker when he foresaw Kitty's judgment: "Why bother when there are so many unusual lives to write about?" She'd be right although any man speaking truthfully about his life should be worth reading. Still, no sense thinking about it until he had completed the Lawrence he was, after years of research, about to start writing. "My God, whatever brought me to him?" After several steps he ran on, a little in fright.

He was running lightly, forearms loosely lifted, watching a wheeling flight of birds—grackles?—when an orange VW with a battered door and a soiled cracked windshield—it looked as though it had passed through the bird flight—roared out of the covered bridge, came to a halt, abruptly started forward, at last pulled jerkily to a stop at Dubin's side. He felt a flash of recognition on beholding the driver but it came to nothing: she was a stranger.

The young woman begged his pardon in a voice he would surely have remembered, vaguely drawing down her skirt over bare thighs. She was braless, her face attractive; he had noticed a few darkish blond hairs on her chin. Her loose fair hair she wore long; the well-formed sturdy body was feminine, appealing. A half-eaten yellow pear lay on the seat beside her but if she had enjoyed the fruit it no longer showed. The girl's curious eyes, he thought, were uneasy, as if she was staring at last night's dream instead of only good-willed Dubin. She wore wire-framed blue-tinted glasses that muddied her green irises, he saw when she removed them. Her smile was nervous, mouth sour in repose. From habit he tried to imagine her past but made no headway. Her first glance at him had seemed tight, as though she was calculating whether his visible interest went beyond what the moment required; or she wanted not to be quickly read by anyone who could possibly read; then her focus shifted, gaze eased; she asked if she was on the right road to town. She had, out of the window, touched his arm.

Dubin, pleased by the gesture, pointed a helpful finger in the direction he had come. "Take the left of the fork."

The girl nodded. This was no comfortable lady despite nature's favor of an impressive body and on-the-verge-of-beautiful face. Whatever she had she seemed to want less of. He was about to walk on but she was still unsure where to go. Dubin gave her a good word: "A lovely day." He was a deep-voiced man with a tentative laugh.

"Some would say so."

"Not you?"

She did not reply.

"Be kind to yourself." He had stammered as a child, and the impulse to on occasion converted itself into a mild hoarseness of expression, sometimes a self-conscious laugh. Dubin cleared his throat.

She gave him an almost sullen look.

"Why do you say that?"

A man behind them, in an Oldsmobile with Jersey plates, honked to pass. "Whyn't you make love in bed?"

The girl burst into a nervous laugh.

Dubin told her he had no idea and hurried on.

It later occurred to him that the disquiet lady had been wearing a Star of David on a thin gold chain around her neck. If they had spoken names might they have touched lips?

Ah, Dubin, you meet a pretty girl on the road and are braced to hop on a horse in pursuit of youth.

There he stood by the tree that had wounded him.

The blow on the head and broken bones were not the wound; they had evoked the wound, he had thought a minute after his car had struck the tree—the aftermath when one cursed himself for suffering the wound. Dubin had tramped through the booming bridge, where the muddy stream turned west and he east, and was again at the point of the road he still shunned, twenty feet from the highway: it had iced up during a freezing late-fall rain last year and Dubin, on a trivial morning errand—a container of milk Kitty had forgotten to buy—slid into an accident. His thoughts had hardly changed. The car spun like an arrow on a board and the biographer—as if trying to foretell the future: what begins with a wound?—had struck a tree, the last lining the road—another foot and he'd have skidded to a stop in the dead grass.

He had not at first felt pain as blood streamed down his face. He had stumbled to the highway waving his left arm, the other cracked at the wrist, bloody nose broken, right knee cut. It had seemed to him hours before anyone stopped to pick him up. Three drivers had seen him and sped by—"Fools!" Dubin had cried in astonishment. She who had stopped for him was a girl in her late twenties in a red Pinto, on her way to work. He had felt ashamed to be bleeding in her car. It was years since he had seen his own blood flowing and he wondered if it was a portent; but nothing came of it except a week of pain and a mild depression for not being able to work.

Through his bleeding nose he could smell her incisive blooming perfume. Some responses have no respect for circumstances, characteristic of Dubin.

He told her his name. "I'm a biographer." And laughed embarrassedly. "Sorry to be messing your upholstery."

"It'll wash off—do you feel much pain?"

"Curiously not. I will, I'm sure."

"I'm Betsy Croy."

"Charmed. What do you do?" Dubin asked her, mopping with his handkerchief the blood dripping down his head. Better to talk.

"I bookkeep. What did you say you do?"

"Write lives—Mark Twain, Thoreau—others." He smiled foolishly; she didn't know the name.

Betsy drove awhile in concentrated silence, then said hesitantly, "I married this boy from my high school class when we graduated. Now he's twenty-eight and has got impotent."

"A shame," Dubin replied. "The composer Mahler was helped in similar circumstances by a long walk with Freud in Leiden—that's in Holland. If he hasn't already, your husband ought to talk to a doctor."

"He has but it did no good." She said nothing more.

Dubin was moved to offer his services but surely not now; he bled quietly.

Afterward he had stupidly forgotten to thank her, express heartfelt gratitude for her kindness; he had wanted to send her flowers. Dubin had visited the State Police, hoping her address might appear on the accident report. It did not. Occasionally he dreamed of her. He had for an instant thought this was she whom he had just met on the road; she was another.

The bark of the oak had been obscenely skinned for months after he had hit it. Although an accident on the road was sooner or later almost certain, given the hard wintry weather and frequency of mishap, Dubin had felt insulted by fate. A year later he would still not look at the tree as he walked or drove by.

He ran across the highway when traffic let up, wobbling as his arthritic knee tightened, and limped a minute after entering a theoretically hard-topped road—subject to winter potholes, spring mud—then went on with his country walk. Dubin thought of it as circular although it was in fact an irregular quadrilateral on the county map. He strode on at a steady pace, refreshing his lungs, exhaling with pleasure. He had put this walk together years ago—the long walk—and his route rarely varied. The short walk went to the bridge and back, about a mile each way. He left by the kitchen door; across the back lawn into a grove of tall gray-trunked silver maples with slender sharp-pointed leaves—gave the elegant effect of elms but less lyric, more grandeur—through a broad field with a pliant path he had worn into it; then, past the old barn, into the sunlit, still, pine-scented wood, drama of white birch with evergreen; in addition, sugar maples, aspen, ash. Kitty called it "Kitty's Wood" because she'd been in it first; explored it while he was unpacking his books after they'd moved into the house. And then up the road to the covered green bridge.

The walk he was into now Dubin estimated an additional

four miles, the whole taking about an hour and a half or three quarters, unless he hurried. The way not to hurry—to enjoy nature, not suffer obsession—was to go the short walk; but sometimes he hurried the long. He felt he was taking his time today when he had the thought—sensation—that the road was coming at him counterclockwise—moving as though the journey hastened its end. Dubin's mind ran ahead of itself. What's my hurry to get back? What must I do that I haven't done? The truth was he hadn't meant to take the long hike today and was probably hitting it up unconsciously; he had meant at the bridge to turn back but walked on remembering his accident. And Betsy Croy.

As he hastened on he warned himself to be attentive to what's present, namely nature. If you looked without seeing, the walk was more of the same—the same subjectivity. The good of it beyond exercise was that it changed the mind's scenery after a day's work. He felt uneasy when not observing—the big ones missed nothing, had eyes that remembered. Thoreau: "The perception of beauty is a moral test." More test than moral but one ought to look. The road came at him in slow motion—he tried to explain it but couldn't. What's happening today that hadn't yesterday? Only this moving road, a device of time hurrying me home. Dubin runs to do what's next. The way to counteract forgetting to look was to join up—take courage in both hands, move your ass off the confining road, be involved. Hop a wall; follow a stream through pasture—what's so sacred about private property when it's all God's earth? Walk up a hill; enter sunlit wood; swim bareass in a pond reflecting day's eye. Walk home wet in dry clothes.

When had such happened lately? He could count the times on one finger. I rarely leave this road. Now and then a picnic under Sunday-evening trees. Sometimes I cut in along an old path to the pond in the quarry. Wild flowers scattered in clusters along the way. Once, with Kitty, we climbed Mt. No Name with the kids—walked up the low north flank. They'd been summer people who had stayed on. City people—Dubin from Newark and Bronx tenements, Kitty originally from Montreal; she had also lived in Augusta, Maine, with her grandmother. Dubin, after a decade and a half in Center Campobello, could recognize and name about twenty trees, a half dozen bushes, fifteen wild flowers, a handful of birds. He followed the flight of a crow elated to know who was flying. He had slowly learned to look, name things of nature. When he passed a flower he told himself to take it all in. What he couldn't name, or when names slipped his mind, he asked Kitty. She saw the flower whole—corolla, stalk, the shape of its leaves. He felt for a moment bereft.

In sum, William Dubin, visitor to nature, had introduced himself along the way but did not intrude. He gazed from the road, kept his distance even when nature hallooed. Unlikely biographer of Henry David Thoreau—I more or less dared. Even in thought nature is moving. Hunger for Thoreau's experience asserted itself. Besides, great men are men; a genius in doubt is a man in doubt—I got close to his human nature. Thoreau gave an otherwise hidden passion and drew from woods and water the love affair with earth and sky he'd recorded in his journals. "All nature is my bride." His biographer-to-be had been knocked off his feet on first serious encounter with nature, a trip to the Adirondacks with a school friend when they were sixteen. Before that he had hungrily sought signs—promises?—of the natural world on city streets and found, in walks out of his neighborhood, private houses with flowers on lawns; hedges; trees; and the dead leaves he was surprised to find in summertime. As a young man he had lived much in public parks; had sought, if not his bride, his bride's cousin? The first time in the mountains had turned him on in the manner of the Wordsworthian youth in "Tintern Abbey": "The sounding cataract haunted me like a passion." Dubin, haunted, had been roused to awareness of self extended in nature, highest pitch of consciousness. He felt what made the self richer: who observes beauty contains it. One is stabbed by the miraculous creation and interwoven whole. He wanted nature to teach him—not sure what—perhaps to bring forth the self he sought—defined self, best self? Nature compelled him to feel what he hadn't felt so well before: "the shaping force," Hardy called it. He never forgot this although the experience, infrequently renewed, had diminished as youth had. My God, how nature moved me. Now "that time is past," as Wordsworth had felt it. Now, on the whole, in varying moods Dubin looked at scenery, and scenery, in varying moods, looked at him. But in his heart he still expected something he could not define. If you dared look you earned seeing. Dubin did his walks in nature's presence.

Still, what nature had meant to him, though not only nature, had inspired him to undertake and ultimately complete a fine life of H. D. Thoreau. In his mind he flipped through pages: close portrait of the solitary sensuous man, privately wounded, who lived on wonder, observed the bald fact and spun metaphor and myth out of nature. In his writing he celebrated his consciousness identified with the Absolute. *Walden* was a lied of death and song of resurrection: Thoreau had it both ways. Now and then someone argued the book was not literally true; it was fictitious: In truth, the man went home often to see his mama. If so, Dubin thought, it was nonetheless a masterpiece, nonetheless inspiring. It had stirred the imaginations of Proust and Yeats. How can it be less than it is? You write sentences and men are sensibly affected. Dubin, proud of the biography, contemplated with confidence his present work on D. H. Lawrence. Do the primitive labyrinth of the man, mystic flame-boiled essence, bloody simple human self.

He warned himself then as he often did, although it came to not much, that a good writer adventures beyond the uses of language, or what's there to put into words? Yet the truth is some do not: of them Dubin is one. As though to make up for his limitations, from his pants pocket he dug out one of his impulsive notes to himself: "Everybody's life is mine unlived. One writes lives he can't live. To live forever is a human hunger."

He was running. As the road dipped the hills rose. In spring light-green foliage raced up the rumpled hills and by June covered the scabrous shoulders of the mountains. Dubin trotted on the road going south. In the distance white clouds moving above patches of sunlight on the hills. The land sloped up to a line of trees advancing on him like a marauding army. For a while the wood rode on his head. Dubin rose on the road as the hills sank; he settled into a fast walk. A sparse quarter mile of old houses went by as on a rusty turntable, then broad fields with now and then a stark farmhouse, upright and spare to a point of principle—with weather-beaten barns, red or black silos, Angus and Herefords on cow paths in the pasture.

Dubin liked to come by on rainy late-afternoons to see the steaming swollen-uddered cows lying in the wet waiting to be milked. When he passed in light fog, the ripe hot smell of cow dung from a barn nearby assailed him across the field—he knew where he was. One night, driving the road alone, he saw a cow cropping grass in moonlight. The farmland around gave pleasure: each neat walled field, each shifting shade of brown beige and green; furrowed, cultivated, harvested, plowed under: order of uses of men, animals, seasons eternal.

Robert Frost and his doomed brood had lived a summer on one of the farms not far away, and Dubin, long after the fact, had talked with his neighbors in Vermont and written an article: "Frost, the Season of His Wife's Death." The poet had been hard on her. His will, it had been said, could tolerate no other wills around. "Elinor has never been any earthly use to me." She had kept him from her bedside while she was dying. He waited in the corridor, saw her only when she was asleep, unconscious; dead. He'd had no last word from her. Her defense was silence. "She was not as original as I in thought but she dominated my art with the power of her character and nature." Dubin occasionally visited their anguished grave in a churchyard a dozen miles away. They were together now in the vault under the tombstone; their ashes were, with the remains of those of their children who were not buried elsewhere, although all their names were incised on the stone. "There's only one subject for a poem," Frost had said. Dubin had laid a small white stone on the marble tombstone.

The biographer had once wanted to do a full-length life of the poet and had written him a letter requesting a talk if he was interested. But the old man wrote back he had already chosen someone "to preserve my immortal remains." "I'd rather be in the hands of a man whose spit I'd seen." Dubin, after going through her papers in the N.Y. Public Library, had considered the life of Virginia Woolf, whose intelligent imagination and fragile self had drawn him to her; but her own nephew, Quentin Bell, was already into a biography of her. Dubin had then thought of D. H. Lawrence, a complex type with tormented inner life, if that's who you felt you had to get involved with.

Thinking of the biographies he had written, in particular

Short Lives in a single volume, he felt a sadness come into him. Completed, most lives were alike in stages of living—joys, celebrations, crises, illusions, losses, sorrows. Some lives accomplished much, some very little. One learned, as he wrote, the arcs, forms, consequences of the flight of lives. One learns where life goes. In fact he led them there. When you know the end the rest moves up only too quickly. Therefore, Dubin, what's on your mind? That he was about to create a new life would in the end shorten his own? When the work was done he was that much older—more serious matter than a decade ago. He had sacrificed to his labors that many hours, that many years. Prufrock had measured out his life with measuring spoons; Dubin, in books resurrecting the lives of others. You lost as you gained; there's only one subject for a poem.

The last part of the country walk went west before it turned south again on an upward pitch to the highway, a length of solitary shaded road heavily wooded on both sides. Overhead, lightly laced branches touched and intertwined. The road was cool in the green shade, the air fragrant. Dubin breathed. He tramped on in the light-green dark. No sound except him walking along thinking his thoughts. At one place on the deserted road he broke into a run. He had more than once encountered a dog racing at him across a field, or bursting out of the woods, teeth bared, growling in its belly. His response was sternly to say, "Go home, boy," and hope for the best. Mostly they wandered away as he walked on; but he feared meeting an animal with no respect for human language. A black German shepherd had all but treed him once—his back against a tree, the hound snarling when Dubin attempted to inch forward. He'd been trapped a mad long time but kept the dog off by talking to it, his heart where it needn't be, telling it the story of his life. At last it yawned and trotted off. In afterthought it had seemed that a cardinal's shrill call, sounding much like a man whistling for his dog, had sent the animal on his way. Dubin waved to the invisible red bird in the trees. He's been set running by the thought of the dog and was running now. "Why, then, should man hasten as if anything less than an eternity were allotted for the least deed?" Who says?

As he ran, the road had stopped moving and he slowed to a walk. A reddish-brown bitch followed him, a shaggy Irish setter who sometimes appeared, a friend of the people. Ahead, where the bushes rose fifteen feet high on one side of the road, and the trees moved into the downsloping wood on the other, he observed a moving figure. It was Greenfeld in white cap and shirt, ambling along. He often carried his flute or recorder and would play as he walked. Dubin would hear a song in the trees. The flute got gut-close to primitive lament. "Ach, ich flöte." Greenfeld did one thing and did it well, not a bad way to live a life. Not now in a mood to listen or be listened to—he felt a hunger for solitude—the biographer stepped behind a tree until the flutist had passed by.

Some other time.

He was looking at a grove of evergreens below—a pleasure to gaze down at the pointed tops of trees—and a little farther on turned as the road grew level and approached the highway. Soon country merged into village, not a charming sight. After departing the highway Dubin walked north on an old sidewalk of broken slate. Center Campobello was a town of 4,601 souls in New York State, almost a mile from the Vermont border. He had lived there fifteen years, unknown to most: Wm. B. Dubin, who wrote lives, and who, it said in *Newsweek*, had once received a medal from President Johnson. There was a picture of them shaking hands. He recalled the clutch of the man's big paw. At the courthouse he turned and walked toward a crimson sunset until he came to the edge of town: his three-story yellow clapboard house with black shutters and wrought-iron widow's walk on the roof. A porch with white pillars ran half the length of the rear of the house. Dubin began his daily walk at the back door and returned from it, as from a journey, by the front.

He went around to the rear but Kitty was not in her garden. Dubin studied the dead elm coming down next week. And a skimpy-leaved maple was expiring—"maple decline" the tree man called it. "Save money cuttin' them both down the same time." Dubin thought he'd wait till the maple was properly dead. Emerson had counted one hundred and twenty-eight trees on his property, lamenting they must ultimately fall. Dubin had counted sixty-one on his nine acres. Emerson could name every one of his trees; not Dubin. The biographer entered the house, called his wife, and when there was no reply, walked up the stairs. He stood solemnly in Gerald's old room, then in Maud's. Later he heard Kitty come into the house and she called up that they had a new cleaning person. "That's what she calls herself. I advertised today and she phoned while you were on your walk. Would you like your supper hot or cold? I feel dreadfully hot."

Dubin, in his study, had picked up his marked copy of *Women in Love.* A wasted walk, he had wanted to work.

"Why do you berate yourself in the poor mirror?" Kitty had asked.

"Because I'm handsomer in my mind than when I look in the glass."

"Don't look," she had said.

Rubbing in shaving cream, he was this morning in the bathroom mirror a solemn gent earnestly expostulating. "Next time round I'll do a comic life. Mark Twain's wasn't all that funny."

"Shush," Dubin warned himself, then remembered Kitty had left their bed. He tried to hold down the talk when she was in the bedroom because—if she was awake or it woke her—it made her uneasy; still, after these many years. If you shouted, groaned, or muttered for no apparent reason, or gestured Up Yours in her presence, you were showing loose ends, reminding her of hers. She would rather not be reminded. Kitty, when Dubin rambled on, made clicking noises with her tongue. He would then shut up, though he had more than once reminded her that Montaigne himself used to groan "Confounded fool" in the morning mirror. And Dr. Samuel Johnson was a noisy beehive of crackpot mannerisms.

"I'm not married to them."

"Montaigne's motto was, 'What do I know?' He was a wise man. And Johnson—'winking and blinking,' Blake described him—though he looked like a mad hatter, inspired men to reason and courage. He had learned from life."

"It's your voice I hear, not theirs."

He beheld in the mirror, under stress of course—like this morning beginning a new biography—a flash of himself in his grave, and with a grimace clutched his gut where he had been stabbed. "Papa," he cried, wishing he had done things better, and made unhappy gestures of evasion and shame that irritated Kitty when she observed them. He would strike his chest with his fist, point at the sky; his nose twitched like a rabbit's. Or he would intone a single sentence like: "My daughter never learned to waltz." That, after six times, would awaken Kitty; she asked through the closed bathroom door what it meant. Dubin pooh-poohed it all. But here he was at it again—a relief this particular morning, conversing with himself at length, glad she had got up and gone out, rare thing for her to do this early in the day. Through the window he watched her contemplating her flowers in thinning mist on the ground. Kitty, wearing blue sneakers and faded pink straw gardening hat, though there was no sun to speak of, looked up and casually waved. The biographer lifted his razor like a sword in salute.

When he arose at seven, usually she slumbered on. Kitty slept raggedly and liked to pick up an hour or more at the morning end. Her sleep, after a fairly decent springtime interval, had got worse in summer. She slept deeply awhile, then was restlessly awake for hours; and slept again in the early morning before Dubin awoke. He left her lying on her stomach, wound in a sheer nightgown, the coffee au lait birthmark on her buttock a blemished island, visible when it was too hot for sheet or blanket. Though she tended to deny it—this depended on how well she was presently treating herself—her figure was good, despite large slender feet and thin shoulders. Kitty, brown hair fading, was still an attractive woman. She said she slept best mornings, when he was no longer in bed; and her most memorable dreams were morning dreams.

He had asked her recently what she thought about when she was awake and she said, "Lately the kids again—mostly. Sometimes silly things like a pair of shoes I paid too much for. Or a clerk who said something rude to me. Or I wish I had been born beautiful, or could lose weight. Some worthless things grind on all night." "Hemingway prayed when he couldn't sleep," Dubin said; "he fished and prayed." "If I prayed it would have been to be more purposeful, organized, kinder. One would have liked to do less harm." "To whom?" "Anyone.—To Gerald," Kitty confessed. He asked her if she thought of death. "I think of those who've died. I often play back my life." Sometimes she went downstairs to read if the house wasn't too cold. She'd rather not read because it woke her thoroughly and she could afterward not find her way back to sleep. She lay listening to the singing bird-world in the 5 A.M. trees. Or sometimes wept that she wasn't sleeping. Once in winter Dubin woke to soft stringed music and went downstairs to find her playing the harp in the dark.

Last night she'd waked him to say she had dreamed of Nathanael, her first husband. "This is the second time this month and I don't think I've dreamed of him in years. We were on our way somewhere, maybe to church to get married. He was young, about his age when I met him, and I was my age now. Somehow I was pregnant, though I couldn't tell whether it was with Gerald or Maud—that's what made the dream so weird. I wanted to say I couldn't go with him, I was living with you, but then I thought Nathanael's a doctor, he'll know. What a mishmash. What do you make of it?"

"What do you?"

"You're better at dreams."

"Did it frighten you?"

"Nathanael wouldn't frighten me."

"Then why wake me up? I've got to start my Lawrence this morning."

"I woke up, thought of the kids gone."

Dubin said that could be what it was about. "The kids are gone. You're floating around with time on your head. You want to be young again."

"People are always leaving," she yawned.

Irritated, he tried to sleep—the curse of an insomniac wife. Kitty crept close and held him; Dubin ultimately slept.

The house, she often complained, was all but empty. "Get some kind of work," he had advised, and now after months of unsatisfactory seeking she was reluctantly working as a volunteer in the town clerk's office. "I stop thinking when I go there." "You're overqualified," Dubin said. "I feel underqualified." She complained she had accomplished little in life. "I have no true talents, I've tried everything." He had given up arguing with her about her life.

Mornings she was active, sleep or no sleep, though she dawdled as she dressed. "Thank God, I have energy." Dubin, after half a night's loss of sleep, had to conserve his. Kitty went to the stores before noon, did her husband's errands, phoned friends—always Myra Wilson, an old widow on a farm in Vermont, a mile and a half up the road, whom Kitty shopped for—then she attended her house. She kept it well; sparsely furnished, suiting the cold climate. Center Campobello shrank, seemed to lose streets and people in wintertime. She was good with space, placed it where it showed. Each piece of furniture looked as though it had been set like a small sculpture. She hated accumulation, clutter; yet placed things around it was pleasant to discover: small antique bottles, oriental tiles, lacquered boxes and pieces of stained glass. Kitty was good with flower arrangements, although she mercifully picked them late and the flowers in her bowls and vases were often slightly wilted. She was strict with her cleaning women, yet patiently showed them how to do things she wanted done. Dubin appreciated the order of the household; it went with his work.

Outside, she was continually digging in her perennial border, pulling up bulbs and planting them elsewhere as though transposing the facts of her life. Dubin enjoyed the flowers brightening the back lawn, but when he complimented her on her garden Kitty said she had no real green thumb. He called it a light-green thumb. The biographer appreciated his wife's good taste. He admired her kind nature, her honesty, even when it hurt. Kitty was spontaneously generous; Dubin had to measure his out. She was empathic: a single string bean in the sink was "lonely" to her. One flower of ten, fallen from a vase, had immediately to be restored to its "home." When Dubin was thinking of the gains over losses in marriage, he felt he had honed his character on hers. In all she had helped stabilize and enlarge his life; but he was not so sure, after a generation of marriage, that he had done the same for her or why wasn't she at peace with herself? Though he thought he knew the answer he continued to ask the question.

Kitty, as he dried his razor by the sunlit window, seemed to be dancing on the lawn. The dance astonished Dubin although she had as a young woman thought of becoming a dancer; had taken lessons. Yet he had not seen her perform anything like this before, this flow of movement—giving herself to it so. Shows you can't know everything about those you know best. The soul has its mysteries. Kitty waved to Dubin, he waved back. It was a running dance, very expressive—fertility rite? Her straw hat flew off and she made no attempt to retrieve it. She ran with her arms raised toward the flowers, twirled and ran the other way; then again to the garden. Her arms moved like a bird's wings; she swooped, turned, now hopped sideways toward the trees. He thought she'd duck into the grove of silver maples and dance there—marvelous sight—but instead she ran toward the house.

"Happy," Kitty called.

He opened the window wide. "What?"

"Hap-pee!"

"Wonderful!"

She danced on the lawn, her body bent low, then rose tall, graceful, once more flapping her arms. He tried to figure out what the ceremonial meant: wounded bird, dying swan? My God, Dubin thought. He had seen her in some happy moments but nothing to dance to. He felt how strange life was, then began thinking of his *Passion of D. H. Lawrence: A Life*, before he realized Kitty was in the house, screaming as she sped up the stairs. Dubin opened the bathroom door as she rushed in, shouting to him, her face red, eyes angered, frightened.

"Why the hell didn't you come and help me?"

"What for?"

"A *bee*, William," she cried.

"My God, where?"

"In my blouse. It crawled up my sleeve. Help me!"

"Unbutton it," Dubin advised.

"I'm afraid, you do it."

He quickly unbuttoned her blouse. A dull buzz sounded as the bee flew forth, a fat black-and-yellow noisy bumblebee. It buzzed in the bathroom close to the ceiling. Dubin defensively seized his razor, waved the weapon. The droning bee zoomed down on a course between his eyes, shot up, twice circled his head, and barreling down, struck him on the back of the neck.

He had expected it, he thought, but not, after her gasp and his grunt, Kitty's uninhibited laughter.

Not long after breakfast Dubin sat at his desk in his study about to begin. "What's my opening sentence going to be?

Christ, it may point the way forever." Kitty, without knocking, entered quietly and handed him his mail. "It came early today." She read on a yellow slip of paper on his desk the daily list of things to do and quickly crumpled it. He pretended not to see. Kitty said she didn't think the cleaning person would work out. She was a college student who would stay on only till school reopened in September. "She's competent but I doubt her heart's in it. She's doing this to earn a buck and take off. I guess I'll have to advertise again."

On the way out she paused. "William, why do I have strange dreams of Nathanael at this time of my life?"

"You tell me."

She said she didn't know.

He impatiently begged off. Kitty stepped out of the room.

After calling up, "Goodbye," she left the house to go into town for her groceries, his newspaper. Dubin heard her back out of the driveway. He laid down his pen and waited with shut eyes two minutes till she had returned, easily imagining her strained face, compressed mouth, eyes mourning as she got out of the car. Kitty hastily reentered the house, hurried into the kitchen, fighting herself. Herself won. She approached the gas stove and drew long deep breaths over each of the four burners, as though after a time of drought she was taking in the salt breezes of the sea. She then pulled down the oven door and breathed in, as her chest passionately rose and fell. Slowly her body relaxed. There was no gas leak; there never was. Kitty then sang up, "Goodbye, dear," and Dubin once more picked up his pen. She swept out of the house, briskly, sensually, almost gaily, as he savagely wrote down his opening sentence. The biographer was in business again, shaping, illumining lives.

He had seriously resisted Lawrence, so intricately involuted, self-contradictory, difficult a man. He had traveled so mercilessly, lived in so many out-of-the-way places; had written so well, so badly, so goddamned much; was so vastly written about—someone had said second to Shakespeare; or if not second, third, Samuel Johnson intervening—therefore who needs more by William Dubin? Who needs, specifically, yet another life of David Herbert Lawrence? Kitty, who had conscientiously traveled with her husband four summers as he had researched Lawrence's obsessive pilgrimages, had asked much the same question. But one fantastic day in Nottinghamshire Dubin had discovered, in an old miner's widowed daughter's slate-roofed attic, two dusty packets of Lawrence's unpublished correspondence: eleven impassioned notes to his mother—surly complaints against the father; and no fewer than twenty-six letters—once thought burned—to Jessie Chambers, his boyhood girl, whom he had ultimately rejected because she had too much the genteel spiritual and intellectual quality of the mother—vagina dentata, or so he thought; he had never visited her there. It was she, who by one means or another, became the Miriam of *Sons and Lovers*.

Later, in a London bookshop, Dubin had also found seventeen unpublished letters of Lawrence to J. Middleton Murry, loveless husband of Katherine Mansfield; there'd also been a strange love-hate relationship between the men. "Weasel," "dirty little worm," "rat," the novelist had called him, "I despise you"; and after breaking off their friendship, Murry, drawn to Lawrence and Frieda, time and again returned to try once more. Dubin's elation at his discoveries—extraordinary good luck—had at last resolved his doubts and hooked him firmly to the biography of Lawrence, at the same time apparently convincing Kitty. He had more new material than anyone in recent years and felt he could do a more subtle portrait of the man than had previously appeared. That was the true battleground for the biographer: the vast available documentation versus the intuition and limited experience of Wm. B. Dubin, formerly of Newark, New Jersey.

Sometimes he felt like an ant about to eat an oak tree. There were several million facts of Lawrence's short life and long work, of which Dubin might master a sufficient quantity. He'd weave them together and say what they meant—that was the daring thing. You assimilated another man's experience and tried to arrange it into "thoughtful centrality"—Samuel Johnson's expression. In order to do that honestly well, you had to anchor yourself in a place of perspective; you had as a strategy to imagine you were the one you were writing about, even though it meant laying illusion on illusion: pretense that he, Dubin, who knew himself passing well, knew, or might know, the life of D. H. Lawrence: who seemed not to have stepped beyond his mythic mask—explained himself without revealing himself; created an ur-blood mystique that helped hide who he ultimately was. Beyond that is more: no one, certainly no biographer, has the final word. Knowing, as they say, is itself a mystery that weaves itself as one unweaves it. And though the evidence pertains to Lawrence, the miner's son, how can it escape the taint, subjectivity, the existence of Willie Dubin, Charlie-the-waiter's son, via the contaminated language he chooses to put down as he eases his boy ever so gently into an imagined life? My life joining his with reservations. But the joining—the marriage?—has to be, or you can't stay on the vicarious track of his past or whatever "truth" you think you're tracking. The past exudes legend: one can't make pure clay of time's mud. There is no life that can be recaptured wholly; as it was. Which is to say that all biography is ultimately fiction. What does that tell you about the nature of life, and does one really want to know?

By mid-afternoon he had done two pages and was feeling good when Kitty returned from the town clerk's office to pay the cleaning person. Dubin was sitting in the living room with a drink. The bee sting no longer bothered. The girl had gone after slantedly writing her name and address on an old envelope on the kitchen counter.

"I'll mail her a check," Kitty said. "What do you think of her? The house is fairly clean. Should I keep her for a while or look for someone permanent?"

He had barely caught a glimpse of the girl but felt magnanimous. "What have you got to lose?"

The cleaning person—Fanny Bick—he had read her name on the envelope—who had appeared Tuesday morning, returned to work on Friday—resisting it all the way, Kitty said. Fanny, a nervously active girl, vacuumed and dusted, and was supposed to do a wash but hadn't got to it the first time. Kitty had done the wash on Thursday and had left a pile of Dubin's underwear, pajamas, socks, to be ironed—she had tried to talk him out of ironed socks but he liked them that way. As he worked that morning he was vaguely aware of the girl outside his door yanking the vacuum cleaner from room to room; and he later asked Kitty to tell her not to come into the study, because there were so many note cards laid out on the desk and worktable that he didn't want touched. She could clean his room next time, once he had the cards weighted down. He'd have lunch meanwhile or would read upstairs in Gerald's old room.

The girl had left before Dubin stopped working—he had eaten while she was in the master bedroom and as he went downstairs for coffee, had caught a look at her on hands and knees, shoving an aluminum hose under the double bed. But on the following Tuesday, when he left his study in midmorning to visit the bathroom—he went sometimes to think a thought through—there she stood barefoot, a brush in her hand, grimly swabbing the toilet bowl.

Fanny sweated as Dubin apologized—he would use the downstairs toilet, no trouble at all. The biographer had recognized her; she seemed younger than he'd remembered, possibly because he now knew she was still in college. Or had he suddenly grown older? Her light hair hung loosely down her back, and he was again aware of the random bleached hairs under her chin—counted four or five and wondered why she hadn't had them removed, a matter of esthetics. Fanny wore a faded denim wraparound skirt and black shirt without bra. Her abundant body, though not voluptuous, clearly had a life of its own.

Dubin stood at the bathroom doorway. The girl had retreated to the tub, holding the brush behind her.

"I'm Fanny Bick," she said, in annoyance and embarrassment. "I'm helping your wife."

"She mentioned it. Glad to know you." He spoke gently, sorry for her unease, apparently a persistent quality of her.

Fanny explained her situation—after a moment seemed calmer—and he lingered to hear: that she was working in his house because there wasn't much else to do in town. "I tried the State Employment Office and all the guy there does is show you unemployment figures for the county and shakes his head. Makes you feel zonky."

"That so?"

"Twittery. So I bought the town gazette, or whatever you call it, and put together four mornings of work at three different houses—this and two others. I had no choice but I don't like cleaning." She made a face. "I do an absolute minimum for myself. I'm not a slob but I don't like housework."

He nodded seriously, not entirely approving.

She smiled dismally.

He clucked in sympathy. "You should have gone on to Winslow. It's a bigger town—more variety. You might have picked up something at the piano factory there."

"Not the way things have been going for me lately. My car pooped out after an accident. My fault, and all I carry is liability."

He shook his head at her luck.

She said with a tense laugh, "Please don't tell your wife I don't like this job. I wouldn't want to lose my two mornings here."

"Have no fear."

Her body eased and she brought forth the brush.

Fanny said she was broke and had to settle for whatever she could get. "I've had it with college and have just about made up my mind I'm not going back. Anyway, my father said he wouldn't support me any more, so I'm trying to put together enough to take me to the Big Apple."

"To do what?"

"Ask me when I get there."

"Haven't we met before?"

She regarded him with fresh interest. "On the road? I thought I'd got lost though I guess I hadn't. I was where I was looking for."

"You can't be much more than twenty-one or -two?"

Her glance was friendly yet reserved.

Dubin said lamely, "Maybe I'm intending to prove I know something about people your age?"

"Twenty-two," she said. "Yesterday, actually. My friends say I look older."

It struck him he had almost hoped so. Dubin said he was fifty-six and after a moment laughed huskily.

She mulled over the news, her face impassive.

"Don't cheat yourself on education," he advised. "College is limited but at least it's a beginning. That's what I told my daughter."

"Giving up college isn't giving up your education. Far from it."

"William James, the psychologist and pragmatist philosopher, reflecting on the social value of the college-bred, thought the major effect of a college education might be to help you recognize a good man when you saw one." Dubin laughed saying this; had often said it. I have a one-track mind.

He tightened his belt. "Here I am offering free advice again," he apologized. "I am a biographer is why. I often have this souped-up sense of other people's lives so that I don't always mind my business. Pardon me, I don't mean to offend."

"No sweat." Fanny was amiable. "You feel empathy for people?"

"That's putting it kindly."

He had noticed her Star of David. Nodding abruptly, Dubin broke off and returned to his study. He was surprised at the time he had given her; and it annoyed him a bit that he had felt her sexuality so keenly. It rose from her bare feet. She thus projects herself?—the feminine body—beautifully formed hefty hips, full bosom, nipples visible—can one see less with two eyes? Or simply his personal view of her?—male chauvinism: reacting reductively? What also ran through his mind was whether he had responded to her as his usual self, or as one presently steeped in Lawrence's sexual theories, odd as they were. He had thought much on the subject as he read the man's work. Despite his reservations it tended to charge him up some. Dubin counteracted the effect by recalling the continuous excitement of Thoreau, woodsy dybbuk, possessing him as he was writing his life. The biographer had for a time become the celibate nature lover, or so it had seemed.

He became aware he was leaving his study more often than usual; he would drift down into the kitchen to pour himself a cup of coffee. He'd be restless, Dubin explained it to himself, well into beginning a work—it might take fifty, sixty pages before you were settled in, sure you were working right. He had the sense of having been more quickly into Thoreau, wasn't yet knee-deep in Lawrence. Once he was securely placed in the life he'd stick it out steadily—hours at his desk without a break, except for an occasional visit to the john. Holding cup on saucer he'd wander through the house, sipping absently, standing around thoughtful, probing his problems. If Fanny, on days she was there, happened to appear, Dubin nodded as though in thought and went on thinking.

Once when he lifted his coffee cup in greeting she said "Hi" cheerily and ducked out of the room.

"How come," Kitty inquired one morning, "you're drinking lots of coffee?" Years ago she had tried bringing up a cup of mid-morning broth to his study. This had soon come to an end: not really her style, not really his. It took time and added weight.

"Beginnings are tough."

"But you've begun."

One did not necessarily begin at the beginning, Dubin explained. "Beginnings may be more effective independent of strict chronology—where the dominant action of the life starts, the moment of insight, cohesion, decision. You can search that out or perhaps define a moment as a beginning and let what follows prove it. I'm not sure I'm there yet."

"You will be," Kitty said. "Don't strive for perfection right off."

He ignored the remark. They'd agreed she was not to advise him how to work unless he asked her.

She poured herself a sherry; it was near lunchtime. He was aware how well she looked this summer, her long body retaining its shape, if slightly heavier than last year. She looked younger than fifty-one, but if you said so she tittered, or sadly smiled at all you hadn't tallied.

"How's the girl working out?" He poured from the coffee pot.

"Not badly. She tries. I told you she's off to New York in September. I'll advertise then."

"Has she said anything about herself?" Kitty had long talks with people who worked for her.

"Not very much. She's intelligent, has a mind of her own and the usual dissatisfactions of someone her age, plus a few I can only guess at. Her old man's let her down, but I don't know how or why—the usual crise de confiance, I suppose. She's apparently decided to drop out of college, after a year in, two out, in again into her senior year and now wanting out for sure, she says."

"What brought her to Center Campobello?"

"She was living in an upstate commune, got fed up, and was on her way to New York City when she had an accident coming off the highway outside town. So she stopped off to earn some money to have her car repaired, et cetera. She's hinted some vague other reason, maybe looking up an old lover—I don't know. She's a mild depressive, I'd say."

Kitty analyzed people; she'd long ago been psychoanalyzed.

"She reminds me a little of Maud," Dubin said.

His wife was incredulous.

"Lots of vitality," he offered. "Direct too, wouldn't you say?"

"She's energetic enough when she wants to be, otherwise tends to droop."

"Seems to present herself as sexy?"

"I'd say so—does Maud?"

"Don't run it into the ground. Just an impression."

"Impressions either have or haven't validity."

Dubin was silent.

"She knows Roger Foster," Kitty said. "Apparently she applied for a job in the library but they had none. Now he calls for her after work—waits in his car in the driveway. I've asked him to come in but I think he's uneasy with you."

Dubin grunted.

"What more could you ask for a single attractive slightly blowsy girl who isn't your daughter, or for that matter much like her?" Kitty asked. "Fanny strikes me as not quite put together."

"Is Roger her lover?"

"How would I know?"

He'd never liked him, a sandy-haired large-shouldered insistent young man. When Roger was in college he'd worked one summer for Dubin, theoretically assisting a carpenter who was altering the barn Dubin was in part turning into an outside study that he had since then not much used. Roger hadn't worked well, goofed off. Lazy bastard.

"Maud never liked him either," Dubin said. "He hung around when she was barely fifteen. She had his number."

"With your assistance," Kitty said. "That was years ago. He's a serious man now and a really good librarian. Crawford isn't coming back and Roger, I hear, will replace him."

"He won't get my vote."

"He won't need it."

Dubin was uncomfortable with his judgment of Roger Foster, because he had disliked him on meeting him and forever thereafter. The biographer did not care to be the victim of that kind of response to people. It indicated objectivity missing, a quality he could not afford to be caught short of.

He glanced at his watch and whistled. "I've been talking to you for half an hour. Lawrence will fry me alive."

"Don't regret it," Kitty said. "I hardly see you once you're into a new biography."

"You see me forty times a day."

She wanted a hug before he left. "I've been feeling lonely."

They kissed affectionately as Fanny entered the room and at once headed out.

Dubin would wander through the house with his cold coffee cup, sipping from one room to another: a momentary break from work—he'd return refreshed. He enjoyed coming on Fanny in motion: forcefully stroking the rugs with the vacuum cleaner; the choreography with a mop over the kitchen floor; her intense private gestures of ironing; hurrying up and down the stairs. He enjoyed her hips in bloom, ample bosom—she wore a brassiere now after a glance or two by Kitty—everything in her figure more beautifully rounded because of the dramatic narrowing of waist between bust and bottom. She was gifted in femininity, Dubin had decided. Fanny wore miniskirts; on hot days she appeared in shorts and gauzy blouses—black, orange, yellow—her white or black bra visible through the garment.

Intermission, he called his viewing of her—the serious looking when she seemed inattentive yet had surely invited. Is she flirting with me? Whatever for—a man my age? When she bent it was a gracious act. A beautifully formed female figure suggested ideal form—her ass a bouquet of flowers. Ah, my dear, if I could paint you nude, if I could paint. Fanny as "sexual object" was balanced by the responding thought that he wouldn't mind being hers if she could imagine it. Is she really so tempting a dish, he asked himself, or am I beautifying every cubit of her according to my need? Women move me to deepest feeling, of pleasure and loss. As if they are eternally mine yet never belong to me. He felt at his thought, as it reverberated amid others, a mounting loneliness. Dubin waited till the feeling had passed. Afterward he reflected that this intense unexpected response to her had probably occurred at the thought she would soon be gone—in a few weeks to the omnivorous city. A momentary source of innocent pleasure lost—the beauty of a vital young woman. Too bad she'd never know. My God, how long does this romantic hunger—residue of old forms, habits, daydreams—haunt the blood?

Though he foresaw her departure he might as well enjoy the time she'd still be around. As for interrupted concentration, so long as he produced his daily two pages he had little to criticize himself for. But Fanny, as though to prove that his foreboding of an end was itself an ending, seemed to tire of the entertainment: his seeking her; her unwilling continuous performance. How juxtapositions distort intent, pleasure. She seemed all at once actively avoiding him. Dubin, concerned, looked less her way, would play no wolf to her harried Pamela. Once when he accidentally came upon her in the kitchen as she was ironing his underpants, Fanny's expression was grim. Both were embarrassed as their glances met. Dubin drained his coffee cup and hurried off.

Afterward she hid when he appeared, or attempted to, whatever his amiability or good intentions; she dropped what she was doing and walked off. Fanny ducked into the bathroom or hastened down the cellar stairs and in a few minutes the washing machine was rumbling. Or she slipped out on the porch and had a cigarette, leaning against a white pillar, staring at the old hills; the hills at least were eyeless. But the biographer enjoyed the sight of her: Susanna turned away from leering elder—lovely figure, something lonely about her. What sort of life does she have? Too bad she can't feel my admiration—as admiration—or perhaps she does and still would rather not. We can't all be friends and relatives as the world is; most of us have to be strangers—terrible construction, and here's Moses-Jesus preaching love thy neighbor as thyself. He went back to his study, dejected. Old billy goat—these feelings at fifty-six, disjunctions of an ordered life. We are all clowns.

Dubin resumed work with affection for it—truly working kept one from useless emotion—on keel, more or less content.

The chapter was bestowing more, resisting less. The facts had been laid out easily enough though he wasn't satisfied with all they said or didn't say. But patience: good beginnings, those that assured the biographer they were right and so was he, blew in like spring winds; some like storms. Some you coaxed out of the blue. The sky was in the process of yielding. What grew word by word grew in value. The young Lawrence had appeared, his face in a pool, or the pool his face. That is to say, the boy, from the first, reflected himself. Double self—never, then, recognized as such? Was this one of the hidden keys of the life—explains the sexual things, never at peace—and his love of ideologized metaphor—double image defined as one? The essential broken self?—unity achieved only in the work, his rainbow? Dubin, concentrating sentence by sentence, no longer ventures out of his room when the girl's around. Were she clinging to his door, he'd hold his water.

Fanny, he thought, a foolish name.

Summer was ending.

Winter waits in the wings.

One morning in early September Dubin hurried downstairs for a cup of hot coffee to keep him awake. Kitty had slept badly and borne him along part of the ride. When he returned to the study he found Fanny there, gazing at the pictures and mementos on the wall; she was examining in particular a framed blue-and-white beribboned gold medal.

The girl was standing close by the wall. Nearsighted, he thought, yet she rarely wears glasses, terrible vanity. In any case she was reading the citation of the medal in the frame. Dubin knew it by heart: "Presented by Lyndon Baines Johnson, President of the United States of America; to William B. Dubin, for his achievement in the Art of Biography; at the White House, December, 1968."

"Medal of Freedom," Dubin explained; formal—would not impose.

"Far out," Fanny said, amiably turning to him. "I've seen it here but never read what it said because you like to get back into your room so fast. The reason I came in just now is the door was standing open and I thought you were reading in Gerald's room so I could dust here."

He set down the cup on his desk, trying to keep it from rattling. A puddle of coffee had formed in the saucer.

"It was presented to me after the publication of my *H. D. Thoreau*—you've heard of him?—American essayist, 1817–62, author of *Walden* and other works. He was a disciple and somewhat ambivalent friend of Emerson—idealized his wife Lidian, might have been in love with her but there's no impressive evidence. A biographer can't afford to lean toward guesses of that sort, no matter how sympathetic his nature."

"I've read *Walden*. Some chapters turn me on—the scenes in winter and at night."

"Wonderful." Dubin had been about to say they had much in common but caught himself.

"You may not think so but all my life I've wanted to live close to nature, except I've never figured out how."

She said she had joined a Buddhist commune near Tupper Lake that summer. "Which was to be no sex and very vegetarian, including growing your own lettuce and beans. I liked it at first but one of the swamis there, a secret acid tripper, got on my nerves, so I split."

The swami pursued her with his naked eye? Dubin felt drawn to the girl in a way that saddened him.

He pointed to a small photograph in a hand-carved frame on the wall. "That's Henry—he was called Davy when he was a boy—not exactly a handsome man but people liked his looks. Hawthorne said they became him more than beauty." He beamed at her.

Fanny looked closely at the picture.

"Note the longish nose," Dubin observed. "Emerson said it reminded him of the prow of a ship. They say Thoreau would pretend to swallow it—tried to get his lower lip over it for laughs. He also tooted a flute as he danced with himself. In winter they skated on the frozen Concord, our boy waltzing like Bacchus on ice. Emerson leaned his ministerial face into the wind and self-reliantly shoved off. Hawthorne, his daughter Rose wrote, skated like a Greek statue on runners. Henry clowned on the ice. With luck he might have been a comedian. Mostly he settled for a solitary life in the woods—one makes his fate: he was there in every wind and weather. Some say eventually it undermined his health and shortened his life—but it's the old business of what for which. Out of this experience came his journal, where he appeared as a figment of his own imagination. And from which he extracted many treasures, including much of *Walden*. Or it might have worked the other way: he had started a journal on Emerson's say-so and went into the woods to let it find its world."

Fanny gave him the first warm smile he'd had from her.

Dubin went on, "He was ambitious to be great—become a major American artist. He is said to have felt a guilt-ridden desire to surpass at all costs and did so by turning nature into a personal possession. Perry Miller made him more conscious of every move toward his literary destiny than I. Not everybody knows what his personal metaphors mean or what he's secretly becoming, though one may sense it, of course. To my way of thinking his major concern, given who he assumed he was, was learning how to live his life. 'One doesn't soon learn the trade of life,' he said. He spent years trying, which is to say he lived to learn, to apprehend and control the forces that shaped him. He said he didn't want, when it came time to die, to discover he hadn't lived."

"Neither do I," said Fanny.

"Nor I," Dubin allowed. "Once he accidentally set fire to the Concord woods and burned up several hundred acres. The townspeople were furious. His behavior was strange: he watched the fire and made no attempt to help put it out. Death, one might expect, inhabited the journal. His brother John's short life was something he never ceased mourning. They'd been rivals for a young woman who turned them both down when each proposed marriage."

"I know he wasn't married. What did he do for sex?"

"Apparently he died chaste—as they say," the biographer soberly answered. "He's one of those people who live on sublimated sex. There are more around than one would think. You marry nature and live in solitude, having it both ways. But given how he lived, and considering what he accomplished, who's to say how much he missed, or that he missed much?" Dubin seemed to put it tentatively.

Fanny made a face. "I don't buy that. I don't care what he accomplished in his books, when you get right down to it he missed the most satisfying pleasure of life. I mean we're human, aren't we?"

His glance fell on her bosom. Dubin quickly looked up into her light-green eyes. Fanny observed him with nearsighted intensity. Her expression momentarily surprised.

"One of his best friends," he admitted, "said, 'No man had a better unfinished life.' I'm not attempting to justify his celibacy or whatever part of it he practiced, Fanny. I simply say he found his way. In essence, like many men of his type, he was a happy man. 'I love to live,' he said, and I believe him."

"Do you?" she asked.

He listened for mockery but heard none.

"Why do you ask?"

"Because I ask myself."

"What do you answer?"

"It's my question."

"Affirmative," Dubin replied.

Her eyes, he thought, reserved judgment.

"I have my doubts about how happy he was," Fanny said. "It must be a pretty dry lay, banging nature."

"There are many ways of love," he ventured.

"Not if you have to do it to a tree, Mr. Dubin."

He laughed warmly. "Please call me William."

"William."

To hold her there he went on concerning his medal: "I didn't want to accept it at first because I didn't like what Johnson had done to escalate and prolong the Vietnam War. But my wife said it wouldn't be courteous to turn the medal down if my country wanted to honor me and my book; so I took it."

Fanny mildly grunted.

"After dinner Johnson took me aside and asked me to write his 'truthful biography.' He held my hand in his big hand and said that Lady Bird had loved my book and there was no doubt in his mind that I could do a first-rate *Life of LBJ*. I said I was honored but couldn't accept his kind suggestion."

"Good for you."

"That's what my daughter said. Anyway, I backed off as best I could. I said that though I'd done a life of Lincoln, on the whole I preferred to work with literary figures. 'You son-of-a-bitch,' his eyes said, 'I'm a better man than you.' 'Yes,' I thought, 'I took your medal.' "

"Later he told my wife, 'No man worked harder for peace

than I did.' And when we left he loaded us with presents. She got a green scarf with border designs of a million LBJs strung together, and a glass bowl embossed with the Presidential seal. He gave me a waterproof watch engraved, 'Do Unto Others As You Would Have Others Do Unto You.' The watch never kept good time but I had the medal framed and there it hangs on the wall—I feel a certain affection for it now—and here we are, you and I."

They were standing within inches of each other, Fanny leaning against the wall, breathing audibly, her pelvis casually thrust forward. She seemed relaxed, as if she'd forgiven him for having burdened her with his desire to know her. Now that she was about to quit working for them, perhaps she had decided that he had wanted not very much from her. She's sought after by men, Dubin thought; yet even in the best of circumstances he doubted he would have tried to entice her into bed. She was only a couple of years older than Maud and he sensed in himself something resembling incest taboo once removed—you don't bed down a girl your daughter's age—let alone other inhibitions. I like to look at pretty women, though in her case maybe I overdid it considering I had her cornered in the house.

"Here's a picture my wife snapped of Johnson handing me the medal."

Fanny examined it closely. "You look like a puppy dog who doesn't want to bite the bone."

"That's more or less the way I felt."

Neither of them spoke for a moment. He thought she was about to leave but she wasn't.

"What are you writing now?" Fanny asked, not at all concerned she wasn't doing her work; neither was Dubin.

He responded quickly: "A new life of D. H. Lawrence, English novelist, poet, prophet, superb letter writer, man of genius and rages. He lived almost forty-five years—from 1885 to 1930—just about as long as Thoreau. They both died of TB—short lives."

"Was he as important as Thoreau? I mean why did you pick him after the other one?"

"He'd been in and out of my mind for years," Dubin said, his voice grown gravelly. "One day I woke up in his presence.

Not that he was actually there, you understand, but I couldn't put him aside in my thoughts. So far as I could remember I hadn't dreamed of him, yet I could not shake the sight of this fierce consumptive bright blue-eyed red-bearded man hectoring me. The experience was puzzling because, try as I would, I couldn't understand what he was saying. To answer your question, maybe I decided to write about him because I wanted to elucidate the mystery."

"Which one?"

"Are there two?"

"I wouldn't know," Fanny said.

Dubin said he had read nothing by Lawrence for years. "But he and Thoreau, though they led vastly different lives, had more in common—apart from being major writers—than is apparent. As writers their themes were alike—death and resurrection. As men both were oppressed by dominating possessive women. Both greatly loved and celebrated the natural world. Both were puritans. And both were less than fully heterosexual. Thoreau, as I said, sublimated his sexuality. Lawrence seemed never entirely at peace with his sexual nature. He felt he needed a man's love as well as a woman's to complete him, but he never seemed able—maybe he lacked the good fortune—to realize a bisexual relationship. He apparently proposed a blutsbrüdershaft to Middleton Murry, who though he seemed to be homoerotically inclined, was afraid of Lawrence. He grabbed his hat and ran. Lawrence once said that the idea of putting his arm around a woman's waist and dancing with her appalled him. If it weren't for Frieda, his sexually talented wife, he'd have been a lot more limited. She wrote someone that she had fought with Lawrence over his homosexual inclinations and had won—whatever that meant. She apparently could handle any kind of sexual experience. Ultimately he made a mystique of sex, preaching it as a dark force of blood-consciousness through which man experiences the primal mystery. It's a paradox that his theories occupied him, especially toward the end of his life, more than the physical sex that by then had failed him."

"What about *Lady Chatterley's Lover*? That had a lot of real live sex in it. Didn't he write that near the end of his life?"

"It too is ideologically charged, but you're right—his

sensuous world is real, affecting, no matter what the theories come to."

Fanny, after a moment, wondered if Dubin's coffee was cold.

He thought it might be.

They gazed seriously at each other.

"You sure know a lot about him."

"I wish I knew more. I don't pretend to see him plain. For instance, in his letters he speaks as if he were telling the factual truth but one can't take him at face value—the letters give autobiographical information yet there is a sense of their belonging to his creative work. I hope to figure him out as I go deeper into the life."

"I was thinking what you said about sex failing him—"

"You understand, Fanny, he was never an exponent of free sex? He didn't like people aimlessly copulating. He said sex should come on us unaware, 'as a terrible thing of suffering and privilege and mystery.' "

The girl seemed, then, troubled. "I think we're entitled to have sexual pleasure any way we want. Not worried or afraid, I mean. Why should we be?"

"Why, indeed?"

"I'm not ashamed of the way I live my life, Mr. Dubin."

"William," he said.

"William."

"I should hope not— What I'm saying," he went on, "is that too many people think of Lawrence's sexual doctrine as exactly the opposite of what it was. Though an innovator in fiction, he was in many ways a conservative person. Marriage, for instance: his own with Frieda was rough-and-tumble—there was much they were at odds about, especially her desire to see her children. Katherine Mansfield saw bruises on her body when they went bathing together. In the presence of Frieda's daughter he threw a glass of wine in her mother's face. She once socked him with a stone plate across the skull. Yet, beyond question, it was a vital enduring relationship. A true marriage, he said, established an unconscious connection 'like a throbbing blood-circuit'; and he once wrote a correspondent something like this: 'Your most vital necessity in this life is that you should love your wife completely and explicitly in entire nakedness of body and spirit.' "

Fanny said she couldn't have guessed.

"On the other hand, despite her marriage to him, Frieda sought and had sexual experiences with other men. She thought of herself as a liberated woman. She told people she was close to, that Lawrence, who was always shaky in sex, was impotent at forty-one."

Fanny sighed. "It sort of wipes you out. I mean a man like that. You wouldn't think so."

"What stays with me most from the biographies I write," Dubin went on, "apart from what one learns about the map of human lives—the unexpected turns and dramatic twists they take—the joyous ways they do, and the tragic ways they don't, work out"—the biographer's eyes momentarily misted and he had to cough a huskiness out of his throat—"what stays with me most, is that life is forever fleeting, our fates juggled heartbreakingly by events we can't foresee or control and we are always pitifully vulnerable to what happens next. Therefore what the poets say about seizing the day, dear Fanny, is incredibly true. If you don't live life to the hilt, or haven't, for whatever reason, you will regret it—especially as you grow older—every day that follows."

"Do you regret it?" she serenely asked.

Dubin gazed at her gravely.

"I'd regret it beyond bearability if I were not involved in the lives of others."

"You mean in your books?"

"Largely so, but not only so."

"And that gives you your big charge? To me life is what you do. I want it to enjoy, and not make any kind of moral lesson or fairy tale out of it."

He felt momentarily let down, despondent.

She seemed, however, affected by him, her color heightened, and in her eyes something resembling affection seemed to show.

Dubin impulsively drew a book out of one of the shelves. "Accept," he said, handing it to her, "a copy of my earliest work: *Short Lives.* Nobody in it lives to forty."

After momentary hesitation she took the book and pressed it to her breast.

"You're beautiful, Fanny," Dubin whispered.

She touched his arm with four fingers.

Moved by her, though he told himself he had wooed her falsely with the business of his Medal of Freedom, his refusal to write President Johnson's life, his too long account of the lives of his betters, Dubin drew Fanny into his arms with immense relief. She rose to him on bare toes, with pointed breasts, forceful hips, hairy chin, hungry tongue. They kissed deeply.

They passed on the stairs as strangers—sometimes she brushed against him—he felt her hair graze his forearm. Dubin, returning to his study, forcefully concentrated; let her flow off in a flood of facts. Sometimes he sensed her presence outside his door but did not open it. He thought often of their embrace. It had caused Fanny to reverse direction, stop evading Dubin—gave him satisfaction: the small victories of life. But while he worked his study was a privileged place, really sanctum. He was headily into his chapter and feeling a long sense of future pleasure: savored the joys of accretion, of laboring and constructing order; appreciative of the self who served him best.

One early afternoon a few days after they had kissed, Fanny tapped on his door and Dubin opened it imagining she had finished *Short Lives* and would want to know if they could talk about it. But she apologized for not yet having read the book—had merely knocked to say hello. She seemed unsure of herself calling on him in his study. Her eyes were characteristically tense. Observing this, Dubin invited her in. He had known he would if she came to the door.

Fanny sat in his armchair, crossed her fine bare legs and smoked. Dubin lit a cheroot. She had washed her hair and it hung loose and light. Pendant silver hoops dangled from her ears, a fine touch while working. Dubin turned his chair to face Fanny. He regretted the menial work she did in the house. He knew she typed and had thought of asking her to type for him, but only Kitty typed for him.

Fanny wondered if she could borrow *Sons and Lovers* and Dubin, with a bound, got her his copy from the bookshelf. She said as she fingered the book that she had enjoyed their recent talk. "I also wanted to say—and I'm sorry if I'm taking your time but I don't know how else we can talk—I just wanted to say that the real truth about my own sexual experience, at least as I am now, is that I have become a better person because of it."

"I wish I were a better person," Dubin said.

He imagined she had felt a need to say this and might just as well to an older man. If you said it to a young man he would want to put you to bed to make you a better person.

"I'm not kidding," she said.

He acknowledged it with a nod. "You're gifted, Fanny."

"How do you mean that?"

"Truly. Some people are gifted in life."

Her body eased. She seemed about to reach out her hand but they weren't within touching distance.

Dubin then asked her why she had joined the meatless sexless commune on Tupper Lake.

"I like to try things."

The biographer, touched by her remark, said he wished he had her kind of freedom when he was her age.

"What kept you from having it?"

"I was a satisfied romantic—loved longing. It made an occasional poem for me."

"Did you have any affairs?"

"I enjoyed the presence of women—I'm describing an almost aesthetic need, not saying it was all."

He said that his mother had been a sick woman and he had no sisters. He had had a younger brother who had drowned when he was nine. His mother was a disturbed woman afterward. She had died when he was thirteen. Thereafter his only company at home was his father. "He never remarried and I missed a feminine presence in the house. I missed a woman. I tried to appease this lack by often falling in love."

"Did you sleep with any of them?"

"Not usually those I loved. Not often others. It was a different world in those days, Fanny, though perhaps I was not as daring as I might have been. There was much I missed."

"Not that different," Fanny said. "My father, who is about your age, screwed around a lot."

They were interrupted by Kitty. She had knocked once and walked in. "Oh, I beg your pardon, I had no idea you were talking."

Fanny got up quickly.

"Don't go, please," Kitty said.

"Your husband loaned me a book."

"We were chatting," Dubin explained.

Fanny left the room and, later, forgot the book she had come to borrow, when she went home for the day.

Dubin, that evening, had thoughts of asking her to go for a walk with him sometime, the short walk.

The next time Fanny was in the house Dubin spied her on the porch, taking time out for a cigarette. He went out with his coffee cup and sat on the bottom step as she sat behind him on a canvas chair. Fanny's legs were parted and her lemon underpants were visible at the crotch. Her feet were bare.

Dubin turned to the hills. To the north was the nameless mountain he looked at when he wanted to look at a mountain.

He asked Fanny what her plans were in New York.

She said she didn't know.

He talked facing the hills, his back warm in sunlight.

"Plans are not my strong point," Fanny said.

Dubin, after a moment, asked her where she had got her name.

"My name? My mother was the one who named me."

"After a relative, friend? Who?"

"No, she named me after Fanny Price in *Mansfield Park.* She was on a Jane Austen kick when she was pregnant."

"You don't say," said Dubin, turning to her. "Do you know Jane Austen had a favorite niece named Fanny Knight? She was charmed by the girl, reread her letters the day she was dying. The sad thing was that Fanny later wrote her sister their Aunt Jane had lacked refinement. She was ashamed of her aunt and, in essence, betrayed her memory."

"I don't think my mother knew that," Fanny said.

She had made no attempt, as they talked, to bring her knees together.

Dubin drank up his coffee and went upstairs.

A few minutes later he was jolted, at his desk, by a single swift knock on the door as the girl slipped into the room.

He was about to wave her out when she untied her wraparound skirt and whipped it off. Her blouse and underpants came off and she was naked.

Dubin was struck by her youthful beauty.

He mumbled his gratitude.

Fanny tossed her yellow underpants at him. He caught them and tossed them back. They struck her breasts and fell to the floor.

The girl studied him curiously, nervously.

"Whatever you're offering," Dubin said, "I regret I can't accept."

"Your wife went to the flower farm. It's an hour each way."

"This is her house."

"It's yours as well."

"Under the circumstances I can't accept."

Her face had reddened. She was angered. "All this beautiful bullshit about seize the day and what life is all about."

He hoarsely laughed at the jest.

Fanny pulled her clothes on in a grim instant and was gone. Nothing of her remained that he could find.

Dubin reached for his pen and after a while slowly began to write.

Fanny quit. She had told Kitty she was off to the city, although Kitty had heard she was still in town, living with Roger Foster. Dubin one day at lunch asked his wife what she had thought of the girl.

"She is sexy," Kitty said, "but I'm better proportioned."

Kitty had waked that morning saying she ought to go to Montreal to see her father's grave, then possibly her mother's in Augusta, on her way back.

"I owe him a visit. I've never really made my peace with him. Will you come with me, William? We could do it in a day there and one back."

"Is something bothering you?" When Kitty thought of visiting graves she was asking her life questions.

She seemed distracted. "I wish you'd come with me. I hate long drives alone."

"Why didn't you suggest it before I began my chapter?"

"It wasn't on my mind then."

Dubin said his work was going well. "It'll take me a week to get back into it if I go off with you now."

Kitty, as she dressed, thought it through at the bedroom

window. He watched her watching a flicker in the chestnut. A maple, barely missing the house, had fallen in a storm shortly after they had moved in, and Kitty had planted a chestnut there, now a luxuriant tree.

"I guess it's something I'll have to do myself."

He tried to persuade himself to drop his work and take off with her. But the journey was to cemeteries and he wasn't in the mood. He had his own graves to visit, that he hadn't been to in years.

Kitty said, "I have to go, why am I lingering?"

After lunch she slipped on two silver bracelets and a large ring. She painted her toenails, packed an overnight bag, and drove off toward the Northway.

They had kissed at the door—goodbye, not for long. She squeezed his hand. He regretted he could not go with her. She asked him to check the burners and Dubin promised but forgot.

On occasion he liked eating a meal out of a can—spaghetti, baked beans, carry-over from boyhood, youth—eating alone; but he prepared instead a hamburger Kitty had left defrosting. The meat burned in the pan, so he called a cab and went downtown. Dubin ate a plate of soup and a roast-beef sandwich at a restaurant counter, and since light still glowed in the evening sky—early fall had run a cool hand through the air—walked home. The stars appeared in misty swarms, Dipper brilliant. The biographer pondered the mystery of north—direction of death—white, silent, frigid, sans soul. Where was Kitty now? He hoped she would not drive at night. The moon had not yet risen. Walking alone in the dark he felt sadness of a sort. He thought he would listen to Schubert lieder, then decided, forget it, I'll go to a movie. Schubert, dead at thirty-one, was the first life Dubin had written for *Short Lives*. No one had written a good long life of Schubert. He had lived long in music and short in life.

The house, once he was inside—he had hesitated at the door—was surprisingly empty. Dubin was staggered, as he entered, at the surge of loneliness he felt, like acid invading the bone. Ridiculous, he thought. Standing at the foot of the stairs the biographer, shaken, tried to puzzle out what was affecting him. As a rule he enjoyed solitude. Being away from home, or occasionally remaining alone there, awoke moods he rarely experienced when his life was geared with Kitty's. What he felt now was more than a melancholy sense of being alone, or perhaps remembrance of that feeling in the past; this seemed a spontaneous almost soiled awareness, more apparent than ever, of one's essential aloneness: the self's separate closed self-conscious subjectivity. Dubin defined it for all time, as previously defined: death's insistence of its presence in life, history, being. If so, nothing new but why once more at this moment?

What had set it off? The absence of his children, a constant remembrance? One day their childhood, and your enjoyment of it, was over. They take off as strangers, not confessing who they presently are. You tried to stay close, in touch, but they were other selves in other places. You could never recover the clear sight of yourself in their eyes. They had become, as though by need, or their own definition, distant relatives. Dubin thought he had got used to the thought. Therefore it must be mainly Kitty's unexpected going to her father's grave? Perhaps he should have gone with her? He switched on the light, waiting as if expecting more light, then trod up the stairs, uneasy still, as though he were a man with three legs who remembered having only two. He wandered in the silent empty house, avoiding his study. What was Lawrence up to when Dubin was away: magicked the circuits of his dark blood? The biographer went up to the third floor to Gerald's old room, sat on the boy's bed. The pall of loneliness hung close—negates the sufficient self. Who rides Dubin's back? It occurred to him it wasn't so much he was missing his wife as being oppressively aware of himself.

In Maud's room he put in a person-to-person call to Berkeley. She wasn't in; he left a call-back message. Dubin was looking up Gerry's number in Stockholm in Kitty's address book when the telephone shrilly rang—Maud returning his call?

It was Kitty saying she was in Philadelphia.

He listened very carefully. "Weren't you going to Montreal?"

"When I left the house I felt I wanted to see Nathanael's grave. I've not been there for years. I hope you don't mind?"

He didn't think there was any reason he'd mind.

"I honestly almost never think of him any more. But when I got to the highway I had the impulse to see his grave, and drove south instead of north."

"I don't mind."

"You're easier on me these days," Kitty said.

"One learns," Dubin said. Then he said, "One thinks he does."

"You sound constrained. Are you all right?"

He was fine.

"I'll go to the cemetery with some flowers in the morning, then drive home."

He said he was surprised to hear her in Philadelphia as he was thinking of her in Montreal.

"Your voice sounds distant. Has something happened?"

"I called Maud. I thought you were Maud calling back."

"Give her my love," said Kitty. "I wish they weren't so far away."

Dubin said he'd go out for a short walk before turning in, and Kitty said she was sorry she wasn't there to walk with him.

When he hung up she called back.

Dubin said he'd thought it was Maud again.

"I'm not Maud, I'm me. Please tell me what you're worried about. Is it the Lawrence?"

He said no.

"He's a hard person to love."

"I don't have to love him. I have to say truthfully who he was and what he accomplished. I've got to say it with grace."

"Then is something else worrying you—money, for instance?"

He confessed he worried about money.

"Are we spending too much?"

"We'll be all right for another year and then we may be tight."

Kitty said if she had to she would look for a paying job. "Good night, love, don't worry. I'll be home tomorrow." She was tender on the phone when either of them was away.

The night was dark deep and starlit, and Dubin walked longer than he thought he might. He was standing at the poster window of the Center Campobello Cinema when the last show broke and he saw, amid two dozen people straggling out, Fanny Bick in bluejeans and clogs, carrying a shoulder bag. She was wearing a white halter tied around the midriff, her hair bound with a red cord. Dubin sensed her before he saw her. He watched, thinking she would look up and see him but she didn't. She seemed to be still into the film, conscious of herself; he recognized the feeling. He had not expected to lay eyes on her again and now he felt he would have regretted not seeing her. Roger Foster was not in the crowd. To make sure he hadn't stopped in the men's room, Dubin crossed the street and let Fanny walk on; when he was sure she was alone he recrossed the street and followed her.

No more than a diversion, the biographer thought. He doubted he would talk to her; then he thought he *must* talk to her. His odd loneliness still rode him—a discomfort he wanted to be rid of, something from youth that no longer suited him. He felt a hunger to know the girl, could not bear to have her remain a stranger. The lonely feeling would ease, he imagined, if he knew more about her. Crazy thing to feel it so strongly, as though he'd earned the right to know. Here I am hurrying after her as if we are occupying the same dream.

Fanny sensed something. Her pace quickened, the clogs resounding in the shadowy lamplit street. At the next corner she nearsightedly glanced back nervously.

"Wait up, Fanny—it's William Dubin."

She waited, austerely, till he caught up with her. If she was relieved she hid it. But her face, pallid in the street light, and restless eyes, offered no welcome.

Dubin was about to tip his hat but had none. He hoped he hadn't frightened her by pursuing her.

Fanny denied the importance of it.

He explained, with a gesture alluding to the loveliness of the night, that he'd been out for a stroll before going to bed. He was, this evening, alone in the house. "I happened to see you leave the movie and thought I'd say hello. Do you mind if I walk with you?"

She said it was a free country.

"Come on, Fanny—you'll have to do better than that. I'm sure you know I enjoy your company."

She seemed to hesitate. "I don't mind if you don't, Mr. Dubin."

"Was it a good film you saw?"

"Good enough—sort of a love story."

"Anything I ought to see?"

They were walking together, her clogs setting the rhythm.

"It's better than nothing."

He laughed at that, felt awkward, as he had in his house when she was conscious of him observing her, imposing himself.

"I'm sorry you left without saying goodbye," Dubin said. "I'd bought you a copy of *Sons and Lovers*. Would you like me to bring it to you?"

"Thanks anyway."

"Where can I send it? I heard you were living with Roger Foster. He used to do odd jobs for me when he was in college. He wore a green sweater and his beard had a green cast. I confess I never liked him very much. Perhaps the fault is mine."

"Well, he has a blue sweater and a dark beard now and doesn't do odd jobs any more, and neither do I, certainly not house cleaning."

"It seemed to me a curious experience for somebody like you. I hope I conveyed my understanding, my respect. I regret we hadn't met under better circumstances."

"Who said I was living with Roger?"

Dubin cleared his throat. "My wife happened to mention it."

"She sure is all over the place. I live in a room in his house but not with him. His sister and brother-in-law live there too."

"Fanny, I'm sorry about the incident in my study," Dubin said. "I regret we couldn't be congenial."

She made no reply.

He asked her if she had left because of that.

"Not that I know. I just got awfully tired of the cleaning crap. I'll never do anything like that again."

He asked her if she had read *Short Lives*, the book he had given her.

Fanny said she hadn't.

"I've wondered," he remarked a moment later as they were walking along the store-darkened street—he had no idea where she lived—"why you wear that Star of David?"

"I wear it because I own it. A friend of mine gave it to me

and I wear it when I think of him. I wear other things too." Then she asked, "Your wife isn't Jewish, is she?"

He said she wasn't.

"How did you happen to meet her?"

He said he'd tell her the story sometime.

"What was she doing when you met her?"

"She was a widow with a child."

"She sure is conscious of everything."

"She has a sensitive nature."

"So have I," Fanny said.

The stores were thinning and there were more private houses. At the corner she turned and he followed her into a short street. In mid-block an orange VW was parked in front of a dour narrow wooden house with a thin high gable. The two-story house was dark, its window shades drawn.

A bright half-moon shone through a copper beech on the lawn. The dark-green house in dappled moonlight looked like a piece of statuary, or an old painting of an old house. Dubin had on a light sweater and loafers, Fanny her jeans and white halter.

He told her D. H. Lawrence used to go wild in the glow of the full moon.

"I'll bet it doesn't do that to you."

"I'm a controlled type," he confessed.

She yawned.

Dubin pointed in the sky. "Look, Fanny, the Big Dipper. And that's Andromeda, really a galaxy, like ours heading into infinity—if there is an infinity and not just a finite wheel with no apparent end, if we crawl forever around its rim. In this universe, finite or infinite, man is alive amidst an explosion of gases that have become stars in flight, from one of which we have evolved. A marvelous privilege wouldn't you say?"

Fanny, momentarily silent, said she thought so too.

"Lawrence called it 'the great sky with its meaningful stars.' "

"Does he mean besides astrology?"

"Besides that."

"Does everything have to mean something?"

"Where there's mind there's meaning. I like the idea of the cosmic mystery living in our minds, and that enormous mystery reflecting our small biological and psychological ones. I like that combination of mysteries."

"Like our minds are the universe, sort of?" Fanny reflected.

"Yes," he told her. "Perhaps we were invented to see the stars and say they're there."

"That's not why I was invented."

"Tell me why."

"I wish I really knew. Why do you bring all that up now?"

"So that I shan't appear naked when we meet again."

She smiled dimly. "I guess I better go in now. Thanks for the astronomy lesson."

Dubin asked her when she would be leaving for New York.

"Next week I plan to go."

The biographer had had a thought: "I've got some research to do at the New York Public Library. Can I drive you down?"

Fanny said she'd be driving her own car. "Roger's going with me."

Dubin had to conceal his disappointment.

"He's coming for the ride and going back by bus. You can tell your wife I'm not living with him. He wants to marry me but I don't dig getting married just yet. I have other things to try out before I do."

"Marvelous. What sort of things?"

Fanny raised her arms in the moonlight. "I'm young yet. I don't do everything for a purpose. I do some things for fun."

"Fun is a purpose."

"It's a purpose that doesn't take away your fun."

"May I hope to see you in the city, Fanny? Couldn't we have dinner together?"

She gave it a moment's reflection. "That's fine with me."

"Good. Where shall we meet? Where will you be living in New York?"

"I don't know yet. I haven't looked for an apartment. Do you want me to come to the restaurant?"

"Would you care to meet me at my hotel?"

She said that was as good as any other place.

They arranged a meeting a week hence. Dubin said he would be at the Gansevoort. "That's Melville's mother's maiden name."

Fanny stifled a yawn. "This night makes me sleepy."

"I won't keep you," he said. "I'm happy we're going to meet again. I was inept the last time we were together. In afterthought I realized how kind you were being."

"Forget it."

"I don't think I want to."

They had parted friends, he hoped.

The house, when he returned, had lost its lonely quality, although Maud, if she had telephoned, did not call again.

Dubin, standing at the darkened bedroom window, looked up at the wash of stars in the night sky. In the universe even the dark is light. "Why should I feel lonely?" Thoreau had asked. "Is not our planet in the Milky Way?"

He would tell that to Fanny.

Dubin talks to his mirror: he weighs how some things happen to happen: Kitty's letter, many years ago, had crossed his desk shortly after he began a new job.

There were two handwritten letters in green ink, the second cancelling the first: "Please don't print my recent 'personals' note. I should have known not to write that kind of letter when I was feeling low. Could you kindly destroy this with the other I sent you?"

Having read it because someone had mistakenly laid it on his desk, Dubin searched through a folder in the next office for the first letter. It read, "Young woman, widowed, fairly attractive, seeks honest, responsible man as friend, one who, given mutuality of interests and regard, would tend to think of marriage. I have a child of three."

Dubin would tend to think of marriage.

After a night of peering into his life, of intense dreams; of being tempted to take a chance because the time had come to take a chance—he was past thirty and neither his vocation nor his relationship with women satisfied him—he wrote her in the morning: "My name is William Dubin. I'm an assistant editor at *The Nation*. Your letter happened to cross my desk. I've read it and would rather not destroy it."

He had had the job a week and had recently also been writing obituaries of literary figures, on assignment for the *Post*. Dubin told her he was thirty-one and unmarried. He'd been in the army two years. He was Jewish. He was responsible.

He wrote that he had practiced law for a year, had finally, like Carlyle, decided it was not for him, and was no longer practicing. He said he loved law but not practicing it. His father had lamented his giving up his profession. He had for a while felt lost, a burden of loss. Wherever his life was going he did not seem to be going with it. "People ask me what I'm saving myself for. Whatever that may be—I want to change my life before it changes me in ways I don't want to be changed."

He said he had never written to anyone as he was writing to her now. "I am touched that only you and I know about the letter you sent and withdrew. I know something I have no right to know; in that respect I'm privileged. I sense you understate yourself. You seem to be capable of a serious act of imagination: to be willing to love someone willing to love you. Plato in the *Republic* says that marriages between good people might reasonably be made by lot. I assume we're that kind of people. Obviously, for whatever reason, you've been flirting with the idea yourself. I have the feeling I've been predisposed to it all my life, although I can't say why. Your letters have excited me. Mayn't we meet?"

She wrote: "Dear Mr. Dubin, Yours disturbs me. It does because it moves me terribly. I am—at least at the moment—afraid to go further. Let me think about it. If you don't hear from me, please forgive me. It will be best not to have said no. Ever, Kitty Willis."

Another letter from her came in less than a month. He almost tore it apart as he tore it open.

"Dear Mr. Dubin, I am twenty-six, my little boy is three and a half. I wish I could believe I know what I'm doing. I thought I ought to say I don't think life will be easy for anyone living with me. I sleep poorly, fear cancer, worry too much about my health, my child, our future. I'm not a very focused person. It took my husband years to learn what I'm telling you in this short letter. I want at this point to get these things down: My father was a suicide when I was four. My mother went abroad with a lover when I was nine. She died in Paris of lung cancer and is buried in Maine. I was brought up by a loving grandmother—my rare good luck. My poor husband died of leukemia at forty. It's such a chronicle of woe I'm almost ashamed to write it."

"Of course I'm more than the sum of my hangups and traumas," she wrote. "Nathanael and I were reasonably happily married, and I ought to make someone a decent wife. I can't say my emotional season is spring but I love life. Fortunately, I have a strong reality element that keeps me balanced against some of my more neurotic inclinations. You have to know if we're going to be serious about each other. I had hoped to write earlier, but it took me some time to put my thoughts together. I don't want to ensnare you with my unhappy history, Mr. Dubin. I sense you lean to that tilt."

They had met at the Gansevoort bar. Each recognized the other. Kitty looked as though she was looking for him. She was a tallish slim-figured woman with bright brown hair and luminous dark eyes. Her eyes, as she greeted him, were contemplative, unsure, not very gay. She hadn't, Dubin thought, fully joined her resolution.

"I'm glad you came."

"I had to."

He agreed they had to.

"How serious we are," she said after a moment. Kitty laughed breathily. "I admit I ask myself why I'm here."

"What do you answer?"

She looked at him with a vague smile, shook her head.

He tried to tell her why, a way of telling himself.

She listened as though she had come to believe in him and all he had to say now was what he had already said in his letters.

This he managed to do.

They ordered drinks. It was not a bad meeting, though they were constrained. Kitty studied him, not seeming to care that he saw her studying him. Dubin was not at all sure of her, much more the gentile lady than he had supposed. Then he placed his hand on hers and Kitty did not withdraw it. She looked at him holding her hand, then withdrew it and pressed it to her cheek. He remembered that gesture for years. One night they went out and enjoyed themselves, enjoyed each other, gambled a kiss. She kissed with passionate intensity. They were hungry kisses he thought of many times. Not long afterward they agreed to be married.

"Let's be happy," she said.

He was willing.

"I hope you know what you're doing."

"Don't you?"

"I don't want you to be disappointed in your decision, or in me."

Dubin said he thought it would be a good life. He had gone through it often in his mind and thought they were doing the right thing. "All it takes is character."

"That's not all it takes."

"Whatever it takes I think we have."

She laughed as though he had said something very witty. Her dark clear eyes were eyes to dance to, he thought. Sometimes she looked older, less pretty. She sometimes looked as though she didn't want her looks to influence his decision.

"I trust you, I think," Kitty said. "You seem to say the right things. In a way you remind me of my husband."

He hoped not too much.

Her eyes grew anxious. "Let's not get married until we know and love each other."

"Let's get married and know and love each other." He said it with doubt like a cold stone in his gut, yet felt he had to say it.

"Where do you get your nerve or whatever it is?" she asked.

He said he had drifted enough in life.

They were married one cold day in spring. Dubin felt inspired. The bride wept at the wedding.

"That isn't how I remember it," Kitty said behind a yawn in the bedroom. "A lot happened that you've forgotten."

Dubin drove to New York with Evan Ondyk, the Center Campobello psychotherapist, who'd been practicing in town for two years. Ondyk had heard through a patient, a friend of Kitty's, that Dubin was driving to the city. He had called him to ask for a ride. His Buick was in the garage for a new transmission. The biographer respected Ondyk's poker playing but not his mechanistic judgments of people, as though possibility did not go beyond Freud. On the other hand he read a lot and talked well about books.

"Why did you pick D. H. Lawrence to write about?" Whoever knew Dubin sooner or later sprang that question.

"Someday he'll tell me."

"Why didn't you try Freud?" Ondyk asked. "We could use a good biography of the man—nobody's done very much past Ernest Jones unless he goes at Freud to attack psychoanalysis. It would be useful, for instance, if someone could find out how he felt about analyzing his daughter Anna. Or from her how it went. Also what his relationship was to his wife's sister. That's ambiguous territory. Jung, in an interview, is on record as saying Minna told him that she and Freud were intimate. Freud himself said—I think to Fliess—that he was forty-one when he gave up sex with his wife. Why, if true? It would be interesting to know."

"I was considering Chekhov," Dubin replied. "He died at Lawrence's age of the same disease, tuberculosis. There were other similarities: problems of loving, impotency, what-all."

"Why didn't you do him instead of Lawrence? He's a much more sympathetic person."

Dubin said he didn't read Russian.

He pondered Ondyk, wondered about his judgment of him. Is there more to him than I think? One has so few facts to go by. He had the reputation of being a good practitioner. He was a deliberate effective card player, peering over his hand to psych out who was holding what. He often called when Dubin bluffed. Eyeball to eyeball, who would best understand the other? the biographer wondered. Someone said Ondyk was not content in his marriage and went off periodically to the city for his sexual pleasure.

Dubin would have liked to be alone but the ride was pleasant. It was a fine autumn day. His vision was stereoscopically sharp, his heart light. A resurgence of sadness had occurred and gone. Here I am, a single man on a date. He felt at peace, serene, had in the mirror that morning looked youthful. He hadn't talked to himself. Fanny had been in his thoughts. It was early October and on the Taconic many of the sun-filled trees, although in high color in the hills above Center Campobello, were yellow-green and growing greener as they drove south. This was a rented car because Kitty needed theirs. She'd been surprised that he had not asked her to go with him but Dubin reminded her how rarely he got out of the house alone. "Being married doesn't mean being tied like cats by our tails." Afterward he recalled the simile was Montaigne's; and Kitty reminded him that lately he'd been making remarks about marriage. "Have I?" Dubin asked. He explained he liked a long drive alone once in a while and she said she understood. He wore tartan slacks and a blue blazer, and in his briefcase carried a bottle of perfume and a Schubert record as presents for Fanny.

"Well, have a good time," Ondyk said. "What are you here for?"

Dubin said he hoped to relax a little from work.

"How's it going?"

"Not badly."

"How's Kitty?"

"She's well," said Dubin.

"Attractive woman," Ondyk said.

He didn't say what he was in the city for.

After Dubin had left the psychotherapist at his hotel and checked into his own, it seemed to him he could use a brighter tie so he went out and bought a yellow one, and while he was at it, a new belt with a heavy silver buckle. He had got to the Gansevoort shortly after three. At four he showered, changing into fresh underwear although he had changed into fresh underwear that morning; and he dressed again. Dubin imagined Fanny would appear at about five. He would order drinks sent up—no, it might be better if they went down to the bar. Afterward he would invite her up and she could say yes or she could say no. They'd go to bed, have dinner late, and let the evening find its way. They would not have to decide one minute what they were going to do the next. If Fanny liked, they could either go for a walk along Fifth Avenue or see a movie. It would be a nice thing to do between twice in bed.

It was a long wait doing nothing, so Dubin unlocked his briefcase and read several of his notes about Lawrence and Jessie Chambers, a good companion but bookish and apparently not much interested in sex. It was a stillborn affair, hard on them both. Lawrence had wanted to love her but couldn't. It was said she reminded him of his mother. The girl had a broad tremulous mouth and uneasy eyes. "I could never love you as a husband should love his wife," he had frankly told her. Lawrence never kept bad news from anyone. The letters Dubin had discovered showed him at his hardest to her.

The biographer thought it must be close to five when he discovered it was close to six. He hurried down to the lobby to see if Fanny was there. Dubin waited for her amid a crowd of new arrivals. He had not waited for her before; it was difficult to say how late she was when she was late. The lobby was afloat with men, single and married, meeting pretty women in bright dresses and pants suits, single and married. Dubin admired an Indian stewardess in a golden-red sari, standing with a white-turbaned bearded Sikh pilot; they were waiting for a limousine to the airport. In the bar the pianist was playing an aria from Puccini. The lobby stirred with expectancy—a sense of adventure, sexuality—Faust ascending, but no Fanny. Fearing he had missed her—perhaps she had gone up as he was coming down, Dubin entered an elevator and rode up to his floor; but she was not in the corridor by his room, nor had he expected she might be. The years I've wasted being on time.

He descended in the elevator, then stood for a while in front of the hotel, trying not to dislike the girl for desiring her. At seven he waited outside till eight. Dubin felt his age. When one is my age the old and maimed stand out in a crowd. One recovers of youth only what he can borrow from the young. Perhaps this is not my privilege. It was a pleasant evening. He eyed passing couples, young with young; and young women with older men—these he envied most—looking as though they had been intimate or were about to be. The young ones did not look at him. Those his age knew whom he was waiting for. Waiting Dubin thought he did comparatively well. It was a matter of temperament, perhaps. He waited not so well for the small things of life but better for the important. Some wait badly. Kitty waited badly. "Un bel di vedremo," the Puccini went in the bar. Puccini, the cantor of longing. Kitty sometimes plucked the aria on her harp. But waiting in expectation is easier than waiting in doubt. It was easier to wait for one who was coming than one who was not.

At nine Dubin ordered a roast-beef sandwich on rye and a bottle of ale sent to his room. If she still came the long wait would have been worth it. He had decided that Fanny had planned not to come because he had not taken her when she had offered herself. There are some things one ought not to do. There are some chances one ought to take.

Looking in the mirror over the bathroom sink, Dubin disliked the yellow tie he had bought. He changed it for a purple one before going down to the bar. He washed his hands and face and went downstairs.

At the bar Nixon was lying on television. His expression was sincere as he sincerely lied.

Dubin ordered a brandy, sipping as he observed the middle-aged bartender.

He told the bartender he seemed sad.

"You look kinda wiped out yourself."

The biographer confessed his lonely nature.

"I have my daughter dead about a year," said the bartender. "She took an overdose when she was twenty."

Dubin was sorry to hear it. "I have a daughter myself."

After a while he said, "Mark Twain lived in heartbreak after his daughter Susy died: 'The mind has a dumb sense of vast loss—that is all.' "

"They stay in your thoughts," said the bartender, rubbing the wood with his cloth.

Dubin in his heart of hearts mourns Dubin.

Two

A LIGHT FOG lay on Venice that end-of-October late afternoon they arrived via an hour in Rome where it had been sunny and warm. Dubin and Fanny after debarking the vaporetto—terribly slow but he was eager to point out hazy sights, mist-enshrouded palazzi—were following a porter wheeling their luggage up a narrow calle. There, as the mist thinned and they could see others approaching, it seemed to the biographer that a red-haired girl clinging to the arm of a gray-haired man—both backed against the wall to let the newcomers and their baggage go by, Fanny and the elderly gent momentarily stood between Dubin and the redhead half hidden from him—was his daughter Maud. He, startled, his legs beginning to tremble, had been about to cry out her name, but the need for concealment was inexorable so he turned from her, pulling his hat brim low over his eyes, and when, no more than a minute later, he gazed back at the couple they were shadows in the fog. The bronze hair had disappeared like the flaming sun sinking in a cloud-massed charcoal sunset.

Anguished, regretful, feeling imperiled—Dubin had the impulse to chase after them to determine if she was indeed Maud, but how could it be during the academic term at Berkeley where he had telephoned and talked with her only a few nights ago? He was surely mistaken, had more than once confused Maud with another redheaded girl nearby. One is struck by the color and recognizes someone who isn't there. Fanny, wearing her blue shades, had noticed nothing and chattered amiably. The porter pushed ahead with the bags. Dubin was still shaken though he had for the most part recovered his calm when they entered the courtyard of the Hotel Contessa. Behind them the setting sun appeared as a fiery half disk in the silvery fog and the evening promised pleasure.

"What's the weather saying for tomorrow?" he asked

the black-suited segretario at the desk as he examined their passports.

"Improving, professore." His nose had twitched: that swinging single with this ambitious vecchio? Dubin felt he must look older with her than when alone.

"I have no university connection. I'm a professional biographer."

"Please pardon me, I meant as compleement."

He nodded genially, not altogether displeased by the man's curiosity nor by the aura of expectancy Fanny stirred up around her wherever she appeared. He'd been mildly surprised by her unseasonable getup—a voluminous violet dress, not her best color, and a wide-brimmed straw hat—though summer, although it could be said to be lingering in Rome, had departed Venice. She wore her wire-framed dark glasses, jade earrings, and a small gold crucifix in place of her Star of David.

"For the fun of it," Fanny had said. "I like to feel at home where I am."

"Will you feel at home with yourself?"

"Some people are freer than others."

That, Dubin granted. Fanny on holiday surprised, had overturned his expectations. She'd be a beautiful woman if she saw herself as one. This is she, Dubin reflected. Let her be.

With her unfurled by his side who would have noticed him in a foggy Venetian street? He was certain it hadn't been Maud they had passed yet wondered: if I was hiding, was she?

The portiere beckoned two bellmen. One, a vital youth, gathered Fanny's three bags as if by instinct, none of which he would yield to an older man who lugged Dubin's worn suitcase; and together with the assistant secretary, they all rose slowly in the wire-doored wood-paneled lift.

The assistant secretary, a closely shaved and powdered man with a sculptured black mustache, led them twice to a wrong room before leading them to the right one. "I deed not recognize eef it was a three or a seven on my paper."

"It's on the key," said Dubin. "But you are absolutely right," said the astonished young man, his eyes mostly on Fanny. They had entered an attractive double room through an adjoining single that Dubin wanted locked on their side. The assistant secretary offered to return immediately with the key but Dubin said he would ask the maid to take care of it in the morning. The man unhappily assented, though a thousand-lire note seemed to settle his nerves.

Their room on the top floor of the Contessa was a magnificent high ornate-ceilinged one with French doors leading to a small balcony overlooking the Grand Canal. The fog had lifted and the view before them—Venice afloat in a rising sea on a serene late-October early evening—and the anticipation of his amorous adventure, filled Dubin with satisfaction at the rightness of his decision to do what he was presently doing.

They had met by chance, after the Big Apple fizzle, on Grand Street in Center Campobello. Dubin, at the tail end of his country walk, had intended to slip past her; but Fanny, approaching as he hesitated, abruptly explained she had returned to pick up a lamp she had bought but hadn't been able to carry in her overloaded VW.

"I was hoping I would see you. I lost the name of the hotel I wrote on a piece of paper, and you weren't registered in the two others I tried."

"Which did you try?"

"I went to the Brevoort, also the Plaza."

"I was registered at the Gansevoort. Why didn't you telephone or at least drop me a line afterward?"

"It was on my mind," Fanny said, "but I thought your wife mightn't like it. Also I was annoyed at myself for losing the name of the place."

Dubin said his wife didn't open his mail. He searched her eyes, she seemed contrite.

Two days later he telephoned Fanny in New York and proposed a week in Italy.

"Why not," she said after momentary hesitation. "I haven't found a job yet so it's okay with me, if you can make it."

On the plane he had asked himself, "What am I doing here, a man my age with a young woman hers?" The answer came easily and happily: "Enjoying myself. I have it coming to me."

Fanny was affectionate, buoyant; they joked. She sat snuggled close, straw hat on her lap, head against his shoulder, her hair spread like a flag across his chest. She had shown nervousness before the flight, which had disappeared after they had ascended. Dubin's difficulty was afterthought: he regretted deceiving Kitty. There ought to be a better way. He recalled Lawrence's remark: "Honesty is more important than marital fidelity."

"—Kitty, I'm going off with a chick for a week. A night out in life. I want the experience before I'm too old to have it. Don't fret, I'll be back soon as good as new and as loyal as ever."

Fat chance. She'd probably have told him she'd be elsewhere when he returned. Kitty was vulnerable, why upset her? He had lied to protect her.

Fanny and he embraced on the Venetian balcony, Dubin nuzzling her neck. Her hot floral breath drew his mouth to hers.

"In a little while," she murmured after a long kiss. "We've been traveling all day and I could use a bath."

"Should we get into the tub together?"

"I'll be out in a sec, lover."

While she was bathing Dubin tried on a pair of striped pajamas Kitty had not long ago bought him. After a moment of reflection in a closet-door mirror he removed them and changed into fresh underwear. He did not admire his girth in boxer shorts, or his thin legs, so he drew on trousers and buttoned up his shirt.

Fanny, as the tub gurgled and toilet flushed, stepped out of the bathroom in a short white nightgown. Her body glowed. She had brushed her hair full and bright. Dubin, like a man about to be dubbed knight, sank to his knees, his arms clasping her legs as he pressed his nose into her navel.

She reacted in surprise, momentarily stiffening, then with affection ran her hand through his hair.

"I have my suitcase stuff all over the bed so I'd better finish unpacking like I see you have."

"I thought I'd get my things out of the way."

"So will I. It won't take long."

"'Had we but world enough and time,' dear Fanny," Dubin, rising, sighed.

"We have all week."

"You're a practical type."

"I'm not romantic, if that's what you mean, though sometimes I have romantic thoughts."

"It lingers in me, perhaps it's my generation."

"Forget your generation. Even if you are older than I you act young when you want to."

"L'chayim," said Dubin, holding aloft an imaginary glass.

"It's cool," she laughed.

She was sorting the contents of a small store: casual clothing—piles of it—and plastic containers of creams, lotions, deodorants. This consumer's side of her was new to him—he barely knew the girl—and he wondered how it squared away with her abstemious stay in a Buddhist commune.

"It's no ripoff. I happen to have this uncle who owns a drugstore. And my mother sends me clothes she doesn't want."

Amid her possessions he noticed a rubber diaphragm in a worn plastic case.

"Don't you use the pill?"

"My uncle says it can give you breast cancer."

"My wife never approved it."

Fanny also carried a traveling iron and portable clothesline she could rig up in any bathroom. "Anything you want to hang on the clothesline, please do it, Bill."

He was helping her put away things into drawers and the medicine cabinet.

"Why don't you call me William, Fanny?"

"I don't like to call you what your wife does."

That hadn't occurred to him, but he preferred William to Bill.

She fell, with a comic groan, into an armchair, her nightie billowing.

"What do you say we get into bed, Fanny?"

"If you wish, Will-yam."

"Call me Bill if you like. What do *you* wish?"

"Are you worried I might call you Bill and your wife would hear it?"

He was startled, could not foresee circumstances in which Kitty and Fanny were likely to meet. Don't consider yourself her equal, Dubin thought.

She regarded him cunningly. "Is something bothering you?"

"My mood at the moment is, as they say, macho, but you are being coy."

"No, I'm not. What did you tell your wife was the reason you were going away for a week?"

"I indicated I had some unexpected bits of research to do in Italy to settle a few things on my mind. But since she knows I'm presently working on Lawrence's early life, she may have wondered whether I wanted to get away for some other reason—possibly so I could see my work in perspective."

"Will she believe what you said—about going to Italy?"

"She believes me," Dubin said soberly.

"This isn't your first affair since you were married, is it, William? I wouldn't think so."

He thanked her for saying his name. "No, but it is with someone—if you'll pardon the expression—as young as you, a long trip involved, and some elaborate deception. Kitty happens to be easy to lie to, which makes it harder to do. I don't like not to be honest with her."

"Sometimes you sound innocent."

"I'm not innocent though my experience is limited."

"Like to some one-night lays with older-type ladies?"

"Not exactly grandmothers."

"How many?" she asked curiously.

"A few affairs—none prolonged."

"In how long a time?"

"I've been married twenty-five years and have been adulterous the last twelve."

"Adulterous? What were you afraid of?"

"There was no special fear. I was largely satisfied as things were. I was married after thirty and had for years too much to do to go actively looking for extramarital sexual experiences. I was working well and had a family to take care of."

"But nobody has to go actively looking—it's there. It always is."

"It may be there but in a way I wasn't," Dubin explained. "I'm only recently a visitor to the new sexual freedom. How many affairs have you had, Fanny?"

She started at the question. "I never counted."

"Often with married men?"

She nodded. "I was into that a lot for a while but less so lately."

"Good," said Dubin, noting a contradiction.

"Why did you pick me to go away with?"

He asked her if she was looking for compliments.

"Not really but I am kind of curious, William."

"Your warmth," he said, "—good looks, womanliness, openness. Because you touch my arm with your fingers when we talk. You're a little larger than life, Fanny. I mean you make life seem larger. I felt that before you tossed your underpants at me."

"What about your wife? I never really got to figure her out."

"What about her?"

"She looks sexy for her age but is she? My mother does but is limp as a rag."

"Fanny, ask anything you please about me and I'll answer, but let's not talk about my wife—she wouldn't like it."

"What is she—the Queen of Sheba? Are you afraid of her?"

"There's no reason to say that. Kitty's a private person with a complicated personal history. That's her business."

"I'll bet she worries a lot."

Dubin admitted it. "The night before I was to leave she asked me to call the trip off. She felt she didn't want to be alone in the house for a week. I said I wouldn't go if she felt that way in the morning. But by morning she had changed her mind: 'You've got to go,' so I went."

"What's her real problem?"

Dubin hesitated. "Let's say she's going through a prolonged glandular thing. That's as much as I intend to say about her."

"You don't have to tell me any more—I don't want to know," Fanny said, drawing up her legs and clasping them with both arms. "Just do you love her?"

Between her ankles her blond pelt was visible. As his eyes rose to hers she lowered her legs.

"I loved her," the biographer responded. "I love her still but differently. Time passes, needs and feelings change. One tries, with others, to recover past pleasures, past privileges. One looks for diversion."

"Is that what I am to you?"

"What would you want to be?" Dubin asked.

"I am not a hooker."

"My God, why should I have thought so?"

"Attitudes don't always need words."

"What attitudes? I assure you of my respect, Fanny."

"How much respect does a diversion get?"

"Forgive the word, I might have chosen better. In any case there are always possibilities. The course of a relationship is unpredictable."

"Well, what is possible?"

"I suppose it's possible to love one woman one way and another another."

"Which way do you think you could love me?" Fanny then asked.

He answered slowly: "I am drawn to you. Surely that's obvious? Anyway, it's as much as I want to think of or define just now. Let's stop analyzing our relationship, dear Fanny, and get into bed. An act defines itself."

"I would really like to," Fanny answered, "but my stomach is rumbling like ape. When I am this hungry I can't concentrate on anything, not even going to bed with someone. But I will if you want me to."

"Let's eat," Dubin said.

Fanny pulled off her short nightgown—her breasts were beautifully formed. She wiggled into black bikini underpants, then drew on a short deep-pink minidress. Her hair she wore attractively up and slightly messy, though the effect was splendid. Her nipples were imprinted on the dress. He considered asking her to put on a bra but didn't. Fanny then draped on the small gold crucifix and slipped on her blue glasses.

"Do you have to wear those?"

"Don't you like them?"

"They blank your face."

"I hate the glare," Fanny said.

"You are the glare."

She liked that, laughed.

When Fanny, in her fuchsia dress—not Dubin in his silk suit—appeared in the Contessa dining room, it burst into life. The vast elegant room, with gold-decorated white walls and a flight of cherubim in blue tones across the ceiling, fronted the dark canal. Before them, as they entered, a multitude of tables draped in white cloths extended into semi-darkness. Only a brightly lit rectangular section under two crystal chandeliers was roped off with a thick white silk rope and lavishly set for dinner. Into this dining area of about two dozen tables, none presently occupied, Fanny and Dubin were led and courteously seated by the maitre d'hôtel.

"I guess we're early," said Dubin.

He had seen the man's discreet yet momentarily stunned glance at Fanny and had noticed that the four waiters who had been standing impassively at the doors had stirred and risen, if not to military attention at least to animated interest in her. Though her young legs were outstanding in short dresses, Dubin, if he had had his wits upstairs, would have suggested a more discreet garment for the dining room.

"Not at all, sir," the maitre d' responded. "The season is at the end. Only a few guests stay."

He was a handsome heavy-eyed man who, as Fanny smiled and he bowed to her, let his eyes rest fleetingly on her bosom; he lingered on the crucifix and recommended the pesce. Dubin felt a stirring of mild jealousy but kept it down. The reaction surprised him.

After studying the menu Fanny ordered brains and Dubin bass. She had shrimp and he melon with prosciutto. Fanny had turned down a drink—too many on the planes—and Dubin signaled the steward and ordered a bottle of wine.

He urged her to remove her sunglasses. "They put you at a distance."

"I'll come nearer." Fanny dropped them into her stuffed purse. He had noticed she had tucked her diaphragm box into the bag before they left the room.

"What for?" Dubin had asked.

"Just a habit."

As he pondered her reply she gazed around the room, her eyes alert, comfortable, eyebrows slightly ragged. The nails of Fanny's efficient plain hands were bitten to the quick. When the wine was poured she gulped it as if it were water. She was affectionate, chummy. "What were you saying when I was in the bathroom? You were saying something."

"Encouraging myself."

"Do you have to?"

"More or less, when I'm away from home and operating adventurously."

"Once you said you would tell me how you met your wife."

How she harps on my wife. "I told you she was a widow then," he said. "She was married to a doctor who died young. He was apparently an unusual man who influenced her strongly. I had trouble competing with him in her memory but that changed after the birth of our daughter."

Fanny, listening with interest, chewed absently.

Dubin then said, "I'm sure you understand, Fanny—I won't bring this up again—that she mustn't know about us, not have the remotest suspicion. Her life hasn't been easy. I wouldn't want to hurt her."

"Would you hurt me, William?"

He swore no. "I feel tender to you, Fanny, and hope you feel something similar for me."

She felt she did. Her wine-flushed face was lovely. Her eyes, more intensely green, looked gently at him. Dubin was enjoying the food and liked the half-hidden glances of the waiters and the concern of the heavy-eyed maitre d', who came by often to see how things were progressing.

"What about you?" he asked: "For instance, what does your father do?"

"He imports," she said doubtfully.

"You don't get along with him?"

"It's very mutual."

"May I ask why?"

"He's self-centered and doesn't have much respect for me or my mother though he gets along with my sister. My mother is a gutsy lady but I don't want to ta!k about her either. I'm enjoying this meal."

He lifted his glass in agreement. Dubin drank wine freely and loved the evening. Fanny relished the brains. One or another of the young waiters appeared from time to time, ostensibly to replenish bread or pour wine. All, Dubin thought, came to view Fanny up close, who seemed to radiate nudity and was, she confessed, very happy. Dubin felt she was one of those gifted people who give public pleasure, not a bad thing in life.

As they were waiting for dessert, the biographer felt a hand on his knee, then as it slowly traveled up his thigh, decided he was dealing with Fanny's foot. She had removed her shoe and was caressing him under the table.

"You make my foot warm."

"Warm or cold, it's a marvelous instrument. Is this what is called footsie?"

She smiled affectionately. "Do you like it?"

"Won't the waiters know what we're doing?"

"They don't give a shit. It goes on forever in restaurants."

"I should be more observant."

He poured the last of the wine as Fanny, her face composed as she stroked his leg, after a paradise of expectation touched his aroused organ. Dubin made no objection. This was Venice, this was Italy. This, according to the arts and humanities, was what it was all about.

He felt in his pleasure a loosening of ties, concerns, restrictions—a sense of trumpets blaring in the woody distance. Here's William the Bold, with upraised sword on a black charger, galloping onward under the bright blue sky. Stepping out of his shoe he began gently to move up Fanny's calf with his adventurous right foot. Deadpan above table, impassioned below, he felt her thighs yield to his insistent gentle probing. Fanny gazed at him dreamily as at last he pressed the soft flesh under her bikini panties. Dubin experienced a desire to pull off his black sock but the perspiring maitre d' fortunately came by, inquiring if they had enjoyed the meal. The biographer, with dignity, said they had indeed, and could he have his check. Fanny nodded. Dubin felt drunk and embarrassed as they got up and walked past the waiters at the French doors, all silently aware of them, one regarding him with a connoisseur's approval; but other patrons were coming in and it was not too bad. Yet he felt he had overeaten and overdrunk, the weight of food and wine antipathic to self and spirit.

"I like you," she said in their room. "Can we go out tonight, William?" Her things were still strewn all over. He felt he knew her well.

"Where for instance?"

"Someplace lively, where we can dance."

"This is off-season," he told her. "There are no night clubs in Venice. We can look for a movie, if you like."

"Let's have some real fun."

"What about a walk in St. Mark's?"

"Could we go to Harry's Bar?"

Dubin agreed. "Put on something warm."

The night was dark, damp, the streets still. Houselights went on as they walked up XXII Marzo. Fanny touched his arm and they stopped in mid-street. He put his mouth on hers. They kissed with wine-soaked tongues.

"I'm wet through my pants," she said. "Let's go home."

"Wonderful," Dubin said.

In their room he undressed her, brief episode—fuchsia dress, underpants, shoes.

Fanny had trouble getting his undershirt over his head.

"Why do you bother wearing them?"

"My wife buys them."

"Tell her not to."

"They help in wintertime. She shops for me, I hate to."

"I wish you wouldn't praise her to me—"

"I wasn't aware I was—"

"Lift your arms."

She drew the undershirt over his head.

"Pardon this bit of belly. You wouldn't think I exercise."

"You wouldn't have the belly if you stood straight."

"Exactly what Kitty says."

"I really don't care what she says. Step out of your shoes."

"I wish I were younger for you."

"Fuck your age."

"Well put," Dubin laughed.

When she bent to remove his socks there was a tearing noise.

"What was that?"

Fanny laughed wildly. "I farted." She ran with a sob into the bathroom, flushed the bowl.

After five minutes, when she failed to answer his inquiring knock, Dubin turned the knob and cautiously looked into the bathroom.

"Are you all right, Fanny?"

She was standing at the toilet bowl, retching, a blob of diarrhea dribbling down her leg.

Afterward she was sick, vomited raucously, spilling her supper, spitting, weeping.

"I feel awful."

"Poor baby, what can I do for you?"

"I also feel I am tripping. 'Seize the day,' hump your lay."

After he had cleaned her with paper, when after sobbing awhile she lay asleep, her mouth open, breathing noisily, Dubin washed her legs and buttocks with a warm soaped cloth but could not wholly remove the odor of her illness.

The biographer recalled Yeats on love's mansion in the place of excrement; but not much came of it.

As he was falling asleep Maud appeared in his mind; Dubin awoke. Was it she he had seen in the fog with a man old enough, ironically, to be older than her father? Whoever he was had seemed past sixty. "My daughter is not for thee": Brabantio. Yet, could Dubin despise an aging man who desired the company of a young woman—endless insistent hunger? The old gent, he guessed, would have to be one of her teachers—maybe someone from her Mexican dig last summer? So soon out of the crib, so quickly grown—bleeding, breasted, gone—lost to me. Out of the house at eighteen; at nineteen as deeply as he into amorous intrigue? How is it possible—the hunger to adventure in contravention of time's good sense? He figured her age with her friend's would average a good forty; his with Fanny's, less. Himself less culpable—if one were to use the word—than Maud's male friend—if it was Maud—because Fanny was three years older than his daughter and no innocent. Life responds to one's moves with comic counterinventions.

He dressed in the dark so as not to awaken the girl.

"I don't want to die," Fanny moaned in her sleep.

A universal lament.

Dubin went down in the cage elevator and through the dimly lit lobby, though it was not much past eleven, into the street. Where does a concerned father seek his erring daughter? The sky was clouded, no sign of moon, the night air hazy, cool; he crossed a stone bridge over a narrow canal exuding mist. In an alley he passed a blind black man touching the wall with his fingers. The biographer drifted through a maze of crooked streets around La Fenice, peering into lit places, staring at elderly men with young women. Though his search, if it was one, came to nothing, he fantasied meeting Maud—she wandering alone wanting to find him—their encounter, embrace. Afterward they'd walk together. He wanted to tell her why he was in Venice though she'd probably not want to know. Perhaps they had experienced similar disappointments and might, tomorrow morning, leave together for the States. Dubin doubted it in afterthought. He doubted Maud was in Venice.

Entering Harry's Bar he sat at a table in a corner. An old waiter with long gray sideburns brought him a brandy. Dubin was moved to speak to the man but did not. He sipped his brandy, watching those at the bar and tables, smart-looking men and sensuous women, even when oddly dressed, beautifully dressed. He sought among them a woman with a sense of past: past time, past pain, awareness of the difficulty of loving. Only the young, the raw young, were present. He did not want to be among them.

Dubin wandered into St. Mark's Square, through the piazzetta to the water. It was a square walk he was making in a circle. There were a few tables in front of Florian's—three or four people sitting quietly in the dark. The other cafés were closed, their tables set top on top, chairs stacked in columns. Some of the summer tables were piled up under the gallery arches. On the embankment by the mooring poles several gondolas lay like dead fish out of water, to be stripped and stored in back canals and there await the end of winter. Two gondolas were still moored in the dark water. The tide was rising and the undulating water slapped the boats and sucked at them. A narrow plank boardwalk on carpenter's horses had been laid across the piazza for the winter floods.

Over the water the night was starless. A string of dim lights ran along the misty shore of the Giudecca. Behind the shore lights rose a dark mass of houses, lit windows here and there in a sparse ascending diagonal. Behind this island other islands floated in the sea. An island is a mystery, he thought. A man is an island in the only sense that matters, not an easy way to be. We live in mystery, a cosmos of separate lonely bodies, men, insects, stars. It is all a loneliness and men know it best.

Dubin stood at the low wall overlooking the water in front of the small tufted umbrella pines in the giardinetta. A half dozen starved cats were consuming the remains of somebody's spaghetti supper on a spread newspaper. An old man in a light coat approached and asked him for a cigarette.

"I have forgotten my own," he said.

Dubin thought it was the waiter he had seen at the bar but this was another man. He handed him his pack of cigarillos.

"Thank you, signore."

"For not much. They're bad for your health."

"I have no health." The old man touched his hat and walked slowly along the embankment. He crossed the steps of the small stone bridge and disappeared.

The biographer thought of that other waiter, his father, who had waited all his years for life to catch up with him. He was waiting when he died. He died waiting.

Papa, his son said, you died before much had happened with me. I wasn't married. You only once met my future wife, never saw your granddaughter. I am a biographer. I want you to know that President Johnson—he was also after your time—gave me a medal for a book I wrote about someone called Henry Thoreau, a large-souled man in the natural world. That's what I do: write books about the lives of men.

He looked at his hands as he spoke. They were his father's.

What do you know about people's lives? said the waiter.

I'm not a kid any more, Papa. Some things I know.

So what kind of a medal you got?

It's called Medal of Freedom—an award for accomplishment.

It would be better if it was from President Roosevelt.

I was only a child then.

Believe me, if I could write a book it would be a wonderful book. I saw a lot in my time. I'm not a waiter thirty years for nothing.

I wish you'd been alive when they gave me the medal. There was a dinner in the White House.

This I would enjoy. I would also donate my services if they needed an extra waiter.

I hoped you would live till I began to earn some money. I wanted to make your life easier.

A living I always made. Not much a living but I made a living. Enough to take care of your mother.

I wish she had lived.

In good health, said the waiter.

He was a round-shouldered man of medium height with purple-veined legs and an overly patient nature. Waiting was congenial to him; not much changed as you waited. He had wet blue eyes and a puffy pinkish face. His eyelids itched and he rubbed salve on them. At work he wore an alpaca jacket whose stains he rubbed out by brushing them with a rag dipped in hot coffee; a daily washed white shirt, snap-on bow tie, black wool trousers. He wore white cotton socks he changed twice a day and knobbed ankle-length shined black shoes. The shoes, when at last he abandoned them, looked like misshapen baking potatoes. He carried a yellow pencil stub on his right ear and worked mostly in Jewish dairy restaurants.

Charlie Dubin was an infinitely patient man, not known for his humor. He did not endear himself to his customers as other waiters did, with their bantering, wisecracks, jokes. He did not do as well with tips as some of the other men. The bosses said you could depend on Charlie but he made no great effort to make those he served happy.

I give good service, said Charlie Dubin. Let the food make the customer happy.

While his customers were eating he withdrew to the coatracks and waited. He waited earnestly, attentively, patiently.

Whyn't you crack a smile once in a big while? a patron asked.

Give me your order and I will deliver to you right away, Charlie said. Smiles I am not serving.

The man left a nickel.

One boss said he depressed the place, the customers complained.

Mr. Goldfein, said Dubin, I am a good waiter. I write down right the order and deliver quick from the kitchen. I don't want to be a vaudeville entertainer. Don't ask me I should be Pat Rooney or Smith and Dale. If the customer wants vaudeville let him go to RKO.

Take a walk, said the boss.

Charlie Dubin took another walk. A month later he was working elsewhere. But he told no jokes, seemed to know none. His life had made him a deadly serious man. He had seemed to want little, made do, lived a meager life. All he knew was being a waiter. When he was a boy William had found it hard to approve him. He gave me all he could, more than I wanted of his: an inclination to a confined lonely life. It was mine before I knew it; for years I held it against him.

Charlie winked at him.

Hannah Dubin, a thin small once redheaded whispering woman, cracked her knuckles against her breast, whispering, Siz mir nisht gut. She had, in her late thirties, not long after the death of her nine-year-old son, become mentally ill. She was afraid of the white window shades and of the long dark hallway of the railroad flat. She was afraid of footsteps on the stairs in the hall. She hid in the back bedroom, coming out to clean; or cook a chicken, then hid in the bedroom. Her face tightened against old friends visiting. The waiter feared sending her to a hospital; he feared she would suffer there. The doctor who had talked to her told Charlie Dubin that keeping her home wouldn't help; still she might recover, remissions were possible.

One winter morning, alone in the house, she swallowed half a bottle of disinfectant, and William, sent home from school because he was running a fever, came upon her lying on the clean kitchen floor, the acrid-smelling uncapped bottle of CN sitting in her shoe. He rushed downstairs to the drugstore and afterward induced vomiting by getting her to swallow the contents of a bottle of citrate of magnesia he had bought in panic.

Yes, she whispered, yes, yes. She drank from the bottle as though famished, as though she had wanted all her life to drink the miraculous potion he served her. It would make her sane again, healthy, young—would restore her chance to have everything she hadn't had in her life. She drank her own everlasting hunger. When she recovered, her graying hair coiled in braids on her head, she promised she would never—never again.

Willie, don't tell Papa I am crazy.

Mama, don't say that.

She warned him: Don't go in the rain, Willie, not in the rain. You will catch a cold, the doctor will come, you will get pneumonia. Don't go, Willie, out in the rain.

Hannah sat in the darkened bedroom, shades drawn, whispering to herself. She was meek in the house but when she ventured into the street to buy something to eat she shouted at those she said were following her.

The steak is in the bathtub, she whispered in the dark.

The doctor thought she ought to go to the hospital but

Charlie, waiting for her to get better, cooked, and cleaned when he could and talked to her in whispers. Hannah, he said, get better or your whole life will be wasted. When her eyes were wet she lifted her skirt and wiped them with her cotton petticoat.

Look how clean she is, the waiter said to his son.

She was dead at forty, of pleurisy and anguish. She did not thank her husband for waiting for her to get better; she did not thank her son for having kept her from taking her life.

He hid from his memories of her.

William and Charlie Dubin lived alone in the house.

After William had met Kitty he told his father about her, and the old man said miserably, Why do you want to marry a goyish widow with a goyish child that he will someday call you names? She won't be comfortable with you.

Dubin said he would take his chances.

William, said the waiter passionately, you know what we went through with Hitler. Don't marry somebody that she will take you away from the Jewish people.

He wrote his father a note: Dear Papa, How can a man be a Jew if he isn't a man? How can he be a man if he gives up the woman he wants to marry?

His father kept his letter in his pants pocket and Dubin found it there when Charlie died. He tried to have him buried in a grave near his wife's but there were no plots, so they lay in different cemeteries.

"Go look for your daughter," the waiter's voice said.

In a street near the embankment a long-faced girl in sweater and jeans sat on a stool bowing a cello clasped between her legs. The music she played was from a Bach suite for cello unaccompanied. Dubin had the record but stayed to listen. He listened, standing to the side, not to distract the girl. It was late. On the ground lay a small cardboard box with a few lire in it. The girl did not play all that well but he listened till the end of the movement. Dubin liked the harsh-sweet gutty bowing. He liked the sensuous dignity of J. S. Bach, husband of two wives and father of twenty children, jigging in a state of grace, his music flowing like water falling in an iron fountain. The pouring fountain was the music. The cellist was not a beautiful girl—her face was long and her figure meager; but she looked handsome playing the cello in the Venetian night and Dubin felt he loved her.

In the morning Fanny said she was so much better, though her gut felt tender. "It was all the wine that did it. I always overreact to wine." Dubin had hovered over her like a mother duck. He had given her a pill that stopped diarrhea and another that diminished nausea. They were pills that Kitty brought along when they traveled. He fed Fanny dry toast with sugarless tea. She was hungrier than she had any right to be but he wouldn't let her have more food. "I'm dying of hunger," Fanny complained. She still felt queasy and had cramps but they weren't bad and she was decently comfortable and even "cozy."

It was raining on the canals. They watched the rain through the window, Fanny lying propped against two pillows in their double bed, her legs covered with a blanket. She wore a light black nightgown. She was reading *Sons and Lovers* and said she liked it.

"I'm up to here," she read aloud: " 'He only knew she loved him. He was afraid of her love for him. It was too good for him, and he was inadequate. His own love was at fault, not hers.' Why is he such a shnook?"

"She reminds him of his mother. He senses it."

"Don't tell me the end, I don't want to know."

"The end is there already."

"I don't want to know it." For a while she stopped reading, seemed depressed.

"Anything the matter?" Dubin asked.

"I was thinking about myself. I'm not the world's most stable woman."

He said, after a moment, that the feeling was not an unnatural one at her age.

"Yes, but why now?"

"You tell me."

"Just a mood, I'm tired of being in bed." Sighing, she went back to her reading as he flipped through a guidebook of Venice. He felt close to her, easy in his mind—at home; he was glad he had suppressed his doubts and gone off with her.

She told him about her life—the usual happy unhappiness of childhood. She had an older sister she called a bitch and a father who thought of Fanny as one. "My mother is the only friend I've got."

"You've got me."

Playing with her long hair, she observed him. "I like to be with you, William. I also like the vibes you have with what you're doing. I wish I could do more with my life."

"More what?"

"More good," she said hostilely.

He said he had often had the same thought.

Dubin got up and kissed her dry lips, and her ears and eyes. She pressed his hand to her breast.

She had tossed her blanket aside and lay in bed in a nightgown that touched her body like an enduring kiss. Extraordinary the grace a bit of draping gives nudity. Her every casual movement stirred him.

"But I still have cramps that come and go," Fanny said.

Dubin went into the bathroom and briskly brushed his teeth.

She said she could eat half a horse and, when he advised her nothing solid yet, said she would settle for some ginger ale. "Ginger ale is what my mother used to spoon us after an upset stomach."

There was nothing in the midget-refrigerator in the room but hard liquor and mineral water. Dubin called down for a bottle of ginger ale but the waiter offered only Pepsi. Fanny made a face: she had this thing about cola drinks—they gave her hives. Dubin said he would hunt up a bottle of ginger ale. He put on his raincoat and borrowed an umbrella from the porter.

He walked in steady rain from their hotel to the Rialto before he was able to find the soda. He was happy he had found it for Fanny. He imagined her saying, when he returned, that she had bathed and wanted him to undress and get into bed with her.

"I think you'll feel better after we make love," Dubin, speaking to himself, said to her.

When he returned to their room she was lying in bed wearing sunglasses. "Jesus, William, I thought you were dead and gone." She said she had ordered a sliced chicken sandwich because she was painfully famished, had eaten every bit of it, and held it down.

He was happy to hear it. He thought he'd take a shower.

She came into the bathroom as he was standing in the shower and, retching, threw up the bread and chicken into the toilet bowl; her diarrhea returned; and hours later he began to spoon-feed her some warmish ginger ale, which, by God's grace—if not her own—she was able to retain. Fanny promised not to do anything equally stupid. "Please don't hold it against me."

Before falling asleep she whispered, "Tomorrow, William, I promise."

Tomorrow appeared exquisite—warm, clear—"inspiring," Dubin said. Fanny awoke glum, as though she'd long worried in her sleep; but after chancing—against his solemn advice—a continental breakfast without suffering consequences, she took a bath with salts, vigorously shampooed her hair, opened windows and doors to air the room, and though still pale, was energetic, vitalized.

"Let's zap out and see the sights."

He readily agreed. She put on the crucifix, then removed it and dropped it in the drawer. Fanny took it out again and draped it around her neck.

He felt at times he would like to be rid of her.

They hurried to St. Mark's, she—after shedding a cardigan because of "the heat"—in white jersey over black bra and in denim swing skirt, carrying her suede shoulder bag. Though she wore heavy-heeled shoes there was a ripple in her walk and people on the street seemed to like to watch her go by.

Fanny and Dubin hurried on in the brilliant sunlight, she keeping pace with his practiced long strides. The biographer wore his blue blazer, with flared reddish plaid slacks, and blue striped shirt with watermelon-pink tie. He was growing longer sideburns whose dominant color was gray. Dubin had occasional thoughts of dyeing his hair. Venice, absolved of fog and rain, had let a golden day rise like a balloon over its annealed islets. The sky floated azure over the green canals of antiquity. The effect was of island, plage, seashore—once more of holiday.

"Fanny," Dubin advised, "take those silly glasses off and look around. Some extraordinary painters took their light from this sky."

She blew a kiss to the sky, removed the glasses and slipped

them into her bag. She walked close to Dubin, their bodies touching. He had never felt younger.

Pigeons rose, wheeling, fluttering over them in the Piazza San Marco. There were a dozen tourists on the Square. Dubin, showing the girl around, pointed out artifacts, objects of interest in and around the Cathedral, reading to her from his guidebook what had been plundered when and where. She listened, looked where he pointed, walked on.

Kitty, on first seeing the Cathedral, had cried out in delight. Coming to a new city, she walked on air through its streets. Fanny gazed around almost without curiosity, looking back as though she did not trust either what she saw or her response. He was not dissatisfied. She would learn; he enjoyed her company. Fanny liked to lock fingers as they walked—what pleasure the simple gesture gave, what a compliment, flesh on flesh.

She had a Kodak in her bag and pulled it out to snap his picture. Dubin threw a hand up before his face.

"Oh, come on—what's a picture?"

"Let's take yours." He snatched the camera and snapped one of Fanny, her knees bent, extending a palm to a curious pigeon. Another alighted on her head. "Get off me, you shitty bird." She swatted at it, laughed in embarrassment as the pigeon fluttered away.

A priest in skirts and biretta, carrying a briefcase and rolled umbrella, perhaps noticing Fanny's crucifix if not her vital good looks, inclined his head in courteous greeting.

He offered to take a picture of them with his Polaroid.

"Let's, William—"

Dubin thanked the priest, said it wasn't necessary. "Are you from the states, Father?"

"Newark, New Jersey."

"Small world, I was born there."

"I was born in Trenton," said Fanny.

"Were you?" Dubin asked in surprise. "We're all from the Garden State—maybe the same garden."

The three laughed.

"Where was your wife born?" she asked.

"Montreal," he answered, clearing his throat.

The priest tipped his biretta. "Blessings on you, my child," he said to Fanny.

Later she squeezed Dubin's hand.

"What made you ask about my wife just then?"

"Just then I wanted to know where she was born."

They wandered on the Piazza, along the galleries toward the Campanile. He asked her impression. "Does this city get to you? Some who see it for the first time wonder if they're the victims of their imagination."

"I like it all right though it isn't Fat City. I can smell smog. It's like a whiff of L.A., only oilier."

"That's from the mainland. Still, not everybody loves the Square or Venice itself. Montaigne did but thought it stank. So did Lawrence. In a letter he called it écoeuré—without heart; in a poem he speaks of it as 'the abhorrent green slippery city of Venice.' "

"Then why have we come here?"

"To be together."

"But why here?"

"I thought it might rouse up a bit of magic and blow it around."

"Did your wife like Venice?"

"Encore my wife?"

"It's an honest question."

"She loves it, although we've never been here but a short time before something nasty happens."

"What did?"

"Once I had a manuscript stolen out of my suitcase. I got it back a year later. It was mailed to me in the States and when I reread it I was glad I had lost it."

"Why?"

"It wasn't a good piece of work—a blow to my pride."

"Did anything else happen?"

"Kitty got awfully sick here."

"Like me—the trots?"

"She ran a high fever—she almost never does—and wanted to leave. She was afraid the plague was back for a visit, but as soon as we were on the plane she recovered and that was that."

"What bugs her? Why does she go around sniffing the gas?"

"It's not important."

"Man, it's weird."

"Forget it. Anyway, here we are together."

She said she wished they had stayed in Rome.

"We'll be back in a day or two. I wanted to scoot up to see if Venice affected you as it does me. Obviously it doesn't."

She momentarily rested her head on his shoulder.

They had stopped in front of a small jewelry shop. Dubin, noticing something in the window, asked her to excuse him.

"Can't I go in with you?"

"It won't take more than a minute. I'll be right out."

When he came out of the jeweler's a moment later, Fanny was earnestly engaged in conversation with a taut-bottomed erect red-haired young man in front of a lavish glass shop a few doors down.

"This is Amadeo Rossini. He wants us to ride in his gondola," she said to Dubin.

"I thought they were mostly stacked away till spring," he said genially.

"Not his," Fanny said.

"I am steel een my beezinez, signore," the young gondolier said. He resembled a matador in black T-shirt and jeans. His pants were tight, buttocks elegant.

"Care for a ride, Fanny?"

"I wouldn't mind."

The gondolier led them, Dubin carrying Fanny's cardigan, up a narrow street to a mooring pole where a single battered gondola, its prow spotted with bird droppings—the boat looked as though it had barely escaped a drastic fate—lay in the green water at the dock, lapped by ripples a parting vaporetto made.

After assisting his two passengers into the bulky boat—he seemed charmed by the vision of Fanny's black bra through her jersey—Amadeo, wearing his professional red-ribboned yellow straw hat, pushed off with a long oar and the ride began pleasantly in the warmish early-November sun. Fanny, her color restored, lifted her face to the light. If there were Indians in Italy this was an Indian summer's day.

Amid the decay what beauty! Many of the palazzi were façade-eroded yet stately, graceful, despite asymmetry of windows and columns. Some houses were boarded up—pigeons nesting in the grillwork—in need of restoration; but their shimmering reflections in the greenish water—salmon, orange, aquamarine—excited Dubin. He lit a cigarillo and smoked contentedly, at times beset by thoughts of Venice subsiding in brackish water at the sea's bottom to be nibbled at into eternity by bony pale fish. The gondola was gliding toward Ponte Accademia and as he watched the reflections in the water it was no great effort to think himself afloat in an insubstantial world. With open eyes Dubin dreamed of passionate love in a fantastic city.

The gondolier broke into song. In a pleasant high tenor he celebrated love in a gondola. His eyes, when Dubin turned to look, were anchored on Fanny. Hers, dear girl, were shut as she listened. Perhaps he was singing to her black brassiere? Or was it her gold crucifix that had inspired his song? No doubt simply Fanny herself, sexy Pippa passes. Dubin experienced no jealousy. What he felt in her presence no doubt the young gondolier also felt, but me first by prior contract. I met her once on a country road, wooed her by wanting, flew away with her over the sea. She's with me—my girl. No point feeling sorry for the gondolier. He has youth; I am momentarily graced by her presence. Next week it's into my long work again.

"Two bits for your thoughts," he remarked to Fanny musing as she watched the water.

She smiled affectionately, pinched his nose. He bent to her. They kissed in the gondola as the youth sang. She lightly ran her fingers up the inside of Dubin's thigh.

"We're highly visible, should we go elsewhere?"

"I dig this ride," she softly sighed.

The battered gondola with blue seats and faded green carpet glided on, the youth singing still, confessing passion and pain to an unknown ear, Trident maybe? Though he did not understand the Venetian dialect, Dubin made out "jealous husband" in "Le bele toseta ga el mario gelosa," and was tempted to advise the young man to rest his voice but refrained.

The boat was in mid-canal after rounding the bend toward the Rialto before he noticed people staring at them from palazzi windows; others from small craft on the canal. It then occurred to Dubin that theirs was the only tourist gondola out that morning. The Venetians were, from old, commercial types, but he beheld no other sightseers around and felt momentary apprehension which he ridiculed but it was there. Had the gondolier on his fat nerve taken them out at a forbidden time? He had waked that morning short of cash and decided it was still summer? So he hauls his banged-up boat from a back canal and goes hunting for belated tourists? Summer anyone? Fanny with Dubin had walked into his practical needs? What a nuisance if they were stopped by the police motoscafo. He looked around and saw the municipal garbage scow, trailed by floating lettuce leaves and a few boiled onions bobbing in the wavy water.

There was also a sand barge and a variety of rowboats, blunt- and sharp-nosed, plus assorted topi delivering produce, meat, cases of beer, even a small coffin for a child or midget.

A hairy-chested man called to them from a barge filled with gray sand.

"What's he saying?" Fanny asked.

"Get off the canal, they need the water."

"Va fan'gulo," chanted the gondolier.

The hairy bargeman cupped his palm over his upper arm, thrusting the free fist into the air.

Unaffected, Amadeo went on singing his love songs. Now he celebrated a petite blonde in a gondola, who out of exquisite pleasure went to sleep as the gondolier rowed. Dubin had asked him what the song was about. To what end he did not sing. A few people crossing the outer stairs of the Rialto stopped to look at the boat. A woman with flowers waved at them. Dubin, facing an audience, felt self-conscious: glad-ragged goat of fifty-six courting a chick of twenty-two who'd be better served, at least in appearance, by the youth who rowed them. I should be rowing them.

Why, he asked himself, didn't this happen to me when I was twenty-five and had less to be self-conscious about? Why was I studying law when I should by some miracle have been in Venice? He felt false and hungered for privacy.

"Pull over," he said to the gondolier. "We want to get off."

"Oh, not yet, please," Fanny said.

"Pull over to the dock," Dubin said. "If the police come we may be ordered off the canal."

"You mak' meestake, signore," the gondolier replied, angered. "No one 'as the right to tell me when I weel work or what to do, if ees summer or weenter."

But Dubin, still uncomfortable, insisted and paid him off; to placate Fanny he included a healthy tip over an exorbitant fee. The handsome gondolier lifted his straw hat, bowing stiffly. His copper head of hair remained an enduring vision.

"I wish you hadn't done that, William," Fanny said on the embankment, her face tense. "So what if the guy was singing at me? It did no harm."

Dubin denied the singing had bothered him. He said he was restless. "There's so much to see in the city. We'll do better on foot. Distances are deceptive here."

He insisted on showing her where some extraordinary people had lived and worked. Close by, near the Goldoni Campo where Venetians gather in talky droves each evening, he pointed out the cortile where Marco Polo's house was supposed to have stood.

"He left Venice when he was a kid of seventeen for a fabulous journey throughout the East that ended a generation, plus a Venetian war, later, in a dank prison in Genoa. There he dictated a book of his travels, which is, among other things, a masterpiece of observation of an anthropological sort. In folklore he's become Marco Millioni, the comic liar, but in truth he said what he saw in a precise Venetian way, without poetry or passion, yet he saw well and kept the Asian world in his head until he was able to record it on paper, via the help of a literary hack he discovered in his cell. Two centuries later Christopher Columbus read the book and had one more reason to take off for what was to be the new world. Isn't it marvelous, Fanny, the way things tie up and turn out?"

"I read about it when I was a kid."

They then hurried, by ways Dubin knew, over stone bridges arching quiet canals, to the Moorish neighborhood where Tintoretto had lived and painted. Fanny and Dubin entered the church of Madonna dell'Orto to see his frescoes. Tintoretto was buried by the side of his favorite daughter Marieta. The biographer told Fanny about the painter—a self-educated imaginative man of genius.

"Some say he painted too much and wasn't as good as the Venetian best, but many of his pictures knock me cold. His miracles have the mysterious force of the miraculous. Marieta was herself a fine portrait painter who used to help in his studio dressed in the then equivalent of dungarees. She died young, at thirty, and he mourned her the short rest of his life. There's a legend that he painted her portrait as she lay dead."

"Didn't he paint her when she was alive?"

"Probably. This was something else—a last act of love." Dubin, as he talked, perspired.

"Maybe he flipped," Fanny said.

Reversing direction when they were once more outside, Dubin led her back to St. Mark's and then along the embankment to the Chiesa S. Maria della Pietà. Fanny was showing fatigue. He asked her if she wanted to rest but she said she would stay with it if this was the last of the sightseeing that morning. Dubin assured her it was.

In the church he said: "Here once stood a church orphanage with a music chapel for girl foundlings. Rousseau said there wasn't one of them without some considerable blemish but when they played their beautiful music he saw less and heard more. Vivaldi was known as 'il prete rosso'—he had auburn hair; he taught them to fiddle and sing, and confessed himself in waterfalls of stringed music. He worked there, off and on, for forty years, composed in a hurry, and earned thousands of ducats. Kings came to hear his concerts but in the end he ran afoul of the Pope's nuncio and fell out of favor, presumably for neglecting to say Mass; not to speak of his friendship with a singer and her sister who had traveled with him for fourteen years. He spent money like water and died a pauper. Like Mozart's, his grave has vanished, but given his music who needs it?"

Her face was weary. "Jesus, all you think about is biography."

"Not all," he said with a light laugh.

Dubin explained that since they were so near where men of this kind had lived it was only right to stop by and pay their respects. "I get this mind-blowing sense—as you say—of their lives and quality. I'm taken by those who celebrate life by making much of their own. It's a subtle altruism."

"If genius is your bag."

Dubin thought their genius made their humanity more clearly apparent. "One learns easily from their ordinary lives."

"I've got my own to live."

"To live it well—"

Though her mouth drooped, Fanny assented.

She said she was dead tired and could they now go home? "At least in the gondola it was a ride."

Dubin led her by short cuts back to the Hotel Contessa, but not before he had stopped off at the jeweler's he had visited earlier, to pick up a bracelet for Fanny, a twenty-two-carat gold band overlaid with a spiraling coil, which surprised and delighted her. She kissed him warmly as she admired the handsome bracelet on her extended arm. "I am really genuinely happy."

After a light lunch at the hotel, spaghetti al burro with a small bottle of non-gaseous mineral water for her; fettucine with red wine for Dubin, they went out again. Fanny, after the meal, had complained of cramps but they quickly disappeared. The day's beauty persisted: the flawless sky flared blue; canals encrusted with green sparkling light; and aura of Venice: expansive, enlivened—sense of island, sense of sea, of voyage.

To Dubin's surprise, though not Fanny's, a small fleet of pleasure gondolas appeared on the Grand Canal as though a carnival had been declared. Dubin offered to make restitution for the aborted ride of that morning by taking her out again but she, after seriously surveying the scene, shook her head. He suggested, if her cramps were gone entirely and she felt refreshed, the Accademia Gallery so she could see some paintings of Tintoretto's after the frescoes of that morning. But Fanny wanted to do some shopping first and Dubin went with her. She bought discreetly—a few modest presents for friends, which he offered to pay for because she had only fifty dollars with her. She would not accept.

Wherever they went she cast occasional glances behind. Dubin, looking where she had looked, saw bright sunlight between palazzi. If you saw through dark glasses would that people the world? Fanny removed her shades only to examine the colors of objects in the shops.

"You feel all right, Fanny?"

"I guess so. I guess what's on my mind is that I better have a bath and get some rest instead of tracking along with you to the museum. That is, if you expect me to have energy for this afternoon." She smiled affectionately.

"In that case do rest, my dear."

She asked him not to stay too long, and Dubin promised to be back at five.

He took the gallery picture by picture at first, viewing slowly; yet not always seeing: thinking of Fanny as Venus bathing, Venus revived. He stayed until half-past four and considered remaining longer to give her more time to herself—he had thoughtlessly worn her out with walking that morning; but Dubin hadn't the serenity to wait longer. He left the gallery and as he was recrossing the Accademia bridge, observed below, in a long black gondola on the sunlit canal, an auburn-haired girl with a gray-haired man, his arm draped around her shoulders. They were sitting with their backs to him, the girl resting her bronze head against the old man's breast. Dubin, watching in a confusion of emotion, called down from the bridge, "Maud—it's your father! Maud, it's me!" She did not turn. He hurried down fifty steps and ran, as Venetians watched, across the Campi Morosini and S. Angelo, then into Calle de la Mandola toward the water. After ten minutes he emerged at the Grand Canal close by the Rialto. Dubin arrived before the gondola and waited, winded—not sure what he could say or do or not do—for the boat to catch up with him. But when it floated toward the bridge, the gondola had in it only the gondolier poling it. Could this be the one he had seen? Another that followed contained two young women and a boy. Dubin looked into the distance and beheld no others.

He called in Italian to the gondolier: "Where are your passengers?"

The man blew his nose in the water and waved vaguely with his hand: "Al sinistro."

Dubin went hastily up the bridge steps and down the other side into the market streets. He hurried through crowds and on the first side street spied a red-haired girl about a block before him, but not the man. Was it his daughter? Though now fatigued Dubin hastened toward her. When he reached the corner she had disappeared, but the first house as he turned into the street was a pension, and he was convinced that was where she was. He thought of entering and seeking her out, then decided not to. If it was Maud it would be wise to talk to her alone. The last thing he needed was to confront his daughter in the presence of her lover—who else?

Seeing a bakery across the street, Dubin went in, tempting the reluctant baker with a thousand lire to produce a telephone book; then he called the pension number.

"Is there a signorina Maud Dubin registered there?"

The padrone wasn't sure and who was calling?

"Tell her her father, William Dubin."

"I can't tell her a thing if you're really her father because there's nobody here by that name."

"She's red-haired," Dubin explained, and the padrone laughed and said, "We've got two different redheads this week. Eh, signore, they're a deceptive lot. You can't tell what they really are until you've looked up their legs."

"I'm much obliged." Dubin lingered at the corner to see if either of the women came out and in less than thirty minutes both did; one a girl with hair dyed orange, the other a strawberry blonde with a middle-aged spectacled escort, neither so much as resembling Maud. Dubin, relieved, though irritated with himself for wasting time he could have used to better purpose, hurried back to the Rialto; since a vaporetto was about to depart and he was weary, he hastened up the gangplank.

It was an interminable trip. He arrived at San Marco at close to seven and broke into a hurried run. What a stupid waste, he thought in anger.

Dubin absently got off the elevator at the fourth floor and ran up to the next flight. Fanny was not in their room. He began to undress for a shower when it occurred to him that the adjoining room was giving off percussive sighs. As he tried the door it easily opened: the bed was made and unoccupied; but not the floor.

On the rug, crouched on hands and knees was the red-haired Amadeo, his fiery hairy ass not so handsome as it had seemed in tight Levi's; and under him, alas, lay Fanny. Dubin observed her gold-braceleted arm around the young man's strong back. Her eyes were shut, her face drawn; she looked, he thought, before slamming the door, like a woman of fifty.

The biographer felt as though he had wasted every cent of a large investment and stood on the verge of desolation. Afterward, when he forced himself to go back to the hotel room late that night, Fanny, in a man's workshirt and denim pants, taut-eyed, pale, her expression ill at ease, fearful, said she had waited hours for him to return, had got anxious, and decided he was simply not interested in her, when the gondolier knocked on the door.

"Why didn't you tell him to go fuck himself?" Dubin shouted. "Why did you so quickly and easily demean us?"

"Don't think you own me because you brought me to this phony city," she wept. "I did it because I was sorry for him. Because he's young," she said cruelly, "and I like his ass. And because you don't deserve me."

She accused him of loving his wife. "Why do I always get hooked with these married shmucks?"

After a dismal night when he woke often—listened for sobbing, a voice begging forgiveness, but heard silence, her breathing—hungry to embrace her, to blot out betrayal by making passionate love, Dubin slept as though awake and woke early. What will it profit me to fuck her in anguish? Fanny, her face in a pool of moist hair on her pillow, lay heavily asleep. In sleep her expression was dull, the face and aspect of a stranger. And what, my God, am I doing in the same bed with her, back to back, four thousand miles from home and work? He detested himself for falling into the hands of a child. Dubin felt in himself a weight of mourning he could not shove aside, or otherwise diminish. He was, he thought, ashamed at having offered himself to her to betray. He sensed a more intense commitment to the girl than he had guessed, or perhaps permitted, and wondered if he had been almost in love with her—sad pattern of long past. If that's so I'm glad to be done with it. Love—given who she is—given her promiscuity and my bad judgment—would have led to something enduringly miserable. Better momentary pain than long heartbreak.

She woke as he was dressing, looked at him with one eye and reached for her tights. "I am," Fanny said, "just as moral as you."

"How would that work?"

"Don't give me that apeshit sarcasm."

He said he had asked an honest question.

"He needed me more than you ever did."

"His needs, assuming you're right, hardly constitute a requisite of morality."

"I have no obligations to you."

"Maybe you should have thought you had. Listen, Fanny," Dubin asserted, "I'm going out for a walk to air my brain. I'll have your breakfast sent up. You needn't get up yet, it's early. Maybe you ought to think a bit about yourself."

"All you wanted was cunt."

"If that's all I wanted I deserved what I got."

"What else did you want?"

"Passion, beauty—I want the world," Dubin shouted.

She fell back in bed and wept.

When he returned after two hours of aimless walking, aimless thought—not much relieved, conscious once more of his years, appearance, pain—Fanny had eaten and was reading in bed.

"What will you do?" he asked her dully.

"What do you mean?" Though her face was calm her voice wavered.

"What are your plans?"

She studied him unhappily. "I think I want to go to Rome and maybe Naples but all I have on me is less than fifty in traveler's checks and about ten in bills and change."

"And your air ticket home." He handed it to her.

"And my air ticket home."

"I've packed," Dubin told her, "and we're checked out. Why don't you dress and meet me across the street in Alitalia at eleven? I'm told there are two flights to Rome today."

"What time is the first?"

"I think at noon. If you decide not to go there you can have your ticket changed to the Air France late-afternoon flight to Paris and from there to New York."

"I have to see a friend in Rome." She said it as though the friend was female but he suspected a man.

He said he would meet her at eleven.

She arrived at eleven-fifteen in a tight black dressy dress and black pumps—a stunning woman, or so it seemed. Dubin resisted a resurgence of desire—"Carmen, il est temps encore"—born of frustration, the overthrow of his late happy adventure.

They greeted one another courteously. Fanny, before looking at him, glanced at the floor. Dubin nodded formally. She had on her blue glasses reflecting ceiling lights, and her Star of David—Jewish type she was meeting in Rome?—and still wore Dubin's handsome bracelet. Her hair was full, thick; to his surprise she had plucked the offending blond hairs on her chin. The girl could not have looked more attractive, or more innocent. Why? My need to absolve her? He was moved to say: "Let's forget it, Fanny—a serious mistake, no doubt of it, but not fatal. The moment's mistake; not for all time. Let's talk it over and maybe stay together the rest of the week? Perhaps there's something for us both to recover."

But he couldn't bring himself to say it. Pain is divisive. It spoke one word: shmuck.

At my age, Dubin modified it, all young women are desirable. I will keep it in mind and not hastily forgive her.

She paid for her ticket to Rome but the biographer insisted she accept a hundred in cash. "It isn't much, still if you're careful you can make it last a week. I suggest you not track around without money."

"You don't owe me anything."

He said he owed himself.

"Do you want the bracelet back?" She had slipped it off her wrist.

Dubin with a flip of his fingers refused to have it. "It's yours. I bought it for you with pleasure. Do what you please with it."

"You could give it to Maud."

"Maud will have to inspire her own bracelets."

"Do I deserve it?"

He laughed hoarsely.

"Are you punishing me with kindness?" she asked bitterly.

"That wouldn't be kind."

"I did it to hurt you," Fanny confessed.

"You hurt me."

She slipped her hand through the gold band. Fanny dug into her suede bag and returned *Sons and Lovers.* He accepted the book.

The baggage porter wheeled her suitcases to the dock on the canal. Dubin waited with her for the water taxi to return. It was another beautiful day, sky and water combining light; in the lagoon a scattering of islands they had planned to visit but never would. If one could embrace the day.

"You'll like Rome," he said.

"Where are you headed?"

He wasn't sure.

"I'll bet you hate me?"

"I wish we had done it differently."

"It was your fault as well as mine." Her mouth was firm.

He nodded gravely. "What will you do when you get back to the States?"

"I don't know. I might get married, maybe not."

"What do you believe in, Fanny?"

She reddened. "Do you mean do I believe in God?—I do."

"Do you believe in yourself?"

"I try."

Dubin, after a moment, advised her to go on with her studies.

She said they didn't teach in college what she wanted to learn.

"What do you want to learn?"

"I'm not sure."

"I see." He saw nothing.

The motoscafo was approaching.

"Take care, Fanny."

"Ciao. I appreciate what you did the night I got sick."

After hesitation they kissed lightly. Not better than nothing.

The motorboat slowly docked backward, piloted by a young capitano in lavender pants.

He wore a damp cigarette in the corner of his mouth and a white French sailor's cap with a red pompon. With gallant care the capitano assisted Fanny and her luggage into the chugging boat and seated her on a bench behind the wheel outside the cabin. There were no other passengers. He raised the accelerator, twirled the wheel, and at once they were off in the water in a wide churning arc.

When the boat hit mid-canal, Fanny, her hair flying around her shoulders, light in the sun, turned to wave goodbye to Dubin—to Venice? He lifted his hat, feeling as he did, glad at last to be alone, and had then his moment of elation.

Three

Q. What makes a clown sad?
A. Other clowns.

Dubin waits in the Swedish rain.

Marriage was his Walden—act to change his life; and what's past but persists. Change you change your past, they say. I was the waiter's true son, shared his inertia, fear, living fate—out of habit, compassion, impure love.

Who am I, Pa?

What do you mean who you are? You are an educated boy.

Years after Hannah Dubin's death he seemed not to know what to do with himself. If your train's on the wrong track every station you come to is the wrong station. The wrong stops, year after year, were vocation and women he couldn't make it with. It seemed to William Dubin he was not prepared to invest a self in a better self—give up solitude, false dreams, the hold of the past. The train chugged on: the wrong train.

In his twenties he was a half-reclusive too subjective romantic youth; yet fed up with self-indulgent falling in love, living in reverie, trafficking in heartache; worn out by what didn't happen: what he could not, or dared not, make happen.

Q. Why did it happen?

A. Who knows for sure? One day I took a chance, made a move, got involved. Life is to invest in life.

Dubin hadn't intended to fly to Stockholm. He'd been there with Kitty after Gerald had deserted the army in West Germany, and had fled to Sweden two years ago. After Venice the biographer had wanted nothing more than to take himself home and immerse his head in work; but that he was in Europe with Gerald nearby—a few hours into Scandinavia—made him want to see his adoptive son. Dubin had loved him as a child; he had intensely returned affection. The death of his father showed; the mother trying to be father had trouble being mother. It wasn't hard for her new husband to imagine himself the child. That was the first step to father. He had rescheduled his flight home and in a little more than five hours, shortly after an astonished view of Norway's fjords, had registered in a small Swedish hotel on the Skeppsbron, at the edge of the blue cold Baltic.

Strangers approaching each other in simple good faith: an act of trust was the imagined beginning. Though neither considered her/himself adventurous, each adventured. Kitty had invented a self-advertisement; and Dubin, though it was none of his business, had imaginatively responded. To that extent it was an arranged marriage: they had arranged it—he to escape his rooming-house existence, repetitive experience, boredom; he was thirty-one with little to show but fingers crossed, a self-critical Bronx Jew with no vocation he was pledged to. She was a troubled lonely ex-Episcopalian lady, a once and former doctor's wife, wanting a husband and protector of her child.

That's not all I want. I want joy, I want to live.

William Dubin promised life.

They promised love.

Kitty came to him with more than modest beauty; it was beauty she qualified. And the clinging remnants of trauma: modified mourning for the young dead, her ongoing burden, derived from a father a suicide at thirty-four, and a husband in his fortieth year destroyed by leukemia—informed in September, buried before Christmas. Kitty, telling herself it needn't be, feared more of the same. She feared her son's imagined fate; soon the child held it against her. Against the will she taught him how to miss a dead father.

Let's call it half a widow she still was when I met her. She had shed deep mourning but mourning lingered where it knew the ground. And there's a presence besides the self, the self that opposes the self: she forgets where she is. Or what's to be done next. She unwinds very slowly from sleep or lack of sleep. Her level of frustration is low: she stamps her foot in a high wind. Or at a sudden blast of an automobile horn. Sometimes at a missed stitch in her knitting; or when she's misplaced her purse again. And laughs when she finds it. And praises her humor as though to defend it: You can tell from the way Gerald laughs that there's fun in me. She laughs at that; and laughs when she is embarrassed. Watching a movie she laughs twice to Dubin's once.

I took the chance. She took hers with me: an oldish youth in his long letters—man of appetites and hungers, yet the stranger who had responded. I was, to her surprise, in her cast of characters.

Kitty said she trusted him but feared the future—nothing personal. The day before their wedding they walked in silence in Central Park. Searching his eyes at parting she said, I hope we aren't making a serious mistake. It isn't hard to.

Simply mistake would be serious enough.

Marriages can be difficult.

Was yours?

I was in love then.

Love is in life, in living, the bridegroom hopefully says. One gets in marriage, I imagine, what he earns.

Do you think so?

If she had asked out he thought he'd have let her go.

They were married in her best friend's living room; the bride, laughing breathlessly, wore a Mexican dress with flounced sleeves, pearls in her ears, and a gauzy rose shawl on her shoulders. It was a cold spring day.

Do you think I can wear a white sweater, I feel shivery?

Would you want a drink?

Later, I think.

She held in her hand a bouquet of white violets and wept silently during the ceremony, performed by her friend's father, an amiable judge. Kitty told Dubin afterward she always wept at weddings. Tears fill her eyes on ceremonial occasions. And when people go forth to distant places. Everyone's loss of someone's presence, significant or small, wakens a sense of prior loss.

Q. How did you feel?

A. Inspired.

Q. In truth?

A. I could come up with no other feeling.

Q. I'm sure. What of afterward, what we used to call the honeymoon?

A. We spent the first week moving into a new apartment. She had asked me to consider living in hers and I thought it was better not to: Let's both start with something new.

Not long before the wedding Dubin had made the acquaintance of her obsolete birthmark: for a while appeased, revived for him as a living fact. Kitty permitted, suppressing apology, yet managing to suggest damaged goods—if not impaired passion. He accepted the given.

As she undressed, she confessed the blemish: a dark skin discoloration that runs up my left inner thigh and spills out on my buttock.

Why do you call it blemish?

Birthmark, she said, with half a smile. It inhibited me sexually when I was young.

Does it now?

Not since Nathanael. He ridiculed me for making so much of it, called it an error in pigmentation. Inverse pride to make much of it. He told me to walk around naked in the bedroom with the shades up. When I wouldn't he pulled my underpants off. I was as angry as relief let me be. Once when we were alone on a beach in Maine he asked me to strip off my bathing suit, and eventually I did.

Dubin said it was a birthmark, not the Scarlet Letter. Why should you think you had earned it?

It's my nature. I don't understand why it should bother me in your presence, William, but it seems to. I have to tell you. They kissed and slid into bed. After a while Kitty said she didn't think she could come. Dubin held on. She begged him to satisfy himself; then cried, Harder, William, I'm coming.

The waterfront, through his hotel window, was lined with white craft: sailboats, sightseeing launches, a two-masted schooner; an ice-breaker waiting for winter. A smoking one-stack steamer was leaving for Finland. The whistle boomed.

How easy it is to go away. He watched the boat move slowly out to sea.

What would I do alone in a foreign country?

Dialing Gerry to say he was in Stockholm, he got back a high-pitched busy signal; so he slipped on his raincoat and walked out into the narrow high-walled streets of the Old Town. The biographer asked at the address of a Mrs. Linder for Gerald Dubin and was told no one by that name lived there. There had been a Gerry Willis.

"That's his name," Dubin told her. "Willis was his father's name—he's entitled to it. I'm his adoptive father, William Dubin, a biographer."

The Swedish lady had begun speaking English at his approach; she said Gerry Willis had moved out a month ago. Her daughter might have his address. She might not. He could try returning at seven, when she came home from work. The lady shrugged. Would he excuse her now? She had supper to prepare.

Did she know whether Gerry was short of funds? "Was that why he moved?"

"I can't say if this is true. I think he likes to move, he has that nature. Our socialist government provides well the American deserters. It comes from our taxes."

He lifted his hat in apology. Dubin said he would return at seven and went back to the hotel.

Restless in his chilly small room, he went again into the city. Stockholm, where he explored, exhibited an austere dignity of space and proportion. He liked the well-formed stately buildings of past centuries. He liked the broad clean canals between sections of the city connected by street-level causeways and bridges. Dubin felt the melancholy of the gray-blue mid-autumn sky, as though some hidden Norse God, if not Ingmar Bergman, pointed eternally to winter, warning Swede and stranger it was more than a season; it was a domain.

Having little to do but wait and think more than he cared to, the biographer embarked on an hour's excursion by launch on the waterways. The boat passed along canals, under bridges, sailed by villas close to the water, old redbrick factories, parks lined with yellow-leaved maples and yellowing pines.

He had been idly watching a man and woman a few rows in front of him in the all but empty motor launch. The man was a middle-aged Indian sitting with a long-faced attractive white girl of twenty-three or so. She might be English, a darkish blonde, motionless, reflective, as though she might think them into an embrace. They looked at each other and looked away. He seemed self-conscious, shy. The girl smiled gently. Neither moved close to the other though their feeling was intense. They talked in whispers, then sat silent. The biographer watched until it grew dark and raindrops splashed on the window of the launch. It seemed to Dubin that there were only three on the boat, the shy couple and himself. They hadn't touched though they wanted to. When the boat docked he left quickly.

Once she went to Montreal to visit a friend hurt in a ski accident. Kitty traveled by train and when she returned Dubin was waiting for her at Grand Central. Coming up the ramp, she walked right at him, yet passed without seeing him. Angered, he called her name. It took her fifteen seconds to recognize her husband. I'm sorry, I got very little sleep on the train. They kissed formally.

Dubin, carrying her bag, asked her if she knew she was married. How can I forget? she said, and laughed. They stopped to kiss.

He asked her to sew a button on his trench coat. Kitty took the button and put it in her plastic button box. She said she would sew it on one morning if he left the coat home. Dubin left it there for two weeks, then wore it without the button.

She quietly talked of her first husband in a seemingly detached way. In Gerald's room there was a picture of Nathanael taken by a *Daily News* photographer: of an intern in an oilskin raincoat attending a man lying on his back after an accident in a wet street.

That was taken years before I met him. In college I cut my leg in a fall off a bike and he stitched and bandaged it. I still have the scar. I was an undergraduate when we were married. Nathanael knew a lot and taught me to think a little. I'm naturally skeptical and he helped me to a more solid intellectual base. He had me reading philosophy for a while; he used to read it the way I read fiction. Though I loved him I wasn't sure about getting married at twenty. I married him, a pretty uncertain woman, but he helped focus me. I wish he had encouraged me to do something serious about a vocation.

I had Gerald when we were three years married. I was nervous with a baby, but it wasn't hard to calm down with a doctor around. Afterward there was a time I thought the marriage was on the rocks. We were both irritable and I felt I was a bad mother. Then we got along well and I was not a bad mother. You can imagine how I felt when he died at forty. I know I've told you this often, but every time I tell you I have to.

Dubin said he was listening.

One rainy morning he shouted, Why the hell don't you sew the button on my coat? If you can't, or don't want to, bring it to a tailor.

Her eyes were shut as though she was concentrating on the button. I have it in my button box. I *will* sew it on. But she didn't.

One winter's night Gerald was sick with the flu; his temperature hit 105° and Kitty was frantic. She telephoned the doctor but couldn't reach him. Fearing the child would go into a convulsion, she ran with him from one room to another. Dubin, also made anxious by the illness of children, said they ought to call an ambulance. Kitty thought it would take too long to come. She wanted to wrap the child in a blanket and get him to the hospital in a taxi. Dubin then looked up fever in a medical adviser she had bought after her husband's death, and began to rub the shrieking child's naked body with alcohol. Kitty held her hands over her ears. Within minutes Gerald's temperature had dropped. Kitty sewed on Dubin's button.

In sex she needed, Kitty said, a man of patience. He provided, plus whatever other talents a man like Dubin had. They were both limited sexually; so apparently had Nathanael been. What she had solved with him she had to resolve with Dubin. There were times he lived on little and ate desire. What she missed seemed not to rankle her.

In bed one night Kitty said, You mean a lot to me, William.

How much?

Because I haven't put Nathanael out of my mind doesn't diminish my feeling for you.

Is it love?

That was the wrong question: She said, I'm not sure what or how much of something is something, philosophically speaking.

Speaking simply, like now in bed?

She admitted she couldn't say she loved anybody without qualification. One had to be honest.

When she asked him, Dubin said he loved her.

Without qualification?

With love.

Sometimes as she was saying one thing he knew from the way she looked at him that she was reflecting on another.

Dubin waited in the small hotel lobby until ten to seven, then walked back into the Old Town and got Gerry's address from his former landlady's plain and distant daughter. He went in the rain to the number she had given him, also in the Old Town, a heavy-shuttered stone house in a curved badly lit cobblestone-paved alley; though he rang repeatedly and rapped on the heavy wooden door, no one responded. He vainly called Gerry's name. He called for Gerry Willis and Gerald Dubin and got no one. Dubin waited in the low wet dripping doorway for someone to come into the alley. He watched the water pour out of the iron downspout of the house and run along a stone drain into the street.

There were better nights for waiting, yet he felt not bad about it. Here he was with nothing else to do. If he gave time generously maybe the waiting would end well. He'd been thinking of Gerald as a child, their mutual need: he needed a father, I wanted a son. Dubin nostalgically remembered their affection. He wondered if Gerry did. But what can he know of me as I am now, or I of him? One guesses at essences—identities. Maybe love is a means of making a useful assumption about another person. Yet once I was his father; he let me be.

He rang, listening in the drumming rain to silence within, then left the alley and sought a telephone in a bar. Dubin opened his address book and dialed the American Deserters Committee. The secretary, a Texan, answered. He looked up Gerald Dubin and said he was registered but hadn't visited the office for a year. "He wrote and asked us to stop sendin the newsletter."

"Any address for Gerry Willis?"

"Not that I have iny record of. Some men get depressed here," the Texan said. "They hate the cold climate and the cold Swedes, not to mintion the government bureaucracy that has you fillin out forms every time you want to pee or lose a pound of weight."

The man said that not everybody got acclimatized to Sweden. Some could not get used to the weather, or the language, or find a satisfactory job, or get on with their education. "They git druggy or go ape and are locked up in prison. I tell them if they can't make it here they sure as hell aren't goin to make it in the U.S. of A."

"You don't remember Gerry?"

"I honestly wish I could."

Dubin returned to the shuttered house, rang again, and waited until he was tired of waiting. He slipped a damp note under the door and left the alley.

The rain had turned into a cold drizzle. The biographer momentarily removed his hat to feel the wet on his face. If he doesn't call tonight I'll try again in the morning.

He felt he hadn't minded not seeing Gerry tonight; he was not much in a mood to. Dubin wondered if he had come to see the boy so he could tell Kitty he had stopped off in Stockholm to visit him. He wanted her to be grateful to him before he lied to her about Venice.

She woke him to explain herself: her father had killed himself when she was a child—after his wife had betrayed him. Yet I loved her till she deserted me for a lover she went to Europe with. I could no more do that to a child than I could destroy it. My grandmother disliked her. I've only once been to her grave. I want you to know what my young life was like. There's a gap in me I will never fill. I've never slept well since I was little. Either a gene is missing or I'm afraid to for understandable reasons. But the world is very real to me and I don't want to make it seem unreal. I've always been honest with myself. What you won't admit, you never understand.

Nathanael loved me more than anyone else ever has.

Including your grandmother?

You know what I mean.

Q. She mythologized him?

A. Whatever it was, there were times I felt I had married him.

Mimosa, she said, is always the beginning of spring.

One spring morning she suffered a miscarriage.

My dear baby, Kitty wept.

It was a fetus, he said, astonished by the depth of her grief, guilt, mourning.

No more death, *please*, no more.

He did not ask her to define death but promised no more. Nathanael packed his suitcase and moved down the street. She spoke of him rarely now, perhaps to make a point about a short life, or something about the nature of marriage. Simply a sufficient time had passed.

A year later Maud was born; Kitty was very happy to have a girl yet promised Dubin a boy of his own. He said he thought of Gerry as his son. She said she believed him.

He delighted in his daughter. Went often to look at her as she slept in her room; enjoyed her childhood. She called for him when she had had a nightmare. He pressed her warm shivering body to him. He kissed her head; she kissed his lips. He read to her; loved her red hair, often combed it.

Kitty slept better. The house was in order. There were parties, house guests, visitors. She was good with the kids: sewed their clothes and knitted them woolen hats. She lived easily in their world. And she baked, made jellies, put clothes in garment bags, watered the house plants, nightly wiped a round oak table with soaped sponge to give it a driftwood quality.

Having a family satisfied a harsh hunger in Dubin. He relished his wife's warm womanly body. And Kitty played the harp for him. She drew it down on her shoulder and with dancing movements of the arms plucked the strings.

Though she said she hardly had time to think of herself, she kept herself informed, judged public events well. She defined things accurately—Nathanael had insisted on careful definitions. She was analytic, skeptical—questioned what Dubin too easily accepted or inaccurately explicated. She hated obfuscation, hypocrisy, ignorance. She praised clear thinking and tested his thought the way Nathanael had tested hers. She analyzed Dubin's behavior aloud as Nathanael had analyzed hers.

Q. You resented him?

A. I resented her.

She lived with her fears—could not live without them—lived above them. She did not indulge in self-pity. What she had to do, ultimately she did. He gave her credit. Kitty wished she was a braver person; he said she was brave enough. That day she deposited what remained of Nathanael's life insurance in their joint savings account. Dubin said he didn't want Nathanael's money there. She withdrew it.

One morning she was formal with him, caught in uncertainty, trying to be calm. Kitty stood by the bedroom window in her nightgown.

He asked her what was the matter.

She smiled no smile to speak of, looked at him as if she weren't seeing him. It took her a while to reply in a strained voice. William, you have to palpate my breast; I think I felt a lump.

She slid into bed, drawing her nightgown over her chest, and he, trying not to think of it as a momentous act, pressed his fingers into her left breast, then gently into the right. He did not like to be doing this.

What am I supposed to feel?

A hard little lump the size of a pea.

Is that what you felt?

I thought so.

Kitty shut her eyes as he tried again to locate the lump, then, without expression, watched his face. Dubin dipped his fingers into her flesh, his eyes growing wet at the thought of the fragility of life. After a while he had found no lumps.

She then felt both breasts carefully; her mouth trembled in relief. Thank you.

He shaved with a mild erection.

At night as they lay together after making love, Kitty confessed her life with Nathanael hadn't gone all that well. He could be very hard on me.

Dubin said he had understood that; had put it together from things she had told him about Nathanael.

Once he hit me, she confessed; he said he hadn't meant to.

Dubin muffled a laugh.

Would you hit me, William?

If you hit me.

Kitty, laughing, later whispered, Don't ever leave me.

Q. It was about this time you got into biography?

A. He was still doing obituaries for the *Post* and book

reviews for *The Nation.* He was tired of the obits but stayed with them because he liked summarizing people's lives. The editor had asked him to emphasize successful careers but he sometimes managed to slip in a failed life.

After Maud was born Dubin had to make a better living. Kitty, concerned about their finances, suggested he go back to practicing law. He felt it made her nervous to think her husband had given up his profession. He'd consider it, he said, if he could be in law without being a lawyer. She then suggested teaching. He doubted he knew enough to face serious students.

One morning as he was typing out the obituary of a poet who had killed himself by jumping from the George Washington Bridge into the icy Hudson—a fragment of ice floe, like a bloody raft, carried his body down the river—Dubin felt as he wrote that the piece had taken on unexpected urgency. The dead poet was terribly real. He felt an imperious need to state his sorrow, understanding, pity—wanted with all his heart to preserve the man from extinction. Dubin, you can't relight lives but you can re-create them. In biographies the dead become alive, or seem to. He was moved, tormented, inspirited; his heart beat like a tin clock, his head aching as though struggling to pop through the neck of a bottle in which it had been enclosed, imprisoned. He felt for a brilliant moment as though he had freed himself forever.

Afterward Dubin knew he had discovered—affirmed—his vocation: the lives of others, there was no end to them. He sensed a more vital relation between books and life than he had allowed himself to feel in the past. He felt that the pieces of his own poor life could be annealed into a unity. He would understand better, be forewarned. He felt he had deepened, extended his life; had become Dubin the biographer.

A month later he showed Kitty his short life of Schubert. She said it was a moving piece of writing but oh so sad. Dubin told her Schubert had once said he didn't know any cheerful music. He wasn't listening, Kitty said. A short life is a short life. He was dead at thirty-one. I'd rather not think of it, she said.

He searched for a restaurant amid a block of stores along a sidewalk that ran level, as the cobblestone street sank in a slant below the sidewalk. Dubin, thinking his thoughts, failed to notice he had to go down a double step before crossing the street. On the unexpected step he lost his footing, groped in the air, fell in disbelief; therefore with a semblance of calm. As he lay in the wet gutter the pain rose so thickly he had to struggle to keep from passing out. He had hit the cobblestones with his knees before pitching forward. Through the nausea and dry retching Dubin felt he had broken both legs. He lay in the street shivering and writhing. If someone had touched him he would have shrieked.

It seemed to him a man appeared in the rain, staring distantly at him, then walked off.

"Gerald," he called.

The man did not look back.

"Help me, I'm in pain."

"Who are you?" someone said in Swedish but did not wait for an answer. In a moment he had vanished. No one assisted him. He wasn't sure anyone had gone by. Dubin lay in the street until the cold wet penetrated his clothes. Fearing he would be run over, he managed to pull himself up. His trousers were shredded, knees dripping blood. He got up the steps, limped into a bar and found the men's room. There, after removing his soiled raincoat and torn pants, Dubin cleaned himself as best he could. He felt depleted, dizzy. In the mirror he beheld a stone-gray face disgusted with him for having fallen; for being in Stockholm rather than home; for having gone through the waste of Venice.

Kitty had said the city was no place to bring up children. When Dubin received an advance for *Short Lives* she added to it from Nathanael's insurance and they put down earnest money on the house in Center Campobello. She had for years wanted to go back to living in the country. Dubin hadn't wanted to leave the city but afterward felt he ought to shake up his life—get out of New York and do differently with the self. Afterward he became a good husbandman: cleaned, painted, repaired. Once he kicked the dead furnace into life; Dubin Prometheus, bringer of heat in a cold house.

There were weekend drives with the kids into small towns in the Adirondacks, around sunlit dark forests. They crossed

Lake Champlain by ferry, into Vermont, and rode through quiet country towns with slender white-spired churches. Dubin enjoyed the sight of white rocks scattered in the beds of swift-flowing mountain streams. On secondary roads they passed long grasslands, dairy farms, groves of sugar maples. Once they drove to the top of a lookout mountain and beheld around them clusters of ancient mountains boiled up all over the state. Present at the creation, said Dubin. I love to see these sights with you, Kitty said.

At home the children were into physical lives, she called it. Their schooling could be better but they read at home and didn't seem to be missing much. Dubin's work went well; he was earning a living. He was glad they had left the city, felt he had played it right: a marriage could start anywhere and grow into a marriage. They talked in bed in the winter dark, confiding to each their lives. They embraced in the house when they chanced up on one another. He was at peace in his mirror.

There were, on the other hand, serious differences of temperament, reaction, rhythm: Dubin's wife could be overly intense, reserved, impatient under stress, punitive, too often anxious. He could be egoistic, time-bound, impulsive, defensive, too often anxious. Though they were alike in more ways than they had guessed; or grew to be alike; often the unmatched elements of their temperaments and tastes—disjunctions, he called them—caused tension, disagreements, quarrels. Her senses were highly charged conductors. She knew before she knew; he got the message more slowly.

Another self, a different self: unexpected noises irritated her. Kitty could hear water dripping in nearby rooms through locked doors and thick walls. In an unfamiliar house or hotel room she would lie awake listening to sounds that had waked her. Sometimes her restlessness woke Dubin and he joined her in the long trek to daylight. She shifted to the edge of the bed and lay still as he lamented his loss of precious sleep, then his fate. She sweated in mild heat and shivered in mild cold. An eyelash she could not quickly pick off her tongue would make her momentarily desperate. She was assailed by the smell of decaying things: food in the refrigerator, old shoes, old clothes, old closets. A close room compelled her, gasping, to throw open a window. A whiff of cheap perfume in a crowd set her teeth on edge. Kitty disliked body odors—abolished her own, kept Dubin informed of his. She passed gas immaculately; after an emission by him she sincerely asked what the smell was. Nathanael, he imagined, had never farted. She was touchy when her vitality was low, the biographer, when his biography was failing him. Her fears diffused her energy, scattered purpose. She regretted a lifetime of part-time jobs. Diligently she smelled the burners, complaining that the gas dried out her throat.

Don't smell them, for Christ's sake.

I can't help it. Don't humiliate me.

Her familiar insecurities made him impatient, preachy; Dubin's incensed her. They argued about taste, habit, idiosyncrasy. Both guarded their defenses. There were differences concerning timing, efficiency, sex. Don't explain sex to me, Kitty cried. Then explain it to me, Dubin shouted. Don't be hysterical, she said. He felt confined by her limitations; she was diminished by his smallnesses.

You yell so you don't have to reason.

You listen with your tongue.

You have a tin ear. You keep your mind in your pocket.

You talk like a bitch.

I'm glad, I always wanted to be a bitch.

When he nitpicked past the point of no return she smashed a dish on the kitchen counter and stalked out of the room. Dubin slammed doors. She repaid slow burn with cutting silence. Once she flung a small flower pot at him, a single geranium. It broke against the wall and the pink flower landed on his hat on a chair. Both laughed at the sight. After he had taught her the magic language Nathanael had failed to teach her, she stopped throwing things: they could swear at each other. Don't give me that shit, Kitty cried. If he swore she stamped her foot. You're alienating the children.

When she explained him to himself Dubin would yawp. Nor did Kitty want to hear who she was as he saw her. What may have begun as a disagreement became a quarrel. They sometimes tore into each other, going farther than they wanted. Each, then, suffered.

More or less, they educated one another concerning their

natures. As a rule, not always, their arguments ended with apologies. He had a sense of not having been wise, of having stupidly got into a useless situation. Apology was a continent Dubin slowly explored. Kitty apologized more rarely: he made more mistakes.

As time went by he persuaded himself not to feel excessive guilt for not feeling total affection for her in every circumstance; and he taught himself, after an argument, to recover affection more quickly than he had in the past; she could be persuaded by a show of feeling. He had noticed she recovered evenness of temper faster than he: when Kitty had thought through a quarrel—understood cause and effect—she communicated by quietly asking what he wanted for supper. Or asked his opinion about something. Each learned to skirt the other's more touchy sensitivities. Dubin studied what most upset her and gave up attempting to justify himself under certain circumstances. The key to a quick end to a quarrel was to cut out accusation. He taught himself to accept her as she was; she lived according to her construction. He grew better at making peace after he began writing his biographies. Kitty characterized their marriage as "fairly good." He did not ask her to say how good it had been with Nathanael.

Whatever concessions she made about the quality of their relationship she went on defending "the real"—said she had to, as though a false fact was a poisonous snake in the living room. She still had to define, delineate, measure, weigh the truth of idea, issue, experience. She pointed at inexactness as though unmasking an illusion—a monster—seemed at times the undying foe of metaphor: I can't help it, have to say a thing's a thing. For her Dubin learned to count accurately, tell the time right, recall a number nearly correctly. If he slipped—if he said, Today I saw an eight-foot sailor, she nervously countered: *I* never saw one—as though her statement eliminated a threat to existence. Now the stars would not fall. From time to time she defined the true nature of their relationship, still regretting—five, ten, or more years after their marriage—that she hadn't been in love with him when they were first married—not *truly* in love. If they had been in love, certain things would have been easier, might have gone better. There would have been fewer spats—bad for the children. We would have been gayer, certainly less tense. I was gayer with Nathanael. And more carefree in sex.

Dubin doubted it: Love, once you have it, whether it comes with intensity and stays, or in slow building and stays, is love. He said he hadn't much use for the kind of honesty that crapped on experience because it had occurred one way and not another.

Kitty's color deepened. I say how I see things. Nathanael appreciated my honesty.

I wish to hell he'd stay in his grave.

She strode out of the room.

Later she returned, distraught. Forgive me, Kitty said, slipping her arms around him—I love only you. Do you love me?

Q. You felt it was love?

A. I loved her, or thought I did. In any case I felt I had become the kind of man who could love her.

Q. A self-flagellating type?

A. I'm speaking of love.

Q. That you can't swear was there?

A. Nothing is ever always or entirely there.

Q. You sound like Kitty.

A. She taught me.

In her middle age, when the children had departed the house, Kitty Dubin was an attractive woman with good features, a slender slightly heavy body, the flesh on her belly striated by three pregnancies. Her slim legs were veined, the long feet still elegant. She painted her toenails. Her dark hair was lightened by strands of gray. After wearing a topknot for years she cut her hair short, often talked of touching it up but never did. That seemed pretense to her. Her voice had dropped an octave. Her eyes were spirited, the left more reflective; the right more uncertain. She drank more freely than she had as a young woman, and was less concerned about the use of four-letter words. He had hoped she would kick smelling the gas burners, but she hadn't. She doubted she would. Kitty regretted growing older, and though she was not unreasonably pessimistic about life, seemed not unhappy. She would touch a handkerchief to her eyes when she looked at old snapshots of the children. Apropos of nothing, or seemingly so, she said to Dubin, I'll never forget how unhappy I was as a widow. Do you consider yourself happily married? he asked. More so than many; not as happy as some, was her judgment. She predicted she would die before him and Dubin vehemently denied it.

He swallowed a brandy and left the bar. Sickened by his fall, he wanted nothing to eat. This is not my night. Dubin thought he would go to the hotel, smear ointment on his knees, get into bed. No taxis were visible as he limped down the dark street. Approaching the alley where Gerry lived, Dubin saw a man in a long army coat emerge in the rain; he wore a flat-topped wide-brimmed hat and heavy shoes. The biographer thought he recognized the stride but couldn't believe the hat and long hair tied in a ponytail. The man stepped into a darkened shop doorway to light a cigarette and Dubin was at once moved by him: it was Gerald. His face uneven, eyes deep-set, dampened by life. The back of his neck had been scarred by boils when he was a boy. Kitty said Gerald resembled her, but Dubin couldn't see it. Whoever he looked like it wasn't William Dubin. They had drifted apart. I wasn't as attentive as I should have been.

At twelve, as though he'd had a prevision of the complexity of life, Gerald had become quiet and secretive. He had grown up a loner, not much responding to those who tried to tempt him into sociability. What have I done to that child? Kitty wanted to know. What have I done to him? I wanted him to be a man before he was out of diapers. Because of me too much of his childhood was a time of mourning. I dealt with him with a self I had little sense of. How selfish I was, how inconsiderate.

She blamed fate that she and Dubin were both without parents, relatives—a family to be part of. The children had no grandparents to visit, confide in, learn from; no cousins to play with, or remember. My grandmother meant the world to me. She made the difference.

They had no religion in common. Dubin said they had. I don't mean humanism, Kitty answered. That's not enough for kids. God is for those who find him, Dubin said. No, he has to be taught. Some people have to be helped to religious discovery. Gerald is one.

Q. Tell me, Dubin, what did the boy really mean to you?

A. I saw myself, in his eyes—a fatherly type. He seemed to trust me. I taught him to play chess. We walked together. He fed me mathematics, I described the new astronomy, as much as I knew it. He listened to every sentence. I told him jokes. I sometimes thought I had taught him to laugh. He was a tall boy with a well-formed head and uneasy thoughtful eyes. One day he asked me to adopt him and we kissed. His name was legally changed to Gerald Dubin. Kitty approved but I worried about it. He was so much his father it may have seemed like betrayal.

Will the earth explode, William?

We won't be around if it does.

I'm afraid to die, aren't you?

Dubin said he wanted his allotted time.

Do you love me? the boy asked.

Yes. You must know that.

As much as Maud?

Yes.

He seemed to doubt it.

Does Mother love me as much as Maud?

Yes.

He seemed to doubt it.

One day when he was fifteen Gerald accused them of not understanding him: I'm different than you think.

Why don't you explain yourself to us?

I try but can't.

You can't explain?

You don't understand.

He seemed fearful after he had said it, ran up to his room; stayed there much of the time. When Dubin came up to talk with him, he listened in silence, staring out of the window, then formally thanked him for coming.

He needed a lot more time than I gave him.

Q. Dedication makes displacement?

A. Important things to do, especially in work, reduce or nullify others. I tried to balance things off—father with children, my needs with Kitty's, not always well done. You think you have three balls in the air but when you count there's one.

Kitty criticized him for withholding himself from them.

Every time I suggest something to do you resent breaking away from work. I'm not so sure you want a family.

He swore he wanted a family.

Maybe you oughtn't to have got married, so you could give your life to your biographies.

Marriage was his constitutional right.

We hardly talk any more.

They talked at long length in the dead of night.

Don't be sarcastic. You're obsessed with work.

Better than with alcohol.

When will you take time to live?

Writing is a mode of being. If I write I live.

Hemingway at least fished after he wrote.

I walk.

Why can't we all walk together?

We can on Sundays.

You don't have to work so hard or long, Kitty argued. I doubt you really enjoy being with people. I have needs other than solitude, certainly the kids have. You're either reading or writing biographies, or thinking your biographical thoughts.

The kids know their father loves them.

Love is being there; it means giving affection.

Much of his past had been badly used, Dubin often had to explain. Don't begrudge my taking time to do difficult work. To do it well one has to do it many times. You have to make time or steal it.

You steal it from us all.

He read her a note about Thomas Carlyle from a biography he was reading. His wife, Jane Welsh Carlyle, wrote to a friend: "All he asked, was, simply, that his wishes come first, his comfort be put before all else, the household so arranged that his sleeping, walks, hours of work or reverie should be when and how he wanted them." Think of that when you criticize me.

What a disgusting man, said Kitty.

Then there was Gustav Mahler.

She covered her ears with her hands: I don't want to hear.

She complained there was little conversation at the table unless she initiated it. You can listen to us speak and hear nothing. I can tell from your eyes you've gone for a walk in your book.

He mistreated holidays, she said. After Christmas-morning exchange of presents—Christmas was for Gerald and Channukah for Maud; Kitty said she wanted her to be a Jewish child out of respect for her father—Dubin went back to his desk to work.

He wrote a note to himself: I do few things perhaps to do one thing well.

Gerald kept a loose-leaf diary whose pages he occasionally tore out and burned in the fireplace. Once he handed Kitty a poem and she wept to be given the gift. He never gave her another.

He fed his words into the fire, telling his parents little or nothing of what he was thinking or doing; as though, if he did, he had betrayed himself.

But he talked to Maud, who kept his secrets. When they were talking together they stopped at Dubin's approach. Maud, he wanted to say, don't be corrupted by him. I am your loving father.

Yet there were times when Gerry seemed to want an adult to talk to. He would appear in Dubin's study before going to school, his book bag strapped to his shoulders, to say why last night's TV news had sickened him. Not why his flight had begun and where it was taking him.

If Dubin spoke about himself as a boy Gerry would listen and leave without comment. One lonely youth was all he could abide.

Dubin asked him to say what was troubling him. He wouldn't say why he didn't say.

We were once close—tell me what happened?

The boy stood stiffly silent, the back of his neck inflamed. With impassioned silence he answered nothing.

If we don't talk I can't tell you what I know, Dubin said. What good is my experience if you won't let me share it with you?

That's your problem. I don't have any interest in autobiography. That's your problem.

If Dubin extended his hand, Gerald stepped back.

He had unwillingly become distant to the boy, matching a distance equal to his own from Dubin; as if he had held up a mirror to a mile and made it two between them.

I overdid mourning, Kitty lamented. He backed away from me. And from you because of me. I know he loves you, William, but I can't explain the change in him, except that at a certain point the person I was—I am—weighed too heavily on him. You're your screwy self a day too long and one or another of your kids takes off without telling you why or waving goodbye. Once he began to change he changed as though he was pursued by change.

Dubin, standing silent on the stairs, overheard her talking to Gerald in his room when he was home from college at Thanksgiving, during his freshman year.

She was asking him in a loud whisper to trust her, confide what ailed him.

My pain in the gut, Gerald replied. I hate the stupid war. I know I'll have to fight in it sooner or later. I hate the goddamned stupid military. I hate how America is destroying the world.

Things will improve, Kitty pleaded. Don't take everything so brutally hard. One must live, the world goes on. A man should enjoy his life or what's it for? Please, Gerald.

He rushed down the stairs.

Dubin, embarrassed to be standing there, stepped to the wall as he ran by.

You've got to live, Kitty, leaning over the banister, shouted after her son.

At lunch she smiled at Gerald, her lips compressed, eyes uneasy. He dipped chunks of bread into the soup and sucked them. Dubin, peacemaker, rattled on about the miserable youth of Edgar Allan Poe; his mother had died young. Kitty asked him to change the subject.

My son the stepson, early exile from self. He is contemptuous of war but won't, after quitting graduate school, register as a conscientious objector, because he can't define himself as one. He insists on accuracy of definition.

You're close to one in spirit, his mother says. You certainly are in principle.

Close enough is not good enough, says the honest lad. Dubin dislikes the mother for her son's passionate honesty.

Gerry considers flight to Canada as a war resister but decides against it. He is drafted and shipped to West Germany for training prior to Vietnam. He is kept on in Germany as a Signal Corps instructor. Three months before his term of enlistment is over, the night before he's due to be flown in an army transport to a jungle in Southeast Asia, he goes AWOL in a Cessna to Sweden.

Whose fate is he running after?

Gerald Willis stepped out of the dripping doorway, exhaling wet smoke. He was a broad-shouldered tall man who walked with a heavy-footed tread. Dubin had last seen him still wearing part of his army uniform and a short haircut going to seed. After crossing the narrow street walled by old houses, the biographer followed him a few paces along a thin strip of sidewalk, then called his name.

The youth swung around in alarm as Dubin, his arm extended, hastened forward. Gerald peered at him in disbelief. "Jesus, William, is it really you?"

"Who else?" He offered his hand. Gerald shook it vaguely and Dubin pumped his. The youth, in his odd hat and long hair, looked like no one he knew.

"What are you here for? What do you want?" His voice had the tone of a man objecting.

Dubin said he had flown in from Venice a few hours ago and had been looking for him since.

"What for?"

"What for, he says." He tried to laugh.

"Sweden isn't next door to Italy. It touches the North Pole. What's on your mind, William?"

"Not much. I was in the vicinity, you might say, and decided to come to see you."

"Why didn't you wire? I might have been in Lapland."

Dubin explained he had come on impulse.

"Is my mother with you?"

"Not this time."

"Anything wrong?"

He didn't think so.

Gerald, working his shoulders, blew his white breath on his wet hands.

They stared at one another. Dubin asked him if he wanted a drink.

Gerald shook his head. "You look like hell."

Dubin described the spill he had taken near a square with a church. "I missed my step and hit the street on both knees and my belly. I'm not comfortable. Is there somewhere we can sit? Have you eaten yet?"

He knew the question was useless: Gerry would not sit and talk. With him he felt as he often had: a man trying to finish a puzzle with a piece that never fitted. Here was this haunted house needing a door or window and the last piece he had was a hand holding a wilted flower.

"I have to do something. Give me your number, I'll call in the morning."

Dubin said what had to be done had to be done. "Did you find my note under your door?"

Gerald shook his head.

"I see by your nameplate that you've changed your name."

"It's my name." He seemed not to be sure. His breath misted, vanished.

"I wish you the best, whatever the name. I'm not taking offense. I consider you my son, or why did I adopt you when you were a kid?"

He felt off-balance, annoyed with his defensive tone. If I have any eloquence, in his presence I lose it. Those who don't approve me diminish me.

He diminished those who diminished him.

"I'll walk over to your hotel in the morning," Gerald said.

"Fine. I'm at the Skeppsbron. But why not take another minute to tell me what you're into these days. I'll probably be telephoning your mother and would like to say I saw you."

"You can say it."

Dubin said last time they were there Gerald had talked of taking some courses in biology and maybe going to med school.

The youth shot his lit butt into the gutter. "I don't think of that as a viable alternative any more."

"Alternative to what?"

"Other alternatives."

"Why don't you name one?"

He said nothing.

"How's your Swedish coming?"

"On stilts, on little cat stilts."

"You were considering studying Russian."

"I'm still considering it."

"Are you still working on the docks?"

He said he wasn't working.

"I'm sorry. Could you use some money? I have some traveler's checks I can cash."

Gerald shook his head.

"Are you living alone?"

"Alone." The word tolled.

Dubin compulsively went on: "I gather you're not much satisfied here?"

"You've gathered what there is to gather." From under his dripping hat he stared at his adoptive father. His eyes were expectant, expecting nothing.

Someday he'll change, Dubin thought. We'll sit together and talk with ease.

"Have you heard from Maud recently?"

"A card I couldn't read."

"Where was it from?"

"Ask Maud."

"Not from Italy?"

"Ask her."

"If you answered a letter once in a while," Dubin said testily, "it'd be easier on both of us than standing in the rain in a foreign city, asking and not answering questions."

"Neither of you approved of what I did when I screwed the army, so I don't care to inform you what I am doing."

"We didn't agree with your timing. You were about to escape the army if you had just been patient."

"It was my own fucking timing."

"Let's walk," Dubin said. "We may be going in the same direction."

Gerald bolted off. Dubin followed him.

The hazy wet street sloped down to the Baltic. Dubin talked to the youth's back and Gerald talked to the night.

"What we didn't like was your going AWOL three months before you were due for discharge. That wasn't a rational thing."

"The army's no place to be rational," Gerald said to the

night. "If I had stayed in it another month I'd have killed somebody, not necessarily a Viet Cong."

"You'd have been free in a few short months."

"The months were short in your head, not mine."

Dubin said it was possible there'd be some sort of amnesty soon. "Congress is talking about it. Nixon will have to go along."

"It's bullshit."

"Some deserters are already coming home. They are making deals with the government."

"That's bullshit. It's handcuffs at the airport, court-martial, Leavenworth. I'm not going to prison."

"Where do you think you are?" Dubin asked Gerald's back.

"I am where I choose to be."

They trudged on in silence, singly, along the narrow sidewalk.

Dubin said he hadn't meant the prison thing the way he had said it.

"That's the way I heard it."

"Gerry, a father is a man who treats you like a son. At least walk with me. I'm the only father you've got."

The youth took off in a heavy-footed run.

Dubin awkwardly trotted after him.

At the Skeppsbron bridge Gerald slowed to a fast walk. The biographer limped along behind him. It was a bleak night, the lights of the long bridge glowing foggily in the freezing drizzle.

"Wait up, Gerry. I can't go fast."

Gerald told Dubin he had passed his hotel a block back.

I have to follow him, the father thought. It's the only way to be with him.

On the bridge a man with a soaking burlap sack on his head was fishing at the rail. Nearby stood a girl in a white cloth coat with a hood, yellow shoes, and a soggy yellow muff.

"Ett nyp?" she said to the biographer as he limped by.

"I beg your pardon?"

"Lof?" she asked him.

Dubin followed his son across the bridge, haranguing his back, and for a while the girl in the yellow shoes followed him.

Four

ON THE ROAD a jogger trotted toward him, a man with a blue band around his head.

He slowed down as Dubin halted.

"What are you running for?" the biographer asked him.

"All I can't stand to do. What about you?"

"Broken heart, I think."

"Ah, too bad for that."

They trotted in opposing directions.

Dubin dropped his bag and embraced his wife. His arms stiffened as it seemed to him hers did. Kitty was nothing if not intuitive, sensed change of emotional weather before it was weather. He had considered telling her he had holed up for a few nights with a young woman in Venice—wouldn't say who because it would humiliate, wound her, more than if it had been someone other than Fanny Bick—anyway, it had come to nothing, if not less.

Kitty seemed constrained, preoccupied. He wondered whether she sensed something not quite right, off-balance—something wrong? Dubin said nothing about the trip, wouldn't unless she asked, would then say the necessary lies. It was painful not to be honest with a woman who did not lie. He was, on arrival, heavyhearted.

"You're late," she said. "Let's eat, I'm ravenous."

He unlocked his bag and produced a sculptured silver bracelet he had bought her in Stockholm. As she admired it, after a moment of hesitation he unwrapped a pair of antique gold earrings he had chosen for Maud and handed them to Kitty. She inspected the bracelet and earrings with interest. "They're beautiful, William, but one or the other would have been enough. Do you mind if I keep the bracelet and give the earrings to Maud?"

"Suit yourself."

They kissed affectionately, sat down for a drink, enjoyed dinner. She had prepared a tasty coq-au-vin. Kitty had the wishbone and when they broke it she won the wish.

"For Gerry?"

"For your new biography, and I guess for him too."

Dubin thanked her.

"How was he?"

He told her in detail; said Gerald had changed his name back to Willis.

She shook her head, eyes distant. "You were so loving to him. It was thoughtful of you to go see him; thank you."

He asked her not to thank him.

He built a fire in the living-room fireplace and they talked as they sipped coffee. The worst is over, Dubin thought, sitting by the fire, looking forward to his work in the morning. Kitty played the harp, some songs by Mahler. She sang in a small sweet voice.

Dubin woke that night relieved to be rid of Fanny. The week abroad had seemed a year. He sensed his wife was awake and drew her to him. Soon they made love. He would not admit the girl to his mind.

Before she slept he asked Kitty how she had fared while he was away.

"Not badly. I kept busy. The house behaved."

"You weren't afraid to be alone at night?"

She said she was.

"Why didn't you sleep at Myra's?"

"It doesn't bother her to be alone day or night. I want her to respect me."

"She respects you."

"I want her to."

"Well, I'm home now," Dubin said. He asked her if Maud had called.

"I called her. She had a nasty cold but is back in class now."

"Anything new with her?"

"Not with her but there is with me," Kitty said in the dark bedroom. "I've been working part-time in the library. Mrs. Eliscu is sick and Roger Foster rang me up the day you left to help him out. At least I get paid for work I do. I put in four weekday mornings and one afternoon. I'd prefer afternoons, but they need me most in the morning. I hope you don't mind? I can do your errands after lunch. I'll bring back the paper when I come home at one. Roger asked me to work a full day, but I said I simply couldn't."

"Let's get back to sleep, we both have to work in the morning."

"When we were first married I always got up with you."

Dubin remembered.

After flipping through a folder full of outlines the biographer began his working day. Rereading what he had written before he took off with Fanny, he was satisfied although a mild sense of waste lingered. Now he felt he'd soon complete the opening chapter and wrote well all morning. Dubin wrote listening to Lawrence's high-pitched insistent voice in his ear, to some degree resisting what he passed on as truth. He had to distance himself from the man to see what he must see. Lawrence wore a coat of many colors, pretending to wear nothing.

Dubin liked what he was writing. Nothing like interrupting the course of daily life to get the mind flowing, enjoying. At least he'd been to another country and had gone through something intense and different; now he lived his life writing another's. He felt for his wife a rush of affection.

On the Saturday morning following the Monday of Dubin's arrival from Sweden, Kitty came upstairs with an airmail letter. "From Italy." He went on with his typing. "Thanks." After a minute she left.

He thought he would finish the page.

When he had completed it, Dubin reached for the letter. It was addressed, as he had guessed—his thoughts of her already were fatiguing—in Fanny's large open slanted writing. Dubin's impulse, after a flash of self-disgust, sadness, remembrance of desire, was to destroy her letter without reading it. He had sensed he would hear from her, although not so soon. Standing apart from himself he tore open the envelope to get it over with so he could go on with his work.

The girl wrote: "I'm in Murano now with the capitano of the motorboat you waited for with me. I changed my mind about going to Rome. I'm writing this after midnight. The stars are out. I love the late hours when nobody but me is awake—feel closer to myself. I'm smoking as I look out of Arnaldo's window across the lagoon where Venice is. I like it a lot more than when you and I first came here, have got used to it.

"William, I've been thinking of you a lot and just got out of bed to write to you. I'm wearing the black nightie you liked me in. Over that I have on Arnaldo's sweater. He isn't a bad guy. He has a sense of humor and makes me laugh. He also cooks for us and I don't have to do very much although I wouldn't mind. Anyway, I had this urge to write you. Try not to think too badly of me if you can. Though we aren't the same kind of people in some ways, I think we are alike in others. I wear your bracelet even in bed. Maybe it will bring me luck. I hope you are less angry now—not that you don't deserve to be—and will write me sometimes. William, I would honestly like to hear from you. I remember some of our nice talks. I'm sorry it ended the way it did. Kind regards, Fanny B."

Dubin, as he tore the letter up, felt a punitive sense of disgust. From the gondolier to capitano in a short hop over his head. Another promiscuous lover to make her a better person. "I wear your bracelet even in bed."

Curbing an impulse to lay on sarcastically, the biographer typed out a plainspoken note. "You're right, Fanny, we have fundamental differences of values, not to speak of simple taste. Life is cheapened when there is no basic consideration by people of others. You've cheapened and shamed me. Please don't bother writing again. Yours most sincerely, William B. Dubin."

He tore her letter to shreds and burned the mound of paper in an ashtray.

In the afternoon he walked with Kitty to the green bridge.

The weekend was pleasant—unexpected visitors from New York City, an old law-school friend with his wife. They drove to Great Barrington to see a mutual friend.

On Monday morning, after quickly putting down a solid paragraph, Dubin felt as though he had walked into a wall. His thoughts were scattered. He felt vapid, vague, something pecking at the back of his mind, as though he'd forgotten to do what he had meant to. Nothing he could think of except to be joyfully into his biography. After a half hour of trying to concentrate he realized there'd be no second paragraph, good or bad, that day. It was a darkish November morning. Dubin turned on the desk lamp but that didn't help. He set aside his notes and spent the rest of the morning on business correspondence.

In the afternoon he went for his walk and after returning got into the car and slowly drove the same route, as though searching for something he had lost on the road.

"You look like someone holding his breath underwater," Kitty said as she came down the stairs. "Would you like me to fix you a drink?"

"Too early." Dubin remarked he'd had a poor day.

"They come and they go," she said.

"They come and they go."

"Sometimes I feel I'd like to see you give up that freaky D. H. Lawrence."

Dubin said he couldn't, had invested years in him. His voice sounded throaty.

Kitty, at the window, cheerfully said it was beginning to blizzard. She called any snowstorm a blizzard.

Fanny beats my brains, he said to his looking glass.

Mad, this reaction. He recalled her for the thousandth time in her black dress and pumps of that last unhappy morning together. She had been at her most desirable—why not if what you're playing with is loss?—as if she had finally become focused as a beautiful woman, defined in a way that had evaded her until the last moment. How else defined? As a bitch? Or a woman who had made a serious mistake and perhaps regretted it? Otherwise promiscuity is narcissism; identity lacking, probably something to do with her ungiving father. I would have been good for her. No use thinking these things, Dubin thought: they took you nowhere. Nowhere was an intensity of not having.

He stood at the bathroom window, staring at the mist-streaked distant mountains. The Vermont mountains, tying up with others in flanking ranges in New York, ran in a broken semicircle creating small valleys, one of which contained Center Campobello. Lawrence hadn't cared for mountains "intruding" through his window. Dubin liked them drawing his gaze into the distance; he made no symbol of them. The nearest peak was due north, a scraggy mass of twenty-eight hundred feet, in summertime covered with pines up its low sloping left flank. It had no name he could locate on the map and he called it Mt. No Name. The first snowfall of November had amounted to a thin inch. Most of it had melted. No Name wore on its pate a crooked white crown. The wooded New York hills were dusted with snow—the woods in their winter underwear. He had to tell himself to quit looking. What a fool I was, when it was going well, to take that little hooker to Venice.

For two days the sunlit study resounded with the pounding of his machine as he retyped his opening chapter. Now I'm traveling again. He felt at the same time wild little thoughts, small fires of Fanny he managed to damp down: Dubin out-thought them. After he had stacked twenty-three newly typed pages he consulted his notes and wrote a fine paragraph; but when he reread it twenty minutes later the paragraph grinned through broken teeth. Lawrence was a stiff boy, walked on stilts. His phallic mother was stiffly withdrawn. Who's the problem, him or me? The way I work or how he evades me? Dubin felt like a sculptor working with hardened clay.

Why the foreboding? He hadn't for years felt himself at fate's mercy but here she was doing her belly dance. A thoughtless girl, careless of him, had made a jackass of Dubin, shamed him as he hadn't ever been. During which time—before and after—almost anything I say to Kitty as truth is a lie: "Did you miss me in Italy, William?" she asks at breakfast. "Yes and no," I say, and she laughs at something she isn't laughing at. Then with a reflective look she says, "I sometimes have the feeling you'd get along well without me." "Yes, but why would I want to?" "I don't know," she says. He felt himself cut down a bloody inch. Doubt Dubin, doubt the biographer. Diminish the man, the writing suffers. He felt short of something he had had before he took off on a wild-goose chase for experience with Fanny.

Trotting downstairs later to heat the coffeepot, he took a minute to listen to the news on the radio: Nixon in press conference. Dubin shut it off in embarrassment.

He recalled Emerson's remark: "All that is clearly due today is not to lie." Emerson, liar? Everyone lies. Why am I making so much of it? Bad business, tying up behavior with writing biography.

After pouring his coffee he telephoned Kitty at the library. "Aren't you working?" she asked.

He understood the anxious question. If your husband or children ducked duty her boat rocked.

"You know the answer before you ask the question."

"You never call me in the morning," she explained.

"I'll see you at lunch, my coffee's cold," Dubin said. "Don't forget the paper."

"I almost never do." She hung up.

Kitty rang back. "I didn't mean to be impatient. If something's wrong, for Pete's sake, tell me. Was there anything in the mail that bothered you?"

"No. You know how it is at the beginning of a long work."

"You began months ago."

"It's a long beginning."

He awoke the next day in unease. As Dubin shaved he considered calling Maud but it was 4 A.M. in California.

He wished Kitty were staying home; they'd talk. What would he tell her? Not that he had had the girl but she had had him. Why bother telling her anything if there are no laughs in the story? What good will it do either of us if I make myself, in her eyes, a rare ass?

At breakfast he suggested he might want the car. "Roger will drive you home, I'm sure."

"I can call a taxi." Her eyes were tired. After sipping her coffee she asked, "Are you still having trouble?"

"Everyone's accounted for but isn't particularly present."

He thought of telling her truly about Fanny—get himself balanced again. No, he thought, if the writing were going well my conscience would be calm.

"Maybe you're pressing too hard?" she asked.

"Maybe."

"Shouldn't you try working before giving up for the day?"

"Please don't tell me when to work."

"Would you like me to read the chapter and give you my opinion?"

He said he would not.

Kitty examined her eyes in a pocket mirror. She had on the blue batik dress she had just bought and an attractive pair of black single-strap shoes.

"I could call Roger and say I wasn't coming in," she suggested. "We could drive into the Berkshires for the day?"

But Dubin thought she was right: he ought to reassess his priorities.

"Which ones?"

"I might give up on Lawrence. If the book's wrong for me, it's wrong."

Kitty set down her coffee cup and studied him. She got up, rinsed a dish, put it away, sat down. Her expression was calm, her voice even.

"William, don't make so much of this. You've had dry periods before and you'll have them again. I'll tell you what: let's goof off. I can ask for Monday off. We'll drive to Lake Champlain, and if we feel like it, go on up to Quebec City for the weekend."

He said, after a long moment, he wouldn't know what to do with himself once he got there.

"Is that how you feel?"

As of now it was how he felt.

She took a last quick swallow of coffee, rinsed her cup and placed it in the dishwasher. "I'm late. Do you want to drive me to work? I really don't mind if you go for a ride by yourself."

But Dubin said she could have the car.

Kitty buttoned her coat and tied on a head scarf. "Please air the kitchen if you think of it. The house is smelly."

"What does it smell of?"

"Burnt toast."

"I think it smells of us."

She drove off. He realized she hadn't returned to breathe at the burners.

Moved by a variety of useless impulses, he went through the house listing things that needed tending to. You skip work, trivialities assail you. Still, any activity is better than none. Dubin aired the kitchen. He went through the refrigerator—threw out two rotting lemons, moldy butter, cheese rinds. Sometimes she didn't know what the hell she had there. He arranged bottles, like with like, and separated butter bars from margarine.

In the cellar he discovered a puddle under the hot-water tank and phoned the plumber. He swept the cellar floor, emptied the kitchen garbage container into the can outside. He tried reading a detective story but couldn't stay with it. Dubin plucked at the strings of Kitty's harp.

In his study he thumbed through his second-chapter notes, looking for a compelling opening idea. If he found one he'd write a sentence. Sentences bred sentences. But the notes tensed him: they were only notes, separate, discrete, like seashells in a box. It was stupid, he thought, to try to work when the idea was not to; to give the brain a rest.

On a card he read, D. H. Lawrence had said to his girl: "I don't believe in the idea of one man for one woman, do you? I mean, there just isn't one woman and one only that a man can marry." Cunning question, foreshadowing the brushoff; she never got over him.

Dubin climbed the stairs to the third-floor unfinished room they called the attic, where the kids had often played. He flicked on the light, moved by a sense of past time rooted in his children's childhood, and poked around in their abandoned toys, books, folders of drawings and correspondence Kitty had saved. She tore up letters she answered but those she saved were from the children and Dubin. That made family history. He had never been able to find Nathanael's letters.

On an impulse he searched in a footlocker for Maud's white wool hat with blue band. Was it still alive or had it been given away? He could not find it, nor any of the dolls she had played with. He remembered a valentine she'd drawn and searched for it. Dubin found the one he'd had in mind, a red-crayoned heart addressed to "Willyam, Be My Valentine," but it was signed "Gerald" in black letters. In apology he touched the paper to his lips.

He kept hunting for something of Maud's, perhaps a note from summer camp when she was nine or ten. Maud still wrote rarely, once in a while a satisfying letter, then months of titbit phone calls. Some were talky calls, others little more than formalities: she was checking in, and what she really said was what she didn't say. She didn't say what most affected her. That ran in the family, began with his mother. Dubin left the attic room. He had wanted one of Maud's affectionate notes as a child to keep in his pocket. The uses of the dwindling past.

The biographer walked downtown in his galoshes, mackinaw, long tan-and-black scarf Kitty had knitted him; took her a year to do the thing. The day was crisp, the wind whipping by, snow flurries scattered through the leafless trees all morning. After withdrawing cash from the bank, having nothing better to do he crossed the street and paid the gas bill, groaning inwardly at the uselessness of the act on a perfectly good day. Since it was already close to one, he thought he'd stop off at the library and let Kitty drive him home. As he came up the street he saw her standing with Roger on the library steps; Dubin could tell as she spoke—the way her body moved—that she was emotional. Roger, since Dubin had last seen him, wore an Edwardian haircut with long sideburns. The biographer considered turning quickly and walking back before they spotted him. Kitty seemed troubled. Dubin worried that Roger, having heard from his friend Fanny about the asinine Venetian adventure, had told his wife the happy news.

But they had seen him and instantly stopped talking. Dubin had paused to retie his shoelaces and pull up his socks. He approached with tight gut, concerned that he had lost first chance to tell her himself; that the librarian, whose business it was not, had informed her in his place. Roger thrust forth his hand and Dubin unwillingly took it.

"Kitty said you've been abroad, Mr. Dubin."

"For a week. What else have you heard?"

Kitty gazed at him with surprised wet eyes. Before he could speak again—to utter what idiocy?—she broke in: "Mrs. Eliscu has cancer of the breast. Roger heard from her husband a half hour ago. They have three small children."

With a hidden sigh Dubin expressed regret. He also regretted his stupid remark to Roger but no one had made anything of it.

"Have a good time?" Roger asked. He'd never been comfortable with Dubin, and wasn't now, in his green suit, blue tie, field boots. Roger rarely wore an overcoat. He had hot blood, he had once told Dubin. Where? Dubin had almost asked. With a nod, Roger walked down the steps to his car at the curb.

"Anybody I can give a lift to?"

Dubin said Kitty had their car.

"He knows," she said impatiently.

"Then why did he ask?"

Roger waved and drove off.

"Why aren't you nice to him?" Kitty asked.

He said he had nothing against Roger. I feel like a jackass and he acts like one. Kitty seemed apart from, almost uncomfortable with him.

If they weren't talking about Fanny, I ought to be, he thought.

"What brought you here?" Kitty asked as though expecting bad news.

He said he had walked into town to get some cash.

"I could have done that easily."

"I needed something to do."

"Are you giving up on your book?"

"Not as of right now."

They kissed as though greeting, then got into the car and drove to the supermarket. Twice, as they walked the long grocery aisles, Kitty dropped a can he had picked off the shelves.

"My hands are small," she explained to her husband.

They hadn't for years shopped together for groceries, and Dubin enjoyed it despite the wasted day.

Though the biographer felt he was dealing with a literary as well as a psychological problem, obviously one tied up to the other. There were too many reverberations of Fanny, too much static in his head, too much guilt. He had reacted as though his character had failed him; the true failure was one of judgment. Dubin wanted to put his thoughts in order by getting to work and doing it well. To not work regularly was to fall into the condition he was out to avoid: purpose sidetracked, the mind adrift; Dubin left on the pier, the ship gone. Montaigne had believed his effective judgment was instrumental in keeping him in good physical health.

He had returned heavier than he'd left, as though misery had paid interest in flesh. He disliked the bounce of his belly as he briskly walked or ran. He disliked the naked sight of himself in the closet-door mirror; pictured youthful slimness, not impossible. He figured he'd cut out brandy after dinner—drink less wine at the dinner table, eat smaller portions. Kitty had a booklet of low-calorie foods; he'd ask her to watch his intake. To get himself effectively together he had to put himself in shape. In fooling with Fanny he'd allowed desire to overflow the workaday life. A pipe had broken, the psyche was flooded. He must rid himself of his ongoing half-jealous thoughts of the girl—these irritating intrusive two-bit emotions—make the floodwaters of the unconscious recede. He had once more to be the man he'd been; *who Dubin was.*

Besides starving his belly he wrestled it off. From youth he had exercised daily—shades of Gatsby—his personal need, in accord with controlling, shaping. But after Maud was born, though Kitty approved calisthenics, he performed superficially—too much to do to earn a living. And he was walking more after they had moved into the country; had invented his long course in nature, part of which he trotted. Now Dubin revived the old setting-up exercises, not easy to go back to at age fifty-six: pushups, bending, pedaling, pulling his knees into the offending gut. In his striped shorts he danced around Maud's room as Kitty slept, the floorboards creaking, a squeak for each shift. He worked resolutely a half hour each morning, protesting in the pit of the self at the effort one had to make, the inertial strain of fabricating monotonous movement, as though he were dragging a carcass of himself back and forth across the floor, frightful bore if present necessity. Indeed necessity. Dubin fought the possessed self.

Afterward, although Kitty was rising early, for her, to go to the library, he had breakfast alone. He'd got into the habit when Maud was an infant and Kitty, when she could, slept later. Dubin liked being alone at that hour, enjoying morning light, morning quiet, thinking whatever thought; relaxed. Now breakfast, given diet, was a chore. He kept the repast simple: fruit followed by sugarless black coffee, with half a slice of bread. For lunch the food made little difference; he ate minuscule portions. Kitty shook her head. But dinner, in principle, satisfied—if that was the word—where there wasn't that much satisfaction. Kitty broiled fish or lean meat, served one green or yellow vegetable, offered sugarless dessert. She clicked her tongue at his modest helpings. Dubin finished the meal hungry—praise moderation, though little after not much all day was hard to bear.

It wasn't easy, after rising from the table, not to dip his fingers into a Swiss chocolate bar he had hidden in a desk drawer; but if he went quickly upstairs and brushed his teeth he brushed away the compelling hunger. He learned to eat slowly, let each forkful of food, each permitted sip of wine, ride the length of the tongue. He savored well the little he ate; and still smoked an occasional cigarillo though he'd given up serious smoking long ago.

Kitty, although friendlier to less rather than more, disliked seeing him at diet's mercy.

At his own mercy, he insisted.

"But isn't the diet what you went on mainly because of your trouble working?"

He more or less nodded.

She said no more; nor did he.

The day's work, if it comes to something, burns out night's dross; night craps in your pants. For the investment the biographer makes in gathering himself together on cold hard mornings, in coming drearily to life, he expects some accomplishment during the day—a good deed, it helps. Dubin felt he was getting nothing much. But though change took its time he daily expected signs of a forthcoming visit. He watched for it out of his better eye, two might scare it away. After Thanksgiving, when winter set in with a wind and a bang, he sat regularly at his desk, promising himself he would stay with it if something good evolved; but day after day very little did—an aimless page or two; so he went—after three prescribed working hours—for a routine walk in any weather, the next sequential imposition on the poor self; a man had to conjure up some relief from nothing much achieved.

Work generally pulls me out of the clutch of the subjective self; but since I'm not working well I have to spring myself another way, if I know another way. S. Johnson, unable to work, would walk twenty-six miles to Birmingham, to shake himself into shape. Dubin was not prodigal with miles, limited himself to four or five each day. "The safe and general antidote against sorrow is employment," Johnson said. Dubin hopes to find an antidote growing in nature.

In December he switched to walking after breakfast, then trying to initiate prose after pouring out on paper a bag of thoughts gathered on the road. He entered his study at about ten and stayed for two and a half hours, his pen at the ready; then lingered at the window, staring at the unnamed mountain; or read and reread his meager mail. Or paced back and forth in the room to shake things in his head into place. At length he laid out a page of notes, concentrating on surprise in arrangement, but too often settling merely for changing the language of the initial note, not going far beyond that; and felt textual thinness, that he was adding little to the naked facts. Go, Dubin, back to obituaries. How can my small brain light up the dark forest of D. H. Lawrence's psyche? He felt distant from the action, from growth of character, inner motivation; sat peering at young Lawrence, handsome youth, floating off in pale water amid lily pads; or trotting into the white-flowered bushes with his mum as pale-faced Jessie peeks through the leaves; Dubin, secondary voyeur, not really knowing what they were up to, barely able to guess. He was not with it, whatever it was. It was—whatever—with Fanny. He lived on memories of her; Lawrence would have scorned him for the little he'd had yet lived on.

Among other cures he added hydrotherapy: re Carlyle, daily on arising—his wife's advice—dumping a bucket of cold water on his head. In Dubin's case a cold shower in winter, hot turning gasping cold—each morning, to get him up and onto the daily merry-go-round; the icy water beating blood into his dull brain as he snorted and pranced in the tub. And at night hot to tepid water to ease a bit, he hoped, a deepening frustration. Though he slept during long intervals of night—vaguely sensing Kitty's controlled restlessness—he dreamed he wasn't asleep, hadn't dared to sink into deep sleep, as though he might be murdered there; Dubin awoke fatigued. His sleep pretended sleep, cheated itself. Some mornings he stayed forty minutes in the hot shower before he could bring himself to turn the cold knob; or if he dared not, to step out of the tub, get into underwear and begin exercise. And if the long day was especially long, therefore especially unproductive—too many hours to count the ways—he went to bed directly after supper.

"I've never seen you this way," Kitty worried.

He had had bad times before, Dubin says.

"Never quite like this. You managed always to do something you liked. At least a little." She looked at him with feeling. "Would it help if we got into bed and kept ourselves company?"

He doubted it; thanked her.

"Sleep well, darling."

Dubin left her sitting in the living room with yesterday's newspaper and a handbook of psychiatry Nathanael had owned. She also consulted a medical adviser.

He got into his pajamas and hurried to sleep. He slept quickly, trying to dawdle. When he went to bed this early he was up at five and fought to sleep again—on principle—but couldn't. Sleep had for a few hours possessed him, not he it. Dubin tossed aside his blankets and staggered in the dark to the shower. Afterward as he diddled with breakfast, the sheer stretch of morning ahead weighed heavily on his imagination. He left the house early, earlier after each early bedtime, to lose himself out of doors; to not think despite the turgid flow of thought: how to get back to productive work, without which his ego was more savagely self-obsessed.

He went through the bare pewter-trunked silver maples, away from the house—sometimes whistling, pretending God's not too far off his heaven, in case anyone's listening—then hurried through Kitty's silent wood, trotting now, the will rampant. Dubin jogged the short walk to the bridge but if it brought no relief—there were times it did—he traveled the long route. Nothing like a little "agitation," Johnson had said, to escape misery. He ran from his gross belly, from Fanny in all her guises, naked to not quite. She flung her underpants at him for the thousandth time; tempting him, betraying him. He ran from heartbreak revived, his dreary discipline, loyal wife, depression afflicting him. Sometimes his legs went faster than his body cared to go.

What a miserable price to pay for unpleasure! My God, whatever hit me so hard? She meant at first not much to me—almost nothing; she gave me little, only what I took, why do I so unwillingly mourn her? Now he regretted his stiff-assed frigid letter to her basically warm one; considered writing another canceling the intent of the first, but would not. He felt—shame on Dubin—jealous of her jape of a lover who had wooed and won her with his red-pompommed sailor's cap and lavender pants, fifteen minutes after he had handed her into his motor taxi on a Venetian canal. The capitano had driven his passenger to Murano, put her safely to bed, and banged her madly. The gondolier had taken her fancy the day before with his manly ass and a lilting love song; the capitano, a day later with his pompommed pitch in a splashing speedboat. For shame, Fanny, what are you doing to yourself? She had canceled out Rome and settled for amiable fornication on an isle of glass. That Dubin would so often replay his humiliation with her was an astonishment to him. It's she who sent me into this tailspin, though not only she. I blame me for offering myself as victim. What was he doing to himself?

Kitty had her theory: "You hit the jackpot with *H. D. Thoreau*. You want, naturally, to repeat with D. H. Lawrence. It's inhibiting—you're afraid you won't. You must think of yourself as being off the Rock Candy Mountain, plodding along a plateau, hunting another mountain. What an honor it was that night, not to mention President Johnson asking you to write his life. God, I wish you had. I'll bet you could have said anything you felt you had to about him. After that a letdown was bound to occur, William, and you'll have to ride it out. Patiently, I hope." She laughed breathily. "Don't you think so?"

Dubin nodded. What she said was true enough, yet not the truth. At meals he sat opposite her, looking out of the window behind her, saying little, agreeing with her, pretending things might be worse; wearing a mask. Nietzsche had said the profound man is he who needs a mask. Dubin, if not profound, was profoundly disgusted with Wm. Dubin, which calls for a small disguise in the presence of your believing wife. Kitty now got out of bed after he had done exercising, drew on her black and burgundy African robe, and yawning, followed her husband downstairs to prepare breakfast as she had used to almost every day when the kids were young. She kept him company, a gracious gesture, for which he saw her plain.

He plunged into the snowy woods. The bleak landscape gave forth bleakness; he gave it back. Though his flesh diminished the paunch persisted.

In the evening, after a long day and subdued supper, unless she could persuade him to go out with her to see a movie, or turn on TV, they sat in silence in opposing armchairs, Kitty knitting as she talked from one thought to another, or sat regarding him above her slightly lowered newspaper as he pretended to be reading a book. I am in my thoughts a detached lonely man, my nature subdued by how I've lived and the lives I've written; subdued by the dyer's bloodless hand.

Dubin was fifty-seven on the twenty-seventh of December, 1973, and the last thing he wanted, or needed, was to celebrate the dismal occasion, but Kitty had urged, insisted. "William, let's get out of the rut we're in. We haven't had a dinner party since before you went off to Italy." He was born in a cold season yet liked to think he had been conceived in spring. Dubin dragged his feet because he had forgotten Kitty's birthday, last April, and wanted her to forget his.

Kitty, who had been a poor cook for her first husband, was an excellent one for her second. She roasted two ducks, produced three bottles of Cabernet Sauvignon and five of Lanson champagne, and arranged masses of red and lavender anemones and bronze chrysanthemum daisies in white vases. He decided her favorite color was white.

She had invited, for this festive occasion, the Greenfelds, Ondyks, Habershams, and, of course, Myra Wilson. The Habershams were old friends, Fred, an activist civil-rights attorney; his wife, Ursula, also a lawyer, was a Vermont Senator, one of three women in the legislature. The Ondyks came, Evan, the psychotherapist, and his wife, Marisa, an insecure lady with a nervous nose she often blew and lips drawn at the corners. If you kissed her on the cheek she said, "Mmmuh," meaning a passionate kiss in return. Her passion was a play-reading group she had formed that Kitty sometimes attended. Marisa preferred tragic roles; Kitty read comic ones.

She and Flora were currently amiable and though they were never entirely at ease with each other—one coveted "more," one "less"—greeted the other cordially. It was, through the years, an ambivalent relationship. Flora was an animated woman of regal bearing, a violinist without professional career or children. Kitty pitied her for not having children, not because she hadn't had them, but because she had wanted them and Oscar hadn't. Dubin had always responded to Flora; they kissed on meeting. Kitty called her "born dissatisfied."

"She pretends, hides so much. When you talk to her you can sense all she's holding back."

"We all hide," Dubin confessed.

"Obviously," she said sadly.

"Then why blame her?"

"She pretends not to."

Myra Wilson, at seventy-eight, was a still vital self-reliant white-haired farmer's widow. Living alone had not soured or scared her. She lived competently and said little about her ailments, poor circulation, arthritic pains in shoulders and neck. "So long as I have my bottle of aspirins." Kitty admired her independence and invited the old woman to her dinner parties; she almost daily attended her. They talked often and at length on the phone. Kitty was genuinely fond of old people, perhaps women more than men: she had been brought up, she often said, by a loving grandmother. Dubin, for this birthday and this mood, would have wanted some young people around, but only Flora was younger than fifty. Not that much younger. But she was womanly and attractive in a low-cut black dress. She was the one woman Dubin was drawn to that night.

"We hardly ever see you, William," Flora said. "Oscar says he meets you on his walk once in a while. I hear you're into your new biography?"

"Deeply," he sighed.

Oscar Greenfeld and the biographer embraced after skirting each other during drinks.

"What's wrong, old boy," Oscar asked.

"Does it show?"

"A strained swimming against the stream."

"My work, I guess."

"Not going well?"

"No."

"If I'd known I'd've brought my pipe to flute you up."

"Too bad you didn't," said Dubin.

He went through the evening with a show of having a good time. Knowing he wasn't, he ate too much too quickly, tasted little, shoveled down more food, grew irritated with himself. He hurried upstairs to brush his teeth, then flung the brush into the sink bowl.

Dubin slogged through the night in a saddened mood. There he was, not being who he was or felt like. Kitty, taken in by his pretense—mask?—seemed to assume the party was working for him. For dessert she sailed in with a birthday cake she had baked from scratch, lit with a flickering white candle; and the guests toasted the biographer with champagne as he smiled with his head bowed.

Kitty would not play the harp when Flora asked her to, despite the applause of her dinner guests. "No, no," she laughed and almost cried, "I'd spoil the fun."

"Oh, come on," said Flora.

"Let her alone," said Greenfeld.

Afterward Maud called. Dubin, sitting in the downstairs bathroom that morning, had heard Kitty dial Maud and quietly ask her to remember to telephone her father that night. He assumed Kitty had also called Gerald but doubted she'd been able to persuade him to put in a collect call.

"Hi, Papa," Maud said, "happy birthday."

Dubin said he missed her and was counting on her coming home for the winter vacation.

"I miss you too. I will if I can."

As he sat at the phone in the hallway he was watching Kitty in the kitchen by the sink, both faucets running, talking seriously with Ondyk.

If she's consulting him about me, I'll break her ass, Dubin thought.

Maud said she'd be home in early February. "I'd like to take off a few days after finals. I hate to leave the sun."

"It would help me to see you," he told her.

Her voice grew serious. "Is something the matter?"

"I like to look at you," he said. "I like you around."

"Don't put more pressure on me, Pa. I'm taking five exams."

He said there'd be no pressure and felt low. She had changed. If a man needs his daughter so much, Dubin thought, maybe he needs somebody else more.

Maud's voice was tender when she said goodbye.

In their bedroom, later, Dubin thanked Kitty for the party.

She was sitting in a chair, her skirt hiked up over her knees, legs raised, looking long at them.

"I have pretty good legs," she said. "Not bad for my age."

Dubin agreed.

"Did you like the evening?"

"Yes. Thanks for going to all the trouble."

She got up to undress. "I don't think of it as trouble, but you don't look very happy."

"I haven't pretended to be," he said, though he had.

Kitty asked whether he might care to talk to Evan Ondyk. She said it doubtfully.

"Were you talking to him about me?"

"No. About myself."

"What would you like me to say to him?"

"Stop being ironic. He might be able to help you pinpoint what's bothering you—to figure out where you stand."

"I know where I stand. He doesn't know. I doubt he knows where he stands."

"I know people he's helped. He's an excellent psychotherapist."

"I don't need his advice. His view of life is reductive. With him a lot more is determined than with me. I know how free I am. I've picked the horse I ride."

"Never mind the horse. How free do you feel?"

"Once I asked him his interpretation of Thoreau and he came up with the usual can of oedipal worms. There's that but there's more."

"He's not a literary critic."

"He's not wise."

"Neither are you," said Kitty.

"That's true," Dubin answered after a pause, "but I know as much about life as he does. Once I didn't, now I do."

"No, you don't. Maybe you do about the careers of certain accomplished literary figures, but not necessarily about yourself and not necessarily about the unconscious."

"Biography—literary or otherwise—teaches you the conduct of life. Those who write about life reflect about life. The unconscious is mirrored in a man's acts and words. If he watches and listens to himself, sooner or later he begins to see the contours of the unconscious self. If you know your defenses you pretty much understand what it's about. In my work I've discovered how to discover. You see in others who you are."

"Mirrored is right. You ought to hear yourself in the bathroom."

"I hear, I listen. That's the point I'm making. I've lived fifty-eight years."

"Fifty-seven."

"Fifty-seven. I think I know myself reasonably well. No one knows himself entirely. There's a mystery in knowing. The big thing is what you do with what you know."

"You exercise? You lose weight?"

"Right now I'm saying to myself that I *can* exercise and lose weight."

"Where will it get you?" Kitty asked. "You're still a depressed man who has trouble working. William, I feel there's more to this than either you know or have said."

She's clever, he thought, but I won't clobber her with honesty—not hers or mine.

He said he had real literary problems with his book. "So far it's a dry piece of work, a compilation of facts rather than a living life—it reads like de La Grange's *Mahler* or Blotner's *Faulkner*. I want the juices of life in it. My reaction to it is not, simply, neurosis."

Kitty had never said it was. "I feel in the dark," she said, her voice strained. "In the dark I'm afraid. I feel you can't work well for a reason, William. If you know what it is please tell me. Don't keep me in the dark."

Dubin told her he would tell her when he knew.

"Losing weight won't do it," Kitty said, looking at him with moist dark eyes. "Nor what you think you know about life because you write biographies. Working it out with someone usually helps. If you don't want to talk to Evan, why don't you go see Dr. Selensaal in Winslow? I hear he's very good."

"I haven't got that kind of time. Winslow is seventy miles one way and seventy back. It'll kill a day to go there."

"Go once and talk to him instead of frittering the morning away getting nothing done."

"Once leads to twice, then twice a week. I haven't got that kind of time."

"Stop yakking about time, for Christ's sake. You're not doing much with it."

"Life is what I'm thinking of," Dubin said. "I know its structure and spin and many of its ways of surprise, if not total pattern or order. I know enough, in other words, to take my chances. I want to run my life my own way, not like yours or

Nathanael's. I don't want to go on sharing with you to my dying day the benefits of your previous marriage."

"That's cruel."

Kitty drew her dress over her head. He looked away from the mark on her buttock through her white underpants. When he looked again she was slipping on a nightgown.

"Don't be so fucking proud," Kitty said in bed.

My pain is tolerable, Dubin thought. All I can not do is work.

He fought winter as if it were the true enemy: if he tore into it the freeze would vanish, his ills be gone, his life, his work, fall into place. He would overcome belly, mood, joyless labor—lust for Fanny, the burden of his unhappy experience with her. Dubin assailed winter by daily testing himself: running through its icy womb to demonstrate he was not afraid of the dead season. Not fearing it, he would fear less the dysfunctioning self—what was or was not happening. He ran in rain, slush, in end-of-December fog—to show weather, winter staring at him as he went by, the quality of Dubin's self, his premise, the thought he ran by. As a youth he would hold a burning match till the flame touched his fingertips: if you held the glowing matchstick until the very end, the girl you loved would love you.

It was as hard a winter as Dubin feared it would be. He had to force himself, after breakfast, to open the kitchen door and step into the frozen morning, facing his icy breath. The cold struck him like a blow of a fist. His face tightened; he could tell every stroke he had shaved—a cut on his chin burned like acid. Dubin walked three steps and broke into a run, his spine touched by chill; across the inert grass, through light snow, along the solitary path of the icy-damp morning wood. Thoreau had called winter a resonant instrument that twanged its own music. Dubin, as he ran, heard branches creak in the cold; once on an icy day a dead tree exploded. The listening wood, animistic, druidic, recalled Stonehenge. Occasionally he saw a small animal stirring, rat or weasel scuttering through the brush; or a dark bird in flight, unrecognizable. Dubin thumped alone along the path in the wood.

He left the trees, trotting on the dirt road to the bridge, the stream misting by his side, his breath flowing behind him. If a car appeared this early in the morning, neither jogger nor driver dared look at the other. He slowed down at the bridge, limped through the booming snow-covered construction, crossed the highway, and at the fork relentlessly ran into the long route. There were times he turned back at the wooden bridge: temporary cure: felt he could get into writing if he tried. Dubin turned back rarely. He went on if when he thought of himself it touched pain. The trick was to get into the winter world and out of within—shift the weight of inner conflict to outside. The cock's tail turns where the cock's head had been. His thoughts therefore were images of gnarled broken-fingered oaks, naked birches—imagine a white tree! And there were more winter birds around than he had guessed—the flyways were overpopulated, the South crowded; some birds remained in the snow. And the frozen circular road.

It took him a half hour to turn the shivery clinging cold in his clothes to warmth gained in running. He slowed to a fast walk, past farmhouses with monumental barns looking like forever; cows in winter pasture as still as statues, their breaths flags in motion; frozen fields undulating up the mist-streaked hills. He pushed on in winter silence, every step striding against the force of nothing, aware of roadside mustard-yellow willows, their long yellow strings limply dancing in the cutting wind. He plodded breathlessly up the road, conscious of the weight of ascent, dismal cold, the unhappy task he had set himself. Walking uphill, Dubin stared at his feet lest the hike to the top slay him. Trotting down, he kept his eyes on the beckoning distance. The ascents were endless. Segments of the road he had once thought level, he realized, were pitched up from five to ten degrees. He tried not to stop on the walk up; it was hard to get started again. Ravenous for summer, for an end to the barren season, he hurried on thinking of the next rise or bend. He felt with each step resistance of the long long walk-run, monotony of self-inflicted cure. Climbing is not ascending. My will is my enemy. It restoreth not my soul. Yet he stayed with it: if he overslept he ran faster.

The flutist remembered him at this time as a strained, almost haggard man in motion, heavily bundled up, a grim-faced man who had lost weight, or might, without knowing it, be ill. He wore a red wool hat his wife had knitted, a long striped scarf his wife had knitted, galoshes with unbuckled buckles that clinked as he ran, and a poplin fleece-lined coat with a brown fur collar. Dubin ran slowly, heavily, in snow or slush, as if his boots were lead and each step an ordeal, his sober inward grayish-blue eyes set dimly in the distance. What he saw there Greenfeld hesitated to guess. When they met, although the biographer appeared to be drowning in all there was to say, he was mute. Sometimes in passing he would stammer half a sentence, break off, and hurry on.

William, Oscar cried, let's not forget our friendship. William, it's a lonely world!

Greenfeld was haunted by the expression of Dubin's eyes as he looked back—embittered?—as though the fault was the flutist's that he did not then know what his friend was living through.

When he had returned to the house, after resting awhile he sat at his desk. Dubin never did not work though he stayed with it for shorter intervals of time, down to an hour and a half each morning. He wrote long swirling sentences on sheets of yellow foolscap and reflected on each. Kitty, one Saturday morning, brought up a cup of consommé. He took a grateful sip and thanked her but did not finish it.

"Don't you like it?"

"Warming—after that long haul."

"Why don't you eat the rest?"

He did not want to eat between meals.

"You're mad," she said.

After she left he went back to his tortuous sentences. It was a bright sunny day after the New Year. Later she brought up the mail. Kitty bent to kiss him as she handed him an airmail letter.

Fanny hoped to hear from him.

"It isn't easy to write to someone who won't answer you. I know you're there, William, because my letters aren't returned to me. At least your first letter, I had the pleasure of opening it before it hit me in the face like a bucket of ice.

"As you can see by the postmark I have left Murano. Arnaldo

wasn't easy to get along with. He was good in bed though not much more than that. When I said I was leaving he begged me to stay. He wanted to marry me but I don't want to be married yet. He got awfully angry, beat his stringy cock on the table. I felt terribly depressed. I hate myself for this kind of thing—I mean going to bed with the nearest guy when I am anxious. In my mind I don't seem to be that kind of person. In my mind you are my friend.

"I am now in Rome, staying with this old friend of mine I mentioned to you that day we broke up. Harvey says I am genuine, whatever mistakes I make. I'm the only woman he knows who can be easy with him when he is impotent. He's sixty-two and was once a singer. He knew my father in L.A. and didn't much care for him. My father used to say I was oversexed and I used to feel awful until one day I realized what *his* problems are.

"Recently, when Harvey and I were standing in a movie line I passed out. In the hospital I thought I was pregnant—that Arnaldo had knocked me up, but it turned out I had developed a cyst in a fallopian tube because of the IUD I had changed to. I hate the Pill because it makes me bleed. Anyway, I was operated on and lost a tube. I felt deathly depressed until the doctor said I could still have children. Harvey has been kind to me. He says I am independent and enjoy life, which is partly true.

"I've been thinking of going back to the States to find some sort of steady work—don't ask me what. I have ideas about what I ought to be doing but am afraid of the next move. I don't want to get into something I can't get out of if I make the wrong choice. Or into something that won't come to much, and will make me feel, again, that I am up Shit Creek in a leaky rowboat. William, please advise me about my life. I like the way you talk to me about myself.

"I wish you would sometime write me a letter saying things I could think about. What happened at the Hotel Contessa between us wasn't all my fault, if you've stopped to think about it. You were kind in your way but your mind wasn't really on me. And not everybody can be lovers—I'm sure you'll agree with that. But I have the feeling we could have been good friends. Could you specifically say what I ought to be thinking about in the way of a job or career, or recommend books that might be helpful? Or give me the names of courses I could take when I get back to New York City?

"I'd like to be better organized and enjoy my life more, but Harvey isn't that well put together and has problems that remind me of my own, so I don't think I ought to stay here. I don't think I'm so good for him either. I'm afraid of my day-to-day life. A day scares me more than a week or month. But the truth of it is I want to be responsible, to work my life out decently. Couldn't we at least talk about that? Affectionately, Fanny B.

"P.S. This is my last letter unless you answer it, gently."

Dubin burned the letter.

She wrote once after that: "I'm not writing to humiliate myself but to show you I have respect for you though you don't seem to have much for me. F."

He kept this letter, her last. She had enclosed a snapshot of herself in jeans, sneakers, and embroidered blue blouse, her long hair stringy, her sad face plain. She was not an ideal woman. Why was he so drawn to her?

In the woods, later, he thought if he had had her in Venice he might not have wanted her afterward. Yet he thought he wanted more than just wanting her.

Dubin awoke in moonlight, unhappy to wake. He'd gone to bed after supper, too intent on sleep to draw the shades. What was that song of Schubert's about a man who was awakened by starlight? It was late January and the ground was covered with snow. Kitty had been sleeping in Maud's bed, not to disturb him. Dubin, moonlight spilling on his face, thought he ought to get up and draw the shade. He lay there, trying to rouse himself. At last he flung the blanket aside. At the window the moon was full, the somber hills bathed in a darkish bronze glow. He stared at his wristwatch on the night table: it wasn't ten yet. He looked again in disbelief, watched the second hand move. He had slept a few hours and now it felt as though today was tomorrow. He felt a sadness of waste. Dubin dressed and went down the stairs.

Kitty, reading in bed, called to him through Maud's closed door. "Is there something you need, William?"

"I waked and can't sleep. I'm going out for a short walk. It's a full moon."

After a minute Kitty asked, "Would you want company? I'll get dressed."

He didn't think so.

Dubin drew on his overcoat and wool hat and buckled on his galoshes. He took along a thick stick that had once belonged to Gerald. Maybe he would go to the bridge.

"It's a freezing night," she said through the door, "don't go far."

He didn't think he would.

He was at first afraid to enter the wood. Then he went through it, dimly lit trees casting shadows on the darkly lit snow.

At the road he turned left instead of right toward the bridge. A few fleecy clouds floated in the night-blue winter sky. After some minutes of careful walking on and off the snowy road he passed the Wilson farmhouse, a narrow two-story white frame house with a sloping addition on the left side. It lay off the road about two hundred feet. An orange light burned in the upstairs darkened bedroom. It was Myra's night light, an old woman alone in a farmhouse in the dead of winter. He imagined her sleeping in a bed she had lain in with her husband for fifty years. Ben, the dog, growled as Dubin went by. He gripped his stick.

Oscar Greenfeld's house was a half mile farther up the road, a two-story spacious red clapboard with a large lawn. Dubin thought of their friendship with regret. How strange to love a man and rarely see him. Dubin had enjoyed coming to Oscar's house in the past—walking along this road in summer, driving the front way through the streets in winter. They played chess, talked and drank. The flutist had come less often to Dubin. He never came with Flora. If you're not alone with a friend there's no friendship, he said. In his company Dubin drank more than he was used to, and Kitty worried when he got into the car at one or half past one A.M. to drive Oscar home. The flutist didn't drive. Flora drove him there but wouldn't call for him that late at night, though she stayed up waiting. That was one of the things about her that antagonized Kitty: Kitty went for Dubin when she had to. Neither of them cared for the drinking, and driving on icy streets. Oscar Greenfeld stopped coming to Dubin's house; then Dubin stopped going to him.

After an evening together hitting the brandy bottle, Oscar when he woke the next morning could reach for his flute and move to Mozart on the music stand. With Mozart dealing out the notes Oscar could toot away most of his hangover. Dubin, working with words, felt he was pushing rocks with his nose, so he stopped visiting the flutist although they talked on the phone. But a telephone conversation now and then could not be called friendship.

He drank, Oscar told Dubin, because he was not a better flutist.

"You're one of the best, Oscar."

"Not in my ears."

"Rampal says so."

"Not in my ears."

"That's not the only reason you drink," the biographer said.

"I never said so."

As Dubin entered the driveway he heard Oscar's flute, clearly, limpidly, deep within the house. He listened: Schubert's "Serenade." Lately Oscar had been transcribing lieder into flute songs. The song was like a lit candle in the night. In his "Short Life of Schubert" the biographer had written that the composer, on hearing the song sung at a concert, was supposed to have said, "You know, I never remembered it was so beautiful." How moving a simple song is, Dubin thought. How often they go to sadness. It's as though the sad song was the natural one, the primal song. Someone sings without knowing why and it's a song expressing hunger for love, regret for life unlived, sorrow for the shortness of life. Even some of the joyful songs evoke memories of something lost that one hopes endures.

The moon bathed the birch trees on the lawn in liquid light. There were several white trees in an irregular circle, inclined in different directions, looking like white-clad dancers in the snow. Oscar had written a flute song called, "The Birch Dancers." He said he wrote it one night when he couldn't sleep, after looking out the window at the white trees.

Listening to the serenade, this lied of yearning, he reflected that Schubert had often intertwined themes of love and death. In a certain time of his life the two experiences had become one. He had died of typhus at thirty-one. A few years before, at twenty-six or -seven, he had been infected with syphilis. "Each night when I go to sleep," he wrote to a friend, "I hope I won't wake again; and each morning reminds me of yesterday's misery." Love, he told his friend, offered only pain. The doppelgänger seeks the mystical fusion of love and death.

Dubin did not go into the house. When the song had ended he left the driveway and walked toward town.

in diesem Hause wohnte mein Schatz;
sie hat schon längst die Stadt verlassen,
doch steht noch das Haus auf demselben Platz.

It looked in the garish moonlight like a piece of stark statuary, or an old painting of an old house. Ah, Fanny, what if you had found me in the Gansevoort that night in the city, would a different beginning have made a happy end?

A window went up with a rasp on the top floor of the house under the high-gabled roof, and Dubin was too surprised to duck into the shadow of the beech tree. A naked large-shouldered man leaned out into the wintry night and stared down at the astonished biographer. This was not the Eve of St. Agnes, nor was Dubin Porphyrio, so he could not have expected to be gazing at Fanny, naked or clothed; but it was a strange surprise, and not unrelated to his mood, to behold Roger Foster's bare curly-haired chest and moonlit thick-sideburned handsome face.

"Good Christ, Mr. Dubin, is that you down there?" the librarian said in surprise.

On a freezing night in January he talks to you naked from his window without a shiver.

"I'm afraid so."

"Anyone in particular you're looking for?"

Dubin calmly replied, "Nobody in particular. I couldn't sleep and am out for a short walk."

"Sorry about that. Anything I can do for you? Would you care to come in for a drink or maybe a cup of hot coffee?"

"Thank you, no."

He wanted to ask about Fanny but dared not.

"How are things going, Roger?"

"Pretty good. All's well at the library, what with the help of your kind wife."

"Wonderful," said Dubin.

"Has anybody heard anything from Fanny?" Roger asked.

"She's in Rome, I believe. Haven't you heard from her?"

"Just a postcard a couple of weeks ago, that she was in Venice having herself a ball."

"You don't say," said Dubin.

"She sure gets around."

"She seems to."

"You know, Mr. Dubin," Roger then said, "someday I hope we get to understand each other better. We have things in common—bookwise, I mean to say. We keep your biographies, every one of them, on our shelves. I know you've never liked me all that well but I'm not such a bad egg, if you ask around, and I hope to accomplish more than you might think."

"You put it well, Roger, I wish you luck."

"And I wish *you* luck, Mr. Dubin."

He breathed in the cold air, exhaling his steamy breath.

"Well, good night now, it's getting chilly."

Roger shut the window and pulled down the shade.

Dubin waited a minute perhaps for Fanny to peek through a slit in the drawn window shade. She did not.

After walking home he listened to a recording of "Death and the Maiden." It was after midnight. Kitty came down in her robe and had a drink as she listened.

They went to sleep in the same bed, Kitty wearing a black chiffon nightgown. She offered herself and he accepted. Afterward she changed into a white flannel nightgown and got back into their double bed.

"I want to travel again soon," Kitty said. "There's so much of the world we haven't seen, so much that's varied and beautiful. Let's have more fun than we've been having. When do you think we'll travel again?"

Dubin didn't know.

It seemed to him he'd been sleeping deeply when he heard a shrill ring and sat stiffly upright in bed. At first he thought the doorbell had sounded and was about to run down the stairs when it shot through him that the phone had rung piercingly once and stopped.

No one answered his insistent hellos.

"Maybe it was Maud," Kitty said. "Or Gerald."

If it was Fanny calling from Rome he was glad she had rung off.

Kitty had snuggled close and fallen asleep.

Dubin lay awake.

Middle age, he thought, is when you pay for what you didn't have or couldn't do when you were young.

The man trudged diagonally across the snowy field to the slushy road. Dubin watched him as he came, listing to the left. He seemed insufficiently dressed for the cold—had on a ragged jacket, thin pants, wet boots. He wore no hat, his thin black eyes expressionless. He was a burly man with heavy ears and small features, face unshaved. He waited in the road till Dubin had caught up with him without trying, and then walked along at the biographer's side.

"Good morning," Dubin said.

The man grunted. Once he hawked up a gob of phlegm and spat at the snow. Every so often, as they went on, he lifted his arms as if pointing a shotgun at a sparrow flying overhead. "Bang bang." The bird flew off. The man lowered his arms and trudged on with Dubin.

Who the hell is he? Does he think he knows me because he's seen me walking here? They were alone on the road and he was uneasy with the stranger.

"You live nearby?"

The man barely nodded.

They walked on, saying nothing. Dubin, after a while, would point at something in the distance and say what it was: "Frost's farmhouse one summer—the poet. His daughter Irma went crazy that year."

The man trudged along with him, scanning the sky. Is he an escaped convict, Dubin worried, or just some poor bastard looking for company?

Suppose he knifes me? He saw himself lying dead in a pool of blood in the frozen snow. There's Dubin lying in the road with a gaping wound in his chest, his gray-blue eyes staring at the gray-blue sky. It's a long hard winter.

The man hung close by, their arms bumping as they walked.

Dubin reconciled himself to his company. After all, it's a public road. He's picked me to walk with, though who he is he's not about to say.

"Neither am I," he said aloud.

The stranger, tight-eyed, scanned the sky.

Suppose a man like him clings to you forever? You try to shake him and he follows you home. You have him arrested and he convinces the judge he's your uncle and moves in. Suppose, by one means or another, he stays forever? Who is he to you then? Dubin talked to himself sub voce.

As he was experiencing these thoughts two crows flew overhead in the white sky. The man dropped to his knee with a grunt and raised his arms as though sighting up a gun barrel.

"Boom boom." To Dubin's astonishment one of the black birds wavered in flight and plummeted to the ground. The stranger let out a hoarse shout and plunged into the white field to retrieve the crow. Holding it up for Dubin to see, he pressed the dead bird to his chest and awkwardly ran, kicking up snow, diagonally across the field in the direction he had come.

Can a crow have a heart attack?

One of us is mad, the biographer thought.

Dubin ran in his rectangular circle.

He remembered, when he was twelve, one day walking home from school with his seventh-grade teacher, a broken-nosed knowing nasally talkative young man. As they were walking, this strange reddish-haired woman wearing a green hat trimmed with brown felt flowers approached in excitement from down the block. When William saw his insane mother coming toward them he said goodbye in the middle of somebody's sentence and hurried across the street. When he looked back she was standing alone on the sidewalk, sobbing, crazily waving her fist.

"*In diesem Wetter, in diesem Braus, nie hätt' ich gesendet die Kinder hinaus!*" Kitty sang at her harp.

As Samuel Johnson, at the top of the stairs, was turning the key of his chamber at Pembroke College, he heard his mother distinctly call, "Sam!"

Willie.

Leo!

The child had been sucked by the waves beyond the ropes. Willie screamed at the lifeguard who jumped into the boat and rowed in the choppy green water to where the child had drowned.

Leo, she called, Willie.

Willie, she wailed, *Leo.*

Q. Why don't you keep a journal?

A. I'm afraid what it might say.

At night they sat in opposing armchairs, hers a wingback against possible drafts, reading in separate pools of light. He had offered to build a fire, but she said she felt hot. He watched her pulse beat on her neck.

"This is one of those nights I keep sweating, then getting cold."

"Don't open the window."

"I will if I want to."

As they were reading, Kitty, a day behind with the day's news, read him humorous snippets from yesterday's papers.

"Don't," Dubin said. "I find it hard to concentrate."

"Why bother?"

Afterward she said, "We used to talk about everything in the world. We talk about nothing now."

He got up to put on a record, not because he wanted to listen to it, but because he must think of Fanny. His thoughts of the girl were a gluey collage representing an unalterable desire to be with her.

Why don't I tell my wife and maybe the misery will yield?

It seemed to him he had not told her because Fanny was still possible. If he answered her letter they might meet.

Mad, Dubin thought, after the treatment she had dished out in Venice. What can I anticipate, given who she is, but more of the same? What fantasy am I living? What imbecility?

He was, in his thoughts, living with Fanny, living it as they hadn't before. Dubin was in Rome with her, in the same rooms, eating with Fanny, enjoying her, enjoying life. They walked through the Borghese Gardens in winter sunlight; wherever he turned he felt her warmhearted embrace. Before his eyes the girl changed: had become loving, loyal, protective, kind. She loved Dubin and he, in his right mind, loved her.

"Tell me about Lawrence," Kitty sometimes said as they sat alone in the room, and Dubin would make the effort to relate episodes of the man's life.

"You tell it so interestingly. Why is it so hard to write?"

"It resists the pen. The second thought hides from the first."

"Why don't you try dictating?"

"That's not for me."

"Why not?"

"I've tried it," Dubin said. He was on the verge of shouting.

"I feel cold. Is there a draft?" she asked, looking around.

"It's you, the house is warm."

Shivering, she tried to read. She glanced at the book she had opened, took in a few sentences, then stole a look at him, or looked away. She read slowly, every word of every sentence. She wanted to know in toto what each sentence said. He knew what book she was reading.

She had suggested cards but he had declined. He had never felt, he thought, this much apart from her. There were two houses and she was in the other. Kitty sat huddled in the Queen Anne chair, wearing pants and two sweaters, a rose cardigan over a black pullover. She's hurt by what she doesn't know.

From behind his book, held to his face, he reflected on his silence. He had nothing to say because he hadn't said it when it was his to say. What you don't say grows into not saying. A locked house is full of locked rooms.

He was, in his silence, elsewhere. He was not who she thought he was. Whoever he was, wearied by sticky fantasies, he wanted escape from his dream-drugged existence. He did not forever want to go on dreaming of Fanny Bick as she wasn't now and never would be. Dubin waited for his drawn-out steamy reverie at last to come to an end. He waited for it to wither, die in the mind. Until it died he was separate, alone, a small fog in a chair, pretending to read. He chilled the room with his presence. Kitty hugged herself against the cold.

At ten o'clock she glanced at her wristwatch, yawned, and shut the fat book.

"You've been whispering to yourself all night, William. Why don't you let me in on it?"

"What have I been saying?"

"I wish I knew. Will it help," she asked, her hands clasped white between her knees, "if I were to stay home mornings—I mean from the library?"

God, no, he thought.

He didn't think so, Dubin said. He wanted not to say it. He tried to say he needed her but felt no need.

"Is there something I can do for you? Some other way I can help?"

He said he was grateful for her patience.

"Patience is minimal. I'd like to do more for you if you'd let me."

Only patience, he urged. The misery could not go on forever.

She spoke firmly: "You're splendid with your gymnastics, William. You take brave walks in every weather. You diet as planned—I give you credit, though I'd go mad if I had to do it if I were feeling like you. You do what you've set yourself to, although I don't know what it comes to except you've lost weight, your clothes droop, your face is strained. You're out on your private little black sailboat in the rough green sea and here I am alone on a dreary lava-like shore. I don't know how to comfort you. I've never seen you so low so long. It has me frightened."

He asked her not to be.

"I can't help it," her voice wavered.

He spoke these words: "I've lost weight and move more easily. I feel lighter, a change at least. Something good may be happening. One day you wake and whatever it was that was sitting on your head has flown off. You feel yourself again."

"I hope so." She seemed doubtful. "Nathanael wasn't a psychiatrist—he almost became one but wouldn't because he enjoyed physical medicine. But he read a lot in psychotherapy, possibly because of me. I remember his saying that a sudden depression usually had a specific cause—you lost a job or love object—some specific disappointment or loss would set it off. William, did anything unusual happen to you while you were abroad?"

Dubin thought, Right here I could get off the train. I could walk out from under the pile of rocks I wear as a hat.

"I saw Gerald," he said. "It wasn't a happy time."

The train chugged on. There was no station. He had not got off.

"I don't mean Gerald. I mean something in Italy."

His eyes would not meet hers. "Why Italy?" he asked irritably, not wanting her to guess what was his to say.

"Just a feeling I have."

He said, believing it, the trouble was his work. If he solved that he'd solve everything.

She vehemently denied it. "It isn't your work that's doing this to you. It's you doing something to your work. I know your doubts about Lawrence as subject but you had similar doubts about Thoreau. You always have doubts at this stage. Please don't put it ass-backwards. It's not your work that hurts your work, it's you."

"Why would I need Evan Ondyk if I have you?"

"I'm not trying to sell you anything," Kitty said with hauteur. "But I think you need help."

He said he was not a child any more. "I don't deny I could have been helped by analysis once but I've lived my life without it. Now I have to go on what I know."

"I've been reading about depression and I think you've had it more often than you think, sometimes simply as lack of joie de vivre—"

"Does the book explain why you sometimes lack joie de vivre?"

"Not as much as you. Sometimes I think you've never felt young in your life; you've almost always interpreted it as obligation or lost opportunity. I'm basically a more carefree happier person than you."

He hoarsely denied it.

"There are times your nature dampens mine," she said.

"That works both ways."

"Let's drop it," Kitty said. "Forget the joie de vivre. I know you know a lot about people, William, because of the way you contemplate human lives, but I'm saying you could cut out a lot of unnecessary suffering if you consulted with someone. The will isn't everything."

"It keeps me going," the biographer shouted.

"If you know what's wrong with you," she said, her voice thickening, "for Christ's sake, tell me."

He said things changed in time; he needed time.

"But what about me while you're dieting and exercising for wisdom? I feel like shit when you want nothing I have to give."

"I want everything," Dubin shouted, waving his arms.

"You seem to want nothing *I* have to give. You hide your life, whispering what I can't hear. You're not affectionate. We never really talk to each other."

"What the hell are we doing now?"

"We aren't talking. You're yelling, we are not talking."

"You have no confidence in me. You insult me by giving me psychiatric advice. Spare me Nathanael's textbooks. I don't want to be his posthumous patient. I don't want to be yours."

Grabbing her *Handbook of Psychiatry*, Kitty ran up the stairs.

To quiet his self-disgust for renewing, replenishing the deceit, Dubin sniffed the gas burners for her.

He found the brandy bottle and poured himself a glassful.

He drank with his hat on in the cold house, his coat draped on his shoulders. The wind clattered down from the mountains. He drank, listening to the roaring wind blowing snowflakes through the straining groaning cracking branches of trees. After midnight he felt himself go to bed in a blizzard. Dubin wound the clock gloomily, unable to look it in the face. The wind wailing around the house seeped in through storm windows. He felt it like a live presence in the room. Undressing, he got into the lonely bed, compounded by two. Kitty slept soundly at first, her breathing heavy. Dubin lay awake listening to the storm: primordial blast blowing from the beginning of the world. If it could only change a man's life. Snowflakes spat at the windows. He slept and woke heavily, resisting waking. The drinking had added to the weight of the heaviness. It was a black heaviness, iron on the soul. Or you were drowning in nothing and this stone arm forced your head under; the arm was your own.

He rose in the live morning dark and stumbled groggily, step by step, through the brutal routine of the day. I must go through it. It is to show the depression it is not all. It is to show I fear it only so much, only so far. It is depression, an entity, it is not all. I know its black heaviness. I must be detached. I will not lock hands with it so that it becomes an adversary, another self; an ax to strike me with. I will wait for it to go its way. If I daily do what I have to, go through the motions, it will leave the house. It wants me to be its love, fuck it, marry it, but I won't. I welcome the white blizzard. It is a thing to think of, to be in other than depression. Thoreau was wrong in saying nature doesn't sympathize with sorrow. It does because it interrupts; it flings its frozen self at you, assails the plots and conjurations of my bleak brain.

He was old in the bathroom mirror. Dubin was afraid not to shave. He told himself not to but didn't know what else to do. This was the wrong day not to shave. He had rarely not shaved when he wasn't sick in bed.

In the lusterless mirror his left eye was fixed, distant, cold; contemplating his frightened right eye.

Dubin felt himself groan.

"Hush," said Kitty from the bedroom. "It never ends."

"Stupid bastard," Dubin groaned.

"Who?" she wanted to know.

He groaned in silence.

"Be silent," Carlyle writes himself in his journal, "be calm, be not mad."

Dubin tries to get a religious thought going.

"Love," Lawrence wrote, "is a thing to be learned through centuries of patient effort."

Where can I find the time?

"Please come out of the bathroom."

She was up early, dressed, studying herself in the long mirror. A night's decent sleep had helped her mood, looks; had brightened her eyes, quickened last night's lank hair.

"I wouldn't go on the long walk if I were you. It's going to blizzard."

"I thought it was."

"So far it's been only the wind with snow flurries. The radio says a blizzard is coming."

"I thought it had begun."

"That was the wind," Kitty said.

He'd come back to the house if it snowed heavily, Dubin said.

"No further than to the green bridge," she cautioned. "And put on long johns and your wool socks or you'll catch cold."

He looked away from her. They ate breakfast in silence. He listened to her chew her crisp toast.

Kitty left for the library. She returned to sniff the gas burners. "Ta ta," she called as she left.

He looked at his work, tried not to think how he felt. He held the misery off, kept it at bay with a stiletto as he wrote out his long yellow page of snaky sentences, reflecting on each, trying to connect them; by some act of grace to weave a tapestry, a life, a biography. Then on a white page he wrote a dozen new sentences and read them with care to see what they said; to find out if they were taking him seriously. He read them with dignity to show the sentences he had written and respected them, and must himself be respected. They were not to crawl or slither or flop around. They must go somewhere seriously into the life of Lawrence, revive, re-create, illumine it. But the last sentence, when he read it, said, "I am trapped." Dubin with a cry flung his pen against the wall. Disgust rose to his gorge and he fought the approach of panic. I've got to get out of here. I've got to get away from my fucking mind.

He left the kitchen door and ran through the trees into the field. Here the wind leapt at him, struck him, clawed his face. He gasped, choked, stood immobilized by the wind. His eyes teared, breath ached, as he tried to push on. The wind was a gorgon with an armlock on his stone head.

He retreated into the house, waited shivering in the kitchen, to recover his strength. He wanted not to go anywhere, to stand there till the weather abated, winter disappeared, the world changed. But he was afraid, if he stayed, of nothing, heavy, painted black. He was afraid of the silence ticking. After endless minutes he went out the front door, stumbled down the steps, hurried along the street. A heavy wind tore through the tops of moaning trees. He made his way downtown, icy snowflakes stinging his face.

Dubin hurried to the library. If he bought a newspaper he could read it there, forget himself; he dared not return to the empty house. Could he sit in the library reading the paper? Not with Kitty around, concerned to see him there. It was best not to buy a paper. He'd be better off into his routine, part of it rather than nothing. Not doing what he had to added to the misery of not doing. He would walk in the weather rather than do nothing.

Dubin went slowly in the falling snow to the outskirts of town, past the thermometer-assembly plant, the auto graveyard, two gas stations, then a motel and a tourist house. Along the wet highway he trod, approaching the long route by the back way. He had never walked it this way before. If Kitty asked why he had taken the long walk after all, he would say he had never done it this backwards way before.

Whatever diverts the mind from itself may help. What else is there to do? The wind-driven snow was now falling heavily. Dubin tramped on quickly a quarter of a mile in a world growing white, then had to tell himself it was no use, to turn back. For a while the wind had been thrusting him forward and it was no great trouble plodding on. Now it shifted, blew at him from the east. The wind, wailing, blew the coarse snow in blasts across the field, assailing him like a cluster of arrows, as though he was its only target. His field of vision was luminously white. He had turned tail and had trouble walking back to the highway. He inched on, stopping every several steps to discover if he knew where he was. When the blustery freezing wind momentarily died down and the snow thinned he was able to stride along. Once he beheld in the distance winter fields growing white, a wall of whitening black trees, and beyond, the misted fields flanking the snow-laced hills. Extraordinary sight: he felt a moment of elation before it vanished in the snow. Dubin peered around for a shelter but saw none. Most of the houses were behind him, toward the midpoint of the long road. He expected he would soon reach the highway. The wavering wind came at him again. He stiffened, staggered forward, then realized the ground had softened; the earth had roughened, he was no longer on the road. The snow, blowing in veiled gusty waves across the uneven fields, had wiped out every sign of the familiar road.

He felt fright, an old fear: his mother frightened by winter; himself stranger, where he oughtn't to be. Dubin found himself moving on a slope propelled downward. With fear in his gut he then diagonally ascended the incline, following his tracks disappearing as he sought them. The snow came down momentarily slowly, the flakes hanging in air before touching earth. He was standing in a hollow in an unknown field. As he tried to think which way to go he saw a rabbit skittering through the snow pursued by a dog; Dubin realized it was a fox. The rabbit slid up against a rock. The fox pounced on it and in a moment tore the screeching creature apart. The snow was covered with blood. Dubin stumbled away. The wild begins where you least expect it, one step off your daily course. A foot past the road and you're fighting with death. He had changed his black inner world for the white outer, equally perilous—man's fate in varying degrees; though some were more fated than others. Those who were concerned with fate were fated. He struck his boot against the dazzling white ground to get a fix on where he was but could not tell one part of the frozen earth from another. Dubin could see nothing in the distance, had no understanding of direction. Then he kicked up some threads of dead grass and knew he was still far off the road.

He waited for the wind to die down so he could see more than snow whirling around him. But the blustery wind continued to blow strongly. Pushing into it, assuming it was coming from the east and he had probably gone off the western side of the road because he had not been walking facing traffic, he wandered amid ridges that rose at last to a level surface. Dubin, in gasping relief, stumbled onto the road. He chose, after a moment, what he thought was the direction to the highway and plodded on, holding his arm above his eyes, trying to see the way ahead. Now and then he could make out a utility pole streaked with snow, and overhead, glimpse the white-coated thick utility wire. Lowering his head against the wind he pushed on, stopping often to peer around through his snow-encrusted eyes. The snow snowed in his ears. He brushed it off his face with his wet mitten. He had gone perhaps an eighth of a mile farther when he felt his galoshes sink into soft snow as a grove of trees opened before him. Disheartened, he knew he had lost the road again.

Panic went through him in a lightning flash. He pictured himself running in circles, but managed to bring himself under control. Dubin stood motionless, breathing heavily, trying to work out where he was. The woods opened upon the light. No tracks of his own he could see beyond ten feet. Probably the road had turned, though not he with it. He must be somewhere near it, surely not far from the highway. Backtracking, he was once more in the open. He thought for a moment he knew where he was: the road had curved to the right as he had walked on level ground straight ahead, gone into the trees. If he had turned with the road and stayed with it he'd soon have got to the highway. After about a mile, possibly via a ride he might hitch in a passing truck—if there was a truck in this wild weather—he'd be safely into Center Campobello.

To find his way he had to make the right next move. Dubin trudged along, stopping at intervals to listen for traffic sounds in the distance; or perhaps a car on the road he'd been walking. Sooner or later a clanking snowplow would come by; sooner on the highway, later on this country road. He heard only the soughing wind. The storm was increasing in intensity, the wind blowing flowing sheets of snow over the road. Dubin turned from the wind. Snow crackled on his clothes. He heard a shrieking bird but could not see it. He thought of running but dared not—would break his leg if he stepped into a hole. A moment later overhead became strangely light but there was no sky. The wind abated. He pushed on. Why haven't I learned more about nature? Which way is north? He had seen moss on all sides of a tree. How can I keep from walking in circles? You can't if you live in them. He felt a chill of fear, an icy trickle on his head, his brain pierced by cold. With a cry Dubin tore off his hat and slapped it savagely on his arm, beating off the wet snow. The red wool hat in his hand startled him.

He was tired. Coming to a low stone wall—would it be bounding a road or dividing a field?—farmers sold their fields with walls running through them—Dubin climbed over it, following until the snow-covered wall ended in a spill of rocks amid trees; then he slowly traced it back the other way. The wind had decreased in force but the coarse wet flakes were falling so rapidly he could barely see five feet ahead of him. He thought he might follow the wall, touching it with his hand; but it was not there to be touched. He was into a grove of sparse trees once more. The woods were gusty with wind, impossible to go through. Now I am really lost. Should he cry for help? Who would hear him in the wailing wind? If a car passed nearby its windows would surely be shut. Who could hear his shouts?

As Dubin came out of the trees he pictured an abandoned house. He pictured the kind of hut children built and left in the fields. After walking up the long flank of a rise and then down, he was again at a gray lichen-covered stone wall—the same?—another? He must stay with it, see where it led. The wall crumbled as he climbed it. Dubin, after a while, got up, brushed off his pants, limped on. He went through a grove of knee-high pines, then beheld a stand of tall whitened Norway pines. Where were these trees? He was almost certain he had seen them close to the road before the bend to the highway where the road sloped on the right. But there was no downward slope he could feel, let alone see. Are these pines where I think they are? Am I where I think I am? What a mad thing not to have stayed home with my small stationary miseries. Now I risk my life. He thought he ought not move until he could think of something sensible to do next. How few choices there are when the weather is white, wind fierce, snow thick. I am mad to be here. He jabbed a finger at the sky. There was a man in his mind wandering forever in deep snow. Dubin beat his breast. He heard his mother's voice. *Leo*, she called. I could drown here as my brother did in the ocean.

Exhausted, he sank to the ground and crawled under the branches of a spruce. Here was room to sit, perhaps rest. Above, the drooping branches were heavy with snow, the lower ones dry tufts of green. The beige spruce needles that covered the ground between trees were dusted with patches of white. He sat with his back to the broad spruce tree, waiting for fatigue to ease, trying to restrain fear, to stay alert.

It was quiet where Dubin sat, though he could hear the wind still groaning in the swaying trees, and every once in a while a clump of snow fell, sifting like mist through the spruce. He would wait till he had recovered his strength to get up and go on being lost. His lungs seared his chest. He could feel his mouth trembling. Despite the cold he felt sweaty; he felt his age. It was easy enough to sit under a tree but he feared the woods filling with snow. He saw himself buried amid trees in snow up to his neck. Embarrassing to die so close to the road; like drowning in a bathtub. Dubin let out a shout for help but the strange cry frightened him, so he sat with hard pounding heart, silent in the still spruce grove. He whispered to himself.

What a mad thing to happen. What a fool I am. It was the having I wanted more than the girl. Who is she to me? She doesn't deserve the feeling I give her. See what I've done to myself. I'm like a broken clock—works, time, mangled. What is life trying to teach me?

The woods were growing dark. He sat unable to decide whether to stay longer under the trees; wait the storm out. Suppose it snowed till nightfall and throughout the night until morning—Dubin frozen stiff, snowman. Death's scarecrow. He heard a sudden heavy plop in the branches overhead and cried out as lumps of snow showered on him. His first wild fear was that a bobcat had seen and leapt at him. But when the powdery mist settled he beheld a hook-nosed white owl perched on a swaying branch over his head staring at him through the leathery slits of its cold blinking eyes. But the owl as if frightened by Dubin flew off into the wind-driven snow with a hoot and great flapping of its long wings. It disappeared into the trees. Dubin rose to his knees, crawled out from under the spruce, walked into an open field.

The wind had quietened, the snow falling silently. It was now more than a foot deep, deeper in drifts. He floundered around the fringe of a stand of bleak ash trees. Two of them had fallen. Dubin picked his way over the fallen trees. Through the brush ahead he made out a snow-covered stone wall about a foot higher than those he had already encountered. Separating him from what fate? He was cruelly fatigued; could barely keep his eyes open. He saw himself lying in the snow. Then he climbed the wall because it was the next thing to do. Dubin lifted himself over the rock wall. He found himself wandering on the recognizable road; assumed he had crossed and recrossed it.

The narrow road had been plowed, plowed narrowly, though he hadn't heard the truck go by. Since then another two inches of snow had fallen, but there were earth-streaked mounds of plowed-up snow banking both sides of the road, and he felt with relief that he could easily follow it. Yet snowflakes continued to pelt him thickly so that he could still not tell direction; was still not sure which was the way to go. It begins again: which is the nearest way to the highway? What side of the road did I go off? Where did I come out of the field? Did I cross the road without knowing it? Why is it I don't remember the high stone wall I just climbed? Has it always been there and I have never noticed, or have I seen it but am too frightened to remember? Is this the long hard-topped road I usually walk, or have I gone somewhere I have never been before? It must be more than a secondary road or they wouldn't have plowed it so soon. Unless a farmer cleared his own access road and I am on it? If so where does it go? Is there a farmhouse or barn nearby? He saw no light. Now how shall I go? Am I already into the turn of the road, therefore head west, then south and I hit the highway? Or should I go north and if I'm lucky I ought to sight a house in twenty minutes; unless I don't.

Dubin turned left where he had been standing at the wall and after tedious and forgetful walking, as dusk grew darker, he was convinced he was on the right road plodding the long but wrong way back. Wrong because long. He stopped, deathly wearied, trying again to decide whether to go the other possibly shorter way. He was dully cold, his clothes wet, face stiff, hands and feet freezing. His back teeth ached with cold. The wind had died down and it was beginning to rain as well as snow. He could feel the icy rain through his soaking hat and see it snowing. Dubin trudged on. After a white wet timeless time it seemed to him something was approaching, a truck, or car, its wheels churning in the slush, brights on, wipers flapping as it loomed up like a locomotive out of the raining snow. The biographer flailed both arms, frantically waved his red hat as he stumbled toward the slowly moving vehicle. It then shot through his frozen head that the white-faced woman, her head wrapped in a black shawl, who sat stiffly behind the wheel, peering nearsightedly through the fogged windshield; frightened, perhaps already mourning, was his wife.

Kitty held the door open as Dubin numbly got in beside her.

"I saw a white owl."

Crying silently, she drove him home.

Five

KITTY'S OLD FRIEND, Myra Wilson, died in her farmhouse of heart failure. She knew she was dying but would not be moved to a hospital. She died a week after her seventy-ninth birthday, a woman more vital than her body permitted. She had rarely mentioned her age or ailments. In her presence Kitty spoke little of hers. Myra would kiss Dubin mouth to mouth when they met, a way she saw herself. Kitty had wired her daughter that her mother was dying and wired again the next morning to say she was dead. Mrs. Meyer flew in from Milwaukee late in the afternoon. With Kitty's help she completed the funeral arrangements.

Mrs. Meyer was a restrained bulky woman in a brown felt hat and black cloth coat. She was about Kitty's age but looked older. Her right eye was tearing—the effect, she said, of a cold. She stayed with the Dubins for two nights and was restless to be home with her family. "Mr. Meyer said Mama could live with us," she told them. "She had her choice." Her youngest child was a boy of thirteen. The girls were nineteen and twenty-four. "My daughter is nineteen," Dubin told her. "Twenty," Kitty said. "She was twenty in October." Dubin felt he had misplaced a year of Maud's life.

There were eight at the graveside: the Methodist minister; Kitty and Dubin; Flora Greenfeld, moody handsome lady—Oscar was on a concert tour in Australia; Ursula and Fred Habersham; Craig Bosell, carpenter and handyman, who had looked after the house and barn for Mrs. Wilson; and there was Mrs. Meyer facing a leafless elm, holding the family Bible. It snowed at the graveside. It snowed lightly into the open grave. As the casket was lowered and the prayers recited, Kitty wept brokenly. Mrs. Meyer darted her a startled glance and wiped her wet eye with a handkerchief. Kitty tried to suppress her sobs, squirmed, bit her lip, but couldn't stop. She walked away from the grave and sat in the car. Dubin, when the ceremony was over, drove her home.

"I couldn't help it," Kitty said.

Mrs. Meyer telephoned them from the Wilson farmhouse. She was shutting up the place and would return in the spring.

"Your mother was a courageous woman living alone in that big house, I couldn't have done it," Kitty said.

"She didn't have to but that's the nature she had."

Mrs. Meyer delivered the farmhouse keys to Kitty in case someone had to get in. "Bosell is closing the house," she said. "He's drained the pipes and when the company takes out the phone he'll lock the doors and shutters. There's no stock left in the barn or henhouse and the dog she had ran away."

Kitty regretted it. "I should have remembered Ben."

"When I come back in the spring I'll put the place up for sale. We sold off seventy acres after Pa died. Now there are twenty-four left, and the house, barn and henhouse. Thanks kindly for your kindness and consideration to Mama and me."

"Myra was a favorite of mine." Kitty quickly turned away.

Mrs. Meyer left for Milwaukee.

"Why am I always crying?" Kitty asked Dubin. He praised her generous nature while disliking her for outdoing Mrs. Meyer at the graveside.

Kitty, after mulling it awhile, had quit her job at the library. Dubin had urged her not to, but she said she had to think of Roger Foster: he needed a professional librarian who could work full-time. "I'm no great help to him."

"That wasn't what he said to me."

"What did he say to you? When did he say it?"

"He said you were doing a very good job or words to that effect. I met him by chance on a walk in town."

"What else did he say?" she spoke casually, studying him.

Had Roger mentioned Fanny? Was Kitty alluding to her? "Nothing I can recall," Dubin said.

"I quit because the work was becoming a bore," Kitty said, looking bored. "I'd rather give you the time I gave them."

Dubin said she gave him as much time as he needed. He spoke gently and she was gentle with him.

Her first morning as housewife resumed she spent showing the new cleaning woman, a bulky French-Canadian of fifty-five, how she liked things done. Kitty also sewed on the sewing machine, typed and filed recipes she had torn out of newspapers and magazines, arranged and catalogued their old travel slides—Dubin often studied the villas and farmhouses Lawrence and Frieda had lived in—and energetically wrote letter after letter, some of which she tore up and at once rewrote. "I owe to everybody, especially the kids."

She started something new with a burst of energy. She had begun a reading project: to read a book on contemporary philosophy and all of Jane Austen. She had never read Lawrence's poetry or Thoreau's *Cape Cod*, which she thought she would do.

Shortly after leaving the library she suffered a spell of indigestion and for a while was worried about her health. "I've not been feeling well. My color has been poor for weeks. You don't think there's anything wrong, do you?" She was nervous and pale, her eyes troubled.

He didn't think so. "You're on edge about something. Just watch your diet. That usually does it for you."

She said she would. When the indigestion disappeared so did her worries about cancer. She kept busy and had few complaints.

Once more Kitty slept late to make up for weary periods of wakefulness in the pit of night, but she would come down in her robe for coffee with Dubin if she was not sleeping when he rose at some outrageously early hour.

Afterward she got back into bed. She still experienced flashes of feeling hot and cold. When she was hot her face looked as though she had just stepped out of a hot shower, or was deeply blushing. She blushed scarlet; so did Maud. When Kitty felt cold she raised the thermostat and went to her dresser for a sweater.

She was not content when she looked at herself in the mirror. Recently while standing without clothes in front of the full-length glass in the bedroom, she had touched her hair, then lifted her breasts and said, "Don't you think I look reasonably young for my age?" She confessed, "I'm mourning my losses. If only one could get used to it. But one doesn't. I see it so clearly, the loss of my looks."

"Du bist noch die alte Marschallin?"

"I wish I were, she was thirty-eight."

"You don't look your age. You'd easily pass for forty-five."

"I wouldn't," she said. "I don't think I would. I'm fifty-one and look every bit of it."

He left her standing sadly naked before the glass.

It was a long white winter—leaden skies broke, spilling snow endlessly on snow. Sometimes it snowed lazily half the day, sometimes savagely for a day or two in flowing waves of white. The biographer stood at his window watching the snowflakes flying, white curtain lowered, ending no play, beginning none. When it stopped snowing for several days, or a week, the scene, the drama, was the endless white world mournfully searched by an eyeless wailing white wind. The monochrome white dulled the mind, restricted movement, experience. Yet the roads were continually plowed, salted, sanded; and Dubin, heavily coated, scarved, booted, against the weather, walked, the one man in town visible on the snow-rutted roads. The temperature rarely rose above zero. The stringy willows in the dead fields were a greenish mustard-yellow. Pines and bent spruce bristled with icicled snow. Once as he tediously walked—it seemed to him nowhere—he plunged into a snowy field up to his gut and waited for his life to change.

The long walk-run was still routine. He had fitted himself for the task: you did it daily and therefore could do it. The experience proved you could. He was compelling a willed experience to contend with another, unwilled, that lingered. But as soon as it became easier to do, the wind, freezing cold, and the icy earth, made it harder to do. If you stopped for a single day, much you had accomplished—at last got used to—you had to accomplish again. For two days at the end of the month the temperature rose and it rained steadily, drearily, foggily; then the weather again turned frigid, the snow stiffened, slush froze; the roads were inches thick with ice. There was a week of twenty below, two awesome days of thirty below. The rumbling clanking snowplows only thinly shaved the stony ice-ruts on the road. Dubin gave up the long walk, against the insatiable will. Now when he left the house he picked his way along the glistening slippery ice only to the covered bridge and back. Even a mile seemed a mad thing to do. People offered rides and shook their heads when he waved them off. They sensed his creation: his trial.

The radio called it a hard winter. It was desolate; and in his study the windows were frozen over. Icicles hung from the deep eaves of the roof and grew thick and long. One long icicle was a four-foot spear before it broke in sunlight and crashed below.

Kitty was sick of being housebound. "Let's, for God's sake, get away to a warm place. We've never been to the Caribbean. What have you got against a warmer climate?"

He offered to let her go alone.

"I don't want to go alone, don't ask me to. Let's both go for a week. I'm married to you, not your book. I want to be free of it."

"You are free of it."

"I want you to be."

He had to hang in. She thought, he guessed, that he might be getting back to work and said no more about going away. Dubin kept to his room for long hours each day, letting her think what she might be thinking. He let her think so but sat at the desk reading. He read one biography after another, famished for lives.

From his window he watched the sunset reflected on the nearby hills. As the winter sky darkened the hills were suffused in rose, lilac, mauve, and these colors, in contrast to freezing daylight, seemed warm, warming the bluish-gray outcroppings on Mt. No Name. One evening the icy mountain blazed in rose flame. From this illusion of warmth he traveled to another: the rosy winter sunset was the promise of spring. Hadn't Thoreau said the mind was the only stronghold against winter: it could, at least, anticipate spring. Good, but not if spring held out to the end of spring: it shunned the anticipating mind. The outside thermometer read six below and winter had far to go before it yielded to reason or mercy—or to the thunder of the wheeling earth: through February and March into the teeth of cold April. In the Northeast, at the thin edge of New England, it sometimes snowed on the flowers of May. If spring comes can spring be far behind? Anticipation admits there is tomorrow, not much more.

Kitty, nursing a cold, was too restless to stay in bed. She wandered in the house, straightening things: ashtrays, vases, flowers. She wiped her oak table. "When I have nothing to do I do everything." She wore a voluminous robe over her bed jacket and nightgown, and a pair of Dubin's black socks he hated to see on her, to keep her feet warm. In another mood she wore a brown housecoat and silver slender mules; and a kerchief to warm her head. Her hair fell in strands on her shoulders. Colds, she complained, made her hair lank and darkened her complexion. Her nose ran, her eyes were rheumy; she was like a small animal he couldn't name. Kitty pulled up the living-room window and poured sunflower seeds on the bird-feeder shelf, then sat sniffling, sneezing, waiting for a winter bird to appear. After an hour a blue jay landed on the feeder with a thump, saw her watching, and flew off scattering sun seeds.

She sat in the kitchen, grooming her housecoat, picking off long hairs. "I seem to be shedding." She jumped when Dubin coughed, then apologized for being startled. She sighed restlessly, seemed someone's lost self—his fault, he thought. Dubin was burdened by his lack of affection; knew she felt it.

The telephone rang. When she picked up the receiver a boy's voice said, "Why don't you go get yourself fucked?" Kitty flung the phone against the wall.

Sometimes when she answered the ring the telephone clicked off. She gave up a call reluctantly. "Hello, hello," she called. "Hello!—Hello!" she insisted to the telephone.

"Who are you trying to hear from?"

"That's a stupid thing to say."

One night she waked from a dream and woke Dubin to tell it to him. She said she would not have minded his waking her.

"I dreamed I was menstruating again. I was flowing profusely and was frightened. I said in my dream, 'William, what shall I do, I'm bleeding so heavily?' And you impatiently said, 'Cut it out!' "

"I apologize," said Dubin. "Now let me sleep."

"I'm burning tonight," Kitty sighed five minutes later. "Is the house overheated?"

"No. Don't open the window or the wind will blast us out of bed."

She turned on her bed lamp and changed, panting, from a white flannel nightgown to a pink sheer sleeveless one; then fell instantly asleep, while he remained awake thinking useless thoughts until the alarm rang in the dark and he groped his way to the shower.

"Drop dead!"

She woke. "Who?"

"Nobody you know."

"I'll bet I do."

"I spoke to the mirror, don't take credit."

"Jesus, Mary, and Joseph, the goddamned things you say."

In the bathroom she gargled loudly, ferociously cleared her throat, coughed on and on. He could hear her in his study. She discovered a large black moth on the wall and socked it relentlessly with a rolled-up towel.

Kitty misplaced her diary and asked Dubin whether he had seen it. It was an on-and-off affair in a spiral notebook, rebegun recently in black ink. When they were first married her diary was written in green ink and he occasionally glanced into it when she wasn't around. He felt she left it in sight so he could read what she wanted him to know, but would rather not talk about. A diary was a punitive instrument.

She had begun a book on modern philosophy and after twenty pages set it aside. That afternoon she drove to Winslow to shop for a dress. She couldn't find one she wanted and drove to Albany. There she bought a pair of shoes and a green dress. She returned the dress the next morning. "Green offends me," she said to Dubin. He had said he didn't care for the dress. She kept the cross-strap elegant black shoes. She had also tried on several hats, but none suited her. Sometimes she bought things to return them.

That night she informed Dubin she had been seeing Evan Ondyk. "Not about you," she said uneasily. "About myself."

He knew why but asked anyway.

She said nothing, then went to the bird-feeder window and looked out as she talked. "Since Myra's funeral I haven't felt right. You remember I couldn't stop crying at the cemetery? A sense of loss has stayed with me."

Dubin remembered.

"Since then I've been thinking of my life—with you, and with Nathanael. That seems to be starting again, though I haven't done it in years."

"You were dreaming of him last summer."

"Not as often as I used to. I have no intense feelings about him, but he's still a familiar stranger who keeps standing on the street corner, expecting me to come over and say hello. I remember the most trivial things of our life together, for instance buying him a pair of tennis sneakers one Saturday afternoon while we were out wheeling Gerald in his carriage. Isn't it strange the way we're constituted—I mean about the past? Jesus, why are we?"

He felt again as though he had married her marriage.

Once when she used to talk about Nathanael, herself, Gerry as a baby, Dubin had felt a sense of being out of it; he no longer felt that.

"Don't make too much of it," he said.

"I honestly don't want to, but certain things keep bothering me. I don't mean Nathanael. Now I think of Myra alone in that empty farmhouse and I scarcely gave her the time of day."

He reminded her she had visited the old woman almost daily. "When you couldn't you telephoned. Sometimes you'd shop for her in the morning and also call at night."

"I could have done more for her when she was sick. She was alone too often. And I feel terrible about Ben running away. I should have paid attention to him."

Dubin thought it might have been better if she hadn't given up the library job. "At least it got you out of the house half the day."

"Lay off about that job," Kitty said in irritation. "I think you'd like it if I was never in the house."

He denied it.

"All you want is to be alone. If I died you'd get along very well without me."

"I'd want you to get along without me."

"I hate your beastly love of solitude."

She had again been playing the harp. Kitty pulled the gilded frame down on her shoulder, pressed her feet on the pedals, and began to pluck the strings, her hands moving like birds flying at each other. When she sang in a soft mezzo her singing voice was small. One day she played for hours and whatever she played—Chopin, Schumann, Hugo Wolf—sounded lonely. The next day she played as though she were in love or wanted to be; and wanted him to know.

He heard the harp as he sat upstairs at his desk, and found it impossible to read. She never played while he was at work. Dubin was angered, then thought she must be certain he wasn't writing. Yet as he listened to her playing he felt the possibility of life with feeling. He thought, as he listened, of meeting someone with whom he might fall in love, a woman of thirty perhaps. He wanted another chance in marriage; he could do it better than he had done it. And he'd be his bride's first husband.

Kitty tore the strings into a reverberant jangle, then went out for a drive.

When she returned she gaily told Dubin that a young man had tried to pick her up in the parking lot of the supermarket when she came out with her bundle of groceries. "He had a heavy mustache and wore bell-bottom trousers. He looked like a New York actor," she laughed.

"What did he say?"

"He called me Cutie and asked me to come for a ride. I said I had a ride and took off. He knew I could see through him."

She then regretted her nature. "I should have flirted with him." And said she had frittered away much of her life. "I find it distressing not to be better pulled together at this time of my life. I should have done more for myself and not depended so much on my husbands. I'm upset about your problems and the way we are. I'm also upset because I feel I've been a lousy mother, or my kids would write once in a while. I'm tense about Maud coming home—if she ever does."

She approached a mirror to look at herself and turned quickly away. She went into the kitchen to brew herself a cup of tea and deeply breathed above the burners before setting down a pot and lighting the gas.

The next morning she misplaced her wedding ring. "I can't find it anywhere, it's lost." It was an inexpensive thin band. She had always liked its design, its simplicity. Kitty could not find it after taking her shower and spent the morning grimly going from room to room—unmaking beds to hunt for it. She pulled up rugs, opened drawers, stood on chairs searching closet shelves, feeling along every inch. In the afternoon when after an hour's restless rest she went on relentlessly looking, Dubin offered to buy her a new wedding ring if this didn't turn up.

"I want my old ring," said Kitty. "It took you a month to find the one you wanted. It was your first real present to me."

She went on vigorously searching and at last found the ring in a plastic glass in the bathroom.

"Bravo," said Dubin.

They faced each other in hatred.

Maud Dubin, who had come home only for short stays last year, appeared at the house in early February, her beautiful long red hair shorn and dyed black. Her brows were lined black. Her light eyes seemed to have darkened. "Maud, for God's sake!" Dubin cried. Her eyes appealed to him not to say more. He momentarily turned away, then put his arms around her, kissing the cheek she offered, and after an attempt at casual talk, trotted up the stairs. For a while he stood at his study window watching the leafless swaying trees in the windswept field near the side of the old barn. In ten minutes he trotted down once more to greet his daughter, but Maud had called a friend and had driven off in Kitty's car. Dubin stared out of his window.

She'd kissed full on the lips as a child, it was her way. She gave feeling so naturally he thought he had earned it. Maud had a raucous laugh and high voice and seemed a little girl until she opened her mouth and spoke in full sentences. She grew according to his vision of what she must ultimately be. Maud resembled Kitty more than Dubin although her red hair derived from his mother, whom he rarely remembered as other than gray-haired. Charlie had told him that as a girl she had a deep-red head of hair. "So people came miles to look on her." Maud's bronze hair had hung thickly down her back. Kitty had knitted her a white wool hat with a blue band that she wore for years in and out of the house. One night Dubin entered her room as she slept wearing her hat. As he tried to remove it she had lifted her warm arms and held him in sleep.

At fifteen Maud plaited her long hair into a pigtail; and when her father heard the front door shut in the morning he would put down his razor and go to the bedroom window so he could watch her on the back lawn striding along in brown boots, white hat, blue coat, the wooden-barretted pigtail swinging as she sturdily walked toward the woods on the way to the bus stop at the covered bridge.

He would sometimes stand in her room after she had left for school, or was away for the summer, to reflect in it, reflect on her. He would look over her books, surprised by some he had given her. He liked the many volumes of poetry she had collected; her small desk; the flowered coverlet on her prim bed in a soft-yellow room; throw rug on the floor; colored pictures of savage and saint taped on the wall above her head. Dubin looked out of her windows to see what she saw. She was a handsome lanky active girl—swam, backpacked, skied—with a slender firm body that grew lovely, after a crisis of fat, as she matured. She had a quiet handsome face with light-blue eyes, uneven lips—they were Dubin's—and a small bony chin. Maud had unexpected qualities and did unexpected things. By Kitty's edict she was Jewish and she called herself a Jew. Kitty had said, "There are only five in town and no house of worship, how can she learn?" but Dubin said, "If she thinks of herself as Jewish let's see what she makes of it."

Her parents' marriage had been best to her teens; she knew when it was at its less than best. Though Gerry, in his private world, had given her short shrift, she spoke up passionately for his rights. Among her own, apparently, was a curious impatience with childhood. She seemed to want to live life in contravention of time—before it permitted. Whatever you're running after, her father thought, wait a bit, it'll catch up with you.

"What's her hurry for experience?" he asked his wife.

"I was never like that," Kitty said. "I played with dolls long past the time she'd given them up. Maybe she's read *Short Lives*?"

She had, in fact, years ago.

Maud had departed her room and house in what had hardly seemed sufficient time. After going away to Berkeley she returned comparatively infrequently. She had spent one summer on a dig in Mexico. Another, she worked as a professor's research assistant. She preferred to work when she could, earn part of her keep. "Not that I don't miss you but there's a lot to see and get done."

Dubin saw the connection with himself yet could not fully comprehend it. "Why should you be gone so long so often?"

"It's not as though I'd left the house, if I keep coming back." She said in afterthought: "I think of you both a lot." Perhaps she shared his hunger to live many lives? In imagination he lived hers. She had eased in him a wanting of much he hadn't had as boy and youth. Kitty, it seemed to him, had loved him in part for his love of the girl.

Dubin was disheartened that he had only this ragged self to offer on her short visit home. And that Maud had appeared almost unrecognizable, the fiery flame of her dyed black. She had walked into the house masked. What is she hiding? Had she seen him, after all, with Fanny in Venice? Had it been she in the gondola with the old man? Who is she, nervously clumping around in boots and poncho, who comes as my child, though I can hardly recognize her? What have we become to each other, who were once so much more than we presently are?

When they were alone during the evening after her arrival, Dubin asked his daughter why she had dyed her hair black.

She answered, "Because I'm me"; then said, "I wanted to see how I look in black hair, I know how I look in red."

"How do you look in black?"

She was for a moment uneasy. "Pretty much as I expected."

"Couldn't you have imagined it?"

"I'm not good in imagining. I'm good in seeing."

He said he sensed a symbol in her mask. "This sort of thing a bit extended could hurt you."

She was annoyed. "Please don't read symbols in everything I do, Papa. I'm not a book. And if I'm masked I'm not the only one."

"Am I?"

"Maybe. Anyway, let's not go ape on this. Everybody overanalyzes in this house."

He called it an occupational problem.

"If you want a symbol, be satisfied with something simpler—maybe somebody looking for herself."

Dubin therefore apologized.

He recalled, the week she was there, other dissatisfactions of hers: she had, for instance, from childhood, complained about her name. Kitty had suggested her own grandmother's name—Christina—for her, which Dubin had doubted. After considering Crystal they had settled on Maud, later discovered it derived from Magdalene; but Maud was by then Maud. Her middle name was his mother's, Hannah. Who's in a name?

"Maud, Maud, the birds cawed," she had parodied Tennyson when she was in high school. "Boy, what a jackass name."

"On you it sounds good."

"It sounds like a cow call. I'm maudlin is what it amounts to. In grade school the kids made it 'Muddy' and now all I hear is 'Moody.' What a shitty thing to do to your little girl." She laughed at that.

Once as he followed her on a trail in the woods, she complained, "Too many of my habits are like yours."

Dubin would not apologize.

"You were always yawking about work, going to bed early so you could be early to work—all that sort of thing, and it took me years before I stopped being afraid to waste time."

"Waste what you want," he said. "I do what I have to. If Mark Twain had applied himself to his writing instead of piddling time away trying to make money on things that didn't work, he'd have been a greater writer. F. Scott Fitzgerald, before he caught himself near the end, had wasted much of his talent. I'm telling you what I learned from their lives."

She laughed scornfully. "Why didn't you learn about some of the fun they had, especially Fitzgerald?"

"Someone once said, no valuable work is accomplished except at the expense of a life."

Maud bet it was Thoreau. "I'm sick of him. Also it depends what you mean by valuable."

Dubin said one had to make choices.

"I'm trying to," she shouted.

He remembered having run over her black-and-white cat in the driveway and hastily burying the animal before she could see its maimed body. When he told her later what he had done she was inconsolable he hadn't given her the kitty to bury. He sometimes felt she had never forgiven him.

One day she had accused him of having favored Gerald over her.

He told her not to believe it.

She reddened, yet insisted it was true. "He was the interesting one you were always going up to talk to, and I was fluff and yum-yum." She complained he had never really understood her. Dubin looked at her to see if she was kidding; she wasn't. It hurt. He thought he had communicated with her better than with almost anyone. Another illusion. When she was fifteen he had sensed a growth of antagonism in her without being able to define it more than generally. Perhaps she had changed faster than he had imagined? It happens so quickly with kids. While I was out for a walk she became someone else.

"You were a good enough father," she once defined it, not noticing the tense or qualifier. "You cared and provided but we could have been closer as a family."

"Propaganda—we were close and attentive to each other."

"Not that close."

Who remembered better? Close? He sometimes thought his life had pressed hers too strongly. He was too intensely aware of Maud, had made her self-conscious.

He wondered what kind of father he had been. A decent one, Dubin had thought, but who was he to say? God, the impression one made without knowing it. What had he ultimately given them? —Much willingly but they made unconscious choices from his daily offerings—or non-offerings, simply being who or what he was. Some take from that what they will never be able to use. The father of Maud's childhood and Gerald's, being in essence little known to them, ultimately a mystery because other—love to the contrary notwithstanding—had left his mark as mythological father; but the historical Papa they had discovered and felt some affection for as they grew was, as self, recognizable, measurable, predictable, vulnerable. They knew reasonably well his strengths and limitations and sensed how they themselves were bound by them. By definition he was as parent—more than Kitty—the opposing self; and in subtle ways they opposed him. They opposed him best by changing. —Ah, fooled you! Overnight, it had seemed, they had changed and gone, each to pursue an unpredictable destiny. —Who would have thought so, contemplating them as kids? Yes, you said love, they said love, but each lived a world apart. They saw him differently as they changed, and against the will he was a changed man. Dubin felt, as much as he could, that he had been himself to them, defined himself as he was; and they would therefore, sooner or later, return to claim his friendship. But either they hadn't listened, or had and forgot; or hadn't he spoken?

Yet every so often the father had the feeling he had lost or misplaced his daughter at a specific time in another country, a foreign experience. Had he, indeed, lost her in Venice, although he did not, in truth, know whether she'd ever been there?

Kitty, after a quiet devastation over the dyed hair, had revived her good spirits in Maud's presence. "She's home rarely, let's not be so critical of what she did. She's been a good kid." She and Maud had got along well. Kitty admired her good looks, independence, sense of adventure; she wished she had been similarly endowed. Maud respected her mother's taste and strength. Kitty pooh-poohed "strength" but the girl insisted. "You do what you have to even with your doubts." Kitty looked emotionally away.

Now they were shopping together, Maud mostly to please her mother because she wanted no more than a pair of bluejeans and two pairs of socks. And Kitty loved cooking for Maud though she had asked her to go easy. "I'm into organic foods and brought a batch with me." "Then let's cook them up," said Kitty. Maud laughed till it hurt.

About her dyed hair Kitty said to Dubin, "It's not forever, the black will grow out."

"What have you told her about me?" he asked. "I'd rather she didn't know what a mean winter I've had."

"She always complained we keep secrets from them."

"There are some things I'm entitled to keep private."

"I've told her nothing she wouldn't guess on laying eyes on you."

He asked her what.

"I said you were having some trouble with Lawrence. I also said you had lost twelve pounds on your diet—was that all right?"

He thanked her.

Maud went to see a high school friend living with an unemployed mechanic in a shack up the side of Mt. No Name. They had rapped about Eastern religions. She had also cross-country skied with Roger Foster—Kitty's dubious arrangement; Dubin had, as usual, his doubts about the librarian. And Maud was restless, prowled around the house; tightened water taps; lowered the thermostat if Kitty permitted; convinced her mother to use cloth napkins instead of paper. "We have got to save trees, Mother." She spent hours looking through things in the attic, searching for something she couldn't find.

One morning when Dubin came downstairs, Maud was eating a granola she had mixed of rolled oats, wheat germ, sesame seeds, other ingredients. Formerly she had eaten a soft-boiled egg almost every morning of her life. The world had changed. He pictured her with red hair.

She studied him as he sipped his coffee. When he looked at her her gaze shifted.

Dubin asked her if she had heard from Gerry lately.

"A card. He's working on an excursion boat. He's moved, I think."

"Again?"

"He can move if he wants." Her voice wavered angrily.

"What's with you?"

She filled her teacup. "Why did you walk away from me the minute I came into the house, Papa?"

He said her black hair had upset him. "I sensed you had changed in a way that excluded me. I guess I didn't want you to see how bad I felt."

"Are you used to me now?"

He said a stupidity had got into him; he regretted it.

She rose, washed the cup and cereal bowl in the sink, then sat down and lit a cigarette. She eats health foods then smokes, Dubin thought.

"Just one," Maud said. "It's snowing," she said, looking out of the window. "I love winter. I don't think I want to spend my life in California."

That seemed good news. Dubin imagined her home again: they were sitting at this table talking and Maud had red hair.

"You haven't said what's been happening to you."

"Not much." She listened to herself say that, then put out her cigarette and said, "Not very much." After a moment Maud asked him if he would like her to recite a poem. She often recited to him poems she had learned. Once she had tried to write verse but had given it up, though he had asked her not to. She said they weren't very good poems; and sounded like Kitty.

Maud recited gravely, her voice expressive, face softened, seriousness deepened:

O Thou whose face hath felt the Winter's Wind,
Whose eye has seen the snow-clouds hung in mist,
And the black elm-tops 'mong freezing stars,
To thee the spring will be a harvest time.

Moved, Dubin said, "Keats."

She went on, ending: "'To thee the spring shall be a triple morn.'"

He thanked her for her kindness.

"Do you remember reading me 'Bright Star' after I had read about Keats in *Short Lives*?"

He remembered. Keats spoke in youth's voice and Dubin had listened with youth's ear.

She seemed gently embarrassed.

Each then left the room. Dubin worked upstairs for a while. The snow had stopped and it was white and still outside. He knocked on Maud's door and asked her to walk to the bridge with him. They trudged along the snowy road, Maud in ski pants and boots, wearing a white padded parka. Dubin had on his black galoshes and red wool hat.

As they stood under the snow-covered bridge, resting, their white breaths intermingling, Maud quietly began another sonnet of Keats'. It was "To Fanny." She spoke the poem feelingfully.

That warm, white, lucent, million-pleasured breast,—
Yourself—your soul—in pity give me all,
Withhold no atom's atom or I die,
Or living on perhaps, your wretched thrall,
Forget, in midst of idle misery,
Life's purposes,—the palate of my mind
Losing its gust, and my ambition blind!

His voice was heavy when he asked her why she had recited that particular poem.

"I loved it when I was sixteen."

"So you recite it now?"

"I just thought you might be in a mood to hear it; I am."

"It's appropriate," he offered. "It helps."

"Helps what?"

"My mood." He thanked her for the poem.

"Mother says you're having trouble with your work?"

Dubin confessed he had been writing without authority.

"Do you really like Lawrence? You're not much like him."

"I like him well enough; he's an interesting man. Not all his books are good, some are very good. He had genius. I doubt he loved mankind but he relished life though he explained it insufficiently."

"But isn't it hard for somebody like you to write about somebody like him?"

"Nobody I've written about is like me though they all are."

"Aren't some more congenial than others? I don't think you had much trouble with Thoreau."

"He came at a better time."

"Why did you pick Lawrence to write on?"

"He picked me. There's something he wants me to know."

After studying him a minute, she said, "You've had bad periods before. You'll soon be back into your rhythm of work."

"It's been a long time."

The next morning at breakfast Maud said she had learned her first poem by D. H. Lawrence. She recited it with eyes closed.

Desire may be dead
and still a man can be
a meeting place for sun and rain
wonder outwaiting pain
as in a wintry tree.

She treats me with poetry, he thought. "Bravo," Dubin said.

Maud reddened.

He worked in his study later in a calm mood.

On Friday of the week Maud was home, as they were again returning from the short walk, he considered telling her what had happened to him in Venice. He had wanted to all week. Dubin said his trouble with work had started after an experience there.

"What kind of experience?"

"Unexpected. I thought I was fairly good facing up to what happens unexpectedly, but apparently less than I thought."

He did not elaborate; she didn't ask him to.

As he was following her along the path through Kitty's Wood Dubin stopped and said, "Maud, I love you."

She turned to him. "I love you."

"I love you more than anyone."

"Papa," Maud said, "I'm not your wife."

Dubin said he hadn't asked her to be.

"You neglect Mother. She's lonely."

"It's a long story," he said, "but I'm addressing you. You're my daughter, I need you. Let's stay more closely in touch."

"You have me."

They embraced on the path in the white wood. Maud kissed him quickly.

Though he had warned himself not to, Dubin asked her if it was she he had seen with an old man in Venice.

"Please don't ask me questions like that."

The next day Maud flew back to California.

One freezing night Dubin drove through the white silent streets to Oscar Greenfeld's. He had had to get out of the house, could not stand being alone with Kitty.

Flora had called a week ago. She said she had wanted to talk with him about a book she was reading, but they had never got to it. On the phone Dubin wasn't sure what they were talking about. Oscar was in Europe.

"Are you all right?" he had asked Flora.

"More or less. Listen, William," she said with mellifluous intensity, "you and I ought to be better friends."

"How would that work?"

Flora hung up on him.

"Who was that?" Kitty had asked. She'd been in the bathroom. Dubin rarely answered the telephone; it was her instrument.

"Flora."

"What did she want?"

"She wanted to talk about a book she was reading."

"What book?"

He said he had forgotten to ask.

"I think she's been lonely since she's given up traveling with Oscar," Kitty said. "I had that feeling when I saw her at Myra's burial."

"Should we invite her over?"

"If you want."

"You don't want?"

"God knows I've tried, but I simply don't take to her."

That very cold night, a week after Flora's call, Dubin parked his car in the driveway by the birch trees, and rang her bell.

"What a nice thing to do," Flora said.

"This isn't the wrong time to come?"

She insisted it wasn't. Flora was wearing a tight pleated white blouse and a long burgundy skirt. Her voice was chesty, throaty, musical. She said Oscar was in Prague.

"Are you dressed to go out?"

"I dress to practice." She took up her bow and went on with a Bach violin sonata. She played zestfully, a little wildly, her body swaying. The Bach was lively, vibrant, earthy. He had heard her say Bach should not be played like Bach. "He should be played like a gypsy."

Flora then went into the first movement of a Vivaldi violin concerto, playing him like a gypsy.

Afterward they sat in silence, he in a rocker by the fireplace, Flora on the sofa.

"Were you angry when I hung up on you?"

Dubin said he wasn't.

She laughed throatily. "Dear William, how little surprises you. Your understanding surpasseth surprise. Don't you sometimes feel cheated?"

He said he sometimes did.

"You look low," Flora said sympathetically. "You looked like hell at your birthday party."

"It was Kitty's party."

"It certainly wasn't yours."

"How long has Oscar been gone?"

"Three weeks tomorrow. He'll be back in a week."

"Why don't you travel with him any more?"

"Travel keeps me on edge. Besides he's happy to go alone."

She gazed into the fire. Dubin watched the small flames along the glowing log.

"Would you like a drink or what would you like?"

He asked for brandy. Flora poured herself a full glass of red wine.

"I hear Maud was home."

"For five days."

"What is she up to besides her Spanish?"

"She didn't say."

"I wish I had a daughter," Flora said. "I'd call her every night."

"No you wouldn't," Dubin told her.

"The music was lively, the talk is sad," Flora said. "Let's not talk sad, William. Let's surprise each other joyfully."

She went to her bedroom and returned in a white flowing caftan and jeweled sandals. She had pinned up her hair and her neck was long and lovely. She had light hair and high cheekbones.

"Do you know what we're doing?" Dubin asked her.

"Don't you?"

"You're my friend's wife."

"Your friend is away more than he's home. We've not been getting along well. Oscar is an egoist. And I'm honestly hard up."

"We've been good friends for years."

"You're not that much friends nowadays and I've never been friends with your wife. Come, we're not children. You and I have touched looks and fingers in many homes. We've loved each other lightly. Somewhere in a lifetime that calls for a consummation." She held out her hand.

Dubin rose. "Not in his bedroom."

Flora led him up to a guest room on the second floor. She removed her caftan and underpants and slid into the bed. Dubin undressed and got in beside her.

Flora's eyes were wet as they kissed. "Bodies are kind, other bodies. Passion is priceless."

Dubin said she was kind.

Afterward in the quiet dark she asked what he was thinking about.

"Oscar. Kitty a little."

"Think of me," Flora said. "I'm fifty today."

Dubin, at fourteen, would cross off on the stiff little calendars his father brought home from the Waiters Union the days and weeks of winter. He crossed off the dark days, slush, freeze, rain/snow, wind wailing. One by one he crossed off the icy mornings he dressed in the cold. His mother filled the kitchen stove with balls of newspaper and strips of wood from egg crates Charlie Dubin had got from the grocer on the corner; and when they were lit, spread on them small shovelfuls of pea coal from the pail on the floor. He would dress fast in front of the tepid stove. As a youth he crossed off loneliness. When will winter end? When will it go where winters go? He breathed the January wind, testing it for change, mildness, promise of spring. He was moved by the sight of dead leaves caught in the branches of leafless bushes. He crossed off the cold season as though he were crossing off an unworthy life. In his room he wrote, many times, a single word: "Will i am."

Now, in Center Campobello, he crossed off nothing. If you mangle time it mangles you. Winter, ancient operator, deaf and blind to his mood, lingered long after Maud had gone. The white sky reflected the white landscape. He hungered for change, change of him. But the iron season would not budge. Mornings were still dishearteningly cold. It snowed almost daily in March, a half inch, quarter inch at a time; the snow melted for a day or so, then it snowed again although rows of maples along the road already wore spigots over metal buckets, and the sugar house near the bridge was pouring white clouds of sweetish steam from its roof vents. There had been a momentary scent of sap and spring. The snow turned heavy-wet, melting as it touched ground. One day when Dubin awoke it was gone. The next morning it covered woods, hilltops, earth.

Again the snow receded, left soiled streaks of white on the hard ground. Except for evergreens the massed bare-branched trees were still winter-gray. The melting snow uncovered meadows wet with grass in soggy clumps and swaths, as though the earth was strewn with soaking rags of brown, yellow, faded-green. After a long rain the bare tree trunks turned brown or black. When the sun reappeared through morning mist some trees flushed rose, some shone an opalescent green. The silver maples, after rain, looked as though they were wrapped in wet brown blankets. Willows were suffused in bright yellow-green. At the end of the month there were tiny seed clusters on maple branches, but no leaves. It was gently snowing.

March he had given up to winter—who claimed choice?—but

a wintry April tormented him. Yet the frozen dancer invisibly danced. One day he discovered snowdrops amid traces of snow in the woods. The snow vanished in the sun; earth dried or tried to; it got to be mud season later than last year. The sun grew stronger daily. On the long walk Dubin saw a darkly plowed field that shone with a greenish cast to its turned soil. Birds appeared in clusters on Kitty's feeder—jays, robins, house sparrows, starlings Dubin recognized; now and then a purple finch. And when they had flown off a mysterious black-masked loner, a crested red cardinal who had been in and out all winter, popped its beak at grains of corn, stopping as it ate to stare at invisible presences. When a sudden shower struck the earth the birds burst off the ground, flying in crazy arcs. Minutes later they were pecking in greener grass in a soft rain. Then from nowhere—from its grave—a mournful dark wind arose trailing bleak streamers of snow. Moments later the sun flared in the bright blue sky. Dubin, on Thoreau's advice, stopped loitering in winter and called the season spring.

He felt, oppressively, the need of an action to take. To do something differently—create a change that would lead to others. Why hadn't he moved beyond the weight of winter? He was bored sick with expecting something to happen. He felt a hungry need to simplify his life, to see what he could do differently. He felt, before long, the need of a new place to be, observe from, reflect in—after the gloom of these past months and his uneasy compromises with Lawrence. Dubin at length decided to move his study from house to small barn, where years ago he had built a room to work in, and for one or another reason never furnished or occupied it. Kitty had liked the idea of his having another place to work nearby. She had foreseen a time when Maud and Gerald would come for summer visits with their children, who would not have to be quiet, because Dubin was out of the house.

When the biographer inspected the study in the barn one day in early April it was damp—smelled distantly of silage and manure; and was abuzz with green-bellied flies that had hatched in the walls. The roof had dripped under the stress of heavy snowfalls, and several feet of top bookshelf were discolored. The smell was dank—winter's corpse. But the electric heat worked and soon baked out dampness and attendant odors. A roofer replaced a section of cracked rotting shingles. Dubin killed off the green flies with a spray gun although Kitty had offered to shoo them with a newspaper. He had bought a rectangular pine table for a desk and transported two chairs from the attic room. Kitty gave him a floor lamp she had got as a wedding present when she married Nathanael; and Dubin bought a sofa that converted into a bed in case he felt like sleeping out in the heat of summer. She suggested putting in a phone but he resisted: "It costs money."

"Suppose I need you in a hurry?"

"When have you since the kids grew up?"

There was no telephone.

Before installing himself Dubin went to the barn in work clothes and galoshes. He swept the study floor and with rags wiped everything within reach. Kitty offered to help but he said he had been wanting for months to do something with his hands. The study was a walled-off quarter of the rear of the barn, a two-windowed room with a long interior wall of shelves halfway to the slanted ceiling. A lavatory with bowl, sink, and a small window had been put in. Dubin lugged boxloads of books across the field in Kitty's garden wheelbarrow. He enjoyed arranging the books, packets of note cards, folders full of manuscript pages, typed and retyped, on the shelves, carefully putting things in place after the disorder of the winter. He hung his picture of Thoreau on the wall by the window where the pine table stood, and near the picture, his Medal of Freedom.

Kitty hoped he wouldn't think of this room as his permanent place to work, though she conceded a change might be helpful now; and Dubin did not tell her that the move had seemed a little like permanently leaving the house.

The morning he tried to work he was assailed by the shrilling of birds in the barn. Dubin knew that a family of starlings had been in the eaves inside the barn but there were no signs of nests. They had got in through a missing windowpane, and when he was cleaning the study he drove them out simply by appearing in the barn. He had opened the double doors and the birds rose with short frantic whistlings and whirring of wings, and flew out into the trees. They sat in the high branches shrilling raucously at him. Dubin replaced the pane and kept the barn doors shut. But the birds slithered in through a two-inch gap under one of the doors; he heard their noisy chirping when he sat down the next morning. He then nailed a long board to the bottom of the barn door. The starlings, after being driven out again, hung around complaining in nearby trees, then, in a week, disappeared.

Kitty called him heartless.

It had led to an argument about his character, their life together, who had failed whom.

Ten days ago they had been to the Wilson farmhouse with Mrs. Meyer, who had come from Milwaukee to clear out her mother's effects and put the farm up for sale. Mrs. Meyer had seemed stricken at all that had to be done and Kitty did much of it. She had asked Dubin to go along. While Kitty, in head scarf and coat, and Mrs. Meyer, in her black overcoat and brown hat, in the cold farmhouse, were sorting out and packing into small cartons the old woman's house dresses, faded underwear and worn shoes, Dubin went through the trunks in the attic.

In one old trunk he found a half-dozen jars of petrified seed, a shoebox full of family photographs, and two bundles of letters, of James to Myra Wilson, and Myra to James, dated around the First World War. Dubin read several of the letters by candlelight. None could be called a love letter. Through the years of marriage they were pretty much the sparse same; little changed, little grew, little was revealed. Contemplating them Dubin felt tired of marriage, wanted to be alone. Solitude was a clean state of being. He wished he'd had less of it when he was young and more now. He thought Kitty and he would have got along better if they were with each other less often. They were too intent on what each did and said. Even when they spoke lightly each heard more than was said. Even when you were not saying it you were saying it. You sat there with the self your wife saw, not necessarily the self you were into; more comfortable with. He felt the long wear and tear and was glad he had decided to work in the barn, where he was away from her. One thing that wore on Dubin was the eternal domesticity of Lawrence and his wife. They were almost always together unless Frieda went to England to see her children; or detoured to indulge in a short affair. They rarely stopped traveling. Their way was to rent a villa or cottage for a season or two, move in, wash it down, paint where necessary; and live tightly and inseparably together. Lawrence cooked, scrubbed floors, sewed if he had to. Describing his intense domestic life wore on Dubin.

He brought the letters downstairs to Mrs. Meyer. Kitty, after reading two, asked if she could have them if Mrs. Meyer didn't want them; and she, with a little laugh, handed both bundles to Kitty.

The visit to the farmhouse, especially packing Myra's clothes, affected Kitty for days after Mrs. Meyer had gone. She was down again, she confessed. "I still feel bad that I wasn't able to do more for her when she was dying." Dubin said, "There are some things one has to forget."

"I can't forget. I regret what I should have done and didn't do. And I have the feeling that in her death I am diminished. I'm afraid I won't easily get over this. Oh, why did you ever marry me?"

He advised her to skip that one.

"It's the same useless guilt," Kitty confessed, "and it bores me stiff. If Myra is in my thoughts, along comes Nathanael to join us. 'Ah, Nathanael,' I say, 'why don't you go see someone else, please? My name is Kitty Dubin and I've been remarried for years to a man who writes biographies, so please leave me alone.' But he looks at me with his trusting intelligent eyes, the true color of which I am no longer sure of, and seems terribly alone. Then I think of his vulnerable son, far away somewhere in Sweden, doing his thing alone, never writing a word, never getting in touch, and I feel a failure at the way I handled him. If I could only shove him up and make him over."

"The same water under the same bridge. Why do you bother?"

"Because I am Kitty Tully Willis Dubin. Because of my stupid nature. Because you know very well why and keep asking me the same stupid questions. Because I feel you don't love me."

"Resist—fight it, for Christ's sake!" Dubin was waving his arms.

She said quietly, "I do, I am." Kitty looked into the distance through the window. She seemed someone on an island with no boat nearby. "I'm seeing Evan," she said. "He's helping me." She began to cry. Dubin put his arm around her and she wept briefly, her head pressed to his shoulder.

Let her go to Ondyk, he thought. I've done what I can.

Kitty blew her nose and nasally said thanks.

The next morning, with a last wheelbarrow-load of books, Dubin completed his move from the house to the barn.

He had set his writing table at a window that looked out on a mountain ash. Kitty had offered to make curtains for the windows but he wanted none. As he sat at his table he could see on his left Kitty's Wood, ragged and sparse after winter, just beginning to be green in spring. He sat alone in the silence of the barn and the surrounding land. It was at first oppressive: he did not want this much quiet, so much space for thought. Then he began to enjoy it. And he was on the move again in his work, perhaps even on track; certainly on the move.

Dubin had at last completed the opening section of the biography, to the death by cancer of Lawrence's mother, and his own illness a year or so after that; and apparent recovery. Then came the watershed year for him, 1912, when in a burst of creativity, among other things he eloped with Frieda Weekley. He had come to consult his French professor; she was his wife, mother of three. Lawrence arrived to have lunch, "a long thin figure," she thought, "quick straight legs, light sure movements," and in a sense he never left.

They took off for the Continent together. David Garnett described him as "a slightly-built, narrow-chested man, thin and tall with mud-colored hair, a small moustache and a hairpin chin." Frieda was "a noble and splendid animal," a tall woman, blond, with high cheekbones and gold-flecked green eyes. Her movements made you think of a lioness. She had never lived, she once said, before living with Lawrence. She had abandoned husband and children. They fled to Germany and later lived in Italy. But she mourned her children; it enraged him. If she loved them she was not in love with him. He wrote a poem, "Misery." Frieda was happy and miserable, vivacious and gloomy. "She has blues enough to repave the floor of heaven." "Nevertheless, the curse against you is still in my heart / like a deep deep burn / The curse against all mothers." But she was present, day and night, and he woke to the beauty of her body and the sensuous delight and self-celebration it roused in him. "She stoops to sponge, and her swung breasts / Sway like full blown yellow / Gloire de Dijon roses." He wrote poem after poem and also finished *Sons and Lovers.* "My detachment leaves me and I know I love only you." "Frieda and I have struggled through some bad times into a wonderful naked intimacy all kindled with warmth that I know at last is love." "Look, we have come through!" They were "two stars in balanced conjunction." They had lived it well and Dubin was writing it well.

Kitty came over to see the furnished study. "It's grand. Is there some way I can help you—research, type, anything at all?"

He said he would let her know when there was. She then went home, pausing to ask if he wanted the mail brought over when it came, and Dubin said no.

"You used to love to have the mail the minute it came."

"I no longer do."

"I guess I think of the past."

When he was through for the morning she had a light lunch waiting and afterward went to Ondyk, or to work in the Youth Opportunity program in town. Ondyk wanted her to keep busy and had persuaded Kitty to take on a voluntary job three afternoons a week.

"All I do is type. I wish I could counsel, but I can't. Still the cases are interesting. The youth are the maimed."

"What about the middle-aged?"

"The middle-aged are the maimed," she said.

At home she pottered around, played the harp, tried to organize her reading. She had started Thoreau's *Cape Cod.* She had dipped into Lawrence's poems but had found the early ones not to her liking; she liked some of the love poems, "though it's his love mostly." She was occasionally in her garden. The weather was cold. She got down on her hands and knees and weeded a section of the perennial border. Kitty read the newspapers for hours. They went out to dinner to celebrate her fifty-second birthday.

The birds, given cold spring, sang in cold trees. Dubin knew the phoebe's call—it sounded like "see-bee"; blue jay's aggressive scream; "tisk" of cardinal, its near voice. He sometimes spied the red bird in the mountain ash. It stayed a minute and flew off. He could afterward hear its shrill whistle, its other voice, in the distance. The cardinal appeared in the mountain ash, barely showing itself, hiding its presence as it hopped on the branch, tisking, trying to have a look at him. Whatever he was doing or not doing, whenever the bird lit on a white-blossomed branch of the tree Dubin sensed it was there.

One morning he laid out some sunflower seeds, from Kitty's feeder, on the ledge of the window in front of him. But only when he left the table and stood elsewhere in the room would the cardinal float down. It pecked at the seeds, then flicked its head up, its beady eye watching, until it flew off. Once when Dubin was at work, to his surprise the cardinal flashed down from the tree to peck at the seeds on the window ledge. For an instant he was caught by the bird's eye, black, mysterious. He marveled at its immaculate beauty. Where had it come from? Why is it so magnificent? To civilize man to protect the bird? "Don't ever die," Dubin said. The cardinal flew off and he listened for its distant song. He pictured it hidden in the tree in midsummer when the berries of the mountain ash had turned orange-red.

Dubin became aware of a presence, something within or close by, like a disturbing memory waiting to occur. Was the red-bearded ghost of D. H. Lawrence, risen in contempt of the biographer's desecrations of his life, haunting the place to revenge himself? One day the feeling grew so oppressive he was drawn into the barn to look around. The old barn was dark, gloomy, wet-cold. Dubin, picking up a hammer handle from the floor, went cautiously among the boxes, garden tools and machines, fertilizer bags, the furniture junk there. He found nothing unusual and was about to return to the study when he was struck by the sight of a pair of glowing eyes. He heard a thud and the eyes disappeared. The biographer was momentarily frightened—had a wild animal got into the barn? After a minute of frozen silence he decided it wasn't likely; yet it could be a stray dog or raccoon. He hoped it was not a skunk. As he approached the corner of the barn, still grasping the hammer handle, an animal hissed. Dubin raised his arm protectively. Behind a barrel he beheld a long black cat lying on a moldy burlap sack. The cat hissed thickly, then mournfully yowled, but was too sick to move.

He considered prodding the animal with the hammer handle, to force it out of the barn.

You mean bastard, he thought, the cat's sick.

The black cat got to its feet, its yellow eyes glaring. It snarled weirdly, its matted soiled fur thickened by fear. The cat stank of shit. Bile leaked from its mouth.

Dubin went back to his table, found he could do nothing, then left the study, walking across the field to the house. He thumbed through the yellow pages of the phone book and called a vet. He said he had a poisoned cat in his barn. "What can I do for him?"

"If it's poison," the vet said, "not much, depending what poisoned him and when."

"Would you want to see the animal if I can get him to you? Could you pump its stomach?"

"No, I handle horses and cows. We had a small-animal man in town but he died last year."

Dubin hung up. What was he doing this for? He had to work.

Going back to the barn he poured some water into the tin top of a jar he found. The cat, yowling low in its throat, let him approach but made no attempt to take the water. It coughed sickly, then tried a few licks. The cat choked, coughed hoarsely, then began to vomit, moving backwards as it regurgitated part of a rabbit or bloody rat. Dubin later flashed a light on the mess; the cat had gorged itself sick.

The next morning he went with Kitty to the barn. The black cat was better and lapped a little of the water she gave it. "Don't feed it anything, William. I'm pretty sure it will get better by itself and then I'll hose it to get rid of the smell."

Squatting, she patted the cat's head. He recalled how she had handled the kids when they were sick. She was affectionate and competent and tried not to be anxious.

The next day she arrived with some milk in a glass, and a saucer, and brought a box of dry cat food. The black cat lapped up the milk and chewed a little of the dry food.

In a week it had recovered. It was a long-bodied lithe almost lynx-like male, with an upright head and twitching tail. Kitty thought they ought to take it to the house. Their old cat had died, but Dubin wanted this one for the barn.

He called the cat Lorenzo. At first it showed no affection for him, then began to rub its head against his legs. Sometimes it jumped up and lay in his lap as he sat on the sofa reading. It's become my cat. He thought of the cats that had come and gone in the family.

Lorenzo lived in the barn and roamed the fields. One day it scratched at the study door, and when Dubin opened it, to his disgust the black cat held a broken-winged bloody cardinal in its mouth.

"You bastard." He tore the red bird from the cat's jaws. But the cardinal was dead. Dubin drove Lorenzo away.

An hour later he went searching for the animal far into his neighbor's field.

Kitty said she had liked helping him with the cat in the barn. "We do so little together." Dinner was quiet. She seemed like a clock listening to itself.

"What would you like us to do that we aren't?"

"I'd like you to respond to more than my voice. Why do you never think of putting your arms around me without my having to ask?"

"Other than that?"

"Other than that, I'm alone in the house. You live by yourself in the barn."

"I don't live there. I'm sorry you feel lonely. It doesn't raise my spirits, but at least you're seeing Ondyk. I'm glad of that."

"Are you?"

"If you are."

"I'm tired of 'seeing' someone. I'd like not to have to. I'd like my life to take over."

"Give it time."

"I have. Something's wrong with the way we live. We take no joy in each other."

"I like the way you look," Dubin said, trying to take joy. "Often I look at you and like the way you look."

"Thank you. You know what I mean."

"My work is mainly what's wrong. But I'm having better days. It's not easy to see Lawrence whole, but I'm closer to it.

You can't explain him till you see him whole. It's hard to do that, but there are good signs."

"I'm glad of that. I'm glad something is good."

Dubin said he was reading a new biography of Freud. "This seems to get closer to the man than any I've read, with his neurotic qualities—hypochondria, constipation, anxiety, bladder difficulty. I've told you about his fainting, usually in Jung's presence. He was tied for half his life in an unexplained triangle with his wife and sister-in-law. But the neurosis, such as it was, led in part to his own self-analysis and thus to his life's accomplishment. His work shrived him."

"I'll bet you like that thought."

"Don't you?"

She admitted she did. "I wish I could work steadily at something I liked."

"Why don't you?"

"Because I never could."

"Don't blame yourself," Dubin said.

"For years I never did, now I do. Being home when the children needed me was a time of privilege and grace. Now that they're grown I wish I had some useful work to do."

After they had gone to bed she was still restless. "Listen to that wind, you'd think it was early March."

"April is March." He tried to sleep but couldn't and felt himself grow worried. Then for a few minutes he fell heavily asleep against Kitty's warm scented back until she moved restlessly and woke him.

The wind had died down. Kitty was sleeping. Dubin, worried about being able to work in the morning if he did not sleep well, got up and dressed in the dark. He wanted a cigarillo but had none and was unable to find Kitty's cigarettes. From the linen closet he got two sheets and a blanket. Then he returned to the bedroom for a flashlight.

Kitty awoke and switched on the bed lamp. She sat up.

"What are you doing with those sheets and blanket?"

"I'm going to the barn."

"What for?"

"To get to sleep so I can work in the morning. I've got a lot to make up. I need every bit of my energy to be sharp. You can do only so much on your nerve."

"I promise to lie very still," Kitty said. "Or you can go up to Gerald's room or sleep in Maud's. Please don't go to the barn. I won't sleep a wink with you gone."

Dubin said it would be best if he went.

"Why?" Kitty asked. She was on her knees in bed, in a flowered nightgown.

"To be alone—I have things to think of."

"I thought you wanted to sleep?"

"That's what I want to do first."

She said, "I don't know why you ever got married."

"You know why I got married," Dubin said.

He zipped up his windbreaker, went downstairs, and left the house. The spring night was austerely cold, and the sky, like a lit ceiling that had been lowered, teemed with jeweled stars. It had been a long time since he had seen so many bright stars so low in the sky.

Dubin dropped the sheets and blanket on the sofa. He got out the bag of kibbles and fed Lorenzo, then gave him some water. The cat wanted to stay but he tossed him out and shut the study door. He unfolded the sofa into a double bed and covered it with the sheets and blanket. He had forgotten a pillow and pajamas and lay on his back in his underwear, relieved to be alone. The cat scratched on the door, then gave up.

Dubin lay in the dark thinking what he would do in the morning. As he was dozing off, a tapping on the window woke him. He listened, wide awake, knew who it was and rose, angered.

He flicked on the light. From the sofa he could see her at the window, peering in, her eyes searching, face strained, white. Under his anger he felt concern for her.

Dubin got up and let her in, irritated by her appearance, by her constant interference in whatever he planned, whatever he did. Kitty had no flashlight. She had found her way to the barn by the light of his toilet window until she had got halfway across the field; then it had gone off. She had fallen once. She was wearing Maud's old hooded yellow oilskin over her flowered nightdress, wet below the knees. Her bed slippers were soaked by the wet grass. When, after she had tapped on the glass, his light went on, she had looked as though she hadn't expected it to. She acted now as if she had never been in this room before.

He gave her a towel to wipe her legs.

"I had to come," Kitty said. "The house was beginning to go at me."

He told her to get warm in bed. "I'm going back to the house."

Kitty looked at him vacantly. "You don't have to," she said. "I'll go back after I tell you what I have to. William, I've been holding back something I feel guilty about, not because of what it came to, which was zilch, but you probably sensed something and it might have made things harder for you than they should have been. I feel ashamed and sorry."

He asked her what she was talking about. Her eyes were restless, dark, her fists tight.

"While you were in Italy that week in the fall I had a sudden very brief and unexpected involvement with Roger. I was involved, not he. I think I was momentarily in love with him. I don't know what else to call it though it came to nothing—and I never told him how I felt. If it sounds slightly crazy that's what it was."

"Roger Foster?" Dubin said in disbelief.

"It was a crazy thing to happen. He's only a year or two older than Gerald. I felt tender to him. I also felt as though my wits were leaving me. When you came home I wanted to tell you but was too embarrassed. In the winter, when you were depressed, I felt awful. I imagined you had sensed a change in me and were let down—perhaps I was foolish, I don't know. I asked Evan what to do and though he said I wasn't what had caused your overwhelming change of mood, my guilt was like salt corroding my thoughts and I knew I would have to tell you. I held back until now because the whole thing was senseless and trivial, and I didn't want you to lose respect for me."

"Did you want to sleep with him?"

"I would have."

"But he wouldn't oblige?"

"I hate the way you distance yourself from me," Kitty said bitterly. "Why do you put it so meanly? I said nothing came of it. I told you he never knew how I felt."

"Maybe you should have told him."

Kitty looked at him coldly. "If I should have I didn't. I'm sorry to say I couldn't arrange it. I wasn't about to begin an affair with someone twenty years younger than I by apologizing for the birthmark on my ass and my flabby breasts."

"Did he ever show in any way that he was interested in you?"

"That's my business." Her voice wavered. She wasn't crying but she looked as though she had cried. One sensed old tears. He thought of his bad time in Venice and felt compassion for her.

Dubin then began a story of his own.

"Kitty," he said, "don't blame yourself for what happened to me. I made my own misery. I had a girl with me in Venice and it turned out badly. I give her little, she gave me less. There was more feeling in the aftermath. When I came home I wanted to tell you but couldn't, partly because I didn't want to hurt you, partly because I was unable to say—out of pride—what a beating I had taken because I had done it badly, or she had done it badly and I let her."

"I'm sorry, terribly sorry." Her eyes were lit with feeling. "I knew something was troubling you but thought I was wrong—mixing up my sense of you with what *I* was feeling. It took me a while to understand how unhappy *you* were."

They went to each other and kissed.

"Please let me stay with you tonight, William."

"Stay with me."

"My nightgown is wet."

"Take it off, wear my shirt."

In bed they forgave themselves; had done it before. That he had told her what had happened in Venice only after she had confessed her feeling for Roger did not seem to bother Kitty, but Dubin regretted he hadn't told her long ago. They talked into the night, watching the low stars out of the window.

"I feel as though we were away somewhere, don't you?" Kitty said. "I feel like a young bride snug in bed with her husband in a faraway country, with cables of stars glowing in the sky. I feel so much relieved."

Dubin said he felt better.

"You're the one I really love," Kitty said, "though I sometimes feel you ought to have married a different kind of woman—someone closer to you in temperament, who might have given you more than I seem to be able to give. Someone less concerned with keeping her own life together."

He said he had never had a better friend. "You don't always give me what I want but you give."

She laughed embarrassedly. "I wish I had given you more. I wish you had given me what I wanted when I wanted it. Sometimes I wish I could have met you before—I mean, instead of—Nathanael."

Dubin thanked her. "But I don't think you would have married me if you hadn't been married to him first. You had to have at least a touch of marriage, perhaps with someone like him, before I could mean something to you."

"What you have to know before you *know* is hard to understand," Kitty said. "Maybe I shouldn't have said that about Nathanael."

"Thanks for thinking it."

They then made love and slept heavily. Dubin felt eased, the self annealed, until he thought of Flora in his sleep and awoke. He felt he oughtn't to tell Kitty about her. He would hold it for another time, for Flora's sake as well as his.

Kitty, moving spasmodically in her sleep, opened her eyes. "What do you think was the happiest time of our lives?"

"When we began to know each other, when we were secure in our trust of each other."

"When the kids were young and needed us. I felt used, useful."

"I was completing *Short Lives* and then did *Lincoln* and *Mark Twain*. I was content, and even the lousy things that happened seemed to fit harmoniously into life. I went to sleep wanting it to be tomorrow."

"That's the time I most remember."

But after lunch that day, perhaps because Kitty had asked him who the girl in Venice was and he hadn't answered, Dubin told her he had once slept with Flora; and Kitty, trying to master it in her thoughts, passed out.

One Sunday morning in late April Dubin was in a stationery store on Grand Street, picking up his newspaper. As he was fingering an adventurous cigar at the counter, through the window he saw—peace to the day—Fanny Bick as large as life and enjoying it, across the street with Roger. He had had a recent card from her: the fountains of Rome: "Hi." The girl, in morning sunlight, was vivid, familiar, as though he'd been with her yesterday, a sad blow to experience. She had cut her hair; it fell barely to the shoulders. Dubin saw her without desire or regret, yet envied her and her friend their youth. So what else is new?

Thinking they might be coming in for a paper, he retreated to the phone on the wall in the rear of the store.

But they did not come into the place, had better to do than waste a Sunday morning reading the newspaper. He felt a saddened pleasure in thinking of her. She had joined the mythological types who lived in his mind: she who had deceived his desire, more than desire, a sort of belle dame sans merci, invention of the self intending to treat itself badly. No, he thought, I'm off that kick. No more slogging in the mud of jealousy; let me act the age I've earned. He was well rid of her. After remaining several more minutes at the phone with the receiver held protectively against the ear, Dubin left the store with his newspaper, got into his car at the curb, and lighting the cigar he had bought, drove off.

He drove a roundabout way home but to his startled surprise got onto the highway going the wrong way and was forced, amid visions of disaster, to crawl in embarrassment along the outer lane for half a mile, his brights on, horn blasting as the drivers in oncoming cars rushed at him in contempt, fury, or glee, before swerving to the next lane; until Dubin, ashamed, could at last make a turn between dividers and swing around to the other side of the highway.

He went to the barn to calm down before Kitty saw him. He decided he would stay out of downtown until he could be reasonably sure Fanny had left.

Before returning to the house he wrote to each of his children.

"Dear Gerry, we miss you, talk of you often. The amnesty issue is coming up in Congress soon. Where mercy arises in society I can't say, but there are good signs. It wouldn't at all surprise me if an offer of conditional amnesty is made to deserters. If the situation changes, as it may overnight, and you can leave Sweden, why don't you come here and stay with us until you decide your next move? We'd all like to see you. I know our relationship is difficult, sometimes no relationship at all, but that can change with good will if we stay in touch. Yesterday needn't be tomorrow. I wish I knew more about your nature but the key to mine, so far as you're concerned, is that I love you as I did when you were a boy. Your father, William Dubin."

A month later Gerry wrote on a postcard that the U.S. knew where it could shove conditional amnesty. He wanted unconditional amnesty and a public apology.

"As for who loved who and when, I never think of it."

Dubin also wrote to Maud. In the late spring she returned home and stayed the summer, a surprise to all.

Spring defined itself: present against odds. April rained in May; the early days poured. On the twelfth of May snow fell on white tulips. Kitty could not get into the soggy garden she had unveiled on a hopefully sunny April day. A flock of glistening wet crows, each a foot long, jabbed at the wet grass. One huge beast flew from a redwing blackbird circling in pursuit in the rain—to account for what crow-crime? A jay, screeching, hit Kitty's feeder with a seed-scattering bump, scaring flickers, two robins, a grackle. Lorenzo, watching from inside, threw up his breakfast. After mid-month the rain rained lightly. May showers brought May flowers: yellow trollius, feather-cusped red tulips, iris, white and purple; dandelions were scattered in the fields, buttercups; a blue haze of forget-me-nots; golden mustard in the green grass. In Kitty's Wood there were violets. The grass, come to life, thickened quickly. Dubin raked away last year's dead leaves from under trees and bushes. The new leaves had, on the thirtieth of April, burst forth like light-green lace on bony fingers. The green spoke a dozen green tongues, foliage covering hills and rising in lighter shades on the stony shoulders of Mt. No Name. In the morning, mist lay like a deep sea on the hills, their tops breaking through like green islands in white water. Sometimes clouds in gray and black masses were piled above the distant mountains, towering like Alps into the sky, a line of golden flame burning at the highest edges.

He welcomed the softened warming days; broke out the tractor mower on Saturday afternoons and drove himself in narrowing circles over the front and back lawns as Kitty sunned herself in a one-piece bathing suit on a strawberry beach towel in the grass. She wore her straw hat and sunglasses and read *Cape Cod* when she wasn't napping in the sun. Or she watched the flowers in her garden. They drove into small towns in the Berkshires, walked in each, sometimes picnicked on roadside tables. They played shuttlecock on Sunday mornings; once in a while tennis. Kitty disliked the game. Evenings they went more often to visit friends, driving with the Habershams or other couples to restaurants in nearby towns. After returning from his latest trip abroad, Oscar Greenfeld called and asked them to come for drinks. Kitty nervously begged off and Dubin, of two minds, wouldn't in the end go without her.

During the week, one afternoon she wasn't working he asked her to go along on his long walk and Kitty, after changing into sneakers, walked with him.

"We haven't done the long walk for a long time."

At the end of the walk, close to where he had been lost in the snow, Dubin felt an urge to leave the road and attempt to retrace his circular wandering, wherever it had been; but one stone wall looked like another; and the woods were full of green trees and flowering bushes, the farmland growing grains and grasses. Where he had been was in truth no longer there.

"What are you thinking of?" she asked and he answered: "D. H. Lawrence."

"Why did I ask? I was thinking of you."

She had given up Ondyk with Ondyk's blessing.

"So long as we have each other."

He told her he had been working well. "I think it will be a good biography."

One morning Dubin, slim man—he had stopped dieting—instead of cutting an orange in quarters and eating it at the breakfast table, peeled it, and stood at the morning-blue kitchen window chewing it in pulpy sections. He sucked each juicy piece. He enjoyed fresh coffee, putting on a clean shirt, listening to Kitty playing her harp. That night he was struck by the splendor of the spring sunset bathing the hills brightly crimson, then mauve. The biographer determined to be kinder to his life.

Now as he briskly strode along the road it was May-become-June, a touch of summer in the mild breeze, nice reversal of running time. If you're into something—this lovely day—you're in it, not longing for it. Dubin wore buff cords, striped T-shirt, blue sneakers with loose white laces: he had been shopping; Kitty had said he needed summer things. He bowed to an ash tree, slender, virginal, but didn't linger. Its young leaves were light-green, seed pockets lavender, like a girl's spring dress. In the fall it bloomed green-gold; then the windy rain came and it was bare, broke the heart. The biographer hurried on. It could get dangerous loving trees, drive you wild. H.D.T. had wanted to embrace a scrub oak "with its scanty garment of leaves rising above the snow . . ." Lush fields were sprinkled with wild flowers; shrubs in bloom. The maples were dropping spinning white seeds into the breeze. Poplars reflected changing sunlight. The lyric greens of first spring had darkened and sights of field and wood enticed the eye: meadows sloping upward toward a descending line of trees; and above sprawling woods upland fields rose to groves of evergreens surging over the hills. Mt. No Name, behind him, was covered with foliage except its stony top. The day was broken by patches of bright blue sky through gaps in cottony clouds sailing like slow ships. At intervals the sun, looking through, lit the landscape. Dubin loved what he observed: nature rather than scene. For nature he *felt*—had earned in winter this beauty of late spring.

A new world, he sighed. In a new world he looked for a friend—scanned the road for Oscar Greenfeld—but the flutist, when you wanted him most, was elsewhere fluting. Dubin had regrets about his affair with Flora.

A white Volvo passed from behind, swerved suddenly—it had drifted too close to the walker's side of the road. Gave Dubin a turn; sped on in the risen dust.

Ten minutes later, as he was inhaling lungfuls of air at the verge of the road, the white car, long past its prime, drove by a second time, skirting the opposite shoulder of the road. It slowed down and, a hundred feet on, parked in the grass. Tourist stopping to view the view? She seemed to hesitate, head bent as though considering the odds, then opened the door, set a doubtful foot down and came toward him. Dubin knew the slender-waisted abundant body, her sturdy stride, female presence. He reflected it was inevitable they would meet again. He knows life.

Fanny, wearing sunglasses—he remembered the short denim skirt, her bare legs in sandals—walked toward him in deep focus, on her face an apprehensive smile. She was in no great hurry, taking her time, might never make it. Perhaps she didn't want to. People do impulsive things they immediately regret, Dubin for one. He might have trotted off the other way; she'd never have caught up once he was on the run—as if to prove he lived in his era, she in another. But here we both are. He'd give her short shrift.

Fanny smiled amiably, or tried to; obviously there were difficult emotions to contend with; maybe she was groping for one he couldn't match. The man had learned his lesson.

Now they touched hands, Dubin lightly.

"I thought it was you but wasn't sure," she said breathily, as though surprised.

"How are you, Fanny?" His voice was subdued, manner polite. Dubin saw clearly what she had and what she lacked; was unmoved by her. She lacked, he thought, experience of a necessary sort; certain mistakes are wrong to make.

"I hope you don't mind me stopping to say hello."

"Hardly." Why would he mind?

"I'll bet you thought you'd never see me again?"

"There were times I hoped so."

She paused to breathe, her lips moving as if she was searching for a new way not to wince. Fanny looked down, then directly at him, her pupils tight, mouth toward sour. He remembered the expression, tried to remember less, remembered all. Dubin was tempted to say a quick goodbye but after a momentarily shaky sense of wasted effort, a feeling quickly banished, objectivity returned. Mustn't make any more of the experience.

Neither spoke for a minute, he observing the small locket she wore, a gold heart with red ruby at its center. Gone six-pointed star and/or naked crucifix, whatever they had signified. Here was another sign. She looked sensibly older although less than a year had gone by since they had first met. She would be, he remembered, twenty-three come August.

A child, he reflected, recalling her face in sleep. Mad he had felt so much for her all winter. A sort of love; he knew the feeling, an old one, indulged in often in youth. Kept one young, he supposed. But how could I put my fate in her hands?

Dubin wondered what she had learned from the experience. It seemed to him a commentary on himself that he expected her to have learned something.

"I finally had electrolysis done on my chin," Fanny explained as though he had asked. "One morning in Rome I waked up anxious and made an appointment. The creep used an unsterilized needle and my face blew up but after a week I was okay."

"You've cut your hair?"

"Don't you like it?"

Dubin thought it looked fine. "Visiting Center Campobello?"

She examined him vaguely. "Only for a week to take it easy, but I'm driving back tomorrow. Roger invited me up when I got back from Rome and I came up for the day about a month ago. This time I was here a little longer."

"Thinking of getting married?" he courteously inquired.

She shook her head. "We're friends—as my mother says—Platonically; I don't sleep with him."

He nodded politely.

"I'm capable of it."

"Is Roger?"

"He's really a great guy."

"How was Rome?"

"Not that good, in fact flaky. My friend who I wrote you about—Harvey—died."

Dubin grimaced sympathetically. Fanny sadly smoothed the road with her sandal.

"And I told you about my operation—the cyst I had?"

"Yes, I'm sorry." He remembered she could still have children and tried to think of her as a mother but it came to nothing.

"My father's been sick. I visited him last week in L.A. Otherwise I'm still living in New York. I had a job for a month that I lost when I went to California. And I take an evening course at the New School."

Dubin approved.

"How are you doing?" Fanny wanted to know.

"Fine, now, after a difficult winter."

She was for a moment neither here nor there, then said, "I'm sorry for whatever of it was my fault."

Fanny had hesitantly raised her hand as if to sympathize

with at least his bare arm but Dubin had instinctively stepped back. She was again uneasy.

He spoke kindly. He had, now they had talked again, nothing against the girl. She was who she was, no doubt her own worst enemy. Caveat emptor, or words to that effect.

"No need to be," he finally replied. "We make our own fates."

"That might be, still people hurt each other without wanting to. Could I give you a ride somewhere?"

"Thanks, I'm on my walk."

She remembered, with a smile.

Dubin, after gazing in the distance as though estimating tomorrow's weather, after a confident minute of self-scrutiny, remarked, "Care to walk a little instead?"

If the invitation surprised her it didn't surprise him—normalizing things. For his sake if not hers: helped put the past in place. Calm now made experience then easier to live with. What still rankled still hurt. Better seeing in perspective, not always possible, but where it seemed to be occurring, let it. He didn't want the girl to be uncomfortable—scared of him. Suppose something similar—he doubted it—happened to Maud?

Fanny said she wouldn't mind. "Just let me get my bag out of the car. It's got everything I own."

She reached into the Volvo for her shoulder bag and car keys. He noticed a bit-into peach on the front seat.

Dubin advised her to lock the car; Fanny did.

They strolled in the direction he had been going. The afternoon sun, having escaped the steamy clouds, was now in full bloom.

"Why don't we get off this road and walk in the grass? I dig that."

Fanny stepped up on a stone wall and before Dubin could warn against it had hopped off on the other side.

"Private property," he said.

"I don't think anyone's going to arrest us for walking in the grass. There's endless miles of it."

Dubin stepped up on the wall and jumped down.

Fanny removed her sandals and dropped them and her glasses into her bag, swinging it back on her shoulder.

"Careful of poison ivy."

"I've never stepped in any that I know of, though I guess I've stepped in everything. I don't even know what it looks like, do you?"

He told her the plant had three shiny leaves.

For a moment Fanny proceeded cautiously, then walked on without concern.

It occurred to him he was more a comic type with her. With Kitty, their anxieties meshed, highlighting the serious life. That's the way it is: you marry a serious woman the chances are increased of a serious fate; a lighter type laughs every ten minutes and takes you with her.

He said he knew a better way to walk, led her diagonally across the field. A brown cow wandered in their direction. Fanny quickly moved toward Dubin, who shooed the animal away.

"At first I thought it was a bull."

"With those teats?"

"I'm not wearing my contacts."

They climbed over another low wall into county property, walking along an overgrown broad path, remnant of a former road. Nearby a narrow brook flowed through the matted grass, turning where some two-trunked silver beeches grew. Fanny thought it would be fun following the water; Dubin said if it was water she liked there was a pond in a quarry not too far from there. Beyond those trees he pointed to.

It seemed, she thought, a good way to go.

Fanny, as they were walking amid a scattering of bushes and small trees on the overgrown path, as if they were now far enough away from Europe to talk about their late mutual misadventure, asked, "Why didn't you answer my letters? I honestly regretted what happened and said I respected you but the letter you sent me was a mean son-of-a-bitch."

"Mean was how I felt and the winter was freezing. I was in no mood to correspond with you."

"Is that the way you still feel?"

"Detached," Dubin told her solemnly. "I think I've earned it." He said he hadn't felt too bad when he had left Italy but once he was home self-disgust came down hard on him. "After your letter, and for other reasons I won't go into, I was depressed and couldn't work. I've never lived through a worse winter."

"I said I was sorry," she said sullenly. "I did a stupid thing but a lot that led to it was your own stupid fault."

"In Venice you said you did it to hurt me; you did a good job."

"Because you made it pretty clear to me that you wanted only so much of me and no more. I wasn't to interfere with you or crawl into your life. I was to be invisible."

"I was protecting my wife."

"Who was protecting me?"

He didn't say.

"I'm not saying you weren't considerate and kind in nice ways that I really appreciate. But when I was having a bad trip in Rome and wrote for some advice and understanding, you didn't even bother to be civilized. I felt pretty bad."

"That's what I was hoping."

"You got your hope."

"For your sake—"

"Whosever," Fanny said bitterly.

If it was only her body I wanted, why the long heartbreak? And if I was in love with a child how could I have been?

"Are you still sore at me?"

"I told you how I feel, I've lived the experience, lived through it."

"I don't bear grudges either," Fanny said quietly. "I don't have that kind of nature."

He complimented her on her nature.

He would give her, Dubin reflected, fifteen minutes, then walk her to her car and hit the road.

Fanny, her mood amiable, strode on freely. That she should now be walking by his side after the winter he had experienced seemed to him almost laughable, one of life's little jokes. Yet better so than having the memory of her as she was in Italy locked in the mind forever as his last view of her.

The biographer told her they were passing an abandoned orchard. "Nobody sprays the trees or picks the worm-eaten apples. They stay on the branches into winter, looking like red bulbs on a Christmas tree. I've seen crows peck at them through snow."

Fanny said she had never seen anything like that. "Why doesn't somebody spray the apples?"

"There was a house here belonging to the people who owned the orchard. When the man died the widow had it moved away on rollers. The land, I understand, later went to the county for non-payment of taxes."

They arrived at a clearing—before them in the long fields a spangling of wild flowers, soft islands of blue, yellow, white, violet in the hazy green grass. He remembered Lawrence had said wild flowers made him want to dance. Dubin felt happy but kept it to himself.

The flower-stippled meadow extended to a crescent of oaks a quarter of a mile away.

"Do you know wild flowers, Fanny?"

"Just a few. Most of my life I've lived in cities, first in Trenton, and when I was seventeen we moved to L.A. I like the country, though, and have since I was small and was sent to camp. I once thought of majoring in environmental studies—preserving animals, forests, the land, you know."

"Why didn't you?"

"I got good enough grades but my heart wasn't in staying in college. I was restless with myself."

He pointed to buttercups, then daisies. "Those are oxeye daisies. Do you know what the word means?—the day's eye, Fanny—beautiful, the sun in a flower."

She fished a plastic case out of her bag—her contact lenses. Fanny wet them with the tip of her tongue, then pulled her eyelids apart and dabbed in each lens with her index finger. "Jesus, what pretty flowers!"

He pointed to a cluster of light-blue tiny flowers. "Do you know those?"

"Yes, forget-me-nots, I know them."

"Do you know the red ones there—trillium? They're also called red rooster."

Fanny clucked like a hen.

Dubin picked a flower and handed it to her.

At first she looked as though she didn't know what to do with it, then held it in her left hand.

"The bright yellow flat open ones are celandine," he said. "I once knew a girl by that name."

"Did you sleep with her?"

"I loved her."

"Is there a Fanny flower?"

"Not that I know but there is a sweet William."

"Male chauvinism," Fanny laughed.

Dubin chuckled huskily. He waded into the grass and plucked a white blossom. "This could be wild lily of the valley. I'm not sure, I'll have to look it up when I get home." He slipped the flower into his wallet.

"Do you have a flower book?"

"My wife has a dozen."

Fanny thought she would buy herself one next time she went into a bookstore. "It's about time I got to know some of them." Then she asked, "What about the blossoms on those bushes? Do you know the names of them?"

Dubin said it was odd about the shrubs there. "They're cultivated, not wild. The only way I can explain it—I figure this from the depression in the earth—is that once the house I mentioned stood here. The woman had shrubs growing around the place. That's bridal wreath you asked about. It's beginning to wither."

"How pretty some of those names are. What do you call those?"

"Mock orange. You have to smell the blossoms to be sure. There are others that look like them but have no scent."

"I can smell the orange," Fanny said. She had picked a blossom and touched it to her lips.

"It's mock orange."

"How do you know them all?"

Dubin said he didn't know that many. "Lawrence seemed to recognize every flower in creation. Thoreau catalogued anything he saw or met in the woods, literally hundreds of flowers. I know few."

"Man, you know all these."

"My lucky day. Some fields I pass I don't know more than Queen Anne's lace. My wife taught me most of them and some flowering bushes. When I forget their names I ask her again."

"How is she doing these days?" Fanny wanted to know. "Are her glands still bothering her?"

He said she was fine.

"You mentioned her yourself just now," she said slightly stiffly. "Roger happened to tell me she was good in her library work."

He affirmed his wife was fine.

"Does she still go around sniffing the gas burners?"

Dubin said he was used to the burners. "I try not to say anything when she smells them, and for that I expect her not to comment when I yell at myself in the bathroom mirror."

"She and I never liked each other much."

"Cleaning house wasn't your act, Fanny."

They were walking a few feet apart, Fanny kicking the flowers. "I'm not criticizing or anything like that but did you know she'd go around smelling the gas before you married her?"

"You can't know everything in advance or what's marriage for? You take your chances. Whoever marries you will be taking one."

"You can say that again. But I may not want to get married."

"It's not so bad. In a marriage, after a while you learn what's given: who your wife is and you are, and how well you can live with each other. If you think you have a chance you're married. That's your choice if nothing else was."

"It's not much of one."

"We met in a curious way," Dubin explained. "Once I said I'd tell you about it. It was like not really meeting until we were ready to. She had written a letter more or less advertising for a husband."

"And you answered it?" Fanny said in pretend-astonishment.

"I happened to read it, though it wasn't addressed to me, and another she wrote canceling the intent of the first. To make it short, I became interested in her. We corresponded until we had developed some sense of each other. If a man and woman stay around trying to define themselves, at a certain point they become responsible one to the other. So we met, looked, talked, and after a while arranged to be married."

"What do you mean 'arranged'?"

"That's how I think of it. Kitty may have a better word."

"Were you in love with her? Like with Celandine?"

"She was someone I wanted to love."

"Did she feel that way?"

They had gone through the flowers and were approaching

a small wood of thick-armed dark-green oaks whose trunks were spotted with mold.

"I imagine there was an expectation of love. If you feel that, it doesn't take long to happen."

"Why didn't you live together first and try it out?"

"In those days," he explained, "few did that, Fanny. You got married. Those who didn't were rare birds and not always happy ones. Kitty was a widow with a child. I needed to be settled."

"Do you love her now? When I passed you on the road before I thought you looked lonely."

"Some are lonelier than others. My mother, in her sad way, was very lonely; my father had to be. I suppose I'm more than ordinarily a solitudinous type. It's not a curse if you learn what the pleasures of it are. But that's another story."

"I can't stand being lonely. There are no pleasures in it for me."

"You shouldn't have many worries, you seem to make friends easily."

She wanted to know how he meant that.

Dubin said he was not saying she was promiscuous.

"You'd better not because I'm not. If I was once I'm not any more." She looked at him intently. "Do you believe that?"

He wasn't sure but said he did. "What are your questions asking, Fanny?"

"About marriage. Everybody talks about it differently. I like to know what it is."

" 'Bear and forbear,' Sam Johnson defined it."

"That's not much."

"He was very sensible about marriage as he was in most things."

"What about you?"

"In the best of marriages you give what you can and get back as much or more. With the right people it's a decent enterprise. It gives pleasure."

"It sounds too much like work to me."

"Thomas Carlyle, who had an awful marriage, called it 'a discipline of character.' "

"I wouldn't want that kind of marriage," she said impatiently.

"What kind would you want?"

"I don't think I want to get married. It wore my mother out. She hates my father."

Dubin said he understood.

"What do you understand?"

"A little more about you."

"Maybe you do and maybe you don't."

"I think I do."

"What I mean is do you really understand what I'm like—what my needs are, for instance?"

He had some idea. "You've described yourself in your letters."

"I didn't tell you everything."

"I've seen you in action. Some things I can guess."

"I bet you'd be wrong."

"Possibly."

"Possibly," she mimicked him.

Fanny dropped the red trillium he had given her into her shoulder bag. "Did you ever want a divorce?"

He said he and his wife had discussed the subject more than once that past winter.

"What did you decide?"

"Nothing new. We were married, we stayed married."

Fanny reached down and plucked a blade of grass to suck on. "Like she expects you to go on forever protecting her?"

"Like she has character," Dubin answered. "Like I respond to it."

She threw the grass away. "Maybe I have character too."

Dubin hoped so.

After a wet morning and overcast late morning a warm sunny afternoon evolved. Large long clouds slowly sailed by.

"Oh, shit," the girl suddenly cried, hopping on one leg. "My foot is bleeding. I stepped on something."

She had cut the ball of her left foot on a piece of slate. Fanny sat down in the grass. The cut bled. Dubin got down on his knees to examine her foot.

"It doesn't look deep but it ought to be bandaged so you can get back to your car. The pond is close by. I could wet my handkerchief, wash the cut, and bandage your foot."

"You don't have to wash my foot, William. Just tie something around it so I don't get my sandal sticky with blood when I put it on. I just bought a new pair."

Dubin tried finger pressure to stop the bleeding.

"Here's some kleenex," Fanny said, pulling a wad out of her bag. "Use it and don't get your hankie bloody."

But he insisted on binding his handkerchief around her foot, knotting it on the arch. "The cut should be sterilized."

"I have a tube of first-aid cream in my glove compartment."

"I'll go get it."

"Not now," said Fanny. "I won't get blood poison. Or will I?" she asked worried.

"I'll get the cream."

"No," she said. "It's not a bad cut."

"Is the bandage too tight?"

"It feels comfortable."

With Dubin's assistance she got up. "Every time I see you I get some kind of free medical treatment. Did you ever want to be a doctor?"

"A lawyer," he said, "a drastic mistake."

The biographer suggested they turn back to the car but Fanny still wanted to see the water in the quarry.

"Can you go where it's rocky?"

"I'll take it easy. I think the bleeding has stopped."

They went on in the grass, Fanny hop-walking on her heel, and passed through the warm leaf-dappled mildewed oak wood; then ascended the sloping granite rock to look down at the green water in the jagged deep basin.

"It's a lot bigger than I thought. Do you swim here?"

"I come to look at the water."

"Want to try?"

"It's dirtier than I thought. Besides, we have no towels."

"You could dry yourself with your underwear."

"Why don't you go in yourself?"

"Never mind," Fanny said. "It might start my foot bleeding again."

They sat at the edge of the water, opposite them a palisade of earth and marble debris out of which some alders and white birch grew and many thick ferns; below, the granite wall was stained tan, gray, black.

The granite had been almost totally mined and the pit left to weather many years before Dubin came to Center Campobello. He had found the quarry in an adventurous jaunt with Kitty and still came every season to observe the reflection of the trees in the water. In the autumn Dubin watched yellow leaves floating in green water.

Fanny, piling her hair on her head, tried to see herself in the pond.

"Do you like my hair this way? It's not too short?"

Dubin didn't think so.

She let her hair fall and combed it, looking for herself in the water.

Fanny, with her bandaged foot and shorn hair, sat close to William Dubin as if they had no prior history. Her thighs were bare, bosom relaxed. The day was high and quiet.

Dubin recalled Venice dispassionately. Ah, William, nature's child, who would remotely have guessed you'd find your way to this spot in her company this day? He sat listening as the girl, her fingers interlocked behind her head, unshaved armpits visible, talked about her travail in Rome.

Harvey's death had seriously got her down. "He was always kind to me, sort of kidded me out of the blues I got into. I met him through his shmucky son Mitchell, who was an orthodontist in Jersey City. Mitch misused me when I was a kid and Harvey found out in a stupid letter I wrote that he had left around. I mentioned the sexual things he had taught me and told him those I liked. After he read the letter Harvey got pissed and warned him to leave me alone or I might get him thrown in the can on a statutory-rape rap, plus impairment of the morals of a minor. Harvey said if I or my father didn't bring charges he just might."

"How old were you?"

"Fifteen when I met him, sixteen when Harvey broke it up."

She said she had met Mitchell at her cousin Mildred's wedding. "He was built, with a good ass and strong shoulders. He had brown hair, reddish sideburns, and came on very macho. Anyway, he gave me a lot of attention and a wedding is where you want to feel good. He turned me on by talking about sex in a way that made me feel it was very mysterious and only he knew how to make it happen.

"I was having hot thoughts and went with him to his apartment after the wedding. Then for the next year almost, till Harvey found that letter, we were in bed or on the floor every

Sunday afternoon. I took the bus in Trenton to Jersey City, then a cab to his apartment. He gave me the carfare. Mitchell taught me all the joys of sex and some that were kinky."

"Bastard," murmured Dubin.

"When I finally got away from him I was pretty much scared of sex for years. I bet you never guessed that? The best thing that came of my experience with Mitchell was that night Harvey called me when I was feeling low, and we got to be friends, and I have never regretted it."

"Why did you let the affair with the son go on so long?"

"Because I wasn't sure about it and thought the more I learn about sex the better for me. I thought everybody had to know what I learned from him. Besides, he said he loved me and I thought he really did. He even filled my cavities and straightened my front teeth. The first thing he did when I got there on Sundays was to take off my braces so that kisses wouldn't hurt."

"An ape," Dubin ventured.

Fanny said he wasn't such a bad guy. "I liked certain things we did. Outside of his habit of screwing whenever he wasn't working his heart was in the right place. He practiced a day a week in a free clinic and wouldn't charge poor people. Harvey said he was the narcissist of the family. When I understood his nature I felt sorry for him. He's been in psychoanalysis about twenty years."

Dubin grunted.

"I had a shaky time after we broke up. When I was seventeen I felt fifty years old. I wasn't getting much out of school but hung in because somehow or other my grades were decent. I went to college. About then I began to sleep around. I was afraid I might become frigid after Mitch, and was scared. I got anxious and slept with people I shouldn't have slept with. I was depressed and used to pray. Then one day I read a book by Havelock Ellis and it helped me orient myself differently. I also was seeing a shrink although my father begrudged every nickel. Anyway, by the time I was twenty I began to enjoy sex again and I want to go on enjoying it, like forever."

"Once you told me your sexual experience had made you a more moral person. Does that relate to the experience with Mitchell or its aftermath?"

"I said a better person." She looked him full in the face. "I'll bet you thought of me as a hooker?"

"If I did, I don't."

"I'm not. I was ashamed of what happened in Venice. It was freaky, I was confused."

Fanny had opened her bag, found the trillium, and tossed it into the water.

He asked her why.

"I wanted to see it float."

They watched the three-petaled red flower floating in the green quarry water.

Fanny, after a while, asked Dubin what his first sex was like.

"With an older woman," he replied, "doing a repair job."

"On you?"

He nodded. "She was married, a teacher of mine. I had read *Sons and Lovers* with her."

"How long did it last?"

"Not long. Long enough."

He asked her about Harvey. "Was he your lover before we met?"

"Not really. He was into marijuana and pottery, never quite putting it together. I stayed with him for weeks just to be with one man. There were times when we wanted to love each other but couldn't. I tried to help him keep up his confidence."

"You were kind to him?"

"We were kind to each other."

Fanny's arms were wrapped around her knees. She extended her left hand so he could see the bracelet he had bought her. "I wear it for luck."

"How so?"

"You let me keep it."

The light on the eastern hills was dark gold as the sun descended in the west.

"It's late," Dubin said.

"I'll bet you don't know why I first came to Center Campobello," Fanny said.

"Was there a particular reason?"

"I read your book *Mark Twain* when I was staying in the commune on Tupper Lake. The way he was at the end of his life after Susy died, and then his wife, and he also felt miserable for treating his epileptic daughter like an idiot all her life—that part wiped me out."

"At the end of his life he lived in a theater of shmalzy misery," Dubin said.

"Shmalzy?"

"He enjoyed cigars and being a celebrity. He was deteriorating physically and mentally, but maybe in the book I laid on his aging and loneliness a bit much. *Thoreau* is a better-proportioned, more objective work."

"I read it in Rome. Harvey bought it for me as a present when I was in the hospital. I like Thoreau but wouldn't want to live his kind of life, although I liked the way he felt about himself at Walden. What I mean is that after I finished reading *Mark Twain* somebody said you had a house in this town and I decided to see if you would meet me if I came here."

"Extraordinary."

"I hoped we could really talk, that you would want to. I wanted somebody other than a shrink to advise me about my life, how to get it together better than I did. I had the feeling you could tell me useful things about myself. I never thought we would end up going to Venice. When you asked me I felt let down."

"What did you expect after undressing in my study?"

"I don't know what I expected. I was afraid of you and didn't want to be, so I went with you."

"I'm sorry I didn't respond more appropriately to your needs."

"You did in your books. The only one I don't like is *Short Lives*."

"Is that so? It's awfully popular in paperback."

"Oh?" Fanny said nervously. "I don't want to read about people ass backwards. I don't dig death hanging over everything they do or created. Are you afraid of death?"

"Not of death but maybe what leads to it."

"Doesn't life lead to it?"

"I'm speaking of sickness, accident—being incapacitated; unable to run my life; that can be worse than death. I'm afraid of the unexpected. What I expect I can deal with. On the other hand these short lives show how intensely and creatively life can be lived even when it is early aborted. In terms of years lived, they missed little; they weren't counting."

"If you're dead you're dead," Fanny said. "Nobody has to tell me what to do with my life, only how to get it together. I know all I want to about death. I don't want my nose rubbed in it."

"It's late," Dubin said after a minute, "let's go home."

She stared at him.

He helped her up, noticing she stood firmly on the cut foot.

Fanny promised to wash the blood out of his handkerchief and mail it to him.

He asked her where she had got the locket she was wearing.

She fingered it. "Harvey gave it to me about a week before his heart attack."

"A whole heart for a broken one?"

"He liked me a lot."

Fanny asked him whether Dubin would answer if she wrote to him once in a while.

He was not much a letter writer, he said.

Why waste what the winter had taught him?

As they were moving down the granite slope half a dozen black birds rose from the oak trees and flapped off toward the reddened sun. The dark rays of the dying sun touched the tips of the trees. Overhead, massive bronze clouds in long convoys were moving east. As Fanny and Dubin came out of the wood a softened early-evening light lay on the long field of wild flowers.

Fanny began to name them. "There's celandine, oxeye daisy, red rooster—what a ball those names are." Farther on she said, "There's forget-me-not, which I knew, and those bushes are bridal wreath."

She plucked a red trillium and thrust it into her shoulder bag, then began to collect a bouquet of daisies.

The clouds were crimson, those close to the hills were violet ships voyaging to black mountains.

Fifteen or more billion years after creation, the biographer thought, here's this sea of wild flowers on earth and amid them this girl picking white daisies.

"Look," said Fanny as they were walking in the grass, "there's wild lily of the valley, if you guessed right. I've learned the names of them all."

She touched Dubin's arm.

He touched the curve of her back. Fanny, letting her bouquet of daisies slip from her hand, turned to him.

The biographer, assailing doubt, took her in his arms. Fanny sank into the warm grass, arching her hips as he drew down her underpants.

This evens it, Dubin thought, for the cruel winter.

Six

DEAR FANNY. In the movie that August night she reached for his hand and kissed it, a gesture that stirred him. Ponce de León had galloped in the wrong direction: the fountain of youth is the presence of youth. In her company he enjoyed the sense of fountain within, experienced flowers of splashing water.

He had seen her in the city twice in June and again in July; had come to New York for two-day visits. This time he arrived for a week one late afternoon on a Saturday in August, a warmish pleasant summer's day, Fanny's twenty-third birthday. She had written, "I want to spend my birthday with you." On the train Dubin had opened his paper, anticipating their meeting, going to bed with her. Soon a thin gloom stole over him and he lowered the newspaper to track down why. Easy enough: Kitty and Maud had driven him to the train station. There were kisses goodbye. He was on his way to the city, he had announced, to complete a contract for three articles he'd write to earn some needed cash; have a look in at the Public Library; maybe visit an old friend or two. "Have a good time," Kitty had said. "Lots of fun," Maud affirmed, not at her best that day. Her hair was still an unhappy mix of red streaked black. She looked as though she hated to see him go, and for a moment he wanted not to leave her. When he looked again she needed someone else and he thought that natural.

Everyone wants Dubin to enjoy himself. They were planning a few days on the Maine Coast. Maud, to tell the truth, was mostly bored, a summer at home less than satisfying as she dealt with an excitement within, now apparently on, now apparently off. Kitty had suggested a drive up the coast to cheer her up and Maud had consented to go if she did the driving. He wished, considering the circumstances, they hadn't insisted on taking him to the train, but they knew he disliked buses. Well, life isn't ideal. He loved them both and tried to put them out of mind. They returned at once through predictable doors and windows. One can't easily dispense with the actors of his personal history. The biographer, as he read the newspaper, hefted and measured guilt, yet managed to sidestep it: I'm not twenty, nor forty—I'm fifty-seven. Surely these years entitle me to this pleasure. In life one daren't miss what his nature requires. Only the spiritually impoverished can live without adventure. After a while the sweep of the broad silver-blue sunlit Hudson, from the window, the smoky Catskills in the distance, helped him cast off the subtle net on his spirit and he listened to himself thinking of being, soon, with Fanny.

Dubin, as the train sped on, reflected without nostalgia how it had been when he was a young man with a prearranged date—rarely with a girl one might meet by chance in park or museum, want to be with, and *is*. But prearrangement had the advantage—it seemed advantage—of buildup in imagination, anticipation of pleasure. As the time of meeting approached, nature improved, the evening expanded, stars were jewels in the sky. As he shaved, dressed, waited for the last minutes to go by before he left the house, enjoying reverie, expectation; he felt a sense of well-being so intense it could only taint, perhaps spoil, the experience: there were times the girl wasn't—couldn't possibly be—as much pleasure as his expectation of her. He would envision more than she was; wanted more to give than he ultimately gave. The occasion therefore became self-defeating, Dubin trying to squeeze out of prevision, desire, something it was not prepared to yield. He had expected more than reality entitled him to—defense against an ordinary fate: an extraordinary woman. Out of hubris, if not fear, young William Dubin had felt an unwillingness to risk himself with someone whose experience was too much like his own. When, years later, Kitty Willis appeared in his life, he felt he had met his equal in possibility, someone who could give him not only what he hadn't had, but hadn't thought of having; Dubin had then stopped sidestepping marriage.

Dear Fanny: He had told her when he was coming but hadn't expected her to be waiting for him when the train arrived. There she was at the rope barrier. Men looked at her as they passed by and she was modestly reserved although her body seemed extrinsic to her clothes, a natural gift Dubin approved in principle. Fanny had changed her hair style since he had seen her last, her thick hair now drawn above her ears and pulled through a silver ring into a loose light mane falling to below her summer-tanned shoulders. She wore a yellow skimp, her bosom snug in the fabric, her legs bare, always good to see in short dresses. She had put on a pound or two and was relaxed, her face womanly. Neither was on probation in the other's eyes. Dubin felt heartened to have recovered her. He felt himself a gifted man, an excellent biographer.

When they arrived in Fanny's apartment on West 83rd Street she unbuttoned his shirt and began quickly to undress. Dubin helped. In bed they loved each other generously. He, after a catnap, lay restfully on her pillow, gazing at a gardenia that looked like three gardenias in a water glass on top of her bookcase.

"I put it there for you to see because you like flowers."

"Dear Fanny."

The evening grew in pleasure, serenity, magnitude. She took ten minutes to brush her hair as Dubin watched each stroke. They dressed and hailed a cab to a bistro she knew on First Avenue. At a bar with its back to a curtained window, Dubin, man of the world, drank brandy and soda as he talked with the young bartender about the merits of Lawrence's early novels, and Fanny, sipping Scotch on the rocks, seriously listened, her warm side pressed to his. The bartender, when Dubin began to explicate D. H. Lawrence on sex—a much misunderstood question: "And I who loathe sexuality so deeply am considered a lurid sexuality specialist. Mi fa malo allo stomacho"—let his eyes rest seriously on Fanny's handsome bosom. Dubin felt expansive, amiable, personally wealthy. "Sex to him, you understand, despite his ideology of blood-being, was a metaphor for a flowering life."

The bartender gravely nodded.

Fanny, her arm around her middle-aged lover, nudged her head against his chest. Dubin kissed her ear. She had a gift of closeness, could almost not bear not being in contact with whomever she felt affection for. She touched, stroked, quietly pressed. Few men had it so good.

"Let's dance," she said. A combo of piano, bull fiddle, and drums in a far corner of the room had begun to play.

Dubin tried to beg off, swore he couldn't—not this new mode of dance. He had been brought up on fox-trot and waltz, could lindy a little, not more. "I don't know the steps."

"Make them up. Hop like a monkey. Peel a banana."

"Then what?"

"Climb a tree."

He did as he was told. Fanny danced to his movements in a way that made him look good. She danced deadpan with wide-open myopic eyes, inventing steps and graceful movements of her arms. When she came close he could smell her through her scent and felt he was dancing off the floor. A blonde of thirty or so dancing nearby with a man of Dubin's age winked at the biographer and told him to save the next one for her. Fanny laughed merrily.

After a supper of omelette, green salad, white wine, Fanny asked him where he wanted to go. Miraculous question: here's Dubin with nowhere to go except where he pleased. Nothing scheduled, appointed, expected. He was this evening, in truth, a free spirit. Dubin, the single. There were a dozen things to do and he might do them all.

"You name it," he told her.

"Disco? I know a good one."

"If you wish."

"Or we could see friends of mine in the East Village?"

"Young people?"

"About my age. They have two kids. Or we could go to a picture I hear is great."

"Fine."

They walked to a movie on Third Avenue. It was there Fanny kissed his hand in the dark and Dubin kissed hers. One did not have to guess with Fanny: she was there, gave instinctually; he easily gave in return. After the film he looked for a bookstore. Dubin remembered how happy it had made Kitty, one evening not long after they had met, when he bought her a book of poems.

Fanny had never read Yeats; he bought her the *Selected Poems*, exactly what he had got Kitty; and at the florist's up the block, a white rose. Fanny carried it and the book solemnly in one hand, hugging his right arm with her left as they walked on the Drive, refreshed by the cool air of the river. They walked until it occurred to them that the streets were no longer safe. Dubin felt a melancholy regret at the way the world had gone; and she, sensing his mood, fell silent.

At home Fanny put on the coffeepot while Dubin examined her bookcase and found in it hardback copies of each of his biographies. She had managed to get even the out-of-print *Abraham Lincoln*—probably had cost her twenty bucks. On the wall above the bookcase hung a medium-enlarged framed colored snapshot of Fanny, pigeons circling her head and shoulders, that Dubin had taken with her camera one morning ages ago—was it really less than a year?—in the Piazza San Marco. He remembered the picture of her in jeans and lank hair she had sent from Rome last winter and asked if he could have a print of the one on the wall.

"Sure, but suppose your wife sees it?"

"She doesn't poke into my things, and if she did she'd know who I was in Venice with."

"How is it you never told her?"

"An anonymous woman hurts less."

Fanny regarded him silently. She began to nibble the nail of her middle finger but there was no nail to nibble. Her fingernails were, as a rule, ragged. "Where does she think you are now?"

"Not where I presently am."

Dubin moved from the bookcase to get away from the thought. She followed him. "In one way I don't mind that hassle in Venice we had."

"Which way?"

"It made me feel closer to you than I might have if everything had gone right. Do you feel close to me, William?"

They kissed.

Fanny drew herself a vitabath. She got her diaphragm out of the bureau drawer and took it into the bathroom. She had been advised after her operation not to take the Pill, she had told Dubin. He was enjoying the thought of sleeping with her again tonight; it had been years since he had slept with a woman twice in a day. He undressed, glad he had slimmed down, tamed his pot belly, a shadow of itself. The telephone rang. Fanny got rid of whoever it was before the guy could seriously unburden himself. Dubin had heard a man's urgent voice; she didn't say who. He felt uneasy. As Fanny bathed he thought of her lying nude on her double bed and imagined a line of men coiled around it, a long line of types and ages extending into the hall and down a flight of stairs; from Mitchell the orthodontist to William Dubin the biographer. How many men had she had in her young life—fifty? eighty?—a hundred and fifty? How many diaphragms had she worn out in her comparatively short sexual lifetime? Did she have one on—was it possible?—when he took her amid the wild flowers? Or did she take me? He felt a momentary distrust of her; but as Dubin, lying on Fanny's sheets, reflected on the course of human lives—on desire, error, pain, understanding, change—he exculpated her in his mind; forgave Fanny her sexual past. And when they were lying in bed after her fragrant bath it seemed to him as if they had come together in innocence. He had re-created her virginity.

Fanny, with her nail scissors, snipped the thorns off the white rose and wound its green stem around his erect cock. She kissed the flower. Dubin wished her a happy birthday.

Kitty, before sex, lowered the shades; Fanny had none on her windows. She came out of the shower naked, dressed in the sunny bedroom and walked around with wet hair, barefoot in cotton underpants. Kitty sneezed when her hair was wet. She was trim. Fanny's rump was heavier than he had thought, her waist narrower. "Why don't you get yourself some window shades?" Dubin asked her.

"I have nothing to hide, do you?"

"What about the synagogue across the street?"

"That's on the second floor and even when I stand at the window with my clothes on nobody down there looks up at me. Even when I don't have any clothes on they don't look my way. Or if somebody does he's searching for God. I don't need window shades."

Dubin often watched the elderly Jews at prayer, or as they sat at study around a long table in a brown room on the left side of the synagogue. He bought two large white shades for Fanny's bedroom windows.

Her apartment, in an old six-story graystone, was not especially attractive, needed painting, bathroom repairs. Roaches haunted the area around sink and range. Dubin sprayed disinfectant liberally, diligently, until no limping survivor remained. Fanny had two medium-size rooms and a small kitchen but the windows, in heavy flaking frames, were large, the apartment light; and she got it for two hundred a month. She had a new job that wasn't bad—the work interesting—as secretary to an executive secretary in a law office. She didn't like nine-to-five, found the hours restrictive, yet had time to think of herself, her needs.

During the week he lived with her, Dubin slept later than usual. Her alarm rang at 7:30. He awoke alert and began his modified exercises; Fanny, into Yoga when she came home, stopped to look on as she dried herself after her shower. Dubin fried an egg and made coffee to get her off on time. She ate slowly, hungrily. She was slow in the morning but not distracted. Fanny was clean but not, like Kitty, neat; he realized how alien to her nature it had been to houseclean for others last summer. It took her about an hour to shower, brush and fix her hair, then select and screw on earrings, a variety of single and double circles of silver mostly. She said, "I'll hit the can and be right out." As she slipped on her dress she seemed lost in thought. She left the house anytime from ten to nine to a quarter after, predicting she'd be fired by the end of the month. On his way to pick up a newspaper, he hurried her to the Broadway bus. She was usually in good humor, laughed when he was witty, kissed him slowly at the bus stop, to Dubin's self-conscious concern, because people were looking and he was embarrassed by his age; but he would rather be kissed.

Afterward he read the Watergate news with intense interest. Nixon had resigned. During the impeachment proceedings Dubin had trotted his walk holding a pocket radio in his hand. Fanny and he looked through the papers every night and talked about the case before going to bed. He wondered what sort of life one might write of Nixon, provided one could stand the monotony of his mind and character. The man made him uncomfortable. It occurred to Dubin how lucky he was to be working on someone of the rich complexity of D. H. Lawrence and felt affection for him, for his self-respect.

Dubin wrote on Fanny's kitchen table after he had cleared it off and washed the breakfast dishes. He put away the freeze-dry coffee and found a box of sanitary napkins in the food cabinet. In the bedroom he hung up her slight black nightgown on a hook behind the closet door. He liked the sight of her bright short dresses hanging in the closet and thought of buying her one or two on his own. He tossed her used tights into the hamper, gave up on the rat's nest of bottles, tubes, containers in the bathroom, but took a minute to mop the tiled floor. Dubin then put the plastic garbage bag out; he had bought her a new garbage container. And he enjoyed the happy surprise with which she greeted the order he had made.

Once he had cleaned and straightened up the place—Fanny hastily made the bed before leaving—he was in a mood for work. It did not bother him that he was not in his study; this was, after all, a holiday, and allowing himself to work, gravy. He laid out his cards, jotted down notes, and began to write careful sentences. Dubin loved sentences. He worked all morning, getting up every so often to watch the elderly Jews reading or at prayer.

After lunch he rode the Fifth Avenue bus to the Public Library and read in the reference room. One day he took the train to Newark to see where he had lived as a child; he felt no nostalgia; but it occurred to him he hadn't visited his father's and mother's graves in years. Charlie Dubin had bought his wife's grave in a cemetery in the Bronx and his own in a huge graveyard in Queens. "I got a bargain for my plot." Most often in thinking of him Dubin saw the father of his childhood, younger than he himself was now. His mother he usually thought of as she had looked after she became insane. Only once had he been to his drowned brother's grave in Newark but could not bear to go that day. After the library, he usually walked home—up Fifth, through Central Park to West 96th, then back on West End to Fanny's on 83rd. That was almost the equivalent of the long walk in Center Campobello. He did not dwell on other equivalents of his New York experience.

Fanny lived in a walk-up graystone with a partly semicircular façade. A fenced yellow steam-stack on the far side of the street spouted a cloud of white steam all day and night. Diagonally across the street were a few stores; and above a florist's shop, the second-floor synagogue, under a roof with a raised skylight. It was not a hot August, and Fanny, if Dubin shopped for her, would rather prepare supper than go out. She fed him large quantities of food. Fanny wasn't a talented cook but she was not a bad one and dared cook fish, giggling and groaning. Dubin liked fish but Kitty rarely cooked it. Kitty loved snails, clams, mussels, and frog's legs; but Dubin did not. Fanny avoided snails and oysters but enjoyed lobster. Dubin had mastered shrimp and crabmeat and stayed clear of other shellfish. He had had none as a child. Fanny, one night in a fish restaurant, got him to share her lobster.

After supper if the apartment was stuffy they usually went out. They saw *A Comedy of Errors* in the park; once attended her weekly summer evening class in government at the New School. On Saturday afternoon Dubin took her to the Metropolitan Museum and told her what he knew about painting. He explained what Kitty had told him about Chinese pottery. She listened as though memorizing. Her bookcase was varied: he noticed books on psychology, political theory, music, ecology. "Fanny," he said, "you're a hidden intellectual." "I'm smarter than I look," she answered, "but not always organized. I'm fairly well organized at work but not when it comes to making decisions for myself. That's where I am missing a cylinder. I wish you could help me make up my mind what I ought to be doing with myself." Dubin said he would. "I am better controlled when you're around," she said. "Do you know what I mean?"

On a framed bulletin board in the kitchen she tacked up snippets of sayings: "Be kind to yourself." He remembered.

"Morality begins when one can control experience."

He wondered if she had once that week thought of Kitty. Probably she would say that was his business. Dubin had attended to his business.

From his *H. D. Thoreau* she had copied this sentence: "There is no other land; there is no other life but this or the like of this."

He gave her credit.

He was careful with her, considerate of her pace and qualities. He liked to do things she suggested. At twilight, one evening, they walked into Central Park and listened, amid a circle of people in a variety of dress, some standing there with their dogs, to the steel drums played by two West Indians who beat up high haunting melodies in their gleaming pots and let them flow into dusk. Afterward they walked to the east side of the park; there were lovers lying in the grass. Fanny slipped her hand into Dubin's back pocket and felt his ass as he walked. They wandered, as the street lights came on, up Madison, seeing themselves in store windows when they stopped to look. There was this fine-figured girl in a light-orange summer dress; and with her an erect slightly self-conscious middle-aged type, smoking a cigarillo, in bell-bottoms, blazer, and Panama hat. Each stared at the reflection of the other as though neither could believe they were together. They locked fingers as they walked.

She called him Bill, tried Will, went back to William. William could sound funny when she said it. When he read poetry to her she sat close in a chair, her bare legs resting on his thighs. She told him personal things: why her periods were late; confessed to occasional problems of constipation, for which he advised her to cook up a pot of prunes with lemon rind and have a plateful each morning. She wrote left-handed, he discovered to his surprise; was otherwise right-handed. She typed beautifully, retyped his Lawrence pages for him. Fanny created little favors for Dubin. At night she drew down the white shades and they turned to each other with passion. She slept heavily. He too slept deeply, lying against her strong young sweet-smelling body.

One night he woke from deep sleep to find himself being sucked off. The pleasure was all but unbearable. Fanny moved her moist mouth patiently until he came with a cry, almost of protest.

"What was that for?"

"I woke up and wanted to."

In the morning they woke making love. Fanny stayed home from work and they slept till noon. He had tried to break through sleep to get up but couldn't. Afterward they rose, showered, ate leisurely, went back to bed. Dubin loved her body, was conscious of her sensuality, aroused by the force of her sexual being. She was embarrassed by nothing, named her pleasures. He responded to her desire by running his tongue along her pudgy clitoris as she squirmed happily. A first for Dubin; he felt like a god.

Fanny asked if he had liked doing it. She was sitting cross-legged in bed. How intimate strangers can be.

"For the effect it has on you, yes."

"Don't do anything you are not comfortable with."

That night she massaged his back with lotions, unguents, kneading his shoulders, pressing her strong fingers into his flesh, working down his legs, rubbing, stroking. His heart beat like a drum. "Does your wife massage you too?" "No." "Never?" "Never." "Too bad," said Fanny. She was subtle, cunning, gifted in touch, wet him exquisitely. She seemed to watch her effect on him. Dubin cherished their intimacy.

But when he asked whether she was teaching him the orthodontist's repertory, Fanny denied it.

"What he taught me has got nothing to do with what I want to give you or want you to give me. One man is a hunk of wood in bed, another is a fire. At first I thought you'd be a loaf of rye bread but now there's something wild in you that I like."

"A wild rye bread or wildfire?"

"A wild flower," Fanny laughed. "I want you to have a lot of fun." Dubin replied it was what he wanted. He felt satisfied in a way he hadn't since early in his marriage. The intensity of pleasure, of possibility, was greater now. Live and learn.

I want her to teach me, he thought. I want to know everything she does. I'm more than twice her age.

Her orgasm, she swore, spaced her. "It's like coming full blast out of a cannon." She let go in surprise. "Will-yam," she sang as to a friend far away. His ended in a slow drop from the bursting sky; knowing it would end safely in a warm bed. He was fulfilled, relieved, as though he had feared what had happened to them might never have; then magically it had happened. Something good, fortunate, had come into his life. With this girl I know the flowering pleasure, heathen innocence, of the natural life. I live in her sun-strong garden. He was grateful to her; they held each other close and kissed affectionately.

As Fanny slept Dubin lay awake thinking of his *Passion of D. H. Lawrence.* He was glad the pleasures of this week had come to him as they had: this long careless giving of oneself in sex. His experiences with Fanny, in variety, intensity, excitement heightened by her watchful curious knowing, sureness of her sexual self, willingness to give, couldn't have come at a better moment. He understood Lawrence more fully, his religion of sexuality: a belief in the blood, the flesh, as wiser than the intellect. I think I know what he means by "the unknown God brought into consciousness"—"the slow invasion in you of the vast invisible God that lives in the ether"—"the old Pagan vision." "This is very important to our being, that we should realise that we have a blood-being, a blood-consciousness, a blood-soul, complete and apart from the mental and nerve consequences." I can't say I fully believe it, Dubin thought, but understand more clearly where it came from in his nature and why he said it in these words. I think—I feel I understand him.

Unable to sleep, he rose hyped up, his imagination pouring ideas like rain. He felt like working but had better not if he could work longer later. He stood at the bedroom window, one shade raised, gazing above the steaming smokestack at the synagogue. The building was darkened except for a small candlelit room where a black-bearded black-hatted Jew, his white shawl glowing on his shoulders, bent back and forth in prayer. Once in a while Dubin prayed. It was a way of addressing the self; God had a tin ear. Who wanted to listen to human complaints within the heavenly music?

Whom shall I pray for?

He thought of Gerald and Maud but this time prayed a moment for Fanny, then got into bed with the girl, who did not stir. He moved close to her sex-scented body, and as she sighed, fell into sleep.

He was awakened by the sound of rain, or a distant sobbing, as though someone was lost and he wasn't sure who. Dubin fought against waking but it sprang out of him like an idiot tearing at the roots of sleep. Protesting the task, he ascended a ladder, rising step by gluey step until he miraculously thrust his head through a foggy hole. In his confusion he called her Kitty. He lay with eyes open trying to understand what Fanny was complaining about. He felt her twisting in her sleep. With an effort he turned on the bed lamp. Her eyelids were twitching, arms moved in spasms, her mouth tormented; she seemed to be locked in a nightmare.

"Fanny." He shook her gently. "Take it easy." She whimpered yet drunkenly slept on. Dubin shook her again. With a groan Fanny quickly sat up, astonished to see him there. She fell into his arms in relief.

"Jesus," she shuddered, "I had this mind-blowing god-awful dream—it was one of those awful ones with blood and shit in it—that I'd been killed in an accident. I saw myself dead and couldn't wake until you made me." She wept in bed. "I don't want to die young. I hate that book you wrote. Why did you give it to me?"

"Forgive me," Dubin said.

Afterward she was depressed. Dubin got up to brew her a cup of tea. As he was waiting for the water to boil he looked uneasily out of the window for a sign of dawn. Wanting to sleep, he did not want it to be dawn; neither did the night—black, heavy, inert. Across the silent street the candlelight was out in the synagogue. Fanny sipped tea in bed. For a while they talked, then put out the light and quietly talked. She turned on her side, resting on his arm.

"I dreamed I saw someone with a crazy crippled face watching us from the fire escape."

"What fire escape?"

"I dreamed there was one. I feel scared about something, I wish I knew what it was. I'm afraid something bad might happen to me. I don't want to do the wrong thing with my life. Advise me, William. I'm afraid I'll be anxious again. Tell me what to do about myself. You're so serious about life, tell me what to do with mine."

He said it wasn't so simple, he didn't know her that well.

"You know me well enough," she said fiercely.

"You're a late bloomer, Fanny. I was too. Keep your eye on yourself. Find out who you are. Watch what you do and tell yourself why. Try to use yourself well."

"People have been saying something like that to me all my life. It drives me up a wall. Suppose I *never* find out who I am?"

"Then you'll have to find out why or pay for it."

"I don't want to go back to a shrink."

"I wasn't talking about shrinks."

"How did you find out you wanted to write biographies? If I knew what I wanted to do that would be half of it for me."

Dubin said trial and error plus good luck. "I was writing

obituaries. Finally I read someone's life of somebody else and thought I could do better. My wife thought so too."

Fanny yawned and grew quiet. For a minute he thought she had fallen asleep. "What about her?" she asked.

"What about her?"

"Did she know what she wanted to do when she was my age?"

"At your age she was about to be a widow."

"I mean before that?"

"She was interested in music but not much came of it. She wanted to teach, she wanted to be a concert harpist, but she didn't do either. She met this doctor and he asked her to marry him."

"I don't want to get married—at least not yet."

"Not yet," Dubin agreed.

"When did she start being afraid she would die of cancer, or something like that?"

"Before I met her."

"Is that the reason she goes around smelling the gas burners?"

"I suppose so. It's a kind of ritual against death."

"Do you think I have one?"

"I don't know. Do you have many nightmares?"

"I used to have more when I was a kid."

"Maybe they're your gas burners."

"Maybe. What are yours?"

"I don't know."

"What about those long walks you always take?"

"I thought a walk was a walk."

Fanny was silent a moment. "Did Thoreau have a ritual? I don't remember whether you mentioned it in your book."

"His journal was his ritual. For all I know he may have thrown handfuls of snow over his left shoulder as he was walking in the woods."

"What about D. H. Lawrence?"

"Maybe his tuberculosis was psychosomatic, I don't know. He would never admit he was seriously ill till after he finished *The Plumed Serpent* in Mexico. He called his sickness catarrh, bronchitis, influenza, a bad cold, finally malaria—everything but the deadly thing it was. He used to say it wasn't his lungs, it was his bronchi; but his lungs were rotting."

"Are you afraid to die, William?" Fanny asked in the dark.

Dubin drew up his knees. "My God, Fanny, how many times are you going to ask me that? I don't want to talk any more. I'm worn out with all the sex we've had. I need sleep desperately. For God's sake, let me sleep."

"Are you sorry about us now?"

"No."

"Are you glad?"

"Yes."

"Is your wife good in bed, William?" Fanny then asked.

"Lay off, Fanny," Dubin said irritably. "She wouldn't want you to know."

"Oh, come off it."

"Obviously she's different from you."

"How different?"

"That's none of your business."

"Do you love her—this minute?"

"Yes."

"Do you love me?"

"Yes."

"Bullshit."

He waited for her to start punishing him but she had fallen asleep. Dubin couldn't till dawn.

In the morning Fanny apologized for having kept him awake during the night. She was menstruating heavily. "That's what gave me those lousy dreams," she said almost gaily. "I always have nightmares before I get the curse."

Sunday morning Dubin called his wife in Center Campobello from a public pay phone while he was out getting the newspaper. Kitty was angered.

"Where in Christ have you been? I was frantic. You weren't registered at the Gansevoort. They had no idea where you were."

Dubin said he was at the Brevoort.

"Why the Brevoort? You've never liked it there."

"For a change," he lied. "Were you calling from Maine? Is something the matter?"

"We never got to Maine. Maud couldn't make it. The night before we were to leave she got a long-distance call from a man she said was a friend, then asked out. She packed a bag and took a bus to New York. I can tell you she stopped being bored in a hurry."

Dubin was worried. "Is she here now?"

"I would imagine so."

"Where is she staying?"

"She hasn't called. I don't know where any of my family are."

"I'm standing here talking to you. Did she say when she'd be home?"

"Vaguely—about a week. She apologized for having to go. I'm certain she's having an affair."

"You don't know who he is?"

"No. Questions about her personal life annoy her."

"There are some questions one has to ask."

"Who she may or may not be sleeping with? You ask her."

"Maybe I will."

"When will you come home?"

"Tomorrow morning."

"I thought you said you'd be home today?"

"I want to visit my father's and mother's graves this afternoon."

"Yes, go," she said.

Dubin asked her to meet him at the train tomorrow noon and Kitty said she would.

He said he was sorry he had forgotten to give her the name of the hotel he'd been staying in.

"That's all right. Did you have a good time?"

"On and off." Hearing that, he laughed nervously. "Pretty good."

Kitty said she was glad.

After he had brought the paper to Fanny, Dubin hailed a cab to take him to the cemetery in the Bronx where his mother was buried. Her grave was overgrown with thick grass.

"Mama," he said, "rest in peace in your grave." Where else could she rest? He thought of her jumble of mad fears; of those he carried in his flesh. He wondered which of them Maud carried in her.

Dubin left a stone on the tombstone to let his mother know he had been there. Maybe it was to let himself know. The white stone he had left more than a dozen years ago when he had taken Kitty to visit the grave was still there, the color of rust. It had begun to rain. He stopped off at the cemetery office and told them to cut the long grass on his mother's grave.

Dubin then rode on the subway to Jamaica and at the station took a taxi to his father's cemetery. Charles Dubin had divorced himself from his wife in his grave. Let God take care of her now. His son carried a small leather-bound book and read from it a Hebrew prayer for the dead transliterated in English.

"Rest in peace, Papa," he said to the wet grave. "You did what you had to."

Dubin imagined nine other men standing at the grave with him, saying Kaddish.

He left the endless cemetery and rode the long subway ride back to Fanny's apartment. When she had returned from Rome she swore off smoking and had taken up Yoga. She wore black leotards with a run down her left thigh as she did her exercises. Fanny had got to a modified headstand, her head resting in a pool of her thick hair, when he entered the apartment.

She fell to her knees. Dubin pulled her up and they kissed with open mouths. Her breath was like the scent of a tropical flower. Her hand went to his fly.

"Not now," Dubin said.

"Because I'm bleeding?"

He said he was not much in a mood. He had just been to the cemetery.

"Did your wife ever want it when she was bleeding?"

"Ask her."

After a while Fanny said she was sorry she had asked. Her face was pallid and worried. "I was happy all week," she said to Dubin. "I don't want to spoil it."

He said he didn't want to spoil it either.

"Do you honestly like me?"

"Most honestly."

Her eyes softened. "I had a fine time, did you?" She touched his hand with her finger.

"Never better."

"Let's have more good times, lots of fun."

He said that was what he wanted.

"I will give you a key to the downstairs door and one for my apartment."

Dubin said he had better not take the keys. "If I left them around or they fell out of my pocket, Kitty would want to know what they were for."

Fanny reluctantly saw the point. "Anyway, when will you be back? I miss you already."

He promised soon.

"Oh, make it sooner. We're lovers now, aren't we?"

Seven

THEY MADE love on a sunny Sunday morning, the moving white curtains enfolding warm light. Afterward Kitty, lying on her side, said the early-fall anemones were especially prettily colored. It was a bright August day thinning toward autumn. He had made love with her, trying not to think of Fanny. Dubin was conscious of himself lying beside his wife, his left arm around her, hers draped across his belly. Kitty was slender, taller than Fanny, felt lighter, weighed less. Her face was at peace and pretty. Her skin shone in the morning light. He was glad she was satisfied; wanted her to have what she was entitled to.

Forgive me, he thought.

"What for?"

He asked, after a minute, what he had said.

She laughed to herself. "What shall I forgive?"

"Who I am."

She had heard it before. "I forgive who you are."

Kitty ruffled his hair, yawned, sat up and reached for her robe. "Let's have breakfast."

Sunday's was the breakfast they almost always ate together. On Sunday she fixed other than ordinary fare. Today she cooked an omelette aux fines herbes. The buttery golden omelette with greens looked succulent in the omelette pan. Biscuits were hot, creamy, coffee tasty. Mt. No Name, through the window behind Kitty, became more clearly visible as summer heat and haze diminished. There were a few yellowing leaves in the silver maples, not many. After a blow of wind a handful of dead leaves lay scattered on the grass. Dubin watched a single leaf, half-green, half-yellow, part from a branch and drift and twirl to the ground. He had always been affected by the sight. Now he thought of Fanny. He tried not to.

Kitty, after pouring second cups of coffee, asked him what his impression had been of Maud's summer. "What did you talk about with her?"

"Politics often. She was excited by the impeachment proceedings. We both were."

"I mean what did she say that was personal?"

"Not much about herself," Dubin told Kitty. "She wasn't giving much though there were moments she seemed to want to. Once in a while I said something that brought her close—not close enough—to saying what was on her mind. I had this sense, on her part, of gesture."

"What do you mean?"

"Her visit as a kind gesture to her parents."

"I hope to God she isn't having a bad time. If she's in love I'd hate it to be unhappy love."

"Do you think she's in love?"

Kitty said she thought so. "She's been reading Spanish love poems in her room. I hear her as I go up the stairs."

"Which poems?"

"One I asked about she copied out for me. It's Mother Juana Inés de la Cruz. She copied it and I learned it:

> Al que ingrato me deja, busco amante;
> al que amante me sigue, dejo ingrata;
> constante adoro a quien mi amor maltrata;
> maltrato a quien mi amor busca constante.
>
> Al que trato de amor, hallo diamante,
> y soy diamante al que de amor me trata . . .

When Kitty recited poetry her voice was sincere, soft, hesitant. Maud recited in a sweet emotional fluent voice.

"What does it mean?"

"She says she lovingly seeks the one who ungratefully abandons her; and he who lovingly pursues her she ungratefully abandons. "Him whom I treat lovingly I find to be hard, and I am hard for him who treats me lovingly."

"It sounds rocky."

"It has a Spanish quality. Her voice sounds Spanishy."

"Castanets, black hair, and throaty voice?"

"She's a surprising girl."

"Has she said who the guy is—somebody Spanish or Mexican?"

"Didn't you ask?"

"No."

"He may be, maybe not, I'm not good at guessing. I hope she's happy with him. Being in love at her age was a happy time for me. When I woke in the morning I ran to see myself in the looking glass."

Dubin said it wasn't a happy time in his life.

"When I first met you, you said it was."

"In a way it was. I enjoyed hurrying to their houses with little bouquets of flowers."

"You haven't brought one home in years."

He said the garden was full of flowers. "I felt happy in love until I had to contend with feeling come back to earth. I was by then disenchanted with the one I'd been in love with and was waiting for the next experience. After a while I felt the waste of the affair."

"Why was it a waste?"

"Nothing had come of it."

"Does something have to come of everything?"

He said that was not a bad idea.

"What happened to the girl?"

"She went elsewhere."

"I sometimes am surprised that you wanted to marry me."

"I was ready for you. You were right for me with your kind of experience. I felt we were in the real world."

"I wasn't so sure of that in the beginning."

"I wasn't sure of myself as your step-husband."

"Oh, cut it out," Kitty grimaced.

Dubin changed the subject: "I sense Maud has a lot to learn."

"If I could she will, maybe Gerald will too. I hope he's happy someday."

"I doubt he thinks of happiness. I don't think it's on his agenda."

"What does he think of?"

"He does his tightrope."

"Where to?"

"To the next tightrope, from the one over rocks to the one over water."

Kitty's dark eyes showed concern. "I liked his last card. He seemed to be having a better time. But he never tells us what he's doing. I hate that kind of gap between son and mother. Do you think he'll want to come home soon?"

"It'll depend on what President Ford offers the deserters. He isn't a man with much moral imagination."

"Gerry Willis insists on an apology. He has an intense moral imagination."

"He's got the makings of a revolutionary."

"What a strange way for one's own son to be," Kitty said. "Before you know who he is he's someone other than you think."

Yet she gave the impression she might square things with Gerald if only he returned to the house for a visit. "I have a lot to say to him. I see things more clearly than I used to. I'm not as guilty as I used to be."

Despite the uncertainties of Gerry's life and Maud's, the worries they kicked up as they defined themselves, lived their experiences, mysteries, Dubin always enjoyed talking about them. Talk was a way of conjuring them up and bringing them close. He often thought of them without worrying about their fates, reflecting on the twists and turns their lives might take before they had settled into vocations—when one could see, if not a completely matured self, at least the self's direction. He wondered what they would ultimately want to work at, or work in. Maud was interested in many things, none strongly defined except her Spanish. Would she teach? Ask her what she hoped to do and she grew impatient. "I'll do something, don't worry. But don't expect me to get married after college or go to graduate school." "What shall I expect?" "Expect nothing and be surprised." Gerald, on the other hand, had always had strong specific interests—his math, astronomy, chess, music. Dubin could imagine him in a Swedish institute doing mathematical research. Or moved perhaps by some indefinable impulse, he might, like his father, become a physician.

They confided little and asked little, Dubin thought. I hoped they would want to know what I could tell them. I wish I had told them more about my life.

"Were we good parents or half-ass ones?" Kitty said. She asked it in a way that seemingly answered the question. She asked it often.

He thought they weren't bad parents but what seemed to count most was who parents were as people, not what they said they were. The more self-conscious or insistent or private they were, the quicker the kids made tracks into space.

"Who you are is the lesson they ingest, resist, live by."

"I can't do much about that," Kitty said, "but I do wish I had tried now and then to explain myself to them. I wanted to but couldn't freely. I hid my fears and they knew. But I love them and want their love. I know it's there, behind the clouds, but I'd like to feel it on me like the living sun."

"What's there will show as they come to terms with themselves."

"Let's not depend on them," Kitty said. "Let's depend on each other."

They went for a drive into the mountains that afternoon, Dubin driving. Fall was advanced there. Some branches of sugar maples had turned color from trunk to tip. In a few weeks trees would glow like jewels. He loved the softness, quietude, before the assault of color, the rage of winter. There were blue holes in the changing foliage—the sky flowing through trees. "Do you feel how sexy the mountains are as we drive through them?" Kitty asked. He said he knew what she meant. "Do you still think of me as sexy?" Dubin said she was.

That evening they had dinner at the Ondyks', with Oscar and Flora. Evan dug out his alto sax and played some songs of the forties. His eyes retained an almost expressionless quality—at most a fixed nostalgia—but the playing was lively. Kitty sang along with him. Then Oscar went to the piano and played Chopin for a while. He apologized for his piano playing. Flora, sitting close to Dubin, whispered she was sorry she hadn't brought her violin. "I sensed I'd want it with you here."

Kitty, when they arrived home, sat down at her harp and played intensely for ten minutes. In their bedroom she looked at herself in the mirror and said this had been one of their happiest days.

Dubin promised many more.

The biographer, while settling the business of his articles, had managed another short visit to Fanny at the end of August. He had registered at the Gansevoort and spent most of his time in her apartment. He would call the hotel for messages and telephone Kitty from a phone booth if she had called. She called once. Dubin and Fanny were immediately intimate. He was perhaps surprised at how quickly and comfortably they came together, as though he wasn't sure he had earned the privilege. He had and he hadn't, as when strangers become lovers they remain in part strangers. Or as when married men, having affairs with single women, expect less than total commitment. But Fanny had pronounced them lovers, and coming together in felt acceptance and desire was a happy circumstance. He enjoyed their familiar life together. They were friends, more to their relationship than sex; but happily there was sex. Dubin worried that he was seeing her so infrequently. How long would they go on being lovers if she had to wait for him to show up—with luck—once or twice a month? He knew she was seeing other men—how could he ask her not to? She had told him, "We go out but I honestly don't sleep with any of them. I pick guys who won't give me a hard time. One is almost your age, and reminds me of Harvey. I hope you don't mind? I also see women I know, one from work, if I feel lonely." Looking at him openly Fanny asked, "Do you believe me?"

Dubin said he did.

They squeezed hands and with serious faces kissed seriously.

She hesitantly showed him a term paper she had written for her government class and sat on the bed clipping her toenails as he read it.

Dubin told her it was informed and well written. Fanny respected facts and reasoned well. The term paper revealed qualities he had not often observed in her: of knowing more than she seemed to; of being organized as she thought things through. He said that to her.

"Are you surprised?"

"Only a little."

"Are you glad?"

He said he was.

"You like me to be a good student?"

"I like you to be a good whatever."

She laughed happily and offered to go to bed. When he asked her why, right then, Fanny said she felt sexy when he complimented her. They went out for dinner and for a while talked of courses she might take in the fall. She intended, she said, "really" "finally" to get her degree. Dubin ordered a bottle of champagne.

Champagne made her feel high, Fanny said. So did music, bright colors, a witty evening, a happy time. They hurried home; she loved hurrying home to make love. He did too. It was a good way to be.

Dubin left on Sunday morning, promising his earliest possible return, thankful she hadn't insisted on a secure date to write down.

"Let's say I'll be back the first chance I have, Fanny. It isn't always easy to get out but I'll manage."

"It's cool," Fanny said. She knew the game, the rules, the odds.

He traveled home thinking of her; putting her out of his mind when the train, its whistle like a sustained organ chord, approached the station where Kitty, sitting in her car, loyally awaited the bull's return. Dubin lifted his Panama, opened the car door; they kissed. As they drove home he had to restrain himself from talking about the girl, as if he were expecting his wife to appreciate Fanny's contribution to his well-being, good life. What "on balance" he owed his wife he would soon repay. He treated her tenderly.

These visits to Fanny sparked his work. Ideas swarmed in Dubin's mind. He was still writing of Lawrence and Frieda during their slow journey on the Continent after their elopement; their deepening love, celebrated in poems and letters written in Germany, Italy, Sicily, as they lived in a villino amid olive, almond, and lemon trees; or in a farmhouse on a mountainside.

> And at last I know my love for you is here;
> I can see it all, it is like twilight . . .
> Strange how we suffer in spite of this!

Dubin worked in the barn study, writing securely and rapidly. Kitty said she would rather he was in the house but would settle for a phone in the barn, "just in case."

"In case what?"

"In case I need you in a hurry. One never knows."

He had a telephone put in. She called rarely—once when the tree man wanted to see him: another elm was dying; once or twice when he had worked long past lunch and she was beginning to be worried.

He labored steadily. There were no serious distractions. Now and then he would put down his pen to pursue a thought of Fanny—usually to relive her looks or body; or simply enjoy the marvelous fact that William Dubin had, at his age, a vital vivid young friend. Sometimes he searched amid the papers in a folder on his desk for the picture she had recently given him—to contemplate Fanny. He kept it hidden in a box of photocopies of the Lawrence correspondence he had discovered in Eastwood, with her short affectionate letters beginning "Dearest William," and closing with four x's in place of love. Her handwriting slanted downward. A triangle of bare paper was left at the bottom. Dubin thought he could write a whole letter in it.

"When are you coming?" she wrote. "I am waiting in bed."

She mailed her typed letters without a return address, his name purposely mispelled; and varied the size and color of the envelope as if to indicate the letters were coming from different people in different places. Dubin remembered that Jonathan Swift had instructed Vanessa to have someone else address her letters to him; but the biographer wanted no part of that. He was surprised by Fanny's machinations; hadn't asked her to join the deceit; did not want to share it with her, nor be reminded or informed of her experience with other men.

"When are you coming? A lot is going to waste—I mean not using what you have is wasting it."

Once she wrote, "Suppose you got sick, how would I know? What could I do to see you? Sometimes I feel as though you aren't in my life."

He wrote her an affectionate letter. In it he said: "I'm happier now than I've been in years. There ought to be a way of having other selves to be with those we love."

Now was a new season, unfortunately without her. He would love to point out changes in nature, share them with her if only in Central Park; but he could not get off to the city. Kitty had insisted she'd go with him the next time round—they'd drive down together, as he had promised. She knew how thoroughly he had done his research; how trivial to voyage to New York to squeeze out a minor fact or two in the Public Library when there'd be many to check after he had completed a full draft. She knew he'd signed his contract for three long biographical articles. If he went to New York now it was mostly as a break; "for fun," Kitty said. She could use a little herself.

When she asked when he might be going he said he wasn't sure. She could go by herself if she liked—shop, visit friends, take in a play; but Kitty said she'd wait for him. It was more fun going together. Dubin waited: the work was flowing. And he was enjoying hoarfrost mornings before warm tangy autumn days; burning-leaf smell of trees yellowing in afternoon sun; a failing luminosity at twilight—most beautiful time of year. Melancholy too: signs of winter's fingers in woods and fields. Landscape as metaphor. Nature repeating the same old tale, usually with same effect; it plays in memory: what dies is present, what's present dies.

Although he missed Fanny he sometimes thought that so long as they cared for each other, admitted the reality and importance of their relationship, he did not always have to be with her. She was his in principle; he had somehow earned the privilege of her. The mild sadness that went with it—dominant emotion of his life, he often thought—touched but did not taint his desire for her. Unless it was the unyielding presence of Kitty in his thoughts that salted in the sadness.

Then Fanny drove up to Center Campobello one Saturday morning and called from her motel as he was working in the barn. There had been talk she might come up but Dubin had hoped he would be in the city before that.

"I'm here," she announced, "to see the color and whoever wants to see me." Her laughter was strained and he imagined her sober expression.

Dubin had called her at the beginning of the week to say once more why he was finding it hard to get away; told her Kitty had insisted on going with him. "I'll have to drive down once with her and not see you. After that I'll try to come back alone."

"But couldn't we see each other for an hour after I get home from work? It's better than not at all."

"I wouldn't want to leave you with the evening in your lap after we'd been to bed."

"Let's take what we can get, William," Fanny had said. "I feel very generous after I've been with someone who means a lot to me."

He had said he'd tell Kitty they'd be coming down next week.

But Fanny hadn't waited. She had felt like driving up, she said. "Can't we meet tonight? I'd love to eat with you, then come back here. I have a nice room in this motel. They have cotton sheets on the bed. Some private people own it. It even has curtains and white window shades. I'll bet you like it."

He said after a minute he would try to arrange it. "One way or the other. But I won't be able to see you tomorrow, Fanny. Don't plan on that. I'm usually home all day Sunday."

"Not even in the morning? I plan to leave by one o'clock. I'm having dinner with my friends in the Village who I told you about."

In the afternoon Dubin went for a drive and called Kitty to say the car had broken down. He was at a garage in Glens Falls and would have to wait until they got the part they needed from a neighboring town. "Don't wait for me. I'll pick up a sandwich across the street."

"I hate to eat alone," Kitty said.

Dubin felt shame; he said nothing.

"Maybe it's time to trade in this lousy car for a new one?"

He said they ought to consider it.

He met Fanny at the motel. They ate an early dinner in a nearby inn and returned to her room. She pulled down the shades and asked to be undressed. They made love impetuously, sensuously. She loved lavishly. He was excited by the aromas of her hair and flesh. She liked him to kiss the dark aureoles of her nipples. "William!" she cried as she came. Dubin fell through the sensuous sky into a mountain of leaves, bounced once, and fell peacefully asleep.

"Won't you see me for a little bit tomorrow?" Fanny asked. "Even an hour would be all right."

He promised he would.

She held up her hands to show him she was growing back her fingernails. He kissed both hands.

On Sunday Dubin rose early, left Kitty sleeping heavily and drove to the motel to have breakfast with Fanny. He had scribbled his wife a note saying he had written something that had come apart during the night and he had to puzzle out why. He was taking an early drive and would be back in time for lunch. He disliked what the note said but left it anyway.

After they had made love, as she was sitting cross-legged in bed, Fanny remarked, "I don't know exactly what we're doing, or what you're doing, but whatever it is hits me right. I felt this one today way up my ass."

"Bingo."

Fanny laughed. "We're good together."

"Is that what it is? Hasn't this happened to you before?"

"Not often. Only once or twice I can remember."

"I'm glad it happens when you're with me but I marvel a little."

"Maybe it's because of the way you want it. I dig the hungry way you go after me."

"You make me feel hungry. I have a long pleasure with you, on the edge of pain. Is it simply that we physically suit each other?"

"It has to be more than that," Fanny replied. "I think I come the way I do because I like myself better when I am with you."

Dubin kissed her knees.

"If we have it this good," Fanny said, "don't you think it's crazy not to see each other a lot more than we do?"

He said they would. She placed her warm palm on his.

He did not have to lie to Kitty when he arrived home shortly before noon. She hadn't seen the note and he tore it up. She had taken a sleeping pill in the middle of the night and was awakening as he came into the bedroom and raised the shades.

"Why didn't you wake me to eat with you?" Kitty said drowsily after glancing at the clock.

He said he had wanted her to sleep.

She shook him out of solid slumber. He woke with a long-drawn groan. She had had a mad dream—could not remember worse: She was a young woman with a baby in a crib. The crib was in flames. It had taken her an endless time to find the burning child's room. She had heard it shrieking and raced up the stairs. Kitty grabbed up the baby, its bedclothes afire, and ran to the bathroom to hold it in the shower, but the door was locked. William, let me in! She hastened from room to room, trying to find him, sick with fright. It occurred to her the child was Nathanael's and she ran to the telephone to call him but Nathanael was in his grave. Kitty had wakened, trying to remember whether she had fainted in the dream.

Dubin held her till she stopped shuddering.

He asked her what was worrying her.

"I don't know," Kitty said, "except a confusing lot of ongoing things. Neither of the kids is nearby or settled. I worry about them. I also worry about Vietnam. I hate the goddamn war. I think I will stop watching the news at night—those burning children running across the road. No wonder I have nightmares."

Dubin told Kitty in their austere high-ceilinged room at the Gansevoort that he would meet her for dinner at half past seven, or eight. Would she want to see a movie afterward?

"Make it half past seven," Kitty said, "I'm famished by eight. We'll see about the movie. We might want to do something else."

He told her he was having a drink with a biographer of Frieda Lawrence.

"Anyone I know?"

"Have you met Fritz Halsman?" He knew no Fritz Halsman and was surprised and irritated by the sincerity of his question.

"No. Why don't you invite him to dinner with us if he's free?"

"Maybe next time. He's not that interesting. I'm only checking a point with him."

Kitty was wearing a new fall dress with a cloche hat. She looked good in hats that framed the face. She had enjoyed the drive and said they ought to come into the city more often.

"Why bother living in the country?"

"New York was no decent place to bring up children. We both thought so years ago."

Dubin left quickly to say nothing else. When he lied he talked too much. In the cab he sat silent as the driver talked.

Dubin got to Fanny's as she was arriving in a taxi. They kissed in the street. "How much time do we have?" she asked.

"About two hours."

"Then we don't have to hurry."

She had her diaphragm on, had been wearing it since that morning. Upstairs she showed him a pair of lace-edged underpants she had bought during her lunch hour. "Let's get into bed," said Dubin. "I knew you'd like them," Fanny said.

Dubin was back at the hotel at 7:40, going on about the war ending soon. Then he warned himself to shut up. He had showered at Fanny's and was about to change his underwear when it occurred to him the shorts he kept in her dresser drawer were striped, whereas the pair he had been wearing were a solid blue. When he got back to the hotel he changed his underclothes and shirt in the bathroom to be sure Fanny's scent wasn't detectable on him. He used Kitty's soap.

Their dinner was excellent. He enjoyed his wife's wit and flushed good looks. She wanted to return to their room after dinner but he talked her into going to a movie that had just opened.

On their way home the next morning, Kitty driving, chatty, Dubin quiet, barely aware of scene or sight, he worried about the spreading dishonesty he was into. Awful, if you thought of yourself as an honest man. You spoke pebbles and pieces of metal and when you determined to say honest words you kept spitting out bits of brackish metal.

Since lying was beyond Kitty, or she beyond it, lying to her tainted his pleasure with Fanny, at least in afterthought. Kitty was trustworthy; Dubin hated to think he wasn't. Of course he could tell her the truth and hope for the best. Some men were able to inform their wives and still manage to carry on an affair. But Kitty wouldn't tolerate it; Dubin didn't see how they could go on living together if she knew. She wasn't constituted for an emotionally, not to say morally, ambiguous relationship. To protect her peace of mind he had to lie though he wanted to protect her from his lies. Nor did he intend, at least yet, to give up Fanny. At times he wondered if his deceit to Kitty might induce dishonesty in his work. The thought bothered him although he knew enough about the lives of writers to understand that even the morally deficient might write well. So he kept his sad secret, recalling that Freud had said no one could keep a secret forever. "If his lips are silent his fingertips give him away."

Yet he concealed his thoughts of Fanny; disguised details of other trips to the city; received letters from her in a post-office box he had recently rented. He called her once a week and she, him, more often, on his barn telephone; but there were times she would try to reach him in the house at night if she'd been unable to make a morning call. Dubin only rarely telephoned her at work. At night, if Kitty answered, Fanny hung up. Kitty reached for the phone when it rang. If he answered but couldn't speak to Fanny because his wife was there, Dubin hung up.

"Who was that, William?"

"Wrong number probably, somebody rang off."

"We've had a spate of hang-ups lately."

"They come and go. There seems to be a season for them."

He asked Fanny not to call him at home. "Then when can we talk?" she asked angrily. "If I can't get you in the barn in the morning because I am too busy to sneak in a call, that means I can't talk to you at all when I have something to tell you. I save most of my news to tell you. I'm taking environmental studies and psychology at N.Y.U. three nights a week. I wanted to talk about what I was writing in my psych paper and see if you like my ideas. I also think of us in bed. Do you suppose we could go to Europe again? I'm getting two weeks off this winter—they're not giving me a summer vacation, because I am new. But my boss says they like me and I make up time when I come in late. They like it that I'm going to school at night. I might get a raise the first of the year."

"Europe would be different this time," Dubin felt.

"If there hadn't been a last time there wouldn't be a this time," Fanny said.

He said he wasn't thinking of last time. "I was thinking we might go to Athens if I could come up with a good enough reason why, like maybe a cache of unpublished Lawrence letters had been discovered there—"

"Why don't you put your mind to it?"

He said he would think about it.

They arranged he would telephone her from the barn twice a week before she left for work, and she would not call him unless it was absolutely necessary.

When he phoned before eight she was usually alert, eager to talk, had much to say and said it warmly. Dubin would walk across the hoarfrost field to call her, then return for a second cup of coffee and to shave. He would afterward trot off to the barn to do his day's work. Fanny once in a while phoned in mid-morning to say a quick hello.

One early morning when he thought Kitty was sleeping, she was watching him cross the field to call Fanny, as a crow circled overhead cawing at him. At lunch she asked why he went to the barn so early, then returned to the house before going out again.

He said that if he first set up the day's work it made breakfast more serene.

Dubin groaned softly in her presence.

"What's up, William? Is something troubling you?"

He did not at once reply but, when he saw the worry in her eyes, shook his head, smiling, then dimmed the smile.

"I thought I heard you say 'deceit,'" she said.

"That was the word on my mind."

"Did Lawrence ever deceive Frieda?"

She often guessed where his thoughts were. Dubin told her that with Lawrence the deceit went the other way. "Frieda had deceived Weekley, her first husband, with at least two lovers. Lawrence she deceived mostly with Angelo Ravagli, their Italian landlord, who became her third husband. Once she traveled on the Continent with John Middleton Murry, but he said he turned her down because he didn't want to betray Lawrence. Some say they did sleep together. My own guess is they didn't while Lawrence was alive. I don't think Murry lied when he wrote he hadn't slept with her then because he didn't want to betray Lawrence."

"How complicated it is."

Dubin said it was.

"Do you think I might be deceiving you?" Kitty asked with a faint smile.

I wish you were, he thought.

Dubin was leaving, that end-of-October weekend, for New York, a year almost to the day when he and Fanny had flown to Venice.

"This is a quickie trip," he explained to Kitty. "I'll be gone Friday and part of Saturday. I should be back by early evening."

"Why can't I come?"

"I'll be going again in two or three weeks to attend other business. Come with me then, it'll be a longer weekend."

"Why are you going now?"

He said he wanted someone who knew wills to look at theirs and suggest changes. "We wrote it when the kids were young."

"Don't you remember enough law to read a will?"

"Not as much as you think."

"Why don't you do the will when you go next time? What's so important right now?"

"Offices are closed on Saturdays and Sundays. I can see someone late this afternoon."

"You could also telephone from here."

He didn't want to. "I've mailed the will out, a friend of mine has read it, I want to talk to him about changing it."

Her eyes were troubled. "Why are you suddenly concerned about a will? There's nothing wrong with you, is there?"

"No," Dubin said, sweating. "I happened to come across it in our safety deposit box and thought I ought to have it checked out. A legal instrument should be kept up to date."

She said talk of the will had worried her.

Dubin swore there was nothing wrong with him. He was irritated with himself for fabricating the will.

Ultimately he was able to lie with less guilt. He geared himself to it: had to protect his relationship with Fanny, at the same time not hurt Kitty. Still, he wouldn't eat his heart out over every fib he told. Not all evil is pure evil. Not all lies are forever.

When William Dubin returned from his youth-renewing short visit to Fanny, for which he blessed her, he felt a surge of love for his wife, followed by a saddening sense of loss—awareness of an illusion he seemed to favor: that as he fulfilled himself he did the same for Kitty. That was not true in any way. He had experienced pleasure he would like her to experience, dish her out a bit of pure lustful joy; but if another woman was the source of his pleasure—if you lived on her body—that diminished desire, affection—obligation—for the other, the wife. He continued to hide from Kitty his feeling for Fanny, his happy involvement with her; but it did not hide well. The Freudian fingertips showed: because of Fanny he was a different man, had grown new attributes, elements of a new self—how could you hide that? You pretended you were your old self, but the old self had changed. You pretended it hadn't, adding to pretense.

Kitty, he knew, sensed something. She had embraced him on his return almost with compassion, as if he had come back with a wound and only she knew it. She asked him again if he was well. Dubin said that next time a will or something of the sort came up he'd take care of it without mentioning it to her.

"No," she said, "you must tell me."

Nothing was wrong with him, Dubin insisted. "Don't worry about what doesn't exist."

"I won't if you promise not to hide from me what does." She laughed breathlessly, her eyes not looking at him. If she believed him with reservation, what, Dubin wondered, did she not believe?

Had she sensed some sort of withdrawal from her? Something more serious—of another kind than had happened last winter? It was months since Fanny and he had become lovers; doesn't an experience of love produce a newly experiencing self? All the exciting new sex diminishing the less exciting sex, the lesser pleasure? Something added, therefore something elsewhere subtracted? Kitty and her husband lived as married, but Fanny had joined the merry company. Dubin has two wives? Here's Kitty gazing out of a window reflecting herself, and beholds, in the wood in the distance, the shadow of a presence; aware of something not fearsome but a source of fear? Dubin, staring through the same glass, sees himself in view, Fanny, in white, standing dimly by his side, all but invisible. He searches the glass, amidst images of leafy trees and darkening shallow clouds, for Kitty, expecting her to be reflected nearby; but she stands alone, amid tall trees, in the deeper distance. What it amounts to, the biographer thinks, is that one may be able to mask dishonesty but not its effects: the diminution of libido, ebb of feeling for a woman, love for her. Deceit distances. He dreamed of Kitty pacing the black-railed widow's walk on the roof.

Dubin had caught a cold that became heavy bronchitis and he could not get to the city in mid-November. He called Fanny very early one morning, as Kitty slept, to say he couldn't possibly be going down this week. Fanny said she would drive to Center Campobello, but Dubin in his laryngitic voice told her he was reasonably sure he could make it to her after another week. Kitty then caught Dubin's cold, and since the trip was promised to her, he felt he oughtn't to go alone this time. It snowed a few days before Thanksgiving, a light snow that melted in a day as though a dropped handkerchief had been snatched up. Fanny urged Dubin to come by himself—he had a perfect excuse with Kitty ill; but he said it was getting more difficult to lie his way into the city so often.

"What's so often about coming here a month ago? I thought you had the excuse of talking to a lawyer about something?"

He said it wasn't a good one. "And it isn't like me to take off for New York in winter weather to talk to a lawyer when the woods are full of them here. I don't travel much in wintertime."

"Wouldn't it be groovy if we could fuck by phone," she said bitterly.

Dubin was silent.

"What I mean," Fanny said after a moment, "is I miss you. When I get lonely I feel like crawling up a wall. If you can't come here, William, I'll zip up there. I bought snow tires and I'd like to come up this next weekend."

"There's at least one dinner date this weekend. Could you make it the one after?"

"Are you sure you really want me to come? Sometimes I have the feeling you don't care all that much."

"You'd be wrong," he said.

"I'm ready to drive up any weekend if you can't come to me. If we don't get together one way we have to another or what's our life all about?"

"The experience of the absent loved one has inspired some beautiful poetry."

"I don't write poetry, I never could."

"Let's try to be together every third weekend or so, though please keep in mind I have no good reason suddenly to be out alone any given night of any particular weekend, let alone two nights in a row. It's not usual."

"I think you have a damn good reason."

"I know I have, but unfortunately not one I can give my wife."

"Unfortunately, old boy."

"I don't want to hurt anyone, little girl."

"I'm not your little girl and you are hurting me."

"I don't want to hurt you, Fanny."

"Other men get out from under their wives—why can't you?"

Dubin explained that he'd worked home for years. "It's hard to find excuses to get out alone when circumstances change. Though in a way it's mad, Fanny, what it amounts to is that one works in a room with the door shut and everyone knows where he is and expects him to be there for all time. Between biographies I am freer."

Fanny's tone softened. "Couldn't you please try to come here? You said your wife's cold is about gone. I'd rather have you come here than go to that lousy motel."

"I thought you liked it?"

"I like it when you're in my apartment with me—in my bed. I like to share my home with you as well as my ass. Why don't you move to New York so we can see each other easier and more often?"

"I've thought about it but it's not feasible right now. Kitty dislikes the city."

"Why don't you do what *you* want?"

"Some things you want to do you don't."

"I wouldn't live that way."

But she called him in the barn the next morning to tell him, happily, that she had got a week of her vacation shifted from January to December and had decided to spend the time in Center Campobello. "Can you swing that in mid-week for a day or two or three—not next week but the one after?"

"Make it for the one after," Dubin said. "We'll see each other as often as we can but I imagine you realize we won't be able to meet every day while you're here? I hope you'll be understanding and flexible about that."

"We could also meet in the afternoon. We can go on your walk together. I'd meet you at the bridge and we could walk together most of the way."

He said he would enjoy that. "But what about seeing each other intimately?"

"Couldn't I stay in your barn with you—not when you're working but at least part of the time?"

Dubin was about to tell her he couldn't risk it, then felt a frustrating sense of confinement; how tightly fenced in he was; could go nowhere without informing someone.

"Let's try," he said. "I've got a sofa convertible to a bed in my study. But we'll have to be very careful."

She promised she would be.

In the week she was in town Fanny and Dubin spent more time together than he would have predicted. She registered at the motel but at night would leave her car on the road to the old Wilson farm by Kitty's Wood. After Dubin had walked the snowy path with her once, she would go along it alone with a flashlight, to the field where the barn stood. He left the study heated for her and she waited till he had trudged back from the house after supper. They were happy to see each other. In dungarees, flannel shirt, boots, she looked like another Fanny, a young woman he had just met he was about to fall in love with. She grasped his hands; they kissed, fumbled with each other's clothes.

Fanny said she enjoyed the adventure of going through the wood, of being with him here. It didn't bother her to be near his wife in the house, although it worried Dubin. To get out tonight, he told Kitty he had reached a crucial point in the biography—he went into a discourse of how bad the marriage of Frieda and Lawrence was when they were fighting about her desire to see her three children. Lawrence jealously wanted her not to see them. They quarreled, were murderous to each other. Frieda broke a plate over his head. Lawrence smashed one phonograph record after another on hers. Dubin said it would be helpful if he could put in a few nights of steady work and knock off this chapter—write four or five pages a day instead of the usual two or two and a half.

"You're crazy," said Kitty, "to work all morning, then work again at night."

"Just this week—less than a week. I've done it before."

"But not every night. Please—it's mad."

"Why don't you pick a couple of nights for whatever you want me to do with you and leave the rest for me?"

"Have some nights," Kitty said. "I'm Queen of the Night and dispense them like peanuts."

"Don't get sore."

"Why don't you at least work in the house?"

He said she knew why: everything was in the barn—his books and notes.

Afterward Kitty quietly said she was sure she could find something to do with herself and Dubin thanked her.

He felt more daring than he'd been in years. One had to be daring before it was too late. He was almost fifty-eight hurrying toward sixty. Every year was a cheat, piling up age, reducing vitality. Still, he felt youthful and was sorry Kitty did not.

After Fanny and he had made love and had listened, as they lay warmly in bed, to music on her portable radio, or talked of their lives, she dressed and went through the woods to her car. Fanny said the woods scared her but she wouldn't let Dubin accompany her to the road.

"It's easier to spot two people than one."

"Nobody can see us walking through the woods from the house," Dubin said. "From the bedroom one can barely see the barn and not much of the woods. From Maud's room and my study you can see more."

"Can she see me leave the barn?"

"Not if you go out the study door. Certainly not in the dark."

"Let's don't take the chance," Fanny said.

After she had gone Dubin removed the bedsheet and reassembled the sofa. He looked for articles of dress or jewelry Fanny might have left behind, discovered her comb, hid it, and went back to the house. Before getting into bed with his wife he took a shower. Dubin lay up against Kitty's warm body, his arm over her hip, her back to him.

"What time is it?" she yawned.

"Toward midnight."

"Are you smiling?"

"No."

"I thought I could feel you smile on my shoulder. How did the work go?"

"Fine."

"Why do you shower every night?"

"It relaxes me."

"Do you want to make love?"

"Do you?"

"I will if you want to."

"No."

"You're not depressed?"

"No."

She fell asleep. In a few hours she would wake, counting the failures of her life. Holding her, Dubin slept. He felt her waken but slept on.

Fanny had arrived on Monday. He did not see her Tuesday but they talked on the phone. On Wednesday night Kitty went with Marisa Ondyk to a high school chorale, and Dubin met Fanny at the motel. They had drinks and later went through the wood to the barn and set up the sofa bed.

"Do you love me?" Fanny asked.

"You know I do."

"Why don't you say it?"

"Because you know."

"I like you to say it," Fanny said.

Dubin promised he would.

"Why do you love me?"

"Because you're a lovely lay."

"Is that all?"

"Because I love you."

"Why?"

"Because you're Fanny, named out of Jane Austen. Because of your affectionate nature. Because you want to make something of your life."

"You make me want to, William. You make me take myself seriously."

He said that was good.

"We are good together," she sighed. "Don't you think so?"

He said he did.

"But I'm not living my life to learn lessons," Fanny said. "Most of all I want to enjoy it."

He wanted her to.

"What are you thinking about?"

"You."

"Doing what?"

"Enjoying your life."

"Are you enjoying it with me?"

"All the way."

It was snowing heavily and when Dubin saw it come down he was concerned about her driving in the snow at night. He asked her to sleep in his study and leave early in the morning. "You ought to leave before seven. I'll drive around to the road and shovel you out if you're blocked in by snow after the road's been plowed."

"I can shovel myself out, I'm strong."

"Have you got a shovel?"

Fanny laughed to herself. "I'll bring one next time."

"I'll shovel you out at seven if you're blocked in."

Dubin slept badly. He worried about her but when he got up at six the next morning he saw through the bathroom window that the snow had stopped. Later he found Fanny's path from the barn and ran in it to the edge of the wood, kicking up her tracks in the snow. On the road her car was gone.

On Thursday it was snowing as they lay in the sofa bed. Lorenzo was with them. Dubin had him in the barn because some field mice had chewed up several of his note cards. Lorenzo lay on the bed, noisily licking himself. Fanny said she was leaving Saturday morning. He wasn't sure he could see her on Friday night but they would meet in the city in two or three weeks.

Their relationship had deepened. Each probed the other's needs. What he desired she gave him; she got what she seemed to want. After they had made love Fanny got out of bed and went naked to the sink. She drank a glass of water and brought him one.

"What for?"

"To drink, lover. Aren't you thirsty?"

" 'Lover' is an old-fashioned way of addressing a lover."

"In certain ways I am old-fashioned. Do you want the water?"

Dubin drank it. Neither Kitty nor he brought each other water after sex; he got her a tissue. Kitty took a hot shower; Fanny drank a glass of water and used the wet corner of a towel to wash herself.

In the dark he thought of her as his wife. They'd live in New York. He would work in their apartment while she attended school. She could prepare for serious work of some sort once she knew what interested her. Maybe she could do something part-time if they were married. She could have kids if she wanted; he imagined she would. She had said she would in one of her letters. It might be hectic but she was a young woman and he would help where he could. Dubin wouldn't mind having young children again. He thought he'd be better with them than he'd been the first time. Children were strangers you loved because you could love. If they gave back love when they were grown you were ahead of the game. You had had them because you thought you could love. He felt Fanny would be happy with him, as happy as a second wife might be with a husband thirty-five years older than she. He would value her as she ought to value herself, perhaps help her unravel some of the distortions of her life. He imagined what she would look like at thirty, when he was sixty-five. Dubin liked what he imagined.

Lives ought to begin again around fifty, he thought. Middle age can stand new enterprises, new beginnings. Some marriages go on too long. If they ended by mutual consent after twenty-five years, or when the kids left the house, that might be refreshing for both partners. Getting into the world again to find out what was going on might do them good. Maybe Kitty would worry less about herself if she had to work; would sleep better; think less of illness, the garbage of the past. She'd get the house, of course. Fanny and he could live in Europe for the first year—maybe to try out living together. That might ease the transition into a new life for them all.

"What are you thinking about, William?"

"You are a loving friend."

"We are more than friends now."

"We are also good friends," Dubin said.

"We really could be," said Fanny.

"I thought we were?"

"If we were living together. I liked coming home from work and you were there."

"We can't now, I'm married."

She said after a minute, "Suppose you weren't any more?"

"But I am," Dubin said.

Fanny got up for a glass of water and did not bring him one.

He asked if she would care to see him tomorrow night.

"I thought you didn't think we ought to meet Friday?"

Dubin said he had changed his mind. "We can be together without going to bed."

After a few minutes Fanny asked, "Should we have another lay before I go?"

He didn't think so. Dubin kissed her mouth and she kissed his, then his eyes, and then again kissed his mouth.

Friday was a clear cold night. As they were comfortably together in bed Dubin got up to go to the toilet. Standing there, he saw through the freezing window a flicker of light amid the silver maples and watched with concern. The light disappeared at intervals and grew brighter as it moved in his direction.

"She's coming," he called hoarsely to Fanny. "Grab your clothes—everything—get into the barn."

Fanny leaped out of bed, hastily gathered her clothes, boots, and portable radio, then hurried naked into the barn.

Dubin had his trousers and shirt on. He stepped into loafers, pulled the sheet off the bed, threw it into the barn after Fanny, slammed the door shut, and closed the sofa bed. He saw her sweater on his worktable and tossed it behind some file boxes on one of the bookshelves.

"William?" Kitty knocked on the door.

"Yes?"

"It's me. Can I come in?"

He took his time getting to the door to unlatch it.

"The furnace has pooped out," Kitty said, stepping into the study. "I was reading in bed, wondering if you'd ever come home and felt myself getting awfully chilly. When I looked at the thermostat it was fifty so I came to tell you."

"Did you call the furnace guy?"

"He comes faster for you."

"You could have phoned me from the house and not frozen your ass coming here in this cold."

Kitty looked around the room. She was wearing a heavy cloth coat, boots, and Dubin's red wool hat.

"Was your light out for a while? I was in Maud's room and could see no reflection of light in the snow."

"I had a headache and was resting my eyes in the dark."

"Why didn't you quit, for Pete's sake? It's mad to work as much as you've been this week."

"I've got only one paragraph to recopy."

"Can't it wait till tomorrow?"

"I want to get it done."

"What's that strange odor in here?" Kitty asked, breathing in, exhaling.

"I passed gas."

"It's not that."

"I smoked a cigarillo."

"It's not that either. The room smells sexy."

"I was thinking of Faye Dunaway. I was also thinking of Marilyn Monroe."

"Don't take your headache out on me, William," Kitty said. "It's your own bloody fault."

He said he was being funny.

The cat meowed in the barn.

"Is Lorenzo hungry?"

"I fed him."

Lorenzo meowed as though wailing.

Kitty pulled the door open and shone her flashlight in the dark.

"What's that sheet doing on the floor?"

Dubin tried to think but couldn't. He was watching Kitty's light move along the sidewall of the barn to the bolted double doors. She then shone the light on the clutter of garden tools, furniture she had discarded, tractor-mower, bags of peat moss. "Was that something moving?"

He didn't think so. "Lorenzo's been sleeping on the sheet. It needs washing. I was going to bring it home."

Lorenzo, eyes glowing, came running in the light. If he says anything, the biographer thought, I'll bash his head in.

"What's the matter with him?" Kitty asked.

"He wants company, he's tired of mice."

Dubin had picked up the phone and was dialing. He told the repairman his furnace had gone on the blink and he was afraid the house pipes would freeze if something wasn't done quickly. The man reluctantly said he would come over.

"He'll be over in ten minutes," Dubin told Kitty. "Please let him in. I'll knock off my last paragraph and go home."

"I'd still like to know what the smell in this room is."

"You know them all," he said.

"You're not exactly endearing tonight."

Dubin rubbed his eyes.

Kitty left the barn, slamming the door.

Through the toilet window he watched her going back in the snow until the light disappeared. He wondered if she had noticed Fanny's boot tracks.

Then he sat down on the sofa, sickened. He felt cold.

Fanny came into the room with her dungarees and bra on. She was barefoot and cold, her face without color.

"I was scared shitless," she said. "I thought I had broken my ankle. It hit something and hurt like hell."

He inspected her bruised blue ankle. "Does it still hurt?"

"It feels as if someone drove a nail into it."

Dubin said he was sorry. He still felt nauseated, half frozen.

"I don't want to have to do anything like that again, William," Fanny said. "I don't want to have to hide from her. Next time I swear I won't. I mean it, William."

"There won't be a next time," Dubin said.

"I won't hide from her again," Fanny said, her eyes taut.

He said he would see her in the city.

One Sunday Kitty rose early, dark-eyed and tight-lipped. She stretched her arms limply. When she had left the bed she removed her nightgown, slowly scratched her blemished buttock.

At breakfast he noticed her lusterless eyes and formal anxious altered voice. Her tight control tightened him. Kitty mulled over things till she had something: she put two and two together and usually came close to four. Had she now come up with Fanny in his life?

He asked if she had had a bad dream.

Kitty was gazing at the fried egg on her plate. She'd hardly touched breakfast. They were at the table together but she sat at the table alone.

Dubin spoke soberly: "Why don't you tell me what's bothering you?"

She said she hated to. "I really do."

"Then it's something physical?"

She looked at her plate. "I'm sure you'll say it's nothing."

"You think it's cancer?" he asked, beginning to eat his fried egg.

Kitty told him her left nipple had altered in size and she had found a mucus stain in her brassiere.

"Do you think it's cancer?"

"It could be," she said unhappily.

"What else could it be?" Dubin dipped his bread into the egg yolk.

"I don't know. For God's sake don't start preaching at me. I hate it when you righteously preach." She was frightfully tight.

He changed his tone. "Have you felt a lump?"

"No," she said tensely.

"Is the breast sore?"

She nodded, not crying, though her eyes were moist.

He sipped his coffee. Dubin then put his cup down and got up and kissed her. He said he was sure it wasn't cancer.

She studied his face to see if he thought otherwise. "What makes you say so?"

"No lumps." He said she ought to see the doctor anyway. "Once you're on a cancer kick, it's wise to."

Kitty said she would, then confessed that even the thought of a mammogram frightened her.

"I'll go with you," he said.

"No, I'll go alone," Kitty said. "I always have."

On Tuesday she visited the surgeon in Center Campobello, who said it was not cancer. He said it was a papilloma, a nodule he located close to the surface of the breast near the nipple.

Kitty afterward told Dubin that the surgeon had said a papilloma was usually benign and he thought he could treat it in his office. A week later—she had been calm since seeing him—he made the incision. After a biopsy, which revealed no sign of malignancy, Kitty gave out a sob of relief. Later she bought a new dress. Arriving home, she embraced Dubin and said she loved him very much. She moved gingerly but freely, as though she was free of dread yet was worried for having once more tried her fate. How many more times could she do it and still escape cancer?

Dubin, as he combed his hair before the mirror, said he was glad it had come to nothing.

"It wasn't exactly nothing," Kitty said. "He removed a nodule that was blocking the duct. That wasn't nothing, and it wasn't my imagination."

He admitted it.

"You look critical?"

"I'm not but it wasn't cancer. The average is still in your favor."

"I'll bet you weren't in the least worried," Kitty said, brushing her eyelids with a tissue. "You didn't seem to be. I'll bet you were thinking about your friend Lawrence and the mystique of the female breast in Indian cow worship. Or maybe you were thinking of Lady Chatterley's handsome ass and well-shaped healthy teats."

He'd been thinking mostly of Fanny.

"That was your sixth or seventh cancer scare since I've known you," Dubin said. "I expected nothing serious."

"My mother had cancer. You may be wrong someday."

He said he hoped he wouldn't be.

Kitty that night suggested making love "in celebration," and he offered the next night, said he was worn out.

"My problems?"

"Mine."

In the morning she seemed distant to him. He felt distant from her. It seemed to Dubin he felt more affection for her when Fanny was around. When she was, Kitty was often in his thoughts, tenderly at times.

With Fanny gone he was constantly thinking of her. That he was working well was not surprising because his mood was good. He lived much in his thoughts of his developing work and in long reveries of Fanny. Dubin invented and discarded reasons to take off for New York. It irritated him that he had to go through so much fantasy to experience the girl.

The next night he made love to his wife. She hadn't wanted to, but responded to his impulse. He was careful not to touch her healing breast. To heighten their pleasure Dubin tried one of the things Fanny had taught him.

"Where did you pick that up?" Kitty wanted to know.

"Do you like it?"

"I'm not sure. I think so."

"Do you object?"

"No."

Afterward she asked, "Where did you pick up that little adventurous bit you tried tonight?"

"From a book I read."

"What made you read that kind of book?"

He was about to say he was human. Dubin said, "To bring something new to our sex lives."

"Do you have any complaints about me?" Kitty asked.

He said he hadn't.

"I'll bet you do. Nathanael thought I was pretty good in bed. He thought me a passionate woman. I *am* passionate."

"One responds differently to different people," Dubin said. "He was your first husband. I'm your second and for too long I was your step-husband."

"If you say 'step-husband' again I swear I'll leave you." Her voice quavered with anger.

He pictured her leaving; probably she would ask him to leave.

The next day Kitty, as she was dressing, quietly asked Dubin if he wanted a divorce. "I don't think you want or need me any more. I sense it. If something has gone wrong why don't you tell me? Have you met someone you'd rather be with?"

Dubin said he hadn't.

"Is that girl you went to Venice with still around?"

He said she wasn't.

"Who was she?"

He would rather not say.

"Do I know her?"

He would rather not say.

"Then I do and she's around," said Kitty.

"I sleep with her twice a day."

"Then what *is* the matter with you. What's made you so unresponsive these last few months? Are we about to go through another awful winter? Why has my husband become my second cousin once removed? Removed is the word. We never talk any more. I don't really know what's happening to you. Tell me what's happening to you? Have you been sleeping with Flora?"

He said that had happened once.

"Then what's eating you, for Christ's sake?"

"Maybe it's marriage. Sometimes I feel boxed in, unfree."

"Boxed in, how?"

"A long marriage gets hard to take. You must feel it yourself."

He was thinking of her sameness, dissatisfactions, eccentricities. He was bored with her fears, her unforgotten unforgettable past.

"What do you mean 'unfree'?—unfree for what?"

"To forget for ten minutes that I'm married."

"That sounds like more than a whim. You must have a reason to want to feel unmarried. What is your need?"

Dubin didn't say.

"Wouldn't a divorce make you feel happier, freer?"

"No," he said, but his heart was gladdened by the thought.

Kitty criticized his nature—Dubin's sobriety, sameness, inability to enjoy life. She said she enjoyed life. "Until we met, you lived on romantic dreams, on nothing really. Now your devotion is work. Your work is all you think of and then you complain you aren't free."

Kitty spoke bitterly, her hands nervously in motion. She had slept with a bracelet on he had once given her. She had dressed and looked good though her eyes were angry.

Dubin, raising his voice, accused her of having depreciated his love for her. "You weren't satisfied with what I had to give—what I gave you. You had to define it to death. The day we were married you began to educate me. You defined love. You defined marriage. You insisted on telling me what I was giving and what I wasn't. I gave with feeling and you gave it a name."

"I wanted it to be a strong enduring love, in and of this world. I had experienced a strong loving love. I wanted what I needed. I had to tell you."

"Love was love to me. It needed not defining but nurturing. It wanted a life of its own. It didn't need Nathanael for company or comparison, or you dissecting it."

He wasn't certain what he was saying, that he was telling the truth about the past. He was trying to but it seemed, in their quarrel, impossible to recall exactly; to say what had truly happened to them. Or exactly what was happening now. How can you define the truth if you can't tell it? How can you tell the truth if you begin with lies?

Kitty said, "I wasn't doubting you—for the sake of doubt—or comparing your love to Nathanael's. I was trying to understand your feelings, your nature, my own. I wanted deep whole lasting love. I can't keep myself from analyzing or defining. I am not Frieda Lawrence. I am not your earth mother."

She wept copiously, in a low wail. "You'll leave me, I know in my heart."

Dubin told her not to cry. He racked his brain thinking how not to fail her yet go on with Fanny.

Then he put his arms around Kitty. "Let's get into bed."

She raised her tear-stained face. "Why?"

"I want you."

"I just got dressed." She slowly removed her clothes. He tried not to notice her aging body, tried not to think of Fanny's youth.

In bed Dubin's flesh failed him. He was unable to perform. He lay back frustrated, told himself not to be alarmed.

Kitty, lying on her pillow, wondered if it was her fault. "I mean maybe all this talk of divorce upset you?"

He said it wasn't her fault, yet hoped it was.

"These things happen. Don't be upset."

"It hadn't happened to me before."

"It's an incident, it's not for all time."

He said he hoped not; he was too young for that. "Lawrence was impotent at forty-two, but he was a sick man."

"Don't think of it."

Afterward Kitty told him she'd been seeing Evan Ondyk again, and Dubin was sorry for her and for himself.

"I was thinking of going away for a while," she said. "Maybe for a week—at the most, two. I'll go see Gerald in Stockholm."

He thought it would be a good thing for her to do. "I should be myself when you get back."

"Don't worry about it," Kitty said calmly. "You've been ever so much better than Nathanael that way. It started with him around thirty-eight, yet on the whole he functioned well."

Dubin said he wasn't worried.

The cold rose in an almost invisible haze from the icy ridged road. The low still polar sky was white as far as he could see. A light snow had struck the hills and whitened the surrounding fields. Nature shrouded, playing dead. Dubin, as he walked, lived in his frozen thoughts. Was that Oscar Greenfeld ahead, plodding past the abandoned farmhouse down the road? The biographer walked on, heavily clothed, not attempting to catch up with the flutist. Dubin wore two scarves, his tan-and-black over a thick black scarf, waffle stompers, earmuffs under his red wool hat.

He tried to think what he'd been thinking of but now and then his thoughts froze. The shrunken afternoon was already into dusk on this Saturday in a below-zero January. Dubin was fifty-eight. That was not Oscar ahead, no wooden flute he held in his hand. It was a man with a double-barreled shotgun resting on his forearm as he trudged on in the dusk. He wore a plaid hunter's cap, heavy sweater, sealskin Eskimo boots. Dubin lingered to see what he shot at from the road but the hunter, from time to time stopping to survey the field, shot at nothing.

The biographer made up his mind to pass quickly and the hunter let him hurry by. A minute later he called his name: "Mr. Dubin?"

It was Roger Foster.

They walked together, Dubin at a loss for something to say. Roger embarrassed him.

"What's the gun for?" he finally asked. "I thought the hunting season was over?"

"Not much really, Mr. Dubin," Roger said. "I thought I'd like to take a potshot at a rabbit or two but haven't laid eyes on one. You can hardly see them this time of the year but sometimes you can spot a cottontail against a tree or rock. No harm done because I generally miss when I shoot. My heart's not in it. I guess I went out with Dad's gun because I felt sort of down. Thought I'd stir up a little excitement for myself but haven't so far."

Dubin grunted.

Neither spoke as they walked on, then Roger said in a tone of regret, "I don't guess you like me all that well, Mr. Dubin. I really don't know why. I grant you're a good biographer, but so far as understanding live people, I honestly don't think you know the kind of man I am."

Dubin nodded. Who knows the passing stranger, or the stranger you pass, he thought, even if your wife in a desperate moment aberrantly falls for him.

"I'll bet you still think of me as a sort of stud because I had that reputation in my early twenties, though I am honestly not that way now. Give me credit for growing up—people do."

"Roger," Dubin said, "I admit I don't know you very well although every so often you unexpectedly enter my life. I have no plans for you to be in it, but now and then you suddenly are—as though you'd stepped out of the pages of Dostoyevsky and begun tracking me. I've come across this fateful phenomenon more often than one would think in biographies I've read or written. Somebody looks around and there's this guy tailing him, for good or ill. I suppose it's different when it's a woman—it's as if you'd been expecting her. Anyway, when you least anticipate or want it, a stranger appears, generally an unlikely person, who for one or another reason attempts to define himself to you, and against every expectation, not to mention your resistance, insists on assuming a role in your life. I have no idea what yours is in mine, but I don't want you to feel I am antagonistic to you in principle or that I am angry about something I am not at all angry about. The older I get, the less I hold people's pasts or past relationships against them—or, for that matter, against myself."

"To tell the honest truth," Roger said, "I made no reference to anybody but myself, but since you might be thinking about the time Mrs. Dubin, who I happen to greatly respect, was working in the library, all I want to say is that if there's anybody I was interested in, and still am, it's Fanny Bick."

Dubin blew on his icy gloved hands, his breath pure white. How much does he know? He thought: I will tell him nothing.

"The fact of it is, Mr. Dubin, I happen to love Fanny and hope to marry her someday."

"Ah?" said Dubin. "And does she hope to marry you?"

Roger laughed throatily, wryly, his moody eyes drawn to the white field. "I've asked her at least four times, including when she was visiting here in December, but she told me she was interested in somebody else, and though she honestly didn't mention your name, the message I got was whoever he was is you."

Dubin did not for a minute speak. "What makes you think so?"

"I know Fanny admires your biographies and yourself. Also I sort of know that you helped her put herself together after she had a shaky time in Europe last year. She has a different emphasis than since I first met her. She's a lot more serious about herself in a way she didn't use to be. I also know you have this mutual friendship that means a lot to her."

"Did she tell you that?"

"Not in so many black-and-white words but it's what I guess. At first I thought it might be something sort of non-sexual, only now I don't think that any more, if you don't mind me saying so, Mr. Dubin. I don't think of you as that kind of a person."

"What kind of person am I?"

"I wish I really knew."

"What do you want from me, Roger?"

They had stopped walking. Each peered into the other's face.

"I admit you've been helpful in advising Fanny, but otherwise the fact is you're married, Mr. Dubin, with two grownup kids and a wife who happens to need you," Roger said, looking down at Dubin's galoshes. "What's more, you're a good thirty or more years older than Fanny. When we first met she liked me an awful lot, and I honestly and sincerely think she still has a real affection left that might get to be permanent under different circumstances. I figure if you weren't around I might stand a good chance to marry her, although I also admit she has this affinity for older men. Mr. Dubin, I'm speaking to you as if I were your own son—I'm not proud. I thought I would respectfully tell you how I feel about her, hoping you might make some decision that would give me a fair shake, or at least a halfway decent chance in the future."

"To marry her?"

"To marry her if I could—if she wants to get married. Not everybody does nowadays, though I and both my sisters honestly do. What I'm trying to say to you is I love Fanny very much." His voice shook.

"So do I."

Roger, to Dubin's embarrassed surprise, sank down on one knee in an awkward gesture of supplication, or despair. In his left hand he still held his shotgun.

Dubin walked on, then broke into a trot.

He hadn't seen Fanny in weeks, felt inertia, lassitude, stasis, wanted not to see her. Was he therefore feeling less for the girl?

Less what? He had got used to her, knew her too well? Some of the excitement, the surprise, was gone? Only her presence, in truth, surprised and she was not present. Though Kitty and he had resolved his temporary mishap and were again comfortable in bed, Dubin felt he wasn't that much interested in the sexual life. She had postponed going away because of him. She didn't seem to understand how much he wanted to be alone, left alone; he wanted to be, at least for now, without challenge to emotion, attention, thought; if possible, also, without desire. Who needs that forever goad? Fanny seriously complicated his life. Having one major problem was enough for him—the Lawrence biography. That continued to go well: at times it carried Dubin aloft as if he were in a balloon with a spy glass surveying the floating earth. It was the "complication"—the task he wanted most to be concerned with. Gerry and Maud were an ongoing other; he was used to their problems, and to Kitty's tangled skein. But Fanny was a complication coming on too fast and strong. She was, in his life, unique; still he didn't want her pressing him to go abroad with her, urging him to move to New York; he didn't want her suggesting they live together, implying divorce. It was all right for Kitty to bring up divorce but not Fanny.

Was what he felt for Fanny love? It wasn't the way he had felt toward women in his youth. Do men of more than fifty love less keenly than young men? He thought the opposite was true: the years deepened the need, the force, the channel of love. At fifty there had to be more at stake: love as a breakwater against age, loss of vital energy, the approach of death. Dubin enjoyed the girl's feeling for him but how much was he offering in return? Obviously not too much at the moment although they shared a real enough friendship. He sometimes felt as if he was waiting for her to say it didn't seem to be working and why didn't they simply call it quits? There were moments when he thought breaking it up now might be a relief—a lot less to worry about; he'd be freer to concentrate on his work. Maybe she was expecting him to make a decision—more Fanny, less Kitty; or vice versa; or simply no Fanny at all? There was a real problem, did he have a real choice?

She hadn't telephoned lately, nor he her. He thought she might still be annoyed by the barn incident with Kitty though her two or three short letters hadn't mentioned it. He had more than once expressed regret. Her letters outlined what she was doing, reading, experiencing; they made no request nor persuasion. She was, she said, "tired," but not of what. What good am I for her? the biographer asked himself. Her letters were contained, muted, saying nothing very personal. She did not say, lately, that she loved him. He wrote innocuous replies. Let's be friends, Dubin thought, and from time to time, lovers. That would diminish complication and make life easier to manage. He never broached this to her. Lawrence had distastefully spoken of "merely companionate sex."

But with the change of season Dubin was glad he had made no serious negative statement to Fanny. Winter broke, retreated, cold waning although greedily lingering; spring was immanent—tied hand and foot but softly exhaling its herbal breath; mysteriously freed, spying out—stalking—the land as well as memory. Spring lights spring within. My spring gives birth to yours—to you. The girl blossomed, bloomed, in his thoughts. Dear God, what have I done? Why have I allowed myself to doubt my true feeling for her? He missed her company, easy laughter, warmth, intimate voice—whatever it said was intimate—her touch, vibrance, their acceptance and enjoyment of each other. He missed her desire, giving, the flower of their embrace in bed. He thought of her, trying not to, between stitches of biographical sentences; on his long and short walks; as he lay in bed with his wife. He thought of their best times, joyfully together. He wanted, he spoke it aloud, to be with her; but heard no sound. He did not visit her in the city; she did not come to him, one way or another, in Center Campobello.

As the season advanced Dubin grew restless, irritable; life was unchanged, confined, reduced. He tried unsuccessfully to hide his mood from Kitty. "You aren't with me," she chided him; "you are elsewhere. Where are you?" He didn't say; flipped his fingers as if there was no answer, why ask? He wanted her to sense his abstinence; instead she sensed his absence, still said they seemed to be drifting apart. It took two to drift together; Dubin was in no mood to. They disagreed, argued, sometimes bitterly over trivialities: he had forgotten to remind her, though he had promised he would, when a television program began; she had sent out special delivery a letter he had wanted certified. He did not listen when she talked, Kitty complained. She could not follow directions, he said. He listened, Dubin responded, past all possible listening. "Who the hell are you to give *directions*?" Kitty said. She walked out with her fingers in her ears.

She accused him of destroying their social life by turning down every invitation; he accused her of not offering any. She did little entertaining. They went at each other face to face; but Dubin noticed she no longer threatened divorce, as if she had sensed it was now, for him, a viable option.

His sleep became surface-thin; he dreamed endlessly: how can one swim in shallow water? One night Kitty woke him out of a dream of Fanny to say she smelled something. Was it a fire? Gas escaping? Had she left a burner on?

Half asleep, he sniffed the air and smelled nothing.

"Are you sure, William?"

"What can I be sure of?"

Barefoot, he plodded dully through the house but could smell no smoke nor locate any. Dubin, muttering, sniffed at the burners in the kitchen, bitter to be awake at this miserable hour engaged in idiotic sniffing. A mad woman makes a man mad.

Kitty was standing at the bedroom window in her nightgown, inhaling the night air. It had rained.

"It was the wet earth I must have smelled—it's so refreshing. Forgive me, it waked me out of sound sleep. How fresh, how fragrant the earth is."

He got into bed, chilled. Fanny did not reappear in his dreams. In the morning they quarreled over what he called her punitive sense of smell. Kitty said she thought a vacation from each other would do them both good. She'd been thinking of Stockholm again, wanted to see Gerald. Maud was writing more often lately, but from Gerald, during the winter months, had come wintry silence. She was worried.

Later, her eyes uncertain, downcast, Kitty asked Dubin, "Would you care to come with me?"

He had expected it. "What's the good of it if I go with you? We need time away from each other."

He had had, that morning, a loving note from Fanny:

"Lover, father, friend—love me, I love you." The self-conceived defensive ice had broken; the river of feeling flowed.

"I'll go alone," Kitty said.

He approved, shame contained. She had rarely, since she'd married him, traveled by herself. It would do her good. What if she were widowed again and had to travel alone?

He knew she'd go—felt admiration for her, affection. On Friday of that week—the first in April—Kitty packed a suitcase and flew to Stockholm.

There were green shoots in her garden, shades of yellow and green, flowers to follow. He waited a day, called Fanny at 8 A.M., on Saturday. She was at once alert, had been expecting a call. Dubin told her Kitty had gone to Stockholm. "Your note meant a great deal to me."

"I'll bomb up there right away."

Fanny arrived shortly after twelve, expansive, happy, vital. Every time he saw her, especially after weeks gone by, she seemed more womanly. She stepped out of her Volvo, carrying a tote bag, her purse slung over her shoulder. Fanny entered the house unself-consciously. "I know this place like the palm of my hand." It excited Dubin to have her with him where he had first desired her. He said they would sleep in the guest room on the third floor.

"Should we go up now?"

"We've got two days together, Fanny. Let's eat first."

"It's just that we haven't seen each other so long."

He put his arm around her. She nuzzled close, reminded him this was their first spring together. "And not our last."

He had prepared lunch—asparagus, a salmon salad, white wine. They ate at the dining table, knees touching. Afterward she rinsed the dishes as Dubin stacked the dishwasher, conscious of her in Kitty's kitchen, domain. Having her in the house was part of the adventure.

"Don't sweat it, William," she said, sensing something. "I've handled nearly everything in this kitchen and will put everything back in place."

He trusted her instincts. They went outside. The silver maples were still leafless and the grass hadn't come to green life but the blue-skyed day embraced the earth. They went through the field into the warm wood. Dubin pulled down branches of opening tree buds. They found white hepatica in bloom and full-grown purple and gold crocus and one paper-thin narcissus amid last year's dead leaves. He thought of the wild flowers they had lain in.

"Come on," Fanny said, taking his hand. They left the woods and she began to run ahead of him on the path. Dubin trotted amiably after her. In the house she ran up the stairs. He followed, thinking she was heading for the third floor. Instead she darted into the master bedroom.

He called to her. "Not in that bed, please, Fanny."

"Why not?" she laughed, her face flushed, eyes very green.

"Kitty wouldn't like it. Come upstairs."

"I want to sleep with you in your bed. You sleep with me in mine."

She tugged down the bedspread. Dubin grabbed and held her. Fanny, twisting in his arms, pulled down the zipper of his fly. He drew off her shirt. She had nothing on under her jeans. Dubin undressed. Fanny, naked, flipped down the blankets on the double bed.

"I said no." He pulled her to him, holding her tightly. She struggled forcefully but he maneuvered her away from the bed. Fanny tried to shake him off. She was strong, sweated. Dubin, enjoying the struggle, forced her to the floor, lowering himself on her on the rug. Fanny squirmed, rocking from side to side, trying to fend him off with her knees.

"Get off me, you ape."

Dubin froze. Her body smoldered under his. Neither of them moved. As he was getting up, Fanny, grasping his shoulders, pulled him down. They kissed to their teeth. She bit his lip, drawing blood, then as he cried out, yielded—he felt her thighs grow soft, part. Dubin went in hard; she received him gently.

Afterward when she asked if she could lie—simply lie—in the bed he permitted it. He slid under the blanket with her, lying on Kitty's side as Fanny lay in his place.

They lay together, palms touching. Dubin felt a great gratitude to her—to life for all it offered. He tried to think of a gift for Fanny, something durable, valuable, beautiful. He wished he had a ring to give her. Perhaps he would have something made. Fanny slept heavily; Dubin slept with her.

In his dream a storm woke them. They woke in a thunderstorm. Through the east window they could see lightning streak through massive clouds, bathing the black sky in forked flickering light. Thunder rumbled, ripped through the cloud mass, crashed over their heads. Fanny clung to him.

"Are you afraid?"

"I would be if I were alone."

The white curtains were blowing, whipping in the wind.

"Jesus, the windows!" Dubin hopped out of bed. He ran to Maud's room to close hers and was about to race upstairs but remembered those were shut. Naked, he hurried down to the living room to close the open window there. Dubin wiped the sill and wet floor with a kitchen towel as thunder roared overhead. Excited by the storm, the biographer watched through the window as lightning flared in a circle. He saw himself pursuing the storm to catch it in a basket.

Rain hissed in the fireplace. He shut the vent and ran up the stairs.

Fanny was not in the double bed.

"Are you in the bathroom?"

She was not. A crackling explosion lit the bedroom. Dubin waited for thunder to crash but heard it rumbling in the distance.

"Fanny, where are you?"

No answer. He pulled open the door of Kitty's dress closet and found the girl, in his wife's African robe, crouched against the wall. Dubin offered his hand but Fanny refused it and rose awkwardly, her complexion pale. "Please don't ask me any questions."

"I won't except are you all right?"

"It's a question."

"Come to bed."

Fanny stepped out of Kitty's robe and slipped under the bedcovers. She was shivering. Dubin held her. As her body grew warm a calm settled in him.

It rained steadily, heavily, still poured. He listened to the water gushing from gutter spouts. Soon it rained lightly and as the storm departed he listened to it lessening; then to the raindrops dripping from the eaves of the roof and to the plop-plop of drops from the chestnut tree in front of the house.

"Are you feeling better?" he asked her.

"I want you to know I don't hide in a closet every time there's a storm."

"Why did you now?"

"I don't know. Let's don't talk about it."

Her hand caressed his thigh. "I'm in the mood, are you?"

"I could be but upstairs—not in this bed."

"You can have the sheets laundered. Also the rug cleaned where we fucked on the floor, and her bathrobe dry-cleaned."

"Don't be angry, Fanny. I never mentioned the robe."

"Scared as I was, I could see you didn't want me to wear it."

"Kitty's senses are sharp. She might know if someone had worn it."

"I never heard of anyone who goes around smelling everything."

"You have your thing, she has hers."

Fanny, after a moment, in a quieter voice spoke of Athens. "Do you think we can go there this month or maybe in May, William? I have another week of vacation coming to me. They might give it to me in May."

"Don't push it. I'll go if I can—it's on my mind."

Fanny sat up in the dark. "I really can't understand where we stand," she said angrily. "We have been through a lot together—some of it wasn't so good but a lot has been fun for both of us. We're happy when we are together, natural, relaxed—we really are. And we get along swell in bed—we enjoy each other in good ways. Sometimes the sex is fantastic. Then why do you let so long go by before we meet again, William? There are times I think all you want is a lay every couple of months or so, just to change the scenery."

Dubin denied it.

"Don't you love me?" she asked.

He said he must.

"What do you mean by that word?"

"I do."

"Then how can we go on like this? I had to hide from her in the goddamn barn, and now I can't even love you in your bed. Why are you so tight-assed?"

Dubin didn't say.

"When do you think you will leave her?"

He said, after a moment, that he had no plans to.

"What plans do you have?"

"Mostly to get on with my Lawrence."

"You expect us to go on as we have been—as we are right now?"

"If possible. I confess I worry about you. I have more than once asked myself whether I ought to let you go—for your sake."

"What do you answer yourself?"

"I honestly don't want to."

"Are you afraid to leave her?"

"It's not fear I feel."

"Then why do you stay with her?"

"There are commitments in marriage. It takes a while to reconsider each."

"I don't think you reconsider anything," Fanny said. "You may want to but you don't. You keep what you have and use anything else you can get."

Dubin said he was not only for himself. "My dear Fanny—"

The telephone rang shrilly.

He grabbed for it in the dark.

"Hello, dear—" Kitty was on the phone, her voice affectionate. Though he had been expecting her call Dubin was displeased to have it come as he was lying in bed with Fanny.

His wife sounded distraught. "Gerald has disappeared. I spoke to everybody I could locate who might know him, but nobody would say where he is now. I can't tell you what yesterday was like. Finally I met a young Swedish couple who said he had joined the Communist Party and gone into the Soviet Union. I'm told other deserters have. I feel desolate."

She wept on the phone. His teeth were on edge.

"It's so dreary here," Kitty said. "It's been raining since I got off the plane. I've had almost no sleep. The hotel room is drafty. The Old City is beautiful and I was hoping to see it in the sun with Gerald, but he's not here."

"Why don't you see some of it yourself, anyway, by bus or launch? See something, for Christ's sake. Gerry may show up if you stay around a few days."

"I'm going to the American Embassy Monday morning to talk with them about how to get in touch with him, although

I imagine they aren't much interested in deserters. I wish you had come with me."

Dubin said he hadn't been able to.

"What's the matter with your voice?—You sound as though you'd got a cold."

"I haven't."

Fanny coughed; Dubin cleared his throat.

Kitty worriedly asked, "Should I go to Moscow? I don't really know what to do next. Will you come with me? Shall I wait for you here?"

He advised her not to rush it. "We'd better go to Washington first. After we talk to a lawyer we may want to see someone in the State Department. Find out all you can about Gerry, then come home. Could he be in another city? He told me he liked Uppsala."

"Nobody I talked to seems to think he's in Sweden."

Dubin doubted anyone knew with certainty. "He may write soon. He could be with the Eskimos in Lapland. Better come home."

She said she'd fly home Tuesday, and Dubin said he'd pick her up at the airport.

"Goodbye."

He turned on the light. Fanny had got out of bed—he thought to go to the bathroom but she had pulled on her underpants and was buttoning a blouse.

"Good God, Fanny, what are you getting dressed for? We've got the whole night before us."

She sat at the edge of the bed. "Listen, William, I've told you how good I think we are together and I mean more than in bed. I want you in me but I also want you by me. I feel happy when we're with each other, sometimes like we were blessed. I know I am good for you but not on the run."

Dubin said he was sorry Kitty had happened to call just then. "I'm worried about Gerry but that doesn't mean we can't go on with our plans to enjoy ourselves alone here. She won't be back till Tuesday. We've got two and a half days to ourselves."

"I've been thinking about us and still can't explain what's happening," Fanny said. "One thing I do know is I'm not someone who's around just to keep your mind off old age.

I have got to be more to you than a substitute for your lost youth, whatever the hell that is. If you want to know something, William, everybody feels they have lost some part of their youth. I know I have, and maybe that's what it's for. Maybe if you lose it you make up by learning something you have to know—the way I imagine you have, and the way I'd like to. But I have to be myself, Fanny Bick, a woman living with or married to a man who wants her—wants to live with her and enjoy their life. I am sick of hiding myself, of not being who I am. It drives me up a wall. I am entitled to an open ordinary and satisfying life of my own."

She stepped into her sandals.

Dubin urged her to stay. The storm had swept the clouds away. A wet sunset hung in the trees. "Tomorrow will be a lovely day. We'll walk in the woods; we'll do anything we please and we can talk out our problems and see what they add up to."

"I know what they add up to and what they will go on adding up to if you don't make a decision. Besides, you will be edgy about where Gerald is and that's not what I want to deal with when I spend a weekend with you. Not this weekend if I can help it."

She had collected her underclothes, diaphragm box, toilet things, and dropped them into her tote bag.

Dubin, barefoot, in striped pajamas, followed her downstairs. "At least stay till Sunday. Let's have breakfast together. Fanny, it's obscene for you to be going off like this. We mean more to each other than that."

"I don't want to be in this house any longer," Fanny said. "I feel your wife's presence all over the place. I really don't like her. I don't think you do either."

"How would you know?"

"I know what I feel in my gut."

He grabbed her arms. "Fanny, you've got to stay. We're friends—genuinely friends. That has to mean something, no matter how our friendship is limited. We have to yield to circumstance for the time being."

"I can't any more."

"I beg you—"

"I can't," Fanny said gloomily.

"When will you be in touch with me?" Dubin asked as she slipped into a raincoat. "When shall I come to the city?"

She didn't want to think about that now.

"You're making a mistake," he told her.

She studied him solemnly without replying.

He put on the driveway light and watched her back her car out and turn on the road, eyes fixed before her. She had barely returned his wave.

Dubin watched till Fanny had gone.

"Maybe I've done her a favor to let her go." He listened to himself talking to himself. He heard himself groan.

Eight

DUBIN AND his daughter walk the wet strand of dark shore. A fast step or two and she will lose him in the fog. He hears the mewling of invisible gulls.

A droning wind blowing from the dunes of this sliver of San Francisco beach had driven them from the cold sand where they had tried to picnic, then from the rocks. They shared a sandwich and gulp of tepid coffee and wandered along the gray shore. Long white-capped waves, flowing from the mist-hidden swelling sea, broke in froth at their feet. Hers were wet, slender, rosy; his corded, purple-veined, sticky with sand. Dubin, in green sweater and dark trousers rolled to his knobby knees, trailed Maud in the thinning rising fog. Years ago, in Cuernavaca, he and Kitty had got her the off-white peasant dress she was wearing; it looked like a wedding dress but she did not look like a bride. In the wind it clung to her back and wet legs. Her shoulders were thin, hair brownish-red. She had snipped off most of the edge of streaky black. Maud as they walked seemed, in Dubin's eyes, to be looking through shadows. Her face had spilled its bloom; she was twenty and seemed thirty. Kitty, after rereading her last letter, had announced the end of an affair.

Dubin had said he must go see her.

"Yes, do," Kitty said. "I can't, I've had one very long trip this spring."

On the beach they walk apart.

He asked her to tell him what had happened.

Maud spoke a Chinese poem: "I am not disheartened in the mindless void. / Wheresoever I go I leave no footprint. / For I am not within color or sound."

"I asked a simple question."

"My response is not hard to understand."

"Are you into Zen?" her father asked.

"If Zen will have me" . . .

After Fanny had left he waked, that Sunday morning without her, to a cardinal's shrill whistling. Dubin at length got out of bed, drew up a shade, and peered into the trees. The red bird, at his glance, flew off. After a woodpecker had stopped rattling away—he often ticked when Dubin typed—the biographer listened to another birdsong: wood thrush warbling a fluting melody. Does the bird hear music or does it hear noise? Will I ever hear a nightingale? He went back to bed and tried to sleep, remembered it had felt late, and at once rose. The clock said past noon. He hadn't slept so long in years. Had it coming to him.

He had liked that day alone: the company of Wm. Dubin, who'd been with him all his life—nobody's father, husband, or lover. He was a man in a house getting himself breakfast; enjoyed scrambling an egg. He thought he'd skip the Sunday paper—too heavy, too long—and drew out of the bookshelf *Far from the Madding Crowd*, had liked it when he was seventeen. Though Lawrence had called Thomas Hardy "a bad artist," Dubin tended to favor his work and the kind of person his fiction seemed to say he was. Lawrence had had his Frieda; he bedded her and yawped. His passionate love for a woman had sprung his ideology of wise blood, as though passionate love could be thus contained, reduced. Hardy, although strongly moved by a variety of women, had flitted from one to another, not daring much. For years he'd been sexually attracted—one after another—to three female cousins, "lower-class" women, none of whom he had appeared to have had an affair with. Then he contracted an essentially loveless marriage to a tough overweight childlike woman, who ultimately freed him from their prison by dying. Hardy was of course of his late-Victorian time; but time or none, he was not as frank or honest about himself as the miner's son. Hiding his knocked-up cook of a mother, and his unaccomplished simple relatives, Thomas Hardy fabricated a "biography" "by" his second wife and former secretary, Florence. "If I get you here," he wrote her after the death of his wife, "won't I clutch you tight." The book for years had misled its readers about his nature and experience. Lawrence, though he admired Hardy's sensibility, and his "instinct," could not stand the way the sexually repressed characters in his novels maimed and ultimately destroyed themselves; failed "life's plenitude" by succumbing to the stupid blind power of the community. Yet Dubin, sympathetic to the older writer, considered he might someday write a biography of Thomas Hardy. He wondered why he wasn't doing it now instead of the one of Lawrence.

Hardy and Dubin both had blue-gray eyes.

Flora had called. She had seen Kitty at the airport the day she delivered Oscar to a flight for a concert in Salt Lake City.

"If you're free, come over."

Dubin, after a moment, doubted he could make it.

"Have you given me up, William?"

"I find it hard to poach in Oscar's domain."

"I am my own domain." She hung up.

He had decided on a bath for a change. Lying, afterward, in his bed, he fell asleep. When he awoke it was night, a crescent moon in the lit sky. He lay in bed wondering if he was lonely.

He ate supper out of a sardine tin with a squeeze of lemon and a sliced tomato. After rinsing spoons, forks, and cup he put in a long-distance call to Maud. The girl who answered said she was in San Francisco. He sat down and wrote her a letter; he owed her several. And he was glad Kitty was getting back Tuesday. He worried on and off about Gerald; but in bed at midnight, when he thought back on the day, it hadn't been a bad Sunday.

After a good morning of work Dubin had driven into town for a paper, conscious that he had dreamed heavily during the night, though he could remember nothing of his dreams. He tucked the newspaper under his arm and experienced something stronger than an impulse to walk a few blocks to Roger Foster's house, although a hand in his head was waving him back. Dubin hurried on, possibly to see what he hadn't come here yesterday for fear of seeing. "What's fate for?" He had thought while shaving: if she went to Roger's house after leaving me she'd be gone now—has to be at work today. If for some reason she's still with him, I don't want to know.

Yet here's Dubin spying her out; and as he had imagined he might, without surprise, came upon Fanny's white Volvo parked in the street in front of Roger's house. His reaction was quickly to flee; instead he circled her car to be certain it was Fanny's; and on the back seat spied a yellow apple and her sandals. It was as though the apple bled. Wait up, Dubin, a hoarse voice advised, but his thoughts raced on. He pictured clearly and in living color a scene from the past: Here's Dubin and Fanny at odds in Venice though he had left it for good a year and a half ago. When the performance was over he was convinced he had made a mistake in letting the girl go. How could he, in his right mind, have done it? He ought by some means or other to have persuaded her to stay. His legs wobbled.

Dubin had considered going for a drive to mull over what to do but couldn't bear to leave the spot without having talked to Fanny. He felt he had misplaced something, an arm or leg. Let me be sane, the biographer thought: nothing very serious has happened. There's been no irrevocable break—of course we'll meet again. We are important to each other. Why should I think she's slept with Roger because she may have stayed the night in his house?—perhaps slept in a room there as she'd done when she first came to this town. Even two nights. How unkind I am to her. Suppose she did sleep with him—hadn't she every right to, given the situation and how I mishandled her? Besides, they're friends: the guy loves her, wants to marry her, and Fanny's warmhearted response to feeling is one of her talents. I mustn't think of it as another betrayal. If anybody's to blame it's me.

He'd gone home thinking he'd telephone Fanny and ask to see her. The phone rang for a full five minutes. He then called the library, asked for Roger, and when the librarian said hello, Dubin remained silent. Roger hung up. Still, he was at work, not in bed with her. Dubin then picked up his Hardy novel but reading it felt unreal. Boldwood's morbid jealousy of Bathsheba embarrassed him. He drove again to Roger's house, went up the porch steps, rang the bell. No one came to the door. As he was driving home Dubin turned in mid-block and rode back to town. It was now almost five o'clock. He waited fifteen minutes under a locust tree up the street from the red-brick library building. When Roger came out and locked the door Dubin trailed him from a block behind, then lingered in his parked car, hoping Fanny would come out of the house—if she ever did—and drive off to New York City. He'd follow and signal her in her mirror to pull over so they could talk.

An hour later, Fanny, in skirt and red blouse, left the house with Roger. She was not carrying her worldly goods, not even the shoulder bag. Roger double-locked the front door as she waited on the porch—they looked like a young couple on their way to dinner out. They went down the steps, Roger's face lit by a happy smile, Fanny talking animatedly—no mourner she—and got into his Chevy. Was her car out of commission? Was that why she had stopped off momentarily, and then it grew to a visit? Dubin swiped at this straw—wanted it to be so; but her car was in the street—not at the garage. Not very likely. They drove away—where Dubin could not know unless he took off after them. The thought was degrading though he favored the action. Where would it get him? He did not follow them.

Instead he drove home; he'd considered Flora's but quashed that. He felt like a man trying to keep something evil, indecent, from breaking out. This will pass, he promised himself. Don't go on reacting like a child to a threatened loss of affection. I've had my morbid little experiences—no more of that. If I have to give Fanny up I will. This is as good a time as any—better, in fact: I'm into the act. But when he thought of her bestowing on Roger that warm affection she had so often expressed for him, those intimate pleasures she had shared with William Dubin, the floor under him seemed to sag. A spurt of jealousy spread like acid in the blood. He resisted the feeling, as if it was a wild animal he was giving birth to. My God, why is this happening to me? Why should it be? In the shower he thought: she's had Roger before and nothing came of it. He can't give her better than I gave—give. She's bound to come back if I'm patient. Just don't do the wrong thing. The wrong thing is to suffer needlessly.

So Dubin informed himself, but his thoughts did not appease or console him. He was heavy with desire of her, his penis as if salted, swollen. "Control yourself," he warned himself, and didn't like the sound of it. Could Fanny have planned this: had guessed he would check her out at Roger's—had foreseen his reaction, possibly to force him to define his commitment to her; decided once and for all how genuine, compelling, it was? That wasn't much Fanny's way, yet who knew for sure? Whatever her way was he had to have her back—at least till he could sanely reason it out and come to a sane decision.

Reason's the word: see the situation as is—no one had said goodbye forever, so why jump the gun? Of course Fanny would call him—a question of time. This self-created crisis—his sense, surely illusory, of their affair having ended badly, had hit him in the head upon discovering her car at Roger's curb. He had once more to contend with the shame of supposed betrayal: Fanny reacts to frustration by sleeping with the nearest guy in sight—had the bitch learned nothing? No, Dubin thought, this is something else again, in truth more serious. Roger is not the gondolier; he wants to marry her, an altogether ultimately more perilous situation for me. This fear tips Dubin's unsettled self and jealous bubbles bubble forth. My God, what else am I capable of that I didn't know? How many more hollows will I uncover in myself? How can this sort of thing, not at all admirable in youth, go on happening to a grown man? The biographer warned himself: It's one thing for a man not to know, not to have learned; it's another not to be able to live by what one does know. That's sure danger.

The next day Fanny's car had disappeared. Dubin had discovered this on his way to the airport to pick up his wife. He'd felt a short-lived relief, until he learned in a long-distance call he made later that Fanny wasn't at work; was not expected in until Wednesday morning. Roger, he then learned, wasn't at the library. Where in hell were they?

Kitty's plane was delayed several hours. Dubin had to return for her that evening. Subdued, worn dark with fatigue, she embraced her husband. On entering the house Kitty cautiously sniffed the burners, interesting reversal. After he had poured her a cup of tea she talked at length of her search for Gerald, ending with her litany of regrets. He observed her carefully, after a while excusing himself to sneak in a call to Fanny via the phone upstairs, leaving Lorenzo to comfort Kitty. No one answered at the girl's apartment. He wondered where she was and what they were doing. The original misery played its dirty little tune. That night he persuaded Kitty, despite her fatigue, to make love, exchanging an overwhelming desire for momentary release—the small brain of the shmuck was without conscience. But the act eased the acid-eating self: Fanny, wherever she was, Kitty's grace kept at bay.

Let her go, he told himself as his wife slept. It wasn't meant to be more than an affair, a short adventure and quits. I've had a good time with her. She isn't the kind of woman I would have thought to marry, although people do change: we aren't who we were; she is matured, shows more control, wants better for herself than she's had. And we've seriously affected one another. Obviously she means more to me than I'd supposed. I've learned that in winter and summer, at home and abroad. She lives in my blood and neither will nor reason can wring her out. Myself, my self's heart, aches for her, for a glowing fundamental pleasure that comes with and from her, an easeful enjoyment of life.

That night the biographer loved and violated her in sensual and perverse ways. He tore at her every sexual stirring, gratified every fantasy. In steaming dreams and torpid reverie he sought satisfaction on her now familiar, though always surprising, pleasure-yielding body. When at last he fell into a grating half sleep he spoke her name aloud.

Kitty abruptly awoke. "Fanny who?"

"Fanny," Dubin confessed, "must be the girl who worked for us summer before last."

"Why are you dreaming of her now?"

"What shall I tell my dreams to dream?"

Kitty yawned. "She must have caught your fancy."

She got up to go to the bathroom. Dubin waited for her to come out and then went in; he fumbled in his pajamas for the offending member.

In the morning a letter had come from Fanny: "Once you said be kind to yourself. I am trying to be. That's why I think we ought to stay broken off. For about a week I didn't think we really were but now I do think so. You wouldn't have let me split that night if in your heart you weren't glad I was going. Maybe you didn't actually want it to happen but you took the out I gave you. I gave it to you to be kind to myself. I was tired of the punishment I was taking. I want someone who wants me. I don't care if we get married or don't but I won't live alone, it hurts too much. I can't see any future for us the way things have been going—sometimes I think you're blind, William—so we'd better not see each other any more. I appreciate certain things you have done for me—some my father might have done but didn't—although with one hand you take away what the other gives. I hope you know what *I* have done for *you*. Sincerely, Fanny."

Dubin wrote an impassioned plea: "Dearest Fanny, Let's not make a hasty mistake. Let's not end what may have barely begun."

Such was the biographer's commitment. He had mailed his letter and also called her from the barn but now her home telephone was disconnected; and at work they said Fanny had quit.

"If she really hasn't, kindly tell her it's William Dubin on the phone, with much good will and an expectation of kindness."

"Why would I want to lie to you?" the operator asked. "I've often been in love myself."

Dubin had then telephoned Roger Foster, with a wretched stirring of jealousy, to ask if he knew where Fanny could be found; and Roger said, without sorrow or laughter, he thought she'd gone back to Los Angeles.

"Do you happen to know her address, Roger?"

"I actually don't, Mr. Dubin. Not that I didn't ask her, but Fanny wasn't all that certain where she was heading. Maybe L.A., or to San Francisco, and she said she'd send me a postcard once she knew for sure."

"Would you kindly let me know where she is when you get that card?"

"I will if she doesn't object."

Dubin had felt an irrational impulse to tell him to stay the hell away from Fanny but had no right to say it.

A few days later he had made up his mind to go to New York to see if he could find her. Kitty, alternating worry about Gerald with a nagging concern for Maud, who seemed to have stopped writing or calling, said she was in no mood to be left alone in the house.

"The house won't hurt you," Dubin said.

He had thought of telling her he was intending to get legal advice about Gerald's case but ultimately said nothing. She hadn't asked him why he was going to the city. Kitty hadn't offered to drive him to the station, so Dubin drove himself. He parked at the depot and boarded the train before realizing he had left her without a car.

In the city he went at once to Fanny's apartment. The door stood open. The flat was empty—the floor covered with paint-spattered drop cloths. The landlord and a painter standing on a ladder were talking inside.

"Excuse me," said Dubin, "do you happen to know where the young lady who lived here has moved to?"

"Who knows," said the landlord, "where they go."

"Where they want," said the painter, "they go. These are different times."

Dubin, at the window, gazed down at the synagogue. An old Jew was praying. Where they want they pray.

At the Gansevoort he sat at the desk in his room and wrote Fanny a note, to her at the law office—to be forwarded. "My dearest Fanny, I wish I had done it better. I wish I were a single man—or perhaps more daring. I wish . . . Life is so varied, sweet, sad. Think of me thinking of you. Surely we'll see each other again? My sense of it is that you're handling your life with purpose. Go on as you are. Ever yours, William Dubin."

As he addressed the envelope he was running through his mind the winter without her.

The morning in San Francisco he met Maud in the hotel lobby and drove in her VW to the beach. Maud is drawn, distant, lonely. He is tormented to see her so . . .

In her last letter she had said she wasn't intending to return to college for her senior year. Her father was at first angered, but rereading her several letters of the past year had filled him with regret: she had been signaling something less than the joyful life. He had let her down, Dubin had felt, in not more insistently trying to discover what was eating her. He had asked superficial questions and accepted casual replies. In one letter she had spoken of an interest in Eastern religions, not before a serious concern of hers. With Maud much happened in little time. In another letter she wished she had her life to live over. "Before you've begun to live?" No response to speak of. He tried it on the telephone: "Before you've begun to live?" "Who's to say how much anybody else has lived?" Fair enough, though not enough. Kitty still theorized that Maud was having her ups and downs in love. Dubin hoped it was that simple. So did Kitty.

Two weeks ago Maud had telephoned and asked not to be called by them.

"Why not?" Dubin asked.

"I need time to think things through."

"We won't interfere with your thoughts."

"I'm asking a favor," Maud wept.

Granted.

Last summer when she was home and bored, beyond occasionally asking her out for lunch or a drive, or to walk his walk with him, he felt he had given her not much. Yet she was, after all, home: they talked at the table; had shared the drama of Watergate—it was interesting to see Nixon, perennial loser, like a magician fabricating his losses. Maud read, played tennis, backpacked with the couple living on Mt. No Name; but it was obvious the focus of her life was elsewhere. Dubin and she seemed to resist each other—no explanation he could think of except they were interested in others. His thoughts had lain in Fanny's lap. One would think that if a man loves, the fountain flows: all may drink, no limit. But in truth the feeling of love for those one has loved was not boundless—it was bound. One loved according to his capacity but capacities differ. If you loved someone with deepening passion the love of others was effectively reduced, perhaps even paid for the passion. No, love was not boundless—not more than a pailful—barely enough for one at a time. You pour love out for a single self: in theory, no; but in practice other selves get less.

Not that Maud had wanted more from him than he ordinarily gave of affection. She had seemed, last summer, to want less; but that he hadn't offered more in a time of need bothered Dubin. It worried him that he never really had known what was going on with Maud once she was past sixteen, as if this fact, natural enough, embedded in their history, was itself the major cause of what was presently lacking in their relationship. He had thought of telling her about Fanny—being honest—but hadn't because he didn't want her to think of him as her mother's betrayer. Reasoning it thus was how Dubin balanced the construction in his mind: in loving Fanny he withheld love from his wife and daughter.

Fanny had, on her last birthday, waited for him at the train; he searched for her face in the crowd awaiting arrivals at the San Francisco Airport. Neither she nor his daughter appeared.

On the beach he impulsively drew her to him. Maud, shivering, stooped to pick up a shell. Dubin thrust his hands into his pockets. "I remember," he said, "when you were a little girl. Once you asked me to marry you."

"Oh, Papa," she said with an impatient gesture.

"Sentimentality has its moments."

"Not just this minute, please."

"Maud," Dubin said, "why don't you tell me what's going on with you? Are you in love? Is it going badly?"

"I'm always in love. Sooner or later it goes badly."

He did not know what to reply.

Maud then said she wouldn't be going back to college in the fall. "I've had it with school. I want something else—something more satisfying."

"Like Zen?"

She wiped her eyes as though she were wiping away tears. The wind blew her hair into her face. Heartache, he reflected, became her age, not his.

"Why don't you call it a day here," Dubin advised, "and do your senior year in the East? You've never greatly liked California."

"I don't think so. I'm tired of intellectual studies, tired of intellectuals."

"Who in particular?"

"No one you know."

"You've always had intellectual interests."

"They're not very relevant to my life any more."

"It's a temporary feeling, believe me."

"Maybe. Maybe not. Buddha gave up books entirely at a critical time of his life."

"Lawrence never did, although I suppose it could be said he was an anti-intellectual natural intellectual."

"I wouldn't mention them both in the same breath."

"What makes you think so? In Sicily, when the peasants saw him with his red beard they cried out, 'Look! Jesus Christ!'"

"What are you trying to prove, Papa?"

"I wish I could tell you what I know about life."

"Don't get on that kick, please, not now. I've read your books."

Dubin, after a while, asked her if she wanted to try psychiatric counseling.

"I've had six months of that at Berkeley. It leaves me cold."

He laughed dully, looked at the ocean, looked away. "I've made the traditional suggestions. What I'm really saying is trust me, confide in me."

She said she had been talking to a Zen Master in South San Francisco. "When I came into his house he said he'd been waiting for me to appear. I'm thinking of entering a Zen commune if they consider me worthy. I've met some of his disciples. People in serious meditation have such clear luminous eyes. I'd like to be one of them. I expect to become a Zen disciple."

Dubin said he understood the rules were strict and the formal training no picnic. "It takes, I understand, years of disciplined effort. I'd like you to enjoy the youth of your youth."

He had read in Zen after rereading her letters.

"I'm not out to bliss it, Papa. I want discipline."

The word drew a tear to his left eye. He felt a sorrow of sorts for what she had of him in her.

Maud said she expected first to be instructed in meditation. "During the formal training I'll support myself by working in the commune—whatever they want me to do is worth doing. I want to live on my own labor, not yours. Please don't send me any more money, though I'm grateful for what you've done for me. I'm fed up with my ego. I want, eventually, satori—true enlightenment, an end to confusion and pain. I'd like to be different than I've been. I'm not looking for, quote, happiness. I want to be in the *Is*ness of the Great Self. I will begin with emptiness."

"Emptiness I know about. It's nothing. Take something, you're only twenty."

"Twenty-one."

"Twenty-one," he said hastily.

"My age makes no difference. I feel like forty. I'd like to step out of time."

"Maud, come off that goddamned fantastic horse."

"That will get you nothing."

"My child," Dubin urged, "take your clear luminous eyes in your hand, as my father used to say, and look through them to see life clearly. In life fulfill yourself."

"I want fulfillment in Zen."

"Why don't you come home and think things through before you make your next move?"

"What's home?" she asked. "Two lonely people trying to get along."

"*Use* us, for Christ's sake, we'd be less lonely."

"I have my own life to live."

"Then *live* it. Don't be a nun, Maud. You've always called yourself a Jew. Jews live in the world. Don't hide from pain, insult, fear of failure. Don't expect perpetual serenity. It's not that kind of life or real world."

"How do you define the real world? All things share in the Buddha nature if one can find it in herself. I want to live in Buddha, that's where it is for me and I wish you wouldn't try to dissuade me now that I know where I want to be. Frankly, Papa, Zen would be good for you too."

She was walking in the surf.

He followed her along the ribbed hard sand. The wind was down; the fog had lifted but not the fog in Dubin. Of himself he had said nothing; she hadn't asked.

Maud strode on; Dubin followed. He was tempted to say, "My child, I understand your pain. I live with my own. Let me tell you about it." He didn't say it; he was, he thought, the father.

She walked on, eyes in the distance. My daughter, the stranger. He looked back: the waves washed the smooth shore and flowed into the sea. When he looked again their footsteps had reappeared.

Maud walks in Dubin's dreams.

It was a quiet long summer, two alone in a big house. The weather had turned humid-hot, and in the evening they sat on the porch facing the long-trunked graceful silver maples. Kitty's garden showed bunches of red phlox within a border of late-blooming yellow lilies. She served salads in white bowls, or cold sliced meats and cheeses they carried out on earthenware plates, with brown bottles of Alsatian wines. As they ate they watched the reflection of dull-gold sunsets on the heavy hills. The grass yielded light at dusk. Swallows darting in broken circles above the trees swooped low over the green lawn. Lorenzo, after long watching the birds, slept on the warm planks by the porch rail.

"He sleeps his life away," Kitty said.

"It's his to sleep."

At dark she lit a three-candle candelabrum he had bought her in Venice their first time there. Kitty smoked to keep the mosquitoes away. The biographer would watch the candles melt until the stars appeared. Afterward they read downstairs until their bedroom had cooled off, and then read in bed. Kitty was into Lawrence's poetry again.

"My God, listen to this—he's talking about his lonely erect phallus: 'How beautiful he is! without sound, / without eyes, without hands; yet flame of the living ground. / He stands, the column of fire by night. / And he knows from the depths; he quite / alone understands.' Isn't it just like D. H. Lawrence to write that?" Kitty laughed.

Dubin said he knew the poem. "He loved his thing."

"Don't you?"

"Yes."

He was reading the *Confessions of St. Augustine*, often putting the book down when he could not concentrate. "Love means that I want you to be," Augustine had said. As Dubin read he heard the *ping* of the moths hitting the window screens and saw lightning bugs flash in the trees in the outside dark. There was no breeze through the open windows; the curtains were limp. Kitty lay with her eyes shut, fanning herself in long strokes with a magazine.

"Lord, it's hot."

"Not that hot."

"I feel hot. Don't tell me it's only me."

"It's cooling now," Dubin said.

It was cooler at midnight, but they were restless in bed. Kitty said it looked like another uncomfortable summer. "Whatever's happened to Northeast weather? Where are the east winds and cool summers?" Dubin didn't know. In the warm dark when they moved apart to try to sleep, Fanny crept close to him, Dubin lay close to her.

Sometimes as he wrote he felt lust arise from nowhere, tempting him at his task. That morning he had gored Fanny on his horn. Fanny pressed her fleshy firm breasts to his lips, caressed his buttocks. Her experienced tongue traveled up his inner thigh to the head of his cock. She dipped it again and again into her mouth. Then she rose on her knees, placing herself above his erect flesh and locked it in her moist vagina, riding rhythmically, enacting an ancient legend in sweet time. Seizing her, he held her motionless, pumping upward until she burst into flame. William, she groaned in silence. He came, at length, extravagantly.

Dubin felt the shame of lust at his age.

"Clouds arose from the slimy desires of the flesh and from my youth's spring. They clouded over and darkened my soul, so that I could not distinguish the calm light of chaste love from the fog of lust."

Augustine's youth's spring; Dubin's late wasteful autumn. Not that flesh is slime, but some emotions are outworn. The expense of spirit: not because he had had her in his wife's company, but because he had had her when he hadn't; when she was no longer his to have.

He turned to Kitty. "Will you sleep with me—make love?"

"In this heat?"

"It's cooler now."

"All right." Her arms were warm, bosom soft.

After a while she asked, "What's the matter?"

"I don't think it's going to work."

"Are you sure?"

He said he was sorry.

"It's too hot," Kitty said. "I wouldn't worry about it."

Better this way, Dubin thought.

She fell asleep. He slept an hour and awoke, indecently mourning the girl. He had done it badly. They'd been friends, better friends than he'd had any right to expect, given the restrictions he had laid on her. With Fanny he had felt a dozen years younger, had acted like a young man, a young woman's lover. Not having her increased his not having. The mourning was harder to bear than the lust. They were two faces of the same loss, not having her you wanted most.

Dubin slept through the ringing alarm, aware of Kitty trying to rouse him and then letting him sleep. He woke heavily, with an increasingly burdensome sense of having mishandled the girl. He felt a gross hollow rooted in himself. The biographer played back the loneliness of his youth. There was more to their lives than he had allowed to happen. Out of the confusion caused by Kitty's call from Stockholm, Gerry's disappearance, his own guilt for being at that moment in bed with Fanny—he had botched it with her; had—without thinking it through—let her walk out of his life.

Perhaps he had allowed it to happen because it had momentarily seemed to simplify life. Dubin felt he had blown it finally when he went looking for her car, expecting to find it where he had found it; to feel justified in letting her go; to be betrayed again so that he could blame her rather than himself. He had indulged in jealousy to re-create the wound of mourning, lust, loneliness. What he ought to have done once she left and he regretted it was to get into his car, drive to New York, and there await her return even if it meant living a few days in a hotel and working in his room. He could have wired Kitty he would pick her up at Kennedy instead of Albany and then stayed with her at the Gansevoort until Fanny had come back and they had talked. I'd have promised her more. More what or more how he couldn't say, but more better. If he had been there waiting for her they would easily have made it up. Instead he had allowed himself to be eaten, undermined, by his jealousy.

He sent off another letter to Fanny via the apartment on West 83rd Street. It was returned in two weeks. He mailed the same letter in another envelope to the law office and then had a very good day. By the end of June he had heard nothing from Fanny yet went on writing to her. It was not a bad way to keep her present: about to reply; therefore in his future. It was a good way to keep his mind at peace and protect his work. He felt so until, one by one, his letters came back stamped "Return to sender." They hadn't been forwarded; she must have requested that: "Don't forward anything return-addressed Center Campobello, I want to get rid of that shmuck." Dubin worked at forgetting. No sense trying to kick the corpse of farewell into life. She left me before and I beat it out of my system. It shouldn't be so hard to do again in summertime. The season is easier, gentler—in my favor. There are green-leaved trees and many flowers around. Yet he had a self-conscious intrusive sense of himself abandoned by a girl, left exposed in his emotional long underwear, if not bare ass. He was embarrassed to have intruded on her youth. Dubin's nose twitched. He felt less vital than a year ago. His face was smaller, wrinkled, pouched under the eyes. He was losing hair, hated the sight of his comb after combing. His belly was expanding—if not in cubits, in eighth-inches; but growing in the long haul. His thick toenails were hard to cut. He had one pink foot and one white. He was adamantly a late-middle-aged gent. One paid for the pursuit of youth—from Faustus to Wm. Dubin. Wanting that much to be young was a way of hurrying time. The years ran forward backward. He counted on two fingers the time to sixty, obscene age. They say an old man dies young, back-slapping myth.

Dubin recomposed the old diet; rising at daybreak; water therapy; jogging the long walk in rain or shine, principally humid heat. Nothing to celebrate but discipline as evasion of a larger pain—ducking from that before it laid on with a bludgeon, insult he was sick of; indulged in to protect the self, self that lived the Lawrence. The dieting was strict, a pleasure-denying effort he was in no mood for. He came to the table with small appetite and left hungry. As in a former time he gobbled squares of chocolate hidden in a drawer. In bed hunger burned in every capillary. Not to brood or tear at himself he went quietly down the creaking stairs to the kitchen. Dubin made himself a liverwurst sandwich on rye, then one of cream cheese and jam smeared on white bread; he devoured both and still was hungry. He ate, he figured, Fanny, her live flesh. He drank wineglasses full of heavy cream—her breasts vanished. He ate her bare-boned; she no longer tempted. No aphrodisiac skeletons. Afterward he savaged himself for her hold on him.

But as the weeks went by his painful discipline fed him. It compels order; is order, he thought. I wish I could do it more easily, but if I can't I will do it this way. If, as in the past, he went into the bathroom to rinse his mouth after eating, he cut out desire for chocolate, feasting at night. If he still felt hunger he drank a glass of skim milk, sometimes two. Dubin lost weight without gaining virtue. Kitty wanted to know how much more he intended to shrink. He said he felt better: loss of flesh lightened the mind.

"You're not depressed again, are you?"

He was trying not to be.

"Then what's eating you?"

He felt her eating him and rose from the table. "I don't want to account for every move I make. Stop asking so many goddamn questions."

She studied him impassively; then Kitty got up and stalked out of the room.

His heart sank. Cutting off contact with her, such as it was—as he had caused it to be—punished him most. Not that he blamed her; it was an effectual defense. Dubin considered apologizing but decided not to. It would be a relief if she didn't talk to him for a few days.

He walked-ran day after day although it was a living bore, the sameness, the ritual. This extraordinary world—is this how life wants me to live it? But he ran to keep himself on keel, to wind himself into work the next morning. Dubin arose at the alarm ring, strayed into the bathroom, stepped blindly into the shower. Hot water poured on his head. He modified it to tepid, cold, colder—till it attacked and he gasped, ran in the tub. He held his head in the cold spray until he was numbed; then toweled himself at the open steamed window, feeling wet when dry. He exercised in his underpants in Maud's room, bent touching toes, pedaled on his back, pulled his knees into his bulging gut, willed pushups, other self-savaging. If the day was hot he exercised just out of bed, then showered, and went down to breakfast at least awake. He heard Lawrence scream *murder*.

The biography was going comparatively well, considering that Fanny, a more accomplished sexual person than Connie Chatterley, haunted his thoughts, rode like a witch astride each sentence he wrote. If the afternoon was impossible he jogged at dusk, at times having to rest against a tree, or lie on his back in the warm grass in the shade of maples grown thick with summer leafage. Dubin began in a walk then upped it to a slow jog. The idea was not to think but let momentum carry him. His spine loosened as he moved, hips and shoulders relaxed, bound energy came unbound. Going uphill in the heat, sweating, breathing laboriously, he stared at his feet as he plodded on. Downhill, he gazed into the shimmering distance. Sometimes a ring of gnats circled his head. Fanny floated in and out of the mind, invisibly kept him company. A short affair and long mourning. Having gone, why didn't she go? What kept her imprinted like a burn on the brain? Yet his sense of loss was more than loss of Fanny. What you dug out of left a hole deeper than the hole. He disliked himself for having twice succumbed to her, and twice to this self-inflicted punishment.

One Sunday morning as he was backing up on the driveway to get the car closer to the house so he could hose it, Dubin heard a savage yowl, hiss, scream through the window. He jammed the brake and frantically hopped out of the car. He knew what he had done. The wheel had crushed Lorenzo lying asleep on the warm asphalt. The cat vomited his tongue, his legs twitched as he died. Dubin, moaning, hid his eyes in his hands. Ten minutes later he furtively entered the house, stole a bath towel from the linen closet, and wrapped the remains of Lorenzo in it. He carried the bloody bundle to the barn, found a shovel, and buried the dead cat in Kitty's Wood. He remembered secretly burying Maud's black-and-white kitty there many years ago. Why does every misery happen twice? "Forgive me, Lorenzo," but the dead cat had nothing to say. Dubin buried him in a hole three feet deep, then returned wearily across the field, hoping Kitty hadn't seen the accident; but when he approached the house she was standing at the window observing him; her face dark, mourning.

The old house gave forth sounds at night—more, recently. It groaned, banged and creaked, without apparent cause. The biographer had long ago heard that the man who had built it had killed himself in the barn. Were his miseries adrift in the house at night? Was he? Dubin had never told Kitty about the suicide.

Kitty, one night, sat up suddenly in bed. "What was that?"

"What?"

She had heard gnawing scraping noises in the ceiling above their bed. He thought a field mouse or chipmunk might have come up inside the wall.

"If only Lorenzo were alive."

"If only."

That night Dubin listened to slow steps on the driveway, but when he got up to peer out of the window, could see no one, nothing in the pitch-dark.

"Should we call the police?" she whispered.

After a time he realized the "footsteps" was water dripping, after rain, from a leak in the gutter.

"What was that?" she whispered as he was falling asleep.

They listened sharply.

"Nothing. What did you think you'd heard?"

"Nothing."

"It was nothing," he said.

Sometimes when the furnace, heating water, rumbled, an upstairs door near the chimney shook.

Once Dubin woke to lonely secret steps coming up the stairs, but as he strained to hear, heard only his heartbeat drumming against the mattress.

When the wind blew, the house sighed, moaned, made sounds like living presences. One summer night Kitty, waking in fright, said she had heard a window slowly go up. Dubin listened sitting up, then pulled a sock on, and dragged himself throughout the house from floor to floor, turning on lights, inspecting window screens to see if one was slashed or missing. All were intact.

"It's mad to get up," he told her. "If I met someone I'd be a dead duck if he hit me on the head. We're safer putting the light on but not getting out of bed."

"I'd never get back to sleep," she said, "if someone didn't check the house."

When he returned to bed after his ritual exploration Kitty locked arms around him and fell asleep. Dubin, his senses alert, lay awake listening for noises in the night.

The window shades rattled. A door slammed in a cross-draft.

"What was that?"

"Nothing. Go back to sleep."

"If I can."

When he urinated, the toilet bowl sounded faintly like a ringing bell.

"Is that the phone?"

"What phone?" she wanted to know.

He was tired of the house—of living in the country. He'd had his fill of housebound cold Northeast winters; of short savage springs; increasingly hot humid summers. Kitty was right, the weather had changed for the worse: cold was colder, hot hotter. He wouldn't mind once more living in the city, chancy as the city was. Millions lived there in peace; millions who hadn't been insulted or mugged. One day on a bus, or as he walked along Madison, he might meet Fanny.

Dubin worried about Maud, chaste in Zen; and Gerald, in

the Soviet Union—to what intent, purpose, future? They were into fates he couldn't have foreseen. He felt at times embittered by his worries about them. And he was fed up with his work; of the endless effort it took to keep going.

And tired of living with Kitty. He was bored with the bounds of marriage; would like to be free before he was too old to enjoy it. Sherwood Anderson had one day escaped from his paint factory, left one or another wife to go to Chicago and write in a rooming house. Gauguin, taking years to sever himself from wife and children, frantically traveling wherever he could, at last made it to Tahiti. Could Dubin do what they had done?—take off and live as he pleased? He preferred, at his age, more solitude, time to himself. When he said something of the sort Kitty's knee-jerk response was: "If you want a divorce you can have a divorce. Don't stay for my sake." He would have to take off before pity restrained him; pack some necessary things and go to New York. One day while she was out of the house he would drive up in a van to collect his clothes, papers, books, and the pine table he liked to write on in the barn. Kitty would get along one way or another.

She now worked two afternoons a week at the Youth Opportunity Center. She saw Ondyk once a week and stayed on after their session for a drink. Considerate of Evan, the biographer thought. Kitty had returned from Stockholm muted, nervous. She wrote long explanatory letters in behalf of Gerald to the State Department and a letter of inquiry to the American Embassy in Moscow. She wrote she had heard that her son, a deserter, was in the Soviet Union—where she couldn't say—and would appreciate it if they tried to find him and put him in touch with his parents. She received official letters in reply—they were looking into the matter—from Washington and Moscow. She wrote every week to Maud in her commune in South San Francisco. "What ails my children?" Kitty asked. She stood at the edge of her garden, regarding her flowers. She rarely played the harp—now and then for five minutes. She had again taken to reading her *Handbook of Psychiatry*, the second volume. Her or me? Dubin thought. He expected, if he looked, to find his name in the index. She seemed forlorn, abandoned by her second husband, such as he was. Her voice was dry; she was thin, distant, out of it somehow. She would look long at her extended legs as she sat in a chair. Whatever she had bought to wear lately seemed wrongly styled or colored. She had bought a fall hat with a bright green ribbon and returned it the next day. "I thought you didn't like green?" Dubin said. "I wondered if it might work this time." She needed, she said, a pair of reading glasses. Lately as she read she had seen floating black spots, but would not go to an eye doctor. "I'm not in a mood to tempt fate." "What do you get out of waiting but anxiety?" "I dislike running to doctors." "Do you think you're being brave?" "Oh, let up, William, I'm being myself."

One evening she asked, "Don't you think it's time we had sex?"

He said perhaps it was.

"You never court me any more."

It's because in a long marriage your wife becomes your sister, he thought. Dubin asked her why she didn't court him.

"You never exactly encourage it."

Kitty brushed her teeth and got into a nightgown he liked. Tonight she lay in bed, waiting for him to begin. He asked her if she was tired and she said she wasn't, was he? He wanted, after Fanny, Dubin thought, someone like Fanny. With her the sexual act began long before the sexual act. Dubin was in his wife when to his surprise his penis wilted like a plucked flower. That hadn't happened before during intercourse. He withdrew and fell back in bed. She tried to bring him to life but he did not respond.

"Had you come?"

He said no.

"Do you feel all right?" she asked gently.

Dubin said he had up to then.

"Well, don't blame yourself. Let's try tomorrow. I'm tired myself."

"Then why did you suggest it?"

"It's been a long time."

They tried for three nights but he achieved no erection. He felt his fear on her body.

"Don't be worried," she urged. "I'm sure it's temporary. Maybe the poor thing is bored. I wish I could plant it in my garden and let it grow like an asparagus."

"I wish you could."

"Are you scared?"

He said he was.

She kissed him. "Let's not make ourselves tense. We'll wait a week and try again. Why do you think it happened in medias res?"

"Maybe because you think of it as in medias res."

"Oh, cut it out."

"One day it happens," he said.

"It shouldn't to you yet. Some men even go on into their eighties. One has to stay with it."

"I'll stay with it if it lets me."

"Is it my fault? I haven't felt much like sex since I came back from Stockholm." She looked at him hopefully, then uneasily.

He asked her if she had been reading about impotence in men.

Kitty confessed she had recently read a chapter in a book.

"Maybe that did it. I respond as you expect me to." He felt he was going after her unjustly but couldn't stop. "If you define me from the book maybe that's the kind of man you get."

She said that was totally irrational.

"All I'm saying is if I'm spinach in your thoughts that's what you'll get when you open the can."

"If you're spinach to me it's because you think of *me* as a vegetable."

"You're reading the book, not I."

"It could be physical," she said earnestly. "Diabetes, for instance, can bring it on. Have you had a blood-sugar test recently?"

He said he hadn't.

"Maybe it's something else—I don't mean to wish diabetes on you," she said with an uncertain laugh, "but something seems wrong. You blame me—that's what your wisecracks and ironies amount to—but you've changed in a way I can't really understand. Have you been sleeping with someone?"

"Do you mean Flora?"

"Her or whoever?"

"You're the only one I sleep with."

Dubin wondered if lying, or the habit of lying, could make a man impotent. You lied to someone and could not lie with her.

"You might have no trouble with another woman," Kitty said.

"I might not."

"If you're sleeping with someone and it's working with her when it's not with me, maybe we ought to think of parting."

He felt his nose twitch.

"Unless"—she hesitated—"would you want to go to Evan now—for advice?"

"You go to him. I wouldn't want to."

"There are other therapists not too far away. There's a new man in Winslow I hear is good."

"How do you know who's new in Winslow? How do you know these things?"

"Evan told me." A moment later she said, "If you're thinking of divorce you ought to let me in on it."

"I think of it often," Dubin said.

Kitty, sitting on the edge of the bed, slipping on her mules, turned to him grimly.

"I wish you'd tell me the truth. Do you have a girl in town?"

"Neither in or out of town."

"*Did* you have during this past winter? I had the feeling you did, when you brought those sex-goodies for me to try with you. I'll bet you had a girl then."

He admitted he had.

"That's what I thought," Kitty said with satisfaction. "Who was she?"

"Nobody you know." Dubin was lying back with his eyes shut.

"You can go to her if you like. Why don't you just go to her?"

"She's not there to go to."

"Then find yourself someone who is," she said angrily.

He said he had no plans to.

"Are you ashamed you'd be impotent?"

"I am ashamed. Your question deepens my shame."

"You deepen your shame."

Afterward they were uneasy with each other. In her presence he lacked; because he lacked she lacked. For each negation or strangeness there is an opposing negation or strangeness. They had got into bed as though they were fragile; as though neither thought it would work. When it did not they looked at each other in loneliness and embarrassment. Neither suggested trying again the next night, or in the foreseeable future.

He thought of himself as crippled. Dubin imagined going to New York to look for a hooker on Eighth Avenue to test his virility. But even reverie didn't work. The hooker said she couldn't take him on because she was overbooked; but she offered him a remedy for his trouble:

"You got to boil it in salt water to clean out the pipe."

"Why don't you blow it out?"

"I couldn't," she said. "I have this sore in my throat."

Dubin didn't think he would go to the city.

Kitty suggested a vacation.

"Not just now," he said.

"Then when?"

"I'm not sure, but not now."

"How's the work going?"

"Surprisingly well."

"What do you think we ought to do?"

"Give it time. Wait and see."

"Wait and see what?"

"If we should seriously be thinking of separating."

She turned away from him, her eyes bruised.

"You'd rather think of divorce than therapy?"

He said he would rather work it out on his own if he could.

"How do you expect to do that?"

"I wish I knew," he said, trying to be conciliatory. "You might walk into the room and pick up a pin. The thing might rise and salute."

They laughed, Dubin wheezily; then looked at each other sadly.

"One feels out of it," Kitty said.

He went on working in the barn, living with the slug of impotence in his mind. But as long as he wrote he felt he was not impotent. Kitty tried to arrange her time so she was doing something gainful almost all day. She went to bed early. When Dubin got into bed she stirred but did not waken. If she was awake she did not say so. He was afraid to touch her or himself. He felt for her a terrible pity.

"Oh, come on," Kitty said, awaking happily one morning. "We haven't been hit by the plague. Let's not give in to our moods. Let's have some parties. Let's see friends." Dubin said it was a fine idea. She made breakfast singing, "We'll sail the ocean blue." In the afternoon she persuaded him to help her bake bread. "We haven't done that since the kids were little. Do you remember how it excited them?" The day went well.

She telephoned friends, who immediately accepted her invitations. She'd been, as Nathanael's wife, a less than accomplished cook, but as Dubin's, Kitty cooked well. They entertained at one dinner party the Greenfelds, Habershams, and Morphys. Morphy was an internist, their nearest neighbor before the covered bridge, who grew small evergreens on his farm for the Christmas tree trade. At another party the Ondyks came with Ossie Lapham and his wife. Ossie was an ornithologist and she, Renata, a twenty-eight-year-old pretty American type who was reading Colette for the first time. She told Dubin Colette had changed her life but didn't say how. Later she asked him if he had ever wanted to have an affair. He said he had. "So have I." "Don't fall in love with him," Dubin advised.

Kitty had a sound instinct for parties of whatever sort and people enjoyed them. She was, at the beginning of the first dinner party, constrained with Flora, but carried the evening off well. Oscar wasn't drinking that night. He seemed to be brooding, looked pale, strained; he volunteered no information and Dubin asked nothing.

After dinner he danced with Flora. Neither mentioned her last phone call or his non-response. "I wear my sleeve on my heart," said Flora.

"In regard to what?"

"In regard to my heart."

He regretted not having gone to her when she had phoned that Sunday morning, after Fanny had left. It might have lessened the effect of her departure if he had spent the day with Flora. In Oscar's presence Dubin felt little guilt; he attributed it to his affection for him, and for having been punished enough also to have been punished for betraying a friend. As the guests were leaving, Kitty stood at the door with her arm around her husband.

In bed they kissed affectionately. "We used to fall asleep in each other's arms," she said. Soon they were exploring their familiar bodies, hesitated, pressed on, trying to invent strategies to outwit the failed flesh; failed.

"Would you still rather wait and see than do anything about it?"

Dubin said he had been to a doctor.

"Why didn't you tell me?"

"I wanted to go without fuss."

"What did he say?"

"It's not diabetes, or the Lariche blood-vessels business, or anything like that. He couldn't say what it was."

"Now that we know that," she said quietly, "maybe this would be a good time to talk to a psychotherapist?"

"Whatever I feel I don't feel impotent," Dubin said.

The point seemed important to make. He said he wanted to wait a while longer to try to figure out what was happening. "It's my life, I want it to tell me what it knows."

"Mother of God," said Kitty, "the way you complicate everything twice over. What happens in these cases has been determined. It's cut-and-dried. You can read about it in books. I imagine it would be very difficult, if not impossible, to cure yourself."

"That's a strange tack for somebody who's always trying to cure herself. This may be a temporary thing. I want to try to work it out."

"Don't be a fanatic," Kitty said. "What happens to me while you're working it out? What happens to *my* young life?"

"I can satisfy you in other ways."

"I don't want a satisfaction, I want a functioning husband."

Afterward she told him to work it out anyway he pleased. "I don't want to discourage you."

She tried not to appear worried, though her eyes and mouth worried. She watered the garden for half an hour, and holding the dripping hose, studied it for another half hour. From afar she contemplated Dubin reading on the porch, glancing away when he looked her way. She had probably told Ondyk about his present incapacity. It was her prerogative though he hated having Ondyk know. He hadn't earned the right.

Dubin had avoided him at their last dinner party. He had talked at length with Marisa, an insecure self-conscious woman. She often blew her nervous nose. Marisa spoke of her husband glowingly in his presence, but he did not mention her in hers. Kitty had talked seriously with Evan more than once that night; she seemed uncomfortable without him. If she had discussed Dubin with him, she did not admit it. "I don't want to tell you what I talk about with him," Kitty said. "He is now a member of the family," the biographer said.

"Would you like me to leave him and find someone else?"

"Whoever you find, don't bring him into the house. I don't want to treat as a friend anybody whose business it is to look up my ass, or yours."

She walked away. Kitty seemed to retreat inwardly. She had stopped playing her harp. They ate in silences. When they walked she went ahead of him, as she used to at times when they were first married. She developed a cough and coughed heavily at night.

"Why don't you do something about it?"

"Why don't you?"

He slept in Gerald's room; she slept in Maud's.

They argued as they hadn't in years, nasty arguments, each topping the other in accusation, neither able to forgo having the last word. Kitty needled him; Dubin shouted. The windows vibrated, his force alarming him.

One morning he gave her a list of things he needed from town: "newspaper, typewriter ribbon, stamps, cigarillos." At the door she turned. "I hate your fucking little lists, I've always hated them. Hereafter *tell* me what you want. I won't look at a list."

When she returned to the house to smell the burners he said, "I put things down on paper because you don't. If you hadn't forgotten to buy a quart of milk that day, I wouldn't have hit a tree and broken my bones. Make your own list, but for Christ's sake make one."

The door slammed as though it had exploded. A window shade snapped and rolled upward.

The front page of the newspaper she brought home was torn, and Dubin mended it with diaphanous tape.

"Why bother?" Kitty asked. "Isn't it to show me up? That I haven't the sense to pick up an untorn newspaper?"

"The wire they bale them with tears them," he said. "I don't mind mending the paper. If I pay for it I'd like to be able to read what it says."

"You explain everything—absolutely everything."

"What we're really arguing about is my sexual inadequacy, and that I haven't taken your advice."

Getting into bed that night after he had gone downstairs to make sure he had locked the front door, as Dubin lay back his head cracked against hers. Kitty screamed. He bellowed: "How the hell did I know your head was on my pillow!"

"I wanted to be affectionate." Tears flowed from her eyes.

He sat in the kitchen at the table where she had piled three pounds of ripe tomatoes in a glass bowl. Dubin bit into a blood-red tomato, hungrily sucking its meat and tepid seedy juice. He devoured two large tomatoes seasoned with coarse salt, then went to bed.

Kitty was awake. "What's that rotten smell?"

"My thoughts."

She rolled over on her side.

He fantasied himself on his walk. He tried to see what he always saw, but this time a stranger with dirty eyes sneaked out of the wood and struck Dubin on the head with a lead pipe. The biographer lay bleeding in the road. The man removed his wallet, counted five singles, and again struck Dubin with the pipe.

"Is that all a man's life means to you?" muttered the bloody-headed biographer.

"Fuck you," said the stranger. "I don't owe you a thing."

Kitty came by. She wept aloud for what she had not done with her life but not for what she had done with it.

"Shush," she said the next morning as he growled at himself in the mirror. He knew he frightened her but could not stop talking to the suffering man in the warped glass.

What if I am impotent forever? Suppose it goes from the cock to the brain? What shall I do? What can I do?

The fanatic regime of two winters ago that Dubin had revived to prevent a great misery happening, he continued to practice in order to change the heartbreaking fate that had befallen him.

One night the ghost of the old man who had hanged himself in the barn tramped across the field to the yellow black-shuttered house and trod up the stairs. Opening the creaking bedroom door, he flung his bloody noose on their bed.

"I am not going to be left to Frieda's tender mercies until I am well again. She is really a devil—and I feel as if I would part with her for ever—to let her go alone to Germany, while I take another road. For it is true, I have been bullied by her long enough. I really could leave her without a pang, I believe. The time has come to make an end, one way or another."

Kitty mourned the dead cat. "He liked to keep me company. I loved the way he stretched out on the kitchen floor with the sun on him." After supper she cut up meat scraps for Lorenzo before remembering he was no longer there to eat them. She hid the cat's dish in a drawer. Thinking it might relieve her to know where Lorenzo was buried, Dubin showed her his grave one evening and Kitty planted an iris bulb in it. "We found him and we lost him."

As they were walking across the field she said, "William, let's be kind. Let's not be nasty. I'm not blaming you for the cat's death or anything else. Let's be considerate and kind."

He put his arm around her, wanting to suggest going to bed, not daring to.

They slept badly in the heat although they slept alone. Dubin wore himself out trying to sleep. He could barely drag himself to the shower. August caught fire from July. At 7 A.M. the thermometer showed seventy-four; at noon it boiled at over ninety. The sun for days flamed. The woods were dry. Trees in the morning mist were like gloomy sculptures: a drunken slanted maple; thick-armed oak; bushy orange-berry mountain ash. Crows barked in the tops of furry pines. Dubin, on his way to the hot barn, cawed at the crows.

Although he had a box fan there he decided to stop working in the barn. The sun beat down on the roof, and by mid-morning the heat lay on him like an overcoat. He had considered putting in an air-conditioner, but in this climate it seemed an obscene act. Maybe next year if the summer started hot. The biographer returned to his cooler study in the house. He hung on the wall his Medal of Freedom and framed picture of Thoreau. With the fan on, the room was bearable, though the muted rattle of the vibrating blades was no help. In Kitty's garden wheelbarrow he trundled back boxes of note cards, folders of manuscript pages. He left the barn reluctantly, imagining the telephone ringing, no one there to answer.

Dubin began to write one of the articles he had contracted

for. It was hard to write with his mind on Lawrence; he was impatient to be back to him but was worried about money. He worked on the biography for two hours each morning and then for two wrote the article. Each sentence was like lifting a rock. Exhausted, he went downstairs to make himself iced coffee. Kitty, her hair up, hot face glistening, was sitting on the porch reading the paper as she fanned herself with her left hand. She seemed not to know he was there. Renewed energy lasted perhaps twenty minutes. Dubin tried another shower, dried himself, returned to his desk. When he read what he had written that morning he laid down the pen. Lassitude came over him. If the weather was minding its business this should be fall beginning. Against the will he felt he ought to lay off a few days. I will write faster once it gets cool.

From his bookshelves he plucked an armful of lives and letters he knew well. Dubin thumbed through lives of Jung, Freud, Swift, Samuel Johnson, Chekhov, Goya, Montaigne, Ruskin, Darwin, Hardy, Mahler, Virginia Woolf. On August 21, 1581, Montaigne, after a night of torment, had passed a stone, "having, to tell the truth, exactly the shape of a prick." "My thoughts have been clouded with sensuality . . ." Johnson lamented. "A strange oblivion has overspread me." "I wind round and round in my present memories the spirals of my errors": Augustine. "Why is it so dull here?" asks Chekhov. "It is snowing, a blizzard, there is a draft from the windows, the stove is sizzling hot, I had the thought of writing, and am not writing anything." "I am sometimes so agitated that I can no longer stand myself," Goya told a friend. "I lack force and work little." Freud devastated Dubin: "Anyone turning biographer has committed himself to lies, to concealment, to hypocrisy, to flattery, and even to hiding his own lack of understanding: for biographical truth is not to be had, and even if it were it couldn't be useful." "I shall be like that tree," said Swift, "I shall die first at the top." "But really, for me," Lawrence wrote in a letter, "it's been a devilish time ever since I was born. But for the fact that when one's got a job on, one ought to go through with it, I'd prefer to be dead any minute." Dubin read to learn what he didn't know or might have forgotten. He sought insights as if hunting for burning bushes on Sinai: how men hold themselves together. But the biographies reminded him of the life he wasn't writing; the life he wasn't living.

Lawrence had become impotent in his early forties—what a terrifying loss to a man who writes poems to his erect phallus. Someone had theorized that his condition was related to tuberculosis, which it took him many years to admit he had; but who is to say what pure Greek fate he had wrought for himself in the labyrinth of the Lawrencian mind, in the recesses of the blue-black blood? Frieda had whispered the sad news around, possibly to justify an affair or two. How curious it is, Dubin thought, as you write a man's life, how often his experiences become yours to live. This goes on from book to book: their lives evoke mine or why do I write? I write to know the next room of my fate. To know it I must complete Lawrence's life. He died at forty-four. I'm fifty-eight but if I die now I die young. My concern with aging has made me conscious of death. William Dubin's in his last life, no longer those one lives to learn with—if he learns. In middle age some degree of accomplishment kept me young, aware of youth in me. The future was my next biography; now it's age. Subjectivity sickens me. I fear myself fearing.

Dubin had taken the measure of himself and measured less.

Almost as he was thinking this, the rains swept summer aside and autumn flowed in. The muggy heat evaporated: weather turned crisp cool; sky cold blue; air transparent. Whirring flocks of birds settled on the lawns, pecked in the dying grass, and flew off in rushing flights. The yellowing trees giving off yellow candlelight turned dull-gold.

He went back to his work, pushed on, wished he was writing in the barn.

As he jogged the long walk one wet late-afternoon, Dubin slipped on a stone, fell heavily, and lay in the road in torment. He felt he had broken his ankle. After excruciating minutes the pain let up and he managed to hobble on. He arrived at the highway, where he was able to hitch a ride in a pickup truck to the hospital emergency room.

Kitty came for him in her new apple-green Toyota. They had traded in the Ford; she would not drive the car that had killed Lorenzo. The swelling was reduced with ice and the strained ankle bound with an ace bandage. Dubin was advised to stop walking for at least a week. The effect was depressingly confining. He had given up the article and gone back entirely to the book. Money was becoming a problem, but if he had to borrow he'd have to borrow. Kitty wouldn't like it. He'd try the article later at a chapter break.

The biographer had to cut out calisthenics and set aside his diet. Immediately he gained weight, felt leaden, heavy, unfocused. In the cellar he located Maud's old bike, cleaned and oiled it, and with Kitty's assistance got it up the stairs. He pedaled the bicycle to the bridge, but the ankle was not that much healed and the pressure of pedaling became painful. The next day he was at a loss what to do for activity. He was restive, nervous. When Dubin stopped running he ran within—a running runs within. To catch up with himself he got into the new automobile.

Dubin went on his long walk in Kitty's car. It took not more than fifteen minutes to drive the route slowly, so he drove it several times. He drove at twenty an hour, puffing a cigar, though not much tasting it; trying to see what he usually saw when he was walking: the seasonally changing landscape—rumpled yellow autumn hills and darkening orange mountains. Close by, eternally a scattering of stiff farmhouses, weathered barns, squat and tall silos, cows in spongy pastures. As he drove his route he was surprised by the narrowness of the road he usually walked. It reminded him of the thin long hallways of the railroad flats he had lived in as a child. Ahead the light receded; the road was shadowy, empty. Dubin drove the emptiness. What am I afraid of other than myself? At the highway he turned left instead of right, and in a burst of speed was halfway to Winslow before returning. The next day he repeated the drive until he had lost count of the number of voyages he had made, and a fog descended on the deserted road.

He could think of nothing that was working as he wanted it to. He had returned the biographies and letters to their proper places in the shelves. Dubin thought of all the lives he had hoped to write that he never would. His nose twitched like a rabbit's as he flipped through Kitty's *Handbook of Psychiatry*, Vol. II. He read in it nothing that gave him pleasure or relief, and hid the book in a closet. Dubin, weary of himself, wanted to be better than he was, free of twitches, tics, compulsive gestures. He wanted to be self-sufficient, in control, good to others, good to his wife. He wanted to breathe in the purity of fresh morning. He was disheartened by his monotonous days and nights. I'm like a rock with an iron fence around it. I'm not doing anything for anybody. He got into the apple-green Toyota and drove to the green bridge.

Dubin journeyed the usual way, not seeing much, head constricted, attention wandering. It began to drizzle and he automatically flicked on the wipers, trying not to think though his mind steamed with thought; and when he lit a cigarillo, his hand trembled. On the wet road close to the path to the quarry Dubin passed a man squatting by his car; he had just changed a rear tire and was lowering the hydraulic jack. The biographer passed him in a spurt of speed. A quarter of a mile farther up the road he pulled to the side and shut off the ignition, tensely trying to think whether to turn back, struggling to control the rush of fear he felt at the thought. The man he had passed in the road was Evan Ondyk. Maybe I ought to talk to him? Dubin touched the starter, turned with difficulty, and reluctantly drove back. He felt shaken, unwell. A vital self had walked out of his life, leaving this old bag.

Lowering his window, he gravely hailed Ondyk. "Need any help?"

"I thought it was you, William. No, thanks, all's done." He lifted the flat-tired wheel, then the jack, into the trunk of the car and slammed down the lid.

Dubin parked on the left side of the road, ten feet beyond Ondyk's Buick on the right. He turned off his wipers but left the motor running. He was still in flight.

"Evan," he said with an effort through the half-open window, "I'm not in the best of shape. In fact I'm not feeling at all well. Would you mind getting into the car with me and talking for a minute? Or I could get into yours?"

"A minute is all I have," Ondyk said, his eyes darting at Dubin's. He hesitated. "Oh, what the hell, talk away, William. But I can't get into the car with you. This flat tire has made hash of my schedule. I'll have to skip something. If it's lunch with Marisa she'll be sore as hell."

"You'll get wet out there."

"I have my rain hat in the car."

The psychotherapist was standing in the road in the drizzle, his hair covered with droplets of rain. His damp brow glistened and blond mustache drooped. He was a heavy-shouldered handsome man with a slender nose, cleft chin, moody eyes. A familiar stranger, Dubin thought. Confiding in him was difficult.

The biographer caught a glimpse of himself in his mirror—shock of recognition: eyes tight, shifty, fearful—mouth compressed, uneasy—complexion gray. He heard his own frightened breathing, felt ashamed of what he was into—consulting a man he had never much liked, a psychotherapist—embarrassed by his embarrassment. There were, among recurring others, two known Dubins: the man sitting in the car and someone within writhing in shame.

"How's Kitty doing?" he heard himself ask. The question seemed strange, imperiling, as though he'd left her and had to ask a neighbor for news.

Ondyk, in the drizzle, smiled slightly. "Ask her, William, don't ask me."

"Of course. I'm sorry."

He cursed his nose twitching spasmodically. Ondyk sneaked a sidelong look at him. Dubin forced himself not to avert his glance.

"I'm not myself," he said with a hollow laugh. "I'm feeling off-center, off-base—as if I have two left sides and nowhere to take them. I work little, without concentration. I'm full of odd crawling fears. I may need an assist, Evan. Has Kitty told you?"

"She didn't put it to me like that. She sort of indicated your book on Lawrence might be doing you in."

"Was that what she said?"

"Something like that."

"What else?"

"That's her business. Listen, William, you and I aren't great friends, but it mightn't be a bad idea if I speak to you as one. I'm no literary critic—that's not my specialty—but I could never figure out why a man of your disposition and temperament would want to get so many years of his life involved with a tormented semi-narcissistic figure like D. H. Lawrence.

Thoreau I can understand for you, but not this fellow. Not all of us are congenial with each other, as I'm sure you'll agree. I'm thinking of the wear and tear in the long run—what a ball-breaking strain it must be to have to identify with someone whose nature is so radically different from yours. Isn't objectivity breached by his constant bilge?"

Dubin did not resist the man's approach. It was easier to reply to than something directly personal.

He answered, lowering his eyes, forcing himself to speak: "He's a strange mindful but essentially a meliorist. He wants a better world but on his own terms: reform sex—the passional lives of men—and you reform the world. But he had very little faith in mankind and allowed himself some detestable beliefs. One critic said his philosophy might be that of any thug or moron if separated from the warm intense articulate being he was. He could be a forthright detached critic of his work. He knew and did not always approve his nature. And whatever his excesses he remained an artist. His fiction, though not always successful, was the work of a man of genius."

Dubin, clearing his throat intermittently, said he took no great pleasure in Lawrence's religious primitivism and anti-democratic fantasies. Or in his view of debased social body with its law-oriented degenerate Jews, weak in maleness, leading in the race to total corruption. Or in his hatred of women whose evil power over blood males emasculated them. "He called the public 'stinking humanity' and equated socialism with syphilis. He was engorged with the rage of a failed prophet.

"On the other hand," he said to Ondyk, "I can't say I'm much upset by his hatred of capitalism and outraged sense of the perversion of human life by technology. Finally, he brings his destructive impulses to a life-enhancing end in his books. He lived in a vast consciousness of life. At his best he wants man to risk himself for a plenitude of life through love."

"Why not?" Ondyk asked.

"Why not?" Dubin hoarsely echoed.

"He sounds better than I thought."

"When you write biography you want to write about people who will make you strain to understand them." Dubin said it was like chasing a runner you would never catch up with. "But the game is, I suppose, to make the reader think that's exactly what you have done, and maybe in a blaze of illumination even have outdistanced him. It's an illusionary farce that holds me by the tail."

The biographer tried to laugh but nothing came of it.

"Still and all," Evan said, continuing to observe Dubin, "though I know I am technically out of my depth, you and he are two radically different types, and living every day with the anger, spleen, and hostility of this enraged man is bound to exacerbate your other day-to-day problems."

"He's hard to take when I'm taking myself hard," Dubin admitted. "He's hard to take now, but I've worked on him for years and have to finish the job."

"You have serious problems."

"I know, but if you don't mind me saying so, Evan, I wish you'd drop this approach. If I give Lawrence up I give up a book, and the thought of that—I confess I've thought of it—makes me feel shivery and sick. I don't want that kind of failure to contend with at this time of my life. I would have no confidence in anything I went to next."

The drizzle turned into rain. Ondyk got his porkpie rain hat out of his car, lowered the brim all around, and placed it on his wet head. He flipped up his jacket collar. In the rain he stood patiently at the window observing the uncomfortable biographer. Dubin's motor was still running. He fought an intense urge to step on the gas and bolt.

"What did you mean before when you said you needed an assist? Were you thinking of consulting me professionally?"

"Kitty said it might be a good idea."

"What's your view?"

Dubin scratched himself nervously. "I'm of two minds. I have my reservations."

"I've heard you on that subject," Ondyk said, wiping his wet face with his wet handkerchief. "In any case it doesn't make much difference because I can't take you on, William. Kitty's my patient and though there are therapists who do marriage counseling with husband and wife it's not my dish of fish, so I regret I have to say no." He smiled moodily. "I know someone in Winslow I could refer you to."

Dubin didn't think so. "I respect what you do or I wouldn't

be encouraging my wife to see you. But I'm not so sure it's right for me at this time of my life. Maybe when I was younger, but I couldn't afford it then."

"If you had needed it seriously, you'd have found a means to afford it."

"I assume I needed it. But that was long ago and I found another way. What I'm saying is I think I understand what's happening to me. I've been there before."

"And you may be there again if you don't do something about it. Simply understanding isn't what it's about, William, you know that. Cure is process—working it through is the only way."

"The unconscious," Dubin heard himself hesitantly say, "is not unavailable to those who study themselves."

"So you intend to continue with your Teddy Roosevelt regime of exercise and calorie counting?"

Dubin laughed unhappily. "It keeps me going."

"In your wife's car with your bad ankle?"

"Till I can figure out a new move, or find myself making one."

"In the meantime undergoing a lot of useless suffering. It's pure waste; so is self-obfuscation."

"We judge ourselves, we take risks," Dubin told himself. Staring uncomfortably at Ondyk standing in the rain he felt wet. The psychotherapist sneezed.

"You're sure you won't get into the car with me, Evan?"

"This will take one last minute. I hate to breach confidentiality, William, but you know I know you have a very serious problem."

Dubin knew.

"Impotence is no joy."

"I don't feel impotent."

Ondyk stared at him in disbelief. "Can a man who writes biography afford to delude himself?"

Dubin, after another miserable moment, thanked the psychotherapist for his advice. "I regret you got wet on my behalf."

"No sweat." Ondyk, in his damp clothes, got into his car.

Dubin, releasing his brake, headed north as Ondyk drove south. For twenty minutes he felt intense relief. Had St. George slain the dragon? He drove the circle backward, but could then not think where to go. His relief evaporated. On awakening that morning he hadn't known what to do next; nor did he now.

That evening the phone rang. "It's Evan," Kitty said. "He wants to talk to you."

"Tell him I'm out."

He had been reading in Lawrence: "We ought to dance with rapture that we should be alive and in the flesh and part of the living incarnate cosmos."

"Speak to him out of common courtesy if for no other reason," Kitty said. "You haven't a friend in the world."

"Only you," Dubin, on his third drink, said. "Tell your friend I'm out."

In the night he would regret it. He was alone in the cosmos and desperately needed anyone, even a friend.

As Dubin slowly drove the ascending road a gaunt runner in a gray sweatsuit, wearing an electric-red safety bib, came loping down toward him. He was an open-mouthed jogger with an awkward gait, who looked as though he hated every step he ran. Sweat streamed down his glistening face, drawn, bony. Dubin, recognizing Oscar Greenfeld, had in astonishment braked the car.

"Holy cow, is that you, Oscar?"

The flutist flatly ran on six or seven steps before wearily halting. He was reluctant to. Dubin backed up the car. He knew the feeling: if you stopped you'd never start again.

"My God, Oscar, what are you doing in that sweatsuit and red bib?"

Greenfeld, pressing his hand to his left side, drew two long noisy breaths before replying. Gasping, he spoke: "Have to. Doctor prescribed—de rigueur. Don't know whether you heard—I had a heart incident this past winter. Have been doing three miles every day since I got back on my feet. Run everywhere—drive to a road whose view I like, then go. Used to walk, but now I run. Run for heart and flute. Running, as they say, makes wind."

Dubin moaned in dismay. "Heart attack? Last winter? God in heaven, Oscar, why didn't you tell me in all this time? Have we become such poor friends? I feel dreadful. Why didn't

Flora call or at least say something when you came to dinner? You looked awful, I was afraid to ask. I find the whole thing hard to believe."

Oscar smiled wanly. "I was in Prague for a concert when it happened. Flora flew over and stayed a month till I could leave. I had the attack on her last birthday, about the time you were fucking her in my house. She told me after we last saw you and Kitty. She felt she finally had to."

He glowered at Dubin, his white face dark, jaw trembling.

"Oscar," Dubin, anguished, cried, "believe me, I regret it."

"William," Greenfeld said, raising his breathy voice, "I don't pretend to be innocent of evil to others. I've screwed around in my time, but what I wasn't prepared for, nor will I ever be, is that my former best friend would betray me in my own house, where he had always been a welcome guest, with my wife. Hypocrite! Fool! I detest you!"

Oscar, resuming his run, disappeared down the road.

Dubin could not for a while remember how to start the car.

A horseman in overalls appeared on the downsloping curved road, a thick-bellied unshaved man wearing field boots, his legs dangling down the flanks of a white heavy-hooved work-horse. Dubin had more than once seen them on this road, wondering where he led the horse or the mare took him. A quarter of a mile up, past acres of unharvested corn, they usually disappeared into the fields. Neither Dubin nor the man had ever so much as nodded to each other when they met. It was that kind of world.

But today as the overalled horseman plodded by Dubin's car, he reined in the white mare and in anger and agitation pointed to the glowing hills under light-shedding seas of autumn clouds.

"Look there! Them Jews are crucifyin' the earth!"

Smacking the horse's flank, he darkly trotted away.

Midway up the nearest hill, a long low one to the north, Dubin beheld an earth-colored savage slash through the foliage where half a dozen twenty-ton yellow bulldozers were shuttling and darting, undercutting and uprooting hundreds of ancient trees.

A deep unyielding pain overwhelmed the biographer as

it occurred to him this was part of a highway cloverleaf being built to divert traffic from town. Dubin had been hearing about it for a dozen years, but had never expected to see it built. He looked with heartache at the long ragged gash where the trees had been torn out of the sides of the living hill. Nature itself, inevitably necessary to his sense of who he was or could be, was being disgraced, destroyed. "Willie," he warned himself, "our natural beauty—inspiration, joy, precious possession, goes gurgling down the drain while you sit in your room writing a life of D. H. Lawrence, of which there are presently too many. Awake, you stupid prick. Stop wasting life's sweet time. Do something to preserve the natural world! Do what has to be done before it can't be any longer!"

Struggling to restrain the dimming that assailed him; to cling to his shaky balance, Dubin, for the first time in his life, fainted away.

A riderless white horse galloped by.

The woman with the broken face, her wasted body swathed in voluminous skirts, pursued him heartbrokenly. Dubin, running for dear life along the rocky shore, his heart pounding beyond belief, sank in exhaustion to the ground. With palms clasped he begged mercy; but it was not the pursuing bitch who'd caught up with him: it was a panting sad-eyed man with a hole in the middle of his face. Now the hole slid across the face, now down. But Dubin glimpsed, through a haze of webbed purple capillaries within, a potato nose and downturned stained mouth from which an ancient rotting voice spoke:

"My name is Richard M. Nixon. I am well-acquainted with your distinguished biography of Abraham Lincoln, my fellow Republican, and I offer you a substantial sum to write one of my life, Mr. Dubin. I've got to get the shit scraped off of my good name."

"And who will scrape it off of mine?"

Kitty, for no reason she could relate, unless it was a hopeful letter she had recently received from the State Department, was sleeping better; but Dubin had caught from her, abetted by the breathless summer, the ailment of sleeplessness. Those you live with teach you. Sometimes she woke and asked him in a whisper if he was sleeping. Knowing that the sound of the human voice invariably set her talking, he stayed silent. Kitty fell back to sleep.

The little Dubin slept each night savaged him. Anything woke him if he momentarily dozed. Any new sound in the night. Or her impassioned breathing during dreams. Or the hint of whistling in his nose. Or his heartbeat drumming in his ears on the pillow. Awake, he feared not sleeping. It took him hours to sleep again, as though for not sleeping the magistrate fined you hours of sleep. He slept a ragged dream-macerated sleep. To break the long wakefulness, Dubin read in the middle of the night. He walked miles in a small room. He took long showers in the dark. If he slept afterward he slept on the knife edge of waking. He must sleep or he couldn't work; wouldn't have the energy even not to work. He feared he would never sleep again. Many were thus afflicted. If he tried pills, although Kitty said he wouldn't, he felt stupid in the morning. The drugged sleep wasted the rest of the day. He would rather be sleepless and work a clear hour or two before his eyelids descended like heavy curtains.

One morning after his alarm had rung, Kitty urged him, "Sleep, William, I'll take care of you."

He had to get up.

"No you don't. Stay in bed, it's Saturday."

"I've been in bed all fucking night."

He drew on a sock and after five minutes pulled up his pants. Kitty catnapped for a minute, then got into her robe and followed him downstairs.

"Would you like me to scramble you an egg?"

He tried to think.

"Forget your goddamn diet." Then she laughed. Dubin was standing at the kitchen window. Kitty went over to him and said, "Why don't you laugh?" She tickled him under the arms. "Where's your funny bone?"

"Not there."

She said she wanted to cry. Resting her head on his shoulder she said she loved him.

After a while he put his arm around her. "I'm a pain-in-the-ass, but try to be patient."

"I can be patient, but how much longer?"

Dubin couldn't say.

"Do it your way," Kitty said, "but *please* do something."

He said he would; she did not ask what.

She hadn't said whether Ondyk had told her they had met on the road.

Dubin saw himself sleeping in a single bed in another house. He slept well there. Would he write better? Would his single life be freer, more varied, joyful? He thought it might in the long run. When he felt better he would ask her to divorce him. Not now but when he was himself once more. Or when he could sleep no longer in this house. That would be a clear sign. He would say he had to leave her because he could not sleep in her bed.

He went relentlessly to his work. Nothing happened. Dubin sobbed noisily.

Kitty knocked on his door. "Can I help?"

He could think of no way.

He wept because his memory was bad. He had at first almost not noticed, or tried not to notice. Recently, forgetting had laid hold hard. It didn't help that Dubin knew Montaigne had complained of a slow mind and incredible lack of memory, despite which he wrote works of genius. Emerson, at sixty-five, was closer to how Dubin felt at fifty-eight: the old man complained of a tied tongue; he said he was "wanting in command of imagery" to match his thought. You had this thing to say and the words would not come; butterflies appeared and flew around the thought. Dubin, against the will, actively forgot names, details, words. He was losing them as though they were coins dropping out of holes in his pockets; or out of his raddled brain. They fell like raindrops into a stream—go find them. Usually when he forgot words he would wait for them to seep back into consciousness like fish drawn up to the hungry surface of a stream. He would remember the initial letter of the forgotten word or sense sounds in it; soon the word reappeared in an illumination. Now words rarely returned when Dubin needed them. He concentrated, trying hard to conjure up a word he could not repossess. It had teased him with its closeness, then burst like a bubble. It was not his to have. He couldn't say what he wanted to; he remained silent.

Dubin forgot what he told himself not to. I'll remember it, he thought, but it hid from him. When he went to bed with a sentence to remember, or one that had come to him as he was trying to sleep, although he kept it alive during the night—unless he wrote it down it had disappeared from his memory by morning. And when he wrote down a sentence, to preserve on paper, it seemed to him he at once forgot a dozen germane to it. As if one sentence is all you are allowed—one to a customer. Or as though someone recites an evil incantation, and therefore a potential paragraph turns to dust. Where are the associations of yesteryear? It was a game of disappearances. Here's this man walking on the road but when you meet up it's his shadow; or it's another man on another road whom you don't remember or even want to know.

Dubin forgot what he read as he was reading it, and much of what he had recently read. Books fell apart in his head; or went up in smoke. He could not repeat, step by step, a long argument. He remembered only the bare bones of what he must know to keep working on his biography. He had notes in place of memory; had to reread often to recall what he had forgotten. He forgot the contents of some of Lawrence's novels; he forgot the arrangement of his Trinitarian metaphysic in the novels. He forgot how important things had happened to him, though not the stations of his short life. When he reread what he had written about him, it seemed to Dubin that someone else had written it. Instead of a chisel he had a hammer to cut stone. I am barely a geographer of D. H. Lawrence. How can my small mind encompass his? *He* forgot nothing.

Augustine had discovered God in his memory: he had left Him there, abandoned Him, and there God had remained. "I recall Thee to my remembrance." God had returned. Dubin discovered realms of space in his memory. Am I forgetting life, or is life forgetting me? He feared telling Kitty what was happening to him, although she sometimes looked as if she knew. Had guessed? What are you forgetting? her eyes seemed to ask. You, Dubin thought, I am forgetting you. What one forgot conceived a further forgetting: a hole unraveling. Unweaving Fanny, he had unwoven the tapestry of their experience. His rotting bones lay amid skeins of memories. Memory cannibalized past experience. It was a maw that ate itself.

He had felt there was much purposeful forgetting in his life; now it *all* seemed purposeful. The purpose was to diminish displeasure, or suffering, or mourning; or simply not to live in active remembrance of the sadnesses of the past. Associative links between one unhappy experience and another had expired in pain and humiliation. He remembered comparatively little of his poor father and crazy mother. His dead brother was drowned in his mind. That had happened almost a half century ago. Dubin had misplaced—displaced?—most of his childhood; he often felt he could replay it minutely; but when he pressed himself to, all he could recall were the bare bones of things. He could remember the color of his mother's eyes, but not their true expression. He remembered only vaguely her features, not the sound of her voice; yet he remembered things she had said. He had once, as a child, noticed menstrual blood on her petticoat and she told him she had had a nosebleed. "There on the back, Mama?" "I turned my head to look for something." After school she gave him a peeled apple with a slice of buttered white bread. When he was sick she mashed a plateful of potatoes in hot milk. One day he had asked her to take him to the movies and she had promised. In those days a child had to ask an adult to take him in and Willie didn't like to. He waited all afternoon for his mother to come down and accompany him to the movies. She came down wearing an old hat. They walked half a block, and then she said she couldn't go, and wept, and went back upstairs. He remembered her grief when her young son was brought home dead. He remembered her thereafter as an insane woman with an altered face and voice, although not much of that time of her life because she was dead before he was fourteen. Once she was in the kitchen, talking sanely to him, when on hearing footsteps in the hall she had with a fearful glance put on her insane face. "Don't go, Willie, out in the rain." She entered his dreams sane and left mad. She began with words of love and ended with sounds that frightened him. He loved and feared her. He forgot words, to forget her; but she, with her fears, lived in his flesh.

When she was dead and he and Charlie Dubin were alone in the house sitting shivah, the waiter sat soaking his purple-veined feet as he read his newspaper. William had felt shame for his father, for his ineffectuality, unwillingness to try to be more than a poor waiter—for hiding his crazy wife in the back bedroom. Without knowing why, as he looked at him, he felt then a sudden keen compassion for the old man. It seemed to the son that whatever else Charlie could or couldn't do, he had done what he had to. The boy was ashamed of having been ashamed of him. Years later he forgave his mother for having lived her insane life in his presence. It was the only life she had to live.

He had told his children little about them, because Charlie and Hannah Dubin had never been present as grandparents. Kitty knew them only as legend. She had met Charlie once and he had tried to please her. Only when Maud had said she wanted to know more about them had Dubin told her at length what he remembered. When he tried to write down what he recalled of their lives, he was surprised at how short an account it had come to. His memories of them had fused into few memories. He had once left himself a week to write about them, but had written all he could in less than two evenings. Where was it all? Where had that part of his life gone? Dubin shook blots out of his fountain pen but could not turn them into words.

Forgetting dimmed the remembering self: kept it in hiding. Often he took in experience, half forgetting. He was not always present in the present; was not always attentive to what was there to be experienced, kept in mind, recalled, remembered. Dubin followed his thoughts where they went, elsewhere. He used to warn himself to observe and remember. He listened carefully to what Kitty said she saw, or had seen: color in colors he hadn't noticed; sounds he hadn't heard. Gerry observed interesting odd combinations of things and events. Maud, in any given experience, saw more details than Dubin saw. He thought he saw whole forms better than they, but wasn't sure. Perhaps he had taken to writing lives in part to teach himself what others saw better. Thoreau looked with eyes, ears and hands, wrote down what he saw, afterward reinvented the world out of his journal. Lawrence observed with genius—a dozen eyes in each eye; saw everything at a glance, retained it, had the language to describe, now or years later, whatever or whomever he had looked at. Kitty, too, saw quickly who was who, though not always what was what. Dubin was a slow study: it took him years to understand who any given man was, including some he thought he had known well; for instance Oscar Greenfeld. He honed his observations in nature on Wordsworth's, Thoreau's, Hardy's; now on Lawrence. Eventually he saw better than he had seen, including inscapes of the self. Dubin sensed what he had forgotten, remembered having lived much in reverie as a youth. There were times he had hidden from life; felt himself, after all these years, doing something of the same now—was walking backward; away from living. He feared the consequences; thought, I must stop that. I must change in some serious way or come to grief.

Kitty put her garden to bed. October was cool sunny warming in the afternoon. He watched her from his window, on her knees, cutting perennial stalks, pulling weeds, pruning, transposing plants. She sprinkled pine needles around rhododendron roots, azalea, mountain laurel. The mountain laurel had done well that summer. Something had done well. A boy she worked with at the Youth Center raked dead leaves. The garden was now for next year. She had complained about autumn flowers, said they didn't grow well for her. Even chrysanthemums, usually an easy flower, had not flourished for her. He imagined the garden under snow.

She came into the kitchen as he stood there with his cup of cold coffee and tiredly washed her hands at the sink. Neither spoke. She opened drawers, looked in them for a while, closed them. She put things away, tidied up mechanically. When they passed in the hall Kitty smiled vaguely. She seemed to be elsewhere; he wasn't sure where she was. Dubin was elsewhere. She was listless, scattered; he hardly recognized her. He hoped someone might help her; he couldn't. One morning she entered his study without knocking and seated herself in the armchair. She had come in, Dubin figured, because she knew he wasn't doing much, as if that made the work interruptible. The thought angered him. She never sat down when he was working well; she'd come in for a stamp or something she had run out of and duck out. Now her presence irritated him, her determined unhappy face, her wilting shoulders. He didn't like the greenish pants or brown blouse she wore. They were colors she punished him with.

Kitty seemed not to know how to begin, then began, sitting stiffly upright, her dark eyes excluding him. This isn't how I want to talk to her, Dubin thought. She ought to think of a better way than to come barging in. It takes two to talk at ease.

"I know who the girl is who was with you in Venice," Kitty said.

"Do you?" Once he hadn't wanted her to know, now he didn't care.

"Fanny Bick," Kitty said coldly. "I don't know why I was so dense in guessing it. I could feel you come alive while she was in the house the summer she worked here. Once I heard you talking together in your study as though you were lovers. They sound like lovers talking, I remember thinking, but I forgot about her when she left. Recently I remembered the airmail letters you were getting from Italy after you came home, then I remembered thinking I'd seen that handwriting before."

Dubin admitted it was Fanny.

"Why didn't you tell me when I asked you?"

"I wasn't out to hurt you."

"It doesn't hurt any the less now."

"I told you I'd had an affair. I didn't say who with."

"Were you ashamed of her?"

"No."

"You took up with her a second time," Kitty said angrily.

He said she had nothing to worry about. "I don't see her any more."

"Did you use to see her in town?"

He said he had.

"Weren't you also seeing her in New York? I suspected you were visiting someone."

He said he had seen Fanny in New York, but that was over now.

"You lied to me?"

"Many times."

"Do you still love her?"

"Still?"

"I assumed you loved her?"

He said he had put her out of his mind.

Kitty's voice wavered. "Why don't you go back to her? Maybe you'd be better off."

She wasn't there to go back to, Dubin said.

"I'll bet you wish she was."

"I wish you'd let up. I wish you'd get out of here."

"Think it over," she said coolly. "You're obviously not getting much from me or giving me very much. If I'm the cause of your discontent, and/or sexual problem, I'm willing to let you go. Some men are impotent only with their wives."

"And some with their mistresses. I read the same chapter you did in that goddamn book."

Though he felt any change would be helpful now, he didn't say it.

"You can leave or I will if you'd rather," Kitty said, seeming to pretend detachment. "We can make the other arrangements later." Her eyes were listless, bruised.

Dubin said if anyone ought to go it should be he.

"Then go," she said bitterly, rising, standing by the chair. "Go today if you want."

He said he couldn't go then. Circumstances weren't right.

"It's your own damn fault. You're crippled out of pride."

"Does Ondyk say that?"

"*I* say it," she shouted. "I also say you can be an awfully stupid bastard. Ask Oscar to toot that in your ear." Kitty slammed the door.

One of his problems, Dubin thought, was that he too often saw himself with her eyes.

He stared out of the window at her shorn garden. He saw her buried in it.

Although his ankle was healed he had not resumed his walk-run on the long road. He had given up losing weight; hadn't the strength to go on with it. Dubin was eight pounds heavier than he'd been early that summer and it was a tight fit into his clothes. He'd had two suits altered by the tailor. "You're bulging," Kitty said. "You ought to go on with your long walks." She piled concern on concern. The husband of a full-time wife is an overworked husband. Whatever she noticed she named. He ate what she fed him—more when she wasn't there: cheese, cake, chocolate. He ate in a hurry, hardly tasting what was in his mouth. It came to nothing: repletion, shame of gluttony. What was happening in his life, the world, in this cursed house, rose to his throat.

Dubin tried sleeping in Gerry's room, in Maud's; it did no good; he could not sleep in three rooms. Kitty asked him to return to their double bed. "What for?" "I sleep better with you there." She seemed newly frightened, as though for her life. She no longer sniffed the burners before going to bed. Her harp rusted. At night Dubin poured himself half a waterglassful of brandy, sipping as he tried to read. Kitty stared at him. Was he saying his thoughts aloud? He asked her and she smiled vaguely. Dubin went to bed drunk, then woke at two. He changed beds, not to awaken her by his restlessness, whispered lamentation. If he woke her she talked. He left the bed at 5 A.M. and dressed in the bathroom. The sky was night-dark, the light of the town rising like silver fumes. There were black trees, then the silver bowl of town, then dark hills. At seven the red sun had burned through the morning mist. His hangover nauseated him. Dubin made coffee. Kitty came down in a gray robe. "It's going to be a beautiful day." He carried his dishes to the sink, trod upstairs to work.

"Fanatic," she cried from the bottom of the stairs. "Fanatic!"

He worked without energy but feared not working. He labored, striving not to forget. He must hold on to the facts and to language. He must keep the right thing in the right place. The facts could be preserved by often studying his note cards, thousands of them. My notes are good, he muttered. I must go on stringing sentences. If I put them together in the right order I can rewrite later, when I feel myself; make what I've written come to life. Breathe into dead words. But the wrong words were coming up too often. When he tried to think of a distinctive synonym of a noun or verb he was down to a rare one or two. He felt for words in a fog, so busy trying to remember that he failed to think. He read the dictionary, then shoved it aside. Language is not life. I've given up life to write lives.

The past when he reached for it was not there. It was hard to sustain that illusion, a colorless weightless fabric that dissolved as he felt for it. He forgot Lawrence's past, did not always remember what went where, came first. Was he seriously sick before his mother died, or sick after? A confusion of villas, countries, complaints. But he lives in his work; who needs me to record how or where he lived outside it?

He searched his files for correspondence with old friends, some who'd been dead for years, to recall who they'd been. What his experience with them had been. He reread Kitty's long letters to him and his to her. Marriage had diminished their variety: one moved to monochrome. Forgetting was without color. He wanted to forget they'd been married as strangers holding to strange pasts. In a sense they were afraid not to be strangers. He wanted to forget that love hadn't come to full-flowering sensuality, as Lawrence had preached it, whatever else it had come to. They had been happy but never sensually so, one with the other. He wanted to forget he did not now love her.

As the days went by, the depression he had held off with upraised hands, as though it was a poisonous cloud, slipped through his fingers and smote him with suffocating force. It fell on his head like a smothering garment. To breathe he pounded his chest, bellowed his name. Dubin felt the entrapment, experienced dullness, nullity. He lived within six sheets of glass, shouting soundless pleas for freedom. He could feel himself cry out but was encased in glass to his head. I am distant to all that surrounds me but my dwarfish scaly self. In reflexive defense he read for the thousandth time: "A grief without a pang, void, dark, and drear." He recited Coleridge's pain to lighten his own and sank into the poet's pit, sipping brandy as the melancholy Coleridge savored tincture of opium. Lawrence, in sickness and depression, lay in bed coughing all night as he stared at a black window. Samuel Johnson sat on a three-legged stool in a tiny room, gazing into a vile abyss. He prayed to God and it came back nought: "My memory grows confused, and I know not how the days pass over me." Dubin knitted and purled the fabric of nothing, entirely nothing. His head shrank as he monotonously recited his name. He went through the movements of life but it was like inching forward on a bed of coals. He could not escape the imprisoning consciousness, the fixed self nailed to its past. He sat alone in a drafty house, forgetting.

A shocking multitude of single hairs appeared in his comb. His chest hair was turning gray. A rotting tooth had to be pulled. He held a book two feet from his face to focus the words. His handwriting grew in size: he'd been avoiding glasses. His haggard face was slack, faded eyes furtively hiding. He looked straight at no one. If he slept he was awakened by cramps twisting his feet. In the dark of night Dubin hopped on the floor to unknot his muscles. Kitty prescribed bananas to supply missing potassium. She knew what was missing. She made banana pudding, baked banana bread. He suffered indigestion, feared an ulcer, eructated, farted. He pissed in a limp stream dribbling in his underpants. Dubin had discovered his prostate. St. Paul might have wished it on fornicators. He had entered the age of aging. I shall never recover what I have lost. He feared illness, immobility; the disgrace of death.

Yet he worked. It was not impossible: the movements of life. He moved his fingers, watched them move. The moving fingers wrote sentences Dubin hadn't invented. He copied them from cards. It meant little but he worked. In the window, the sky was heavy with streamers of moving blue-gray-black clouds blown high from the northeast, eerily, mysteriously floating with outstretched wings, not east but west. A flock of honking geese headed not south but north. He feared their voyage. An avalanche of slashing rivers of rain poured into a forest of raised spears of light. In the dark distance stood winter with its white sword. Dubin shut his eyes not to see what he dared not confront.

Time timed; crept faster. He slept with his watch in his hand. Time tightened its iron fingers around his throat. He turned the clock away, struck it, blinded it. If he thought of tomorrow today withered. Time ran in Dubin; he ran in time. Time excoriated the man from his toenails to the hairs of his head. Stuck its dirty fingers up his old ass. Time preached dying. Life was a trace of dark light in a gaseous entity, a darkly glowing sail in an irradiated universal sea of loss.

Dubin feared ineptitude, imbalance, disorder. The sameness of each boring day slowed the effort to go on. Whispering, sighing, moaning, he raged against the yellow mirror: face of cast-iron gravity; against the crackbrained psychic homunculus. He had done it wrong, made the wrong choices: ought never to have married her; ought never to have let the girl go. In one place he found himself in another. In the bathroom in the cellar. Lost self, selves. Dubin feared his mother's fate, saw her go mad in his looking glass. When had not wanting to live occurred to her?

Or should he burn the book? Free himself from dead life.

A spectral face glowed like a candle flame; waxen, with red beard and rancid enraged ice-blue eyes; he cursed in an agitated high-pitched voice: You rat-faced Jew, I am unknown to you—as Christ is Who was born to the Spirit, Word, the Man, the Male. Your Jew mind is antagonistic to the active Male Principle. You dare not live as man *ought*. Sex, to you, is functional, equivalent to passing excrement. You fear primal impulses. Work which should be an extension of human consciousness you distort to the end-all of existence. You write muckspout lives because you fear you have no life to live. Your impotence is Jewish self-hatred. I detest and loathe you! Mudworm! Dog! *Stay yer bloody distance. Th'art blind to the joy of my life. Tha s'lltna touch me. Burn yer blahsted book for s'lltna live t' see it done!*

Dubin waked running, fearing what he might do. He ran to Gerald's room, pulled up the window, called his name. Gerry, come home. No one in the night replied. He heard Maud whisper to a whispering voice. Her room was empty, white shades drawn. My children, help me—remember the hours I sat by your beds. Kitty lay heavily asleep, openmouthed. He must not wake her, she mustn't see who he was. Downstairs he dialed Ondyk—twelve rings and no reply. Dubin cursed him for sleeping with his phone jack disconnected. I'll go to his house and pound on the door. He ran into the night, feared he would destroy himself or his book.

He drove the circular route backward, his lights plowing the moving haze. At the bridge he turned into a curved lane, then skidded along it into a dirt road, and from there to the other way to the bridge. A dozen times he passed Ondyk's white-framed dark-shuttered house and each time warned himself against his own dreadful pride. At the edge of town he crossed a railroad track against a swinging pendulum signal, as a black locomotive dragging a single freight car loomed out of the churning mist and rumbled by. He drove watching his reflection in the windshield, the overhead light on. A stranger sat in the lit car gloomily crouched over the wheel, driving in the circular dark. Whoever saw him would know he was breaking—had broken—down. Hastily he flicked off the interior light, backed up the car, and drove the opposite way, past Kitty's Wood, the deserted Wilson farmhouse, on the long lonely country road. Here I will live out my days and nights riding forever.

The motor *ping*ed, gave out on the descending road. Dubin jammed his shoe on the gas but nothing came of it. He coasted as far as he could, until the car came to a tedious stop near a dead spruce at the side of the level potholed roadway. He inspected the gas gauge with a lit match. Empty. Kitty clung to his every move. He had asked her to get gas. He turned off the headlights and switched on the flasher. Its orange blinkings lit the heavy-shadowed road. His watch had stopped at one minute past three. Dubin waited in the car, fearing to return home; detested being where he was but did not know where else to go. With both bony hands he fought panic.

The moon rose in a glowing saucer of light in the indigo sky; under it the mountains shone luminously black. In the haze of moonlight on the night field a farmhouse was visible—a light in a window, or perhaps in front of a barn. Dubin's fear of himself rose like a river about to flood. Shoving the car door open he plunged into the rutted field, running in the soft earth toward the farmhouse, skirting a section of withering silage corn. Nearby stood a grove of trees. Approaching them, he lost sight of the light. He was not sure where the trees were in relation to the farmhouse, if it was a farmhouse. Then he spied the light through the trees. Dubin trod on dead leaves in the dimly lit wood of maples and oak wearing tatters of brown foliage. If it was a farmhouse he would watch a minute to see if anyone was up before he went to the door.

He would knock, he thought, and tell whoever answered that his car had broken down. He would ask to use the telephone and try Ondyk again. He would rather call Oscar Greenfeld but felt he couldn't. He did not want to go home. He did not want to be near the manuscript. If he called Kitty he would ask her to hide it. Dubin thought that if the farmer would drive him to the bus station he would take an early bus to New York City. There he would phone Kitty and tell her where he had abandoned her car, but not where he had holed up. He would say he'd get in touch with her when he felt himself again, whenever that was. When he had been away from her for a while. He could not imagine what he would do with himself in the city. He wondered if Maud would leave the Zen commune to come see him in New York. He did not think she would. He did not think he would ask her.

He heard a growling bark of a dog and retreated into the wood. His testicles shrank. The thought of a dog to contend with was more than he could bear. Why hadn't he waited in the car till morning, or got a hitch on the highway and tried Ondyk again? What farmer in his right mind would open his door to a stranger's knock at this time of the night? I'd better get out of here before the dog sniffs me. Was the animal leashed? He listened for the clink of a chain but heard none. Nor did he hear a barking dog. Dubin moved stealthily back through the trees. When he came out of the wood he saw no cornfield in the darkened moonlight. It would have to be on the other side of the wood—a larger wood than the grove of trees he had imagined. He must go carefully not to alert the dog, chain or no chain. Once he got to the cornfield and saw his flasher in the road he'd know where he was, at least for the moment.

The moon slowly moved behind a darkly glowing white cloud mass, and Dubin saw by the light of a cluster of bright stars that he was standing in an unfenced small graveyard, perhaps a family cemetery. He sank down to see who his company was. He touched the nearest stone slab with his fingers but the carved limestone letters had been eroded by wind and rain, the snow, the seasons. Whoever lay dead there was not saying who he had been. Crawling to the next grave, he felt the slender long headstone above it, and found it too was effaced. He rose to his feet, and as the clouds broke and moonlight flooded the graveyard, he discovered to his horrified surprise that the stone he had touched had been erected before an open grave. Dubin ran.

As he came into the moonlit wood to try to find his way

back to the cornfield, he heard what he thought was a rushing wind and listened in fright as it became the sound of an animal coming at him through the spattering dead leaves. Dubin stood momentarily immobilized, then with a choking cry tore his belt out of his pants, and as the dog hurtled up at him, swung at it in panic with the belt buckle. The silver buckle struck the dog's skull with a thud-like crack. The animal yelped, withdrawing with a whimpering snarl. Dubin, dropping the belt, rushed to a tree and jumped for a low limb. He lifted his leg over it as the dog with a snarling growl flung himself up at him, fastening its slobbering teeth into his right shoe, as he tried in terror to drag himself up the tree. He was unable to move. The dog, its eyes glowing yellow, clung like a deadweight to his foot.

"Help," Dubin cried. "Help me!"

The door of the farmhouse, twenty feet away, shot open, and through the trees he saw a somber oblong of light as a burly man with a rusty pistol appeared in the lit doorway. The man raised the gun and fired into the wood.

"Git 'im!"

The dog quivered and fell to the ground at Dubin's feet, growling throatily, threshing its legs as though running a race it had long ago lost.

Dubin dropped from the branch and ducked through the brush. With a cry the farmer holding his smoking pistol came charging into the wood. A moan of deep-boweled lamentation rose like slow smoke. Dubin heard a bullet thwack into a tree as several dead leaves fluttered down on his head. For a minute he ran in a circle, then stepped into the crotch of a two-trunked oak with ragged low boughs. Catching one, he managed to pull himself up into the oak's bare crown. He shinnied and climbed, straining, writhing, until he was fifteen feet above the ground, where he watched through the branches the white-faced farmer hunting him with a gun.

"I'll git you for murderin' my dog, you homusexual bastard!" He was a large-faced gray-haired man in a white undershirt, dirty work-pants, earth-stained leather boots. His face poured sweat as he wandered in the gloomy wood. He seemed dazed, frightened, mourning his dog.

Dubin shivered in the cold tree. He was moved to call

out—beg the man's pardon, explain what had happened tonight, perhaps tell him the story of his life—why it had brought him at this moment to this wood. But he dared not utter a sound—felt the farmer would shoot at his voice. He'd be dead before he could identify himself—a madman hiding in a stranger's tree.

The farmer sank to his knees before his dead dog, its head and neck dark with blood. He lay with his cheek on the dog's flank, his shoulders shaking. Dubin, watching from above, thought: At midnight I was in bed unable to sleep, and a few hours later am up somebody's tree after causing him to kill his dog. He regretted there wasn't time to live more than once and maybe do things better another time.

To his dismay, the burly farmer, rising, began to shoot into the trees. He would stand under one, grimly shoot a bullet into it, then pass to the next. "I'll git you, you-Jew-son-of-a-bitch, one way or t'other!"

Dubin, on the verge of calling out who and where he was, held back, fearing the man would fire before he had two words out. He saw himself fall to the ground like an ungainly huge bird.

The farmer aimed his pistol and shot into Dubin's tree. The bullet broke a branch over his head; it brushed his face as it cracked through others on its way to the ground. To keep himself from falling, he clasped the trunk of the rough oak with both arms.

The gun banged twice more as the man aimed at nearby trees. When the pistol was empty, he stumbled into the house, probably to reload. Dubin began hastily to descend, but before he could get halfway down, the farmer reappeared with a quilted blanket and tenderly covered his dead dog. Lifting the animal as if it were a child, he carried it into the wood. Dubin knew an empty grave where he could bury it.

It had begun to rain. The moon had gone; the wood was pitch-black. He slid down the tree, his raw hands bleeding. Avoiding the wood where the farmer had disappeared, he ran in the brush through the trees into the open. Skirting the lit narrow farmhouse, Dubin ran in the wet dark, expecting a bullet in the back of his head.

Then he saw the cornfield. In the rain he trotted alongside

the rows of silage corn, the stalks sighing in the wet. As he turned the end of the sloping field, he beheld through trees the blinking orange light of Kitty's car on the road. In a few minutes he was in it, drenched to the flesh, his teeth chattering. His watch read a minute after three.

Dubin sat exhausted in the freezing car, waiting for morning. He tried to sleep but his consciousness was lit like a lamp. He could not put out the light in the dark. When the sky turned gray he staggered out of the car, came back to lock it, and in the misty drizzle headed toward the highway. As he walked the wet road Dubin thought of the long night. His panic was gone. He knew where he had left it, but not where it would find him again. He promised himself to send the old farmer a dog.

I've had it with testing myself, he thought. Du bist Dubin. I know who I am—well enough to take the next necessary step. I learn best when struggling with the work—with the lives I write. Tomorrow I'll go on with it or I may find myself up another tree, trying to change my life. I must stop running from Lawrence dying. I must act my age.

A dog barked shrilly in the nearby woods, and Dubin began to run. He ran poorly, hardly a trot, came to a stop in a few paces, hobbled on. Until this night he hadn't run in an age. He could not run now. If a dog appeared out of the trees he could do nothing but cry murder. He was holding his pants up with his hand. Blood oozed from the toe of the shoe the dog had torn; he was limping.

As he crossed the wet highway in predawn traffic, a car with blazing lights bore down on him. Dubin waved both arms, crying out a warning. The lights dimmed but the car, after hesitating, again came at him. With a cry he broke into a limping run, holding his pants. A horn honked. The auto stopped with a clonk abreast the biographer running in the highway, a door fell open. "I thought it was you, get in, William." She was wearing her blue-tinted glasses. The car was warm. He slid in with relief and gratitude. Fanny, calling Dubin lover, said she had come back to stay. Was it this, he wondered, he had earned tonight?

Nine

HE REMEMBERED Dr. Johnson in the marketplace at Uttoxeter, standing bareheaded in the rain where his father's bookstall had been. Years before, the old bookseller, ailing that day, had asked his son to go there in his place and the son had refused. "Pride prevented me." Fifty years later Samuel Johnson, an old man, laboriously journeyed to the market and stood an hour in the rain by the stall his father had once used, to do for the dead man what he hadn't done.

Oscar Greenfeld appeared in the hospital room.

He had come to see Dubin because his own brush with death had revived in him a sense of their old friendship.

The biographer, recovering from bacterial pneumonia, thanked him; pointed to a leather chair. He was lying on a raised pillow watching the green-streaked short November sunset. Each was moved. Each tried not to notice how old they were becoming. Both for a while sat in silence.

Greenfeld then told Dubin the joke about the rabbi who when his shammes prayed, "Dear God, I am nothing, you are everything," remarked, "Look who says he's nothing."

Dubin laughed fruitily.

Oscar placed on the bed the book he had picked up on the chair: "I'd have thought Lawrence."

"Montaigne," Dubin said, "premeditating death as premeditation of freedom."

"Why bother?" The flutist coughed raucously, wiping his mouth with a handkerchief. "Not to worry, I am not contagious."

Dubin said that sometime after an accidental foretaste of death in a collision on horses with a servant riding forth to greet him, Montaigne had concluded that death was of minor concern to him. "He felt if we don't know how to live it's wrong to teach ourselves to die and so make the end inconsistent with the whole."

"He's got his nose in his belly button," Oscar said in irritation.

"He had no belly button," Dubin snapped.

"He sounds like Buddha."

"In the end the great sound alike."

"Are you afraid of death?"

"No more than ever."

"After my heart attack I got fed up with the way it buzzed in my mind. To save my sanity I stopped thinking."

"I have to know."

"So much is evasion, illusion. How often do we truly know what is? Do I know you? Do you know me? I thought you and I agreed on that?"

"It's a practical thing," Dubin said gloomily. "I'm tired of the number of times I make the same error. One fails at a certain point when he continues to fail."

"My sense of it," Greenfeld said, "is that there is little serious changing of self in life, no matter what one knows. Who knows how to change? It comes or it doesn't. I don't say one mayn't try to make the wrong thing harder to repeat—sometimes he succeeds, usually no. I'd rather concentrate on improving my fluting."

Dubin said he wanted to know what a man his age ought to know.

"Wasn't it your friend Lawrence who insisted there's no knowing one's way through life?"

Dubin admitted it. "He lived in his own personal mystery, infinitely expanded. I won't relinquish for myself what he failed to know about himself."

"Forgive him: he wrote well and died young."

Oscar had brought with him his leather case and began to assemble his silver flute on the chair he'd been sitting in.

Dubin, as he watched, mused: "I thought biography—the thousands of lives I've read and the few I've written—would make the difference between badly and decently knowing. I thought I would know, at my age, what to do when I had to."

"Still into knowing? Your friend says in an unforgettable passage you read me once to let life invade you. Don't prejudge a flower or the blue sky. Here, William, let me play you, please, a song of Schubert's I've just transcribed—"Seufzer," a good word for "Sighs."

Wetting his lips, he played the lied with silvery intensity, moving his head as he moved his fingers. The notes were light clear liquescent.

In the growing dark Dubin listened to the fluting melody of unfulfilled wanting: "*Denn ach, allein irre ich im Hain.*"

"Not me," the man in the bed insisted. "I've had it with loneliness. I've had it with youth. I'll take only what I'm entitled to."

"A ripe old age?"

"I'm an odd inward man held together by an ordered life."

Oscar unscrewed the flute and placed the parts in its velvet-lined case.

"It's a song, a short song, all I can offer."

He was, at that time of his life, a thin man with saddened eyes and a hacking cough, except when he played his flute. When he played he was a young man with a silvery voice.

Sunset had turned the clouds light-green streaked with charcoal. When Oscar left it was night.

"Will you want the light on?" he asked as he was going.

"It's mad to die," Dubin passionately cried.

"Flora," said Oscar, "sends her best."

"Please give her mine."

They kissed in the dark and parted.

"Can't we go on being lovers?"

If it was the wrong question how do you know till you ask?

Fanny and Dubin were standing at the long narrow window that Myra Wilson used to call "the west parlor window," where she had often watched sunsets; often with Kitty Dubin, who afterward described them to her husband. Kitty collected sunsets. Fanny's hair was loosely braided into a pigtail halfway down her back. Both were wearing coats and wool hats—Dubin his red, Fanny a beige hat pulled down over her ears—in the cold farmhouse as they gazed through the slightly distorted green glass at the long stretch of weedy snow that went on for miles to the dense gray forest rising beyond the fields of Fanny's farm. She had bought it with her inheritance. Her mother had died of a stroke that past summer. "I got half of what she left, my sister the other half. My mother is the only person I feel really loved me."

Dubin did not protest nor deny.

She told him that her father, recovered from his recent illness, had gone with a chick to the South of France. "Don't expect anything more," he had said to Fanny. "Whatever you're getting out of my pocket you got from your mother."

"I don't expect a thing from you, you ape," she said she had said.

Dubin, as father, winced.

She had soon thereafter driven across the country to Center Campobello, not exactly sure why. "Except that I like small Northeastern towns, even if they are too freaking cold. But I love to live in the country and already have friends here. A lot of young people are coming into the area, buying farmhouses, some doing marginal farming as well as things of their own." Not long after her arrival she had seen, bargained for, and bought the Wilson farm.

That's for a long time to come, Dubin thought.

He asked Fanny why she hadn't been to see him at the hospital after delivering him there the rainy morning he became ill. Their present meeting, as they gazed out of the window, one overcast frozen day in December, was their first since he had left the hospital.

"I phoned but wouldn't go because I didn't want to walk into your wife."

Her plain face was serious, light-green eyes distant, calm as they talked; but she hadn't once laid a finger on his arm in the intimate way she had. There was no more than an inch between them where they were standing. It was that kind of window: to see out of it together two had to be standing close. Dubin did not touch her because he sensed she wasn't about to touch him. It was a game of losses: probability annulled possibility.

"About that question you asked me," Fanny at last said, "I don't think I ought to go on sleeping with you as we used to, William. I have my own life to live."

It was the wrong question: he oughtn't to have asked, at least not now.

"I know the good things about you," she said. "And I know you understand me. I even feel you love me in your way but I still can't sleep with you. I have to look out for myself and you're not free to be with me. But I would like to be friends,

William, if you want to be mine if we don't go to bed any more. I came back here to find something different for myself, something that might last—which doesn't mean going on sleeping with a married man. I have to be careful of my future. It's my life and I have to respect it."

He nodded sagely, as though he had put the words in her mouth.

"Still," Dubin said, "if it was over between us, past redemption, what drew you back? Was it Roger?"

"Not really," Fanny answered with a quivering yawn, "although I'm glad he's here just as much as I am you are. I'm not sure why or when I made up my mind to come back. Part of it was because I went to U.C.L.A. last summer and got enough credits for a B.A. degree, which N.Y.U. says it will give me in January. I finally got that done partly because of you—because I wanted to show you I could—but most of all because I want to go on to the next step of my life. I think I have got my head together by now. I wasted all I want to waste of life. If I waste more it's cutting my bone. I feel this is the right scene for me. I've always had a nice feeling about being in the country, as if something good might happen to me here."

"Did you foresee a farm in your life? I never heard you say so."

"Not necessarily a farm but something to do with the earth—with having land. I don't know much about nature but now I would like to. There are new things in my thoughts that tie up with some that are old."

Dubin, in a stray thought, remembered her lying receptive to him in a field of flowers.

"I had this shrink once," Fanny said, "who said because my father was so flighty and unconcerned I had this image of myself with roots in the earth. I've often felt I wanted to dig my hands into soil and make something grow."

Dubin wondered if she felt the sexuality of the earth. "You're a vital sexual creature, Fanny—in a good sense."

She laughed breathily. "Anyway I'm not oversexed, although I think my father thought I was."

"I never thought so."

"I liked it when you once said I celebrate life with my sexuality."

He said so had he with her.

"Craig Bosell's brother-in-law," Fanny went on, as Dubin in silence lamented his loss, "wants to rent twenty-five acres of my land to put in corn and soybeans. I will plant a vegetable garden next to the house and besides that I already have six goats in the barn and a dozen Rhode Island Reds that I handle myself. I had a course in animal husbandry last summer and it's not all that hard if you have patience and don't mind getting your hands in animal shit. I think I can support myself with what I grow and earn on this farm. I'm sure I will get along although all I have left in cash is six thousand of the forty-eight I got from my mother."

"Why did you buy the farm outright? Why didn't you take a mortgage and leave yourself more cash?"

"I felt I wanted to completely own my property when I moved in."

"Fanny Farmer," Dubin said with a limp laugh this winter's day.

She tittered.

Lifting his hat, he said he had to be going.

Raising her arm, she showed him she still wore his bracelet.

Fanny then embraced Dubin and he was about to pull her into a desperate clinch until he realized she was hugging him formally, as if he were her cousin Alfred if she had one; and Dubin felt this was indeed the coup de grace—their affair had run its course.

He trotted all the way home but had to walk back for the car.

That night after supper, Dubin, repossessed by desire, waited in the auto, parked without lights beyond a stand of sugar maples fifty feet up the road from Fanny's farmhouse. The biographer had sad thoughts of free will; of functioning and failing at this time of his life. Greenfeld was right about significant change in a man's life: as you were grooved so you were graved. He berated himself for spying on the girl, fried himself alive. He could not justify his renascent jealousy; lived badly with it. It had, against his will, boiled up, monotonizing feeling, wearying, irritating him; but there was no escaping it. You fled; it grabbed you by the cock and swung you round.

Why be jealous now they had formally buried the corpse of their intimate relationship? No rational answer to an irrational response; yet he waited to see if Roger Foster showed up, not knowing what he would say or do if the youth did. Would a fistfight settle anything more than Dubin's hash?

The light went out in the farmhouse kitchen, then bloomed upstairs in Fanny's bedroom. The girl didn't know that Myra Wilson had died in that room or would she have slept elsewhere? Yet there was something chaste about a young woman sleeping alone in a room where a courageous old woman had died. Dubin, when the bedroom light went out, drove home.

That was Tuesday. He waited three more nights before Roger appeared on Friday after eight, in his father's one-ton truck. The biographer ducked the truck's brights, fearing he would be spotlighted like a hooked fish on the front seat; but the road curved where he was parked and the lights lit up several sparse elms on the other side. Roger drove into the farmhouse driveway and rang the rusty bell on the door. Dubin kept himself out of sight as Fanny's dog, Snowdrop, a golden Labrador that looked almost white at night, came woofing out of the house as she, in calf-length yellow boots and padded jacket, held the door open for her guest.

The dog sniffed at Roger and was let loose. Snowdrop, frisking through the snow, his tag tinkling, found Dubin's car, where the driver sat motionless on the qui vive, ready to turn on the ignition and take off if the beast barked loudly. Snowdrop, instead, sniffed at the left front tire, pissed a steaming stream on it, and trotted up the road. Dubin waited five minutes, then got out of the car and approached the house.

What were they up to in Myra's old-fashioned parlor? He trod in the soft snow around to the back of the farmhouse, sinking to the tops of his carefully buckled galoshes; listened at the narrow window, his cold ear pressed to the side of the house where he could see an avocado plant Fanny had in a white wooden tub a few feet behind the windowsill. She had kept Myra's worn leather armchairs but had replaced the stuffed velveteen sofa with a slim tan one along modern lines.

It was that they were no doubt occupying. He strained to see. What a base thing to be doing, Dubin—at your age a Peeping Tom. He observed himself staring at them through the avocado leaves, a gray-haired old man with thick salt-and-pepper sideburns and jealous eyes. What if they spotted him spying, to his eternal humiliation? His heart raced but he remained rooted there, ears straining, and heard Roger ask, "Are you still seeing the guy?" Fanny replied, "We're friends but nothing more. I told him so the other day."

There has to be more to it than she says, the old man thought.

The Labrador ran up to Dubin with a throaty growl.

"It's me, Snowdrop," he whispered, experiencing excruciating déjà vu. We met Monday. You sniffed me up and down."

Fanny appeared at the window, shading her eyes; peered out. After a minute she left. Would she go to the door? My God, what will I say?

Dubin walked backward, the dog persisting, harrying him, growling, now and then letting out a sharp bark. The biographer instinctively moved toward some trees. The dog, snorting, snapped at his sleeve. Dubin tore it free. The animal jumped for his face. He forcefully shoved it aside, fearing exposure, disgrace. Fanny hadn't yet come out. Dubin was about to make a run to his car but the hound was being playful, so he stopped in his flight to rub its head, and Snowdrop licked his gloved hand. In another minute he had made it into the auto, slamming the door and pressing down the lock button. Saved by Fanny: her affectionate nature conditions the likable hound. If it weren't hers the dog would have mangled me. Snowdrop raised his leg, wet the other tire. Dubin started the car after Roger left the farmhouse. He drove for a while, returning to see Fanny's orange light go on upstairs. He rode home, more or less content.

Two days after, the evil effects of his nature caught up with him. Fanny had seen him through the window. "I know that was you spying on us last night," she wrote. "Please don't come here any more. I don't want to have the shame of seeing you do anything like that again."

Barely able to stand himself, Dubin drove to the farmhouse. Fanny was in the barn feeding a pregnant Nubian goat. Bosell had built stalls for the goats and repaired the henhouse for the dozen Reds.

She stared at a panful of brown eggs she had collected as

Dubin apologized. "To tell the truth, Fanny, I was a victim of a fit of unreasoning jealousy. Forgive me, my feeling for you is immense."

"What would you say if I told you I'd had an abortion last summer?" she asked wearily, grimly.

"I'd regret it."

"I don't. I never really cared for the guy."

"I regret that too."

"What else do you regret?"

"That I wasn't single and closer to your age when we met."

"What are you really saying?"

"Let's go on for a while. Let's see what happens."

"I can't," she said flatly, nasally, her stiffened eyes fixed on his face. "I wish you wouldn't ask me that any more."

"I won't," he said compassionately. Dubin hurried out of the barn and drove at once to Winslow. After searching through a tray of rings at a jeweler's he found one he liked, a hammered gold band with six glowing rubies. He wrote out a check for $450.

Dubin picked up a hothouse gardenia for Fanny and peacefully drove back to Center Campobello. He would give her the gift and depart. At the barn door he met Bosell, who said he thought Fanny had gone into the house to nap.

He tried writing her a note on the parlor table. Dubin wrote two: "From a former lover who never made it as a friend." And since that didn't say much, tried "Goodbye, dear Fanny, with thanks for all *you* gave me." He left neither. He left the ring in its blue velour box and the gardenia in a glass of water. He hurried up the driveway to his car.

A window was noisily raised at the front of the house. "William!"

Dubin trotted back.

Fanny had come downstairs after her nap. Her face was refreshed, softened, flushed by sleep. She was standing at the parlor table, wearing Dubin's ruby ring and holding his white flower.

"It looks like a wedding ring. I feel like a bride."

The flickering red candle Fanny had left on the bookcase gave forth a darkish private light.

She had put on Bach: *Ein feste Burg ist unser Gott . . .*

They had eaten in the parlor and were now in her bedroom, deceptively small in the shadowy light. Fanny, in her see-through caftan, wearing white bra and black underpants, pattered in bare feet from bathroom to bedroom, watering her potted plants out of a drinking glass.

The bedroom was furnished as her city apartment had been, with the exception of Myra's standing lamp with its large orange shade: the same chairs, pictures on the walls, even the colored snap with pigeons in San Marco, the same books in the bookcase; almost everything but the single bed—double in the city. What this meant he seemed to think he knew. Dubin, listening to the choral bang of the cantata, sat in striped boxer shorts and undershirt, his clothes piled on a straight-back chair, black winter shoes stuffed with black socks tucked under it. In the bathroom he combed his gray hair with her slightly soiled bone comb and rinsed his mouth. Fanny had once instructed him to urinate before getting into bed. "You'll come better." She educates me. He was grateful.

Wohl auf, der Bräutigam kommt . . .

She glanced at him momentarily anxiously as he took the water glass from her hand and held it as they kissed. Their first kiss, after a season of separation, loss, before renewing joy, hurt. Dubin set the glass down and began to unbraid Fanny's warm hair. She shook it out, heavy full. Her shoulders, breasts, youthful legs, were splendid. He loved her glowing flesh. Fanny removed her heart-shaped locket and his bracelet, placing them on the bookcase near the dripping red candle. She kept the ruby ring on. Forcefully she pulled his undershirt over his head; he drew down her black underpants. Fanny kissed his live cock. What they were doing they did as though the experience were new. It was a new experience. He was, in her arms, a youthful figure. On his knees he embraced her legs, kissed her between them.

So geh herein zu mir,
Du mir erwälte Braut!

She led him to bed, flipped aside the blanket. He drew it over their hips.

"Hello, lover."

"Hello, my child."

"I'm not your child."

"Hello, dear Fanny."

They wrestled in her narrow bed, she with her youth; he with his wiles. At her climax Fanny's mouth slackened; she shut her eyes as though in disbelief and came in silence.

Mit harfen und mit zimbeln schön.

Dubin slept with his arms around her; she with her hand cupping his balls.

When he awoke that Christmas-day morning he felt, as he stared at the bedroom floor, that weeds were growing between the boards. Kitty, awake, said, "If I am born again I hope it will be with B-cup breasts."

"Don't get up," she said. Sitting, she drew off her blue-flowered nightgown and moved toward him. Dubin lay back. Though he willingly embraced her warm familiar body he felt no stirring of desire. She held his phallus but it lay inert.

Kitty, lying motionless, her head on his breast, shifted to the edge of the bed and lay looking out the window.

Dubin said he was sorry.

"You're doing this to punish me."

"What for?"

"For being who I am. For having married you. Because you lived your life with me."

"I lived with you willingly."

"I think you willed it."

"I will waking up, for Christ's sake. I will my goddamned work. There are times I will living."

"Love can't be willed."

"There is a will-to-love."

"The thought depresses me."

"Don't let it," he shouted at her.

"Oh crap," said Kitty.

"Don't piss on the past. Don't deny the love I felt for you because you don't think I feel it now."

"I know you don't."

"I'm saying not to deny I loved you."

"What good is that to me now?"

"It preserves the past. It keeps you from making something into nothing."

"When I was a little girl I used to fantasy a church bell tolling when someone was advising me to count my blessings if I was feeling loss. I remember the sound."

"Why bother?"

"Don't feel superior to me. You're the one who's impotent."

He didn't say whom he was not impotent with.

You tell the truth, Dubin thought, it stands erect, finds the well. You lie as I lie to her it plays dead. She gets no use of it.

Kitty, on her back, monotonously recited complaints he had heard many times in many voices:

"We were never passionately in love. I suppose it was a mistake to have got married. I should have waited. We had the best of intentions, and hopes, but it was surely a mistake. What you lack of love in marriage, of true passion, if you're me, you never make up. You miss it always, even when, I suppose, you oughtn't to. I went through my young married life telling myself the good things I had—my home, children, hardworking faithful husband—a decent life, surely—but I missed something."

"The bell tolled?"

"Often."

"Tough," Dubin said. "Whatever you missed you'd have missed with any man. Marriage doesn't make up for what life fails to deliver."

"With some it does, the right marriage."

"Yes, for a while, but a time comes when you miss what you've always wanted more of. I would have lacked something with any woman I married."

"We missed more, married to each other. The kids missed something too. They sensed our lack of deep love for each other. Both of them sensed it and I'm sure it bothered them."

"People bother people. If it was there to sense I'd want them to."

"They were hurt by our tensions, irritations, quarrels. We pretended a better relationship than we had."

"Doesn't everyone? You put it together as best you can. You protect it."

"It was not the best of marriages." Kitty wept briefly into the pillow.

Dubin lay on his side, his back to her, trying to tote it up as a fairly decent marriage. Not in this mood.

She blew her nose. Shifting into dispassion, she told him she had dreamed that she had bought a plane ticket to Amsterdam to see the spring tulips but had landed, instead, in Newark, New Jersey, where William Dubin lived with his parents.

"I went up a couple of rickety flights of stairs in a broken-windowed tenement, but when I got to your door I was afraid to ring. Finally I had to. I was a widow with a child, who needed help. I'd been told you were looking for a wife. The door opened, and a woman ran down the hall and hid in the bathroom. I came across you in a small room at the end of a hallway. You were a man with earlocks and dark lonely eyes. You were wearing a yarmulka and studying a book in Hebrew. The letters looked like broken bits of a puzzle. This man is a rabbi, I thought. It would be a mistake to marry him."

"Marry a Jew?"

"A rabbi. Someone who, for obvious reasons, would never be devoted to me."

"What brought you to a rabbi?"

"My peculiar fate. He knew about me when I arrived and said he would marry me. I wept."

"Why would a rabbi marry you?"

"I don't know."

"Why didn't you go home and marry someone else?"

"I couldn't."

Afterward, Kitty said, "I'm sure I failed you more than I thought, but that's just the point—I would have done better with someone more like myself. You should have married a Jewish woman who was better put together and needed less attention, someone who slept nights and wouldn't keep you awake. You'd have waked fresh as a daisy, running to work."

"Who would you have done better with?"

Her eyes were moist. "If Nathanael hadn't died."

"I wish to God he hadn't."

After a long hesitation, Dubin, turning to her, said their talk was self-defeating.

"I'm not afraid of the truth, are you?"

"What truth are we telling each other?"

"That we live side by side but not together. We live in the same house, but I can float around for days yet not make contact with you. After your affair with Fanny in Venice, the feeling we had for one another that we'd kept more or less intact, began to unravel. You speak of a will-to-love. If what I get is what you've willed there's not much to sustain me."

"You make it sound more negative than it was, or is. Will or no will, I've always appreciated you as a woman."

"I want more than appreciation."

"So it was a bad marriage?"

She was observing him gravely, uneasily, sadly. "It's not much of one, I'm afraid. Not any more. I have to be honest."

He damned her honesty, felt at a loss, had not wanted to fail in marriage. "Then I owe you an apology," Dubin said.

"I admit we tried, but we aren't sufficiently suited to each other or there'd be less holding back, much more giving. That has to be said."

"Who I am is not Nathanael?"

"He was in love with me when we got married. I loved him. He wanted me close by. He did not resent me for needing him. He wasn't cold to me, even when I made the mistake of being cold to him."

"Nate the saint, except when he bopped you in the eye?"

"He was dreadfully sorry for that. He was a good man. He gave affection easily."

"Once I had the impression I was giving you love," Dubin said. "It felt like love, but maybe less came across than I thought. Maybe at most I was thinking I was giving love, a rationale or self-deception suiting your needs to my ethic or aesthetics, or both."

He had thought this before but had never said it to her. Kitty listened as though she had often heard it.

"I don't suppose it's very hard to fool yourself about loving," Dubin went on. "It isn't easy to give if you're anchored in an involved subjectivity. Some people complicate their feelings in self-protective ways. I must be one of them. You think you're sailing with a cargo of love, but never deliver because you haven't hoisted anchor, although you have the illusion you had."

"You're erecting a monument to impossibility— Why I never really loved my wife."

"I'm trying to respond to your argument. On the other hand, not all are receptive to those who've taught themselves to love a little. I imagined love for you. To me it felt like love.

I thought you could feel it coming from me—I think you did, but maybe less than I imagined, as though I'd set the thermostat to warm but you, with your nature, never got over feeling chilly in our house."

Dubin said he regretted that. He regretted Dubin, the lacking man. "I regret he comes out meager when he means to be generous, potent, large in love."

"You're not large in love."

"To be honest," he confessed, sitting up with the force of his insight, "William Dubin, the biographer, is grateful to you for having through the years described to him what his lacking love, lacking nature, come to—for having kept him up with himself so that he could be a truthful measure, as well as recorder, of the lives of those he writes about, and therefore a better biographer."

Kitty got out of bed, tight-jawed. "It's more of the same, another denial of me. Everything sooner or later goes back to your biographies. That's your grand passion—if you could fuck your books you'd have it made."

"I'd rather do the same for you."

"No, you wouldn't," she cried. "You could if you wanted to. Your explanation of your rationale is itself a rationale. I sense something unsaid, as though you were evading truth in pretending to tell it."

It's a way of life, the biographer thought. I must stop thinking of myself as a truthful man.

As they were dabbling at breakfast, Kitty, struggling for control, said as she tremblingly poured his coffee, "I hear someone has bought the Wilson farm."

He said he hadn't heard about it.

On New Year's Day night, Dubin trudging up the snowy road to the farm, was caught in the flaring lights of a truck that had backed out of Fanny's driveway. He'd been thinking of his desire for her; it was sometimes only desire. Was it, too, a lacking love?

The driver brought the truck to a stop. "Is that you, Mr. Dubin?" He had poked his head out of the window.

"Dubin," said the biographer, shielding his eyes in the light, as he stood by a snowbank.

The truck lights went off. "Roger Foster here. I want you

to know I intend to wait you out for Fanny. I got a long life ahead of me."

Dubin said his father was a waiter.

He jogged past the truck.

Roger drove on with his lights off.

One winter's late-afternoon Maud Dubin arrived home with her large suitcase and duffel bag and went at once up to her old room to sleep. "For a visit?" Dubin asked his wife when he returned after a quick hour at the farm. "She's pregnant," Kitty said unhappily. He was overwhelmed by a long sense of loss. He had been concerned with Maud rarely lately and castigated himself for it.

"How many months?" he afterward asked.

"Probably two." Kitty paced around the room with her hands clasped.

"Has she spoken of an abortion?"

"She wants to have the baby." Her unhappiness yielded a tender smile; she loved little babies.

Maud slept fifteen hours and in the early morning appeared in her father's study in bathrobe and boots. She laid down on his desk a pack of cigarettes and book of matches. Her face was fresh after sleep and a shower, her eyes trying to be calm.

He knew she had never liked talking to him in his study—he was, she had said, *always* there. "Would you rather talk in your room," Dubin asked, "or maybe go for a walk later?"

She said she would rather talk now.

He thought of the child she had been and was once more aware of loss. Of what? That he hadn't married her? That his love could not control her fate? He hid from her his sense of desecrated life.

Maud lit a cigarette, her hand trembling. "Mother said she's told you? Not much of an annunciation, I'm afraid."

"I hate accidents determining people's fates," Dubin said.

"I've made my peace with it."

He advised her not too quickly to make peace. Maud smoked silently.

He wanted to put his arms around her—his daughter, who ran through experience as though she was slicing bread—but sensed she would rather he didn't.

"It's hard to believe. I pictured you chaste in Zen."

"Believe," Maud said dryly.

"This is what satori came to?"

"Do you really want to know?"

He nodded, wanting to know but not to hear.

She said a letter had come after she'd been four months at the commune—"from a man I've had a long affair with. He asked to see me. I thought I wouldn't—I was the one who had broken it off but maybe the Zen hadn't taken—I was finding it hard to concentrate. And I kept on thinking of you telling me to remember I was Jewish and live in the real world. Anyway, I saw him again and got pregnant."

He sighed. "So I helped initiate the conception?"

"Don't be ironic, Papa."

"I'm bitter."

"Don't be, I'm not. The Zen Master asked me to stay in the commune. He said I could have my baby there and the commune would help me to take care of it. They are incredibly kind people but I felt I had no right to stay because I had failed their teaching. So I went home."

"Does the man know you're pregnant—the father, or whatever you call him?"

"You call him the father, he's a fatherly man."

"Does he know?"

She shook her head.

"Why haven't you told him?"

"It wouldn't do any good—he's married."

After a while Dubin asked, "Any chance of his divorcing his wife?"

Her complexion reddened. "I wouldn't say so. He's about your age and has been married thirty-five years."

Dubin broke into a sweat. "My age?"

"Sixty."

"My God, he's older than I."

"I've often told myself that."

"How in Christ did you ever get involved with an old man at your age?"

He had trouble with the question, thought of himself as hypocrite, except that Fanny, when they had met, was an experienced woman.

"I don't think of him as old."

That drew a mist to her father's eyes.

"Sixty is the age he happens to be," Maud said, rubbing her cigarette out. "For a while I was frightened about the difference in years—that he was three times my age. Then it became a sort of mythic thing in my mind that he was more than lover—he was father, friend, and lover—that there was something extraordinary in our relationship, that it had been happening since man appeared on earth. I stopped being afraid. His age made little difference to me—although it did to him—because in his heart he was young, because he loved me. He seemed to know everything I wanted to know. I valued myself better when I was with him."

"I always valued you highly."

"Too highly, I bet?"

"I never thought so. I thought you valued yourself?"

"I do but with doubt. He was my Spanish teacher in my sophomore year. In class he couldn't keep his eyes off me. When we talked I could see his love. Once he poured a paper cup of water for me in the hall and his hand shook. We began to sleep together. He never asked, it happened when I realized I was in love with him."

She said they saw each other seriously from then on. "Finally his wife found out and had a breakdown. I felt I had to leave college. I joined the Zen commune in South San Francisco but still missed him. When he wrote to me we got back together for a few days and when I woke up in the motel room the morning he left, I knew I was pregnant."

"Didn't he ask if you were protected? What sort of ass is he?"

"If I had slept with a fifteen-year-old boy I still would have got pregnant," Maud said. "I was stupid about my diaphragm. He had no reason to think I didn't know what I was doing. He's a gentle and courteous man. He taught me an awful lot about poetry. We read the classic Spanish poets together. I was happy with him. What's wrong with happiness?"

Dubin didn't say.

"Was he the man you went to Venice with?"

"I don't know how you know that. I never told you or Mother I went to Venice with anyone. We weren't there when you were, without Mother."

"How did you know I was there without Mother?"

"You all but confessed it the winter I was here for a week."

Dubin got up as she rose, kissed her hair, drew her to him. He could feel her pregnant frame trembling. "I'm glad you're home."

"I suppose you feel betrayed?"

"I feel a lot but not betrayed. You're the one who's betrayed."

"I don't think of it that way."

She went to the window, raised it, breathed deeply. "I need a breath of air."

"You won't get any air through the storm window. My God, you've forgotten you ever lived here." He opened a window with a ventilating slot at the bottom of the outer frame.

Maud was sitting again, smoking. He advised her not to if she was pregnant but she continued to smoke.

"Maud," Dubin asked, "what is your life trying to prove?"

"Why do you ask me that kind of question?"

"I wouldn't if you asked yourself."

"I'm trying to live my life without you."

He said he desperately wanted her to.

"Pay attention to your wife," said Maud, rising. "She's not a happy woman." She left the study.

At supper when they glanced at one another they looked away. Kitty served Maud's vegetable casserole. Maud ate poorly, diddled the baby carrots to the side of her plate. Dubin ate hungrily.

"It's not the world's greatest tragedy," Kitty said, looking out of the window.

Maud stared at her.

"I'm sorry, I didn't mean it that way," her mother said. "But I can't help wishing it hadn't happened."

They talked about Gerald. Maud said they had to do more than just write letters to make contact with him.

"Your father has promised to go to Moscow with me," Kitty said to her.

"We'd better know what we're doing," Dubin said. "We can't just pitch a tent in the middle of Red Square."

Chewing listlessly, Kitty asked Maud her plans.

"To have my baby. To support myself with her/him. To make the least do. To live a simple decent life."

"You ought to finish college," Dubin said.

"In time she will," said Kitty. "The baby comes first."

He pictured his daughter as a young widow with a child. What else were you with a fatherless child? They had tipped her life in some odd way.

Maud's eyes would still not meet his.

"What will you do with a little baby to take care of?" Kitty uneasily asked.

"What I have to do. Many women do it nowadays. There are ways of getting together for everyone's benefit."

"Living alone with a child can be trying," her mother said. "I won't deny its pleasures, but it can be quite sad putting a baby to sleep without a father there. It's a double loneliness though the child won't know for a while, a fate I would gladly have spared you. Maybe you ought to consider abortion?"

"You've taught me to value life. I value life. How can I have an abortion?"

If she marries someone to be a father for her child, Dubin was thinking, he will someday hunger for a lover.

"What kind of work do you think you can get?" he asked Maud.

"I have no idea."

"Would you want to consult a psychiatrist?" Dubin then said to his daughter.

"What for?"

"To loosen your fate a little."

"My illegitimate baby isn't my fate."

"Insight may come faster with some help."

"I want it to come slow."

"Leave her alone," Kitty told him.

"Leave *me* alone."

Maud said she'd live in New York City with her baby.

"Why there?" Kitty asked.

"There are more opportunities for a single mother."

"You could live here. I'd help with the baby. You'd be a lot freer."

"I don't want to live here."

"What kind of opportunities?" Dubin wanted to know. "Welfare? Food stamps?"

"That isn't what she means," Kitty said with irritation.

Maud said she would take welfare if she had to. Dubin said she was not being wise.

"Maybe I will be someday, who can tell?"

"I'd expect to help you," he offered. "But things are tight with us now. Inflation isn't helping. I'm worried about money."

"I don't want to be helped," Maud said.

"You ought to notify the baby's father about your situation. He has some obligation to you."

"I will when I feel like it."

"Maud, be reasonable," Kitty said.

"I am reasonable, Mother." She flung her napkin on the table and ran upstairs.

"Be careful with her," Kitty said to Dubin. "Don't be insensitive."

"Tell her not to be. An unwanted pregnancy is no privilege."

They had raised their voices, began to quarrel. Above their heads Maud thumped on the floor with her boot.

They stopped shouting.

The next afternoon Dubin and his daughter walked in the snow to the covered bridge. Maud took his arm. Usually he asked her to walk with him; today she had suggested it. Dubin thought he would say she could rely on his support. She was wearing the antique gold earrings he had bought her in Stockholm. He was moved by them, by her.

He pointed out how many blue jays were around that winter. They counted eight in the snow at one spot.

At the bridge she nervously said, "Papa, my lover was a black man. I may have a black child."

Dubin, even as he was touched by her, groaned aloud.

"Jesus, how you mess up your life, Maud."

"Be gentle, please." The girl looked as if she were drowning. He felt he must keep her afloat, yet could not restrain his anger. "Not only an old man but black in the bargain. Not only a single mother but white with a black baby. What kind of simple life can you have when you complicate yours so incredibly?"

"I happened to love a certain man."

"There are times when love is impossible."

"I never thought of it as impossible."

"Now I understand why you came home that winter with your hair dyed black."

"You understand nothing." Her face was stiff, eyes motionless.

"I understand the misery you're heading into. You'd be better off aborting."

"No one's going to make me abort my baby," she wept.

When they had returned to the house she packed her suitcase and duffel bag and ordered a cab to take her to the bus station.

Kitty canceled the cab. "If you insist on going I'll take you."

Dubin asked Maud not to leave. "I'm sorry I lost my cool. Stay, let's talk it over calmly."

Kitty said stay for her sake.

"I can't, Mother, I'm miserable here."

Her father carried her things out to the car. His breath misted as he kissed her cheek. "We'll be in touch, my child. Things will be better."

When Kitty came back from the bus she accused him of having driven the girl out of the house.

Dubin got into the car and drove quickly to the bus station. A bus had just left and he followed it to Winslow until it occurred to him that wasn't the way to New York.

One night as the telephone rang while Kitty and Dubin sat in the living room, each looked tensely at the other; neither moved to answer. The ringing went on and ceased. They watched it ring and listened to an aftermath of ringing silence.

"Why didn't you answer it?" he asked.

"Why didn't you?"

"It might have been Maud. I thought you would. You usually answer the phone."

"You'd have been embarrassed if it was your girl calling long-distance."

"I have no girl calling long-distance. It might have been Maud."

"She wouldn't hang up after five rings."

"Has she called?"

Kitty shook her head.

"Do you have her address?"

"She said she would write."

"I asked her to stay in touch," he said.

The next day when the phone rang he picked up the receiver and heard it click off after he and Kitty simultaneously said hello. Dubin wondered if it was Fanny signaling him to get in touch with her but when he rang her up from the barn she said she hadn't called.

"Why would I if I promised not to call you at your house any more?"

"Something might have come up so that we couldn't meet."

"I'd leave a note for you on the table inside my front door."

He would rather have her do that than call, Dubin agreed. He hadn't yet told Kitty Fanny had bought the Wilson farm. She'd find it out soon enough herself, but whatever time he had before that he wanted to have. Sooner or later time would evolve a course of action. He wanted it to be the right one; he wanted time on his side.

The next day when the phone rang Kitty answered it in her husband's presence. After listening a minute she seemed puzzled. "You must have the wrong number." She hung up slowly.

"Have you noticed all the wrong numbers?"

"Sometimes the circuits get screwed up."

"It puts me on edge. I mean when there are so many."

"I noticed it a couple of weeks ago but not lately."

"I guess you're right," Kitty said.

She was sleeping better, gaining weight. She complained that flesh was hitting her on the hips and belly. She was having trouble getting into her best dresses, would have to diet. Knowing how intensely she worried about Maud, not to speak of Gerald, Dubin thought that all in all she was in good control. Seeing Ondyk obviously helped her. So did her work in the Youth Opportunity Center; there she could do for others what she couldn't do for her elusive children. At night Kitty carefully creamed her face and hands. She had got a short haircut and looked pretty.

"Do you want to go to bed?" Dubin asked her one evening.

"Let's give it a little longer," she hesitantly said. Her dark eyes were sober.

"Are you afraid?"

"Yes."

He said they could wait a while longer; he felt bad saying it.

She hadn't complained lately about his problem. She seemed calm about it, objective, patient. She treated him, Dubin thought, as if he was someone convalescing; or she hoped convalescing. Kitty would glance into his study or wherever he happened to be when she was on her way out, and ask him how he felt. "Fine," Dubin said. "How's the work going?" "Fine," he said. She smiled and left quickly, returning to smell the burners casually, as though she had really returned to look at the clock. She reminded him a little of the woman she had been when they first met. She seemed more independent lately, able to get along without consulting him. He put her out of his thoughts, yet found himself thinking of her. He sensed her secretly eluding him. He felt some regret, but did not worry about it—wanted her to be on her own, free of him.

Dubin could not recall when he began thinking of her diary. It seemed to him he had lately become curious to have a look at it. It had been around so often he was surprised when it was no longer in sight. When Kitty left the house one morning, he stopped work to search for it. Dubin went from room to room, looking in dresser drawers, amidst her underwear, on closet shelves, behind books in her bookcase, for the worn hardbound blue spiral notebook she wrote in every so often, sometimes late at night—her intense outpourings in thoughtful passages. The tone of the book was self-critical, but often she said things about life that made him reflect on life. He had guessed she might be writing in the diary lately and searched for it continually, half disgusted with what he was doing; yet he felt there had been a change in her he had to understand.

Dubin wanted to know how she defined herself now; and what her degree of feeling or non-feeling for him was. Maybe he had become curious to read the diary when he realized she was no longer leaving it around like yesterday's newspaper. He had often seen it on her dresser or his; or downstairs on a kitchen chair; or in the bathroom. Sometimes it annoyed him to come across it if he thought she had placed it where it would be at hand, his hand. He hadn't wanted to read what she feared or was bored with; or how William Dubin had once more failed her. Why bother reading it when she would sooner or later say openly what she had written? On the whole he knew how she measured him. Too bad he hadn't kept a journal of his own for her to read, though she would never read it without asking if she might. Tolstoy and his wife let each other read their diaries and were both wounded. Total confession was not necessarily pure honesty. There were mean ways to confess whatever one was confessing. However, in Kitty's present mood, whatever it was, Dubin felt he wanted a glimpse of her mind. He had to know what he could freely do next. He wanted to do it the way it would hurt least.

He searched under their bed; through a pile of unanswered correspondence on her desk; in her desk drawers. Nor was there a letter from a lover, if she had one. Dubin had been incredulously wondering if she might be having an affair. With whom? This would be tricky terrain for Kitty. She had more than once remarked she had no objection to extramarital affairs "for some women," those, Dubin gathered, who could find little relief from meager marriages. "But I doubt I'd want to get into that act," she said. "I'm not made for it." Kitty laughed breathily as though she had confessed a serious lack.

"How would you know till you had tried?"

"I know myself," she had said. She spoke with doubt, looking at him as though expecting him to deny the doubt, which he did not do.

She said then with more certainty, "I'm not saying I wouldn't want to try an affair. I've thought about it, frankly, though I don't know who'd be interested in me at my age. I'm not a young woman any more."

He said again, hesitating to say it, that she was, nevertheless, attractive. "Stop remembering when you were born."

"I wish I had been more adventurous when I was young—more daring. I wish I could have let go—I'm a passionate woman—but I wouldn't have been comfortable with an affair while Nathanael was walking the dog, or you were picking flowers. And I don't think I'd care for the concealment and dishonesty that goes with an affair, though my grandmother told me my mother was very good at it, could do it all without blinking an eyelash. But I am not my mother. Somewhere along the line I think I bored her."

Dubin gave her credit: Kitty knew herself not badly, and lived with it, not badly. He thought of her as comparatively untried. Life had fallen on her once like a tree that had cracked and been blown over in a storm. She had crawled out from under a ton of broken branches, shocked, bleeding, traumatized; but after that, life had more or less let her be. A little crippled was fine with life. So long as you're wounded you know you're alive. Yet he felt the more experienced he became, the less she seemed to be. Though Kitty called herself passionate there were areas of sensual experience she had made no attempt to know. She did not play with what might explode in her face. One tree falling on you in a lifetime was enough forever. She seemed always self-protective; had a quality of that kind, therefore that kind of innocence. Besides she couldn't lie. Perhaps he could teach her?

Was she changing—might she have changed? Had she thought it over, decided, at her age, because of her age, to take a chance—in protest of his neglect of her? If she were into an affair now had he forced it on her? But an affair with whom in Center Campobello? Oscar—perhaps evening the score for Flora and Dubin? Not likely: if he'd allowed himself to be attracted by Kitty he'd have gone after her years ago. Only once had he persuaded her to play the harp to his flute. Evan Ondyk? She had said he would not appeal to her as a lover. Roger Foster?—the desire for a young lover revived? Given the failure of their former attraction, Dubin doubted her interest in Roger now. Still, he couldn't say for sure. Women of Kitty's age could be desirable to younger men. She might be willing if he was. But Dubin thought if she was into an affair it would probably be with a stranger to him, possibly one of the psychiatric social-worker types she met at the Youth Center. Kitty admired people who advised others about their lives.

Dubin had noticed a leak in the hot-water tank and one morning went down to the cellar to see how bad it was. The water was dripping steadily. He hurried upstairs to call the plumber and when he picked up the receiver heard Evan Ondyk on the phone. He was about to hang up when Evan quietly said, "We can have lunch and be together."

"Is someone on the telephone?" Kitty asked loudly, nervously. Dubin could hear her voice on the phone; at the same time he heard it coming from upstairs. His heart hammered; he didn't speak and could not hang up lest she hear him.

Ondyk after a long moment said he didn't think so. "Where's William?"

"I think in his study. Let's not talk any more now, Evan. I'll meet you—you know where—and please don't call me here—I get anxious when the telephone rings."

"Kitty, you called me."

"So you wouldn't call me."

He insisted he was being careful. "How else can I reach you when time unexpectedly becomes available?"

"Smoke signals," she said.

They laughed.

"I look forward."

"I too." She hung up.

From therapy to bed with the psychotherapist, an easy next step. The bastard probably tells himself he's doing me a favor—filling in for a friend with a soft cock.

Dubin waited in the cellar till Kitty came down for breakfast. He entered the kitchen, saying there was a leak in the hot-water tank. She said she would call the plumber. Neither of them looked long at the other.

In mid-morning, as she was taking a bath, he left the house and walked to town to rent a car. Dubin parked it on a nearby road on an overcast February day. Before Kitty, wearing flushed-pink stockings, left the house shortly before noon, she said, "The plumber will be here in the morning. I may do some shopping. There's a hamburger for you defrosted in the fridge if you want one for lunch. Coffee is set to boil."

She paused trying to think whether there was something else to say but there wasn't. Kitty did not return to dip her head over the burners. Now she knew what an affair might do for one.

Dubin followed her at a distance in his rented car. She drove to a motel a few miles away, her apple-green automobile turning into its driveway. As he rode by he observed his wife enter the cabin where Ondyk's Buick was parked. Fair is fair. It was the same motel Dubin had been in with Fanny.

He arrived home nervously excited. He felt, too, nostalgic regret. He felt relief accompanied by an oppressive surge of energy. Sitting at his desk with a sheet of paper before him he listed the steps of a divorce. He remembered more law than he had thought. It occurred to him that he had kept up with recent changes in divorce law in New York State.

In the weeks that followed Dubin pretended to know nothing about Kitty's affair. He sometimes felt an embarrassed self-punitive regret when she went off to be with her lover. When she went to meet him she wore the silver bracelet Dubin had got her in Stockholm after he had bought the gold one in Venice for Fanny. And lately Kitty also wore an old locket she had, a medallion of Mary the Mother. She usually left her wedding ring home when she went to see Evan. Dubin pretended not to notice, or seem suspicious. He doubted she could have carried on an affair when she was a young woman. The years, her need, made the difference.

He still kept his eye open for her diary. What was she writing about her affair? He felt a desire to know. In her clothes closet he came across her blue gardening sneakers. They were long sneakers, split at the toes, comic. Her droopy faded orange straw hat looked as if it belonged to somebody's grandmother. He thought of himself and her, a generation ago, as a young man and woman who had just met, and moved by mutual respect and the magic of possibility, were willing to try to know and love each other. It was, in this world, a brave thing to do, and they had for a while done it. There was indeed, Dubin thought, a married state; and if you had lived in it for years with someone who had treated you considerately you wanted to go on thinking of her as the considerate woman she was. You wanted to go on respecting her whether she was still your wife or not. He hoped she would not spoil that for him.

One afternoon Dubin discovered Kitty's diary in the kitchen oven. It had been elsewhere, but now it was in the oven. Kitty sometimes temporarily shoved things in it to get them out of the way. He had asked her not to, but she said she had never in her life caused a fire. Dubin riffled through the last pages of the notebook. She had written little about herself recently, not a word about Ondyk, nothing directly about Dubin. He discovered, not without surprise, that she had been reading biographies of accomplished women. Four she mentioned were Charlotte Brontë, Rosa Luxemburg, Jane Welsh, Eleanor Roosevelt. She commented on how they had fought for strength and resisted the tyranny of lovers and husbands.

Most of her notes in the diary were about Jane Welsh, Thomas Carlyle's wife, a woman of exceptional intellect, character, wit, with vivid powers of literary expression, who might have had, Kitty wrote, "a remarkable writing career if she weren't enmeshed in a miserable Victorian marriage. What an age!" Carlyle, though he could at times be a tender and affectionate husband, especially when he was miles from her, in Scotland or elsewhere writing letters to her, was an almost totally self-centered man of genius; for years bound to, and groaning in his bowels over, the multi-volumed lives of Cromwell and Frederick the Great it took him forever to write, while his unhappy wife was sometimes suffering from illness and neglect in the next room. Once after she had been seriously hurt in a street accident she wrote in her diary, "Oh, my husband! I am suffering torments! Each day I suffer more horribly. O, I would like you beside me. I am terribly alone. But I don't want to interrupt your work." Though Carlyle depended heavily on her, he was all but blind to her loneliness; he gave her little emotionally and nothing sexually. Like Ruskin he seemed to have been impotent throughout his married life. When she died in London, he, in Scotland, dreamed she had died. She was buried in her father's grave and Carlyle's remorse began. For fifteen years he mourned her. "Oh that I had you yet for five minutes beside me, to tell you all."

"About time," Kitty wrote. Her last entry on Jane Welsh read: "She waked between thirty and forty times a night, averaging three hours of sleep, 'all in fractions.' But she was not a defeated person, a victim, thanks to her talent for friendship, writing, self-preservation. She felt marriage was a 'shockingly immoral institution.' And 'an extremely disagreeable one.'" Kitty called Carlyle "a narcissistic, nervous, *obsessed*, *impotent biographer*." Dubin noted the emphasis.

The entry after that in her diary was a despairing one about Gerald. Dubin tossed the notebook back into the oven and seriously considered turning the gas on.

One night she came to Maud's room, where he was sleeping, and standing by the bed in the dark, told him she had had a terrible dream about their daughter: "She had given birth but wouldn't let me see the baby. Then a black man went into the room and stabbed it. I sank into a faint so deep I don't know how I managed to wake up and come here."

"Do you want to get into bed with me?"

She said, after momentary silence, "Would you mind first going down to look at the burners? I meant to but forgot."

There's this hissing open burner in her head, he thought, and I live with it as though it were real.

Dubin got up as she slipped into Maud's narrow bed. Stepping into his slippers he went down to the kitchen to sniff the gas. First he tightened the knobs, then breathed over the burners to make sure no gas was leaking. He felt he had to smell them if she asked him to. It was a responsibility: you lied about your girl but not about the gas. He tried to estimate how often he had smelled the burners since he had married Kitty. How many cubic feet of gas had he inhaled in the hundreds of times he had bent over the burners for her? One married her wounds with the woman. One ingested them. And it worked the other way, he supposed. His wounds had wounded her.

What would I smell for Fanny? Only her body. Her breasts smell like flowers and her cunt like the salt sea.

The bed lamp was on when he returned to Maud's room. Kitty's head lay on the pillow in darkish light.

"Is there something I can do for you?" she asked.

"Nothing," said Dubin, "except please let me sleep if I fall asleep. You stay here, I'll go to our bed."

"Are you sure?"

"Nothing at all."

As he was becoming sleepy, Kitty slid into their bed with him. "William," she said, "I have something to tell you: I've been having an affair with Evan. It started a couple of months ago, and you know why."

"That horse's ass," he said dully.

"No, he isn't. He's considerate and appreciative and a lot wiser than you think. He asked me to go to bed with him and I did. He's not very happy with Marisa, and I was hard up and disgusted with you. But what I want to say now is that I've broken it off. I don't regret what I've done, but I didn't do it easily. If it weren't for you I don't think I would have done it."

"Is he still your therapist?"

"I don't think we'd better. I'm sorry because he was good with me. I don't know what to do about that."

"Would you want a divorce?" Dubin asked her.

She said bitterly she no longer knew what she wanted.

Winter

Dear William, Dear Mother—If this ever reaches you it will be through a contact I had with a friend in the French Embassy when I first came here. I'm in her room writing this as she packs. She's leaving the Soviet Union to marry a medical student in France and has promised to try to sneak this letter out. If she does you will get it from Rouen but won't be able to answer. I have no address to give you. I am in serious trouble—which won't surprise you. I sleep in a freezing shack. I have little to eat. I am worn out and sick.

Here's what happened—I was recruited in Stockholm by the KGB into Soviet espionage. I wasn't sure I wanted to accept but finally talked myself into it. I think I thought I was being true to myself. I was flown into the Soviet Union from Finland after a boat trip across the Baltic. In Moscow I was trained to work with coding and code-breaking electronic equipment. Colonel Kovacol, in charge of my unit, twice cited me for excellent work. As you might expect it didn't take me long to fall out of favor. Whatever reasons I came here for, I didn't come out of a love for communism, and I underestimated the effects of totalitarianism. Men *are* superfluous in this society. The worst things in American life are all here, derived from a terrifying materialism. Everybody eats now but few think independently and those who do and say so usually end up in prison. It depressed me that I always go one worse when I hope to go one better. Finally I made up my mind to ask out, I requested to be sent back to Sweden. That was, of course, a stupid mistake. I should have waited until they had some reason of their own to send me out of the country.

Kovacol told me there was no way out for a foreigner who knew the secrets of their coding computers. He asked me what I thought I was accomplishing by quitting and I said I wanted to rectify a serious error. I didn't say my life was full of them. He said the fate of a bourgeois humanist was bound to be narrow. He said I was lucky he didn't shoot me on the spot and then discharged me from the unit without pay. The friend I had come with from Stockholm, the one who had given them my name originally, wouldn't see me again.

For a few weeks they let me alone, then began to tail me to see if I had any contacts. I had one a short while, a man I met one night in a park. At first he didn't trust me but then became sympathetic. When he told me he was a Jew I said you were, William, and told him about my situation here. Arkady Davidovich turned out to be a dissident. For some weeks he and his wife helped me with food parcels they hid in various spots I had been told to look in, but I stopped picking them up when I realized the secret police were tight on my tail. Arkady and his wife have two kids, a boy thirteen and a girl nine, and I didn't want them to get into worse trouble because of me. We don't meet any more but sometimes they manage to slip an envelope with a couple of rubles to me. I walk into a crowd and when I come out usually there are two or three rubles in my pocket. Lately—now that I am being followed day and night—that happens rarely.

I've tried to get into the U.S. Embassy, but the Soviet guards recognize me and won't let me in. If I wait for an American to come out they shove me along with their nightsticks. I don't know how they do it but when I call from a public booth the call is jammed. I hear a buzz and when I talk my voice breaks into noise. It's as though your self had destructed.

I don't know how much longer I can last. I'm on the move and they are generally close behind but not making the arrest, though I've begun to hunger for it. If I'm lucky I'll end up in a strict-regime labor camp in the Gulag. Frankly, it would be a relief. I wouldn't have to scrounge for bread or try to hide where they watch me hiding. I have a croupy cough and almost constant diarrhea. Maybe that's the punishment they've arranged till I collapse.

I'm afraid of my fate. I'm afraid of myself for the fate I've created. Right now I'd give half my life to be free the other half.

I wish I could say there was something you could do for me. Maybe talk to the press? But if you do they might shoot me at once. I've blocked my exits. All my life I've been walking in a tunnel believing I was out in the open. The only really generous thing I ever really did was to stop taking food from a dissident Jew and his family.

Tell Maud I think of her a lot. My mother is my mother, and you are my father, William. Some simple things take a long time to get thought out.

Gerry.

Dubin mourned D. H. Lawrence.

In a letter to his sister-in-law Else, he said: "It is very lovely, the wind, clouds, the running sea that bursts like a blossom on the island opposite. If only I was well, and had my strength back!

"But I am so weak. And something inside me weeps black tears. I wish it would go away."

Frieda held his ankle as he lay dying. "I held his ankle from time to time, it felt so full of life, all my days I shall hold his ankle in my hand."

After Lawrence's death, Middleton Murry, the ex-friend he detested, came to stand at his grave; and soon thereafter Frieda and he became lovers. Murry later wrote in his diary, "With her for the first time in my life, I know what fulfilment in love really meant."

Kitty could not sleep. Dubin woke and saw her not sleeping.

"Haven't you slept yet?"

"No. When will we leave for Russia?"

"When the visas come."

"What will we do when we get there?"

"Cry out his name."

"Maud hasn't called."

"I know."

Kitty slept, snoring lightly. She spoke in her sleep, "Nat, dear Nat."

Dubin, with sweet pleasure, remembered his mother covering him with a second blanket on a very cold night.

He lay awake, recomposing a letter to Gerry he carried in his head. Then he got out of bed and went upstairs to sleep in the boy's bed.

A breeze blew up in the late afternoon, making sea sounds in the tops of leafless trees; at night winter dipped its cold hands into the wind. But a half-moon brightened the night-blue sky, lit, softened, as though spring might begin as moonlight, a not bad idea in a cold climate.

Dubin again worked in the barn study. Kitty hadn't asked why he worked when or where he worked. He wrote there mornings and returned after supper till almost midnight, except those nights he left the light on and went early to Fanny's farm. If the phone rang, he had told Kitty, he would not answer, wanted no interruptions.

The biographer, carrying a heavy birch stick, trotted through the woods and up the road to the farm. The snow had melted but at night the dirt road hardened and was ridged. In a few weeks it would be mud season. He had given up his afternoon walks and this was his new route, from house to house by way of his barn, Kitty's Wood, the farm, then back to the barn study to be alone a few minutes before he went home. In bed, awake as Kitty slept her early sleep, he considered fasting a day a week.

Dubin ran, this windy pre-spring night, to Fanny's. Where else? The wind buffeted him and he ducked behind trees to catch his breath. On the road the going was easier with the wind blowing behind him. Fanny's large barn was dark and silent. Her kitchen light was on. Through the window he saw her sitting at the table in her padded jacket and beige wool hat, reading the local paper. Snowdrop yawned at her feet. Her boots were muddy. She looked dismally tired. Dubin, concerned about her, knocked the clapper and entered, using the key she had given him. The sink was full of dirty dishes he quickly washed for her.

The farm, Fanny confessed, had seriously been worrying her. She hadn't wanted to give it this much time and labor. Craig Bosell had fallen off a ladder in his cellar and broken his right hip; he was in the hospital. She could not replace him at the modest salary he accepted. The day after he left, one of the Toggenburgs was killed in the goat pasture by a dog that had burrowed under the wire fence. He had torn her udder and chewed off an ear. Fanny had chased the hound with an ax as Snowdrop yelped but the bloody doe was dead. Bawling, she dug the goat a grave. Dubin helped bury her.

The goats weren't easy to handle. The pregnant doe, Trudy, a large-eared black-and-white yammering Nubian that Fanny had bought bred, was a neurotic beast. Left alone in the dark she trumpeted in fear until she learned to flip the light switch with her nose after Fanny had left the barn. The barn light burned all night and she had to fence the goat into another stall. Trudy bleated throughout the night. Fanny returned her to her former stall and let her turn the light on when she wanted to. "I was afraid of the dark myself when I was a little girl." She loved the pregnant goat. "She's about to kid and I almost hate to see it happen she's so satisfied to be a pregnant goat."

She shoveled the goats' hay into the overhead manger and filled with warmish drinking water their rubber buckets hooked to the wall; she also cleaned their stalls, carried out manure; laid new sawdust, and spent an hour every day brushing their coats. Later she collected the warm newly laid eggs from the hens' nests, sold or bartered them in town; had a dozen other tasks that kept her busy till dark. Although she complained she was dead-tired she seemed always to have energy for sex. "Or what's it all about?" In her bedroom she changed into a sheer nightgown before Dubin came upstairs. In bed she was adventurous, exciting, even wise. Afterward they quietly talked, affectionately, honestly. Then Dubin showered, dressed, and trotted back to his study, sitting there contemplatively ten or fifteen minutes before going home.

"How did it go tonight?" Kitty asked.

He told her fine.

One night in February when the temperature had fallen below zero, Fanny's pipes froze and it cost her seventy-two dollars to repair the one that had burst in the cellar and thaw out the others to get the water running. In a driving storm a week later the roof leaked around the chimney. Patching that cost another fifty. She worried about the rising cost of services; Dubin worried with her. She said she didn't know how she would go on doing all she did, plus milk Trudy twice a day after she had kidded; and that summer take care of the vegetable garden she wanted. "Besides that I would like to plant some flowers to look at when I feel like it." Dubin said she had to have help and suggested, to begin with, hiring a high school boy part-time. He offered to pay his hourly wages. "I've lectured twice lately for good fees."

Fanny said no.

"Why not?"

"I'm not your goddamned wife—I don't want your money."

"What can I do for a friend?" he said after a minute.

"I will pay my own bills."

He sometimes came over in the afternoon to work at whatever he could. Dubin sawed wood for the kitchen stove. Once he replaced a broken window. He fixed an electric light socket—little jobs he hadn't done for years. And Roger Foster, Fanny informed him, came on weekend mornings. "He helps me clean my barn."

Though her hips and bosom seemed fuller, Fanny said she had lost weight. Her face was thinner. One night as she unbraided her hair he found a strand of gray in it; and Dubin noticed that the four or five darkish hairs under her chin had once more sprouted forth. Fanny, hopping out of bed to look in the mirror, was incensed. "I spent over a hundred bucks on electrolysis and injections. I thought I'd got rid of them forever." She said angrily: "Even if they grow seven feet long I will never cut those hairs again."

"Lady Bluebeard," he teased.

"Don't you call me that," she yelled at him.

He begged her pardon.

"You also call me Kitty, in case you don't know it."

"Often?"

"Once in a while."

Dubin said he was sorry.

Crawling back into bed she complained about her life: "Nothing is going the way I hoped. I haven't had any time to myself since Craig broke his hip. I have no time to read. I feel flaked out when I look at a page of print. Sometimes the feeling that my life is not turning out right floods over me."

"Do you think taking on this farm was a mistake?"

He disliked his question because he feared her answer, but Fanny said after a pause, "Not actually coming here but maybe my idea of having a barnful of tender loving animals welcoming me with yaps of joy in the morning was out of my childhood books. Still this place is right for me, and I love the house and have been fixing it up, little by little, the way I want."

Dubin said it was tastefully done.

"I wouldn't think of leaving it. My main gripe is I am tied down too much. Everything I do I *have* to."

"Not everything."

"You'd be surprised." Smiling in afterthought she said, "Not everything."

Fanny said she had been thinking a lot about the future.

"Relative to what?"

"To myself—that I still find it hard to zero in on what I want out of my life."

"You know yourself better than you did, not a long time ago."

"Yes, but I am still not sure what I want to do—what I want to work at. Sometimes I say, the hell with that, I'd rather get married. I want to have a baby before I am too old. I want to get settled. I don't want to be a single woman forever."

He said she was entitled to these things.

"With you?"

"With or without me."

Fanny let it slowly go at that, then said, "Other times I think I'd rather stay single and in some career I respect. I honestly think that. I want to work at something worthwhile that I could do well. I want to do something really well, not get lost in the shuffle. I want to like myself up to the hilt sometime in my life."

He asked her what she had in mind to do.

"I've thought a lot about that, and have even thought of selling antiques in my house," Fanny said. "My mother did that once, and I have taste but it doesn't take much of a brain. I thought of teaching but don't want to. I don't feel I have the right to—everybody knows what I know. I've also looked at veterinary-medicine catalogues but there I am fantasizing. What I keep going back to in my mind—ever since I worked as a secretary in a law office—is to study law and practice it. But the trouble is I don't think I can handle law school right now, though I think I could get accepted if I applied. They're taking more women nowadays and I have good grades even if it did take me six years to knock off my B.A."

They had talked before about studying law and talked of it now as they lay in bed. Dubin had told her about his own disappointing experience as a lawyer. "I got little pleasure out of it though perhaps the fault was mine for not being more patient. I could have changed the nature of my practice if I wasn't so anxious about making a living. I lived on cases involving small finaglers and found myself engaged in pisher dishonesties. I told myself the law is not perfect and neither are men, but I couldn't stand what I was doing. Montaigne wanted to get out of public life so he could stop lying for convenience' sake. I wanted to stop lying, period."

"Law doesn't have to be only that way," Fanny said. "What I think I'd like to get into is the law protecting the environment and dealing with women's rights. I'd also like to represent poor people in court. I like that pro bono stuff."

"You'd have to do more than pro bono to make a living."

"I could grow most of my food here and work in the legal-aid office in town. Or if I couldn't get a job there I'd do half of make-a-living law and half pro bono, once I passed the bar."

He asked her if she would go away to law school if she was accepted. "There's an old established one in Albany and a new one in Royalton."

"In the first place I couldn't afford that. In the second place I want to live here."

"It isn't that you're without potential funds, Fanny. Real estate keeps going up. You could sell this farm for a good profit."

"I told you I don't want to sell my farm," she said, sitting up. "I expect to go on living here."

"Don't get angry in bed."

"Stay the night," Fanny said. "I feel lonely."

He said he couldn't.

Kitty, when Dubin got home, was awake, reading. She no longer set up his breakfast dishes for the morning. She no longer paired his washed socks; she dropped them in a heap on his dresser.

"Do you think I could find work as a secretary?" she asked him. "I'm a good typist, all I need is shorthand. I could pick that up in an extension class at night, but who would want to employ a woman over fifty as a secretary?"

"Some people would."

"Not many."

He thought she could make it.

"That won't absolve you from supporting me."

He was not expecting absolution.

"It'll be an empty life," Kitty said.

He said nothing.

After a while she said, "I'm smoking too much. Sometimes when I take a deep breath my lungs seem to be burning."

"Cut down," he advised.

She said her sleep was dreadful.

"Why don't you try a sleep-disorder clinic? There are many now. Maybe they can help you."

She said she just might. "Will you come with me?"

He said he would.

After a restless night Dubin made several morning calls to attorneys in nearby Vermont. He took a tablet for heartburn and drove to Arlington to see two lawyers who had said they could see him that morning.

Dubin returned to Fanny's a few days later—that windy pre-spring night in early March—to tell her it was possible to study law by clerking in a law office and thus not have to go to law school.

"You'll have to decide pretty quickly because the State of Vermont isn't permitting this procedure much longer."

"I'd want to start right away if anybody wanted me," Fanny said in excitement. "What do I have to do?"

"You'd have to be pretty sure of it or it would be an awful waste of time for you and the attorney who had taken you on."

"I *am* sure, William. I know I am."

Dubin explained he had been to see Ursula Habersham, a friend of his wife's. "She's a State Senator who's giving up politics because of her husband's poor health. Now she's trying to revive her law office. When I told her about you out here on a farm, wanting to study law, she was interested. I recommended you as a responsible person with a B.A., who by now would have fulfilled the residency requirements. She said she might take you on as a clerk if you were as apt as I said."

Dubin told her she would read law with Habersham and after four years under her tutelage would take the bar. "If you pass you can practice. There's no salary while you're learning. What you learn is what you're paid."

Fanny hugged him. "It's what I want to do. I will be a good apprentice. It's just the kind of thing I need."

"Four years is a long haul."

She said she wasn't going anywhere.

Dubin said, "I've got you an interview for Monday afternoon."

Fanny said her mind was made up. "Except what will I do with my goats?"

"Sell them."

"All but Trudy and her baby. I can take care of them. Jesus, I'm excited, William. My father will fall on his face when he hears I am studying law. Do you think she will take me on?"

"She liked what I told her about you. She liked the fact you had done secretarial work in a law office. I think you stand a fair chance. I praised all your talents but one."

"I think you like me, lover," Fanny said.

In her bedroom Dubin gave her a packet of notes he had saved from law school. "These are my old notes on contracts."

She promised to read them. "If I get into the law office I will throw a blast to celebrate. I've never had a party in this house."

"Who would you want to come?"

"People around and whatever friends of yours you invite."

As they were undressing in the bedroom—she kept an electric heater going on nights Dubin appeared—Fanny said she had run into Kitty at the grocery market that morning. "We were both picking out loaves of bread and then recognized each other."

White or rye? he wondered.

"What did she say?"

"Only what was I doing in town. I said living on a farm. She has bigger feet than I remembered. I could feel she didn't like me though she was polite. I felt sorry for her. She looks mousy and sort of sad."

"Did you say anything else?"

"She looked at the gold bracelet you bought me in Venice but didn't say anything although she looked as if she had guessed you had given it to me. Then we went our different ways."

Fanny suggested Dubin ought to stay three days with her and four with his wife. "She could have Thursday to Sunday. I'd like you to be with me Monday to Wednesday. There's a nice warm room with a desk for you to work in downstairs while you're here. I'd like to have that to look forward to. It would be less lonely those nights you aren't here."

Dubin said he didn't think Kitty would agree to that.

Fanny smiled vaguely. "Try it and see. I bet she would now. It's only fair."

He said he might.

"I don't understand why you stayed married to her."

"It wasn't so hard," he explained. "I'm a family man. We had kids we loved. I had my work to do. Conditions were good. There are other things."

"But do you love her?"

"I love her life."

"Do you love me?"

He said he did.

She put on softly a Mozart flute concerto. They embraced in bed. "God bless you, dear Fanny." She wet his flesh with her pointed tongue.

Dubin soon heaved himself out of bed, stumbled into the bathroom, got into pants and shirt.

As he came out of the farmhouse Fanny's window went up and she leaned out in the orange light, her hair flying in the pre-spring wind.

"Don't kid yourself," she called.

Roger Foster waited in the shadow of a long-boughed two-trunked silver maple as Dubin ran up the moonlit road, holding his half-stiffened phallus in his hand, for his wife with love.

Works by William B. Dubin

SHORT LIVES
ABRAHAM LINCOLN
MARK TWAIN
H. D. THOREAU
THE PASSION OF D. H. LAWRENCE: A LIFE
THE ART OF BIOGRAPHY
ANNA FREUD (WITH MAUD D. PERRERA)

GOD'S GRACE

FOR DIARMUID RUSSELL
GONE NOW;
AND FOR ROSE RUSSELL

I'm grateful to the Center for Advanced Study in the Behavioral Sciences for gifts of time and hospitality; and to Carol Bain, Del Powers, and Deanna Dejan for secretarial and word-processing assistance; and to Eleanor Moore, who typed early drafts of this story in Bennington, Vermont.

I read many books to write this but am particularly indebted to Shalom Spiegel's *The Last Trial*, and Jane Goodall's *In the Shadow of Man*.

"The Holy One, blessed be He, cast a stone into the sea and from it the world was founded."

R. YITZHAQ NAPPAHA

"I came upon the horrible remains of a cannibal feast."

ROBINSON CRUSOE

"Nobody seemed to know where George's name came from."

JOHANSON, EDEY

The Flood

THIS IS THAT STORY

The heaving high seas were laden with scum
The dull sky glowed red
Dust and ashes drifted in the wind circling the earth
The burdened seas slanted this way, and that, flooding the scorched land under a daylight moon
A black oily rain rained
No one was there

At the end, after the thermonuclear war between the Djanks and Druzhkies, in consequence of which they had destroyed themselves, and, madly, all other inhabitants of the earth, God spoke through a glowing crack in a bulbous black cloud to Calvin Cohn, the paleologist, who of all men had miraculously survived in a battered oceanography vessel with sails, as the swollen seas tilted this way and that;

Saying this:

"'Don't presume on Me a visible face, Mr. Cohn, I am not that kind, but if you can, imagine Me. I regret to say it was through a minuscule error that you escaped destruction. Though mine, it was not a serious one; a serious mistake might have jammed the universe. The cosmos is so conceived that I myself don't know what goes on everywhere. It is not perfection although I, of course, am perfect. That's how I arranged my mind.

"'And that you, Mr. Cohn, happen to exist when no one else does, though embarrassing to Me, has nothing to do with your once having studied for the rabbinate, or for that matter, having given it up.

"'That was your concern, but I don't want you to conceive any false expectations. Inevitably, my purpose is to rectify the error I conceived.

"'I have no wish to torment you, only once more affirm cause and effect. It is no more than a system within a system, yet I depend on it to maintain a certain order. Man, after failing to use to a sufficient purpose his possibilities, and my good will, has destroyed himself; therefore, in truth, so have you.'"

Cohn, shivering in his dripping rubber diving suit, complained bitterly:

"After Your first Holocaust You promised no further Floods. 'Never again shall there be a Flood to destroy the earth.' That was Your Covenant with Noah and all living creatures. Instead, You turned the water on again. Everyone who wasn't consumed in fire is drowned in bitter water, and a Second Flood covers the earth."

God said this: " 'All that was pre-Torah. There was no such thing as Holocaust, only cause and effect. But after I had created man I did not know how he would fail Me next, in what manner of violence, corruption, blasphemy, beastliness, sin beyond belief. Thus he defiled himself. I had not foreseen the extent of it.

" 'The present Devastation, ending in smoke and dust, comes as a consequence of man's self-betrayal. From the beginning, when I gave them the gift of life, they were perversely greedy for death. At last I thought, I will give them death because they are engrossed in evil.

" 'They have destroyed my handiwork, the conditions of their survival: the sweet air I gave them to breathe; the fresh water I blessed them with, to drink and bathe in; the fertile green earth. They tore apart my ozone, carbonized my oxygen, acidified my refreshing rain. Now they affront my cosmos. How much shall the Lord endure?

" 'I made man to be free, but his freedom, badly used, destroyed him. In sum, the evil overwhelmed the good. The Second Flood, this that now subsides on the broken earth, they brought on themselves. They had not lived according to the Covenant.

" 'Therefore I let them do away with themselves. They invented the manner; I turned my head. That you went on living, Mr. Cohn, I regret to say, was no more than a marginal error. Such things may happen.' "

"Lord," begged Calvin Cohn, a five-foot-six man in his late thirties, on his wet knees. "It wasn't as though I had a choice. I was at the bottom of the ocean attending to my work when the Devastation struck. Since I am still alive it would only be fair if You let me live. A new fact is a new condition. Though I deeply regret man's insult to a more worthy fate, still I would consider it a favor if You permit me to live."

" 'That cannot be my intent, Mr. Cohn. My anger has diminished but my patience is not endless. In the past I often forgave them their evil; but I shall not now. No Noah this time, no exceptions, righteous or otherwise. Though it hurts Me to say it, I must slay you; it is just. Yet because of my error, I will grant you time to compose yourself, make your peace. Therefore live quickly—a few deep breaths and go your way. Beyond that lies nothing for you. These are my words.' "

"It says in Sanhedrin," Cohn attempted to say, " 'He who saves one life, it is as if he saved the world.' " He begged for another such favor.

" 'Although the world was saved it could not save itself. I will not save it again. I am not a tribal God; I am Master of the Universe. That means more interrelated responsibilities than you can imagine.' "

Cohn then asked for a miracle.

" 'Miracles,' " God answered, " 'go only so far. Once you proclaim it, a miracle is limited. Man would need more than a miracle.' "

The Lord snapped the crack in the cloud shut. He had been invisible, light from which a voice extruded; no sign of Godcrown, silverbeard, peering eye—the image in which man had sought his own. The bulbous cloud sailed imperiously away, vanishing.

A dark coldness descended. Either the dust had thickened or night had fallen. Calvin Cohn was alone, forlorn. When he raised his head the silence all but cracked his neck.

As he struggled to stand, he lifted his fist at the darkened sky. "God made us who we are."

He danced in a shower of rocks; but that may have been his imagining. Yet those that hit the head hurt.

Cohn fell to his knees, fearing God's wrath. His teeth chattered; he shivered as though touched on the neck by icy fingers. Taking back his angry words, he spoke these: "I am not a secularist although I have doubts. Einstein said God doesn't dice with the universe; if he could believe it maybe I can. I accept Your conditions, but please don't cut my time too short."

The rusty, battered vessel with one broken mast drifted on

slanted seas. Of all men only Calvin Cohn lived on, passionate to survive.

Not long after dawn, a faded rainbow appeared in the soiled sky. Although a wedge-shaped section of its arch seemed broken off, as though a triangular mouth had taken a colorful bite, Cohn wept yet rejoiced. It seemed a good sign and he needed one.

The oceanographic vessel *Rebekah Q*, a renovated iron-hulled, diesel-powered, two-masted schooner, of whose broad-sailed masts one remained erect, drifted unsteadily on the water as the Flood abated—the man-made Flood, Cohn had been instructed, not God-given.

The waters receded. They had risen high enough to overwhelm the remnants of the human race; now were slowly ebbing. He imagined the stricken vessel floating over graveyards of intricate-spired drowned cities—Calcutta, Tokyo; London on the water-swept British island. But he would not be surprised if they (he and the she-boat) were still drifting in the outraged Pacific, under whose angry waves he had sat in a small deep-sea submersible, observing the sea floor at the instant the ocean flared, and shuddered, and steamed; as nuclear havoc struck, causing a mountainous tidal wave that swallowed and spewed forth the low-lying, rusty-hulled research schooner.

Shortly thereafter Cohn had risen from the sea.

His scientist colleagues—he pictured in particular Dr. Walther Bünder departing hastily with his previously packed suitcase, his Cuban stogie clamped in his teeth—and the officers and crew who administered the ship had, seemingly without grace or goodness, disappeared. Their disregard of Cohn had outraged him, though he now admitted that in leaving him behind they had preserved him.

He had descended to the bottom of the sea twenty minutes before the missiles began to fly at each other; and when he rose from the ocean floor, the instant, totally catastrophic war had ended, and mankind had destroyed itself. The lifeboats and most of the life jackets were gone—a few left strewn on the deck. Cohn found a yellow rubber raft that had been inflated and left as though for him; he therefore forgave them their panic-stricken desertion.

He had dangled in the swaying submersible it seemed for hours after the PERIL light had flashed and the buzzer raucously signaled ASCEND. The little submarine swung in insane sweeping arcs. Its pendulous motion churned his stomach and filled it with terror until he felt the steam-powered winch begin to draw him slowly up, stopping several minutes, then drawing him up.

It was a frightful ascent. He watched thousands of maddened fish banging their blind mouths against his lit window. Cohn snapped off the lamp as the submersible moved up luminously in the watery blackness. When he reached the deck on the surface of the sea, no one appeared to secure the tiny submarine and help him out. He had bobbed around in the frothy waves, trying to escape, hopelessly seasick, before he was able to emerge from the hatch and plop, as he vomited, into the water.

Cohn pulled himself up the metal ladder on the hull of the *Rebekah Q*. The four lifeboats were gone, their ropes dangling like spaghetti strings. The sky was smeared with ashes and the reflection of flames. The ocean was thick with channels of fish scum and floating animal bodies. When the smell of dead flesh assailed him, Cohn at last knew what had happened. He felt sick horror and a retching contempt of the human race. Dozens of steel missiles had plunged to the bottom of the sea and lay there like smoking turds.

Why he had survived Cohn could not guess. He had no idea how long he might go on. It seemed useless to take a radiation reading. Some had lived after Hiroshima; some had not. What comes will come.

In the communications cabin he read a scribbled message on a warped piece of cardboard. Cohn learned what he already knew: Humanity had done itself in.

The rainbow, he remembered, was God's sign to Noah that He would not pour another deluge on the earth. So much for signs, for Covenants.

Dead souls floated on stagnant seas. The *Rebekah Q* drifted through shoals of rotting fish, and plowed through blackened seaweed in lakes of sludge.

The oceanographic schooner, its lightning-split mast draped

in fallen sails, drifted close to volcanic shores as Cohn slept the heavyhearted sleep of the dead. It sailed away from the soaking land before he woke.

He awoke mourning human being, human existence, all the lives lost. He listed everyone he could remember, and the names of those he did not know whose names he had heard. He mourned civilization, goodness, daring, joy; and all that man had done well.

Cohn was enraged with God Who had destroyed His own dream. The war was man's; the Flood, God's. Cohn heard thunder when he thought of God and sometimes hid.

The sky was old—how often had the earth changed as the same sky looked on? Never had there been so much space in space. He had never been so desolate.

Cohn diligently pasted stamps in albums, recalling nations lost; he pitched darts at a red-and-white target in the games room. He read till his eyes were blobs of glue stuck to words. He listened to records on his father the rabbi's portable phonograph. He kept, so to speak, going.

The boat's engines had ceased throbbing; there was no electricity. It seemed useless to attempt to activate the rusty generator aboard; but there was bottled gas to cook with in the galley.

On good days Cohn told himself stories, saying the Lord would let him live if he spoke the right words. Or lived the right life. But how was that possible without another human life around? Only God and he "contending," Cohn attempting to evade His difficult nature?

(Thunder groaning, Cohn hiding.)

No way of outdoing the Lord Who had invented Himself into being. The God of beginnings; He wanted to begin, therefore had begun. Spontaneous combustion? Beginnings were far up the line from First Causes. Therefore where had God begun?

Who was He? You had to see His face to say in Whose image man had been fashioned; and no one could. Moses, who had come close, saw Him through fog and flame. Or from a cleft in a huge rock where the Lord had placed him. And God, approaching the rock in his own light, covered the cleft with

His hand, until He had passed by, then removed His hand and Moses clearly saw the Lord's endless back.

Shall I someday see His face? God seemed to feel the need to talk to men. He needed worship, and even faithless men had hungered to worship Him.

Cohn added up columns of random figures. He began and tore up a notebook journal. He trotted back and forth, for exercise, along the 152-foot deck, hurdling obstacles, the fallen mast, yards of canvas sail, instruments of observation, hauling, drilling; tons of thick ropes covered with seaweed, barnacles, starfish, sea detritus; Cohn, despite his small size and slightly bowed legs, had once been an athlete in Staten Island High School.

The radio was dead. He talked to himself. He missed the human voice.

"What can one expect in this life of desolation?"

—More life?

"To be alive alone forever?"

—It takes one rib to make an Eve.

"Do you see yourself as Adam?"

—If the job is open.

Wherever they were it rarely rained. The heavy rains had served, and were gone; the present weather was dry, the flood subsiding; but not Cohn's anger at the destruction God had wrought. Why does human life mean so little to Him? Because He hadn't lived it? If Jesus had, why didn't he tell Him about it? Cohn thought he would bring Them to the bar of justice if he could.

(Terrible thundering; he hid for days.)

Drinking water was short. Part of the storage tankful had leaked into the sea, adding to the ocean water. To the bitter salt sea. Food was plentiful but he ate without appetite.

Cohn, proficient in reading geological and biological time in the microfossilized cores drilled out of the ocean floor, could barely read the visible stars. He did not know how to navigate, and could only guess where in the wet world he was; nor could he steer *Rebekah Q*, though he diligently studied repair manuals of the ship's machinery and electric system. What difference did steering make if there was no dry place to go? He went where the crippled vessel bore him, wondering whether to swim if it sank.

One tedious, sultry day Cohn thought he was no longer in the Pacific. He couldn't imagine where he was. What shall I do, alone of all men on this devastated earth?

He swore he would live on despite the wrathful God who had let him out on a string and would snap him back on a string.

Once he heard an awesome whirring of wings, and when Cohn gazed up to behold a resplendent angel, he saw a piece of torn blue sky shaped like a shrunken hand.

Cohn prayed on his knees. No voice spoke. No wind blew.

One moonlit night, Calvin Cohn, shivering in his sleep, sensed a presence aboard, surely not himself. He sat up thinking of his dead young wife. She had been driving, not Cohn. He mourned her among those he mourned.

He feared that God, in His butcher's hat, was about to knock on the door. For the ultimate reason: "'Kiddo, it's time,'" or hinting, perhaps, to prepare Cohn? He was to be slain, God had said, though not executed. Why, therefore, hadn't it happened in his sleep rather than out of it? You go to bed and wake up dead. Or was Cohn making much of nothing real, letting fear touch his throat?

Or was this sense of another presence no more than anticipation of the land in the abated floodwaters; dove bearing in its beak a twig of olive leaf? Or raven croaking, "Land ahoy! Get your pants on"?

Cohn stared out the porthole glass; moonlight flowing on the night-calm smooth sea. No other sight.

Before reclining in his berth he drew on his green-and-blue striped sneakers and, taking along his flashlight, peeked into each cabin and lab room below the foredeck. There were creakings and crackings as he prowled from one damp room to another; but no visitors or visitations.

He woke at the sound of a whimper, switched on his torch, and strained to hear.

Cohn imagined it might be some broken thing creakily swaying back and forth in the night breeze, but it sounded like a mewling baby nearby. There had been none such aboard, nor baby's mother.

Holding a lit candle in his hand, Cohn laid his ear against each cabin door. Might it be a cat? He hadn't encountered one on the boat. Was it, then, no more than a cry in a dream?

As he was standing in his cabin, a scream in the distance shook him. Bird screeching at ship approaching shore? Impossible—there were no living birds. In Genesis, God, at the time of the First Flood, had destroyed every living thing, had burned, drowned, or starved them, except those spared on the Ark. Yet if Cohn was alive so might a single bird or mouse be.

In the morning he posted a message on the bulletin board in the games room. "Whoever you may be, kindly contact Calvin Cohn in A-11. No harm will befall you."

Afterwards, he heated up a pot of water on the gas stove and then and there gave up shaving. All supplies were short. Cohn piped out the fresh water that remained in the leaky storage tank he had unsuccessfully soldered, and let it pour into a wooden barrel he had found in the scullery. By nightfall almost an eighth of the water in the barrel was gone. That was no bird.

Who would have drunk it? Cohn feared the question as much as any response. He nailed three boards over the head of the barrel. When he wanted to drink he pried one up, then nailed it down again.

He was edgy in the galley as he scrambled a panful of powdered eggs that evening before dark, sensing he was being watched. A human eye? Cohn's skin crawled. But he had been informed by an Unimpeachable Source that he was the one man left in the world, so he persuaded himself to be calm. Cohn ate his eggs with a stale bun, washing the food down with sips of water. He was reflecting on the pleasures of a cigarette when he wondered if he had detected a slight movement of the cabinet door under the galley double-sink.

Who would that be?

The question frightened him. Cohn looked around for a cleaver and settled on a long cooking fork hanging on the wall. Holding the instrument poised like a dagger, he strode forward and pulled open the metal door.

The shriek of an animal sent his heart into flight. Cohn considered pursuing it in space but took an impulsive look inside the under-sink cabinet and could not believe what he beheld—a small chimpanzee with glowing, frightened eyes, sitting scrunched up amid bottles of cleaning fluid, grinning sickly as he clucked hoo-hoos. He wore a frayed cheesecloth compress around his neck.

"Who are you?" Cohn cried, moved by his question—that he was asking it of another living being. A live chimp-child, second small error by God Himself? The Universal Machine, off by a split cosmi-second, allows a young ape also to survive?

That being so, the realm of possibility had expanded. Cohn's mood improved. He felt more the old Cohn.

The chimp, swatting aside the cooking fork, bolted out of the cabinet, scampering forward on all fours to a swing-door that wouldn't budge. Scooting behind a tin-top work table, he climbed up a wall of shelves and sat perched at the top, persistently hooting. The chimp chattered like an auctioneer encouraging bids as he awaited Cohn's next move. At the same time he seemed to be eloquently orating: he had his rights, let him be.

Cohn kept his distance. He guessed the chimp had belonged to Dr. Walther Bünder, had heard the scientist kept one in his cabin; but Cohn had never seen the animal and forgot it existed. He had heard the doctor walked it on the deck late at night, and the little chimp peed in the ocean.

The ape on the shelf seemed to be signaling something—he tapped his toothy mouth with his fingers. The message was clear—Cohn offered him what was left of his own glass of water. Accepting it, the chimp drank hungrily. He wiped the inside of the glass with his long finger and sucked the juice before tossing the tumbler to Cohn. Hooting for attention, he tapped his mouth again, but Cohn advised him no more water till bedtime.

They were communicating!

Sitting on a kitchen stool, Calvin Cohn carefully observed the young chimpanzee, who guardedly returned his observation. He gave the impression that he was not above serious reflection, a quite intelligent animal. Descending the shelves, he self-consciously knuckle-walked toward Cohn, nervously chattering as the other sat motionless watching him.

Then the little animal mounted Cohn's lap and attempted to suckle him through his T-shirt, but he, embarrassed, fended him off. "Behave yourself." The chimp sat grooming his belly as if he had lived forever on Cohn's lap and punctually paid the rent.

He was a bowlegged, bright little boy with an expressive, affectionate face, now that his fear of Cohn seemed to have diminished. He weighed about seventy pounds, a large-craniumed creature with big ears, a flat nose, and bony-ridged curious dark eyes. His shaggy coat was brown. He seemed lively, optimistic, objective; did not say all he knew. He sat in Cohn's lap as though signifying he had long ago met, and did not necessarily despise, the human race. When in his exploration of his body hair he came on a tasty morsel, he ate it with interest. One such tidbit he offered Cohn, who respectfully declined.

He, feeling an amicable need to confide in somebody, told the little ape they had both been abandoned on this crippled ship, to an unknown fate.

At that the chimp beat his chest with the fist of one pink-palmed hand, and Cohn wondered at the response; protest, mourning—both? Whatever he meant meant meaning, comprehension. The thought of cultivating that aptitude in the animal pleased the man.

What would you tell me if you could?

The young chimp's stomach rumbled. Hopping off Cohn's lap, he reached for his hand, and tugging as he knuckle-walked, led him to a cabin in the foredeck, about thirty feet up the passage from Cohn's.

Cohn had cleaned up and dried his own room; this was a soggy mess. Scattered over the floor were pieces of a man's wearing apparel, silk shirts, striped jockey shorts, knee-length black socks, and dozens of blurred typewritten pages of what might have been a book in progress adhering to the waterlogged green rug. Among the clothes lay several damp notebooks, a damaged microscope, two rusted surgical instruments. Many swollen-paged damp books were strewn over the floor. Cohn, out of respect, placed them in the bookcase shelves, assisted by the chimp, who seemed to like doing what Cohn did. Several of the books dealt with modern and prehistoric apes; one was a fat textbook on the great apes, by Dr. Bünder. The subject of others was paleoichthyology.

As he inspected the framed pictures on the white walls, Cohn came upon a mottled color photograph of Walther Bünder, a round-faced man with a rectilinear view of life. Wearing a hard straw hat, the famous scientist sat in an armchair holding a baby chimp in diapers, recognizably the lad now standing by Cohn's side. In the photograph the baby chimp wore a small silver crucifix on a thin chain around his neck. Cohn wondered what the doctor supposed it meant to the little ape. He then tried peeking under the boy's bandage, but the chimp pushed his hand away. When Cohn was a child his mother wrapped a compress around his neck whenever his tonsils were swollen.

Cohn had talked to Dr. Bünder rarely, because he was not an accessible person. Yet once into conversation he reacted amiably, though he complained how little people had to say to each other. He had been a student of Konrad Lorenz and had written a classic text on the great apes before concerning himself with prehistoric fish. He said he had divorced his wife because she had produced three daughters and never a son. "She did not look to my needs." He argued she was just as responsible as he for the sex-type of their children. And he had not remarried because he did not "in ezzence" trust women. He called himself a natural philosopher.

Cohn "had to say" that he had studied for the rabbinate, but was not moved by his calling—as he was by his father's calling—so he had become instead a paleologist. The doctor offered Cohn a Cuban cigar he had imported from Zurich.

Why the doctor had not taken his little chimp with him at the very end, Cohn couldn't say, unless the chimpanzee had hidden in panic when the alarm bells rang, and could not be located by his master. Or the doctor, out of fear for his own life, had abandoned his little boy.

What's his loss may be my gain, Cohn reflected.

Close by Dr. Bünder's berth stood a barred, wooden holding cage four feet high. In it lay a small, damp Oriental rug and two rusted tin platters. The chimp, as though to demonstrate the good life he had lived, stepped into the cage, swinging the door shut, and then impulsively snapped the lock that had been hanging open on the hasp. A moment later he gazed at Cohn in embarrassed surprise, as though he had, indeed, done something stupid. Seizing the wooden bars with both hands, he fiercely rattled them.

Get me out of here.

"Think first," Cohn advised him.

Cohn went through the doctor's pockets, in his wet garments, but could not find a key to the cage. He pantomimed he would have to break the door in.

The chimp rose upright, displaying; he swaggered from foot to foot. It did him no good, so he tried sign language, but Cohn shook his head—he did not comprehend. The animal angrily orated; this was his home and he loved it.

"Either I bang the door in, or you stay there for the rest of your natural life," Cohn told him.

The chimpanzee kicked at the cage and grunted in pain. He held his foot to show where it hurt.

Cohn, for the first time since the Day of Devastation, laughed heartily.

The little chimp chattered as if begging for a fast favor, but Cohn aimed his boot at the locked wooden door and bashed it in.

The chimp, his shaggy hair bristling, charged out of the cage, caught Cohn's right thumb between his canines and bit.

Cohn, responding with a hoarse cry, slapped his face—at once regretting it. But it ended there because, although his thumb bled, he apologized.

The ape presented his rump to Cohn, who instinctively patted it. He seemed to signal he would like to do the same for Cohn, and he presented his right buttock and was touched by the animal. Civilized, Cohn thought.

In one of the damp notebooks whose pages had to be carefully teased apart, the writing barely legible because the purple fountain-pen ink had run—not to speak of the doctor's difficult Gothic script—was his record of the little ape's progress in learning the Ameslan sign language for the deaf. "He knows already all the important signs. He mages egzellent progress." The accent played in Cohn's head as he read the doctor's words. He could hear him mumbling to himself as he scratched out his sentences.

Calvin Cohn searched for a list of illustrated language signs but could not find them. Trying another soggy notebook, he came across additional entries concerning Dr. Bünder's experiment in teaching the boy to speak with him. On the last page he found a note in the scientist's tormented handwriting to the effect that he was becoming bored with the sign-language exercises, "although Gottlob gobbles it up. I must try something more daring. I think he ist now ready for it. He ist quite a fellow."

Gottlob!

That was the last entry in this notebook, dated a week before the Day of Devastation.

Cohn was not fond of the name Dr. Bünder had hung on the unsuspecting chimp; it did not seem true to type, flapped loose in the breeze. Was he patronizing his boy or attempting to convert him? Leading the ape by his hairy hand to his cabin, Cohn got out his old Pentateuch, his Torah in Hebrew and English which he had recently baked out in the hot sun, flipped open a wrinkled page at random and put his finger on it. He then informed the little chimp that he now had a more fitting name, one that went harmoniously with the self he presented. In other words he was Buz.

Cohn told him that Buz was one of the descendants of Nahor, the brother of Abraham the Patriarch, therefore a name of sterling worth and a more suitable one than the doctor had imposed on him.

To his surprise the chimp seemed to disagree. He reacted in anger, beat his chest, jumped up and down in breathy protest. Buz was obviously temperamental.

But his nature was essentially unspoiled. Since his objections had done him no great good, he moodily yawned and climbed up on the top berth where, after counting his fingers and toes, he fell soundly asleep on his back.

His mouth twitched in sleep and his eye movements indicated he was dreaming. Somebody he was hitting on the head with a rock? Except that his expression was innocent.

Cohn felt they could become fast friends, possibly like brothers.

Who else do I have?

He locked Buz in the doctor's cabin, and let him out in the morning to have breakfast with him in the galley.

Cohn observed that the chimp had done his business in his tin dish in the cage. Clever fellow, he suited himself to circumstance. Afterwards they played hide-and-seek and Cohn swung him in circles by his long skinny arms on the sunny, slightly listing deck. Buz shut his eyes and opened his mouth as he sailed through the air.

Cohn enjoyed playing with him but worried about diminishing food supplies. Canned goods, except for five cases of sardines, twelve of vegetarian baked beans and three of tuna fish, plus two cases of sliced peach halves in heavy syrup, were about gone; but there was plenty of rice and flour in large bins. The frightening thing was the disappearing drinking water. There were only a few gallons in the barrel. Cohn doled it out a tablespoon at a time.

What if they went on drifting on the vast ocean without ever landing? The worst was yet to come. Wait till God discovered His second little error—that Buz, too, had momentarily escaped his final fate. Not that he was alive when he shouldn't be, but that he hadn't expired when he was supposed to. Or had He already discovered it and was making plans? The Lord was mysterious. His speech was silence, His presence, mystery. He made life a mystery, problematic for anyone attempting to survive.

In a week the water supply was all but depleted. Cohn considered attempting to distill sea water but hadn't the equipment. Besides, the gas was low. Simply cooking salt water all day and trying to collect its steam would be an impossible task. Still, if they had to they would try.

If only it would rain again, no deluge, just enough to store up some precious water. Maybe he oughtn't to have kept Buz on ship, who ate as though starved, and if given a chance drank twice as much water as Cohn. Ought he to have kicked the ape overboard? Should he—to preserve himself? Could he?

As he was contemplating desperate measures, the sky darkened. Cohn lugged up on deck the all-but-empty water barrel, and Buz carried up a copper frying pan he had found below. He banged the clattering instrument as though summoning a rain God.

And as if the rain God had himself appeared, the wind rose with a wail and in minutes the black, thickened sky poured water on water. The rising waves lifted the battered schooner on swelling seas, then dropped it low. Now the rudderless vessel plunged through fierce, roiling currents, driven southward by the hurricane.

A howling wind raged. Cohn had tightly tied the ashen-faced chimpanzee to the broken mast, as the *Rebekah Q* dipped and rose, from ocean pit to sky, in the hissing waves. They watched the storm with shut eyes, the drenched little chimp whimpering after he had thrown up.

Cohn, shivering within himself, feared they'd be washed into the heaving sea. Drowning would be the end of it, the last wet page of life. Today may be the day He slays us, though why does He complicate it so when He can knock us off with one small lightning bolt? Mission completed, the earth cleansed of living creatures, except maybe an underweight cockroach under a wooden sink in Bombay, that He will knock off with His spray gun the next time it exposes its frantic antennaed head. What makes Him so theatrical? Cohn wondered. He enjoys performance, spectacle—people in peril His most entertaining circus. He loves sad stories, with casts of thousands. Cohn hid his anger at the Lord, turning it low, then hid his thoughts.

After hours of anguished enduring, Calvin Cohn watched the slow night unfold as the wind gently subsided. The sea grew quiet, the storm abated. A white star hung like a lucent pearl in the clearing sky. The chimp had revived and was listening with interest to his borborygmus. Any voice interested him. They had sailed southeast after south and were now drifting north-northeast. Cohn guessed they had voyaged out of the Pacific, but where in the world are we?

In the morning the sun blazed like a flaming bronze mirror. Cohn untied himself and Buz, whereupon the little chimp embraced him in his hairy arms. And they kissed. In his expressive mood Buz inserted two fingers under his neck cloth and tugged at something; he handed Cohn a small silver cross on a broken chain, perhaps as a gift.

One God is sufficient, thought Cohn. But instead of casting it into the water he slipped it into his pocket.

The chimp hastily rehearsed his repertoire of language signs, none of which Cohn knew, though he was able to guess out a couple of the more obvious ones. And the barrel on the deck was brimming with rainwater, slightly salted. It seemed as though the ship itself sought the end of its voyage but had trouble arriving upon it.

The sinking boat was leaking through its rusty hull. If they lasted one more day he'd be surprised. And where was land? As if to say *look!* two violet-blue jacaranda blossoms appeared on the lavender water, trailed by a palm frond and two green-leaved bamboo shoots.

And he spied four dead rainbow fish; had assumed they were alive until he shook out the bottom of a paper bag of bread crumbs on the glazed water. The fish did not flicker. The air was heavily humid. Cohn focused his binoculars into the hazy distance and saw moving fog. No birds present, not an albatross or pelican, or anything smaller.

He inspected their yellow rubber raft and gathered supplies and objects of craft and art to take ashore, granting they arrived at a shore. He collected several precious books, and the water in ten-gallon jugs. Cohn had hand-picked, from cabin to cabin, piles of clothing for all seasons; all the provisions he could carry; also a portable wind-up phonograph with a dozen uncracked records, seventy-eights, long ago the property of his father the rabbi who had once been a cantor; plus yards of lumber and a full tool chest, with gimlets and awls. And he took with him a small off-white urn containing his pregnant wife's ashes. She had been cremated before the universal cremation, her will, not Cohn's; she had seemed always to know what was coming next.

That night, while Buz and Cohn were asleep in their upper and lower beds, the vessel shuddered, splintered, and cracked stupendously as it went grindingly aground. The chimp was pitched out of his berth and began to hoot in the dark; but Cohn got a candle lit and calmed him, saying they would no longer be at the mercy of a foundering ship.

At dawn Buz slid down a rope as Cohn climbed down the tilted ship's ladder, stepping on the blackened surface of a coral reef on whose algae-covered mass the *Rebekah Q*, jaggedly broken in two, was pulled up tight. Across a narrow channel lay a strip of coastal land, possibly an island.

Buz stepped into the water, and to Cohn's great surprise,

began swimming across the channel to the verdant thick-treed shore. A chimp paddling on his back? A genius chimp, Cohn reflected.

They'd be like brothers, if not father and son.

Arriving on shore, the dripping ape thumbed his comic nose at Cohn, and sauntering forward, plunged into the steaming rain forest without so much as a glance backward.

Hours later, having brought in the yellow raft laden with supplies to the green shore, then hidden them in the saw-toothed tall grass, an exhausted Cohn followed Buz into the forest. He figured God had, at long length, permitted him to go on living, otherwise He wouldn't have let Cohn leave the wrecked vessel and make for shore.

The Lord, baruch Ha-shem, had moved from His Judgment to His Mercy seat. Cohn would fast. Today must be Yom Kippur.

Cohn's Island

HIS FIRST NIGHT on the island—the massive silence was unreal—Cohn spent in a scarlet-blossomed candelabrum tree, although there were no wild beasts to hide from. In the rain forest no birds sang or insects buzzed; no snakes slithered on their bellies; no moths, bats, or lizards had survived. No friend Buz, for that matter; Cohn had seen no sign of the young ape. How desolate the world was; how bleak experience, when only one experienced.

Where were the dead? He had come across yards of scattered bones. None were fossils. All were skeletons of animals that had perished in the Devastation, among them an undersize leopard and a lady chimpanzee. He found no bones of men, felt a renewal of abandonment, but kept himself busy exploring the island.

In the morning he discovered—there where the rain forest curved behind a rocky, hilly area, and flowed north—several caves in a striated yellow sandstone escarpment, and Cohn chose the largest, a double-caverned chamber, to shelter himself. The escarpment, as high as a five-story tenement backed against a parapet of green and lilac hills, was a many-ledged bluff topped by masses of wild ferns, mossy epiphytic saplings, and cord-thick vines dripping down its face.

Cohn ascended the escarpment, practically a walk-up. From a terraced enclosure like a small balcony two-thirds of the way up, he paused for a view of the woodsy neighborhood—the rain forest, a wall of steaming vegetation in the west moving north; and toward east a sparser woodland of flowering trees and thick-grassed fields extending to the southern shore of the island, lined with varieties of wild palm.

From the left side of the escarpment, which looked like a fortress from the shore, a waterfall resembling a horse's bushy tail fell, forming a foaming pool where it hit the rocky ground. The pool overflowed into a downward sloping savanna, beyond which the rain forest grew over a section of hills to the northern sea, where Cohn and Buz had landed on a coral reef.

After this initially unsettling yet engrossing view of his domain, Cohn's disposition improved.

He set to work diligently clearing the anterior, and smaller, of the two caves, carrying out shovel loads of black mud; he tore out armfuls of entangled dead vines; and hauled buckets of rocks and wet sand. Cohn unearthed two stone ledges, one along the rear of the cave where it opened into the larger cavern; the other an almost rounded table of sandstone extending from the left wall as one entered the cave, an all-purpose work platform on which he figured he would prepare food, assemble and repair objects he might need; and on which he could build cooking fires.

The cave, surely eighteen feet high, ten broad, and twenty feet deep, showed no high-water line of the Flood. That appeared on the face of the escarpment about thirty feet up. Despite the humid heat Cohn lit a fire to bake out the cave. He had dragged in a quantity of lumber, transported with great difficulty from the reef—a pile of boards of mixed woods and lengths that he managed to fit under the long rock ledge; and in a week he set to work constructing a wall of shelves ten feet by twelve high and wide, and two deep, where he stored his possessions, such as they were, and would keep whatever else he might collect. It occurred to Cohn he seemed to be assuming a future, for better or worse.

Using the fine tools he had carted along from the oceanographic vessel, which included a surveyor's telescope, he built himself a rough small table, sturdy cot, and a primitive rocker with water-barrel staves; then Cohn constructed an outside hut not far from a small stand of white acacia trees about thirty feet from the cave. The hut was walled with split saplings on three sides, and the fourth was left open because he liked to look at a grassy, wooded area that sloped to the sea.

His hut was covered with a bamboo roof insulated from the heat by a thatch of palm fronds interwoven with strips of bark. When Cohn tired of the cave—his bedroom, kitchen, and living area—he sat in the hut, more like an open porch and revery room. There he had strung up a canvas hammock he had made from a sail, where he often lay, reflecting on his lonely fate.

Can I call this a life?

Better than death.

Why bother?

"Because I breathe."

When the humidity grew intolerable he rested in the cool cave, lit at night by a kerosene lamp. He considered constructing a gate across the oval opening, but why get involved if there were no inconvenient animals around? And gate or no gate the Lord knew where he lived, if He felt like dropping in to talk with His little mistake.

A week or two after his arrival on the island Cohn was struck by a nauseating illness, felt ghastly, headachy to the pits of his eyes, shivered feverishly. He vomited continuously though he ate nothing to vomit. Cohn sweated; he stank. He lost hair in dreadful quantities; it fell from his head as he lay on the floor on an old overcoat. He lost his short brown beard, chest and pubic hair, every bit on his body.

Cohn guessed he was afflicted by radiation poisoning, or had been affected—perhaps in addition—by excessive bursts of X-rays trespassing in the shredded ozone. Is it the Swiss-cheese ozone or the will of God that makes me ill? Maybe He knows I'm still angry at Him? Cohn thought he had better watch his thoughts. He who knoweth the voice of the bird way up there isn't above knowing what C. Cohn thinks. I'd better stay out of his ESP and/or Knowing Eye. But sick as I am I won't knock on His perilous door, even if I knew where it is. Let Him look me up if He's in the mood for instant benediction.

Cohn doctored himself as best he could, with aspirin and sips of stale water. To coat his stomach he chewed grains of raw rice, though it did no apparent good. He vomited anything he imbibed; fouled himself disgracefully; felt abandoned, outcast, bleak. Nobody was present to cluck in sympathy at poor Cohn's fate. He could not stand very much more of the same. " 'Live quickly,' " the Lord had said. " 'A few deep breaths and go your way.' " Calvin Cohn, as though in agreement, slipped out of consciousness of the world it was.

During a long night of delirium, with morbid intervals of awareness and no desire to go on, cursing the woman who had given him birth and anybody who had assisted in the enterprise, Cohn woke in the drafty front cave to the sensuous presence (Mama forgive me) of a hand lifting his aching head.

It then seemed to the sick man that a delicious elixir of coconut was flowing down his parched throat.

In the glowing dark he was teased by a thought that he was being assisted and fed by a heavy-breathing, grunting, black god, holding half a fragrant coconut to his wasted lips as Cohn gulped; or was he still delirious and the experience illusion, dreamthought?

"Buz?" he murmured and got no response. Cohn reached forth to touch the god, if god it was, or beast; a hand withdrew and his head struck the ground. The pain, flashing a dozen lightnings, confused him.

In the morning two ripe red bananas lay by his side, and with them four soft oranges. Cohn reached for one, cupping it in his gaunt hands, deeply breathing its orange fragrance as the warm fumes rose in his head. He bit the skin and sucked the fruit dry. Going by this statement of his senses, Cohn lived on. He had one constant dream: he was alone in the world if not elsewhere.

His nausea returned but not the creature (or whoever) that had fed him. Cohn, still seriously ill, heaved up the fruity contents of his stomach and sank into a coma. How long it endured he didn't know. Or whether he had had a visitor or visitors. When he came out of it, he could not separate experience from what might have been. Anyway, here was Cohn lying on the warm ground in bright sun, in open view of the cloudless island sky. Whoever-he-was had dragged or carried him in his soiled overcoat out of the cave into the grass before his hut, where the acacias grew at the edge of the woods and field that led to the sea.

For days it seemed to Cohn he lay there barely able to stir, staring at the sky, hoping to recover health and existence. Whoever-his-protector continued to provide fruit of several sorts, plus acacia leaves for decoration—and as of yesterday, washed rootstocks of cassava. Cohn, having nothing else to occupy him, forced himself to chew the bitter, starchy root, sensing it nourished him. He had lost a great deal of weight and was afraid to look at any part of himself. But he felt a hot breeze wander over him, indicating he had substance; and when Cohn touched his head to see if it was still there, he could feel a growing fluff of hair. Fortunately it rarely rained as he lay outside; at times drizzled.

Each day fruit and washed root appeared. If he awoke early to see who was feeding him, invariably there was no delivery. He fell asleep and when he awakened later his portion was present, together with a broken piece of sugar cane. Cohn daily thanked his benefactor but hadn't the pleasure of making his or her acquaintance.

One morning, after devouring a breakfast of five pieces of fruit, Cohn got up and dunked himself in the fresh-water pool formed by the horsetail waterfall, from which a spring flowed into the savanna beyond the side of the escarpment. Here Cohn had bathed shortly after arriving in this part of the island, as though to celebrate his arrival; and now he bathed to cleanse himself of his illness.

He dried his legs, sitting on a warm large rock in the sun, and drew on a white silk shirt of Dr. Bünder's, his own denims, and blue-and-green sneakers. Cohn liked being dressed; Adam probably had got to enjoy his fig leaf.

Afterwards Calvin Cohn sat in his rocker in the open but couldn't work up energy to read. He shut his eyes and was dreaming of sleep when he heard a rustle in one of the white-flowered acacias. Glancing up, he saw to his happy surprise Buz himself sitting on a low bough, paying no attention to his former friend and mentor. He was eating a small, wrinkled, plum-like fruit with a greenish center. Cohn, an old encyclopedia hand, recognized it as passion fruit. Buz held four bunched in his pink palm. He still wore his decaying neck cloth as though out of affection. His supple toes held to the tree limb. The chimp's phallus and fleshy scrotum were visible, a more than respectable apparatus for a boy his age.

When Buz saw Cohn observing him he let out an instinctive squawk and chattered angrily at the fuzzy creature below; then, as if recognition had lit a lamp, hooted conversationally. Cohn spoke a few words of welcome home, refraining from mentioning the ape's desertion of him or engaging in a complaint of his recent woes.

He had noticed that Buz's shaggy coat adorned him in tufts and patches, and that the hair on his head had thinned out and left him slightly bald. He wasn't as skinny as Cohn but had obviously been ill.

Buz, in courteous acknowledgment of Cohn's greetings,

tossed down one of his passion fruits; it struck him on the head, and though it was a pitless fruit, knocked him cold. The ape, after eating those he held in his palm, curiously inspected Cohn's supine body and at last climbed down to attend him.

Cohn said Kaddish for one hundred souls whose names he had picked at random in a heavily thumbed copy of a Manhattan telephone directory he had snatched from the sea-battered *Rebekah Q.* He kept it for company in the cave as a sort of "Book of the Dead."

He often felt an urge to read all those names aloud. The Dead must be acknowledged if one respected life. He would say Kaddish at least once for everyone in the book, although, technically speaking, to do so one needed the presence of ten live Jews. Yet, since there were not ten in the world, there was no sin saying it via only one man. Who was counting?

God said nothing.

Cohn said Kaddish.

There's a legend in Midrash that Moses did not want to die despite his so-called old age. He was against it, respectfully, of course.

"Master of the World! Let me stay like a bird that flies on the four winds and gathers its food every day, and at eventide returns to the nest. Let me be like one of them!"

"'With all due regard for services rendered,'" God said, "'nothing doing. You're asking too much. That mixes everything up. First things first.'"

Cohn said Kaddish.

If we were bound to come to this dreadful end, why did the All-knowing God create us?

Some sages said: In order to reflect His light. He liked to know He was present.

Some said: In order to create justice on earth; at least to give it a try.

Cohn thought: He was the Author of the universe. Each man was a story unto himself, it seemed. He liked beginnings and endings. He enjoyed endings based on beginnings, and beginnings on endings. He liked to guess out endings and watch them go awry. At first He liked the juicy parts where people were torn between good and evil; but later the stories may have let Him down: how often, without seeming to try, the evil triumphed. It wasn't an effect; it was an embarrassing condition: His insufficient creation. Man was subtly conceived but less well executed. Body and soul hung badly together.

Maybe next time.

Cohn said Kaddish.

When he recovered from his radiation illness, he had acquired a light-brown beard and slim, tanned body, but his short legs, from childhood a bit bent, seemed more so. No cows, no calcium. One day he journeyed with Buz by rubber raft to the coral atoll on the northwestern side of the island to see what they might recover from the wreck of *Rebekah Q.* Many useful objects were too large for transportation by raft, but they could pile up small things, about a four-hundred-pound load each trip.

The cave was a sloping half mile from the southern shore of the island, on the opposite side from the reefs; and it was best to carry in supplies by raft around the island rather than attempt to lug them through the rain forest by tortuous, all-but-impossible routes. Cohn had made five trips to the beached boat, before he became ill, and had gathered many useful objects. Given his uncertain destiny, he felt he ought not pass up any serviceable item.

He paddled at the forward-port corner, and Buz imitated his friend, wielding his aluminum oar in the starboard corner. Or if the chimp dozed off, Cohn, with difficulty, rowed alone.

A breeze had risen and the water was choppy; it took half the morning to arrive at the reef. The grounded vessel, broken in two and lying broadside the sea, was still there, sprayed by waves chopping against the bony atoll.

Cohn had previously taken back with him *The Works of William Shakespeare*, his old Pentateuch, a one-volume encyclopedia, a college dictionary, and a copy—there were eight in his cabin—of Dr. Walther Bünder's *The Great Apes*, a classic textbook containing three excellent chapters on the life cycle of the chimpanzee.

Now he set aside Morris Fishbein's *Medical Adviser*, *The Joys of Simple Cookery*, *How to do Satisfying Carpentry*, and several volumes on paleontology and geology, plus two novels that had once belonged to his wife, may she rest in peace. He had, for entertainment's sake, considered and discarded *A Manual of Sexual Skills for Singles*, found in Dr. Bünder's bottom dresser drawer.

Buz kept for himself a can opener, after he had succeeded in raggedly opening a tin of Portuguese sardines in oil, of which he ate every little fish without offering Cohn a bite.

The ape insisted on dragging along the holding cage he had inhabited and to which he was affectionately attached. They packed the raft as best they could, for fear of overloading leaving behind on the atoll four gallons of linseed oil, a large jar of vitamin C, also Cohn's portable typewriter because he doubted he would write another letter. As for a journal, if he should keep one, he preferred to do it in his handwriting.

He tried to persuade Buz to abandon his silly cage, but the chimp, hooting, on the verge of displaying anger, would not yield. After their return journey in calmer waters, Buz tugged and lugged his cage along the shore and up the long rise to the cave; and he stored it under the stone ledge where Cohn kept what was left of his lumber, a dirty-clothes basket, plus several brooms and a dust mop he had collected.

The next time they returned to the reef—on a cloudy morning after a week of rain—Cohn wondered if they had come to the wrong one, for the vessel was gone. But it was the right reef and the vessel was gone.

The oil, vitamins, and portable typewriter had been washed away. And Cohn felt sadness at the final loss of the ship, the last home he had had in a homeless world. He forgave Buz for wanting to retain his holding cage.

To explore the island, Cohn made trips in stages by raft, and forays into the interior, hiking with Buz. The chimp's ordinary mode of locomotion was knuckle-walking, but he enjoyed brachiating, was talented at it, though no gibbon—hadn't their almost flying skills. He would, however, climb into the crown of a tall tree and fling himself forward, grasping arm-thick liana vines to hold himself aloft before dropping into the next tree. Cohn admired his skill in plunging from one to another without stopping to think about it.

In the rain forest Buz left Cohn behind, a compass in his

hand, trying to hack his way out of the dense undergrowth that made hash of his clothes. Cohn wielded a fine, exquisitely sharp, French saber from the Franco-Prussian War that the chimp had discovered, and borrowed from Dr. Bünder's trunk.

The massive equatorial rain forest was canopied with interwoven branches of leaves festooned with mossy looping vines, through which sunlight barely filtered. The effect was of lit green gloom over a shadowy forest floor. Saplings smothered each other in their struggle to arrive at light.

Parts of the forest floor were covered with flowers. Cohn caught glimpses of vermilion, white, and yellow blossoms. Man and beast had expired but not flowers; the Lord loved their fragrance and color. But who were the pollinators? unless there was a little bee around—God's grace—fructifying the little flowers? How vegetation existed without insects or other small creatures to pollinate plants, Cohn didn't know but could guess: the Lord Himself had creatively taken over. Even the distorted fruits Cohn had found on many trees on his arrival had reassumed their natural forms. "'Grow,'" He said, because that was His nature. And trees and flowers blossomed and bloomed.

The Lord enjoyed beginnings and He usually began by phasing some things out—to make room. Creation soon created crowds. What was He maybe into now? A touch of life without death? Bacteria, for instance, also continued to exist. Maybe this island was Paradise, although where was everybody who had been rumored to be rentless in eternity? No visible living creature moved through the outsize vegetation, only a lone Jewish gentleman and a defenseless, orphaned chimp he had, by chance, befriended on a doomed oceanography vessel.

It took them about two weeks to encircle the island in their yellow raft, camping on land at night, eating from wild fruit trees and root patches, sucking sugar cane; and where there were no streams or waterholes, drinking fresh water Buz found in tree holes. They had begun this journey on the beach below Cohn's cave and had paddled east, then north at the highlands. The island was shaped like a broken stubby flask, it seemed to Cohn. Its bottom had split off in the recent Devastation and sunk into the sea.

On the northern coast as they paddled west, the shoreline was indented by a series of coves and short bays with coarse, sandy beaches; and where the mouth of the flask appeared, a half-dozen atolls shielded the shore.

Every so often they had drawn the raft up on the beach and commenced a fossil dig nearby for a day or so. Cohn kept extensive notes on the bones they unearthed. He was interested in bone movement. And he searched for hominids and found varieties of small ancient animals. He had discovered some surprising samples and felt he ought to knock out an article or two, if for no other reason than to keep up the habit. He wished he had saved his typewriter from the sea, the loss a result of momentary confusion. Buz enjoyed making small holes bigger and breaking rocks with Cohn's hammer. When his eye lit on an interesting bone he beckoned Cohn over to make the identification. To date they had found six teeth of Eohippus—an extraordinary find, two chimp leg bones and a gorilla jaw, possibly from Pliocene times. Also a Jurassic mouse, and an ancient giant raccoon from the Miocene epoch. It was a pretty old island.

Cohn guessed from the vegetation that it lay somewhere in what had once been the Indian Ocean, perhaps off the southern coast of old Africa, possibly over a more or less dead volcano that had bubbled up in the ocean bed. Too bad he had left behind all his diving equipment.

The island, he figured, was about twenty miles in length, and maybe six miles across, except at its midpoint where it seemed to bulge to nine or ten; and at its northeastern end, where it shrank to two across for three miles or so—the mouth of the flask.

Thinking of names, he considered calling it Broken End Island. He also thought of Chimpan Zee in honor of his young friend, and at last settled for Cohn's Island. On a narrow mid-island beach he set up a sign stating the name of the place; but when they were once more embarked on the raft Cohn had second thoughts and felt he ought to remove the sign next time around, lest the Lord accuse him of hubris.

Cohn supposed that the island had been four or five miles longer than at present. On the Day of Devastation an earthquake struck, and a portion of the highland mass split off and sank into the sea. What was left of the land had been overwhelmed by a tidal wave—the first stage of the World Flood, from which it had slowly, recently, recovered.

Perhaps the island inhabitants, in fishing and farming villages sloping down the hills, had rushed in panic to higher ground, and as they ran were swept by the tidal wave into the ocean; as were those who, in panic, had remained where they were.

Cohn, as they had rowed the raft around to the northern coast from the east, had beheld a forest of brown dead-leaved tops of trees rising in the mild waves touching the rock-bound shore. He thought he could see, in the near distance, a drowned village under water.

Could the Lord see it?

The late-autumn rains—cold, pulpy raindrops—poured torrentially; and soon, in a second or third growing season, streams of small orange, pink, and huge purple flowers Cohn had never laid eyes on before sprang up on the earth.

The rain went on, with a few dry periods, from possibly October to December, and March through May—Cohn did not know because he kept no calendar; his watch had stopped, he would not wind it up. It extended time not to hack it to bits and pieces. Perhaps this was closer to the Lord's duration. He was not much concerned with minutes, or hours, and after Creation, with days, except the Sabbath. His comfortable unit of existence was the universe enduring.

In the afternoon, the rain lightened and Cohn would go forth in his woolen brown poncho and rain-repellent fur hat to search for fruit.

Buz, who swam when he had to, could not stand the wet; it depressed him. When the rain was heavy he sat semi-catatonically in the cave, staring at the water streaming down. It poured as a solid sheet of wet, blurring the trees. When it let up they went forth together, and if they happened to be caught in a renewed downpour, the chimp sheltered himself under a thick-leaved tree, his hands crossed on his chest, his head bent, body hair shedding water. It was as though he mourned when it rained.

Cohn wanted to know why.

The ape hooted.

Cohn prepared a map of fruit trees with footnotes saying when and how they bore fruit. The palms yielded oil, coconuts, dates, round hard red nuts. Buz collected coconuts and carried them to the cave—four in his arms against his chest. Cohn, after tapping them open with a claw hammer, milked each and saved the juice in a jug as a refreshing drink and tasty flavoring agent. And then he hammered the coconut pulp into a delicious paste, flavored with vanilla or chocolate, that they relished as candy.

Buz led Cohn to a small grove of yellow banana trees whose plentiful fruit they ate, ripe, and sometimes fried; and that Cohn fermented in a barrel vat into a pleasant beer that Buz was fond of. When available they collected mangoes—to which Cohn had discovered he was allergic; and figs, passion fruit, oranges, but no lemons—none grew on the island—all of which, except the mangoes, he cut up and mixed with chunks of coconut and pieces of cassava into a delicious salad. He built a trap in the cold stream beyond the pool and used it as an icebox. They ate twice daily; nobody suffered hunger.

Despite the mortal insult the earth had endured, it yielded fruit and flowers, a fact that said a good word for God. Cohn had become a fructivore, except when fruit was unripe or unavailable—fortunately not for long, because they picked and stored it for reasonably lengthy periods.

When there was nothing else to eat they opened tins of sardines or tuna fish. Though the young ape relished these specialties, Cohn felt he was violating an ethic if he ate them. He had pledged himself never to ingest what had once been a living creature.

Therefore he boiled up rice, and with the flour from the ship, baked—since there was no yeast—matzo-like unleavened breadcakes on flat stones in the wood fire on the round stone ledge. The large cave acted as a ventilator, and once in a while a not always comfortable damp draft blew out of it.

Buz ate the thin, often burnt breadcakes in small portions, unable to work up an appetite for Cohn's rice and bread cookery unless he added a fistful of leaves to the collation—his little salad.

The late autumn months were a dreary time of damp and

cold on the island. Cohn hadn't expected the chill. He wore long johns, wool socks, and his overcoat on two sweaters; and he permitted Buz to borrow his poncho if he wanted it. Cohn suspected that something unusual had altered the climate, perhaps ashes of the destroyed world imprisoned in winds in the atmosphere.

That meant hotter and colder than ordinary weather; and he sometimes wondered whether vegetation would continue to endure if God looked away a few celestial seconds. And whether the rain forest would turn black and expire. Cohn was concerned that a new ice age might be in the making, not usually likely on an equatorial island of this size and climatology; but the Lord had His mysterious ways and was not about to explain them.

Cohn insulated the cave as best he could, with two sacks of cement and some rocks he broke up with his hammer; he filled the opening between the caves to a height of six feet. That left space for ventilation, especially important when the wood they burned was wet and smoked heavily. But the cave was comfortable and on dry days smelled of grass; and on wet days smelled like a wet forest. For himself he had added short legs to the cot he had constructed, and made of it a bed of split saplings covered with a layer of mimosa leaves, and a canvas sheet with his overcoat as blankets.

Buz, when it wasn't raining, preferred to rest in a nearby acacia; and when it rained at night he slept in his holding cage, despite the fact that he had grown three inches since he and his friend had met. His head, when Cohn pulled him up by his hands, reached to Cohn's chest, appreciably narrower than Buz's. Though his legs were naturally bent, the chimp covered ground rapidly, sustaining his balance with ease, and propelling himself forward with his knuckles touching the ground. When they raced for fun, invariably Cohn fell behind.

They played tag, hide-and-seek, nut-in-the-hole, an aggie game he had taught him that Buz liked extraordinarily well, although he rolled his nut clumsily and Cohn often let him win by rolling his own so forcefully it shot past the hole. Victory, however arranged, made no difference to Buz so long as he won. He grunted as he ate, danced on occasion, and if Cohn tickled him, responded by tickling Cohn. Cohn enjoyed laughing helplessly—it fitted the scheme of things. And he often thought what a fine friend Buz would make if he could talk.

As spring neared, Cohn, wearing an old army cap to protect his head in the sun, worked with rocks and dead tree limbs to divert the stream that flowed from the waterfall across the savanna below the farther hills. Cohn dammed it and fed the water as irrigation to a rice paddy he had constructed after reading an article and studying a picture in his encyclopedia; and he seeded it with rice sprouts he had grown in the cave. Within about four months he harvested a crop of rice and planted another. So long as the Lord was in a genial mood there would be rice forever. Cohn played with thoughts of immortality.

He also planted—from seeds he had collected and saved—yams and black-eyed beans. Unfortunately there was no lettuce or tomatoes anywhere on the island. Cohn relished salad but could not enjoy leaf salads, passing them up when Buz arrived with his offerings. He presented him, too—from his mouth into Cohn's palm—with a chewed-up green gob of leaves; but Cohn was not tempted.

Buz now and then assisted with the gardening. His fingers weren't subtle and he was inefficient in planting, when Cohn, on his insistence, let him help. Buz cupped a small mound of beans in his palm but found it difficult to insert them individually into the soft soil; so he chewed up some and flung the rest away. Cohn thought he might be of more help in harvesting.

But Buz was comparatively handy with a few tools. He liked plunging the point of his can opener into the top of a can, working it raggedly around until the tin was cut and he could get his fingers under the lid. He had learned to slice fruit with a knife and he used a hammer fairly accurately. All Cohn had to do was tap the tip of a nail into wood and Buz would drive it in all the way.

Cohn crafted things. He carved wood with a jackknife and chisel, and made bowls, platters, pitchers. He carved a variety of wooden flowers and animals for remembrance. He wove fibers of cactus into stiff little cloths he wasn't sure what to do with, and gathered and polished stones.

One day he fixed up a small hammock for Buz, converting

a topcoat of Dr. Bünder's. He tied it between two live oak saplings, and Buz lay in it, swinging gently until he fell off to sleep. The chimp liked sunbathing in his hammock. He also enjoyed sniffing Cohn's bare feet as he lay in his hammock contemplating his fate.

Would He have given me Buz if He intended to slay me?

That night in the cave, Cohn said the island was shaped like a short, stubby bottle.

Buz pantomimed he disagreed, a grunt with a shake of the head. He pantomimed peeling a banana.

"A little like one, maybe," Cohn nodded, "but a lot more like a stubby bottle, in my eye."

A banana, Buz insisted.

Cohn had brought from the *Rebekah Q* five of Dr. Bünder's fairly legible, waterlogged notebooks. He had discovered in one of them approximately forty partially blurred small drawings of sign-language images the scientist had taught the chimp. Cohn practiced as many signs as he could read.

One day, as he sat in his rocker with Buz on his lap, he signaled to the chimp: "We—you and I—are alone in this world. Do you understand?"

The chimp signaled, "Buz wants fruit."

Cohn signed: "I feel alone (lonely). Is Buz lonely?"

The chimp signaled, "What is alone?"

Cohn, excited by the ape's genuine question, pantomimed signs that might mean sad, unhappy, oppressed.

Buz signed, "Play with Buz."

Cohn impatiently spoke aloud. "What I want to say is that the situation is getting on my nerves. I mean we're alone on this island and can't be said to speak to each other. We may indicate certain things but there's no direct personal communication. I'm not referring to existential loneliness, you understand—what might be called awareness of one's essentially subjective being, not without some sense of death-in-life, if you know what I mean. I'm talking, rather, about the loneliness one feels when he lacks companionship, or that sense of company that derives from community. Do you read me, Buz?"

The chimp signaled, "Drink-fruit (orange or coconut) for Buz."

"First Buz speak to (answer) what I ask (my question)."

The little ape yawned—a gaping pink mouth and lively tongue within a semicircle of strong teeth. His breath smelled like a fragrant mulch pile. Cohn coughed.

Buz attempted to suckle his left nipple.

Cohn dumped him on the ground.

The chimp bit Cohn's right ankle.

He cried out, at once springing a nosebleed. When Buz saw the blood flowing down his upper lip he scampered out of the cave and knuckle-galloped into the forest.

When he was gone two days Cohn worried about him, but on the third day he returned, not without a smirk of guilt, and Cohn forgave him.

Some nights were lonelier than others. They sat by the fire and Buz watched the shadow of Cohn's creaking rocker on the wall. Pointing at it, he let out a gurgling hoot.

"Shadow," Cohn pantomimed, casting a barking dog on the wall with his fingers.

Buz, after studying it, hooted weirdly.

When, as the nights grew warmer, they dispensed with the fire, Cohn, after supper, waited till it was dark, then lit the kerosene lamp if he wanted to read. He read quickly, the kerosene was going fast. When the cave was sultry he read at the table in the hut. There were no moths or mosquitoes invading the lamp. If one could invent a mosquito, Cohn would.

"The silence bugs me."

Buz produced a shrill hoot.

Cohn thanked him.

One night he read to the chimpanzee, regretting he had nothing appropriate for an equivalent of young teenager. But he sensed Buz understood what was read to him; or he understood more than he pretended to. Cohn thought he would try a touch of Shakespeare to attune his ear to spoken English. That might wake a desire to speak the language.

Cohn tried reading aloud from *The Merchant of Venice*, to no avail. Buz was bored and yawned. He studied an illustration on the page and cautiously reached forth a finger to touch Jessica, but Cohn would not let him. Buz retreated, boredom glazing his eyes.

Cohn then switched to Genesis in his Pentateuch and read

aloud the story of the first six days of Creation. The chimp listened stilly. On the seventh day, as God rested from His labors, Buz crossed himself. Cohn could not believe he had seen it. Was it a random act? Again he read aloud the Creation, and the ape again crossed himself. Most likely Dr. Bünder had Christianized him, Cohn decided. His thought was that if one of them was a Christian and the other a Jew, Cohn's Island would never be Paradise.

With that in mind he searched in his valise for a black yarmulke he had saved from childhood, then decided not to offer it to Buz. If he wanted to know something about Jewish experience he would have to say so. Jews did not proselytize.

Buz, however, reached for the yarmulke and draped it on his head. That night he slept with it on his forehead, as if he were trying to determine where it would rest most comfortably. He wore it the next day when he made his usual exploratory rounds among the neighboring trees before entering the rain forest, but in the late afternoon he came back without it.

Cohn wanted to know what he had done with it, and got no reply.

He never saw his yarmulke again. Perhaps in some future time, Deo volente, a snake might come slithering along wearing one. Who knows the combinations, transformations, possibilities of a new future?

He offered the chimp the silver crucifix he had been holding for him, but Buz signed for Cohn to retain it since he had no pockets of his own.

Cohn figured that when the chimp hit what might be the equivalent of thirteen years of age, he would offer him a Bar Mitzvah. Buz might accept; he might not. If he didn't, Cohn would give him back his silver cross. I wonder if he thinks he can convert me by letting me hang onto it?

In the meantime he would tell him stories, in particular those he remembered from Aesop, La Fontaine, Dr. Dolittle, and *Tales of the Hasidim.* How else educate someone who couldn't read? Cohn hoped to alter and raise his experiential level—deepen, humanize this sentient, intelligent creature, even though he did not "speak" beyond a variety of hoots and grunts and make a few pantomimed signals.

Besides, Cohn reflected, if I talk to him and he listens, no matter how much or little he comprehends, I hear my own voice and know I am present. And if I am, because I speak to him, maybe one of these days he will reply so that he can be present in my presence. He may get the idea.

Cohn then began a story of his own. "I'm not so good at this," he set it up. "My imagination has little fantasy in it—that's why I became a digger of bones—but I am fairly good at describing what I've seen and lived through. So instead of inventing stories that never happen—although some do anyhow—I'd rather tell you a few items about my past. Let's call it a bit of family history.

"Personally, Buz, I'm the second son of a rabbi who was once a cantor. And he was the first son of a rabbi—my grandfather, alev hasholem—who was killed in a pogrom. That's a word you probably never heard, one I imagine that Dr. Bünder gave you no sign for."

Buz wouldn't say.

"Nor for Holocaust either? That's a total pogrom and led directly to the Day of Devastation, a tale I will tell you on the next dark day."

The chimp groomed himself under both arms, seeming to be waiting for the real story to commence.

Cohn said that his father the cantor had decided to become a rabbi, and was a good one, thus fulfilling a pledge to his father, not to mention showing respect.

"For somewhat similar reasons I attempted to go the same route, but for complex other reasons I never made it, diverted by inclinations and events I'd rather not talk about at the moment. It isn't that I'm being evasive but there's a time and place for everything."

Cohn, however, mentioned experiencing a trial of faith—losing interest in religion yet maintaining a more than ordinary interest in God Himself.

"It's like staying involved with First Causes but not in their theological consequences. Creation is the mystery that most affects me, so not unexpectedly I ended up in science. And that—to conclude this episode—is why you and I are sitting here listening to each other at a time when nobody else is, I am told."

Cohn, as the chimp yawned, cleverly asked, "And what

about yourself? Can you tell me something about you? When and where, for instance, did you meet Dr. Bünder? What influence, in the long run, did he have on you? Are you American by birth, or were you born in Tanzania or Zaire? How did you get on the oceanography vessel, and were you at all aware civilization was ending when the lights banged out and scientists and crew abandoned ship without taking you along? I sense surprising gifts of communication in you and would be grateful, sooner than later, to know the facts."

Buz pointed to his belly button.

"Are you saying you *are*, or asking that question?" Cohn, in rising excitement, wanted to know.

The chimp tried to make his mouth speak. His neck tendons under the decaying cloth bulged as he strained, but no sound came forth—no word, no hoot.

Buz grunted anticlimactically, then leaped up in anger, landing on one foot. He stamped the other, stormed, socked his chest, his body hair rising. There was no crying but he seemed on the verge.

To calm him, Cohn wound up the portable phonograph and put on a record of his father the cantor singing a prayer of lamentation. This was a lamentor indeed; he sang from the pit of his belly, but with respect.

The cantor noisily brayed his passion for God, pity for the world, compassion for mankind. The force of his fruity baritone seemed to shiver the cave in the rock. His voice was vibrant, youthful; though he was dead. Cohn was grateful his father had died before the Day of Devastation. For that disaster he might not have forgiven God. They had serious trouble after the Holocaust.

" 'Sh'ma yisroel, ad-nai eloheynu, ad-nai echad—' " sang the cantor, his wavering voice climbing to the glory of God.

Buz listened in astonishment. He orated, as though complaining. The chimp was holding the lamp above his head, peering at the floor of the cave as if he had encountered a snake. Or discovered a mystery. Was he seeking the source of the cantor's voice? Cohn took the lamp from him and held it to the phonograph. He explained the voice was in the record. The ape, without glancing at it, rushed to the cave opening, pulled aside the vines, and stared into the humid night. Buz's head-hair bristled, his canines glowed. He growled in his throat.

"What do you see?" Cohn held the lamp aloft.

The chimp whimpered as a musty hot odor, like a burning tire, or someone's stinkingly sweaty body, with a redemptive trace of mint, flowed into the cave.

Calvin Cohn stared into the primeval night and saw nothing. An essence, unformed and ancient in the night's ripe darkness, caused him to sense he was about to do battle with a dinosaur, if not full-fledged dragon; but he saw neither. Yet he thought he had heard an explosive grunt and had observed a shadow flit out of the hut and into the trees.

Cohn went out in his stocking feet. No stars were visible, but a slender emerald crescent moon was rising. He stood for a while probing the night. When he returned to the cave Buz was snoring as if accompanying a dream of hot pursuit.

In the morning, Cohn returned to his chores in the rice paddy and Buz went exploring. On the way, he played in the acacias and tumbled among the branches of a bushy eucalyptus a little farther down.

He tore off a long leafy branch and leaped to the ground, dragging it up the rocky slope to the escarpment, and then charged down, venting a long scream as he pulled the hissing branch after him. A shower burst on his head as he plunged down the slope. Buz danced like an Indian chief in the rain.

When the rain had let up the next morning, the little chimp went out, stopping to throw rocks at a mangrove tree he didn't like. Before slipping into the rain forest he heaved chunks of coconut shell at two epiphytic trees in the leafy gloom, as if to drive away any lingering evil spirit.

Then he disappeared into the forest, sometimes hooting from trees deep in the green growth. That afternoon when the chimp returned from the rain forest his face seemed gone several shades pale. He covered his shoulders with Cohn's poncho and sat in the chair, hoo-hooting to himself. Cohn squatted, stroking his shoulders, at last quieting him. At dusk he climbed into his acacia sleep-tree and bent some branches back to make a nest for himself, but had second thoughts and slept in the cave.

A quarter moon rose and Buz walked in his sleep. Either

that, or he had been frightened as he slept and walked away from the offending sleep-cage.

Cohn asked him if he had had a bad dream but the chimp made no reply.

The next evening, after they had eaten a supper of yams and black beans and drunk tumblers of coconut juice, Cohn played on the phonograph a record of his father the cantor praying. The chimp yodeled along with him, and Cohn, in a sentimental mood, danced to the music of his father's voice. He snapped his thumbs, shook his hips, and sang in Yiddish, "Ich tants far mayn tate."

Buz also tried a few dance steps, dangling one foot, then the other. Abruptly he stopped, his face a frozen sight. What had troubled him? He was these days a nervous chap. Puberty? Cohn wondered. Simply unfulfilled sexual desire? Certainly he was mature enough to want a female—lost cause.

But if there was a female chimp around, Buz wasn't responding in an attractive fashion. Standing at the cave entrance, he pitched into the night a teapot, two tablespoons, a salad bowl Cohn had sculpted with his jackknife and chisel. He had to wrestle two porcelain dishes away from Buz.

Peering through the vines, the chimp bristled and hooted, then retreated, grumbling. Cohn wondered whether the little ape knew something he didn't and ought to?

It seemed to him he heard someone mumbling, or attempting to sing in a guttural voice. It came out a throaty basso aiming an aria to the night sky, possibly pledging his heart and soul to the song of the impassioned cantor. The phonograph was suddenly stilled—silent. Cohn heard nothing more outside the cave. He carried the kerosene lamp to the hut, holding it high so he could see to the edge of the forest.

Amid the shadows wrought in the uneasy night, he had the startled impression he was gazing at a huge man in a black suit seated on the ground twenty feet beyond the hut.

Cohn almost dropped the teetering lamp.

"Who are you?"

The man, rising slowly, became a gorilla lumbering away. When he stopped to look back, his deep, small, black eyes glowed in the lamplight. Cohn wanted frantically to run.

The chimp at the cave stood hooting at the giant ape,

preaching against his kind. He shrieked as the gorilla, reversing direction, moved toward him, halting, staring with blank gaze all the more frightening because it seemed to be his only expression.

Cohn ducked into the cave, set down the lamp, and instinctively grabbed a shovel. As though he had touched hot metal, he tossed it aside and reached for an orange.

Buz, sounding more like monkey than ape, retreated as the gorilla loomed up at the cave entrance. A musty, rank, yet heavy herbal odor filled the cave.

Cohn in a quick whisper warned Buz to quiet down, but the half-hysterical animal, scooping a coconut off the shelf, pitched it at the gorilla. It bounced with a thud off his sloping skull, yet his eyes did not flicker in the lamplight as he stared at the two frightened inhabitants of the cave.

Cohn, sotto voce, informed Buz that the gorilla would not attack if he did not bother him. "But he will rend you limb from limb if you act like a hysteric."

The chimp protested this strategy, but the gorilla, as if he had decided he would never make a home in this cave, mercifully fell back, turning again to cast an impassive stare at them. Or was it a depressive type they were contending with? As he knuckle-walked to the rain forest he expelled a burst of gorilla gas and was gone.

Cohn wondered how many more apes, large or small, he must confront if the Lord's computer had stopped telling Him the numerical truth.

The next morning the gorilla sat alone under a bearded palm tree fifty feet from the cave.

He seems a peaceful gent, Cohn thought, and I'll pretend he isn't there unless he gives me a sign to the contrary.

He was a burly beast, almost ugly, with a shaggy blue-black head and heavy brow ridges. His nostrils were highlighted like polished black stones, and his mouth, when he yawned, was cavernous. The gorilla's black coat was graying on his massive shoulders. Still, if he was frightening, he was not frightful. Despite his size and implied strength—perhaps because he seemed to have a talented ear for devotional music—there was something gentle about him. His dark brown eyes seemed experienced, saddened—after the Flood?—in a way Buz's weren't. Cohn respected the giant ape.

All morning he had remained nearby, as though listening, waiting perhaps to hear the cantor singing. No doubt he was looking for company. Cohn asked Buz not to disturb him. A large friend in a small world had its advantages. But Buz, though he listened obediently, at least respectfully, on catching sight of the gorilla sitting under his favorite white acacia, persistently banged an aluminum frying pan against the escarpment until it howled like a metal drum. He orated at length, growing hoarse, and barking like a baboon. But the gorilla sat motionlessly watching.

Cohn figured he might put on a phonograph record to test his theory; instead he ventured forth and sat in the grass about ten feet from the gorilla, his heart pounding. One false move—for instance, threatening the beast by staring into his eyes—and goodbye Cohn.

Calvin Cohn then experienced an extraordinary insight: I know this one. I know his scent. We've met before.

"Are you the one," he asked humbly, "who fed me when I was sick? If so, please accept heartfelt thanks."

The gorilla blinked as though he wasn't sure he understood the question. He stared at Cohn as if he might have helped him, or he might not; he had his mystery.

Cohn cautiously approached the huge animal—he weighed a good five hundred pounds—with extended hand, his gaze on the ground.

The gorilla rose on his short legs, as he watched the man coming toward him, and modestly raised his own right arm. But Buz, spying the gesture, ran between them, screeching, before the extended arms could become a handclasp.

Although Cohn tried to restrain the jealous chimp, Buz chattered at the gorilla, taunting him.

The chimp pretend-charged, backed off, lunged forward as if to attack, but the gorilla patiently fended him off with his meaty long arm. Grunting at the chimp, he knuckle-walked away. He lifted himself into an acacia tree and sat on a low bough in the dappled sunlight, peacefully observing the scene below.

A true gentleman, Cohn thought.

"If it's all right with you," he addressed the gorilla in gratitude, "I'd like to call you George, after my late wife's father, who was an accomplished dentist, a wonderful man. He often fixed people's teeth for nothing."

He told the gorilla they three were alone in the world and must look after each other.

George seemed to agree, but Buz had clapped both hands over his ears and was mockingly hooting.

One early morning Cohn, on awaking, stealthily drew aside the vines and let in the light. Since Buz was asleep in his cage, he tiptoed over with a pair of small scissors, and reaching between the wooden bars before the ape was thoroughly awake, snipped off his fetid, decomposing neck cloth.

The wound he expected to see was totally healed, and from it two flattened copper wires grew out of the scar where a man's Adam's apple would be.

Buz, awaking startled, hoarsely protested the loss of his loving compress, but Cohn argued it needed a washing and dropped it into the dirty-laundry basket. Buz then did his business outside the cave, as he had been taught; and when he returned, Cohn, before serving him his banana-rice porridge, got the chimp to play tickle.

As he tickled Buz under the arms, he lifted the hilarious ape into a chair, and deftly twisted together the two exposed copper wires on his neck. There was a momentary crackling as the chimp, grinning sickly, stared at Cohn, and Cohn, smiling sheepishly, observed him. After a rasping cough, followed by a metallic gasp that startled him, Buz spoke as though reciting a miracle.

"Fontostisch/ / / I con hear myzelv speag/ / / pong-pong."

Hearing his words, Buz in joy jumped off and on his chair in celebration. Displaying proudly, he socked his chest with both fists. The chimp, then emitting a piercing hoot, rushed out of the cave, shinnied up a nearby palm tree, tore off a fan-shaped leafy branch, and charged up the rocky slope, dragging the swishing branch behind him.

"Fontostisch/ / /" he exclaimed as he knuckle-galloped down the slope with his palm branch. "I con talg/ / / pong-pong."

Calvin Cohn, flushed with the excitement of unexpected adventure, could almost not believe what he had heard.

"A miracle," he conceded. "But what do you mean by pong-pong?"

"Thot's nod me/ / / Thot's the sound the copper wires mage when they vibrate ot the end of a sendence/ / / I hov on artifiziol lorynch/ / / pong-pong."

His voice was metallic, as if he were a deaf person talking, who had never before heard himself articulate. Buz spoke with his juicy tongue awash in his mouth. His speech, reminiscent of Dr. Bünder's, sounded like a metachimp's, given that possibility. In any case, that the ape could speak had fired Cohn's imagination.

"How do you know what a sentence is?"

"I con understond and speag only words I hov formerly heard/ / / pong-pong. I con say whot I hov heard you say to me/ / / I con alzo say those words thot Dr. Bünder taught me/ / / For instonze, I know the Lord's Prayer/ / / pong-pong."

"How did he teach you that?"

"He taught it to me in sign longuoge/ / / but now I know it is words thot I hov in my head/ / / pong-pong."

"Did he perform the operation on your larynx?"

Buz coughed metallically. "If he hod waited another weeg or two I would hov done it myzelf/ / / I was already talging on my libs but he didn't hear it/ / / I would hov talged oz I do now/ / / pong-pong."

"How—without a proper larynx?"

"Because onimals con talg/ / /" Buz told him. "We talg among ourselves/ / / Maybe someday you will hear our phonemes oz we hear yours/ / / If you con communicade with one living onimal/ / / you con communicade with all his relations/ / / It is pozzible if you will odmid the pozzibility/ / /"

Cohn said it seemed a reasonable possibility. "Belief itself may not be that easy, but I want to believe. In fact, after hearing you in action, I do. I imagine your experience contains an evolutionary factor in it, and I see it as real and believable."

Cohn went on: "What an extraordinary opportunity it provides to understand the nature of communication and development of speech in man. I bet I could make an important contribution in semantics, and I greatly regret there's no one but us, and maybe George, to behold this miracle."

"There's Jesus of Nozoroth/ / /" Buz said.

"Maybe," said Cohn.

Buz said that was beyond question.

Withal a miracle, Cohn felt; he was deeply moved, still amazed, all but overwhelmed. Despite his eccentricities Dr. Walther Bünder had been an extraordinary scientist; and Buz—God bless—was a genius chimp.

Now I will have an intelligent companion as long as we both shall live. Cohn dabbed his eyes with his woolen handkerchief.

The chimp, observing this, tried to squeeze out a tear but failed.

Cohn said not to worry, he would teach him how, among other things.

"Sholl I call you moster/ / / pong-pong?"

"Call me Cal, or if you like, call me Dad."

"Dod/ / /" said Buz, "pong-pong."

Cohn, with a pair of ratnose pliers, tightened Buz's neck wires, and that ended the pong-pong. The chimp said he hadn't minded the redundant sound so long as he could clearly say the rest of a sentence. His articulation improved, and in a short while he lost almost every trace of Dr. Bünder's accent and enunciated consonants and most vowels correctly.

Cohn praised him for being a good lad. They laid arms around each other and affectionately kissed.

Buz began his language studies diligently assisted by Cohn, who read him selected pages in the dictionary. Cohn redefined the definitions, not always to Buz's satisfaction. At first the chimp felt a word should mean what it looked like. He wanted an aardvark to be a snail in its shell, hoping the aard was the snail and the vark its cubicle. Later he accepted the aardvark as a termite eater and called the snail a disgusting slug.

Their dictionary study pleased Buz, and he wondered if it would improve his vocabulary if he ate a few pages now and then, but Cohn forbade that for all time.

Nonetheless he made satisfactory progress. He was not timid in guessing the meaning of words he didn't know, that Cohn used, and asking about others. One day he had a remarkable insight: "What you don't say means something too." Cohn agreed. That was a breakthrough point, and thereafter Buz made faster progress in his mastery of language. Cohn was overjoyed by his semantic talent.

Buz one day wanted to know who had invented language.

Cohn said man. "That's what made him superior to all the other creatures."

"If he was so superior where is he now?"

"Here I am," said Cohn.

"I mean the humon race?"

Cohn, on reflection, admitted maybe God had invented language. "The word began the world. Nor would anyone have known there was a monotheistic God if He hadn't proclaimed it."

Buz said that maybe Jesus had invented language.

Cohn said, "He spoke well but the word was already there."

"He preached to the chimps," said Buz.

Cohn said that Buz had just got close to a metaphor and praised him.

"How close?"

"The chimps as Christians."

"Whot's a metaphor?"

"It's a symbol—sort of," Cohn responded. "It says something not fully expected, through analogy. Like when a banana is conceived to symbolize a man's phallus, and a cave or grotto, a womb."

"I don't agree that a cave is a wombot," Buz said.

"Womb, not wombat."

"I don't believe it. I don't think a phollus is a bonona. I eat bononas, I don't eat pholluses."

"Eating has nothing to do with it. An object, because of a quality in common with another, is taken to represent the other. For instance, Walt Whitman in one of his poems refers to the grass as 'the handkerchief of the Lord'—far out but reasonable."

Buz said he wished his name was Walt.

"Your name is Buz."

"I wish it was Walt. Why does he call the grass a handkerchief?"

"It provides an earthly concept of God: He who walks on

grass with the same ease as he uses His handkerchief. Or He may use the grass to wipe His brow. Anyway, He dwells in our lives. Another similar concept is God the Father."

"Whot about God the son?"

"That's a metaphor too."

Buz said it was the one he liked best.

"You take your choice," Cohn said. "In any case, it's through language that a man becomes more finely and subtly man—a sensitive, principled, civilized human being—as he opens himself to other men—by comprehending, describing, and communicating his experiences, aspirations, and nature—such as it is. Or was." Cohn smiled a melancholy smile.

"Don't forget the chimponzees," Buz said.

He afterwards asked, "If I go on learning your longuoge will I become humon?"

"Maybe not you yourself," Cohn replied, "but something like that could happen in the long run." He said his descent and Buz's from a common ancestor had been a matter of eons of evolution. "And if it was to happen again, I hope it results in an improved species of homo sapiens."

"Whot is humon, Dod?"

Cohn said he thought to be human was to be responsive to and protective of life and civilization.

Buz said he would rather be a chimp.

He wanted to know where stories came from.

Cohn said from other stories.

"Where did they come from?"

"Somebody spoke a metaphor and that broke into a story. Man began to tell them to keep his life from washing away."

"Which was the first story?"

"God inventing Himself."

"How did He do thot?"

"He began, He's the God of Beginnings. He said the word and the earth began. If you tell stories you can say what God's doing. Let's read that one again, Buz." He turned to the story of Creation.

Buz said he was tired of that one. "Nothing hoppons in thot fairy story. Why don't you read about Jesus of Nozoroth? He preached to the chimponzees."

"In what language?"

"I don't know thot. We heard His voice in our ears."

Cohn said he didn't have a copy of the New Testament in the cave. He did have the Old.

"Tell it without the book."

He would, promised Cohn. "But you complain I don't tell you enough animal stories, so how about one of those now? I'll start with the old snake who lived in Paradise with Adam and Eve."

Buz said he hated snake stories. "They crawl on their bellies."

Cohn said God had punished them for getting man into trouble. "Rashi—he was a medieval Talmudic commentator—in other words, somebody who told stories about stories—he said the snake saw Adam and Eve having intercourse amid the flowers. The snake afterwards asked Eve for a bit of the same, but she indignantly refused. That started off his evil plans of the betrayal of man. I've read you the story where he tempted Eve with the apple. She could have said no, but the snake was a tricky gent. He got her confused by his sexual request."

"Whot's intercourse?"

"I read you the relevant passage in Dr. Bünder's book."

"When will I get some of it?"

Cohn said he was sorry but couldn't say.

"If not the snake, how about Cain and Abel?" he asked. "There's action in that one, a stupendous blow on the head."

Buz said he disliked violence and bloodshed. He said he preferred the New Testament.

"There's plenty of violence and blood in the New Testament. Painters worked in red from that for centuries."

"Thot's because they crucified Jesus of Nozoroth," Buz said.

"Who did?" asked Cohn, on the qui vive.

"The Roman soldiers."

Cohn patted his head.

"Tell me the one about the Dod who cut his little boy's throat," Buz then asked.

Cohn responded in annoyance. "Buz, I've told you four times that Abraham never cut his boy's throat. Those who said he did were making up stories that suited their own natures, not Isaac's or Abraham's."

"Tell me again," sighed Buz, climbing up on Calvin Cohn's lap.

Cohn told him again: "This is the story of Abraham and Isaac, his beloved son," he began. "The Talmud says that Satan pestered God to test Abraham's love for Him; and God, to test and prove that love, commanded Abraham to take his boy up to the mountain in Moriah and give him for a burnt offering to the Lord Himself.

"As the story goes, Abraham, not flicking an eyelash, out of love for God, consented. Isaac carried the wood for the fire up the mountain. Then Abraham laid it on the altar, binding his son with leather thongs before lifting the knife to his throat."

Buz said the story was giving him cramps.

"Then why do you ask me to tell it?"

Buz thought maybe it was the figs he had eaten for breakfast that gave him cramps. "But tell the story anyway."

Cohn went on: "Just as Abraham was about to sacrifice his son, an angel called to him out of the blue, 'Don't lay your hands on that boy, or do anything to hurt him. I know you fear God.' And that proves that the Lord, at any given time, may not know all, or He would surely have known that Abraham feared Him.

"On the other hand, if God was testing Abraham to get Satan off His back, He knew what the outcome would be, and I bet Satan did—he has his talents—but not Abraham or Isaac. Still and all, their suffering was limited more or less to intense worry, and had no discernible traumatic effect after the incident when they had confirmed the hard way that they all loved each other."

Buz liked happy endings. "God is love," he said.

Cohn wasn't sure but didn't say so.

"So Isaac's life was saved," he quickly went on, "and a ram caught by his horns in a thicket was substituted as the burnt offering, in that way affirming the idea of an animal in place of human sacrifice. I'm talking now about the time the story of Abraham and Isaac began to be told. It was probably a protest against the pagan sacrifice of human beings. That's what I meant by man humanizing himself—if you follow me."

"Ond do you call murdering onimols a civilized oct?" Buz wanted to know.

Before Cohn, embarrassed, could reply, a rumble of thunder shook the sandstone escarpment. Dirt and small stones sifted down from the ceiling. Fearing an earthquake, or worse, Cohn, cowering over Buz, listened for God's judgment but heard none. He had broken into a chilling sweat and warned himself to be very careful what he was saying. Apparently God wasn't liking every word of it.

"Whot hopponed?" Buz asked, hauling himself out from under Cohn.

"Thunder and lightning."

"Is thot bod?"

"It depends on His mood."

Cohn hesitantly returned to the story of Isaac, saying:

"That ended his ordeal, except that if you reflect on the details at the very end, you figure he must have got lost on the mountain after his life was saved by the Angel, because he disappears from the tale. Exit Isaac. The scriptures have them both going up the mountain to participate in the ceremony God had ordained, but only Abraham came down. So where was Isaac?"

Buz, clearly in suspense, said he had no idea.

Cohn said some Talmudic sages had interpreted it that Isaac had been carried off by the Angel to the Garden of Eden, and that he had rested there, convalescing from the bloody wound his father had inflicted on him.

"Thot's whot I said, but you got mod ot me."

Cohn replied the true reading obviously was that Abraham had not cut his son's throat—God wouldn't allow it—no matter what Abraham's intention, conscious or otherwise, may have been.

"A certain philosopher—somebody called Kierkegaard, whom I haven't told you about, though he's on my list to bring up—he felt that Abraham really wanted to murder Isaac. Freud might have agreed—I'll be filling you in on him in the very near future."

"Do I hov to know everything?" Buz complained. He hopped off Cohn's lap, circled the cave, then climbed back on him.

Cohn loved explication—had once considered becoming a teacher. "Everything that counts," he replied. "Which leads to why the interpretation of Abraham as his son's cutthroat persists through the centuries. That says something about the nature of man—his fantasies of death that get enacted into the slaughter of man by man—kinfolk or strangers in droves—on every possible mindless occasion. But let's not go into that now, except to point out that man paid for who he was—maybe—to my mind—er—somewhat unjustly."

He glanced uneasily at the split up in the ceiling, yet still ran on. "When you bring it all back to basics," he whispered, "it means that God made man seriously imperfect. Maybe what was on His mind was that if He made man whole, pacific, good, he would feel no need to become better, and if he didn't, he would never truly be a man. He also planned it that man had to contend with evil, or it was no go. But the awful thing was that the evil was much a bigger bag of snakes than man could handle. We behaved toward each other like animals, and therefore the Second Flood followed hard on the Day of Devastation."

Buz hooted, "I'm on onimol and hov always been a vegetorion."

Cohn complimented him and hastily returned to Isaac lost on the mountain. "How do you think he got down?"

Buz suggested that maybe a kidnapper had kidnapped him.

Cohn said that might have happened. "But murdered, kidnapped, or whatever, he got to Paradise—some commentators said. There he was resurrected, they say. That's a twist in the story that shows the human passion to bring the dead back to life. Given the nature of death—how long it lasts once it sets in—who can blame us for inventing resurrection?"

Cohn said his personal opinion was that man's will to hang on to life was a worthy reason why God should have preserved humanity. "Call it upholding the value of His original investment."

"Jesus of Nozoroth was resurrected," Buz said.

Cohn said that resurrection was probably related to the resurrection of Isaac. "The New Testament scribes always set the Christian unfolding carefully in the Judaic past."

"Jesus was the first," Buz said. "He preached to the chimps."

Cohn said that whoever was first, neither Judaism nor Christianity, nor any other religion, had prevented the Day of Devastation.

"Well, that's the end of that story," he told Buz, "except that the Talmudists say Isaac returned from Paradise after three years, to his father's house, and soon began to look for a bride. According to the commentators, he was thirty-seven years old when the incident of the burnt offering occurred—and even given the evidence, that's an astonishment."

The chimp, after sitting a moment in silence, asked, "When will I get morried, Dod?"

Cohn, genuinely moved, said he didn't see how that could happen just then. "I'm afraid there's nobody on this island you can marry."

"Con't I morry you?"

Cohn, though he appreciated the sentiment, said it wouldn't work. But he admitted, "We are sort of married in the sense that we are living together and sharing a similar fate."

Buz was disappointed.

Cohn said he hoped Buz had anyway enjoyed his retelling of the story of Abraham and Isaac, though it seemed to get more involved every time he retold it.

Buz said he thought it was a pretty simple story.

During the season of rains, confined to the cave for days, they were often bored. Cohn continued to relate stories of his father—peace on his head. When the old Cohn was seventy-five, he cut into his long white beard to have a better look at his lifelong face. The chimp got a pair of scissors out of the toolbox and began to snip at his own skimpy beard, but Cohn took them away.

On wet days Cohn would sometimes dim the kerosene lamp and, in the shadowy cave, as it windily poured outside, would play records on the wind-up portable phonograph. Despite the force of the gale, George the gorilla sat under a dripping acacia, soaked to the skin, his drenched head bent to his chest as he listened through the wind to the vibrant bray of Cohn's father the cantor.

But when the gorilla, as the downpour lightened, or momentarily ceased, attempted to edge closer to the cave, Buz, who often peeked through the curtain of vines to follow George's movements when he was in the vicinity, flung stones, spoons, bamboo sticks at him. And when he ran out of ammunition, he threw cups and saucers and carved wooden figurines, despite Cohn's ringing disapproval.

Cohn, when the rain let up long enough for him to venture forth in his orange oilskins, occasionally came upon George as they were seeking tubers, or fruit, in the woodland. One day as they stood a short distance apart, Cohn tried to express his apologies to George for the chimp's immature behavior. He said he hoped Buz would soon get used to George; he was a little on the fearful side—despite his intelligence—having been traumatized as a child by being separated from his mother by a scientist who had cut into his neck for reasons of experiment. George raised his hand to touch his throat, then turned and plunged off. That was as much direct communication as they had experienced up to then, but Cohn was not disheartened.

Having George nearby, however, had certain disadvantages. The gorilla, who lived on grasses, roots, bark, bamboo pith, also seemed to relish fruit for dessert, and some of the fruit trees, when he was in residence, were all but denuded after George had been out collecting. He was a connoisseur and would fling aside fifty bitter mangoes to find one sweet one. Cohn couldn't stand the waste.

Yet he felt sorry for the animal—gorillas were polygamous family types, and George had no one to go home to. He was a wanderer in the forest and wandered alone; Cohn could hear him swishing through the vegetation. He often thought, when they passed each other in a clearing, of asking him to the cave for an occasional meal, but when he tried in sign language—pointing to his mouth with his finger—to convey an invitation that George return with him for a fruit-salad dessert plus a cup of banana beer, the wary great ape, his dark brown eyes lonelily observing Cohn, made mournful growling noises.

Cohn had more than once attempted to follow George in the forest, but the gorilla screamed and trumpeted his displeasure, and Cohn hastened away. One day he decided to hold his ground when he encountered the great ape, and for an uneasy moment he watched George approach bipedally. Cohn, as advised in Dr. Bünder's book, lowered his eyes and stared at his toes as George came forward and noisily sniffed Cohn's head and ears, then slunk away as if affronted by the odor.

But he was back as though by appointment, rain or shine, when the cantor was singing in the phonograph. The chimp, after an initial lively response to the old man praying, now stuffed his fingers into his ears and orated against the noise. George, on the other hand, listening outside the cave, after a magnificent Kaddish, rose to his full height and pounded his chest as if it were a kettledrum.

When the chimp heard the gorilla booming his breast he hid in the rear of the cave and covered his head with dirty laundry.

George also liked to be present when Cohn, preferably in the hut, but also in the cave, from which his voice could be heard, was reading aloud to Buz or telling him stories. The gorilla listened as though he understood every word—though sometimes his eyes expressed puzzlement—of Cohn's tales, particularly those about his father the rabbi. George would grunt, perhaps was affected by an act of mercy the old man had engaged in, as when he had labored up the stairs of a cold tenement to deliver a pail of coal to an old woman in a freezing flat.

And Cohn could hear the gorilla breathing in suspense as he read aloud, for instance, of the escape of the Israelites across the parted Red Sea, pursued furiously by hordes of Egyptian charioteers. When the waves of the sea crashed on their heads, and horses and men drowned embracing, George cried out as though in woe. Cohn felt that the gorilla was on the verge of speech even if he hadn't yet learned sign language. There was no saying what the future might bring. Cohn hoped someday to ask George how he had been saved from the Devastation. Had God appeared to him, and if He had, in what language had they conversed?

As the windy, lashing rains diminished, the soaked earth gave forth miniature gold orchids, lilies, poinsettias. And mimosas, acacias, jacarandas burst into yellow, red, purple blossoms. After the rain they listened to water dripping from leaf to leaf in the trees. The chimp sat on Cohn's lap after a sit-wrestle, which was work. Buz was a big lad now, growing taller, stronger. Cohn had begun to build him a rocker of his own to sit in as he listened to stories.

Now Cohn was quietly talking about the gorilla to his boy. He asked Buz to be nice to him. "He's gentle and does no harm to anybody. He hangs around this cave because he's lonely. He's a family type, it says in the ape book."

"He looks mean to me," Buz said. "If he ever cotches me in the forest on a dark night, he will eat me up."

"He wouldn't eat a cockroach. Gorillas are herbivores."

"I don't like his name either."

"What would you have suggested?" Cohn had stiffened a little.

"Adolph."

"Over my dead body." Cohn said he had named the gorilla after a fine dentist he knew, but also after George Washington; and he told Buz the story of the cherry tree. He warned the chimp that the more sticks and stones he flung at George, the more Buz's fear of him would grow.

"Try a little love," Cohn suggested.

"I don't see what love hos to do with thot fot gorilla. You said thot if it didn't work before the Flood why should it work ofter?"

"These are different times," Cohn explained. "As we progress, what didn't work in the past may work hereafter."

"I know thot," Buz answered, "but does thot stupid gorilla?"

Someone close by coughed, and they discovered George outside, sitting against the wall of the escarpment. Seeing himself discovered, the embarrassed gorilla rose and knuckle-lumbered away.

The chimp, hopping on both legs, cried murder. "He's a fot, stupid pig, and besides thot, he stinks."

Cohn warned him not to start that kind of talk. "How often must I tell you of the Devastation that destroyed the world and every living being except you, me, and George? If we expect to go on living we have to be kind to each other."

The chimp, in disgust, climbed the wall shelves and sat on the top, as far from Cohn as he could. He spent most of the day in his hammock outside the cave.

On his return from the rice paddies the next afternoon,

Cohn hunted for a record whose melody he had been humming that morning.

He found the carton of records where he kept them, high on the wooden shelves, but couldn't locate the one he wanted. Counting them, Cohn, to his dismay, found that one was missing—there were nine instead of ten.

Had Buz taken it to punish his dod for something? Disturbed, Cohn rushed out of the cave looking for the chimp. Instead of Buz he spied George the gorilla seated in a eucalyptus, in mid-tree, steadying himself by holding onto an overhead branch, as he chewed on the phonograph record he held in his hand. He had taken a large bite and was trying to savor it as he crackingly chewed. Then George spat it out and flung the record away. It sailed in the air like a frisbee and struck the escarpment, breaking into bits.

Cohn uttered a brokenhearted sob. "Bastard-fool," he shouted, "I'll shoot you dead if you ever again enter the cave without my permission."

George hastily lowered himself to the bottom limb and dropped to the ground. He ran into the rain forest like a runaway locomotive.

During the spring they explored the far end of the island, after beaching the rubber raft near a stunted palm.

"Tie it up," Cohn ordered. "There's nothing in sight, but one never knows."

He was wearing his poncho and rain-repellent fur hat after a chest cold two weeks before. His voice was hoarse. Cohn carried a 30.06 Winchester 70 rifle he had discovered on the last trip to the *Rebekah Q.* Why he had brought it along on his present jaunt into the far country, he wasn't sure. He had overoiled the weapon, and the dripping barrel smelled.

It was a large gun and Cohn was uneasy about leaving it behind just anywhere, as they were exploring. A stupid fear, really atavistic. It should have gone out with the Devastation, but somehow persisted.

Buz wore a Venetian gondolier's red-ribboned straw hat he had found in Dr. Bünder's clothes closet, and was otherwise unclothed. He had recently tried on a pair of Cohn's winter drawers but they did not fit well. In fact, he had burst through two pairs before giving up.

He carried along an aluminum oar, at times resting it on his shoulder in the same military fashion Cohn held the Winchester. As they were exploring a low sandstone outcropping about two miles from shore, Cohn stopped, speechless, his throat constricted, and pointed to a blob of semi-liquid dark matter he had almost stepped into.

Buz raised his oar to kill the creature, but Cohn, gone fearfully pale, grabbed the ape's arm, hoarsely crying, "Don't, it will splatter us. It's an animal spoor."

"Whot's thot?"

"In this case, animal droppings—excrement."

"Shit?"

"More or less, though I don't care for that word on this island."

"It's the gorilla!"

Cohn didn't think so. "A gorilla's dung tends to be a dry, fibrous, three-lobed dropping. This is semi-liquid without sign of fiber."

"I say it's thot stupid gorilla. It smells like him."

"What would he be doing up here in the headlands?"

"He's spying on us."

"What in the world for?"

"Because he's a spy and thot's whot they do. He follows us and hears whot we say."

"Whatever animal this derived from," Cohn said uneasily, "I don't want to think about. Let's get out of here and head back to the cave."

"Suppose it's a lady?"

Cohn, on reexamining the turd, said he hadn't thought of that.

When they returned to the stunted palm at the beach where they had moored the raft, to their dismay and stupefaction it was gone. Cohn, shading his eyes, saw a yellow speck on the distant water, floating away. Buz lamented he had left a bag of dried figs in it.

"I was depending on that raft to get us off this island someday," Cohn muttered. "There has to be another island, maybe a piece of what was once African coast floating around. Given the few tools we have, it will take us months to construct a usable boat."

He turned in annoyance to Buz. "How did it happen? I told you to tie the raft to the palm tree."

Buz confessed he hadn't learned to tie a decent knot. "My fingers don't know how to make one."

"Why in Christ's name didn't you tell me?"

"I didn't wont you to swear ot me."

Cohn denied it in exasperation. "Have I ever sworn at you?"

"I heard you curse thot gorilla."

"There's a difference between curse and curse out," Cohn explained, but the chimp seemed doubtful.

They shouldered arms and began the long trek across the island to their cave.

From time to time Cohn stopped to shoot a rifle bullet in practice. Whenever he fell on his knee to fire, Buz ran for shelter.

The night they arrived at the cave, Buz sat on Cohn's lap and asked for a story.

Cohn told him he thought that the story one heard most probably became the one he would live out.

Buz then said he didn't want to hear one.

But Cohn, in a mood for talk, told Buz that a philosopher by the name of Ortega y Gasset once said that the difference between a man and a chimp is that the chimp wakes every morning as if no other chimpanzee had existed before him.

Buz didn't like that philosopher. "I think of my mother, and I think of Dr. Bünder."

"He was no chimp," Cohn said.

Buz said he could have been one.

Cohn said he was curious about how Buz had managed to escape death on the Day of Devastation.

"I hid in the toilet."

"Why didn't Dr. Bünder take you with him?"

The chimp's voice wavered. "He said in my ear thot he didn't wont me to drown in the ocean."

"So he left you on the ship and took to a lifeboat?"

Buz reminded Cohn that he was the one who was alive and not Dr. Bünder. "But I am grateful for whot he did for me."

He said he thought they ought to change the name of the island to Dr. Walther Bünder Island, but Cohn did not favor the idea.

He said he would rather call it Survivor's Island. "Survive is what we have to do. Thus we protest our fate to God and at the same time imitate Him."

"Whot for?"

"My father said survival was one way we shared God's purpose."

Buz, vaguely fingering his pink phallus, said his opinion was that the true purpose of life was to have as much fun as one could.

Cohn separated his hand from his organ. "Leave it alone, let it breathe."

Buz bristled, hair thickening.

"Leave it alone," Cohn insisted, "until you know what to do with it, sexually speaking."

"Why don't you tell me, instead of twisting my arm?"

Cohn apologized. "Sex ties up with survival," he explained, "not to speak of certain pleasures of creation. For survival the participants need someone of the opposite sex and neither of us is that. Given the nature of things, that limits possibility."

Buz stealthily tried to slip his fingers between Cohn's thighs, and though his dod knew it was meant benignly he would not allow his boy to touch his testicles.

Buz snuggled close and was soon sucking Cohn's nipple through Dr. Bünder's white silk shirt. The tug of the chimp's insistent lips on his dry nipple hurt, but Cohn let him suck.

Outside the cave, George, peeking through the ivy curtain, stared at the sight, but when Cohn looked up he let go of the ivy and scampered off.

Jealous? Shocked? Outraged? Cohn wondered. He gazed down at the little chimp at his breast.

If you had suckled the lad, could you marry him?

The Schooltree

GOD WAS SILENT.

Cohn tried to squeeze out a small assurance. That had its dangers: Would He respond to preserve me, or would that remind Him to knock me off?

Why would He do that? Cohn thought. I'm the only man left—no serious threat to Him. Why don't I simply give notice I'm still around, and hope it helps because He enjoys the attention I give Him?

On the other hand, I could forget the whole business and pray He forgets me.

(I could also ask, if He responds, "Why does God permit evil?"

" 'How could I not?' "

Touché.)

Cohn tried prayer to establish contact but no vibrations occurred, and in muddled desperation he flung a coconut at the night sky.

The fruit ascended and never descended, not as fruit. Something happened on high—perhaps the coconut struck an astral body or itself became one?

Whatever caused what, Cohn couldn't say, but a contained cosmic bang occurred from whose center a flaring stream of flame shot forth. Watching in wonder, Cohn concluded this was no meteor in flight, but a twisting hard fire with his initials on it—for Curse Cohn? Clobber or Castrate Cohn?

He hurried to his protective cave, and though a long day passed as he lay hidden under a rock ledge, Cohn heard no punitive spat of electric, no hiss of flame, boom of thunder, or driving rain. The hidden man imagined the coconut had whizzed past God's good ear, Who wrote in icy letters in the sky, " 'Don't make waves!' " Then more gently, " 'Don't call anything to my attention; I will call it to yours.' "

Cohn remembered: God was Torah. He was made of words.

Cohn suggested a census to Buz, "Of every bug, to see if any are present."

Though they roamed the breadth of the island, poking into

mounds, webs, combs, and dry holes, they located no ants, spiders, roaches—no flies or bedbugs either.

The Lord had wiped the island clean of insects—no buzzing except Buz, who groomed himself under both arms and discovered no single louse or flea.

Meandering homeward, they explored a moist deep cave one would think might harbor a waterbug or two; but it contained no more than a network of labyrinthine galleries, narrow and broad, which led crookedly to others where stalactites hung like icicles from stone ceilings, dripping glowing drops on the limestone stumps rising from sweating floors.

After a long descent through shadowy corridors lit by Cohn's white candle stub in his wax-stippled hand, they discovered that this mountainful of twisting chambers at last opened on a sparkling sand beach by the restless, booming sea.

Buz hopped with joy at the sight, and Cohn fell to his knees in the white sand, ravished by the view of purple waves breaking and spilling over a line of black rocks along the shore, and flowing as lit foam up the beach.

They swam in the refreshing water and afterwards ascended the mountain into a long cave crowded with crystalline columns. The walls gave forth mysterious noises, as though of voices whispering, or muted singing in the rocks; but no living creatures, not even a small fish, dwelt anywhere they could see or hear.

"I say a hundred," Buz swore, panting like an exhausted messenger.

Cohn, cleaning a fossilized spinal column of a small ancient horse, possibly Eohippus, that he had dug up in a rocky field beyond the rice paddy, suggested maybe a dozen?

"Droves," Buz swore, swaggering from foot to foot.

"Would you say ten?"

The ape jumped two feet in annoyance, hitting the ground on his fours.

Cohn, abandoning skepticism, cast aside his leather apron and hurried after Buz into the trees below the cave. These were separated by a grassy sward from the edge of the rain forest.

There in the woodland, halfway up a massive, scarred

baobab that looked like a ruined tree crossed with an abandoned tenement house of a former world, appeared—great heavens!—five unknown chimpanzees huddled together on a bough whose girth was that of an ordinary tree trunk. The five apes had been exploring the baobab, but when Cohn approached, a warning hoot drove them together.

The tree, whose top looked like an arthritic human hand, seemed to have been stripped of its fruit, leaves, yards of bark, by the famished, hyperactive, shabby apes, who looked as if they had been recently released from a prison pit, and had spent their first hours of freedom devouring the baobab. Their bellies had popped out—but their faces were gaunt. On the ground around its trunk lay piles of hard-shelled green fruits spilling their mucilaginous pulp.

Calvin Cohn stared at the strangers in the tree, momentarily stunned. He found the sight, real as it was, difficult to believe. If there was no single live insect on the island, where did five living chimps come from?

Studying them, Cohn discovered a young female holding a pendulous white flower; and a graybeard male with rheumy eyes and a chest cold; also a gorilla-like, sour-faced, youthful male, who bristled at Cohn—and two squatting, skinny male children, apparently younger than Buz, with relatively large heads, low-lying eyes, and short extremities. Both peered stilly at Cohn as he observed them. They were surely twins. He could hear them rhythmically breathing.

"Where are you from?" Cohn asked, and the five startled apes, as if they had been whistled to, broke their huddle and disappeared into the forest.

Cohn, considering hot pursuit, paused to reflect. He must find out where they had come from and how escaped Devastation and Flood. Suppose—as the five chimps unexpectedly were—another human being, possibly female, was also alive on the island? Though Cohn believed that only he, of all men, had been more or less spared—who, on this further evidence of the Lord's occasional inattentiveness to events on earth, could be certain?

If he pursued, they would easily outdistance him. Better he woo them with bananas. Cohn hurried to the cave for a ripe basketful—this was the best red-banana season ever—and then hastened into the forest, trailing Buz. The little ape, having watched Cohn's encounter with the newly arrived chimps, from a discreet distance, now swung on lianas from tree to tree, as his dod, carrying the banana basket, plowed through the vegetation below, depending on Buz to alert him when he sighted the apes.

Within minutes they came upon the newcomers, now dispersed on five limbs of an ebony tree. They were a genuinely tired lot, the female an attractive but wilted creature, the males grubby, their unkempt coats missing patches of hair, their eyes listless, still showing hunger. Only the barrel-chested male seemed energetic. Seeing Cohn, he rose threateningly, but was immediately affected by the banana basket, at whose contents he stared greedily.

Cohn set the basket down under the ebony tree and though the two boys came to life, whimpering in anticipation, none of the apes descended the tree to get at the bananas.

"Eat if you please," Cohn announced, and nobody moved.

Buz tried an encouraging food grunt or two but the apes remained stationary.

Cohn thought they might eat if he left. "Tell them there's more where this came from," he said to Buz. "But please also say we'll have to be careful with distribution because the supply isn't endless. The way they stripped the baobab isn't advisable behavior. In fact, I urge them to be careful how much they eat once they get over their present pangs."

He reminded Buz to bring the basket back with him. He seemed to be admiring the young lady chimp, who now sat timidly at the very top of the tree.

Cohn, on leaving them, stepped behind a tall fern and peeked through it to watch the five chimpanzees climb down the tree in a single line and make for the basket with grunts, squeals, congratulatory back slappings and embraces. While four of them were hugging, the energetic male grabbed the basket and began to devour the red bananas. The rheumy old chimp approached him with extended palm, but the youthful ape, clutching the basket, would not part with even a banana skin.

Cohn was about to come thundering back but decided to let them work it out themselves. The husky one was obviously the dominant male and had certain privileges. Cohn would keep his eye on him to see that none of the others went hungry.

He returned to the cave and ate supper alone, a rice pudding with slices of tangerine baked into it. The food situation worried him. Would there be enough for all? Counting George, the island company now made eight. If eight, why not nine soon, or ten, enough for a hungry minyan?

He unfolded and examined his map of fruit trees. Bananas and figs were doing well; the figs would last at least eight weeks if the chimps were careful. Oranges and coconuts were plentiful, and so were dates, mangoes, and passion fruit. There was enough for all. Cohn thought he might apportion fruit trees so that each chimp would share what was available without trespassing on the rights of others.

And he was concerned what the unexpected appearance of five ape strangers might signify regarding God's decisive intent toward Calvin Cohn. Apparently He had slipped again, or was it His nature to be unable to count? Why should He have to if He contained all numbers, all possible combinations thereof? Or had He planned to develop it thus, individual animals appearing on the island, dribbling in one by one? For what purpose, if there was purpose?

After he had stopped posing himself unanswerable questions, Cohn stepped out of his cave, holding his kerosene lamp, to read in the evening cool. To his surprise, the visiting chimps—Buz among them—were sitting on the rocky ground in an untidy semicircle, as if expecting Cohn to walk over and officially greet them.

He wanted to, this was his chance to become acquainted. And he would take the occasion, after a word of welcome, to say how they could best get along together on this island.

"My dear primate brothers and sister," he began hoarsely. Cohn blew his nose before going on, when George the gorilla, his head helmeted with cockleburs, making him look like Mars himself if not a militant Moses or Joshua, emerged from the forest and cautiously beheld the assembled chimpanzees.

They, catching sight of the gorilla and the gigantic shadow he dragged after him, rose with excited hoots and shrieks and ran up the nearest trees.

When George observed Cohn's exasperated disappointment,

he plunged into an empty cave and did not emerge for two days.

The five apes, perhaps tracking another basket of bananas, appeared at the cave again the next morning, but when Cohn came out in his lab apron, holding a leg bone of a fossilized ape he had been cleaning—screeching, the chimps galloped off and were at once in flight along arboreal ways.

Only the young female remained an instant, as if to satisfy a curiosity about the white-skinned ape before turning tail and flying off with the others.

Cohn was disappointed at not being able to establish contact with them. He looked forward to feeding them at his table. He hoped soon to set up rules and regulations for apportioning and distributing fruit. To have order you had to plan order. He had mentioned this to Buz and explained the American Constitution to him, asking him to convey his thoughts to the visiting apes. He wasn't sure of the range of ape comprehension, but given Buz's recent language experiences, held high hopes for them.

Buz assured him the chimps would understand more than he thought. "They know more thon you think they do. You hov to hov faith." Cohn decided to look further into the matter, so he changed into field boots and protective outer clothing, then pushed off into the rain forest in search of the newcomers.

After an unsuccessful morning, Cohn, on inspiration, came back to the woodland where some mango trees in full fruit grew, and there he found the migrant apes ensconced on a glossy-leaved tree, eating the sweet orange-yellow fruit, after trial bites having discarded dozens of stringy sour ones.

He was disappointed to see, as he approached them, that four of the six mango trees were already denuded of fruit, and the others would soon be. The ground was strewn with rotting fruit and yellow pits.

Cohn, standing under the mango where the apes squatted, addressed them in a cordial voice. "Brother and sister primates, welcome to this island; and if this is your native land, welcome anyway to our corner of this beautiful island.

"I hope you get the gist of what I am saying. If I didn't

think that was possible, I wouldn't be standing here. In other words, I have faith."

He listened for a smattering of applause but heard none.

"What I would hope you understand is the necessity of making a determined effort to learn a common tongue so that we can communicate with each other. Only if one knows the word, you might say, can he spread the word."

The chimps had stopped chewing and seemed to be absorbed in listening.

Cohn said he would like them to enjoy their stay, but if they intended to make this their place of permanent habitation, he sincerely hoped they would not mind a few observations concerning how certain matters might be arranged for everyone's mutual benefit.

"Calvin Cohn's my name, and I guess you can think of me as your protector, if you like the thought. I want you all to know I am not in the least interested in personal power; simply I would like to give the common effort a certain amount of reasonable direction."

He waited in vain for a random handclap. Cohn's voice fell a bit. "Take my word for it, I would accept leadership reluctantly—my oceanographic colleagues used to say I had some talent for administration—however, I feel I ought to take responsibility because I've had a fairly decent education and perhaps a little more experience than most of you—to help establish what I hope will become an effective social community. Also I'm older than most of you, except maybe the old gentleman snoozing directly above me. Not that age is necessarily wisdom, but in certain ways it helps. Much, however, depends on the Lord."

Cohn laughed jovially, but when he beheld the two boys grinning in stupefaction, he told himself either shut up or be practical. He then addressed the multitude on the subject of food—that there would be enough around if they took care.

"Don't, for instance," Cohn seriously pleaded, "eat just to eat, or because you're bored. Kindly eat only when you're legitimately hungry, and then only enough to satisfy that hunger."

Someone in the tree let out a brash hoot whose source Cohn was unable to determine, but there was no other discourteous response to speak of.

"Please keep in mind that others have the right to share food sources equally, as free living beings. That's saying that freedom depends on mutual obligation, which is the bottom line, I'm sure you'll agree."

He heard petrified silence. After waiting for a change of heart, if that was the problem rather than their comprehension of his human language, Cohn felt he ought to shift his approach. "Let me tell you a story."

The apes seemed to lean forward in anticipation.

They understand, he thought excitedly, and went at once into an old tale of a chimpanzee named Leopold, an absent-minded gentleman, somewhat a narcissist, who ate without thought of other chimps' natural rights, until he ate himself into such swollen proportions that, swallowing one last grape, he burst.

Dead silence.

They must know that one, Cohn reflected. Either that or they don't like the way it ended. He asked if there were any questions, and nobody had one.

Wanting to do it better—get it right—Cohn began another story, about someone he knew who fasted days at a time so he could feed poor people who had nothing at all to eat.

This man's wife asked, "How will you give them what you don't eat, if we have nothing to eat anyway?"

"God will take nothing from me and give something to them," said the old rabbi.

Cohn asked if they had got the point of the story.

But the stunned apes were no longer listening. A stream of dung from where the dominant male stood barely missed Cohn's head.

An explosion of derisive sounds filled the dense mango, and the apes, one by one, dropped out of its branches and disappeared into the woodland.

Cohn made no attempt to follow them. Either they hadn't liked his stories, or his language had failed to communicate anything but a monotonous voice. In afterthought he felt it was perhaps overambitious to have hit them with so many new concepts.

He felt that these apes lacked Buz's gifts of communication and wondered if he could learn, by rereading Dr. Bünder's notebooks, how he had performed the laryngeal operation on Buz. Yet what good would the operation itself be if there were no electronic voice boxes to install?

Vaguely stirred, vaguely dissatisfied, Cohn hurried back to his cave and began to draw up plans for a heavy gate for the entrance, but search where he would, could find no strong metal pin to hang it on.

He began instead to construct a wall of split oak logs—very hard work—a device he planned to put on rollers so it could quickly be moved across the mouth of the cave in case of peril.

Since the arrival of the five chimps, Buz had made himself comparatively scarce at the cave. Reasonably enough—he liked hanging out with his new friends, understandable for a creature who had been deprived of a carefree childhood.

Once a week, or twice, he came in for supper with his dod and stayed over. Or he came to hear a story. For months he had asked only for Cain and Abel. "Thot's where the oction is." Once in a while he returned for a swig of banana beer and then was out again till all hours.

One pre-dawn night Cohn woke from a stark dream of drowning, hearing gurgling sounds. He feared another flood but then remembered Buz's borborygmus.

In the dark he could hear the chimp stealthily picking through the food stores for some morsel or other. Outside, the sky lit up in foggy flashes of summer lightning.

Cohn aimed his torch at Buz, who instinctively bristled when the light hit him. He self-consciously climbed down the shelf.

"I hope you aren't monkeying with my phonograph records?" Cohn said.

"I om not a monkey," said Buz. "Ond I don't eat voice records like some stupid gorillas do. Whot I om looking for is a piece of coconut condy for Mary Modelyn."

"Who's Mary Madelyn?"

"The girl chimponzee I om interested in."

"Did you give her that name?"

Buz proudly said he had. He said naming was nobody's monopoly.

Cohn said it had been Adam's task and on this island was

his. "But I have no objection if you name a few names—if you kindly notify me first."

Buz said he didn't see why he had to. Naming names was freedom of speech. Cohn dropped the subject, not wanting to inhibit him.

"Are you romantically interested in her?"

"Thot depends. Om I sexuolly moture enough yet?"

"That's for you to say, Buz. Some male chimps are slower than others. Some attempt to mount a female when they are eight or nine months old."

"I hod nobody to mount when I was thot age, not even my mother to proctice on."

Cohn told him not to worry, he'd get the swing of it when he had to.

"Not with thot loudmouth Esau around. He growls when he sees me looking ot her. He's two years post my age and hos strong muscles."

"Is Esau the aggressive male? Did you name him too?"

"He's the hairy ape. I hov named all the new ones."

Cohn wanted to know the other names.

"Melchior is the old one."

"Named for whom?"

"Dr. Bünder's father-in-law. He used to give me marsh-mollows."

"Who else?"

"Luke and Saul of Tarsus are twins."

"Where did you get their names?"

"Dr. Bünder had two gerbils with those names."

Cohn got out of bed, slipped on his robe, and they sat in their rockers facing each other. He asked Buz if the apes were a family, and Buz replied they had met in their wanderings on the island after the Flood.

"Where did they stay during the Flood?"

Buz said he didn't know, probably in trees. He said that Mary Madelyn liked Melchior and got along with the twins, but not with Esau. "All he wants is sex."

"Won't she oblige?"

"She hosn't yet but con't guorontee whot might hoppen ofter she goes into heat. She says she would prefer me os a lover if I hurried my development."

"You're almost there."

The cave was lit by light flashes in the sky.

"Whot's thot?" Buz asked nervously.

Cohn explained it was heat lightning, also nothing to worry about. "It's caused by a discharge of atmospheric electricity traveling from one cloud to another."

"Why don't I know about thot?"

Cohn admitted he had never told him and guessed neither had Dr. Bünder. "I can't tell you every fact I know."

Buz said he had every right to know what was going on in the world without asking the human race.

Cohn replied there wasn't much of the human race on the island. "But if you stayed home nights and paid more attention to your reading, instead of fantasizing when you can begin to have sexual relations, you'd pick up a lot of useful information about the world around us."

Buz said he had his own life to live and would live it as he saw fit.

Cohn, feeling Buz had become snappish lately, which he attributed to the approach of puberty, wouldn't argue with that. He did say he was concerned about getting the new chimps organized and living by the law of the island.

"Whot law is thot?"

"A law we'll have to put together—all of us—but it won't work unless we can communicate with one another. That means speech. Maybe we ought to begin teaching these recently arrived chimps a sign language. You know Ameslan, and I know a little, and if we can persuade them to show up for language lessons, we can teach them several signs a day. That's at least a beginning."

Buz then sprang an astonishing surprise. "I hov already taught the new chimponzees to speak the English longuoge and hoven't only been fontasying sexuol relations."

"You have what?" Cohn said in amazement. "Is it possible?"

"It is more than possible, it is on occomplished foct."

Cohn felt an overwhelming elation. Apologizing for his previous invidious remark, he kindled the lamp and drew the ivy curtain. When the night was warm he kept the ivy tied in bunches at the sides of the cave opening.

Long shadows whirled on the walls.

"But how can they talk if they have no apparatus for speech?" Cohn asked in a whisper, "no adequate larynx?"

"Their speech is not os well articulated os mine, but they hov ocquired longuoge because they hov faith."

"In whom and what?"

"In whot I hov told them."

"What was that?"

"Thot they could learn if they hod faith."

"Incredible," Cohn muttered. "A stupendous miracle if it has really occurred."

Buz insisted it had. Unusual things were abroad on the island. "Fruit is more abundont and sweeter this season. I heard mogic strains of music in those winding caves we found—prettier music thon you play on thot voice mochine. Ond now my friends hov learned to talk by an oct of faith. If you hov faith you con hear them talk."

Cohn humbly said he hod faith.

Though Cohn, as scientist, could not explain how the chimps had learned to speak English, he was of course gratified that they had learned. If explanation was needed: the world was different from once it was; and what might happen, and what could not, he was not as sure of as he used to be. It seemed to him that after a frightening period of incoherence, there was now a breath of settled purpose in the universe. One could not say for sure where the Almighty stood after the Second Flood; but if He had permitted the visiting chimps to learn one of the languages unique to homo sapiens—had allowed them to go on living through Devastation and Flood in order to learn—one might say—why not similar good grace for Cohn?

In celebration of the miraculous descent, or spontaneous emergence of human speech among the apes, he planned a seder. Cohn figured that the fifteenth day of Nisan had gone its way, but since there were no calendars available, one could not be held responsible for exact dates.

It wasn't, anyway, the date that counted, it was the mood and purpose of the occasion: simply a celebration—nothing extraordinary—a means of bringing together the island company, and at the same time politely thanking Someone for favors received. Nothing wrong with a little sincere gratitude for every amelioration of an unforgivable condition caused by the Creator. He had his problems too. After all, First Causes were not always first causes; and maybe He was having second thoughts about these matters.

Anyway, it was a beautiful early spring. The bright green grass was ankle-high. Fragrant flowers, astonishing ones, were scattered everywhere. Mimosas were abloom in flaring yellow. Oleander was white and bougainvillea royal purple. Each color seemed deeper, more livingly intense, than its ordinary color. It seemed a splendid year ahead. Peace to all, amen.

Cohn diligently cleaned the cave, swept, shined, mopped. And he had built a long teak table that would seat eight—three on each side bench, one at head and foot.

He carried out and hid, according to ritual, all suspected unleavened food, recalling how his mother, holding a candle in her hand, had prayed on this occasion, "May all the leaven in my possession, whether I have seen it or not, be annulled and considered as dust of the earth." In those days dust of the earth was a more innocent substance.

Cohn was the official host and Buz assisted. The guests were the five new chimps, and George the gorilla, if he was in the mood to appear. Any way one looked at it, the gorilla was a permanent inhabitant of the island and had to be encouraged to join the company. Cohn had more or less forgiven him for destroying his father's record—"Kol Nidre," nothing less, a sad loss—probably George had thought the record was a licorice wafer or something equally good to eat.

To invite him personally, since there were no mail deliveries, and since Buz wouldn't go in his place to persuade him to attend, Cohn scouted George's usual haunts. He came across his nests in the flattened deep grass but rarely found a trace of George himself, not even a fragment of fibrous dung where he had recently made camp. Gorillas soiled their nests but were not themselves soiled; chimps, because of their liquid excrement, would tend to perform their bowel functions outside their nests, and save himself who loitered below. Who was, therefore, the more civilized?

Buz said that probably the giant ape's fear of the presence of six lively chimpanzees had scared him away.

Cohn replied George would be welcome if he came. "I'll

put him down for Elijah's seat, but whoever sits there first is the guest of honor."

"Not thot fot ape, in the cave I live in."

"This is a celebration. Be generous, Buz."

"I om but I om not cuckoo. You don't like thot monster any more thon I do. You said thot ofter he smoshed your father's music record."

"I've since had second thoughts. Frankly, I respect him. I feel there's more than gorilla to George."

"Yes, he is bigger and stupider."

"He is a lonely ape. I sense he's had a bad time beyond our late bad times, perhaps a personal crisis. He may look fierce but has a gentle heart. I suspect he was the one who helped me when I was sick with radiation poisoning. And keep in mind that he never had your advantages, Buz."

Buz covered his nose with one hand and tugged at an imaginary toilet chain with the other hand. He could have got that gesture only from Dr. Bünder.

Seder night was a night of full moon. Wearing a reasonable facsimile of a traditional white kitl he had stitched together out of a roll of mosquito netting they had fetched from the hold of the *Rebekah Q*, Cohn prepared the festive seder meal. He had baked a batch of thin, round, crisp flat-cakes, according to the tradition of the hastily baked bread in Exodus.

Cohn covered the teak table with a portion of sail they had recovered from the former oceanographic schooner. Since they had only one candle left, he installed the lit kerosene lamp as centerpiece; and in the shadowy scene on the cave wall the seated chimps looked like wise elders.

On the teak table stood two slender-necked blue vases Cohn had recently potted out of some rare lumps of clay, aburst with white fruit-tree blossoms he had painted on them. And there were three carafes of banana wine, a tasty light wine, something like a gewürztraminer, that required a longer fermentation than the fizzy banana beer.

For baked eggs—nothing on the island could lay an egg—he served pickled red palm nuts. A platter of matzos lay on the table covered with a linen napkin. Instead of bitter herbs Cohn offered cut-up chunks of cassava root.

In place of lamb shankbone, he had served on each wooden

plate a portion of leg bone of a fossil he was almost certain was Eohippus, the fox-size, dawn horse, the first of this species to be discovered outside North America. Cohn, in tense excitement, had dug up the leg bone, embedded in limestone, in a back-yard dig in the field beyond the rice paddy. The bone, hardly kosher, and expendable because he already had two hind right-leg femurs in his bone box—was for ritual purposes only; to be used symbolically, therefore he hoped permissibly. Eohippus, if that's what it was, suited the occasion because it was distantly related to the thundering equi of the Egyptian charioteers.

Mary Madelyn picked up her small portion of bone and cautiously sniffed it; she hastily replaced it on the plate.

"For symbolic use only, not for eating," Cohn explained in a whisper, patting her hand, and she, affectionate creature, patted his.

Instead of haroset, he served a sweet paste of chopped apricots and nuts from a ten-pound bag they had found in the vessel. For lettuce and celery, he placed a small bouquet of oak leaves on the plate before each chimp. For himself he had collected a few rice shoots that reminded him of a Japanese drawing he had once owned.

And for the ritual red wine he poured white banana wine into the rough wooden tumblers he had carved. Bit by bit Cohn was replacing objects he and Buz had salvaged with ones he made himself. Each tumbler depicted an epic scene from Exodus of the escape of the Israelites from their Egyptian oppressors—the symbolic escape that dwelt in the minds of Jews throughout history and inspired them in times of desperation. On his own tumbler Cohn had portrayed the visage of Moshe Rebbenu, with his two-pronged beard. One might have mistaken it for the likeness of God himself, if that was possible.

Cohn sat at the head of the table, opposite the cave entrance, facing the empty seat for Elijah, or whoever appeared in his place. Here he could easily reach to the fireplace ledge where he had baked the matzos and prepared the food.

The appearance of the visiting chimps had improved. Their hair had grown in and their coats were sleek. They were energetic and talkative. Cohn enjoyed hearing them talk among themselves.

On the bench to his right sat trusty Buz; next to him, Melchior; and to his side Saul of Tarsus, whom the old man kept a wet eye on.

On his left, Cohn had seated Mary Madelyn, at her request opposite Buz and as far from Esau as she could be; not very far, for only Luke sat between them. Esau tended to make a nuisance of himself although she tried not to notice each offense. Buz, however, bristled. The situation between the two young apes was charged, and Cohn tried to keep them busy with ritual.

Melchior, the graybeard chimp, oversaw the twins on both sides of the table. What they did not eat on their plates or drink from their cups, he willingly consumed.

Mary Madelyn was an intelligent, attractive young female with silken hair, a somewhat heart-shaped, healthy face—a trifle pale—and an affectionate manner. Her sexy ears lay close to the head. She had almost a real figure, Cohn thought. When Melchior grew too sleepy to fuss over the restive twins, a glance from her would calm them.

Cohn began the seder with a kiddush for wine, and the first two toasts he proposed were the traditional ones to life and to freedom.

Closing his eyes, he recited, "Our thanks to God who kept us alive and sustained us to this moment"—(notwithstanding the fact He had not sustained any others, ran through Cohn's mind, but he banished the thought. Not on this night of celebration).

When he explained who God was everyone at the table cheered.

Buz tugged at Cohn's kitl. "I thought you told me He let the Holocaust ond Second Flood hoppen?"

"I'm thanking Him for what good He did, not for what He did badly," Cohn whispered. "You and I are alive, as are those present, despite the Devastation. Certain grateful thanks therefore are due to Whom they are due. That's how I look at it."

Buz crossed himself and the twins followed suit; they imitated him often.

"Do that later, Buz," Cohn said sotto voce.

"Whot's wrong with now?"

"It's not part of this ceremony. It's another modality."

Buz took a moment to memorize the word and went on eating.

Cohn lifted his tumbler and toasted peace. "Next year on this blessed isle—may we all have prospered!"

"I hope we hov freedom of religion," Buz said.

"Amen," said Cohn, toasting every freedom.

All joined the toast and drank down the banana wine. Buz went around the table refilling the tumblers. Esau tried to trip him but Buz hopped over his foot. Though his hair had risen he kept out of a fight. Mary Madelyn smiled at him.

Cohn knew he wasn't following the sequence of the seder, but what counted was the spirit, and that was running high.

He had explained that the seder was originally a Passover celebration. "The Jews were slaves in Egypt and God brought them out. That's the thing to keep in mind, that He brought them out, although not always quickly enough in the recent past. In any case, tonight we are celebrating the escape from Egypt and our own personal escape from the Second Flood, though our burden of mourning is still heavy. Our present ceremony is also a thanksgiving for our life on this island. We're alive and in good health. Our task is to co-exist peacefully in the future."

Buz crossed himself and Cohn pretended not to notice.

Melchior and Mary Madelyn clapped their hands in approval of his little homily. Cohn hoped he hadn't bored them. Esau was trying to blow bubbles with his banana wine. The twins giggled.

But the ceremony flowed on pleasurably. Then came the Four Questions. Since neither of the twins could be depended on to stay with the script—Saul of Tarsus seemed slightly autistic; he spoke one word at a time after breathy pauses, yet he knuckle-walked steadily, if clumsily, and brachiated boldly; and Luke seemed to lack power of concentration—Cohn had asked Buz to ask the questions.

Cohn had primed him concerning the seder. He had also composed the questions to elicit as much information as possible about the visiting chimps, hoping to understand the Lord's purpose in letting them live after the Flood.

These were the questions:

1. Assuming the proposition is correct, how does this night differ from all others?

2. Please state who you are, that is to say, define yourself.

3. Do you know where you were born? What were your experiences during the Second Flood? How did you save yourself from the rising water?

4. Do you think of life as having a particular purpose? What is it? Please answer responsively.

Cohn had hand-printed the questions, and Buz, now seriously into reading, had memorized them before eating the printed page. He loved the taste of paper. Once in a rare while Cohn gave him a blank notebook sheet for a confection.

Seeming to relish his role as correspondent, Buz recited each question, and Melchior and Mary Madelyn volunteered to answer them. Esau announced that the questions were stupid but he would respond because he had nothing better to do.

Since acquiring speech, he had developed into a self-important overweight ape trying hard to resemble a gorilla. His face was large, his teeth unsettled and wandering in the mouth. Yet he enunciated quite clearly and spoke without hesitation. His eyes were restless, his expression, challenging. Buz obviously disliked and feared him. Esau seemed not to fear anyone and to dislike all.

Cohn considered him a bright-enough chimp, not without native wit, but surely a case of arrested emotional development. He had made up his mind to have a serious talk with him. Esau threatened; he rocked the boat.

Esau declared he would answer first. Buz asked each question forthrightly, yet modestly, and Esau proclaimed his replies.

"For question 1, all nights are the same except when it's raining, or I am having dirty thoughts." He made the sound of a kiss to Mary Madelyn, and she, dear lady, pretended she was hard of hearing.

"For question 2, I am the Alpha Ape of us all. And that's a warning to stay away from my girl."

He stared fixedly at Buz, who, after glancing at Cohn, drank from his tumbler of wine, and asked the next question.

"For 3," said Esau, "I don't remember where I was born. My mother used to say I had made myself out of mud and water. At the time of the high water I climbed to the top of a palm tree, lived on the coconuts, and crapped in the Flood till it ran off."

Cohn asked him not to be tasteless, there was a lady present.

"On the fourth question, my answer is short. My purpose in my life right at this particular time is to slip it to Mary Madelyn as soon as she learns the facts of life. She doesn't know what she is missing."

Mary Madelyn blushed deeply.

"Don't spoil the seder," Cohn warned Esau. "We're expecting Elijah."

Buz whispered in his ear that they would have to get rid of the brute, but Cohn replied they had to have faith. "We can't reject him at first whiff."

He thanked Esau for his frank replies and called Melchior.

Bored when the old ape rose to answer the Four Questions, Esau gnawed on the Eohippus bone. It turned to dust in his mouth. He spat it out with a gasping cough and gurgled down a carafe of wine. In a few minutes he was soundly asleep at the table. No one waked him.

Melchior cleared his throat and warmed up his breathy voice. His speech was slurpy—every word swam in spittle, but he spoke slowly and could be understood. The old ape had trouble breathing and would bang his chest with his fist to move air into his lungs.

He answered thus: "One to two—the weather is dry and I feel fine, thank you. Whether it's day or night I don't think about nowadays." He wheezed wetly, his eyes turning slightly milky. "I feel a heaviness of the chesht but that's the way of age. My mother used to say we exchange ailments for yearzh. We take on one as we give up the other. It doesn't pay to live too long is my theory. Thank you kindly.

"On question 3," he said, "what's that again?"

Buz repeated it.

"One day I woke up in a tree nesht with my mother. She was good to me till the day she went off with a gentleman she had met. I followed them in the foresht and then got losht and did not ever find her again. I will miss her till the end of my days—which is not too far off."

Cohn remarked there was time enough to think of death.

"No time at all," said Melchior with an extended wheeze.

"The fourth question," Cohn reminded him, "concerns purpose in life."

"I have no regretsh," said Melchior.

Cohn said he hadn't told them how he had escaped the Flood.

"I found a big shnow mountain and sat on it eating leaves until the water on the land below disappeared. Then I began to vomit and losht all my hair. I looked like a newborn babe. I was ashamed of my nakedness, but I climbed down off the mountain and went to the lowlands. Your fruit is delicious in this country. Please don't anyone hurt me. I am a pretty old ape."

Cohn said he had forbidden strife. "This is a peaceful island."

"We hov forbidden strife," Buz said.

"Everybody wovs you," Mary Madelyn said to Melchior.

Whenever she pronounced an el it became doubleu. Buz giggled but Cohn liked the sound of it.

The twins cheered Melchior. That woke Esau, gagging. He was about to throw up over the tablecloth, but Cohn got him out of the cave in time. "Horseass," groaned Esau as he retched in the bushes.

Cohn left him there and returned to the cave to serve a platter of bananas flambé, with slices of boiled apricots stewed in brandy, their last bottle from the wreck. All ate heartily.

Then Mary Madelyn answered the questions. Except for her partial lallation she spoke well, though not as fluently as Buz, who, despite the fact he had initiated it, seemed jealous of her swift progress in language.

Cohn had read her the balcony scene from *Romeo and Juliet*, and though she hardly understood every word, she had listened raptly.

She had told Cohn she didn't know her age but suspected she would soon be old enough to bear a child.

"Do you look forward to it?"

"Yes, but not to be in estrus."

"Why not?"

"It's humiwiating to present mysewf every time a mawe approaches. I wish to be independent and free."

"Have you ever been in heat?"

"Pwease," Mary Madelyn said, "I don't wike that word; in fact I detest it. No, I have never been in estrus."

Cohn begged her pardon. "I know how you feel."

Mary Madelyn looked at him with a doubtful smile. She confessed she was afraid of Esau. "He threatens me by shaking big branches in my face and caws me awfuw names. He said he would break my behind if I keep on being sexuawy off-putting."

"How do you handle that?"

"I asked him to wait for my fuw natuaw devewopment."

"Then what happens?"

She said she was afraid to think.

She was an altogether interesting lady chimpanzee. Cohn thought she would look lovely in a white dress, but where would you shop for one nowadays?

Mary Madelyn then responded to the Four Questions:

"Yes, this night is different because we are cewebrating our survivaw now that the wicked water has run off and the vomiting sickness is no wonger in us."

"Bravo," Cohn said.

Buz nudged his arm with his head. "When do I hov my turn to onswer?"

"Tonight is your turn to ask and others to answer."

"I would rother onswer than osk," Buz said.

"Not tonight," said Cohn.

Esau, looking as though he had lost five pounds, had knuckle-walked back into the cave and taken his seat on the bench. He smelled of vomit but none of the chimps save Buz seemed to mind. He privately held his nose.

"I am the best answerer," Esau announced. "I am King of the Trees."

"I think Mr. Mewchior is," said Mary Madelyn.

The twins applauded and Melchior, tentatively chewing a matzo, nodded.

"And you are a bitch-whore," Esau spoke across the table.

She slid as far from him as she could. Another inch and she would be sitting in Cohn's lap—not wise for decorum.

"In answer to the second question," she said, "my name is Mary Madewyn, a femawe chimpanzee who respects hersewf and wishes to be respected by others."

"Beautiful," commented Cohn.

"You praise her but never praise me," Buz complained in a whisper.

Cohn whispered she was their guest. "The third question?" he asked.

"First there was the Fwood and then came the awfuw nights of rain. We wost our poor mother in the rising water before we cwimbed to the headwands. After the Fwood sank, my baby sister and I were sick in a wet cave. She died there and I weft and wandered on, miserabwy awone untiw I met Mr. Mewchior and the twins.

"When Esau joined our group he said he was our weader. He got wost wherever we went, and Mr. Mewchior had to show us the way. Soon we came to this wand of fruit trees and decided to stay. Buz found us and taught us to speak your wanguage. He towd us his dod was a white chimpanzee, and no one bewieved it untiw we met you."

"God's grace," said Cohn.

"As for question 4," Mary Madelyn went on, "my speciew purpose in wife is to wiv."

"Marvelously put," he said.

Buz produced a mild rumble with his lips not unlike that which Cohn in his boyhood had known as a Bronx cheer. And Esau gurgled as if he was swallowing a whole egg, but it was the way he laughed.

No one asked questions of the twins.

"We are too young," said Luke.

Saul of Tarsus nodded sagely.

Cohn removed the napkin from the matzo bowl. "This is the bread of affliction," he recited. "Let us eat to remember who we are."

"Who are we?" Buz said, despite himself, asking.

"The still-alive—those who have survived despite the terrible odds," Cohn said. He passed a matzo to each of them except Melchior, who slowly chewed the broken piece he held in his hand. The chimps bit into the unleavened bread and spat it out, except Buz, who was used to the taste. He got his matzo down with a fistful of oak leaves and a long drink of banana wine. Mary Madelyn politely nibbled hers in tiny bites.

Cohn began the singing—"A Kid for Two Farthings." Though he urged them all to join no one would, so he put on a record of his father the cantor chanting "Chad Gadye" in a way that made the apes dance.

They danced at the rear of the cave and watched their shadows dance. The twins chased after the dancing shadows, slapping the wall with their palms.

At the end of the seder, Cohn poured a tumbler of wine to toast Elijah the Prophet.

The cantor was singing: "God is mighty . . . / Awesome is His mystery."

The chimps at the table were grooming one another. Esau insisted on combing Mary Madelyn's rump, as she groomed Buz. Luke picked among the hairs of Saul of Tarsus's head, and Saul did the same for Luke. Cohn was wondering whether—to be congenial—he ought to groom himself, when a streak of light flashed across the rear wall of the cave as George the gorilla, sweeping aside the ivy curtain, eased himself into the chamber.

A heavy, nose-filling odor of bay leaves and garlic seeped into the cave as he paused at the entrance to stare at the assemblage of apes at the table.

Cohn at once rose to welcome the visitor and offered him Elijah's seat.

The chimps, grinning in fear, froze in their places.

Cohn urged them all to remain calm. "This is a different night. Nobody wants to harm anybody. It's a night of peace and a celebration of life. Sit down, George, and have a glass of wine."

George, sitting bulkily at the table, drank from a tumbler of banana wine. He sat with eyes lowered as if to affirm he was their peaceful neighbor. To prove it he smiled, revealing his fangs.

The chimps slid to the ends of both benches close to Cohn. Even Esau had gone pale.

Cohn asked George to taste his matzo and say a good word to his friends-and-fellow-islanders.

The giant ape, after a hesitant bite he seemed to relish, strove to speak. He coughed, strained, sighed. His throat bulged. Now he grunted as though resisting constipation. His heavy black form trembled as if he was feverish. In desperation, George rose from the chair and beat his booming chest. The cave resounded loudly with the drumming. With a roar of rage he lifted and overturned the teak table. The seder food and wine crashed to the floor.

The shrieking, hooting chimpanzees scattered. They rushed out of the cave into the night and hastily disappeared in every direction.

Cohn's father was singing a hymn in praise of deliverance.

George, slumped in Elijah's chair, listened, moodily munching his matzo.

Cohn, although outraged by the shambles the gorilla had made of the seder—their first communal enterprise—restrained his anger, in keeping with the spirit of the evening, and even attempted to cheer up the unfortunate ape. For as long as he lived on the island there could be no functioning community without George. Outsiders were dangerous; he had to be in.

"George," said Cohn, "for certain reasons I forgive you the mess you made tonight at the end of an unusual occasion, and while I'm forgiving I want you to know I no longer hold it against you that you absconded with, and destroyed, a rare record of my father's. But I have to tell you this: either change your ways or go your way."

George, after a moment of depressed silence, moaned.

Cohn, on impulse, asked the gorilla the Four Questions and, not surprisingly, got no reply. He then related the story of the Prodigal Son, a parable Buz had more than once requested, and the gorilla listened with tears flowing as he consumed large pieces of damp matzo.

"They that sow in tears," sang the passionate cantor, "shall reap in joy."

"Amen," answered Cohn.

George bonged his chest in joy.

After he had swept the cave and put things away, Cohn, as he slept, conceived a white dream. An albino ape had appeared in the mist-laden forest, a fearsome male chimpanzee no one had seen but all seemed to know of.

"Is he for real?" Cohn asked Buz, and Buz replied, "He hos to be, I dream of him often."

Cohn lived in serious concern that the white ape might appear in his cave and make demands. He foresaw trouble.

He felt he would not be at ease until he had talked with the creature, asked who he was, and what he wanted here. If he wished to join the community, let him sign up.

One morning he set out to find the albino ape in the rain forest. He remained there searching for three days and nights, but got no more than a muffled glimpse of a white figure, dimly lit amid misty trees and the green-gloomy foliage.

Exasperated, Cohn flung his iron spear (he had chanced on it in the *Rebekah Q*) to the ground; and in his dream was angered at God for having got him to this island and into this dream. "What kind of God is that?"

At once, above the trees, he beheld a bulbous cloud shaped like a white tulip held aloft by strains of music.

Mr. Cohn? an angelic voice spoke, one so beautiful that Cohn was all goose pimples when he heard it. He sank to his knees. "Yes, sir, or ma'am, whichever the case may be."

Mr. Cohn, please don't utter blasphemous thoughts. Or express childish doubts about the Deity. I say this for your good.

Cohn sincerely apologized. "I'm sorry I misspoke. After seeing that white ape, I felt a dread something bad might happen."

State the nature of that dread.

"Was he really there like a dim light in those trees, or is it all imagined and dreamed by me?"

He is insofar as it seems to be, said the angelic voice.

Cohn groaned at length. "That moldy chestnut encore?"

What there is to use we use, the angel replied.

"What I want to know is: Is he on this island, and others like him in black or brown? Or any like me?" Cohn went on, "Another human being, for instance—perhaps female—anywhere in what's left of the world? I wish to know for my peace of mind. Put yourself in my place."

Where I put myself is not your concern, Mr. Cohn. But I will say in answer to your question that there are none like you anywhere, any more.

"How would anybody know for sure?"

Who knows anything for sure?

"That old saw, too?"

What's usable we use, said the angel with the beautiful voice.

"Then who knows what's happening anywhere? Is this island what it seems to be?"

What does it seem to be?

"At least an island with two on it, conversing."

Whatever I reply, would you in reality believe me?

"Not necessarily," Cohn warily said.

So call it a dream.

"No more than that?" he cried.

But the angel had gone, though the haunting sound of his voice lingered.

Cohn woke holding his spear aloft in a dark-green forest.

He feared God more than he loved Him.

How can I square it with Him for that dream I think I dreamed, if that's what it was, assuming He knows? He must, it is His Name and Nature. I've got to be careful.

It seemed to Cohn he had to be wary, indeed, in dealing with God. Theoretically no, but in truth yes. He was constantly slipping up, speaking and acting in error against his best interests; not containing his dissatisfactions; not therefore protecting himself, considering his hunger to survive.

I have to watch my words, also thoughts and dreams.

They had irreconcilable differences concerning whose responsibility the Day of Devastation was. Cohn still had trouble subduing his rage and grief therefrom; but practically speaking, the event was beyond redoing and one had the future to contend with.

In that matter the Lord held every card in His comprehensive hand; and if Cohn held one it was invisible to him, except perhaps his extraordinary knowledge that God did not know everything. *He* had difficulty with numbers, could not always count accurately; for instance, there were more than only poor Cohn alive on earth. That was the only card Cohn held.

Still if he wanted to go on breathing on this less-than-perfect, magic island, as indeed he did if it was at all feasible, he had to invent some practical means of winning God's favor while not exactly taking Him off the hook for perpetrating His Latest Flood.

Cohn hoped the Lord had appreciated his seder and all the nice things they had said about Him the other night.

What might please God would be some sensible arrangement of the lives of the apes on the island into a functioning social community, interacting lives; and with Cohn as advisor and protector to help them understand themselves and fulfill the social contract. Maybe start with a sort of small family and extend into community? You are not the chimps your fathers were—you can talk. Yours, therefore, is the obligation to communicate, speak as equals, work and together build, evolve into concerned, altruistic living beings.

Not bad if it worked. How would Cohn know unless and until he tried? On this island more seemed possible than one might imagine. A functioning social unit, even as small as seven or eight living beings, would be a civilizing force inspiring a higher order of behavior—to a former lower order of creatures—highest now that man was more or less kaput.

If this small community behaved, developed, endured, it might someday—if some chimpy Father Abraham got himself born—produce its own Covenant with God. So much better for God, Who seemed to need one to make Him feel easy with Himself as Party-of-the-First-Part, even though He found it troublesome, in the long run, to make the Covenant work as it should. One could hardly look after the party of the second part every minute of the day.

It was better to attempt to civilize whoever needed civilizing, the Lord would surely agree—more good that way, less evil. A good society served a good purpose; He would surely approve if Cohn dedicated himself to fostering it.

To do what God might be expecting, now that a common language existed between himself and the chimps, Cohn felt he ought to try to educate them up to some decent level, eventually to make them aware of the cosmos and of mankind, too, who had fallen from earth and cosmos, because men had failed each other in obligations and responsibilities—failed to achieve brotherhood, lost their lovely world, not to mention living lives.

Therefore Cohn established a schooltree for them, a bushy-leaved, bark-peeled, hard-blue-acorned eucalyptus tree exuding a nose-opening aromatic odor, especially after rain, that kept them alert in the grove of mixed trees, some of which were crabbed live oaks not more than sixty feet from his cave.

The apes, including Buz, who was advanced in schooling but liked to listen to others being taught, attended classes regularly, spending two hours each morning getting educated; except on the Seventh Day, when Cohn preferred not to teach because, since he did not keep track of time, he might inadvertently be working on the Sabbath. God was a great fan of the Sabbath, and it was worth anybody's life, it said in Exodus, to work on that day.

So he skipped each Seventh Day to show his respect and good will.

Cohn blew on a brass horn to summon them to class.

The apes, some reluctantly, climbed the eucalyptus and moved out on spreading limbs of the blowsy tree, sitting alone or in two's, chewing leaves and spitting them out; or cracking nuts they had brought along, and eating them out of their palms as they listened to Calvin Cohn lecture; or groomed themselves and their partners as he droned on. When the lectures got to be boring they would shake branches and throw nuts at him. They hooted and grunted, but subsided when Cohn raised his hand, indicating he intended to do better.

He sat on a stool he had assembled at the foot of the shedding schooltree, on a leaf-covered hillock of hard earth he had constructed as a teaching platform, talking fast or slow, depending on the subject. He addressed them on a variety of topics, or inspired thoughts, formally or casually; or he read aloud from one book or another. And Cohn related tales he had made up as best he could the night before as he prepared his lectures; or had culled from memory.

He was no Martin Buber and the apes no Hasidim, though they might someday be, Cohn permitted himself to think. These things needed time. It depended, to some degree, on how one addressed the apes and they played it back.

The chimps seemed, on the whole, to enjoy their schooling although there were occasional truants, Esau, for instance, a prime offender; and Luke and Saul of Tarsus, after a difficult lesson had left them dazed, usually took the next day off. Melchior was steady, he liked to listen; and so did Mary Madelyn, who discreetly applauded certain things Cohn said and some he only hinted at.

Buz, diligently present, sometimes interrupted the teacher's discourse to disagree with a fact. He also corrected Cohn's mistakes in usage, when he caught a "which" for a "that," or "precipitate" for "precipitous." Buz had been immersed in dictionary study lately. Cohn, when corrected, felt some embarrassment, especially when the other chimps broke out in applause for Buz. However, the amateur teacher—he so defined himself—was good-humored about his little errors, and education went on.

George the gorilla was a part-time scholar, listening from a neighboring cedar, because the apes, particularly after the seder shambles, showed they did not care to have him among them. George could tell and had picked himself this tall coniferous tree twenty feet from the eucalyptus. Cohn argued with the chimps, defending the gorilla's human rights, but fortunately George preferred to be by himself.

He crouched on the lower branch of the cedar, at times lay outstretched, chewing a weed, seemingly absorbed in Cohn's remarks and stories, though one never knew for sure because the gorilla did not talk; yet Cohn was almost certain he comprehended what he heard.

However, his attention to the lesson appeared to be fitful, partly because he seemed to be roused, or struck, by certain things, and for a while was not able to concentrate on anything more. At least it seemed so to Cohn.

George would stay in his tree until some interesting fact, or quotation, or tale, excited his fancy, at which moment he lowered himself to the ground and went reeling off into the forest as though high on reflection, to hoots of ridicule by the students in the schooltree. Cohn pictured him lying in the sun-warmed grass, playing with a thought till it arranged itself in his head. Or was that giving the beast more credit than he deserved? Yet there was something "possible" about George. He looked like himself plus something else he might be.

After the daily lectures, the chimps climbed down the eucalyptus to enjoy a cup of fizzy banana beer that Cohn served to all present.

Melchior, as he guzzled the beer dripping into his beard, stopped drinking long enough to say this was the besht part of the day.

Cohn thought he knew more about fossils than anything else he had studied, but with the help, if not collaboration, of his one-volume encyclopedia he would try to inform them about the major doings of the past.

"Knowing what occurred in the world might favor the future. Yours, I mean, rather than mine. Mine looks scarce; yours, at least possible."

He said, "There are gaps in my knowledge, large and small, but I will tell it as best I can. If you listen, there may be some morsels to nibble on. I sincerely hope you won't think I am being reductive."

The chimps in the eucalyptus, with the exception of sour-faced Esau, who sat on his hairy hands, politely applauded Cohn's honest declaration.

So in the days that followed he lectured on the cosmos—from Big Bang to Dying Whimper of man (for whom Cohn asked, and got, a full minute's silence). The apes were curious about practically everything that had happened on earth and heaven. Starting there, the universe expanded.

"What for?" asked Buz.

"Because it's expansible."

(Laughter.)

He detailed Descent, Advent, Ascent of Man, as Darwin and Wallace had propounded the theory of the origin of species and natural selection; adding a sketch on sociobiology, with a word about the nature-nurture controversy.

Only George clapped at that, and Cohn could not figure out if he knew what he was doing or was he trying to crush an imaginary fly between his palms?

Cohn then noted man's ambivalent nature, the no-in-yes, evil-in-good, death-in-life, illusion-in-real, the complex, joyous-heartbreaking way it had worked out. Was the basic split caused by body-soul? Or was it God's withdrawal from His own presence? How would that go? Freud, an unbeliever, spoke of a secret trauma in His mind, converted to pain Everywhere.

"That brings us to evil—wherever it begins or how far goes: a metaphysical dripping, perhaps, we can't account for, resulting in the appearance of Satan himself, whom I will discourse on for a couple of lectures at a later date—in particular, whether the Lord tore him out of His own mind and flung him into the bottomless pit out of which he afterwards crawled as a smoking snake; and has since then taken out on man his loss of angelic form and privilege—anyway, if Satan is allowed to go slithering around in Paradise, there's bound to be serious conflict and conflagration. In essence, the old boy envies man, wants to be him. Didn't he desire Eve when he saw her rolling bare-skinned in the flowers with Adam naked? 'Where's mine of that?' the old snake said when he met her in the wood; and she modestly responded, 'It isn't for you, for reasons I can't say.' He poisoned her apple after that. Broke her tree, it stopped singing hymns."

Cohn then sketchily recounted Freud's work and to prove it apt began summarizing certain aspects of human history, not excluding major wars fought and other useless disasters. "Man had innumerable chances but was—in the long run—insufficient to God's purpose. He was insufficient to himself. Some blame it on a poisoned consciousness, caused, for some chemical reason, by our lunatic genes running wild. More about that in the near future. Anyway, man doing a not-so-hot job, by and large, in his relations to other men—he loves only finger-deep. Love is not a popular phenomenon. Talks and talks but the real thing goes only finger-deep. Anyway, in all those ages he hardly masters his nature enough to stop the endless slaughter. What I mean," said Cohn, "is he never mastered his animal nature for the good of all—please excuse the word—I am an animal myself—nor could he invent a workable altruism. In short, he behaved too often irrationally, unreasonably, savagely, bestially. I'm talking, obviously, about constant overkill.

"And more of the same throughout human history. Please don't say I am hypersensitive—I'm talking at a time of almost total extinction, except us few. I will go into the Historical Past in six lectures I have planned; and the Twentieth Century Up to Now, in another two, the second beginning with the Holocaust that I mentioned yesterday: all that Jewish soap from those skeletal gassed bodies; and not long after that, since these experiences are bound to each other, the U.S. Americans drop the first atom bombs—teensy ones—on all those unsuspecting 8 A.M. Japanese crawling in broken glass to find their eyeballs. I could say more but haven't the heart."

Cohn said it wasn't his intention to exaggerate the extent of man's failures, willed or otherwise. Nor would he slight his capacity for good and beauty. "The reason I may seem to you to dwell heavily on the sins of man is to give you something to think about so you may, in a future chimpanzee society, avoid repeating man's worst errors. The future lies in your hands."

Ongoing hearty applause. Buz waved a green cap of Cohn's he had taken to wearing lately. Esau reluctantly pat-patted his moist palms. Mary Madelyn's eyes glowed tenderly, and Melchior, though he called it "pretty dry stuff," blew his nose and sentimentally frowned.

Cohn took a bow. Here's Calvin Cohn, one man left on earth, teaching apes concerning man's failures. Not bad. His father the rabbi, may he rest in peace, would surely have approved.

(—Listen, Colvin, I never liked that you changed your name from Seymour to Colvin—a big naarishkeit—but what you say to the monkeys, this I like.

—Those aren't monkeys, Papa, those are full-grown primates.

—To me it's all the same, a monkey is a monkey.)

Cohn, unable to slow down his lecture, speculated that man failed because he was imperfect to begin with. "Never mind free will. How can he be free if the mind is limited by its constitution? Why hadn't the Almighty—in sum—done a better job? It wouldn't have been all that hard for Him—whether man appeared first as a gene with evolutionary potential, or as Adam himself and his rib fully formed—to have endowed him with a little more control over his instincts; and if not pure love for the human race, possibly for reasons of natural selection, then maybe at least enough feeling to be moved by their common plight—that many have little, and many have nothing—and that they are alive for a minute and die young?

"Am I wrong about that?"

Dead silence.

Melchior coughed.

"In other words," Cohn desperately ran on, "why should the Lord's imperfect creation have spoiled His originally extraordinary idea? Why hadn't He created man equal to whom He had imagined?"

Thus Cohn had aimed his arrow at God and was invisibly aimed at.

Buz afterward swore it was he who had first seen a Pillar of Fire descending the darkened sky.

(—At the very least you ought to have called it to my attention.
—I liked thot story you were telling us and wonted it to go on.)
The fearful apes sensed something about to happen and were afraid to move or they would have jumped screaming from the tree.

ALL ONE SAW WAS LIGHT.

" 'Why do you contend
with Me, Mr. Cohn?' "

Cohn had shriveled, but wearing his father the cantor's white yarmulke kept him going. "I humbly ask to understand the Lord's intention."

" 'Who are you
to understand
the Lord's intention?
How can I explain
my mystery
to your mind?
Can a cripple ascend
a flaming of stars?' "

"Abraham and Job contended," Cohn heard himself say.

" 'They were my servants.' "

"Job complained You destroyed the blameless as well as the wicked."

" 'Job therefore repented.' "

Cohn shook his enraged fist. "You have destroyed mankind. Our children are all dead. Where are justice and mercy?"

Holy Moses, he thought. Am I deranged? What am I doing to me?

Something knocked him with a bounce off his stool. He lay in a flopping heap on the earth.

"'I am the Lord Thy God
who created man
to perfect Himself.'"

The chimpanzees, crouching on high branches in the schooltree, watched, hushed, as Cohn lay writhing in dead leaves.

Mary Madelyn looked on with her eyes slammed shut. None dared approach Cohn. Nor would Buz move after the Pillar of Fire had ascended the heavens.

A wind wailed, pregnant with forked flashes and thunderous roars. The apes clung with hands and feet to the swaying, creaking, hissing eucalyptus. George the gorilla was seasick in his heaving cedar.

Cohn felt a trickle of bitter rain penetrate his lips and waked, groaning.

"Something hit me on the bone of my head."

He fell back on his stool, holding a book above him to keep the yellow raindrops from pounding his headache.

The drenched chimps held their places—barely—as the lashing wet wind diminished and the storm rose like a yellow balloon someone had let go.

Buz, from the top of the slippery tree, called the lecture a knockout. "When is the next episode?"

Cohn had no idea. His nose dripped ice water. He had caught a heavy cold and must go home. "I may have walking pneumonia. There won't be any school tomorrow."

Sincere, prolonged applause, drowning out Esau's bray of contempt, rocked the schooltree.

And the ground was covered with lemons but no one had been hit except Cohn on his conk.

Melchior said, "My, all the lemonade we can shqueeze out of all those big lemonzh."

The Virgin in the Trees

BUZ SWORE he had spied a black bottle in the frothy waves.

"Where in the frothy waves?"

"There in the ocean."

"Miserable child, why didn't you fish it out? You can swim."

"You said we had all the bottles we would ever need," Buz swore.

"That bottle had to be different," said Cohn.

"How would I know thot foct?"

As the sun broke through the morning mist three strangers appeared on the island beach a mile below Cohn's cave. Cohn studied them through his surveyor's glass, feeling uneasy. Where could they have come from? Is God replenishing the earth, or is the earth replenishing itself? The chimps sat in the sand diagonally opposite one another, touching toes. Buz hadn't slept in the cave that night. Cohn snatched up his full banana basket, plus a half-dozen coconut bars, and hurried to the beach.

By the time he arrived at the water all the other chimpanzees of the island community had assembled to greet the newcomers. Buz and Mary Madelyn, self-engrossed Esau, gentle Melchior, and the twins, were sniffing at or being sniffed by the new apes. They kissed, patted backs, grunted, embraced. None acted as a stranger, as if the world had shrunk too small for that. Cohn's companions had at first frightened the visitors by addressing them in human speech but then reverted to their primate language, which only the twins had partially forgotten.

"Do any of you know any of them?" Cohn, in a straw hat, standing barefoot in the hot sand with his banana basket, asked Buz.

"No," said Buz, "but we like them."

"Well done," said Cohn, "but who are they and where have they come from?"

"They say they don't know thot."

"Was it high ground or low?"

"They say it was either one or the other."

"Could they have got here by boat—maybe our old raft?—I mean from some other island?"

"They hov no boats or rofts. Their footsteps come out of the woods, but not out of the water."

Buz said he would know more about the visitors after he had taught them to speak like the others.

Cohn said the sooner the better. "I am eager to know how they escaped the Second Flood." He cheerfully passed out some overripe bananas and candy bars to the three new chimps, who ate hungrily what he offered them. The two males, good-humored, one tall, the other stocky with bowed legs, had glossy brown coats. The old grandmother chimp sported ragged ears, teeth worn to the gums, and a threadbare behind.

Cohn, before Buz could make suggestions, called the old female Hattie, after an aunt; and the males he named Bromberg—the monkish tall one—and Esterhazy, the short other—after two college friends whose names he liked to be able to say once more.

Melchior enjoyed making the acquaintance of Hattie. He chucked her under the chin. They gamboled in the sand, huffing and panting, pushing each other down on their backs, tickling until they gasped.

Esterhazy, a bookkeeperish-looking ape, swallowed his soft banana without bothering to remove the peel; and Bromberg, a sweet-toothed type, applied himself to a coconut candy bar, teasing it with his tongue. When Saul of Tarsus and Luke begged for a piece, lifting their palms, he broke off two minute bites, handed one to each twin, and grunting, patted their heads. After wearing out the first candy bar he swallowed the second in a lip-sucking gulp.

Esau then informed the newly arrived brothers that he was the Alpha Ape of the island; and neither of them, although they seemed to consider the news seriously, objected.

The brothers watched Mary Madelyn in fascination, and sniffed at her rear, to her acute embarrassment, to determine whether she was in heat; apparently she wasn't. Mary Madelyn climbed a tree and sat in it, hidden by leafy branches.

In the afternoon, Bromberg and Esterhazy sat in a fig tree, plucking and eating ripe figs as they watched Cohn's community going through its varied chores—except for Esau, who was squatting on the ground poking long straws into the mound-nests of nonexistent ants.

And the next morning the newcomer apes sat hunched under the schooltree but refused to join the others in the branches, as if embarrassed by their lack of language, while Cohn discoursed on the first ice age. Those in the tree listened to the lecture in a mood resembling stupefied absorption. Saul of Tarsus broke into shivers, and Luke, after watching him a minute, joined him. Mary Madelyn sat hunched up in anticipation of Cohn's next freezing sentence. Melchior chewed thoughtfully on a leftover matzo from the seder, as he listened.

Buz dangled in suspense by one arm from an upper limb of the eucalyptus; and George the gorilla at length dropped out of his cedar to think something over; he headed, knuckle-walking, into the rain forest, frightening Esterhazy, Bromberg, and Hattie, who hastily ascended the schooltree and at once became students. Sometime afterwards, during a whispered conversation with Buz, they began to speak in a human tongue.

These were productive days. Cohn had taken to throwing and baking clay pots; also to practicing herbal medicine, a development that brought the community closer together because they appreciated having an attending physician.

Always a collector, Cohn liked to take samples of grasses, herbs, leaves, and barks of various trees, some of which he boiled up in water and evaporated, to produce an extract of each substance. He sampled these concoctions, bitter and sweet, and found that one calmed his stomach if he had overeaten, and another lightened a severe headache.

Buz complained his eyes were strained and Cohn advised him to cut down on reading, but Buz wouldn't because he liked the stories he was becoming acquainted with. "Everything gets to be a story," he said, and Cohn agreed. He brewed up a mimosa ointment with boric acid, a concoction that reduced his boy's eyestrain.

For most minor ailments Cohn prescribed a mixture of eucalyptus oil and bicarbonate of soda. Either his patients vomited up the medication and improved in health, or kept it down and got better. With the same prescription he purged Saul of

Tarsus, and Luke, of "worms," which couldn't really have been worms because they no longer lived on earth, though they resembled worms. Whatever they were, Cohn eradicated them. He also calmed Esau's toothache, offering to pull the offending molar with a pair of pliers, at which the Alpha Ape bristled threateningly and hooted sternly. He informed Cohn he no longer felt the toothache.

George the gorilla still loitered in the vicinity of Cohn's cave, usually when the cantor was singing, but he refused to enter and be treated for illness when he seemed to be ailing, though one day he suffered a severe, nose-dripping, eye-tearing, sneezy cold, for which Cohn wanted to prescribe an herb that would clear his breathing.

George refused to accept it.

"If you like to suffer," Cohn said to the gorilla, "that's your choice."

George sneezed seven times and Cohn uttered one "God bless."

Calvin Cohn had baked his early pots in midday sunlight but they hadn't turned out well. In his last large dig in the field beyond and above the rice paddy, he had discovered a muddy vein of white hydrous aluminum silicate clay, with which he began to mold unique dishes, bowls, vases, artificial flowers, other artifacts of decoration. He fired these in a kiln he had constructed in the fireplace, a simple metal "firebox" he had fabricated out of a ship's locker; this he heated with homemade charcoal of ebony wood that got so hot the box glowed vermilion and took hours to cool. Buz was uncomfortable in the presence of the red-hot kiln, yet as he lurked by the cave opening, he liked to watch Cohn remove the fired objects, some severely cracked because there was no temperature control.

Cohn, to the chimp's amusement, had lately begun to design clay masks sculpted with faces of Greek gods, former politicians, famous scientists of the past, some of whom he hung up as a mobile on a tree near the eucalyptus; and he created a few vertebrate animals the chimp had never laid eyes on. Cohn hadn't learned how to glaze his pots, so he painted the white clay masks with features colored in black, green, red, and yellow inks.

Buz saw his first lion's head as a mask produced by Cohn.

Afterwards the artist destroyed many of the masks, fearing that the Lord, if He got a peek at them, might accuse him of worshipping false gods.

The island community was active and flourished beyond Cohn's best hopes. All the chimps, even the newcomers, were gainfully employed, with the exception of Esau, who lived on the fruit of the island. "Why disturb yourself if the fruit is for free? Why spoil our natures to please a non-chimp? Who is he, for instance?"

Cohn wouldn't say.

Saul of Tarsus and Luke helped in the rice paddy, Melchior overseeing them. Sometimes he fell asleep, standing, and the twins stopped working until he awoke and then asked for a banana-beer break, a custom Melchior favored.

Mary Madelyn assisted Cohn in collecting roots, leaves, new samples of bark. She watched him catalogue each item on a 3x5 card.

"I wish I had a handwriting, Cawvin."

"Maybe someday."

"Wiw I someday be human?"

"It's a long haul."

"I would wike to be Juwiet in wov with Romeo."

Cohn was growing a brown beard as he became bald.

Buz was, page by page, reading through the encyclopedia. His dod permitted him to use his personal reading eyeglasses, and they seemed to ease a slight strabismus.

Hattie had for a while looked after the twins, who resisted her motherly ministrations. She then took care of Melchior and he permitted her to build a sleep-nest near his in a low live oak.

Cohn stored away in dry caves full plastic bags of newly discovered sunflower seeds.

The chimps helped plant banana groves and other fruit trees. Esterhazy and Bromberg willingly assisted.

And everyone congregated around Buz and Cohn at their dig in the late afternoon. They sniffed and—to Cohn's annoyance—sometimes chewed on the ancient animal bones he had unearthed. To those who retched, he had to dispense gallons of eucalyptus-bicarb medicine for their dyspepsia.

He had occasional hopes that Buz might ask to be bar mitzvah'd since he was already the equivalent of age thirteen, but the little chimp never brought the matter up, and Cohn did not proselytize.

Life was serene until Mary Madelyn, the jeweled pink flower of her swollen sexual skin visible from the rear, hid herself from the pursuing males by taking to the tops of tall trees, but when the wind hit her dense scent—a compound of night-blooming jasmine and raw eggs, it seemed to Cohn—and blew it around, they went hungrily seeking and could not locate her although they ran through every tree in the vicinity.

Esau sought her relentlessly, sniffing his small-eyed way from branch to branch, breathing stertorously, restless with desire. Once after not finding her, he pounded in frustration on the trunk of the tree they had just explored.

Esterhazy and Bromberg, on the run, were ascending and descending one or another tree where they thought they had glimpsed the tempting flower, or caught an enticing trace of her sexual perfume. One dark day they pounced on someone who turned out to be Hattie, and happily crouched, but they seemed to have lost interest.

After catching an invigorating breath of Mary Madelyn's scent in the headlong breeze, Buz had decided he was mature enough to be interested and had joined the apes in pursuit of her; as had the twins because the chase was fun. They were caught up in adventure, spying out Mary Madelyn and swiftly shinnying up a tree to entrap her, but she escaped, and went squealing through the treetops. They pursued her until, by virtue of her inspired speed, she outdistanced them and disappeared in a curtain of green.

One still morning, Esau, bored with the school lesson, happened to spot her hiding in George the gorilla's cedar; she had been secretly listening to Cohn lecturing on the fossils of the Mesozoic age. Mary Madelyn had been thus engaged for three days, apparently with the connivance or unconcern of George, in an attempt to keep up with her lessons.

Esau, his head hair erect, stealthily climbed higher and higher in the eucalyptus and swung into the cedar on a vine. He descended in a leap and charged at Mary Madelyn as she sat absorbed in Cohn's description of a dinosaur attempting to defend itself in a bloody swamp against a rapacious flying reptile.

Catching sight of Esau, Mary Madelyn let out a full scream, interrupting Cohn's lecture, and at once leaped to the ground, the males in hot pursuit. George the gorilla roared at the contretemps, and the noise seemed to paralyze the other apes in the schooltree, although it had no effect, to speak of, on Esau. Cohn bellowed at him to leave the girl alone.

The uncooperative chimp, chasing her on the ground, caught Mary Madelyn by the arm and hurled her against a tree. She went down with the breath knocked out of her, bleeding from a wound over her left eye. Before Esau, swaggering from foot to foot, could compel her to crouch, she tore herself out of his grasp and swung into a vast baobab, immediately losing herself in it. In a minute she was brachiating like a gibbon through the rain forest, zigzagging in the foliage as Esau furiously hooted after her.

Gaining on her, he was a moment from overtaking Mary Madelyn, when she reversed direction and dipped under him. He grabbed for her where she no longer was, and fell halfway through a tree. Esau hit the ground hard and lay motionless on his back.

Mary Madelyn had disappeared.

Bromberg and Esterhazy had abandoned the contest between the dinosaur and pterodactyl to see what was going on in the modern world. They stopped off to prop Esau up, who would have none of it. He rose on his knees and stomped the earth in rage.

Cohn, after his interrupted lecture, confided to Buz that Esau had become a hazard to a free society and must reform, or they might have to consider getting rid of him.

"Why don't we get rid of her?"

"I thought you were interested in Mary Madelyn?"

"Not when she runs whenever she sees me. It says in Dr. Bünder's book that female chimponzees seek male compony when they go into heat. Why doesn't she do whot the book says?"

Cohn thought she seemed to be resisting her instincts.

Buz asked why.

He wasn't sure. "Something in her. She's an unusual person—which is to say, chimpanzee."

Buz thought she was mad. "How om I supposed to experience sex if she won't stond still for holf a minute?"

Cohn suggested he seek out and persuade her. "My sense of it is she would like to be courted, not gunned down from the rear by an ambitious phallus. Talk to her about *Romeo and Juliet.* She admires the play."

Buz said he disliked it. "They are both goons and so is Mary Modelyn."

"She's a sensitive, empathic, intelligent creature."

That night he was awakened by the rustling of his ivy curtain. Cohn struck a match and held the flickering flame above his head.

"Who's there?"

Mary Madelyn squatted amid the shadows on the floor of the cave.

"I have no safe pwace to go. May I pwease stay the night?"

"Why don't you make yourself a nest in a tree? The males should be sleeping now."

"No, they aren't." She was fatigued, forlorn, disquieted.

"Turn your head till I get my pants on," Cohn told her.

When he had drawn them on he said she could stay, and lit the lamp.

She wanted to rest on some branches on the cave floor, but he said she could have Buz's cage. "He almost never uses it."

Mary Madelyn promised to leave before the sun was up.

He offered her a drink of coconut juice. As he poured, Cohn observed her flabby, wilted flower, and the sight of it made him slightly ill.

"It wiw go away soon," she said apologetically.

"I can't understand why you resist every male who approaches you."

She said it was in part his fault. "You wanted us to wearn your wanguage. Now that I have, I am different than I used to be. If I hadn't wearned to speak and understand human speech, I would have awready presented mysewf to every mawe on the iwand."

She asked Cohn if he would mate with her.

"It is not permitted. I am a man. I am not allowed to copulate with animals."

"You told us you were proud to be an animal."

"Of course. Generically speaking."

"You would be mistaken to think of me only as a beast," Mary Madelyn said.

She said she had decided to sleep elsewhere.

Hairy Esau, lugging a knobby log four feet long and three inches thick, lurched into Cohn's cave the next morning. "Where's the bitch hiding?"

He let out a roar, his yellowed fangs repulsively visible, and raised the log as though to bash Cohn's mind in.

He rose hastily from his unfinished breakfast. "You're mistaken, she's not here."

"Saul of Tarsus saw her sneak in last night."

Cohn swore she had left. His scalp stung as if his hair had turned into needles. How does one reason with a mad chimp who confuses himself with a gorilla? Fearing for his life, Cohn had backed toward the storage shelves—the breakfast table the only barrier between him and the grossly angered ape.

"Don't be overhasty, Esau. This is a desperately serious situation. The world has been destroyed by fire and water. You heard my recent lecture on the subject. I have reason to believe that those of us left on this island are the only survivors of life on the planet. If we expect to go on living we've got to live as brothers. Why don't you put that nasty log down and let's discuss the matter peaceably."

Esau, breathing noisily, his small eyes restlessly roaming the cave, called Cohn an idiot. "Your stupid schooltree has made her too proud to dip her butt for friends."

He swung his log at Cohn, who ducked, barely escaping having his head crushed. Stealthily he felt behind him for his 30.06 Winchester, at the same panicky instant thinking, I mustn't use it.

If he could tease the French saber out of its sheath, the sight of it might scare the beast away. Esau kept his brutal log raised as he inched toward Cohn, who was then assailed by a more frightening thought: Is he the Lord's messenger who has this day come to slay me?

Without waiting for a formal response, he overturned the table between them. Esau was scalded by a pot of hot mint tea.

The ape let out a quavering cry that rose to a scream when he dropped the log on his burnt foot. His mouth dribbled and eyes bled tears of rage.

Cohn, instead of taking up a weapon, grabbed a witch's mask from the shelf and held it over his face, at the same time ululating and grunting.

It was a contorted white mask with watery red eyes, a nose like a bent bone, and wet black mouth. The mouth moved obscenely as Cohn howled.

Esau, erect in fright, stared wide-eyed at Cohn's horrid mask. He let out a whine, as if he had lost control of his bodily functions. Bolting out of the cave, he ran groaning into the forest. No one saw him for months afterwards.

After two days, Mary Madelyn, looking her neat, attractive self, returned to the schooltree to resume her education.

None of the male apes approached, or even seemed to notice her presence, but Cohn, on greeting her, had kissed her fingertips.

He thought he had handled Esau badly and would have to do better in the future, assuming the chimp returned. Esau must be patiently talked to and counseled until he understood what was required of him for the common good.

Cohn sent Buz into the forest to locate the rebellious Alpha Ape and ask him to return to the community, but Buz, after a full day's search, saw no sign of him and figured he had made for the headlands.

He told Cohn, in unconcealed trepidation, that an albino ape seemed to be in the woodland trees again.

"I saw him but he didn't see me."

"Who is this type and is he for real?" Cohn wanted to know.

"A white ape, they can be nasty people."

"Have you ever known one?"

"Dr. Bünder has a long porogroph on them in his book. Sometimes they get schizoid, or like thot."

"He'd better stay out of here."

But on the next dark night the albino, grown a few feet since Cohn had last laid eyes on him, appeared in his cave. Either dawn broke then, or he lit the cave with his white presence.

Cohn hastily retreated to the rear.

Rising on his legs, the albino pantomimed flinging a spear at Cohn, or someone like him.

"That was like in a dream," Cohn explained. "I was attempting to defend myself, not hurt anybody."

To get rid of the ape, he reached for a black witch's mask hanging on a peg on the wall.

The ape tore the mask from Cohn's hand and held it in front of his face, becoming a white ape with a black face, pierced by a red witch's eye. The sight sent a chill through Cohn and he bolted the cave.

In the forest, in an instant, he encountered a black-faced white ape. Cohn squared off in the circling crouch of a grunting Japanese wrestler, to hold the ape off as best he could; but the fierce creature grabbed his arm and yanked him over his shoulder, his large paw grasping both of Cohn's hands, his long ape-arm pinning his kicking legs.

"Let's talk about this," begged Cohn.

The white ape, bumpily running with a struggling Cohn on his shoulders, leaped for a low bough of an ebony tree, and with his free hand, both legs, and a grunt, swung himself and his victim into the tree.

He'll destroy me up there. Should I try prayer, or is the white ape God's messenger come to execute His purpose?

"Are you God's messenger?"

If the ape knew he wouldn't say. He had with a vibrant roar stopped in his tracks.

Above them, holding to an upper branch, stood George the gorilla, his right hand aiming a large black coconut—if not a rock—at the head of the white ape carrying Cohn.

The tree began to shake as if it had conceived a mad thought, but the swaying gorilla held tight to his black object.

The ape released his hold on him and Cohn, freed, felt himself falling through the thick-leaved swaying ebony, bumping his head till it sickened him. He landed, with a swooshing thud, in a bouquet of giant ferns at the foot of the tree.

In the bright sunlight that broke through the forest canopy, the white ape seemed to dissolve, and the ebony stopped its frightful shaking. The forest was hushed.

Buz appeared in the undergrowth wearing a Japanese general's cap and blasting a long tin horn.

The nervous gorilla high in the tree thrust two fingers into each ear as Cohn tried to shake himself awake; but how could you if you hadn't slept?

A disturbing desire possessed him, fortunately yielding affection, not so easy to come upon these days. And affection grew against his will—a difficult way to love.

After the schooltree class they strolled amid the dappled palm trees lining the sea. Cohn walked at ease, Mary Madelyn standing upright or knuckle-walking by his side. When they rested she groomed his balding head. In turn, he groomed her breasts and belly. They talked as friends.

And Buz, forgetting his manners, persistently trailed them, and neither of them could convince him to leave them to their privacy. He hung around, eavesdropping, hiding behind the trunks of trees, or pretending to be asleep as they sat on the ground. Sometimes he brachiated quietly above them, observing their actions. Cohn, when he spotted him, recalled the serpent licentiously regarding Adam and Eve in intercourse.

They liked holding hands as they walked together. Mary Madelyn, after consuming a passion fruit he had picked for her, kissed Cohn full on the lips.

Buz complained high in a tree. He shredded bark with his teeth, obviously deeply jealous.

He had told Cohn he was old enough for sexual experience and wished to copulate with Mary Madelyn. He didn't know by what right his own dod interfered with his courtship of her. She was his kind, not Cohn's.

Cohn said that on this island there was only one kind—sentient, intelligent living beings. "We're sort of affectionately in love," he told Buz, "or something close to it."

Buz wanted to be in love too, and Cohn replied his time would come. He mentioned Hattie, and Buz hooted in ridicule. The chimp stomped away but got over being angry with Cohn in less than a week. Instead of following the lovers, he began to collect rare stones and shells on the beach. Cohn had taught him the rudiments of polishing stones, and had also told him some appealing stories of sublimation. Buz said he didn't like the stories, yet it was apparent he had learned something. On the other hand, he formally moved out of the cave, taking along eight cream coconut bars and an old hat of Cohn's.

Cohn agreed it was time Buz had a place of his own, though he expected him to drop in at the cave whenever he felt like it. If he happened to be busy, he was sure Buz would understand.

On their wandering walks, or as they rested in the warm grass, or sat together in a tree, Mary Madelyn and he talked about *Romeo and Juliet*. Cohn had read her the first act three times, and she greatly enjoyed the balcony scene. She liked to say, " 'What wov can do, that dares wov attempt.' "

She had never seen a balcony and imagined a vine-entangled baobab in which Juliet was confined by two hefty, threatening guardian apes. Then Romeo, a youthful, handsome chimpanzee, appeared, scared off the offensive apes with a display of strength, and released Juliet from her prison-tree. They lived together, afterwards, in his happy flowering acacia.

Cohn didn't tell her about the sad future fate of the lovers. He would let her find that out herself. Mary Madelyn was not the curious reader Buz was, yet she liked to be read to and learned well by ear.

"Am I wovwy as Juwiet?" she asked Cohn.

"You have your graces."

"Wiw you ever wov me?"

He couldn't say yes nor did he say no. Cohn said love was complicated but they were obviously affectionate to each other.

"What is wov?" Mary Madelyn asked.

Cohn said it was a flame that lights a flame. "That's how a romantic would put it." He was eager to educate her.

Mary Madelyn, listening dreamily, wanted to know what other kind of love there was.

"A living-together kind of love, however romantically it may have begun, something trusting, sustaining, committed to life."

"Can I wov wike that?"

"I hope so."

"If I do, wiw you wov me?"

He said he thought so.

"I wov you," she said to Calvin Cohn.

He said he found her engaging. She was even alluring these days, amiable brown eyes, silken black hair; her features approached human. Though Mary Madelyn could not be said to be classically beautiful—facts were facts—still beauty existed, derived to some degree from her intelligent, generous nature. She came to something. Having become aware of her quality, her spirit, Cohn thought, accounted for his growing feeling for her.

Sensing receptivity, Mary Madelyn presented herself to him, crouching low. Her sexual skin, after four weeks, had blossomed overnight, like a repellent flower.

Cohn said he was sorry but he couldn't possibly oblige—couldn't mount her.

"Why not? You said you fewt affection for me."

He admitted he did but could only embrace her face to face. "I wouldn't be surprised if love began that way—evolutionarily speaking," he said, "when two lovers were able to face one another."

She said she was perfectly willing to embrace him face to face, and afterwards they could mate as nature demanded.

Cohn then said the act was forbidden to him—"to copulate with an animal."

"Is that *aw* I am to you?"

"Certainly not. But I have to take other things into account. My father was a religious man. I've been influenced by his teaching, not to mention his moral vision, and also his temperament." Cohn said that as a young man he had broken from his father and gone his own way, but he was still bound to him, although he had been dead for years and Cohn's own world had been destroyed.

Mary Madelyn, getting back to the practical, said she had taken a bath that morning. She told him she was pure. "I have kept my virginity for you ever since you expwained the word to me when you first read me *Romeo and Juwiet.*"

He now understood her frantic flights from the male apes, and admired her for saving herself for him on his terms, an astonishing feat for an animal, even a primate.

Yet he replied, "It says in Leviticus, 'Thou shalt not let thy cattle gender with a diverse kind—' "

"I am not a cattew."

"It also says, 'If a man lies with a beast he shall be put to death; and you shall kill the beast.' And it says more or less the same in Deuteronomy: 'Cursed be he who lies with any kind of beast.'"

"Do you think of me as a beast, Cawvin?"

"Not really," he admitted.

Mary Madelyn asked him if he had a mind of his own; and the next moment she was in flight, having spied a band of males in a nearby tree—Buz among them—who had beheld, and were discussing, her shivering pale flower.

Cohn, shouting and waving his arms, diverted them as Mary Madelyn took off for, and escaped into, the rain forest.

How can I love her? he reflected in his cave, except as I loved my dog?

During the tropical night a haggard Mary Madelyn appeared in the cave, and when Cohn sleepily lit the lamp, she presented herself to him.

He blew out the light and turned toward the wall.

She slept in Buz's cage and in the morning swept the floor with a bramble broom and was gone.

She did not appear in the schooltree, and neither did the young males. Only Melchior and Hattie attended class that day, squatting on a branch of the eucalyptus, holding hands.

And George, in his coniferous cedar, sat alone as usual, cracking palm nuts with his rock-like teeth as he listened, the short hair on his sloping dark skull rising as Cohn lectured on the development of the great apes and ascent of homo sapiens during the course of evolution. He had several times lectured on natural selection—the maximization of fitness, someone had defined it—a popular subject with his students. It promised possibilities if one made himself—or in some way became—selectable.

And the chimpanzees liked to learn where they might have originated. They enjoyed the mysteries of being and becoming, of guessing and knowing. Cohn used some of the fossils he had dug out of the earth to illustrate and trace the anatomical development of mammals. He said he had had great hopes for the future of man, until the Day of Devastation. Cohn had at one time theorized that evolution might produce a moral explosion via a gifted creature, homo ethicalis; but man, as he was, had got there first with a different kind of explosion.

In class the next morning, after a night of sleepless thinking of Mary Madelyn, he was not as carefully prepared as usual, yet he addressed himself to the subject of the close relationship of chimpanzees and the creature who had once lived on earth as man, a closer relationship than Darwin might have imagined. They were descended from a common ancestor, perhaps Ramapithecus, who lived about twenty million years ago, a gifted ape-like primate who may have been struck—it seemed to Cohn—by a crafty desire to improve his lot in life, if not altogether to change himself into something better than he assumed he was.

"The physical similarities of chimpanzee and man show in their blood and brain," Cohn lectured, "as well as in their appearance and behavior. Human beings—this will interest you—and great apes have almost identical genes—more than 99 percent of the amino-acid sequences in human beings and African apes are identical, despite morphological differences. And the African apes' albumin antibody reactions are (let's say) closer to men's than they were (let's say) to Asian apes. All this indicates about five million years since we diverged from a common ancestor on the molecular clock, which is very impressive, I'd say."

Cohn cited Dr. Walther Bünder as his source, and the two old chimps in the tree clapped heartily. The gorilla, still cracking palm nuts with his teeth, listened raptly, sometimes forgetting to chew.

Cohn went on: "Also in their sensory apparatus, the nature of their emotions, and their expressions and grimaces—perhaps even in who they think they are, chimpanzees are more like men than some men, or any other primate.

"Though they can be as nasty, brutish, and mean as men, their natures are essentially affectionate. They kiss and hug on celebratory occasions, and some—I have heard—even die of broken hearts."

Here Hattie dabbed her eye with eucalyptus leaves, and Melchior sniffed once.

But George the gorilla gave his chest a muffled thump, as if in doubt he was hearing good news; and sighed to himself.

"The idea I wish to propound," Cohn suggested, "is that it seems entirely possible that chimpanzees, as they progress in their evolution may, if their unconscious minds insist, incite molecular changes that will sooner or later—sooner, I hope—cause them to develop into a species something like man, perhaps better than man was when he fell from grace and vanished"—Cohn coughed to dislodge a frog in his throat—"from the face of this earth.

"And if these forthcoming chimps do, in the long run, turn out to be more fortunate than man—maybe a little more richly endowed, more carefully controlled, more easily inclined to the moral life; in the larger sense more 'humanly' behaved than the species of which I am the last survivor; then maybe the presently disaffected Almighty Being Who began the creation of us all may bestow on them a more magnanimous fate than homo sapiens achieved—I mean suffered."

Cohn personally felt that the Lord, when He saw such good-willed alteration going on among the chimps who had selected themselves, might once more love His creation.

"God's there, sure enough," he said, "sitting in his judgment seat, but not always attentive to what's going on, as if He has on His mind one of His new concerns—in this case a gob of bacteria He had that day laid under a warm rock on Pluto; and as a result he suffers a cosmic absentmindedness caused by being conscious of *everything* at every instant of existence, or duration, or whatever it is that, among infinite other qualities, we call God's Being—That-Which-Is-Above-Is-Below-and-What-Is-Inside-Is-Outside-Kind-of-Being. Yet surely He will welcome, when He notices, a species of adventurous chimps developing into a species of superior-sort-of-men?

"Amen," Cohn muttered.

Melchior and Hattie, at the conclusion of this inspired address, applauded enthusiastically, and quickly descended the schooltree for their banana beer.

George dropped out of his cedar like a long lump of putty, as if dismayed he hadn't heard a gorilla mentioned once, and he loped away.

Cohn then reconsidered a daring plan that had filtered through his thoughts last night as Mary Madelyn slept in his cave. In the morning he plotted it on a sheet of paper he afterwards destroyed.

He had decided that the extraordinary act he had in mind

might be worth a stab in the dark. Doubts assailed him—contemplating a fantastic act of daring was like a trumpet blast, the soldiers of doubt woke and charged—but Cohn cleverly sidestepped them.

If he and Mary Madelyn, in mutual affection, lay with each other, and however he aimed and entered, he succeeded in depositing in her hospitable uterus a spurt of adventurous sperm: *that*—if it took—might sooner or later have the effect he was hoping for. Assuming fertilization, and carrying her fetus to full term (the odds against that, he had learned from Dr. Bünder, were high), she would, with luck, give birth to a baby in eight months. Whatever happened thereafter was uncertain, but the beginning—without which nothing began but God Himself—would have begun.

In sum, a worthy primate evolution demanded, besides a few macroevolutionary lucky breaks, a basis of brainpower; and commencing with a combination of man-chimp child, the two most intelligent of God's creatures might produce this new species—ultimately of Cohn's invention—an eon or two ahead on the molecular clock.

Let's see what happens now.

Cohn reasoned thus: Already his citizen-chimps had mastered language as speech and foundation of rational thought. Assuming the presence, not too long from now (Look how quickly Adam and Eve, a single couple who did not work hard at it, had peopled the earth), of the necessary females, and as a result of Cohn's "experiment" a rich pool of genes to work with—sooner or later the developing man-apes would inherit larger, more complex, more subtle brains than either now possessed; and who knows what other useful characteristics, also freely bestowed, might be achieved in comparatively less future-time, evolutionarily speaking, if God did not interfere with (indeed, secretly sanctioned and blessed) the process.

Who knows—Cohn let it play in his mind—maybe the Lord had reconsidered His Second Dismal Flood and was regretting it. He Himself, possibly, had inspired the revolutionary impulse in Cohn's head—(His vessel)—that he mate with a lady ape; despite which act He would omit cursing him, and thereafter killing the innocent "beast," such primeval punishment null and void in these ineluctably post-Torah times?

And wouldn't Cohn be playing a role in purpose like that of Lot's daughters, who lay down with their wine-drunk father after Sodom had been smoked off the map, to preserve the future of mankind and its successors, not excluding the Messiah?

If two daughters, in a dark cave on separate nights, lay incestuously with their wine-sotted, love-groaning father, why not Cohn, a clearheaded, honest man, lying with biophilial affection and shut eyes, against the warm furry back of a loving lady chimpanzee who spoke English well and was mysteriously moved by *Romeo and Juliet*?

He considered renaming the island, "Cohn's Lot."

But his doubts were these: he had recalled the fable of the cat changed into a princess, who as pretty princess—to the prince her husband's astonishment—pounced on a befuddled gray mouse who had blundered into the parlor. The next day the cat was back in the cat life.

What's bred in the bones lives there. Similarly, with or without speech, Mary Madelyn had armies of ancient chimp-genes tucked away in her flesh, that might overwhelm Cohn's civilized genotypes trying to make a living in her warm ape-womb. If they perished in the struggle to survive in a semi-alien fetus, how could Cohn contribute anything of lasting value to the child?

Or suppose the child was born a monster and for some inevitable genetic reason developed as King Kong, unless the old monster appeared on the scene as Queen?

Fooling around with evolution—for wasn't that what it ultimately came to?—despite good intentions, was a mad act for a hitherto responsible scientist. Besides, the future was beyond invisible reach, and he would never know what he had stirred up.

On the other hand, with so many doubts and maybes staring him in the face on this broken island, yet with fantastic possibilities on the horizon, or boiling up in the surrounding seas—maybe about to fly at him from another planet—so much one could not begin to foretell—therefore what else to do when there were no practical prospects at hand but "take a chance"? Some good might come of it. What worked, worked; what hadn't, might.

Therefore monkey with evolution? That much chutzpah?

Why not—in these times—if one took into account the eschatological living trauma the Lord had laid on the world?

That decided the matter for Cohn.

After the day's work, he unfolded the portion of stiff sail of the *Rebekah Q* that he had used as a seder tablecloth. Guiding a pair of tinsmith's shears along a charcoal line he had drawn to outline a simple dress pattern he had found in his one-volume, all-purpose, popular encyclopedia, Cohn cut out a portion of the canvas material into front and back panels of a simple white chemise.

With a waxed twine inserted through an eye he had punched into a nail, he sewed together the two halves of the dress; and Cohn considered adding a pair of white drawers, but gave that up when it occurred to him they would only get in the way. When Mary Madelyn, groggy from outrunning pursuing males all day, returned to the cave, Cohn presented the white garment to her as a friendship gift.

She asked what she could do with it, and Cohn said he would like her to dress in it, and he would help if she needed help. Apparently she didn't. She went through the motions of clothing herself and seemed to enjoy dressing, though she swore she had never before in her life worn any garment except a hat of flowers she had once made for herself.

Cohn, stepping back to admire her elegant appearance in the white dress, said she looked like somebody's bride.

"Do I wook wike Juwiet?"

"Sort of, though I'm no Romeo."

"I wov you, do you wov me?"

"Sure enough," said Cohn. "I sure do."

Perhaps her eyes misted, perhaps not, but it seemed to Cohn that she would have cried a little if chimps could. Maybe someday—another step in their humanization.

Turning the lamp low, he proposed that she and he mate, and Mary Madelyn modestly assented.

He lifted her white skirt from the rear, and with shut eyes, telling himself to keep his thoughts level, Cohn dipped his phallus into her hot flower. There was an instant electric connection and Cohn parted with his seed as she possessed it. He felt himself happily drawn clean of sperm. Mary Madelyn was at once calmed. She waited a minute for more to happen, but when nothing more did, she chewed up a fig and fell asleep in his bed.

He lifted down from the top storage shelf the clay urn containing his former wife's ashes, and with his shovel buried it under a palm tree. Buz, in the night-dark, dug it up with his hands and flung the urn into the dimly moonlit sea.

Esau appeared, ghastly, one morning as Cohn was breakfasting in the cave. He rose, wildly seeking a weapon to defend his life with, then realized the dispirited ape was not well. He had lost about twenty pounds, his shaggy coat was soiled, and his left jaw swollen. His eyes were ten degrees crossed and bleary.

Esau said he suffered from a mind-blowing toothache; the pain tore his face apart. He begged Cohn to help him or he would go mad.

Cohn, after slipping on his glasses, administered an herb that put the chimp to sleep, and assisted by Mary Madelyn, pulled out the offending molar with a strong pair of pliers.

Esau, when he woke, was overjoyed the pain had ceased and expressed everlasting gratitude to Cohn. He promised to reform, and volunteered to assist the common effort. And to prove his resolve, he asked to be given a productive task to perform.

Cohn appointed him keeper of the orchard. It was his duty to report those trees that were flowering and about to come to fruit; also to look for fruit trees that hadn't been catalogued.

After the episode with Esau, Cohn wrote down seven Commandments he had been carrying in his head, and tried to think of a way of presenting them to the assembly of apes. He wasn't attempting to rewrite the Pentateuch, he told himself (and God); he was simply restating, or amplifying, some principles he had been reflecting on.

There was no nearby mountain from whose heights to come trudging down bearing two tablets in his arms, so Cohn baked each letter in white clay, assembled them into sentences, and set each up with twine, pegs, nails, and Elmer's glue, on the eastern face of the escarpment near the waterfall, where all who passed by on their way to the rice paddy, or big dig, would see them.

Cohn's Admonitions—he had decided to drop Commandments—read thus:

1. We have survived the end of the world; therefore cherish life. Thou shalt not kill.

2. Note: God is not love, God is God. Remember Him.

3. Love thy neighbor. If you can't love, serve—others, the community. Remember the willing obligation.

4. Lives as lives are equal in value but not ideas. Attend the Schooltree.

5. Blessed are those who divide the fruit equally.

6. Altruism is possible, if not probable. Keep trying. See 3 above.

7. Aspiration may improve natural selection. Chimpanzees may someday be better living beings than men were. There's no hurry but keep it in mind.

On the day the Admonitions were fixed on the wall of the escarpment, Cohn read them aloud to the assembled apes and led a cheer for each. The response to the 7th was moderate but he did not insist on another cheer.

The island colony prospered. All chimps worked, in fields and trees and in caves, collecting and storing food, seeding and caring for gardens, and distributing flowers to those who wanted to adorn their sleep-nests.

The rice paddies were extended, the twins doing much of the planting and harvesting. Melchior directed and Hattie helped. Not all members of the community cared for rice—Buz called it tasteless stuff, though Melchior said it was good to rub on aching gums—but Cohn kept hundreds of sacks stored in nearby caves in case of famine. He was not fearful of famine—hadn't dreamed of it in his dreams—was just being careful.

The schooltree was well attended every day. Esau, his sour face sweetened, sat on a branch close to Mary Madelyn, but did not trouble her. Buz sat on an upper bough, as far from her as he could arrange. On his own, he spent days working out arithmetic puzzles. He had asked Cohn to teach him algebra so he could go on sublimating.

Everyone enjoyed the pleasant weather—cool mornings, hot afternoons, chilly nights; and the chimps—all but the twins—tended to walk upright. George did not change; he was still the old knuckle-walking George, rather than flirt with backaches got from holding his 500-pound body erect. Buz, after chancing on the word in the dictionary, called him pariah; but the gorilla, though he might have crushed the little chimp's skull in his hands, paid him no attention. He kept his dignity.

On the important holidays Cohn played his father's records on the machine, and the apes danced a square dance in the green grass. Holidays came often that year, whenever anyone thought there ought to be one.

They called themselves "men." Esterhazy hooted, "Come on, men, let's get cracking." Cohn felt that evolution was peeking through them. He encouraged being healthy because it felt good, and for purposes of natural selection. He was voted teacher-for-life and honorary chimpanzee.

Mary Madelyn had taught herself to say lwov for wov, and was in her second month of pregnancy.

What was God doing in her womb?

The Voice of the Prophet

EIGHT BABOONS sat like black dogs in a circle on a large, flat, sandstone rock. One male bled from his left eye. The other had lost part of his snout and all but one right toe. If a leaf moved they screamed in alarm, their muzzles showing long mouthfuls of pointed teeth.

Each of the three females mothered one undernourished child. When the males threat-yawned, or snarled at each other, the females rose and paced tensely and gracefully on the rock, their children riding their backs, until the males had calmed down.

On the ground they ate tubers and fruit, and tore at dry grasses. They lapped water at the pond, often raising their heads to stare at the chimps tending the rice. When a baboon male barked in alarm the small troop galloped back to the rock, the females gracefully ascending its ledges, their children clinging to their backs.

Saul of Tarsus had spied the baboons from the rice field, and word by slow word, informed anyone who would listen that he had seen some strange black monkeys around. Melchior said they looked to him like baboons who had lived in a pit or dirty cave. He said they all needed baths. He personally had no use for any of them, and Hattie agreed.

At dusk the baboons were afraid of the dark. They leaped from the rock and fled across the grass to an old madrone where they built their sleep-nests. When night came they were asleep. Awaking, they seemed to fear each other until one day, after a dry season, the drenching rain washed the black out of their patchy coats, and turned them a greenish-yellow. After the rain they sat placidly on the rock, or galloped in the grass, back-flipping, tail-pulling, wrestling. The black stain—dye, mud, or ashes—washed out of their coats in the rain, had discolored the pond by the rice, and Melchior complained bitterly to Cohn, who thus learned of the presence of the baboons. For days he pondered God's purpose.

Mary Madelyn, after a time of doubt, when she bled and it seemed she might momentarily lose her fetus, having become securely pregnant, had one day disappeared from her favorite white acacia. Cohn had searched for her among the fruit trees in the woods, in the rain forest, and in caves in the escarpment, but could not, after several days, locate her.

He asked Hattie to help him find her and if necessary to stay with her while she gave birth, but Hattie said no chimpanzee lady in her right mind would need a midwife.

The next night Mary Madelyn appeared in Cohn's cave, trailing a bloody umbilical cord, and carrying a newborn baby she timidly presented to him.

Seeing a fuzzy white baby with human eyes, Cohn ran out of the cave because he thought he had affronted God; then he ran back because he felt he hadn't.

This was a different world from the one he had been born into. In a different world different things—unusual combinations—occurred. If something wasn't kosher the Lord would have to say so. He had no trouble with words.

The Lord said nothing.

With a pair of small sterilized scissors Cohn snipped Mary Madelyn's umbilical cord, washed and knotted it, then examined the new baby. She was a compact, well-formed, curious-eyed little female who looked, indeed, like a humanoid infant, or chimpanzee-human baby. She wasn't as large as an infant chimp, according to the measurements cited by Dr. Bünder in his book, but she was healthy, spirited, and obviously bright. Cohn counted aloud to ten, and she responded by moving her lips. He was sure she would do well in school.

"Do you wike her?"

"A miracle," said Cohn. "Why wouldn't I like her?"

"I wondered if you wanted a mawe chiwd."

He said the community needed all the females it could get.

Mary Madelyn said it wasn't that easy—chimpanzee ladies bore children only every four or five years.

Cohn said they would solve it one way or another. The birth of the baby made him feel more optimistic than he had been since arriving on the island.

The baby, as she nursed at her mother's breast, regarded him with bright eyes, human eyes. Cohn was thinking of his role in raising the child. With a chimpanzee mother she is technically a chimp, but I will keep reminding her of her human source and quality. A lot depends on which genes have gone where. If the right genes have arranged themselves to their best advantage, she'll be talking soon. In a month or two he would begin reading to her.

"Shaw we caw her Juwiet?"

Cohn suggested maybe Islanda, but when Mary Madelyn pronounced it Iwanda, he said Rebekah might be preferable.

Mary Madelyn liked Honeybunch, a name Cohn occasionally called her, but they settled, at his suggestion, on Rebekah Islanda as her legal first and middle names.

Yet when they talked of her, Mary Madelyn called her Iwanda and Cohn said Rebekah. He then asked Mary Madelyn if she would mind being called another name, maybe Rachel, but she preferred to keep her own name.

That night, Cohn, making a determined effort, finished nailing together the wall of split logs he had begun to assemble when the first new chimps had appeared on the island.

He mounted the wall on rollers he had constructed—slow, squeaky, but workable. To block the entrance, he had to shove with his shoulder to roll the creaking wall across the mouth of the cave. He had dug a narrow trench for the barrier to fit in, making it less likely to topple over if it ever was rammed from the outside. A chimp or two confronting it would have to give up and walk away. It wasn't the most practical bulwark he had ever seen, but Cohn felt it would serve its purpose.

Mary Madelyn wanted to know why they had to have a wall—it would keep the fresh air out that the baby needed; and Cohn replied he was just being careful. Civilization had barely recommenced.

When the chimps arrived in a group to see the new baby, Cohn permitted them all to enter, and served them a mixture of tangerine and mango juice, which they all enjoyed; no one seemed to notice the wall he had built.

Hattie picked up the baby, and Mary Madelyn permitted only her to do so. Melchior was allowed to pat Rebekah on the head; and Esau, to show his love of children, felt her bottom and then covered the child with her blanket, aware of Mary Madelyn's nervousness.

"Trust me," the Alpha Ape assured her. "I am her good fairy."

Buz, on the other hand, showed only a negative interest in the baby girl, insisting on dragging his holding cage out of the cave because he didn't want it to be used as a crib.

"What will you use it for?" Cohn asked.

Buz said, "Storage."

"Why don't you at least say hello to your little sister?"

Buz replied he had never had a relative other than the mother who had given birth to him, and his adoptive father, who had brought him up and educated him in his home in Jersey City, Dr. Walther Bünder, Ph.D., M.D.—the kindest, wisest, most loving person he had ever met in all his life.

Cohn felt unwillingly left out—omitted, deeply disappointed.

"Don't think I've lost my affection or admiration for you, Buz, I haven't."

Buz did say he would be returning for a candy bar now and then, but he seemed still angered, and Cohn felt he must give him more attention one way or another.

When the visiting chimps had left the cave, Mary Madelyn said she hoped their own little family would stay together, and Cohn said they would indeed while Rebekah was growing up.

"She may someday be the mother of a new race of men," he said, "—if they are called that then and not by some other name."

Mary Madelyn wondered if they ought to get married. "I wov the scene that you read me wast week where Romeo and Juwiet are married by Father Wawrence."

Cohn said for his father's sake he would prefer a sort of Jewish wedding.

The baboon males on the rock groomed each other, and the three females groomed themselves and their children. Cohn had named the little girl Sara, and the boys Pat and Aloysius, after two Irish public-school chums of many years ago. Sometimes the children groomed the adult males.

One early afternoon Sara descended the rock with an unpeeled red banana in her mouth, and climbed a lichened live oak at the far edge of the tall grass, where she sat eating her fruit.

Saul of Tarsus, working the far edge of the rice paddy, spied her from the other side of the shallow pond that ran off from the rice, between the growing grain and the grass, and after a few minutes he waded through the pond—pausing from time to time as though he were simply soaking his feet—yet stealthily moving toward the oak tree where Sara sat. He slowly shinnied up the oak, stopping whenever she peered down at him, till she went on nibbling her banana. Saul of Tarsus felt amorous and he felt hungry, yet not at all sure which desire grabbed him most.

The little girl nervously peered at the chimp ascending and at first did not move because he was not in motion, but when he seemed suddenly to be much too close to her, she dropped the remains of the banana and made shrill little cries, showing her teeth in a frightened grin.

Sara climbed into the crown of the oak, Saul of Tarsus sneakily following her, pretending he wasn't. But now she screeched excitedly until the two adult males across the field leaped off the rock and came charging through the heavy grass to the trees.

Hearing their raucous alarm-barks, Saul of Tarsus hastily slid down the oak tree and knuckle-galloped back to the rice paddy, pursued by the barking baboons. The young chimp waded through the pond to the other side, where he sought the protective company of Melchior, Hattie, and his less adventurous brother.

Melchior testily demanded to know where he had been.

Saul of Tarsus swore he had been attacked by some vicious creatures. The old ape cursed out the two baboons at the edge of the water. "You stupid, dog-face monkeys, go back where you came from."

The male baboons barked raucously at the chimps, then scuttled back to the big rock, where little Sara sat among the adult females, grooming her mother. The mother had swatted her hard when she came back from the oak tree, and the child had yelped, but afterwards calmly chewed a tuber.

Cohn had visited the baboon rock, and though his hopes of communicating with these animals were dim, he had asked where they had come from and how they had survived the Flood. The baboons appeared not to be disturbed by his presence, whether they understood him or not, and went on eating and ignoring him as he questioned them at length. Cohn left, feeling he had accomplished little, and was almost certain that Buz, no matter who had faith, would not be able to teach them anything resembling a spoken language.

It was on this occasion that he named the adult males Max—the one with the bleeding eye, and Arthur—the one with the torn snout; and the look-alike females he named the three Anastasias.

Afterwards Cohn spoke sternly to Luke. "Hattie tells me you were working up a sneak-attack on Sara, the little baboon."

Luke said that Hattie didn't know her mouth from a water-hole. "That wasn't me, that was Saul of Tarsus."

"Was that you stalking the little baboon girl?" Cohn asked Saul of Tarsus, and the chimp breathily replied he thought it was his brother who had stalked her.

"Whoever it was," warned Cohn, "I don't want anybody attempting to terrorize her again."

Saul of Tarsus said all he had wanted to do was play tickle with her.

"Playing with her is one thing, scaring her half to death is something else again. If you want to play, play nice—no harm or threats of harm to an innocent child."

"Not me," said Saul of Tarsus.

"What about you?" Cohn asked Luke.

"Not me either."

Cohn smiled through his grizzled beard. "Why would anyone want to harm a little female baboon?" he asked. "This is a peaceful island. Besides, we're moving into the next civilization."

"Esau told us that baboons don't belong to our tribe," Luke said. "He said that all they are is goddam strangers. That's what he told us both."

"Never mind Esau. Strangers are people God expects us to welcome and live with."

"What for?"

"So we stop being strangers."

"Then why does he make strangers in the first place?"

"To see what we might do about it. What you do right improves you. That's the kind of conditions the Lord has imposed on us. You have to think He means well."

He listened vaguely for a whirlwind from the north and

heard only a clear blue sky over a sunlit island of massed trees and multitudes of blooming flowers surrounded by a warm, fragrant sea.

Cohn also spoke to Esau.

"I'm talking to you because you're a chimp of more than ordinary potential, not to speak of unusual physical resources and other useful endowments and attributes. It's not for nothing you're the ranking ape on this island, and since your recent reformation, one of the best workers in the vineyard."

"Which vineyard is that?"

"I use the word metaphorically—this fruitful island as vineyard."

"I am the best," Esau admitted. "Better than Buz or whoever."

Cohn pretended not to have heard "whoever." He told him he was worried about Saul of Tarsus. "He may have been about to do real harm to little Sara, the baboon child who sits with the others on that big rock on the other side of the rice paddy. Somebody said you've been telling him that the baboons don't belong here because they're strangers."

Esau said he had never liked them. "They're monkeys and ought to look like monkeys. Instead, they look like monkeys with dog-heads, I don't go for that."

Cohn then recited the First Admonition, the part about cherishing life.

Esau, after a minute's reflection, said he would try to tolerate the baboons although he didn't naturally take to them. He then asked Cohn if they were expecting a shipment of female chimps in the near future.

Cohn answered it was possible that an unattached female or two—God willing—might one day wander into the neighborhood, but it was impossible to predict when.

Esau said that masturbating gave him a headache and he would prefer something more practical.

"Sublimation is what I advise, considering circumstances," said Cohn. "That's using one's sexual energy creatively—in thought, art, or some satisfying labor."

Esau, after listening with a stunned expression, asked after Mary Madelyn. "How is she doing with her baby?"

"She's doing fine," said Cohn, not liking to talk to him about Mary Madelyn, or the baby.

"You're a lucky prick," said Esau, regarding him enviously. "I bet you get it every night."

Cohn told him to be careful of his language.

Esau rose erect, and with his powerful arms lifted Cohn off the ground in hearty embrace, all but cracking four of his ribs.

Neither of them laughed, though both were laughing.

One day when the sun shone golden, and a summer breeze blew an armada of long white clouds through the cerulean ocean-sky, Sara hopped off the big rock, where the adult baboons had sunned themselves asleep, and Pat and Aloysius were seriously grooming each other, and she danced in the warm grass. She nosed into a patch of bare earth, pushing aside small stones in search of insects but found none.

Sara traveled elegantly through the grass, stopping for a mouthful of dusty water in a small waterhole, then climbed a slender, fragrant, yellow sandalwood and fell asleep in the crook of two upper branches.

Saul of Tarsus, spotting her there, pointed her out to Esau, Buz, Esterhazy, Bromberg, and Luke, who were out prospecting for chimpanzee females, although it was agreed there were none.

Esau at once took charge. He stationed Bromberg, Esterhazy, and Luke at the trunks of three neighboring trees, and ordered Buz to go home.

"Go home yourself," Buz told him.

"This hunt isn't for an intellectual-type chimp. Your brains will get in the way."

"Which hunt are you referring to?"

"You better go home before you fall on your head."

Buz ran off to tell Cohn what was going on, but Cohn wasn't in the cave; he, and Mary Madelyn, carrying Rebekah nursing, were sitting at the beach, watching the waves.

("Suppose a boat came," said Calvin Cohn.

"Could I and Iwanda go with you?" she asked.

"Go where? No boat will ever come.")

Annoyed because nobody was there to hear his news, Buz flung a mango pit into the cave and scampered off when the noise of glass breaking sounded inside.

Esau, his hair thickening as he climbed the sandalwood where Sara lay sleeping on her stomach, as the chimps on the ground tensely watched, with a quick leap forward grabbed the baboon girl. Sara awoke as he touched her, screeching as if she had been set afire, but Esau had her by her hind legs.

He held the screaming, wildly twisting, little baboon, and slammed her head against the tree until the trunk ran blood.

When Max and Arthur, after galloping across the savanna toward Sara's shrill screams, came upon the chimps in the wood, Esau was descending the tree with the body of Sara hanging by its tail from his mouth.

The baboons, with a barking roar, leapt at the apes waiting at the base of the sandalwood, but the chimps, hooting, screaming, fought them off. Luke flung rocks underhand, as Bromberg belabored them with a heavy stick he had picked up. The baboons fled into the bush.

Esau sat on a fallen dead tree, dismembering Sara, the other chimps seated in a silent semicircle, each with his hand formally extended, each getting nothing.

After a solitary meal, relishing every morsel, grunting over the ravishing taste of fresh meat, Esau at length distributed a leg ligament to Saul of Tarsus, a small strip of gut to Esterhazy, the bloody windpipe to Luke, who fruitlessly blew into it; and Bromberg was permitted to suck Sara's eyeballs before Esau began to pry out the brain.

One by one he tossed away the bone fragments of the shattered small skull until he had exposed the pulpy, pinkly-bloodied brain. He plucked it out with his fingers, bit into it, savoring it, chewing slowly, adding a mouthful of leaves Luke had brought him to make the taste of brain last longer. Luke also wanted to keep the delicacy from being too quickly devoured.

At the end of the tastiest meal he remembered since he was a boy in the headlands, Esau handed the remains of little Sara's skeleton to Bromberg—"a nice guy." The other chimpanzees extended their upturned palms, but Bromberg, as he studied the possibilities of the repast, pushed all hands away.

They sat motionless, each concentrating on Bromberg gnawing what was left of flesh on the bones. He handed a few bare bones around, the right arm to Luke, who, Esterhazy complained, had been of no earthly help on the hunt. He got both of Sara's kneecaps. The chimps sniffed the bones, gave them a lick or two, and threw them away.

Esau, lying in the grass, belched resonantly. "I am the Alpha of them all," he murmured as he fell asleep.

His companions sat on the ground studying Sara's naked skeleton.

Cohn, after inspecting the sack containing the remains of Sara that Buz had collected and delivered to him, was horrified, appalled, embittered, saddened.

He thundered against the chimps who had participated in the baboon hunt, calling them depraved killers. For their evil deed he threatened painful punishment. He swore he would flay, uproot, exile them for their brutality, disrespect for the Admonitions; for their insensitivity to the welfare of the Island community, to the changed world and altered conditions of earthly survival.

As Cohn railed against them in hoarse, terrifying tones, Buz covered both big ears with his hands, and Mary Madelyn temporarily hid the baby in the bushes.

When he had calmed down and reflected, although grieved, tormented, still angered, Cohn felt he had to deal more subtly with the apes involved in Sara's murder. Rage and curses would get him rage and curses.

These apes, after all, were not the naïve chimpanzees of the past, many of whose recent progenitors had performed as comedians in vaudeville, television, zoos. The island creatures were privileged characters who spoke, and thought, in a complex human tongue, chimps who had improved themselves, and, one had hoped, their lives and lot.

In the schooltree they had heard, and daily discussed, Cohn's lectures on history, science, and literature; and his stories, maxims, recitations, homilies, exhortations—some of which they had spontaneously applauded. And they had had before them the example of their teacher as moral being, family man, author of the Seven Admonitions. When, therefore, would their education take hold, deepen conscience, help them become better, more responsible, living beings? When would they experience that inspired insight that would wake in them what civilization might mean? Who would have thought that this chimpanzee elite would destroy and devour an innocent child?

Cohn planned a new course of lectures, oriented around the matter of significant values. And he made it a point to talk to each chimp.

"Why did you do it, Esterhazy?" Cohn asked the bookkeeperish ape.

"Esau said to."

"Don't you have a will of your own?"

"Not yet," said Esterhazy.

Cohn sat shivah for a week.

*

He would bury Sara's bones.

A funeral was in order, a ceremony of public mourning and respect for life—though they were strangers to her—for the life of the deceased, a child who would never know what it was to be other than a child. A bare few of the chimpanzee community attended, but of those implicated in Sara's murder, only Esterhazy was present.

Mary Madelyn was there, wearing her white dress, which she had to remove every time she nursed the baby. Hattie sat close by them, grooming Mary Madelyn's arms and happily tickling the baby's pink feet so that it giggled or wailed at serious moments, embarrassing its mother and disturbing Cohn.

Melchior, lips puckered, soberly listened to Cohn's graveside eulogy. Buz, thinking his thoughts, was present. And George the gorilla, sitting high in a neighboring tree, looked down at the services, sobered by them. He seemed to have a natural appreciation of funerals. No official Kaddish was recited for the dead child, but Cohn, to George's pleasure, put on a record of his father singing "El Molei Rachameem," a simple prayer for the dead. Dead is dead, who needs more than a song of remembrance?

Reversing his role as digger of bones, Cohn buried the child's skeleton—he had reconstructed it as best he could—near a small natural garden of flowers not far from the schooltree. None of the baboon relatives was at the funeral although

Buz had been sent to invite them. He said they hadn't let him approach their rock, confronting him with a yapping chorus of enraged alarm-barks and threats. He hadn't stayed to argue with them.

"They are stupid yokels," said Buz.

*

At the schooltree the next morning, with all scholars present, the killers of Sara sitting together in a tight cluster of males high in the eucalyptus, which gave forth—after a night's fresh rain—an expansive aromatic odor, Cohn, his face raised toward the crown of the tree, spoke directly at Esau, saying certain things. For instance: "If you depreciate lives, the worth of your own diminishes. Therefore remember the Seven Admonitions."

Esau coughed dryly.

Waxing poetic, Cohn said a life gone was a gone life. A flower, or sunrise, no longer existed for it. Neither did a cup of tea—if tea was your dish. The gone life knew it not any longer. No one could describe Nothing, but one's life gone was an aspect, a mode, of nothing. Whoever lived even in Paradise—if that's where she/he had gone—was not here where the weather was more interesting because it varied as the seasons changed.

"Or to put it in more practical terms, when you are dead, a fig or sun seed will not tickle your taste buds, and no warm hand will groom you again."

He said that a child—whosesoever—had an inborn, God-given right to grow up to be more than a child. "A life—to be a life—must run its course. Thus it achieves freedom of choice, within the usual limitations, but certainly the freedom to imagine the future. Having a future—or thinking you have—waters the gardens of the mind. As though one lives in two places at the same time. Therefore," said Cohn, "it was an evil act of deprivation to destroy little Sara's future."

The apes, though not unmoved, applauded moderately. Mary Madelyn gave a loud "Hurrah," but Buz, detesting homilies—they insulted his intelligence—snorted.

When Cohn, having expressed himself, sat down in his

chair, Esau rose, expanding his chest and grabbing a bushy branch to steady himself. More and more he resembled a small gorilla, not necessarily a runt, Cohn thought, but perhaps a runt and a half. When Esau's voice boomed forth, George, assailed by it, dropped out of his cedar and walked away. Esau called him a fat pig, and George blew him some gorilla gas.

Esau proclaimed that every chimp he had known "in the good old days in the highland" had hunted small baboons. It was a perfectly natural, naturally selective, thing to do. The hunt was stimulating and the flesh delicious. "Also it gives me a lift to hear the sound of a crunchy skull that you have batted against something hard.

"And besides that, those baboons are dirty, stinking, thieving monkeys, interfering into everybody's business. They breed like rats and foul up all over the clean bush. If we don't control their population they will squat all over this island and we will have to get off.

"And further to that, all of us are mighty sick and tired of eating so much goddam fruit, plus moldy matzos for dessert."

The male chimps clapped heartily.

"Of course," Esau went on almost congenially, "if there was a piece of sex around instead of that horseass sublimation you are trying to trick on us, we would have something to keep our thoughts going, but the way it has turned out, only our Jewish instructor has sex whenever he might want it, with somebody who happens to be related closer to us; and the rest of us have nothing but our dongs to pull."

Buz stood up and clapped loudly but sat down before Cohn could say anything.

Cohn rose and remarked that since the Day of Devastation, followed by the Late Unlamented Flood, this island had become a privileged place, a sanctuary for the few lives that remained in the world. "And it's got to stay a sanctuary, even if that means a certain amount of food monotony and a few other minor inconveniences."

He asked Esau and his hunter friends to promise they would not terrorize any of the other baboon children; and Esau said if that was what the community wanted, that's what they would get, even if it went against his personal grain.

Cohn did not suggest a voice vote, although tempted to; he

wasn't sure he had the votes to win—but he told Esau to raise his right arm and pledge "I will not kill. I will obey the Seven Admonitions."

Esau raised his left arm and solemnly swore he would never again "quote, never again"—kill an innocent female baboon child, and Esterhazy and Bromberg swore along with him.

Pat and Aloysius, groomed immaculate by their mothers, went with them for a root-dig and soon outdistanced and lost the ladies. Climbing a tree to see where they were, they found themselves staring through some branches at Esterhazy, he as astonished as they.

His fur risen, Esterhazy let out a long distress-hoot.

The baboon boys, not waiting to hear the end of it, leaped to the ground and discovered they were being chased by the chimps who had immediately responded to Esterhazy's call—Bromberg, Luke, Saul of Tarsus, and after several minutes, Esau himself. Esterhazy also pursued the baboon boys. Nobody mentioned a pledge of any sort. Besides, that was a pledge not to interfere with a female, and these madly running boys were no girls. Girls couldn't run that fast.

Twisting and darting amid a grove of palms a short distance from the sea, Pat and Aloysius, unable to contend with the speed and agility of the adult chimps racing after them, scuttered up a nut palm, Aloysius behind Pat, both emitting screams as they hastened into the crown.

Esau stationed his men at the base of the bearded date palms nearest the one the boy baboons had gone up, and hand over hand, he climbed the tree after them.

Aloysius, seeing him coming up, flung himself into an adjoining, shorter, broad-crowned palm; and Pat, making a similar large leap, stayed on Aloysius's tail, still scream-barking.

Because Bromberg was stationed at the trunk of this tree, without stopping they jumped into the top of the nearest stout palm—at the bottom of which, they discovered, Esterhazy stood guard.

Esau had plunged after them into the broad-crowned palm.

The baboon children leaped at the trunk of a long palm arced like a scimitar, held tight, and quickly raced up to its feathery small crown. At that moment Max and Arthur, the adult baboons, came roaring into the palm grove with ferocious barking and fangs bared.

They simultaneously attacked Bromberg, who tried fending them off with sharp barks and both arms flailing, but the baboons penetrated his defense and tore at his legs and pink scrotum. Bromberg, shrilly screaming, snarled, and in a moment of pause, hobbled off, then ran, bleeding down his legs.

The adult baboons fought fiercely with Esterhazy, who ran up the long arced palm pursued by Max.

Arthur, noisily jabbing at Luke and Saul of Tarsus protecting each other back to back, snapped at them in feinting leaps, but was afraid to charge two male chimpanzees. They hooted, barked, showed their teeth, and pawed at the jumping baboon, holding him off.

Esau had catapulted himself into the slender curved palm the little boys were in now, both screeching as they peered down at the baboon males on the ground.

Aloysius jumped back onto the shorter palm, lost his grip on a swishing branch, grabbed and lost another, and tumbled twenty feet to the ground, hitting Luke and knocking him out. Aloysius escaped into the bushes, followed by Arthur. Max soon scampered after them.

Little Pat, still in the palms, hopped into a live oak at the edge of the palm grove, and as Esau swung in after him, jumped again into the grove, still chased by the Alpha Ape. Pat, taking a desperate chance, dove into the bushes below, and as he lay gasping on the ground on his belly, trying to breathe, was pounced on by Saul of Tarsus and Bromberg.

Max and Arthur returned on the run, searching for Pat, but Esau, who had snatched the squirming, terrified boy away from his captors, standing erect, his body hair heavily full, swung the screaming baboon by his legs at the adult baboons. They drew back, snarling, and were at once savaged by Luke and Esterhazy. Max and Arthur rushed into the bushes.

Esau, whirling the boy baboon over his head, slammed him hard against a rock. The breaking skull made the sound of a small explosion. Pat now hung limp in Esau's hand.

Squatting on the ground, facing his hungry companions, he began to peel the bone fragments off the baboon's bloody skull to dig at once for the brain.

Bromberg, still bleeding from wounds on both legs, timidly requested the testicles, and Esau promised him one if he behaved while he ate his meal.

The twins, their palms extended, in small voices begged for a bit of flesh; and Esau stopped chewing little Pat's remains long enough to give them both a good tickle until they broke into excruciating laughter.

Esau resumed eating the yummy brain after reminding those present what they already knew—that little Pat could in no way be described as a baboon girl.

While strolling with Buz, as Cohn attempted to explain the Second Law of Thermodynamics and his boy corrected his dod's facts, they came upon four chimps silently observing a fifth voraciously feasting on the boy baboon.

Cohn ran furiously into their midst, tore the partially eaten cadaver out of Esau's bloody hands, and with a cry flung it deep into the bushes. Saul of Tarsus watched it in flight, and when it fell, was about to bolt for it, but seeing the other apes sitting frozen, did not move.

"Each devours his neighbor's flesh," Cohn shouted from Isaiah, swearing he had begged them not to repeat this heinous crime.

"Wouldn't you think you owed me some consideration for how comfortable I have helped make your lives? You have work, leisure, free schooling and health care. You have survived a Disastrous Flood and live in comparative peace on an indescribably beautiful island. We have a functioning community and are on the verge of an evolutionary advance, if not breakthrough. And how do you show your appreciation of these advantages? In the murder of children!"

He accused them of ingratitude. He called them hypocrites. "Wasn't it only yesterday that three of you raised your hands in a solemn oath to obey the Seven Admonitions, yet hadn't the slightest intention to do so? You're a disgrace to decent chimpanzees wherever they may be."

They listened with interest as Cohn castigated them. Only Esau was restless as he rubbed the blood off his hairy fingers with oak leaves. One by one he wiped the fingers, then with a broken twig cleaned under his fingernails.

Cohn ran on: "After all the poems and stories we discussed in class regarding the sanctity of life, and after the homily I preached at little Sara's funeral; to wit, a child's right to experience the awakening of sensibility, thought, the discovery of self, and afterwards to emerge in the world in the majesty of youth—despite that, you have with your hands and teeth torn their bodies apart and cannibalized them."

"What the hell are you—some crazy kind of vegetarian?" Esau asked, still cleaning his fingernails.

Cohn called them corrupt and brutish evildoers, hard-hearted beasts with little understanding or compassion.

"Remember man destroyed himself by his selfishness and indifference to those who were different from, or differed with, him. He scorned himself to death. At least learn that lesson if you want to evade his fate.

"I have no desire to punish you corporally," he announced, "therefore by the authority vested in me as Protector of the Community, I hereby officially exile the three of you—Esau, the falsely redeemed—you fake—and Bromberg, who has no second thought after a limp first—and Esterhazy, coward and fool."

He said he would chastise Luke and Saul of Tarsus at a later date in a manner befitting their age.

They both cheered.

"Quiet," ordered Cohn. "Now, therefore, I order you three to pack your gear and leave this end of the island. If there was another island in the neighboring waters, I would exile you there, provided there was a ferry boat to transport you—but since there isn't another island, so far as I know, I want you to go elsewhere on this, far away and out of sight. If we lay eyes on you again, I warn you of direst consequences."

After he had said this, Cohn felt himself trembling.

The three adult apes glanced uneasily at each other and then Esau rose with a bellow to his full height and advanced on Cohn with four fangs gleaming. Buz, Esterhazy, Bromberg, Luke, and Saul of Tarsus noisily scattered.

Cohn, frozen an instant, began to back up slowly, wishing he had brought along his spear when he had started out for a walk with Buz. What can I do that Esau can't—or doesn't expect? If I try force against his force I won't have much to show, if anything.

He planned at least a quick kick in the groin, and if that worked, to take off for the cave hurriedly, and once there, to shove the defensive wall across the opening. When Esau had left the scene he would sneak out and round up Mary Madelyn and the baby.

Yet Cohn knew that if he got close enough to kick Esau where it hurt, he was close enough to be upended by Esau's longer reach.

The Alpha Ape pounded his chest. "You busybody horse-ass, you stole my natural food out of my mouth. You possessed my betrothed and forced her to bear your half-breed child. I will break every Jewbone in your head."

He advanced toward Cohn, standing erect, both arms extended, hoot-barking, the ferocity of his expression fearsome.

This is no place for me, thought Cohn, wishing for a sling-shot; but he had none, so he retreated, making ugly faces and disgusting noises, but without a frightening mask they had no effect.

"Maybe we ought to talk, Esau. Let's reason together."

He turned to run as the ape pounced on him, snatching Cohn like a fierce lover, lifting him off the ground. Instead of embracing him he flung him down like a dead dog. Cohn grunted in pain and tried to roll into the brush. Esau dragged him forth by his leg and with a snarl fell on him.

"Help—Buz," Cohn cried.

But there was no Buz, until Cohn caught a split-second glimpse of him sitting on an upper branch of a tree, looking down at the combat with absorbed interest, as he peeled an orange.

Life grew dark for Cohn. Death was a white eye centered in a staring black face. That was how he saw Esau, who seemed to be choking him to death. Afterwards he would bash Cohn's skull with a rock and eat his brain as a delicacy. Cohn hoped it poisoned the evil ape.

He himself wandered in Paradise, trying to exit, but all portals were locked. Woe is me, he muttered, how does one get back into life? He had asked this question of the Lord and heard no answer. He heard his own rapid, choked, diminishing breathing.

At this moment of his dying Cohn felt already dead; but

Esau, as though he had heard a telephone ring and had decided to answer, loosened his hands on Cohn's neck and fell to the side like a sack of flour. He lay utterly still.

That was no miracle. Mary Madelyn, holding Rebekah in her arm, had sneaked up behind Esau with Cohn's claw hammer, and as the chimps in the trees gazed in stupefaction, had bounced the tool against his head.

That evening, a throat-bruised, hoarse-voiced Cohn bandaged Esau's wound after sewing twenty-one stitches in his scalp; and in the morning the bandaged ape hobbled forth, with a severe headache and small borrowed suitcase, into permanent exile.

Bromberg and Esterhazy had vanished. And Luke and Saul of Tarsus were let off with strong reprimands. Both promised to mend their ways. Buz swore he had been about to drop like Tarzan out of the tree onto Esau's back to rescue Cohn, but Mary Madelyn had got there first.

He did, however, say he hadn't taken kindly to those nasty curses Cohn had laid on the race of chimpanzees.

In a week Cohn paid a census visit to baboon rock and noticed that Aloysius was missing.

"Where's the little baboon boy?" he politely inquired, and the two males roused themselves with malignant roars and showed threatening fangs. The Anastasias, one pregnant, barked mournfully. Cohn hastily ended his visit.

That evening he found little Aloysius's half-eaten, decomposing body smelling up a fig tree full of rotting fruit, the cadaver lying athwart a branch where it had been tossed.

Cohn felt himself a failure.

I have failed to teach these chimpanzees a basic truth. How can they survive if they do to fellow survivors what men did to each other before the Second Flood? How will they evolve into something better than men?

"Who did that terrible thing to Aloysius, Buz?" he asked, and the chimp, devouring a juicy mango, said he had no idea.

"What can we do to dispel the evil rife in this land?"

Buz said it was Cohn's fault for not teaching love. Cohn said he had tried to teach the good life, but it hadn't come to much.

Buz then advised him to remove the false Admonition he had put up on the face of the escarpment.

"Why do you call it false?"

"Because God is love."

Cohn said he wouldn't feel secure promising a loving God. Afterwards he realized he hadn't said that; he had quietly thought it.

He told Buz he was discouraged and would try anything that helped the cause of peace.

When he came out of the woodland the next day, after a count of new fruit trees, to his astonishment but not surprise, Cohn beheld Buz standing in a balconied enclosure two-thirds of the way up the escarpment, preaching to the chimpanzees assembled below, where the waterfall sometimes sprayed them, but they seemed not to mind.

The chutzpah of that little chimp.

Cohn discovered that Buz, without seeking his consent, had altered the second of the Seven Admonitions on the face of the escarpment. He had removed the "not," and the Admonition read "God is   love, God is God."

Cohn decided he would disassemble the second Admonition altogether, except "Remember Him." God, he thought, would not mind so long as he didn't mess around with basics.

It would take a while, given the present spiritual resources of the chimps, to get a new morality in place and working. Even Moses had had trouble, and Isaiah had all but blown his voice crying out against the ethical failures of the Israelites.

At the foot of the escarpment stood the small band of chimpanzees, among them Mary Madelyn holding Rebekah, now very lively. Melchior smoked a homemade cigar rolled from some tough tobacco leaves he had stumbled on on the island. And Hattie remarked she felt she was now Mrs. Melchior, whether they were married or not, even though Melchior had no great interest in sex anymore.

Then Esterhazy and Bromberg slithered in among the others, like escaped convicts who had been slinking around in the rain forest. Yet when they pressed their palms together and sank to their knees, Cohn considered rescinding their sentence to exile. He might give them another chance, but not Esau, because his nature was close to evil.

And Luke, and Saul of Tarsus, were on their knees, praying, but not George the gorilla.

George wasn't there anymore. He had disappeared a few days ago. The rumor was he had trudged off to the headlands, and no one knew for sure if this was a temporary move or one for all time.

Cohn, not without a pang, had watched him lumbering away in the sunset, carrying a small bundle of his belongings at the end of a stick on his shoulder.

"Blessed are the chimpanzees," Buz preached from the terrace of the yellow escarpment, "for they hov inherited the whole earth."

And the chimps below let out a resounding hearty cheer.

Buz later told Cohn he thought that things would go better hereafter in the island community; but Cohn pessimistically reminded him that Christianity, too, hadn't prevented the Holocaust—"the Jewish one I lectured on most recently in class"—nor had it stayed the Day of Devastation.

Buz angrily accused Cohn of never approving anything, pragmatic or spiritual, that he was interested in or had done; and Cohn vehemently denied it.

For an instant they faced each other in anger, right arms upraised, then turned and walked/knuckle-walked away.

After an early supper, as Mary Madelyn was rinsing the wooden platters in the water bucket, Cohn lit the lamp, and pressing his shoulder to the wooden wall, pushed it creaking on its rollers across the mouth of the cave.

"God is wov," she reminded him. "Why are you shutting the cave off from daywight and fresh air?"

Cohn said he had this feeling that evil persisted in the land, and doubted Buz's sermon would do much to allay it. "It will take a while to get things in order; the atmosphere has been tense since those baboons appeared in the neighborhood. I've been wondering what God is up to."

She asked Cohn when they might get married, and he said they were more or less married. "We must breed daughters."

Cohn held Rebekah in his lap, dressed in a little white sailcloth jumper he had sewed for her; he was about to tell her a bedtime story.

Rebekah, though a half-chimp infant, looked more than

half-human. She liked to sit on the ground on her hard little behind, playing with a straw doll Cohn had made for her, whose head she had eaten.

According to Dr. Bünder's book, she was behind in chimp infant movements, yet ahead in speech. She said dada and mama, and counted to five on one foot and up to ten on the other. She was bright and pretty and chuckled deeply. Her eyes were intensely curious, lively, blue; Cohn was tender to her, enormously fond of his little girl.

He often pondered her fate. Would she live her life out on the island? Was she destined to be the mother of a humanoid-chimpanzoid race if she mated with a full chimp, possibly Buz, someday, if he behaved? Cohn hoped his little girl had been created for a better than ordinary, personally fulfilling, future. At that moment there was a snap-knock on the protective wooden wall, as though someone had thrown a stone against it.

"Open the blosted gate," Buz called from outside. "Whot is there to fear?"

Cohn didn't like the question and would not move the wall.

"Who's out there with you?"

"Just myself."

"What do you want?"

"A condy bar," Buz shouted in frustration, kicking the wall with his bare foot, at once wishing he hadn't.

"Enter," said Cohn.

Mary Madelyn quickly tucked the baby into the crib as Cohn shoved at the wall with his shoulder and slowly pushed it open.

Buz knuckle-limped in. On the way to the candy box on the shelf he peered at Rebekah in her crib. "I hov forgiven her."

Cohn said he was pleased to hear it, especially since the baby had nothing against him.

"We all feel good will to you, Buz, although we rarely see you except in the schooltree or at public ceremonies."

Buz swallowed a vanilla coconut bar and began chewing a chocolate. He said, with mouth full, it wasn't a kind thing Cohn had done to evict him from his long-standing home.

Cohn reminded him that he had left the cave willingly. "You said you didn't want to live with a squalling brat—you had your private thoughts to think."

Buz seemed to be thinking them. He was, as he ate the candy, staring at Mary Madelyn's bosom in a way that made her blush. She covered the baby with a second blanket.

Cohn got Buz's silver crucifix out of his valise and offered it to him. "You've taken all your worldly goods out of the cave—do you want the cross I've been holding for you?"

"Not now," Buz said. "I hov no pockets on me."

"You can put it around your neck."

"My neck is bigger than it was, the chain wouldn't fit."

Cohn told him to try it.

Buz said no.

Cohn was on the qui vive, when a sulphurous odor assailed his nostrils—nothing like George's, this was a dreadfully foul smell—and his heart sank as he beheld Esau, smirking like the Devil himself, standing in the cave.

Cohn cursed himself for having neglected to roll back the protective wall after Buz had entered. "You knew all the time he hadn't gone into exile," Cohn accused his boy.

Buz said he had heard a rumor but wasn't sure. Cohn was angered and fearful.

With Esau, Esterhazy appeared; and Bromberg, Luke, and Saul of Tarsus entered the cave, wearing clay masks stolen from Cohn's collection, all holding sharp rocks aimed at his head.

Esau, his soiled bandage wrapped around his thick skull, had become heavy-bodied, his face bloated. He looked as if he had spent his time in hiding drinking banana beer. His glazed, reddened eyes were mean-looking.

Mary Madelyn, letting out a cry, snatched the baby from her crib and tried to get out of the cave, but Esterhazy, raising the saber he had found hanging on a hook on the wall, barred her way.

Cohn warned Esterhazy to watch where he pointed the weapon or he would be docked a month's fruit rations.

He then said to Esau, "I have treated you well since you appeared at this end of the island. I pulled a painful tooth and bandaged your wounded head. Be merciful, Esau."

Not mentioning who had wounded the head he had bandaged, Cohn tried to move toward Mary Madelyn and Rebekah and found that his wrists were tightly held by each twin.

Esau, with a sneaky deft movement, snatched Rebekah out of her whimpering mother's arms, and tossed the baby to Bromberg. Rebekah gurgled as she went sailing through the air.

Cohn flung the twins aside and sprang forward to recover the child, as Bromberg threw her to Esterhazy. The bookkeeperish ape caught her in one large hand as Mary Madelyn came rushing at him.

He flipped her to Saul of Tarsus, who passed her to Luke, who scuttled out of the cave.

Mary Madelyn made choking noises of grief as she beat off the twins and burst out of the cave on her fours in pursuit of her daughter.

Cohn prayed for Esau's destruction where he stood—let him drop enormously dead—but nothing came of it. The Alpha Ape lived on in the best of health.

Esau and the other chimps scurried out of the cave, Buz carrying the saber in his teeth. They had left Cohn lying on the ground with a mound of rocks piled on his chest.

"Et tu, Buz?" Cohn was heartbroken beyond his anguish for Rebekah.

He lifted aside one rock after another, not without pressing pain, then rising shakily from the floor, grabbed his iron spear from its rack and charged after the evildoers in the gathering dusk.

The apes met in the gorilla's abandoned cedar near the schooltree and curiously inspected little Rebekah. Esau sat on a high branch, tickling her little pink feet and peeking under the skirt of her jumper to see what was there.

The chimps surrounding him looked on with absorbed interest until Mary Madelyn appeared, distraught, and mumbling to herself. She begged them in heartbroken tones to return her innocent baby and she would give them anything they wanted, promising never again to flee at their approach when she was in heat.

As the sun sank, the island sky turned purple, with zigzagging rivers of black. The apes wandered like Bedouins from one tree to another with the little girl, as her mother brachiated after them, and Cohn, having abandoned his massive spear, pursued them on foot, his arms extended as he ran, to catch the child if she accidentally fell, or was dropped to the ground by the apes.

He begged them, as he ran, to be merciful. "You may think me a foolishly fond father, but Rebekah—I give you my word—is a gifted child. She's been talking more than a month, and counts to ten on her toes. She's a child of unusual promise, also musically inclined, and may someday be a concert pianist if we can come up with a piano and get a music-education program going.

"It's no exaggeration at all to say that the future of us on this island lives in Rebekah's being, the future of another and—God willing—better civilization, a more idealistic and altruistic one, I certainly hope. She is, as I'm sure you know, half your kind and half mine, and from the unique assortment of her inherited genes, and no doubt of those from one of you in the womb of her maturity—no more than a dozen years from now—the naturally best species of the future will probably be derived. Think of that, gentlemen!

"Please be careful of her—she is our dear child. I urge you to lay her gently on the ground where we can recover her and take her home. I assure you we will reward you all and treat you as heroes."

The apes in the trees seemed to pause in their game to listen to Cohn; and Mary Madelyn, pursuing them without regard for her safety, after a moment of moving stealthily forward, was able to land in the same tree with four of them and almost had her hand on Rebekah, when the astonished Bromberg, come to life, flipped her across the tree aisle to Esau, erect atop a short flowering palm on the left. Esau caught a bad throw but held tight as the other male chimps dived out of the tree into three palms nearby. Mary Madelyn, moaning, sprang into the crown of a nut palm, but Esau had, with a grunt, already leapt forward with the child in his arm, into an adjoining tree.

Cohn, from the ground, promised that if they returned the baby to her loving parents, to either if not both—no doubt this was their ultimate aim, none of them was an intentional kidnapper—he would happily reward them with gifts of 500 sacks of brown rice, about 200 bananas, 48 of which were pulpy red, 56 sweet tangerines, 3 boxes of dried figs, about a ton of sunflower seeds, 32 coconut candy bars, half a large vat of fizzy banana beer, and/or every other object in the cave, including his books, articles of clothing, not excluding his warm poncho; with the cave itself thrown in, and also the outside hut—a joy in summertime—if they mercifully released the little girl, unharmed.

Esau laughed to himself in the deepening dark.

He slung the baby sideways to Esterhazy, who shifted her from one arm to the other and pitched her in an arc over Mary Madelyn's head to Bromberg. Rebekah, for a while wailing faintly, had now ceased crying. In the early evening light she sailed in slow motion through the air, soundlessly in every direction.

It seemed to Cohn that the apes in the trees had become tired or bored; yet their game went on in the dark, and he felt his last hope for his child fall apart.

"Oh, you barbarian beasts! Who but the heartless would tear a little girl from her parents' arms, and not for a minute respond to their piteous pleading—tearful cries, begging—yet relentlessly go on playing a harrowing game of toss-the-baby, without in the least being moved by their distress?

"A curse on your souls, if you have any, and may the Almighty God forever punish you for your wickedness. I pray there's a Third Flood, higher and deeper than the others."

Then Cohn sank to his knees and prayed to God to save his child's life—but after a while rose, thinking, maybe He doesn't like fifty-percent chimps who are fifty-percent human. Or maybe He can't recall the sound of my voice?

Night had descended. The last of light had disappeared in the palm grove, but he could still make out the small white bundle floating through the air from tree to tree, pursued by a fatigued, desolated, brachiating figure approaching closer to the child in motion—until, as darkness grew profound, Rebekah fell, or was pitched at a glowing boulder below; and the two male baboons, Max and Arthur, waiting in the bush, made off with her bloody remains.

It was Cohn's heartbroken impression that no one had willed the event; it had happened because "it was prepared for this," Rashi had said, "from the first six days of creation."

When the half-moon rose, Cohn found his spear where he had abandoned it. (Would having hurled it at Esau have changed the course of events and saved Rebekah? Would Mary Madelyn, for instance, have caught the baby in her arms if Esterhazy or Bromberg, seeing the spear split Esau's hairy chest, had dropped it in malice or fright?)

Cohn hunted Satan in the nightwood.

He beheld a white bandaged head in the shadowy trees, took aim, and flung the spear with shuddering force. There was a terrible, groaning cry of an ape unwilling to give up life; and a body toppled out of the tree and plummeted to earth.

When Cohn, after spending most of the night searching for Mary Madelyn, came back to bury Esau at daybreak, the ape clutching the spear in his chest, who had bled to death from the massive wound, was not Esau but an albino chimpanzee. Not a god-like mysterious creature—simply a soiled white ape from the headlands, turning black in death; but Cohn felt as though he had murdered a man.

He sought Buz and found him sleeping soundly in a nest in the schooltree. He had forbidden the apes to sleep there, and only Buz had disobeyed. Cohn silently climbed the tree and did what he felt he must.

Buz, awaking with a hoot of fright, found that both his legs had been caught in a noose of vines, and his body trussed to the bough he had built his sleep-nest on. He bared his teeth at Cohn, and Cohn, startled, slapped his face.

"Wot hov I done?" asked the ape. "I om innocent."

Cohn told him he must punish him for betraying his dod, stepmother, and half-sister; he would do it by snapping the wires of his artificial voice-box, depriving him of speech.

Buz, in agitation, begged him not to do *thot*, and Cohn, though grieved, answered he had no choice.

"You betrayed us to those murderous apes. Because of you I unblocked the barrier, and now the child is dead. You were jealous of her and conspired with Esau and the others to kidnap her."

Buz blamed Cohn. "I came for a condy bar for my sweet tooth. You forgot to close the blosted gate."

"You let them lay rocks on my chest. I could barely take a breath, but you did nothing to help me. You left me there in pain. You could have come back but didn't."

Buz swore he had joined their game to spy on them. "I plonned to warn you if they plotted to kill you."

Cohn drew the wire clippers from his pants pocket.

"Please don't take my speech away," Buz begged. "Take anything but thot. Dr. Bünder wouldn't commit thot nosty crime on his worst enemy. He loved me as a father loves his child."

"I was a father and loved my child. The Lord giveth and taketh away."

Pong pong. Cohn clipped the knotted rusty wires through the hairs on his neck, but not before Buz had groaned, "I om not Buz, my name ist Gottlob."

The apes assembled by habit in the empty schooltree the next morning and threw sun seeds and stones at Cohn's head as he sat on his teaching stool.

He had searched in vain for Mary Madelyn, but she was nowhere to be found. Neither was Esau present, nor had Cohn seen Gottlob again.

As he began to talk the twins booed. Hattie shrilly hooted at him. It sounded like "Hoity-toity."

Cohn was moved to talk about Rebekah, tell stories of what she was like—for a moment attempt to undo in language what had been done to her; to bring her back to life. They listened in silence but when he stopped talking, overcome by grief for his little girl, the twins mocked him. They tore out bunches of eucalyptus leaves and, hoo-hooting, showered them on him, together with some sharp small rocks they had carried up the tree in a sack. Hattie and Melchior flung palm nuts at Cohn. He begged them all to fast for the future, and got boos and gurgles in response. It was then he realized the chimpanzees had lost their speech. He hadn't planned it thus. That it had worked out so burdened Cohn's heart.

He hurried to the cave to hide behind his bulwark till things settled down and he figured out what to do next. Was there a way to escape the island? He planned to build a raft on the shore. High tide would float it out.

What if it drifted in the ocean forever? Suppose Cohn and his beard had to live forever on a raft?

As he hastened to the cave, he caught sight of Mary Madelyn

in the field beyond the waterfall, this side the rice paddy, her sexual flower risen like a stiff red flag, her white sail dress torn into rags on the grass. She crouched as Esau, eating a bruised banana, mounted her. He pumped once, dismounted carefully, peeled himself another banana.

Then Gottlob, who had been looking on studiously, entered Mary Madelyn twice. Shutting both eyes he concentrated, as he pumped vigorously and dismounted; then he reentered, pumped eight hard deliberate times, and proudly descended. He seemed to have shamed Esau, who had stopped chewing his small banana and would not look him in the eye.

Gottlob pounded his chest and indicated by raising his fist that he was the Alpha Ape.

Esau did not contest the matter.

"Mary Madelyn," Cohn heartbrokenly called to her. "Here I am!"

Sighting him, the three chimpanzees knuckle-ran for the trees.

"Don't forget Romeo and Juliet," he called. "Love, Wov, Lwov!"

He waited for her response but heard nothing. Cohn wondered for a minute if he had gone deaf. Or hadn't she wanted to hear him? She was lost without words.

That night, as he was stuffing his gear into duffel bags, a gang of chimps rammed down his protective wall with a huge log they carried, and poured into the cave, Gottlob leading the way. Cohn had hidden under the bed.

The chimps feasted on fresh and dried fruit, and on cans of food banged open with a hammer or thrown against the wall—tuna, olives, spaghetti, and beans. They tore apart Cohn's threadbare underwear, patched trousers, poncho, and other wearing apparel; destroyed his writing instruments, platters and tumblers, clay masks and flower vases, books and paper. They broke his saber at the hilt, hitting it on the fireplace ledge, and smashed the stock of the 30.06 Winchester by batting it against the rock wall. All the beer they couldn't drink they poured on the ground and sloshed around in. Gottlob put on Cohn's galoshes and waded in the banana beer.

The apes then pulled down, and shattered with the iron

spear, the wooden storage shelves Cohn had built on first arriving on the island.

Esau, with the claw hammer that had bloodied his head, smashed all the cantor's old records, and in three savage strokes demolished the portable phonograph. Its insides hung out.

The apes apprehended Cohn, binding his arms with a metal chain he had once tied a trunk with, and they looped a rope around his neck. As they tightly tied him up—his arms behind his back, his legs, on Gottlob's insistence, trussed together—they laughed, screamed, barked, hooted, filling the echoing cave with impossible noise. But in the place where the wrecked phonograph stood, a rabbinic voice recited the law.

God's Mercy

IN THE DAY they ascended in sunlight, and at night through a cloud of stars drenching the mountainside.

Cohn's wrists were bound by leather thongs; he carried a bundle of split wood against his chest. A noose hung loose around his skinny neck, its frayed rope trailing behind him as he plodded up the stone mountain. He wore his white kitl, not a warm garment this cold night.

Buz trailed behind him, walking erect, a terry-cloth turban on his head and a pair of Cohn's old sandals on his feet.

At a turn in the narrow road they met a beggar, a surprise to all.

He stretched forth his bony seven-fingered hand, but Cohn said he couldn't possibly reach into his pocket because his hands were bound.

"So say it in words."

"My words are questions."

"Ask."

"For instance, are you the Lord's Messenger? Or possibly the Messiah?"

"I am a beggar who begs."

"Begs what?"

"A blessing."

"I wish I had one to give."

"Oho," said the beggar, disappearing in a cloud of mist as deep as an avalanche of snow.

Cohn had heard of such encounters on mountain roads.

"Who was that?" he asked anyway. "Pong," was all Buz said.

Cohn wondered what would happen if he tried running down the mountain, but Buz ran faster than he and if by chance he stepped on Cohn's trailing rope it could break his neck.

So he climbed the stone mountain in his bare feet, holding the split wood against his chest.

"Buz," said Cohn, "you are my beloved son, tell me where we are going. I think I know but would like you to say so."

"Pong."

At an altitude where five evergreens grew in a bunch they came upon an open cave with an altar gleaming within.

Cohn dropped the wood on the ground and relieved himself against the mountain before gathering up the pieces and approaching the altar.

Buz seemed to look at a watch he didn't have and pointed it was time.

"Where's this ram in the thicket?" asked Cohn with a bleat.

Buz wagged his finger at his dod.

Though he had known, Cohn turned icy cold. "Am I to be the burnt offering?"

"Pong."

Buz laid the wood in an orderly row on the altar and applied a match to the dried logs. He poured spices and myrrh into the smoke. The flames sprang up, crackling in a foreign tongue.

"Untie my hands and I won't move, I promise you. I shan't blemish the sacrifice. If that's what I am, that's what I am."

Buz indicated Cohn kneel. He bent his knees to show how.

"I wouldn't do this if you weren't my beloved son."

Cohn knelt before the fire, waiting for a naysaying angel who never appeared. Unless one had come and gone? You can't depend on angels.

Buz pulled his father's head back by his long hair, exposing his neck, aiming at his throat with a stone knife.

Blood, to their astonishment, spurted forth an instant before the knife touched Cohn's flesh.

"Poong," said Buz, but it came to nothing. Who could tell whether it meant yes, no, or maybe.

Cohn lay still on the floor of the cave waiting to be lifted onto the flames. By the golden dark-light of the fire he could see that his long white beard was flecked with spots of blood.

"Merciful God," he said, "I am an old man. The Lord has let me live my life out."

He wept at the thought. Maybe tomorrow the world to come?

In a tall tree in the valley below, George the gorilla, wearing a mud-stained white yarmulke he had one day found in the woods, chanted, "Sh'ma, Yisroel, the Lord our God is one."

In his throaty, gruff voice he began a long Kaddish for Calvin Cohn.

THIRTEEN STORIES

God's Wrath

GLASSER, a retired sexton, a man with a short beard and rheumy eyes, lived with his daughter on the top floor of a narrow brick building on Second Avenue and Sixth Street. He stayed in most of the day, hated going up and hated going out. He felt old, tired, and irritable. He felt he had done something wrong with his life and didn't know what. The oak doors of the old synagogue in the neighborhood had been nailed shut, its windows boarded, and the white-bearded rabbi, whom the sexton disliked, had gone off to live with his son in Detroit.

The sexton retired on social security and continued to live with his youngest daughter, the only child of his recently deceased second wife. She was a heavy-breasted, restless girl of twenty-six who called herself Luci on the phone and worked as an assistant bookkeeper in a linoleum factory during the day. She was by nature a plain and lonely girl with thoughts that bothered her; as a child she had often been depressed. The telephone in the house rarely rang.

After his shul had closed its doors, the sexton rode on the subway twice a day to a synagogue on Canal Street. On the anniversary of his first wife's death he said kaddish for both wives and barely resisted saying it for his youngest daughter. He was at times irritated by her fate. Why is my luck with my daughters so bad?

Still in all, though twice a widower, Glasser got along, thanks to God. He asked for little and was the kind of man who functioned well alone. Nor did he see much of his daughters from his first marriage, Helen, forty, and Fay, thirty-seven. Helen's husband, a drinker, a bum, supported her badly and Glasser handed her a few dollars now and then; Fay had a goiter and five children. He visited each of them every six weeks or so. His daughters served him a glass of tea.

Lucille he had more affection for, and sometimes she seemed to have affection for him. More often not; this was his second wife's doing. She had been a dissatisfied woman, complained, bewailed her fate. Anyway, the girl did little for herself, had few friends—once in a while a salesman where she worked asked her out—and it was possible, more and more likely, that she would in the end be left unmarried. No young man with or without long hair had asked her to live with him. The sexton would have disliked such an arrangement but he resolved, if ever the time came, not to oppose it. If God in His mercy winks an eye, He doesn't care who sees with two. What God in His mystery won't allow in the present, He may permit in the future, possibly even marriage for Lucille. Glasser remembered friends from the old country, some were Orthodox Jews, who had lived for years with their wives before marrying them. It was, after all, a way of life. Sometimes this thought worried him. If you opened the door a crack too much the wind would invade the bedroom. The devil, they said, hid in a cold wind. The sexton was uneasy. Who could tell where an evil began? Still, better a cold bedroom than one without a double bed. Better a daughter ultimately married than an empty vessel all her life. Glasser had seen some people, not many, come to better fates than had been expected for them.

At night after Lucille returned from work she prepared supper, and then her father cleaned up the kitchen so she could study or go to her classes. He also thoroughly cleaned the house on Fridays; he washed the windows and mopped the floors. Being twice a widower, used to looking out for himself, he was not bothered by having to do domestic tasks. What most disappointed the retired sexton in his youngest daughter was her lack of ambition. She had wanted to be a secretary after finishing high school and was now, five years later, an assistant bookkeeper. A year ago he had said to her, "You won't get better wages if you don't have a college diploma." "None of my friends go to college any more," she said. "So how many friends have you got?" "I'm talking about the friends I know who started and stopped," Lucille said; but Glasser finally persuaded her to register at Hunter College at night, where she took two courses a term. Although she had done that reluctantly, now once in a while she talked of becoming a teacher.

"Someday I will be dead," the sexton remarked, "and you'll be better off with a profession."

Both of them knew he was reminding her she might be an

old maid. She seemed not to worry, but later he heard her, through the door, crying in her room.

Once on a hot summer's day they went together on the subway to Manhattan Beach for a dip in the ocean. Glasser, perspiring, wore his summer caftan and a black felt hat of twenty years. He had on white cotton socks, worn bulbous black shoes, and a white shirt open at the collar. Part of his beard was faintly brown and his complexion was flushed. On the train Lucille wore tight bell-bottom ducks and a lacy blue blouse whose long sleeves could be seen through up to her armpits; she wore clogs and had braided her dark hair to about six inches of pony tail, which she tied off with a green ribbon. Her father was uncomfortable at an inch of bare midriff, her heavy breasts, and the tightness of her pants, but said nothing. One of her troubles was that, however she dressed, she had little to say, and he hoped the college courses would help her. Lucille had gold-flecked grayish eyes, and in a bathing suit showed a plumpish but not bad figure. A Yeshiva bocher, dressed much like her father, stared at her from across the aisle of the train, and though Glasser sensed she was interested, her face self-consciously stiffened. He felt for her an affectionate contempt.

In September Lucille delayed, then would not go to reregister for night college. She had spent the summer mostly alone. The sexton argued kindly and furiously but she could not be moved. After he had shouted for an hour she locked herself in the bathroom and would not come out though he swore he had to urinate. The next day she returned very late from work and he had to boil an egg for supper. It ended the argument; she did not return to her night classes. As though to balance that, the telephone in her room began to ring more often, and she called herself Luci when she picked up the receiver. Luci bought herself new clothes—dresses, miniskirts, leotards, new sandals and shoes, and wore them in combinations and bright colors he had never seen on her before. So let her go, Glasser thought. He watched television and was usually asleep when she got home late from a date.

"So how was your evening?" he asked in the morning.

"That's my own business," Luci said.

When he dreamed of her, as he often did, he was upbraiding

her for her short dresses; when she bent over he could see her behind. And for the disgusting costume she called hot pants. And the eyeliner and violet eye shadow she now used regularly. And for the way she looked at him when he complained about her.

One day when the sexton was praying in the shul on Canal Street Luci moved out of the house on Second Avenue. She had left a green-ink note on lined paper on the kitchen table, saying she wanted to live her own life but would phone him once in a while. He telephoned the linoleum office the next day and a man there said she had quit her job. Though shaken that she had left the house in this fashion, the sexton felt it might come to some good. If she was living with someone, all he asked was that it be an honest Jew.

Awful dreams invaded his sleep. He woke enraged at her. Sometimes he woke in fright. The old rabbi, the one who had gone to live with his son in Detroit, in one dream shook his fist at him.

On Fourteenth Street, one night on his way home from Helen's house, he passed a prostitute standing in the street. She was a heavily made-up woman of thirty or so, and at the sight of her he became, without cause, nauseated. The sexton felt a weight of sickness on his heart and was moved to cry out to God but could not. For five minutes, resting his swaying weight on his cane, he was unable to walk. The prostitute had taken a quick look at his face and had run off. If not for a stranger who had held him against a telephone pole until he had flagged down a police car that drove the sexton home, he would have collapsed in the street.

In the house he pounded clasped hands against the wall of Lucille's room, bare except for her bed and a chair. He wept, wailing. Glasser telephoned his eldest daughter and cried out his terrible fear.

"How can you be so positive about that?"

"I know in my heart. I wish I didn't know but I know it."

"So in that case she's true to her nature," Helen said. "She can't be otherwise than she is, I never trusted her."

He hung up on her and called Fay.

"All I can say," said Fay, "is I saw it coming, but what can you do about such things? Who could I tell it to?"

"What should I do?"

"Ask for God's help, what else can you do?"

The sexton hurried to the synagogue and prayed for God's intervention. When he returned to his flat he felt unrelieved, outraged, miserable. He beat his chest with his fists, blamed himself for not having been stricter with her. He was angered with her for being the kind she was and sought ways to punish her. Really, he wanted to beg her to return home, to be a good daughter, to ease the pain in his heart.

The next morning he woke in the dark and determined to find her. But where do you look for a daughter who has become a whore? He waited a few days for her to call, and when she didn't, on Helen's advice he dialed information and asked if there was a new telephone number in the name of Luci Glasser.

"Not for Luci Glasser but for Luci Glass," said the operator.

"Give me this number."

The operator, at his impassioned insistence, gave him an address as well, a place on midtown Ninth Avenue. Though it was still September and not cold, the sexton put on his winter coat and took his rubber-tipped heavy cane. He rode, whispering to himself, on the subway to West Fiftieth Street, and walked to Ninth, to a large new orange-brick apartment house.

All day, though it rained intermittently, he waited across the street from the apartment house until his daughter appeared late at night; then he followed her. She walked quickly, lightly, as though without a worry, down the avenue. As he hurried after her she hailed a cab. Glasser shouted at it but no one looked back.

In the morning he telephoned her and she did not answer, as though she knew her father was calling. That evening Glasser went once more to the apartment house and waited across the street. He had considered going in and asking the doorman for her apartment number but was ashamed to.

"Please, give me the number of my daughter, Luci Glasser, the prostitute."

At eleven that night Luci came out. From the way she was dressed and made up he was positive he had not been mistaken.

She turned on Forty-eighth Street and walked to Eighth Avenue. Luci sauntered calmly along the avenue. The sidewalks were crowded with silent men and showily dressed young women. Traffic was heavy and there were strong lights everywhere, yet the long street looked dark and evil. Some of the stores, in their spotlit windows, showed pictures of men and women in sexual embrace. The sexton groaned. Luci wore a purple silk sweater with red sequins, almost no skirt, and long black net stockings. She paused for a while on a street corner, apart from a group of girls farther up the block. She would speak to the men passing by, and one or two would stop to speak to her, then she waited again. One man spoke quietly for a while as she listened intently. Then Luci went into a drugstore to make a telephone call, and when she came out, her father, half dead, was waiting for her at the door. She walked past him.

Incensed, he called her name and she turned in frightened surprise. Under the makeup, false eyelashes, gaudy mouth, her face had turned ashen, eyes anguished.

"Papa, go home," she cried in fright.

"What did I do to you that you do this to me?"

"It's not as bad as people think," Luci said.

"It's worse, it's filthy."

"Not if you don't think so. I meet lots of people—some are Jewish."

"A black year on their heads."

"You live your life, let me live mine."

"God will curse you, He will rot your flesh."

"You're not God," Luci cried in sudden rage.

"Cocksucker," the sexton shouted, waving his cane.

A policeman approached. Luci ran off. The sexton, to the man's questions, was inarticulate.

When he sought her again Luci had disappeared. He went to the orange apartment house and the doorman said Miss Glass had moved out; he could not say where. Though Glasser returned several times the doorman always said the same thing. When he telephoned her number he got a tape recording of the operator saying the number had been disconnected.

The sexton walked the streets looking for her, though Fay and Helen begged him not to. He said he must. They asked him why. He wept aloud. He sought her among the streetwalkers on Eighth and Ninth Avenues and on Broadway.

Sometimes he went into a small cockroachy hotel and uttered her name, but nobody knew her.

Late one October night he saw her on Third Avenue near Twenty-third Street. Luci was standing in midblock near the curb, and though it was a cold night she was not wearing a coat. She had on a heavy white sweater and a mirrored leather miniskirt. A round two-inch mirror in a metal holder was sewn onto the back of the skirt, above her plump thighs, and it bounced on her buttocks as she walked.

Glasser crossed the street and waited in silence through her alarm of recognition.

"Lucille," he begged her, "come home with your father. We won't tell anybody. Your room is waiting."

She laughed angrily. She had gained weight. When he attempted to follow her she called him dirty names. He hobbled across the street and waited in an unlit doorway.

Luci walked along the block and when a man approached she spoke to him. Sometimes the man stopped to speak to her. Then they would go together to a run-down, dark, squat hotel on a side street nearby, and a half hour later she returned to Third Avenue, standing between Twenty-third and -second, or higher up the avenue, near Twenty-sixth.

The sexton follows her and waits on the other side of the street by a bare-branched tree. She knows he is there. He waits. He counts the number of her performances. He punishes by his presence. He calls down God's wrath on the prostitute and her blind father.

Talking Horse

Q. Am I a man in a horse or a horse that talks like a man? Suppose they took an X-ray, what would they see?—a man's luminous skeleton prostrate inside a horse, or just a horse with a complicated voice box? If the first, then Jonah had it better in the whale—more room all around; also he knew who he was and how he had got there. About myself I have to make guesses. Anyway, after three days and nights the big fish stopped at Nineveh and Jonah took his valise and got off. But not Abramowitz, still on board, or at hand, after years; he's no prophet. On the contrary, he works in a sideshow full of freaks—though recently advanced, on Goldberg's insistence, to the center ring inside the big tent in an act with his deaf-mute master—Goldberg himself, may the Almighty forgive him. All I know is I've been here for years and still don't understand the nature of my fate; in short if I'm Abramowitz, a horse; or a horse *including* Abramowitz. Why is anybody's guess. Understanding goes so far and no further, especially if Goldberg blocks the way. It might be because of something I said, or thought, or did, or didn't do in my life. It's easy to make mistakes and easy not to know who made them. I have my theories, glimmers, guesses, but can't prove a thing.

When Abramowitz stands in his stall, his hooves nervously booming on the battered wooden boards as he chews in his bag of hard yellow oats, sometimes he has thoughts, far-off remembrances they seem to be, of young horses racing, playing, nipping at each other's flanks in green fields; and other disquieting images that might be memories; so who's to say what's really the truth?

I've tried asking Goldberg, but save yourself the trouble. He goes black-and-blue in the face at questions, really uptight. I can understand—he's a deaf-mute from way back; he doesn't like interference with his thoughts or plans, or the way he lives, and no surprises except those he invents. In other words questions disturb him. Ask him a question and he's off his track. He talks to me only when he feels like it, which isn't so often—his little patience wears thin. Lately his mood is awful, he reaches too often for his bamboo cane—whoosh across the rump! There's usually plenty of oats and straw and water, and once in a while even a joke to relax me when I'm tensed up, but otherwise it's one threat or another, followed by a flash of pain if I don't get something or other right, or something I say hits him on his nerves. It's not only that cane that slashes like a whip; his threats have the same effect—like a zing-zong of lightning through the flesh; in fact the blow hurts less than the threat—the blow's momentary, the threat you worry about. But the true pain, at least to me, is when you don't know what you have to know.

Which doesn't mean we don't communicate to each other. Goldberg taps out Morse code messages on my head with his big knuckle—crack crack crack; I feel the vibrations run through my bones to the tip of my tail—when he orders me what to do next or he threatens how many lashes for the last offense. His first message, I remember, was NO QUESTIONS. UNDERSTOOD? I shook my head yes and a little bell jingled on a strap under the forelock. That was the first I knew it was there.

TALK, he rapped on my head after he told me about the act. "You're a talking horse."

"Yes, master." What else can you say?

My voice surprised me when it came out high through the tunnel of a horse's neck. I can't exactly remember the occasion—go remember beginnings. My memory I have to fight to get an early remembrance out of. Don't ask me why unless I happened to fall and hurt my head, or was otherwise stunted. Goldberg is my deaf-mute owner; he reads my lips. Once when he was drunk and looking for company he tapped me that I used to carry goods on my back to fairs and markets in the old days before we joined the circus.

I used to think I was born here.

"On a rainy, snowy, crappy night," Goldberg Morse-coded me on my bony skull.

"What happened then?"

He stopped talking altogether. I should know better but don't.

I try to remember what night we're talking about and certain hazy thoughts flicker in my mind, which could be some sort of story I dream up when I have nothing to do but chew oats. It's easier than remembering. The one that comes to me most is about two men, or horses, or men on horses, though which was me I can't say. Anyway two strangers meet, somebody asks the other a question, and the next thing they're locked in battle, either hacking at one another's head with swords, or braying wildly as they tear flesh with their teeth; or both at the same time. If riders, or horses, one is thin and poetic, the other a fat stranger wearing a huge black crown. They meet in a stone pit on a rainy, snowy, crappy night, one wearing his cracked metal crown that weighs a ton on his head and makes his movements slow though nonetheless accurate, and the other on his head wears a ragged colored cap. All night they wrestle by weird light in the slippery stone pit.

Q. "What's to be done?"

A. "None of those accursed bloody questions."

The next morning one of us wakes with a terrible pain which feels like a wound in the neck but also a headache. He remembers a blow he can't swear to and a strange dialogue where the answers come first and the questions follow:

I descended a ladder.

How did you get here?

The up and the down.

Which is which?

Abramowitz, in his dream story, suspects Goldberg had walloped him over the head and stuffed him into a horse because he needed a talking one for his act and there was no such thing.

I wish I knew for sure.

DON'T DARE ASK.

That's his nature; he's a lout though not without a little consideration when he's depressed and tippling his bottle. That's when he taps me out a teasing anecdote or two. He has no visible friends. Family neither of us talks about. When he laughs he cries.

It must frustrate Goldberg that all he can say aloud is four-letter words like geee, gooo, gaaa, gaaw; and the circus manager who doubles as ringmaster, in for a snifter, looks embarrassed at the floor. At those who don't know the Morse code

Goldberg grimaces, glares, and grinds his teeth. He has his mysteries. He keeps a mildewed three-prong spear hanging on the wall over a stuffed pony's head. Sometimes he goes down the cellar with an old candle and comes up with a new one lit though we have electric lights. Although he doesn't complain about his life, he worries and cracks his knuckles. He doesn't seem interested in women but sees to it that Abramowitz gets his chance at a mare in heat, if available. Abramowitz engages to satisfy his physical nature, a fact is a fact, otherwise it's no big deal; the mare has no interest in a talking courtship. Furthermore, Goldberg applauds when Abramowitz mounts her, which is humiliating.

And when they're in their winter quarters the owner once a week or so dresses up and goes out on the town. When he puts on his broadcloth suit, diamond stickpin, and yellow gloves, he preens before the full-length mirror. He pretends to fence, jabs the bamboo cane at the figure in the glass, twirls it around one finger. Where he goes when he goes he never informs Abramowitz. But when he returns he's usually melancholic, sometimes anguished, didn't have much of a good time; and in this mood may mete out a few loving lashes with that bastard cane. Or worse—make threats. Nothing serious but who needs it? Usually he prefers to stay home and watch television. He is fascinated by astronomy, and when they have those programs on the educational channel he's there night after night, staring at pictures of stars, quasars, infinite space. He also likes to read the *Daily News*, which he tears up when he's done. Sometimes he reads this book he hides on a shelf in the closet under some old hats. If the book doesn't make him laugh outright it makes him cry. When he gets excited over something he's reading in his fat book, his eyes roll, his mouth gets wet, and he tries to talk through his thick tongue, though all Abramowitz hears is geee, gooo, gaaa, gaaw. Always these words, whatever they mean, and sometimes gool goon geek gonk, in various combinations, usually gool with gonk, which Abramowitz thinks means Goldberg. And in such states he has been known to kick Abramowitz in the belly with his heavy boot. Ooof.

When he laughs he sounds like a horse, or maybe it's the way I hear him with these ears. And though he laughs once in a while, it doesn't make my life easier, because of my condition. I mean I think, Here I am in this horse. This is my theory though I have my doubts. Otherwise, Goldberg is a small stocky figure with a thick neck, heavy black brows, each like a small mustache, and big feet that swell in his shapeless boots. He washes his feet in the kitchen sink and hangs up his yellowed socks to dry on the whitewashed walls of my stall. Phoo.

He likes to do card tricks.

In winter they live in the South in a small, messy, one-floor house with a horse's stall attached that Goldberg can approach, down a few steps, from the kitchen of the house. To get Abramowitz into the stall he is led up a plank from the outside and the door shuts on his rear end. To keep him from wandering all over the house there's a slatted gate to just under his head. Furthermore, the stall is next to the toilet and the broken water closet runs all night. It's a boring life with a deaf-mute except when Goldberg changes the act a little. Abramowitz enjoys it when they rehearse a new routine, although Goldberg hardly ever alters the lines, only the order of answer and question. That's better than nothing. Sometimes when Abramowitz gets tired of talking to himself, asking unanswered questions, he complains, shouts, calls the owner dirty names. He snorts, brays, whinnies shrilly. In his frustration he rears, rocks, gallops in his stall; but what good is a gallop if there's no place to go and Goldberg can't, or won't, hear complaints, pleas, protest?

Q. "Answer me this: If it's a sentence I'm serving, how long?"

A.

Once in a while Goldberg seems to sense somebody else's needs and is momentarily considerate of Abramowitz—combs and curries him, even rubs his bushy head against the horse's. He also shows interest in his diet and whether his bowel movements are regular and sufficient; but if Abramowitz gets sentimentally careless when the owner is close by and forms a question he can see on his lips, Goldberg punches him on the nose. Or threatens to. It doesn't hurt any the less.

All I know is he's a former vaudeville comic and acrobat. He did a solo act telling jokes with the help of a blind assistant before he went sad. That's about all he's ever tapped to me about himself. When I forgot myself and asked what happened then, he punched me in the nose.

Only once, when he was half drunk and giving me my bucket of water, I sneaked in a fast one which he answered before he knew it.

"Where did you get me, master? Did you buy me from somebody else? Maybe in some kind of auction?"

I FOUND YOU IN A CABBAGE PATCH.

Once he tapped my skull: "In the beginning was the word."

"Which word was that?"

Bong on the nose.

NO MORE QUESTIONS.

"Watch out for the wound on my head or whatever it is."

"Keep your trap shut or you'll lose your teeth."

Goldberg should read that story I once heard on his transistor radio, I thought to myself. It's about a poor cab driver driving his sledge in the Russian snow. His son, a fine promising lad, got sick with pneumonia and soon died, and the poor cabby can't find anybody to talk to so as to relieve his grief. Nobody wants to listen to his troubles, because that's the way it is in the world. When he opens his mouth to say a word, the customers insult him. So he finally tells the story to his bony nag in the stable, and the horse, munching oats, listens as the weeping old man tells him about his boy that he has just buried.

Something like that could happen to you, Goldberg, and you'd be a lot kinder to whoever I am.

"Will you ever free me out of here, master?"

I'LL FLAY YOU ALIVE, YOU BASTARD HORSE.

We have this act we do together. Goldberg calls it "Ask Me Another," an ironic title where I am concerned.

In the sideshow days people used to stand among the bearded ladies, the blobby fat men, Joey the snake boy, and other freaks, laughing beyond belief at Abramowitz talking. He remembers one man staring into his mouth to see who's hiding there. Homunculus? Others suggested it was a ventriloquist's act even though the horse told them Goldberg was a deaf-mute. But in the main tent the act got thunderous storms of applause. Reporters pleaded for permission to interview Abramowitz and he had plans to spill all, but

Goldberg wouldn't allow it. "His head will swell up too big," Abramowitz said for him. "He will never be able to wear the same size hat he wore last summer."

For the performance the owner dresses up in a balloony red-and-white polka-dot clown's suit with a pointed clown's cap and has borrowed a ringmaster's snaky whip, an item Abramowitz is skittish of though Goldberg says it's nothing to worry about, little more than decoration in a circus act. No animal act is without one. People like to hear the snap. He also ties an upside-down feather duster on Abramowitz's head that makes him look like a wilted unicorn. The five-piece circus band ends its brassy "Overture to *William Tell*"; there's a flourish of trumpets, and Goldberg cracks the whip as Abramowitz, with his loose-feathered, upside-down duster, trots once around the spotlit ring and stops at attention, facing clown-Goldberg, his left foreleg pawing the sawdust-covered earth. They then begin the act; Goldberg's ruddy face, as he opens his painted mouth to express himself, flushes dark red, and his melancholy eyes under black brows protrude as he painfully squeezes out the abominable sounds, his only eloquence:

"Geee gooo gaaa gaaw?"

Abramowitz's resonant, beautifully timed response is:

A. "To get to the other side."

There's a gasp from the spectators, a murmur, perhaps of puzzlement, and a moment of intense expectant silence. Then at a roll of the drums Goldberg snaps his long whip and Abramowitz translates the owner's idiocy into something that makes sense and somehow fulfills expectations; though in truth it's no more than a question following a response already given.

Q. "Why does a chicken cross the road?"

Then they laugh. And do they laugh! They pound each other in merriment. You'd think this trite riddle, this sad excuse for a joke, was the first they had heard in their lives. And they're laughing at the translated question, of course, not at the answer, which is the way Goldberg has set it up. That's his nature for you. It's the only way he works.

Abramowitz used to sink into the dumps after that, knowing what really amuses everybody is not the old-fashioned tired conundrum but the fact it's put to them by a talking horse. That's what splits the gut.

"It's a stupid little question."

"There are no better," Goldberg said.

"You could try letting me ask one or two of my own."

YOU KNOW WHAT A GELDING IS?

I gave him no reply. Two can play at that game.

After the first applause both performers take a low bow. Abramowitz trots around the ring, his head with panache held high. And when Goldberg again cracks the pudgy whip, he moves nervously to the center of the ring and they go through the routine of the other infantile answers and questions in the same silly ass-backwards order. After each question Abramowitz runs around the ring as the spectators cheer.

A. "To hold up his pants."

Q. "Why does a fireman wear red suspenders?"

A. "Columbus."

Q. "What was the first bus to cross the Atlantic?"

A. "A newspaper."

Q. "What's black and white and red all over?"

We did a dozen like that, and when we finished up, Goldberg cracked the foolish whip, I galloped a couple more times around the ring, then we took our last bows.

Goldberg pats my steaming flank and in the ocean-roar of everyone in the tent applauding and shouting bravo, we leave the ring, running down the ramp to our quarters, Goldberg's personal wagon van and attached stall; after that we're private parties till tomorrow's show. Many customers used to come night after night to watch the performance, and they laughed at the riddles though they had known them from childhood. That's how the season goes, and nothing much has changed one way or the other except that recently Goldberg added a couple of silly elephant riddles to modernize the act.

A. "From playing marbles."

Q. "Why do elephants have wrinkled knees?"

A. "To pack their dirty laundry in."

Q. "Why do elephants have long trunks?"

Neither Goldberg nor I think much of the new jokes but they're the latest style. I reflect that we could do the act without jokes. All you need is a free talking horse.

One day Abramowitz thought he would make up a question-response of his own—it's not that hard to do. So that night after they had finished the routine, he slipped in his new riddle.

A. "To greet his friend the chicken."

Q. "Why does a yellow duck cross the road?"

After a moment of confused silence everybody cracked up; they beat themselves silly with their fists—broken straw boaters flew all over the place; but Goldberg in unbelieving astonishment glowered murderously at the horse. His ruddy face turned purple. When he cracked the whip it sounded like a river of ice breaking. Realizing in fright that he had gone too far, Abramowitz, baring his big teeth, reared up on his hind legs and took several steps forward against his will. But the spectators, thinking this was an extra flourish at the end of the act, applauded wildly. Goldberg's anger eased, and lowering his whip, he pretended to chuckle. Amid continuing applause he beamed at Abramowitz as if he were his only child and could do no wrong, though Abramowitz, in his heart of hearts, knew the owner was furious.

"Don't forget WHO'S WHO, you insane horse," Goldberg, his back to the audience, tapped out on Abramowitz's nose.

He made him gallop once more around the ring, mounted him in an acrobatic leap onto his bare back, and drove him madly to the exit.

Afterwards he Morse-coded with his hard knuckle on the horse's bony head that if he pulled anything like that again he would personally deliver him to the glue factory.

WHERE THEY WILL MELT YOU DOWN TO SIZE. "What's left over goes into dog food."

"It was just a joke, master," Abramowitz explained.

"To say the answer was O.K., but not to ask the question by yourself."

Out of stored-up bitterness the talking horse replied, "I did it on account of it made me feel free."

At that Goldberg whacked him hard across the neck with his murderous cane. Abramowitz, choking, staggered but did not bleed.

"Don't, master," he gasped, "not on my old wound."

Goldberg went into slow motion, still waving the cane.

"Try it again, you tub of guts, and I'll be wearing a horsehide coat with fur collar, gool, goon, geek, gonk." Spit crackled in the corners of his mouth.

Understood.

Sometimes I think of myself as an idea, yet here I stand in this filthy stall, my hooves sunk in my yellow balls of dreck. I feel old, disgusted with myself, smelling the odor of my bad breath as my teeth in the feedbag grind the hard oats into a foaming lump, while Goldberg smokes his panatela as he watches TV. He feeds me well enough, if oats are your dish, but hasn't had my stall cleaned for a week. It's easy to get even on a horse if that's the type you are.

So the act goes on every matinee and night, keeping Goldberg in good spirits and thousands in stitches, but Abramowitz had dreams of being in the open. They were strange dreams—if dreams; he isn't sure what they are or come from—hidden thoughts, maybe, of freedom, or some sort of self-mockery? You let yourself conceive what can't be? Anyhow, whoever heard of a talking horse's dreams? Goldberg hasn't said he knows what's going on but Abramowitz suspects he understands more than he seems to, because when the horse, lying in his dung and soiled straw, awakens from a dangerous reverie, he hears the owner muttering in his sleep in deaf-mute talk.

Abramowitz dreams, or something of the sort, of other lives he might live, let's say of a horse that can't talk, couldn't conceive the idea; is perfectly content to be simply a horse without speech. He sees himself, for instance, pulling a wagonload of yellow apples along a rural road. There are leafy beech trees on both sides and beyond them broad green fields full of wild flowers. If he were that kind of horse, maybe he might retire to graze in such fields. More adventurously, he sees himself a racehorse in goggles, thundering down the last stretch of muddy track, slicing through a wedge of other galloping horses to win by a nose at the finish; and the jockey is definitely not Goldberg. There is no jockey; he fell off.

Or if not a racehorse, if he has to be practical about it, Abramowitz continues on as a talking horse but not in circus work any longer; and every night on the stage he recites poetry. The theater is packed and people cry out oooh and aaah, what beautiful things that horse is saying.

Sometimes he thinks of himself as altogether a free "man," someone of indeterminate appearance and characteristics, who is maybe a doctor or lawyer helping poor people. Not a bad idea for a useful life.

But even if I am dreaming or whatever it is, I hear Goldberg talking in *my* sleep. He talks something like me:

As for number one, you are first and last a talking horse, not any nag that can't talk; and believe me I have got nothing against you that you *can* talk, Abramowitz, but on account of what you say when you open your mouth and break the rules.

As for a racehorse, if you take a good look at the broken-down type you are—overweight, with big sagging belly and a thick uneven dark coat that won't shine up no matter how much I comb or brush you, and four hairy, thick, bent legs, plus a pair of slight cross-eyes, you would give up that foolish idea you can be a racehorse before you do something very ridiculous.

As for reciting poetry, who wants to hear a horse recite poetry? That's for the birds.

As for the last dream, or whatever it is that's bothering you, that you can be a doctor or lawyer, you better forget it, it's not that kind of a world. A horse is a horse even if he's a talking horse; don't mix yourself up with human beings if you know what I mean. If you're a talking horse that's your fate. I warn you, don't try to be a wise guy, Abramowitz. Don't try to know everything, you might go mad. Nobody can know everything; it's not that kind of world. Follow the rules of the game. Don't rock the boat. Don't try to make a monkey out of me; I know more than you. It's my nature. We have to be who we are, although this is rough on both of us. But that's the logic of the situation. It goes by certain laws even though that's a hard proposition for some to understand. The law is the law, you can't change the order. That's the way things stay put together. We are mutually related, Abramowitz, and that's all there is to it. If it makes you feel any better, I will admit to you I can't live without you, and I won't let you live without me. I have my living to make and you are my talking horse I use in my act to earn my living, plus so I can take care of your needs. The true freedom, like I have always told you, though you never want to believe me, is to understand that and don't waste your energy resisting the rules; if so you waste your life. All you are is a horse who talks, and believe me, there are very few horses that can do that; so if you are smart, Abramowitz, it should make you happy instead of always and continually dissatisfied. Don't break up the act if you know what's good for you.

As for those yellow balls of your dreck, if you will behave yourself like a gentleman and watch out what you say, tomorrow the shovelers will come and after I will hose you down personally with warm water. Believe me, there's nothing like cleanliness.

Thus he mocks me in my sleep though I have my doubts that I sleep much nowadays.

In short hops between towns and small cities the circus moves in wagon vans. The other horses pull them, but Goldberg won't let me, which again wakes disturbing ideas in my head. For longer hauls, from one big city to another, we ride in red-and-white-striped circus trains. I have a stall in a freight car with some non-talking horses with fancy braided manes and sculptured tails from the bareback rider's act. None of us are much interested in each other. If they think at all they think a talking horse is a show-off. All they do is eat and drink, piss and crap. Not a single word goes back or forth among them. Nobody has a good or bad idea.

The long train rides generally give us a day off without a show, and Goldberg gets depressed and surly when we're not working the matinee or evening performance. Early in the morning of a long train-ride day he starts loving his bottle and Morse-coding me nasty remarks and threats.

"Abramowitz, you think too much, why do you bother? In the first place your thoughts come out of you and you don't know that much, so your thoughts don't either. In other words don't get too ambitious. For instance, what's on your mind right now, tell me?"

"Answers and questions, master—some new ones to modernize the act."

"Feh, we don't need any new ones, the act is already too long."

He should know the questions I am really asking myself, though better not.

Once you start asking questions one leads to the next and in the end it's endless. And what if it turns out I'm always asking myself the same question in different words? I keep on wanting to know why I can't ask this coarse lout a simple question about *anything*. By now I have it figured out Goldberg is afraid of questions because a question could show he's afraid people will find out who he is. Somebody who all he does is repeat his fate. Anyway, Goldberg has some kind of past he is afraid to tell me about, though sometimes he hints. And when I mention my own past he says forget it. Concentrate on the future. What future? On the other hand, what does he think he can hide from Abramowitz, a student by nature, who spends most of his time asking himself questions Goldberg won't permit him to ask, putting one and one together, and finally making up his mind—miraculous thought—that he knows more than a horse should, even a talking horse, so therefore, given all the built-up evidence, he is positively not a horse. Not in origin anyway.

So I came once more to the conclusion that I am a man in a horse and not just a horse that happens to be able to talk. I had figured this out in my mind before; then I said, no it can't be. I feel more like a horse bodywise; on the other hand I talk, I think, I wish to ask questions. So I am what I am. Something tells me there is no such thing as a talking horse, even though Goldberg, pointing his fat finger at me, says the opposite. He lives on his lies, it's his nature.

After long days of traveling, when they were in their new quarters one night, finding the rear door to his stall unlocked—Goldberg grew careless when depressed—acting on belief as well as impulse, Abramowitz cautiously backed out. Avoiding the front of Goldberg's wagon van he trotted across the fairgrounds on which the circus was situated. Two of the circus hands who saw him trot by, perhaps because Abramowitz greeted them, "Hello, boys, marvelous evening," did not attempt to stop him. Outside the grounds, though exhilarated to be in the open, Abramowitz began to wonder if he was doing a foolish thing. He had hoped to find a wooded spot to hide in for the time being, surrounded by fields in which he could peacefully graze; but this was the industrial edge of the city, and though he clop-clopped from street to street there were no woods nearby, not even a small park.

Where can somebody who looks like a horse go by himself?

Abramowitz tried to hide in an old riding-school stable but was driven out by an irate woman. In the end they caught up with him on a station platform where he had been waiting for a train. Quite foolishly, he knew. The conductor wouldn't let him get on though Abramowitz had explained his predicament. The stationmaster ran out and pointed a pistol at his head. He held the horse there, deaf to his blandishments, until Goldberg arrived with his bamboo cane. The owner threatened to whip Abramowitz to the quick, and his description of the effects was so painfully lurid that Abramowitz felt as though he had been slashed into a bleeding pulp. A half hour later he found himself back in his locked stall, his throbbing head encrusted with dried horse blood. Goldberg ranted in deaf-mute talk, but Abramowitz, who with lowered head pretended contrition, felt none. To escape Goldberg he must first get out of the horse he was in.

But to exit a horse as a man takes some doing. Abramowitz planned to proceed slowly and appeal to public opinion. It might take months, possibly years, to do what he must. Protest! Sabotage if necessary! Revolt! One night after they had taken their bows and the applause was subsiding, Abramowitz, raising his head as though to whinny his appreciation of the plaudits, cried out to all assembled in the circus tent, "Help! Get me out of here, somebody! I am a prisoner in this horse! Free a fellow man!"

After a silence that grew like a dense forest, Goldberg, who was standing to the side, unaware of Abramowitz's passionate outcry—he picked up the news later from another ringmaster—saw at once from everybody's surprised and startled expression, not to mention Abramowitz's undisguised look of triumph, that something had gone seriously amiss. The owner at once began to laugh heartily, as though whatever was going on was more of the same, part of the act, a bit of personal encore by the horse. The spectators laughed too, again warmly applauding.

"It won't do you any good," the owner Morse-coded Abramowitz afterwards. "Because nobody is going to believe you."

"Then please let me out of here on your own account, master. Have some mercy."

"About that matter," Goldberg rapped out sternly, "I am already on record. Our lives and livings are dependent each on the other. You got nothing substantial to complain about, Abramowitz. I'm taking care on you better than you could take care on yourself."

"Maybe that's so, Mr. Goldberg, but what good is it if in my heart I am a man and not a talking horse?"

Goldberg's ruddy face blanched as he Morse-coded the usual NO QUESTIONS.

"I'm not asking, I'm trying to tell you something very serious."

"Watch out for your hubris, Abramowitz."

That night the owner went out on the town, came back dreadfully drunk, as though he had been lying with his mouth open under a spigot pouring brandy; and he threatened Abramowitz with the trident spear he kept in his trunk when they traveled. This is a new torment.

Anyway, the act goes on but definitely altered, not as before. Abramowitz, despite numerous warnings and various other painful threats, daily disturbs the routine. After Goldberg makes his idiot noises, his geee gooo gaaa gaaw, Abramowitz purposely mixes up the responses to the usual ridiculous riddles.

A. "To get to the other side."

Q. "Why does a fireman wear red suspenders?"

A. "From playing marbles."

Q. "Why do elephants have long trunks?"

And he adds dangerous A.'s and Q.'s without permission despite the inevitability of punishment.

A. "A talking horse."

Q. "What has four legs and wishes to be free?"

At that nobody laughed.

He also mocked Goldberg when the owner wasn't attentively reading his lips; called him "deaf-mute," "stupid ears," "lock mouth"; and whenever possible addressed the public, requesting, urging, begging their assistance.

"Gevalt! Get me out of here! I am one of you! This is slavery! I wish to be free!"

Now and then when Goldberg's back was turned, or when he was too lethargic with melancholy to be much attentive,

Abramowitz clowned around and in other ways ridiculed the owner. He heehawed at his appearance, brayed at his "talk," stupidity, arrogance. Sometimes he made up little songs of freedom as he jigged on his hind legs, exposing his private parts. And at times Goldberg, to mock the mocker, danced gracelessly with him—a clown with a glum-painted smile, waltzing with a horse. Those who had seen the act last season were astounded, stunned by the change, uneasy, as though the future threatened.

"Help! Help, somebody help me!" Abramowitz pleaded. Nobody moved.

Sensing the tension in and around the ring, the audience sometimes booed the performers, causing Goldberg, in his red-and-white polka-dot suit and white clown's cap, great embarrassment, though on the whole he kept his cool during the act and never used the ringmaster's whip. In fact he smiled as he was insulted, whether he "listened" or not. He heard what he saw. A sly smile was fixed on his face and his lips twitched. And though his fleshy ears flared like torches at the gibes and mockeries he endured, Goldberg laughed to the verge of tears at Abramowitz's sallies and shenanigans; many in the big tent laughed along with him. Abramowitz was furious.

Afterwards Goldberg, once he had stepped out of his clown suit, threatened him to the point of collapse, or flayed him viciously with his cane; and the next day fed him pep pills and painted his hide black before the performance so that people wouldn't see his wounds.

"You bastard horse, you'll lose us our living."

"I wish to be free."

"To be free you got to know when you are free. Considering your type, Abramowitz, you'll be free in the glue factory."

One night when Goldberg, after a day of profound depression, was listless and logy in the ring, could not evoke so much as a limp snap out of his whip, Abramowitz, thinking that where the future was concerned, glue factory or his present condition of life made little difference, determined to escape either fate; he gave a solo performance for freedom, the best of his career. Though desperate, he entertained, made up hilarious riddles: A. "By jumping through the window." Q. "How do you end the pane?"; he recited poems he had heard on Goldberg's radio, which sometimes stayed on all night after the owner had fallen asleep; he also told stories and ended the evening with a moving speech.

He told sad stories of the lot of horses, one, for instance, beaten to death by his cruel owner, his brains battered with a log because he was too weakened by hunger to pull a wagonload of wood. Another concerned a racehorse of fabulous speed, a sure winner in the Kentucky Derby, had he not in his very first race been doped by his avaricious master, who had placed a fortune in bets on the next best horse. A third was about a fabulous flying horse shot down by a hunter who couldn't believe his eyes. And then Abramowitz told a story of a youth of great promise who, out for a stroll one spring day, came upon a goddess bathing naked in a stream. As he gazed at her beauty in amazement and longing, she let out a piercing scream to the sky. The youth took off at a fast gallop, realizing from the snorting, and sound of pounding hoofs as he ran, that he was no longer a youth of great promise, but a horse running.

Abramowitz then cried out to the faces that surrounded him, "I also am a man in a horse. Is there a doctor in the house?"

Dead silence.

"Maybe a magician?"

No response but nervous tittering.

He then delivered an impassioned speech on freedom for all. Abramowitz talked his brains blue, ending once more with a personal appeal. "Help me to recover my original form. It's not what I am but what I wish to be. I wish to be what I really am, which is a man."

At the end of the act many people in the tent were standing wet-eyed and the band played "The Star-Spangled Banner."

Goldberg, who had been dozing in a sawdust pile for a good part of Abramowitz's solo act, roused himself in time to join the horse in a bow. Afterwards, on the enthusiastic advice of the new circus manager, he changed the name of the act from "Ask Me Another" to "Goldberg's Varieties." And wept himself for unknown reasons.

Back in the stall after the failure of his most passionate, most inspired, pleas for assistance, Abramowitz butted his head in frustration against the stall gate until his nostrils bled into the feedbag. He thought he would drown in the blood and didn't much care. Goldberg found him lying on the floor in the dirty straw, in a deep faint, and revived him with aromatic spirits of ammonia. He bandaged his nose and spoke to him in a fatherly fashion.

"That's how the mop flops," he Morse-coded with his blunt fingertip, "but things could be worse. Take my advice and settle for a talking horse, it's not without distinction."

"Make me either into a man or make me into a horse," Abramowitz pleaded. "It's in your power, Goldberg."

"You got the wrong party, my friend."

"Why do you always say lies?"

"Why do you always ask questions you can't ask?"

"I ask because I am. Because I wish to be free."

"So who's free, tell me?" Goldberg mocked.

"If so," said Abramowitz, "what's to be done?"

DON'T ASK, I WARNED YOU.

He warned he would punch his nose; it bled again.

Abramowitz later that day began a hunger strike which he carried on for the better part of a week; but Goldberg threatened force-feeding with thick rubber tubes in both nostrils, and that ended that. Abramowitz almost choked to death at the thought of it. The act went on as before, and the owner changed its name back to "Ask Me Another." When the season was over the circus headed south, Abramowitz trotting along in a cloud of dust with the other horses.

Anyway I got my own thoughts.

One fine autumn, after a long hard summer, Goldberg washed his big feet in the kitchen sink and hung his smelly socks to dry on the gate of Abramowitz's stall before sitting down to watch astronomy on ETV. To see better he placed a lit candle on top of the color set. But he had carelessly left the stall gate open, and Abramowitz hopped up three steps and trotted through the messy kitchen, his eyes flaring. Confronting Goldberg staring in awe at the universe on the screen, he reared with a bray of rage, to bring his hoofs down on the owner's head. Goldberg, seeing him out of the corner of his eye, rose to protect himself. Instantly jumping up on the chair, he managed with a grunt to grab Abramowitz by both big ears as though to lift him by them, and the horse's head and neck, up to an old wound, came off in his hands. Amid the stench of blood and bowel a man's pale head popped out of the hole in the horse. He was in his early forties, with fogged pince-nez, intense dark eyes, and a black mustache. Pulling his arms free, he grabbed Goldberg around his thick neck with both bare arms and held on for dear life. As they tugged and struggled, Abramowitz, straining to the point of madness, slowly pulled himself out of the horse up to his navel. At that moment Goldberg broke his frantic grip and, though the astronomy lesson was still going on in a blaze of light, disappeared. Abramowitz later made a few discreet inquiries, but no one could say where.

Departing the circus grounds, he cantered across a grassy soft field into a dark wood, a free centaur.

The Letter

AT THE GATE stands Teddy holding his letter.

On Sunday afternoons Newman sat with his father on a white bench in the open ward. The son had brought a pineapple tart but the old man wouldn't eat it.

Twice during the two and a half hours he spent in the ward with his father, Newman said, "Do you want me to come back next Sunday or don't you? Do you want to have next Sunday off?"

The old man said nothing. Nothing meant yes or it meant no. If you pressed him to say which he wept.

"All right, I'll see you next Sunday. But if you want a week off sometime, let me know. I want a Sunday off myself."

His father said nothing. Then his mouth moved and after a while he said, "Your mother didn't talk to me like that. She didn't like to leave any dead chickens in the bathtub. When is she coming to see me here?"

"Pa, she's been dead since before you got sick and tried to take your life. Try to keep that in your memory."

"Don't ask me to believe that one," his father said, and Newman got up to go to the station where he took the Long Island Rail Road train to New York City.

He said, "Get better, pa," when he left, and his father answered, "Don't tell me that, I am better."

Sundays after he left his father in Ward 12 of Building B and walked across the hospital grounds, that spring and dry summer, at the arched iron-barred gate between brick posts under a towering oak that shadowed the raw red brick wall, he met Teddy standing there with his letter in his hand. Newman could have got out through the main entrance of Building B of the hospital complex, but this way to the railroad station was shorter. The gate was open to visitors on Sundays only.

Teddy was a stout soft man in loose gray institutional clothes and canvas slippers. He was fifty or more and maybe so was his letter. He held it as he always held it, as though he had held it always, a thick squarish finger-soiled blue envelope with unsealed flap. Inside were four sheets of cream paper with nothing written on them. After he had looked at the paper the first time, Newman had handed the envelope back to Teddy, and the green-uniformed guard had let him out the gate. Sometimes there were other patients standing by the gate who wanted to walk out with Newman but the guard said they couldn't.

"What about mailing my letter," Teddy said on Sundays.

He handed Newman the finger-smudged envelope. It was easier to take, then hand back, than to refuse to take it.

The mailbox hung on a short cement pole just outside the iron gate on the other side of the road, a few feet from the oak tree. Teddy would throw a right jab in its direction. Once it had been painted red and was now painted blue. There was also a mailbox in the doctor's office in each ward. Newman had reminded him, but Teddy said he didn't want the doctor reading his letter.

"You bring it to the office and so they read it."

"That's his job," Newman answered.

"Not on my head," said Teddy. "Why don't you mail it? It won't do you any good if you don't."

"There's nothing in it to mail."

"That's what you say."

His heavy head was set on a short sunburned neck, the coarse grizzled hair cropped an inch from the skull. One of his eyes was a fleshy gray, the other was walleyed. He stared beyond Newman when he talked to him, sometimes through his shoulder. And Newman noticed he never so much as glanced at the blue envelope when it was momentarily out of his hand, when Newman was holding it. Once in a while he pointed a short finger at something but said nothing. When he said nothing he rose a little on the balls of his toes. The guard did not interfere when Teddy handed Newman the letter every Sunday.

Newman gave it back.

"It's your mistake," said Teddy. Then he said, "I got my walking privileges. I'm almost sane. I fought in Guadalcanal."

Newman said he knew that.

"Where did you fight?"

"Nowhere yet."

"Why don't you mail my letter out?"

"It's for your own good the doctor reads it."

"That's a hot one." Teddy stared at the mailbox through Newman's shoulder.

"The letter isn't addressed to anybody and there's no stamp on it."

"Put one on. They won't let me buy one three or three ones."

"It's eight cents now. I'll put one on if you address the envelope."

"Not me," said Teddy.

Newman no longer asked why.

"It's not that kind of a letter."

He asked what kind it was.

"Blue with white paper inside of it."

"Saying what?"

"Shame on you," said Teddy.

Newman left on the four o'clock train. The ride home was not so bad as the ride there, though Sundays were murderous.

Teddy holds his letter.

"No luck?"

"No luck," said Newman.

"It's off your noodle."

He handed the envelope to Newman anyway and after a while Newman gave it back.

Teddy stared at his shoulder.

Ralph holds the finger-soiled blue envelope.

On Sunday a tall lean grim old man, clean-shaven, faded-eyed, wearing a worn-thin World War I overseas cap on his yellowed white head, stood at the gate with Teddy. He looked eighty.

The guard in the green uniform told him to step back, he was blocking the gate.

"Step back, Ralph, you're in the way of the gate."

"Why don't you stick it in the box on your way out?" Ralph asked in a gravelly old man's voice, handing the letter to Newman.

Newman wouldn't take it. "Who are you?"

Teddy and Ralph said nothing.

"It's his father," the guard at the gate said.

"Whose?"

"Teddy."

"My God," said Newman. "Are they both in here?"

"That's right," said the guard.

"Was he just admitted or has he been here all the while?"

"He just got his walking privileges returned again. They were revoked about a year."

"I got them back after five years," Ralph said.

"One year."

"Five."

"It's astonishing anyway," Newman said. "Neither one of you resembles the other."

"Who do you resemble?" asked Ralph.

Newman couldn't say.

"What war were you in?" Ralph asked.

"No war at all."

"That settles your pickle. Why don't you mail my letter?"

Teddy stood by sullenly. He rose on his toes and threw a short right and left at the mailbox.

"I thought it was Teddy's letter."

"He told me to mail it for him. He fought at Iwo Jima. We fought two wars. I fought in the Marne and the Argonne Forest. I had both my lungs gassed with mustard gas. The wind changed and the Huns were gassed. That's not all that were."

"Tough turd," said Teddy.

"Mail it anyway for the poor kid," said Ralph. His tall body trembled. He was an angular man with deep-set bluish eyes and craggy features that looked as though they had been hacked out of a tree.

"I told your son I would if he wrote something on the paper," Newman said.

"What do you want it to say?"

"Anything he wants it to. Isn't there somebody he wants to communicate with? If he doesn't want to write it he could tell me what to say and I'll write it out."

"Tough turd," said Teddy.

"He wants to communicate to me," said Ralph.

"It's not a bad idea," Newman said. "Why doesn't he write a few words to you? Or you could write a few words to him."

"A Bronx cheer on you."

"It's my letter," Teddy said.

"I don't care who writes it," said Newman. "I could write a message for you wishing him luck. I could say you hope he gets out of here soon."

"A Bronx cheer to that."

"Not in my letter," Teddy said.

"Not in mine either," said Ralph grimly. "Why don't you mail it like it is? I bet you're afraid to."

"No I'm not."

"I'll bet you are."

"No I'm not."

"I have my bets going."

"There's nothing to mail. There's nothing in the letter. It's a blank."

"What makes you think so?" asked Ralph. "There's a whole letter in there. Plenty of news."

"I'd better be going," Newman said, "or I'll miss my train."

The guard opened the gate to let him out. Then he shut the gate.

Teddy turned away and stared over the oak tree into the summer sun with his gray eye and his walleyed one.

Ralph trembled at the gate.

"Who do you come here to see on Sundays?" he called to Newman.

"My father."

"What war was he in?"

"The war in his head."

"Has he got his walking privileges?"

"No, they won't give him any."

"What I mean, he's crazy?"

"That's right," said Newman, walking away.

"So are you," said Ralph. "Why don't you come back here and hang around with the rest of us?"

The Silver Crown

GANS, the father, lay dying in a hospital bed. Different doctors said different things, held different theories. There was talk of an exploratory operation but they thought it might kill him. One doctor said cancer.

"Of the heart," the old man said bitterly.

"It wouldn't be impossible."

The young Gans, Albert, a high school biology teacher, in the afternoons walked the streets in sorrow. What can anybody do about cancer? His soles wore thin with walking. He was easily irritated; angered by the war, atom bomb, pollution, death, obviously the strain of worrying about his father's illness. To be able to do nothing for him made him frantic. He had done nothing for him all his life.

A female colleague, an English teacher he had slept with once, a girl who was visibly aging, advised, "If the doctors don't know, Albert, try a faith healer. Different people know different things; nobody knows everything. You can't tell about the human body."

Albert laughed mirthlessly but listened. If specialists disagree, who do you agree with? If you've tried everything, what else can you try?

One afternoon after a long walk alone, as he was about to descend the subway stairs somewhere in the Bronx, still burdened by his worries, uneasy that nothing had changed, he was accosted by a fat girl with bare meaty arms who thrust a soiled card at him that he tried to avoid. She was a stupefying sight, retarded at the very least. Fifteen, he'd say, though she looks thirty and probably has the mentality of age ten. Her skin glowed, face wet, fleshy, a small mouth open and would be forever; eyes set wide apart on the broad unfocused face, either watery green or brown, or one of each—he wasn't sure. She seemed not to mind his appraisal, gurgled faintly. Her thick hair was braided in two ropelike strands; she wore bulging cloth slippers bursting at seams and soles; a faded red skirt down to massive ankles, and a heavy brown sweater vest buttoned over blown breasts, though the weather was still hot September.

The teacher's impulse was to pass by her outthrust plump baby hand. Instead he took the card from her. Simple curiosity—once you had learned to read you read anything? Charitable impulse?

Albert recognized Yiddish and Hebrew but read in English: "Heal The Sick. Save The Dying. Make A Silver Crown."

"What kind of silver crown would that be?"

She uttered impossible noises. Depressed, he looked away. When his eyes turned to hers she ran off.

He studied the card. "Make A Silver Crown." It gave a rabbi's name and address no less: Jonas Lifschitz, close by in the neighborhood. The silver crown mystified him. He had no idea what it had to do with saving the dying but felt he ought to know. Although at first repelled by the thought, he made up his mind to visit the rabbi and felt, in a way, relieved.

The teacher hastened along the street a few blocks until he came to the address on the card, a battered synagogue in a store, Congregation Theodor Herzl, painted in large uneven white letters on the plate-glass window. The rabbi's name, in smaller, gold letters, was A. Marcus. In the doorway to the left of the store the number of the house was repeated in tin numerals, and on a card under the vacant name plate under the mezuzah appeared in pencil, "Rabbi J. Lifschitz. Retired. Consultations. Ring The Bell." The bell, when he decided to chance it, did not work—seemed dead to the touch—so Albert, his heartbeat erratic, turned the knob. The door gave easily enough and he hesitantly walked up a dark flight of narrow wooden stairs. Ascending, assailed by doubts, peering up through the gloom, he thought of turning back but at the first-floor landing compelled himself to knock loudly on the door.

"Anybody home here?"

He rapped harder, annoyed with himself for being there, engaging in the act of entrance—who would have predicted it an hour ago? The door opened a crack and that broad, badly formed face appeared. The retarded girl, squinting one bulbous eye, made noises like two eggs frying, and ducked back, slamming the door. The teacher, after momentary reflection, thrust it open in time to see her, bulky as she was, running along the long tight corridor, her body bumping the walls as she disappeared into a room at the rear.

Albert entered cautiously, with a sense of embarrassment, if not danger, warning himself to depart at once; yet stayed to peek curiously into a front room off the hallway, darkened by lowered green shades through which threadlike rivulets of light streamed. The shades resembled faded maps of ancient lands. An old gray-bearded man with thickened left eyelid, wearing a yarmulke, sat heavily asleep, a book in his lap, on a sagging armchair. Someone in the room gave off a stale odor, unless it was the armchair. As Albert stared, the old man awoke in a hurry. The small thick book on his lap fell with a thump to the floor, but instead of picking it up, he shoved it with a kick of his heel under the chair.

"So where were we?" he inquired pleasantly, a bit breathless.

The teacher removed his hat, remembered whose house he was in, and put it back on his head.

He introduced himself. "I was looking for Rabbi J. Lifschitz. Your—ah—girl let me in."

"Rabbi Lifschitz—this was my daughter Rifkele. She's not perfect, though God, who made her in His image, is Himself perfection. What this means I don't have to tell you."

His heavy eyelid went down in a wink, apparently involuntarily.

"What does it mean?" Albert asked.

"In her way she is also perfect."

"Anyway, she let me in and here I am."

"So what did you decide?"

"About what?"

"What did you decide about what we were talking about—the silver crown?"

His eyes roved as he spoke; he rubbed a nervous thumb and forefinger. Crafty type, the teacher decided. Him I have to watch myself with.

"I came here to find out about this crown you advertised," he said, "but actually we haven't talked about it or anything else. When I entered here you were sound asleep."

"At my age—" the rabbi explained with a little laugh.

"I don't mean any criticism. All I'm saying is I am a stranger to you."

"How can we be strangers if we both believe in God?"

Albert made no argument of it.

The rabbi raised the two shades and the last of daylight fell into the spacious high-ceilinged room, crowded with at least a dozen stiff-back and folding chairs, plus a broken sofa. What kind of operation is he running here? Group consultations? He dispensed rabbinic therapy? The teacher felt renewed distaste for himself for having come. On the wall hung a single oval mirror, framed in gold-plated groupings of joined metal circles, large and small; but no pictures. Despite the empty chairs, or perhaps because of them, the room seemed barren.

The teacher observed that the rabbi's trousers were a week from ragged. He was wearing an unpressed worn black suit-coat and a yellowed white shirt without a tie. His wet grayish-blue eyes were restless. Rabbi Lifschitz was a dark-faced man with brown eye pouches and smelled of old age. This was the odor. It was hard to say whether he resembled his daughter; Rifkele resembled her species.

"So sit," said the old rabbi with a light sigh. "Not on the couch, sit on a chair."

"Which in particular?"

"You have a first-class humor." Smiling absently, he pointed to two kitchen chairs and seated himself in one.

He offered a thin cigarette.

"I'm off them," the teacher explained.

"I also." The old man put the pack away. "So who is sick?" he inquired.

Albert tightened at the question, as he recalled the card he had taken from the girl: "Heal The Sick, Save The Dying."

"To come to the point, my father's in the hospital with a serious ailment. In fact he's dying."

The rabbi, nodding gravely, dug into his pants pocket for a pair of glasses, wiped them with a large soiled handkerchief, and put them on, lifting the wire earpieces over each fleshy ear.

"So we will make then a crown for him?"

"That depends. The crown is what I came here to find out about."

"What do you wish to find out?"

"I'll be frank with you." The teacher blew his nose and

slowly wiped it. "My cast of mind is naturally empiric and objective—you might say non-mystical. I'm suspicious of faith healing, but I've come here, frankly, because I want to do anything possible to help my father recover his former health. To put it otherwise, I don't want anything to go untried."

"You love your father?" the rabbi clucked, a glaze of sentiment veiling his eyes.

"What I feel is obvious. My real concern right now mainly is how does the crown work. Could you be explicit about the mechanism of it all? Who wears it, for instance? Does he? Do you? Or do I have to? In other words, how does it function? And if you wouldn't mind saying, what's the principle, or rationale, behind it? This is terra incognita for me, but I think I might be willing to take a chance if I could justify it to myself. Could I see a sample of the crown, for instance, if you have one on hand?"

The rabbi, with an absentminded start, seemed to interrupt himself about to pick his nose.

"What is the crown?" he asked, at first haughtily, then again, gently. "It's a crown, nothing else. There are crowns in Mishna, Proverbs, Kabbalah; the holy scrolls of the Torah are often protected by crowns. But this one is different, this you will understand when it does the work. It's a miracle. A sample doesn't exist. The crown has to be made individual for your father. Then his health will be restored. There are two prices—"

"Kindly explain what's supposed to cure the sickness," Albert said. "Does it work like sympathetic magic? I'm not nay-saying, you understand. I just happen to be interested in all kinds of phenomena. Is the crown supposed to draw off the illness like some kind of poultice, or what?"

"The crown is not a medicine, it is the health of your father. We offer the crown to God and God returns to your father his health. But first we got to make it the way it must be made—this I will do with my assistant, a retired jeweler. He has helped me to make a thousand crowns. Believe me, he knows silver—the right amount to the ounce according to the size you wish. Then I will say the blessings. Without the right blessings, exact to each word, the crown don't work. I don't have to tell you why. When the crown is finished your father will get better. This I will guarantee you. Let me read you some words from the mystic book."

"The Kabbalah?" the teacher asked respectfully.

"Like the Kabbalah."

The rabbi rose, went to his armchair, got slowly down on his hands and knees and withdrew the book he had shoved under the misshapen chair, a thick small volume with faded purple covers, not a word imprinted on it. The rabbi kissed the book and murmured a prayer.

"I hid it for a minute," he explained, "when you came in the room. It's a terrible thing nowadays, goyim come in your house in the middle of the day and take away that which belongs to you, if not your life itself."

"I told you right away that your daughter had let me in," Albert said in embarrassment.

"Once you mentioned I knew."

The teacher then asked, "Suppose I am a non-believer? Will the crown work if it's ordered by a person who has his doubts?"

"Doubts we all got. We doubt God and God doubts us. This is natural on account of the nature of existence. Of this kind doubts I am not afraid so long as you love your father."

"You're putting it as sort of a paradox."

"So what's so bad about a paradox?"

"My father wasn't the easiest man in the world to get along with, and neither am I for that matter, but he has been generous to me and I'd like to repay him in some way."

"God respects a grateful son. If you love your father this will go in the crown and help him to recover his health. Do you understand Hebrew?"

"Unfortunately not."

The rabbi flipped a few pages of his thick tome, peered at one closely and read aloud in Hebrew, which he then translated into English. " 'The crown is the fruit of God's grace. His grace is love of creation.' These words I will read seven times over the silver crown. This is the most important blessing."

"Fine. But what about those two prices you quoted me a minute ago?"

"This depends how quick you wish the cure."

"I want the cure to be immediate, otherwise there's no sense to the whole deal," Albert said, controlling anger. "If you're questioning my sincerity, I've already told you I'm considering this recourse even though it goes against the grain of some of my strongest convictions. I've gone out of my way to make my pros and cons absolutely clear."

"Who says no?"

The teacher became aware of Rifkele standing at the door, eating a slice of bread with lumps of butter on it. She beheld him in mild stupefaction, as though seeing him for the first time.

"Shpeter, Rifkele," the rabbi said patiently.

The girl shoved the bread into her mouth and ran ponderously down the passageway.

"Anyway, what about those two prices?" Albert asked, annoyed by the interruption. Every time Rifkele appeared his doubts of the enterprise rose before him like warriors with spears.

"We got two kinds crowns," said the rabbi. "One is for 401 and the other is 986."

"Dollars, you mean, for God's sake?—that's fantastic."

"The crown is pure silver. The client pays in silver dollars. So the silver dollars we melt—more for the large-size crown, less for the medium."

"What about the small?"

"There is no small. What good is a small crown?"

"I wouldn't know, but the assumption seems to be the bigger the better. Tell me, please, what can a 986 crown do that a 401 can't? Does the patient get better faster with the larger one? It hastens the reaction?"

The rabbi, five fingers hidden in his limp beard, assented.

"Are there any other costs?"

"Costs?"

"Over and above the quoted prices?"

"The price is the price, there is no extra. The price is for the silver and for the work and for the blessings."

"Now would you kindly tell me, assuming I decide to get involved in this deal, where I am supposed to lay my hands on 401 silver dollars? Or if I should opt for the 986 job, where can I get a pile of cartwheels of that amount? I don't suppose that any bank in the whole Bronx would keep that many silver dollars on hand nowadays. The Bronx is no longer the Wild West, Rabbi Lifschitz. But what's more to the point, isn't it true the mint isn't making silver dollars all silver any more?"

"So if they are not making we will get wholesale. If you will leave with me the cash, I will order the silver from a wholesaler, and we will save you the trouble to go to the bank. It will be the same amount of silver, only in small bars, I will weigh them on a scale in front of your eyes."

"One other question. Would you take my personal check in payment? I could give it to you right away once I've made my final decision."

"I wish I could, Mr. Gans," said the rabbi, his veined hand still nervously exploring his beard, "but it's better cash when the patient is so sick, so I can start to work right away. A check sometimes comes back, or gets lost in the bank, and this interferes with the crown."

Albert did not ask how, suspecting that a bounced check, or a lost one, wasn't the problem. No doubt some customers for crowns had stopped their checks on afterthought.

As the teacher reflected concerning his next move—should he, shouldn't he?—weighing a rational thought against a sentimental, the old rabbi sat in his chair, reading quickly in his small mystic book, his lips hastening along silently.

Albert at last got up.

"I'll decide the question once and for all tonight. If I go ahead and commit myself on the crown I'll bring you the cash after work tomorrow."

"Go in good health," said the rabbi. Removing his glasses he wiped both eyes with his handkerchief.

Wet or dry? thought the teacher.

As he let himself out of the downstairs door, more inclined than not toward trying the crown, he felt relieved, almost euphoric.

But by the next morning, after a difficult night, Albert's mood had about-faced. He fought gloom, irritation, felt flashes of hot and cold anger. It's throwing money away, pure and simple. I'm dealing with a clever confidence man, that's plain to me, but for some reason I am not resisting strongly. Maybe my subconscious is telling me to go along with a blowing wind and have the crown made. After that we'll see what happens—whether it rains, snows, or spring comes. Not much will happen, I suppose, but whatever does, my conscience will be in the clear.

But when he visited Rabbi Lifschitz that afternoon in the same roomful of empty chairs, though the teacher carried the required cash in his wallet, he was still uncomfortable about parting with it.

"Where do the crowns go after they are used and the patient recovers his health?" he cleverly asked the rabbi.

"I'm glad you asked me this question," said the rabbi alertly, his thick lid drooping. "They are melted, and the silver we give to the poor. A mitzvah for one makes a mitzvah for another."

"To the poor you say?"

"There are plenty poor people, Mr. Gans. Sometimes they need a crown for a sick wife or a sick child. Where will they get the silver?"

"I see what you mean—recycled, sort of, but can't a crown be reused as it is? I mean, do you permit a period of time to go by before you melt them down? Suppose a dying man who recovers gets seriously ill again at a future date?"

"For a new sickness you will need a new crown. Tomorrow the world is not the same as today, though God listens with the same ear."

"Look, Rabbi Lifschitz," Albert said impatiently, "I'll tell you frankly that I am inching toward ordering the crown, but it would make my decision a whole lot easier all around if you would let me have a quick look at one of them—it wouldn't have to be for more than five seconds—at a crown-in-progress for some other client."

"What will you see in five seconds?"

"Enough—whether the object is believable, worth the fuss and not inconsequential investment."

"Mr. Gans," replied the rabbi, "this is not a showcase business. You are not buying from me a new Chevrolet automobile. Your father lays now dying in the hospital. Do you love him? Do you wish me to make a crown that will cure him?"

The teacher's anger flared. "Don't be stupid, rabbi, I've answered that. Please don't sidetrack the real issue. You're working on my guilt so I'll suspend my perfectly reasonable doubts of the whole freaking enterprise. I won't fall for that."

They glared at each other. The rabbi's beard quivered. Albert ground his teeth.

Rifkele, in a nearby room, moaned.

The rabbi, breathing emotionally, after a moment relented.

"I will show you the crown," he sighed.

"Accept my apologies for losing my temper."

The rabbi accepted. "Now tell me please what kind of sickness your father has got."

"Ah," said Albert, "nobody is certain for sure. One day he got into bed, turned to the wall and said, 'I'm sick.' They suspected leukemia at first but the lab tests didn't confirm it."

"You talked to the doctors?"

"In droves. Till I was blue in the face. A bunch of ignoramuses," said the teacher hoarsely. "Anyway, nobody knows exactly what he has wrong with him. The theories include rare blood diseases, also a possible carcinoma of certain endocrine glands. You name it, I've heard it, with complications suggested, like Parkinson's or Addison's disease, multiple sclerosis, or something similar, alone or in combination with other sicknesses. It's a mysterious case, all in all."

"This means you will need a special crown," said the rabbi.

The teacher bridled. "What do you mean special? What will it cost?"

"The cost will be the same," the rabbi answered dryly, "but the design and the kind of blessings will be different. When you are dealing with such a mystery you got to make another one but it must be bigger."

"How would that work?"

"Like two winds that they meet in the sky. A white and a blue. The blue says, 'Not only I am blue but inside I am also purple and orange.' So the white goes away."

"If you can work it up for the same price, that's up to you."

Rabbi Lifschitz then drew down the two green window shades and shut the door, darkening the room.

"Sit," he said in the heavy dark, "I will show you the crown."

"I'm sitting."

"So sit where you are, but turn your head to the wall where is the mirror."

"But why so dark?"

"You will see light."

He heard the rabbi strike a match and it flared momentarily, casting shadows of candles and chairs amid the empty chairs in the room.

"Look now in the mirror."

"I'm looking."

"What do you see?"

"Nothing."

"Look with your eyes."

A silver candelabrum, first with three, then five, then seven burning bony candlesticks, appeared like ghostly hands with flaming fingertips in the oval mirror. The heat of it hit Albert in the face and for a moment he was stunned.

But recalling the games of his childhood, he thought, who's kidding who? It's one of those illusion things I remember from when I was a kid. In that case I'm getting the hell out of here. I can stand maybe mystery but not magic tricks or dealing with a rabbinical magician.

The candelabrum had vanished, although not its light, and he now saw the rabbi's somber face in the glass, his gaze addressing him. Albert glanced quickly around to see if anyone was standing at his shoulder, but nobody was. Where the rabbi was hiding at the moment the teacher did not know; but in the lit glass appeared his old man's lined and shrunken face, his sad eyes, compelling, inquisitive, weary, perhaps even frightened, as though they had seen more than they had cared to but were still looking.

What's this, slides or home movies? Albert sought some source of projection but saw no ray of light from wall or ceiling, nor object or image that might be reflected by the mirror.

The rabbi's eyes glowed like sun-filled clouds. A moon rose in the blue sky. The teacher dared not move, afraid to discover he was unable to. He then beheld a shining crown on the rabbi's head.

It had appeared at first like a braided mother-of-pearl turban, then had luminously become—like an intricate star in the night sky—a silver crown, constructed of bars, triangles, halfmoons and crescents, spires, turrets, trees, points of spears; as though a wild storm had swept them up from the earth and flung them together in its vortex, twisted into a single glowing interlocked sculpture, a forest of disparate objects.

The sight in the ghostly mirror, a crown of rare beauty—very impressive, Albert thought—lasted no longer than five short seconds, then the reflecting glass by degrees turned dark and empty.

The shades were up. The single bulb in a frosted lily fixture on the ceiling shone harshly in the room. It was night.

The old rabbi sat, exhausted, on the broken sofa.

"So you saw it?"

"I saw something."

"You believe what you saw—the crown?"

"I believe I saw. Anyway, I'll take it."

The rabbi gazed at him blankly.

"I mean I agree to have the crown made," Albert said, having to clear his throat.

"Which size?"

"Which size was the one I saw?"

"Both sizes. This is the same design for both sizes, but there is more silver and also more blessings for the $986 size."

"But didn't you say that the design for my father's crown, because of the special nature of his illness, would have a different style, plus some special blessings?"

The rabbi nodded. "This comes also in two sizes—the $401 and $986."

The teacher hesitated a split second. "Make it the big one," he said decisively.

He had his wallet in his hand and counted out fifteen new bills—nine one hundreds, four twenties, a five, and a single—adding to $986.

Putting on his glasses, the rabbi hastily counted the money, snapping with thumb and forefinger each crisp bill as though to be sure none had stuck together. He folded the stiff paper and thrust the wad into his pants pocket.

"Could I have a receipt?"

"I would like to give you a receipt," said Rabbi Lifschitz earnestly, "but for the crowns there are no receipts. Some things are not a business."

"If money is exchanged, why not?"

"God will not allow. My father did not give receipts and also my grandfather."

"How can I prove I paid you if something goes wrong?"

"You have my word, nothing will go wrong."

"Yes, but suppose something unforeseen did," Albert insisted, "would you return the cash?"

"Here is your cash," said the rabbi, handing the teacher the packet of folded bills.

"Never mind," said Albert hastily. "Could you tell me when the crown will be ready?"

"Tomorrow night before Shabbos, the latest."

"So soon?"

"Your father is dying."

"That's right, but the crown looks like a pretty intricate piece of work to put together out of all those odd pieces."

"We will hurry."

"I wouldn't want you to rush the job in any way that would—let's say—prejudice the potency of the crown, or for that matter, in any way impair the quality of it as I saw it in the mirror—or however I saw it."

Down came the rabbi's eyelid, quickly raised without a sign of self-consciousness. "Mr. Gans, all my crowns are first-class jobs. About this you got nothing to worry about."

They then shook hands. Albert, still assailed by doubts, stepped into the corridor. He felt he did not, in essence, trust the rabbi; and suspected that Rabbi Lifschitz knew it and did not, in essence, trust him.

Rifkele, panting like a cow for a bull, let him out the front door, perfectly.

In the subway, Albert figured he would call it an investment in experience and see what came of it. Education costs money, but how else can you get it? He pictured the crown, as he had seen it, established on the rabbi's head, and then seemed to remember that as he had stared at the man's shifty face in the mirror the thickened lid of his right eye had slowly dropped into a full wink. Did he recall this in truth, or was he seeing in his mind's eye and transposing into the past something that had happened just before he left the house? What does he mean by his wink?—not only is he a fake but he kids you? Uneasy once more, the teacher clearly remembered, when he was staring into the rabbi's fish eyes in the glass, after which they had lit in visionary light, that he had fought a hunger to sleep; and the next thing there's the sight of the old boy, as though on the television screen, wearing this high-hat magic crown.

Albert, rising, cried, "Hypnosis! The bastard magician hypnotized me! He never did produce a silver crown, it's out of my imagination—I've been suckered!"

He was outraged by the knavery, hypocrisy, fat nerve of Rabbi Jonas Lifschitz. The concept of a curative crown, if he had ever for a moment believed in it, crumbled in his brain and all he could think of were 986 blackbirds flying in the sky. As three curious passengers watched, Albert bolted out of the car at the next stop, rushed up the stairs, hurried across the street, then cooled his impatient heels for twenty-two minutes till the next train clattered into the station, and he rode back to the stop near the rabbi's house. Though he banged with both fists on the door, kicked at it, "rang" the useless bell until his thumb was blistered, the boxlike wooden house, including dilapidated synagogue store, was dark, monumentally starkly still, like a gigantic, slightly tilted tombstone in a vast graveyard; and in the end unable to arouse a soul, the teacher, long past midnight, had to head home.

He awoke next morning cursing the rabbi and his own stupidity for having got involved with a faith healer. This is what happens when a man—even for a minute—surrenders his true beliefs. There are less punishing ways to help the dying. Albert considered calling the cops but had no receipt and did not want to appear that much a fool. He was tempted, for the first time in six years of teaching, to phone in sick; then take a cab to the rabbi's house and demand the return of his cash. The thought agitated him. On the other hand, suppose Rabbi Lifschitz was seriously at work assembling the crown with his helper; on which, let's say, after he had bought the silver and paid the retired jeweler for his work, he made, let's say, a hundred bucks clear profit—not so very much; and there really *was* a silver crown, and the rabbi sincerely and religiously believed it would reverse the course of his father's illness? Although nervously disturbed by his suspicions, Albert felt he had better not get the police into the act too soon, because the crown wasn't promised—didn't the old gent say—until before the Sabbath, which gave him till sunset tonight.

If he produces the thing by then, I have no case against him even if it's a piece of junk. So I better wait. But what a dope I was to order the $986 job instead of the $401. On that decision alone I lost $585.

After a distracted day's work Albert taxied to the rabbi's house and tried to rouse him, even hallooing at the blank windows facing the street; but either nobody was home or they were both hiding, the rabbi under the broken sofa, Rifkele trying to shove her bulk under a bathtub. Albert decided to wait them out. Soon the old boy would have to leave the house to step into the shul on Friday night. He would speak to him, warn him to come clean. But the sun set; dusk settled on the earth; and though the autumn stars and a sliver of moon gleamed in the sky, the house was dark, shades drawn; and no Rabbi Lifschitz emerged. Lights had gone on in the little shul, candles were lit. It occurred to Albert, with chagrin, that the rabbi might be already worshipping; he might all this time have been in the synagogue.

The teacher entered the long, brightly lit store. On yellow folding chairs scattered around the room sat a dozen men holding worn prayer books, praying. The Rabbi A. Marcus, a middle-aged man with a high voice and a short reddish beard, was dovening at the Ark, his back to the congregation.

As Albert entered and embarrassedly searched from face to face, the congregants stared at him. The old rabbi was not among them. Disappointed, the teacher withdrew.

A man sitting by the door touched his sleeve.

"Stay awhile and read with us."

"Excuse me, I'd like to but I'm looking for a friend."

"Look," said the man, "maybe you'll find him."

Albert waited across the street under a chestnut tree losing its leaves. He waited patiently—till tomorrow if he had to.

Shortly after nine the lights went out in the synagogue and the last of the worshippers left for home. The red-bearded rabbi then emerged with his key in his hand to lock the store door.

"Excuse me, rabbi," said Albert, approaching. "Are you acquainted with Rabbi Jonas Lifschitz, who lives upstairs with his daughter Rifkele—if she is his daughter?"

"He used to come here," said the rabbi with a small smile, "but since he retired he prefers a big synagogue on Mosholu Parkway, a palace."

"Will he be home soon, do you think?"

"Maybe in an hour. It's Shabbat, he must walk."

"Do you—ah—happen to know anything about his work on silver crowns?"

"What kind of silver crowns?"

"To assist the sick, the dying?"

"No," said the rabbi, locking the shul door, pocketing the key, and hurrying away.

The teacher, eating his heart, waited under the chestnut tree till past midnight, all the while urging himself to give up and go home, but unable to unstick the glue of his frustration and rage. Then shortly before 1 A.M. he saw some shadows moving and two people drifting up the shadow-encrusted street. One was the old rabbi, in a new caftan and snappy black Homburg, walking tiredly. Rifkele, in sexy yellow mini, exposing to above the big-bone knees her legs like poles, walked lightly behind him, stopping to strike her ears with her hands. A long white shawl, pulled short on the right shoulder, hung down to her left shoe.

"On my income their glad rags."

Rifkele chanted a long "Boooo" and slapped both ears with her pudgy hands to keep from hearing it.

They toiled up the ill-lit narrow staircase, the teacher trailing them.

"I came to see my crown," he told the pale, astonished rabbi, in the front room.

"The crown," the rabbi said haughtily, "is already finished. Go home and wait, your father will soon get better."

"I called the hospital before leaving my apartment, there's been no improvement."

"How can you expect so soon improvement if the doctors themselves don't know what is the sickness? You must give the crown a little more time. God Himself has trouble to understand human sickness."

"I came to see the thing I paid for."

"I showed you already, you saw before you ordered."

"That was an image of a facsimile, maybe, or something of the sort. I insist on seeing the real thing, for which I paid close to one thousand smackers."

"Listen, Mr. Gans," said the rabbi patiently, "there are some things we are allowed to see which He lets us see them. Sometimes I wish He didn't let us. There are other things we are not allowed to see—Moses knew this—and one is God's face, and another is the real crown that He makes and blesses it. A miracle is a miracle, this is God's business."

"Don't you see it?"

"Not with my eyes."

"I don't believe a word of it, you faker, two-bit magician."

"The crown is a real crown. If you think there is magic, it is on account those people that they insist to see it—we try to give them an idea. For those who believe, there is no magic."

"Rifkele," the rabbi said hurriedly, "bring to Papa my book of letters."

She left the room, after a while, a little in fright, her eyes evasive; and returned in ten minutes, after flushing the toilet, in a shapeless long flannel nightgown, carrying a large yellowed notebook whose loose pages were thickly interleaved with old correspondence.

"Testimonials," said the rabbi.

Turning several loose pages, with trembling hand he extracted a letter and read it aloud, his voice husky with emotion.

"'Dear Rabbi Lifschitz: Since the miraculous recovery of my mother, Mrs. Max Cohen, from her recent illness, my impulse is to cover your bare feet with kisses. Your crown worked wonders and I am recommending it to all my friends. Yours truly and sincerely, (Mrs.) Esther Polatnik.'

"This is a college teacher."

He read another. "'Dear Rabbi Lifschitz, Your $986 crown totally and completely cured my father of cancer of the pancreas, with serious complications of the lungs, after nothing else had worked. Never before have I believed in miraculous occurrences, but from now on I will have less doubts. My thanks to you and God. Most sincerely, Daniel Schwartz.'

"A lawyer," said the rabbi.

He offered the book to Albert. "Look yourself, Mr. Gans, hundreds of letters."

Albert wouldn't touch it.

"There's only one thing I want to look at, Rabbi Lifschitz, and it's not a book of useless testimonials. I want to see my father's silver crown."

"This is impossible. I already explained to you why I can't do this. God's word is God's law."

"So if it's the law you're citing, either I see the crown in the next five minutes, or the first thing tomorrow morning I'm reporting you and your activities to the Bronx County District Attorney."

"Boooo-ooo," sang Rifkele, banging her ears.

"Shut up!" Albert said.

"Have respect," cried the rabbi. "Grubber yung!"

"I will swear out a complaint and the D.A. will shut you down, the whole freaking plant, if you don't at once return the $986 you swindled me out of."

The rabbi wavered in his tracks. "Is this the way to talk to a rabbi of God?"

"A thief is a thief."

Rifkele blubbered, squealed.

"Sha," the rabbi thickly whispered to Albert, clasping and unclasping his gray hands. "You'll frighten the neighbors. Listen to me, Mr. Gans, you saw with your eyes what it looks like the real crown. I give you my word that nobody of my whole clientele ever saw this before. I showed you for your father's sake so you would tell me to make the crown which will save him. Don't spoil now the miracle."

"Miracle," Albert bellowed, "it's a freaking fake magic, with an idiot girl for a come-on and hypnotic mirrors. I was mesmerized, suckered by you."

"Be kind," begged the rabbi, tottering as he wandered amid empty chairs. "Be merciful to an old man. Think of my poor child. Think of your father who loves you."

"He hates me, the son of a bitch, I hope he croaks."

In an explosion of silence the girl slobbered in fright.

"Aha," cried the wild-eyed rabbi, pointing a finger at God in heaven. "Murderer," he cried, aghast.

Moaning, father and daughter rushed into each other's arms, as Albert, wearing a massive, spike-laden headache, rushed down the booming stairs.

An hour later the elder Gans shut his eyes and expired.

Notes from a Lady at a Dinner Party

MAX ADLER, passing through the city in November, had telephoned his old professor of architecture, Clem Harris, and was at once cordially invited to dinner that night at his house in Hempstead to meet some good friends and his young wife Karla.

She spoke of her husband's respect for Adler. "He says about you something he doesn't often say about his former students—that you deserve your success. Didn't you win an A.I.A. national medal about two years out of graduate school?"

"Not a medal," Adler explained, pleased. "It was an Honor Award certificate for a house I designed."

Adler, at the time of the dinner party, was a loose-fleshed heavy man who dressed with conservative carelessness and weighed 210.

"That's what I mean." She laughed in embarrassment and he imagined that she often laughed in embarrassment. She was strong-bodied and plain, in an elegant way, and wore her brown hair pulled back in a twist. He thought she was twenty-five or -six. She had on a short green dress with sandals, and her sturdy legs and thighs were well formed. Adler, when she asked, said he was thirty-two, and Karla remarked it was a fine age for a man. He knew her husband's age was twice his. She was direct and witty, with a certain tensity of expression, and she told him almost at once that friendship meant a lot to her.

It was during dinner that Karla Harris let Adler know about the note in his pocket. They were six at the table in the large wood-paneled dining room, with a bay window containing a pebbled bed of chrysanthemums and begonias. Besides the hosts there was a middle-aged couple, the Ralph Lewins—he was a colleague of Harris's at the Columbia University School of Architecture; and maybe to balance off Adler, Harris's secretary, Shirley Fisher, had been invited, a thin-ankled, wet-eyed divorcee in a long bright-blue skirt, who talked and drank liberally. Harris, pouring wine liberally from a bottle in a basket, sat at the head of the broad neat table, opposite Karla, who was on the qui vive to see that everything went as it should; from time to time her husband smiled his encouragement.

Max Adler sat on her right, facing Lewin across the table, and on his right was Mrs. Lewin, a small luminous-faced, listening person. Karla, when Harris was ladling turtle soup into bowls out of a handsome tureen, and the conversation was lively, leaned imperceptibly close to Adler and whispered, "If you like surprises, feel in your left pocket when you can," and though he wasn't sure at once was the proper time, when she left the room to get the rolls that had almost burned, he casually reached into his suit-coat pocket and felt a folded slip of paper which, after a minute, he smoothed out and read in his palm.

If anybody at the table had noticed that Adler's head was momentarily lowered and wondered whether he were privately saying grace, or maybe studying his wristwatch with a view to catching an early train back to the city, it occurred to him he wouldn't have worried; he was politely reading the lady's note, had initiated nothing. The slip of yellow lined paper, in small printed handwriting, said simply, "Why do we all think we *should* be happy, that it's one of the *necessary* conditions of life?" and for a while Adler, who took questions of this sort seriously, didn't know what to say in reply.

She could quite easily have asked her question while they were having cocktails on the enclosed porch and he would have done his best with it; but she had seemed concerned about the dinner and had been in and out of the kitchen many times; dealing also with the girl sitter who was putting the children to bed, really too busy to sustain a conversation with any of her guests. Yet since she hadn't orally asked her question, Adler felt he had to respect the fact that she had found it necessary to write it out on paper and slip into his pocket. If this was the way she was moved to express herself, he thought he ought to answer with a note. He glanced at her husband, aged but still vigorous since he had seen him last, who was at the moment listening attentively to Shirley. Adler excused himself—he said to get his glasses—to scribble a note on a memo pad; and when he returned, though he wasn't comfortable in pretense, he covertly passed the paper to her, grazing her warm bare thigh, though he hadn't intended to, then feeling her narrow fingers, as he touched them, close on the note.

He had been tempted to say that happiness wasn't something he worried about any more—you had it or you hadn't and why beat your brains blue when there was work to be done; but he didn't say that. He had quickly written, "Why not?—it's a short hard life if you don't outfox it."

Karla glanced at the paper in her hand, a fork in a piece of filet of sole in the other, apparently not disappointed, her color heightened, expression neutral, a bit distant. She disappeared into the kitchen with an empty salad bowl, and when she was again seated at the table, secretly passed Adler another note: "I want you to see my babies." Adler solemnly nodded as he pocketed the paper. She smiled vaguely as her husband, who had once more risen to refill the wineglasses, gazed at her fondly. The others were momentarily quietly eating, not, apparently, attentive. Karla returned a resemblance of her husband's smile as Adler, wondering why she engaged him in this curious game, felt they were now related in a way he couldn't have foreseen when he had entered the house that evening. When Harris, behind him, pouring wine into his glass, let his hand fall affectionately on his former student's shoulder, Max, who had experienced a strong emotion on seeing his old professor after so many years, felt himself resist his touch.

Later he enjoyed talking with him over brandy in the living room; it was a spacious room, twenty-four by thirty, Adler estimated, tastefully and comfortably furnished, draped, decorated, with a glass bowl of golden chrysanthemums and Shasta daisies on the fireplace mantel and some bright modernist paintings on the wall. Karla was then in the kitchen, showing the sitter how to stack and operate the dishwasher, and Adler felt geared to anticipation, though not sure of what. He tried to suppress the feeling and to some extent succeeded. But as Clem Harris poured him a cognac he stealthily felt in his pocket and there were the two notes only.

The professor, a crisp tall man with a clipped grayish beard, faintly red, and thick gray sideburns, who wore a green blazer with an orange shirt and white bow tie, was lavish in his praise of Adler's recent work, some slides of which the architect had sent him; and Max once more expressed gratitude for the interest Harris continued to show. He had always been a kind man and influential teacher.

"What are you into now?" Harris asked. After two brandies he had gone back to Scotch-and-soda. His large face was flushed and he wiped his watery eyes with a pressed handkerchief. Adler had noticed how often he glanced up at the dining-room door in anticipation of his wife's reappearance.

"The same project you saw in the transparencies," Adler said. "How about you?"

"Renovating some slum units for a private low-income housing group. There's very little money in it. It's more or less pro bono."

"I ought to be doing more of that myself."

Harris, after observing Adler for a moment, asked, "Aren't you putting on more weight, Max?"

"I eat too much," Adler confessed.

"You ought to watch your weight. Do you still smoke like a chimney?"

"Not any more."

"Bully. I wish I could get Karla to cut down."

When she reappeared his wife had brushed her hair. The green dress she had been wearing she had changed for a short crocheted strawberry mini, with white bra and half-slip showing through the weave. The warm color of the dress brought out a bloom in her face. She was an attractive woman.

"Ah, you've changed your dress," her husband said.

"I spilled at least a pint of gravy on it," Karla explained with an embarrassed laugh.

"I thought you didn't much care for this one."

"When did I say that?" she asked. "I do like it. I like it very much. It's the purple one I don't like—it's too damn harsh."

Harris, drinking from his glass, nodded pleasantly. Something else was on his mind. "I wish you'd get yourself more help when you need it."

"What kind of help?" asked Karla.

"In the kitchen, of course." His tone was affectionate, solicitous.

"Stephanie's cleaning up—that's the dirty work."

"It was a wonderful meal," said Max.

She thanked him.

"We ought to have a maid to help at dinner parties," Harris insisted. "Sometimes our guests barely get a look at you. I wish you'd be less a puritan about occasional luxuries. I hate for you to be too tired to enjoy your own parties."

"I'm enjoying this."

Max nodded.

"You know what I mean," Harris said.

"Clem, I simply don't like maids around at small dinner parties."

She told Adler that Stephanie was another of Harris's students.

"The father of us all," she laughed.

"Stephanie needs the money," Harris said.

Karla then asked Adler if he liked her in her crocheted dress. He said he did.

"Is it too short?"

"No," said Max.

"I didn't say it was," said Harris.

The phone rang and when he answered, it was one of his doctoral candidates. Harris, good-humoredly wiggling his fingers at Karla, talked patiently with the doctoral candidate.

Adler and Karla were sitting on a love seat facing the flower-laden fireplace, when she whispered there was a note between the pillows. He recovered it as they were talking and slipped it into his pocket.

"I'll read it later."

But she had left the love seat as though to give him an opportunity to read what she had written. Karla plopped herself down next to Ada Lewin on the long beige sofa along the left wall, as Ralph Lewin, sipping a brandy, listened to Clem on the phone. Shirley Fisher then drifted over to talk with the visitor. She wore a low-draped white camisole with a slit midi and was openly flirtatious. When she crossed her legs a long thin thigh was exposed.

"Don't older women interest you, Mr. Adler?" Her voice was slightly husky.

"I wouldn't call you old."

Shirley said she was charmed but then Karla returned. Harris was still patiently on the phone. Adler decided the colors he wore went well with the paintings on the walls. When

Max was his student, Harris had worn gray suits with white shirts.

"Can you spare him for five minutes, Shirley?" Karla asked. "I want Mr. Adler to see the babies."

"Max," said Adler.

"Wouldn't they be sleeping now?"

"I want him to see them anyway—if he'd like to."

Max said he would.

He had managed to glance at her note: "Don't panic but I like you a lot."

"Enjoy yourselves," Shirley said, pouring herself a brandy.

"We will," Karla said.

As they were going up the stairs Adler said, "I wouldn't want to wake them up."

"They'll go right on sleeping."

She opened the door, switching on the light. Two children slept in cribs in a large nursery room with three curtained windows. At first Adler thought they were twins, but they weren't. One was a little girl with light-blond curls in a white crib, and the other was an infant boy in an orange crib. On the floor, in the corner, stood a circular canvas playpen strewn with dolls and wooden toys. A series of small-animal watercolors was framed on the walls; Karla said she had done them.

"I used to do such lovely watercolors."

Adler said they were charming.

"Not those, my watercolors from nature. I just haven't the time to paint any more."

"I know what you mean."

"You really don't," she said.

"This is Sara," Karla said, standing by the white crib. "She's two. Stevie is just eleven months. Look at those shoulders. Clem thought we ought to have them close together so they would be friends. His first wife died childless."

"I knew her," Adler said.

The boy, in undershirt and plastic diaper cover, lay on his side, sucking the corner of his blanket in his sleep. He resembled his father.

The little girl, asleep on her back in a flowered yellow nightgown, clutching a stuffed doll, looked like Karla.

"They're lovely children," Adler said.

Karla stood at the little girl's crib. "Oh, my babies," she said. "My little babies. My heart goes out to them." She lowered the side of the crib and, bending, kissed Sara, who opened her eyes, stared at her mother, and was then asleep, smiling.

Karla withdrew the doll and the child released it with a sigh. Then she covered the little boy with his blanket.

"Very nice children," Adler said.

"My lovely little babies. My babies, my babies." Her face was tender, sad, illumined.

"Do I sound hokey?"

"I wouldn't say so." Max was affected by her.

She lowered the shades, switched out the lights, quietly closed the door.

"Come see my study."

It was a light-curtained lavender room with a desk, portable sewing machine, and a circle of snapshots on the wall before her. Her father, who had sold insurance in Columbus, Ohio, was dead. There he was, fifty, standing in front of his automobile. The sad-faced mother had posed in her flower garden. A shot of Karla taken in college showed an attractive, sober girl with wire-frame glasses, dark eyes and brows, firm full lips. Her desk was cluttered with books, sheet music, shopping lists, correspondence.

She wanted to know if Adler had any children.

"No." He told her he had been married a short time and divorced long ago.

"You never remarried?"

"No."

"Clem married me when I was very young," Karla said.

"Didn't you marry him?"

"I mean I hardly knew what I was doing."

"What was he doing?"

"Marrying me when I was very young."

She raised the shade and stared into the night. A street light in the distance glowed through the wet window. "I always give dinner parties on rainy nights."

She said they ought to go down to the others but then opened the closet door and got out a large glossy photograph of a one-family dwelling project she had done in her architecture class with Harris.

Max said it showed promise. Karla smiled wryly.

"Really," he said.

"I love *your* work," she said. "I love the chances you take."

"If they work out right."

"They do, they do." She seemed to be trembling.

They embraced forcefully. She dug her body into his. They kissed wet-mouthed, then she broke with an embarrassed laugh.

"They'll be wondering."

"He's still on the phone," Max said, aroused.

"We'd better go down."

"What's Shirley to him?"

"A tight-jawed bitch."

"To him I said."

"He's sorry for her. Her fourteen-year-old kid is on LSD. He's sorry for everybody."

They kissed again, then Karla stepped out of his embrace and they went downstairs.

Harris was off the phone.

"I showed him our babies," Karla said to her husband.

"Showoff," smiled Harris.

"Lovely children," said Max.

Shirley winked at him.

I've lost the right to his friendship, the architect thought. A minute later he thought, Things change, they have to.

"Now please stay put for a few minutes," Harris said to Karla. "Catch your breath."

"First I have to pay Stephanie."

Harris went to his den and returned with a box of color transparencies of his renovation project for a slum-housing improvement group: before and after.

Max, his mind on Karla, examined the slides, holding each to the light. He said it was work well done.

Harris said he was gratified that Max approved.

Karla was paying Stephanie in the kitchen. Ralph Lewin, smoking a cigar, also looked at the slides, although he said he was the one who had originally taken them. Ada and Shirley were on the green sofa on the right side of the room, Ada seriously listening as Shirley went on about her son on LSD.

Karla carried in a silver trayful of bone-china cups and saucers.

"I'm always late with coffee," she remarked.

"Make mine tea," said Ralph.

She said she would get the tea in a minute.

As she handed out the coffee cups she slipped Adler a note with his.

He read it in the bathroom. "Pretend you're going to the bathroom, then go left in the back hall and you'll come out in the kitchen."

He went to the left in the hall and came out in the kitchen.

They kissed with passion.

"Where can we meet?"

"When?" Max asked.

"Tonight, maybe? I'm not sure."

"Is there a motel around?"

"Two blocks away."

"I'll get a room if you can make it. If not tonight, I could stay on till tomorrow noon. I've got to be in Boston by evening."

"I think I can. Clem and I are in separate bedrooms right now. He sleeps like dead. I'll let you know before you leave."

"Just give me a sign," Max said. "Don't write any notes."

"Don't you like them?" Karla asked.

"I do but they're risky. What if he sees you passing me one?"

"It might do him good."

"I don't want any part of that," Max said.

"I like to write notes," said Karla. "I like to write to people I like. I like to write things that suddenly occur to me. My diary was full of exciting thoughts when I was young."

"All I'm saying is it could be dangerous. Just give me a sign or say something before I leave and I'll wait till you come."

"I burned my diary last summer but I still write notes. I've always written notes to people. You have to let me be who I am."

He asked her why she had burned her diary.

"I had to. It beat me up badly." She burst into tears.

Adler left the kitchen and returned to the bathroom. He flushed the toilet, washed his hands, and reappeared in the living room. At the same moment, Karla, her face composed, brought in Ralph's tea.

For a while they talked politics across the room. Then the talk went to music and Harris put on a new recording he had bought of Mahler's "Songs of a Wayfarer." Despite the singing,

Shirley talked earnestly to Ralph Lewin, who suppressed a yawn now and then. Ada and Karla were chatting about the Lewins' new house they were about to build in the spring, and Harris and Adler, on the long beige couch, discussed developments in architecture. "I might as well turn off the music," Harris said. After he had put the record away he returned and, resuming their conversation, characterized Adler's latest work as his most daring.

"That's a quality you inspired me to."

"In moderation."

Adler said he appreciated his mentor's sentiments. He felt for the first time he did not know what to say to him and it made him uncomfortable. He was now not sure whether to urge Karla to try to get out of the house tonight. On the one hand he had gratitude and loyalty to Harris to contend with; on the other he felt as though he were in love with her.

They managed to meet alone at the fireplace, when to his strange surprise she whispered, "Something's coming your way," and surreptitiously touched his hand with a folded slip of paper. Turning away from the company, Adler managed to read it, then thrust it into his pants pocket.

Karla's note said: "Can someone love someone she doesn't know?"

"We do it all the time."

"Partly I think I love you because I love your work."

"Don't confuse me with my work," Adler said. "It would be a mistake."

"It's on for tonight," she whispered.

As they stood side by side with their backs to the fireplace they reached behind them and squeezed hands.

Karla, glancing across the room at her husband, excused herself to go up to see if the babies were covered. Adler, after she had gone, tried to think of a reason to follow her upstairs, but the impulse was insane. It was past eleven and he felt nervously expectant.

When Karla came down from the nursery he heard her say to her husband, "Clem, I'm having some anxiety."

"Take a pill," Harris advised.

Adler then seriously wondered whether to tell her to cool it for tonight. It might be better to call her from the motel in the morning, when Harris was gone, and if she still felt she could they would meet then. But he doubted, if they didn't get together tonight, that she could make it in the morning. So he decided to urge her to come as soon as she was sure her husband was asleep.

She wants someone young for a change, he thought. It will be good for her.

Wanting to tell her the anxiety would go once they were in bed together, Max sat down beside her on the green sofa where she was listening distantly to Shirley saying the drug situation had made her frantic. He waited impatiently for one or the other to get up so that he could say what he had to to Karla. Harris, standing nearby, conversing with Ada, seemed to be listening to Shirley. Karla pretended to be unaware of Adler by her side; but after a minute he felt her hand groping for his pocket. Without wanting to he moved away.

Adler, just then, expected his pocket to burst into flame. She'll write them forever, he thought; that's her nature. If not to me, then to the next one who comes into the house who's done something she wishes she had. He made up his mind to return the note unread. At the same time, with a dismaying sense of sudden loss, Adler realized he couldn't read it if he wanted to because the paper hadn't gone into his pocket but had fallen to the floor. The sight of the folded yellow paper at his feet sickened the architect. Karla was staring at it as though reliving a dream. She had written it upstairs in her study and it said, "Darling, I can't meet you, I am six months pregnant."

Before either of them could move to retrieve the paper, or even let it lie where it had fallen, Shirley had plucked it up.

"Did you drop this?" she asked Clem Harris.

Adler's head was thick with blood. He felt childlike and foolish. I'm disgraced and deserve it.

But Harris did not unfold the paper. He handed it to his former student. "It isn't mine, is it yours?"

"An address I wrote down," Adler said. He rose. "I have this early train to Boston to catch in the morning."

Ada and Ralph Lewin were the first to say good night.

"Bon voyage," said Shirley.

Harris brought Adler's coat and helped him on with it. They shook hands cordially.

"The air shuttle is the fastest way to Boston."

Max said he thought that was how he would go. He then said goodbye to Karla. "Thanks for having me."

"Love, marriage, happiness," Karla sang, standing in her crocheted short mini on the stairs.

She runs up to her babies in the nursery.

In Retirement

HE HAD lately taken to studying his old Greek grammar of fifty years ago. He read in Bulfinch and wanted to reread the *Odyssey* in Greek. His life had changed. He slept less these days and in the morning got up to stare at the sky over Gramercy Park. He watched the clouds until they took shapes he could reflect on. He liked strange, haunted vessels, and he liked to watch mythological birds and animals. He had noticed that if he contemplated these forms in the clouds, could keep his mind on them for a while, there might be a diminution of his morning depression. Dr. Morris was sixty-six, a physician, retired for two years. He had shut down his practice in Queens and moved to Manhattan. He had retired himself after a heart attack, not too serious but serious enough. It was his first attack and he hoped his last, though in the end he hoped to go quickly. His wife was dead and his daughter lived in Scotland. He wrote her twice a month and heard from her twice a month. And though he had a few friends he visited, and kept up with medical journals, and liked museums and theater, generally he contended with loneliness. And he was concerned about the future; the future was by old age possessed.

After a light breakfast he would dress warmly and go out for a walk around the Square. That was the easy part of the walk. He took this walk even when it was very cold, or nasty rainy, or had snowed several inches and he had to proceed very carefully. After the Square he crossed the street and went down Irving Place, a tall figure with a cape and cane, and picked up his *Times.* If the weather was not too bad he continued on to Fourteenth Street, around to Park Avenue South, up Park and along East Twentieth back to the narrow, tall, white stone apartment building he lived in. Rarely, lately, had he gone in another direction though when on the long walk, he stopped at least once on the way, perhaps in front of a mid-block store, perhaps at a street corner, and asked himself where else he might go. This was the difficult part of the walk. What was difficult was that it made no difference which way he went. He now wished he had not retired. He had become more conscious of his age since his retirement, although sixty-six was not eighty. Still it was old. He experienced moments of anguish.

One morning after his rectangular long walk in the rain, he found a letter on the rubber mat under the line of mailboxes in the lobby. It was a narrow, deep lobby with false green marble columns and several bulky chairs where few people ever sat. Dr. Morris had seen a young woman with long hair, in a white raincoat and maroon shoulder bag, carrying a plastic bubble umbrella, hurry down the vestibule steps and leave the house as he was about to enter. In fact he held the door open for her and got a breath of her bold perfume. He did not remember seeing her before and felt a momentary confusion as to who she might be. He later imagined her taking the letter out of her box, reading it hastily, then stuffing it into the maroon cloth purse she carried over her shoulder; but she had stuffed in the envelope and not the letter.

That had fallen to the floor. He imagined this as he bent to retrieve it. It was a folded sheet of heavy white writing paper, written on in black ink in a masculine hand. The doctor unfolded and glanced at it without making out the salutation or any of its contents. He would have to put on his reading glasses, and he thought Flaherty, the doorman and elevator man, might see him if the elevator should suddenly descend. Of course Flaherty might think the doctor was reading his own mail, except that he never read it, such as it was, in the lobby. He did not want the man thinking he was reading someone else's letter. He also thought of handing him the letter and describing the young woman who had dropped it. Perhaps he could return it to her? But for some reason not at once clear to him the doctor slipped it into his pocket to take upstairs to read. His arm began to tremble and he felt his heart racing at a rate that bothered him.

After the doctor had got his own mail out of the box—nothing more than the few medical circulars he held in his hand—Flaherty took him up to the fifteenth floor. Flaherty spelled the night man at 8 A.M. and was himself relieved at 4 P.M. He was a slender man of sixty with sparse white hair on his half-bald head, who had lost part of his jaw under the left ear after two bone operations. He would be out for a few months; then return, the lower part of the left side of his face partially caved in; still it was not a bad face to look at. Although the doorman never spoke of his ailment, the doctor knew he was not done with cancer of the jaw, but of course he kept this to himself; and he sensed when the man was concealing pain.

This morning, though preoccupied, he asked, "How is it going, Mr. Flaherty?"

"Not too tough."

"Not a bad day." He said this, thinking not of the rain but of the letter in his pocket.

"Fine and dandy," Flaherty quipped. On the whole he moved and talked animatedly, and was careful to align the elevator with the floor before letting passengers off. Sometimes the doctor wished he could say more to him than he usually did; but not this morning.

He stood by the large double window of his living room overlooking the Square, in the dull rainy-day February light, in pleasurable excitement reading the letter he had found, the kind he had anticipated it might be. It was a letter written by a father to his daughter, addressed to "Dear Evelyn." What it expressed after an irresolute start was the father's dissatisfaction with his daughter's way of life. And it ended with an exhortatory paragraph of advice: "You have slept around long enough. I don't understand what you get out of that type of behavior any more. I think you have tried everything there is to try. You claim you are a serious person but let men use you for what they can get. There is no true payoff to you unless it is very temporary, and the real payoff to them is that they have got themselves an easy lay. I know how they think about this and how they talk about it in the lavatory the next day. Now I want to urge you once and for all that you ought to be more serious about your life. You have experimented long enough. I honestly and sincerely and urgently advise you to look around for a man of steady habits and good character who will marry you and treat you like the person I believe you want to be. I don't want to think of you any more as a drifting semi-prostitute. Please follow this advice, the age of twenty-nine is no longer sixteen." The letter was signed, "Your Father," and under his signature, another sentence, in neat small handwriting, was appended: "Your sex life fills me full of fear. Mother."

The doctor put the letter away in a drawer. His excitement had left him and he felt ashamed of having read it. He was sympathetic to the father, and at the same time sympathetic to the young woman, though perhaps less so to her. After a while he tried to study his Greek grammar but could not concentrate. The letter remained in his mind like a billboard sign as he was reading the *Times*, and he was conscious of it throughout the day, as though it had aroused in him some sort of expectation he could not define. Sentences from it would replay themselves in his thoughts. He reveried the young woman as he had imagined her after reading what the father had written, and as the woman—was she Evelyn?—he had seen coming out of the house. He could not be certain the letter was hers. Perhaps it was not; still he thought of it as belonging to her, the woman he had held the door for whose perfume still lingered in his senses.

That night, thoughts of her kept him from falling asleep. "I'm too old for this nonsense." He got up to read and was able to concentrate, but when his head lay once more on the pillow, a long freight train of thoughts provocative of her rumbled by drawn by a long black locomotive. He pictured Evelyn, the drifting semi-prostitute, in bed with various lovers, enagaged in various acts of sex. Once she lay alone, erotically naked, her maroon cloth purse drawn close to her nude body. He also thought of her as an ordinary girl with many fewer lovers than her father seemed to think. This was probably closer to the truth. He wondered if he could be useful to her in some way. He felt a fright he could not explain but managed to dispel it by promising himself to burn the letter in the morning. The freight train, with its many cars, clattered along in the foggy distance. When the doctor awoke at 10 A.M. on a sunny winter's morning, there was no awareness, light or heavy, of his morning depression.

But he did not burn the letter. He reread it several times during the day, each time returning it to his desk drawer and locking it there. Then he unlocked the drawer to read it again. As the day passed he was aware of an insistent hunger in himself. He recalled memories, experienced longing, intense desires he had not felt in years. The doctor was concerned by this change in him, this disturbance. He tried to blot the letter out of his mind but could not. Yet he would still not burn it, as though if he did, he had shut the door on certain possibilities in his life, other ways to go, whatever that might mean. He was astonished—even thought of it as affronted, that this was happening to him at his age. He had seen it in others, former patients, but had not expected it in himself.

The hunger he felt, a hunger for pleasure, disruption of habit, renewal of feeling, yet a fear of it, continued to grow in him like a dead tree come to life and spreading its branches. He felt as though he was hungry for exotic experience, which, if he was to have it, might make him ravenously hungry. He did not want that to happen. He recalled mythological figures: Sisyphus, Midas, who for one reason or another had been eternally cursed. He thought of Tithonus, his youth gone, become a grasshopper living forever. The doctor felt he was caught in an overwhelming emotion, a fearful dark wind.

When Flaherty left for the day at 4 P.M. and Silvio, who had tight curly black hair, was on duty, Dr. Morris came down and sat in the lobby, pretending to read his newspaper. As soon as the elevator went up he approached the letter boxes and scanned the name plates for an Evelyn, whoever she might be. He found no Evelyns, though there was an E. Gordon and an E. Commings. He suspected one of them might be she. He knew that single women often preferred not to reveal their first names in order to keep cranks at a distance, conceal themselves from potential annoyers. He casually asked Silvio if Miss Gordon or Miss Commings was named Evelyn, but Silvio said he didn't know, although probably Mr. Flaherty would because he distributed the mail. "Too many peoples in this house," Silvio shrugged. The doctor remarked he was just curious, a lame remark but all he could think of. He went out for an aimless short stroll and when he returned said nothing more to Silvio. They rode silently up in the elevator, the doctor standing tall, almost stiff. That night he slept badly. When he fell deeply asleep a moment his dreams were erotic. He woke feeling desire and repulsion and lay mourning himself. He felt powerless to be other than he was.

He was up before five and was uselessly in the lobby before seven. He felt he must find out, settle who she was. In the lobby, Richard, the night man who had brought him down, returned to a pornographic paperback he was reading; the mail, as Dr. Morris knew, hadn't come. He knew it would not arrive until after eight, but hadn't the patience to wait in his apartment. So he left the building, bought the *Times* on Irving Place, continued on his walk, and because it was a pleasant morning, not too cold, sat on a bench in Union Square Park. He stared at the newspaper but could not read it. He watched some sparrows pecking at dead grass. He was an older man, true enough, but had lived long enough to know that age often meant little in man-woman relationships. He was still vigorous and bodies are bodies. The doctor was back in the lobby at eight-thirty, an act of restraint. Flaherty had received the mail sack and was alphabetizing the first-class letters on a long table before distributing them into the boxes. He did not look well today. He moved slowly. His misshapen face was gray, the mouth slack; one heard his breathing; his eyes harbored pain.

"Nothin for you yet," he said to the doctor, not looking up.

"I'll wait this morning," said Dr. Morris. "I should be hearing from my daughter."

"Nothin yet, but you might hit the lucky number in this last bundle." He removed the string.

As he was alphabetizing the last bundle of letters the elevator buzzed and Flaherty had to go up for a call.

The doctor pretended to be absorbed in his *Times*. When the elevator door shut he sat momentarily still, then went to the table and hastily riffled through the C pile of letters. E. Commings was Ernest Commings. He shuffled through the G's, watching the metal arrow as it showed the elevator descending. In the G pile there were two letters addressed to Evelyn Gordon. One was from her mother. The other, also handwritten, was from a Lee Bradley. Almost against the will the doctor removed this letter and slipped it into his suit pocket. His body was hot. He was sitting in the chair turning the page of his newspaper when the elevator door opened.

"Nothin at all for you," Flaherty said after a moment.

"Thank you," said Dr. Morris. "I think I'll go up."

In his apartment the doctor, conscious of his whisperous breathing, placed the letter on the kitchen table and sat looking at it, waiting for a tea kettle to boil. The kettle whistled as it boiled but still he sat with the unopened letter before him. For a while he sat there with dulled thoughts. Soon he fantasied Lee Bradley describing the sexual pleasure he had had with Evelyn Gordon. He fantasied the lovers' acts they engaged in. Then though he audibly told himself not to, he steamed open the flap of the envelope and had to place it flat on the table so he could read it. His heart beat in anticipation of what he might read. But to his surprise the letter was a bore, an egoistic account of some stupid business deal this Bradley was concocting. Only the last sentences came surprisingly to life. "Be in your bed when I get there tonight. Be wearing only your white panties."

The doctor didn't know whom he was more disgusted with, this fool or himself. In truth, himself. Slipping the sheet of paper into the envelope, he resealed it with a thin layer of paste he had rubbed carefully on the flap with his fingertip. Later in the day he tucked the letter into his inside pocket and pressed the elevator button for Silvio. The doctor left the building and afterwards returned with a copy of the *Post* he seemed to be involved with until Silvio had to take up two women who had come into the lobby; then the doctor slipped the letter into Evelyn Gordon's box and went out for a breath of air.

He was sitting near the table in the lobby when the young woman he had held the door open for came in shortly after 6 P.M. He was aware of her perfume almost at once. Silvio was not around at that moment; he had gone down to the basement to eat a sandwich. She inserted a small key into Evelyn Gordon's mailbox and stood before the open box, smoking, as she read Bradley's letter. She was wearing a light-blue pants suit with a brown knit sweater-coat. Her tail of black hair was tied with a brown silk scarf. Her face, though a little heavy, was pretty, her intense eyes blue, the lids lightly eye-shadowed. Her body, he thought, was finely proportioned. She had not noticed him but he was more than half in love with her.

He observed her many mornings. He would come down later now, at nine, and spend some time going through the medical circulars he had got out of his box, sitting on a throne-like wooden chair near a tall unlit lamp in the rear of the lobby. He would watch people as they left for work or shopping in the morning. Evelyn appeared at about half past nine and stood smoking in front of her box, absorbed in the morning's mail. When spring came she wore brightly colored skirts with pastel blouses, or light slim pants suits. Sometimes she wore mini-dresses. Her figure was exquisite. She received many letters and read most of them with apparent pleasure, some with what seemed suppressed excitement. A few she gave short shrift to, scanned these and stuffed them into her bag. He imagined they were from her father, or mother. He thought that most of her letters came from lovers, past and present, and he felt a sort of sadness that there was none from him in her mailbox. He would write to her.

He thought it through carefully. Some women needed an older man; it stabilized their lives. Sometimes a difference of as many as thirty or even thirty-five years offered no serious disadvantages. A younger woman inspired an older man to remain virile. And despite the heart incident his health was good, in some ways better than before. A woman like Evelyn, probably at odds with herself, could benefit from a steadying relationship with an older man, someone who would respect and love her and help her to respect and love herself; who would demand less from her in certain ways than some young men awash in their egoism; who would awake in her a stronger sense of well-being, and if things went quite well, perhaps even love for a particular man.

"I am a retired physician, a widower," he wrote to Evelyn Gordon. "I write you with some hesitation and circumspection, although needless to say with high regard, because I am old enough to be your father. I have observed you often in this building and as we passed each other in nearby streets; I have grown to admire you. I wonder if you will permit me to make your acquaintance? Would you care to have dinner with me and perhaps enjoy a film or performance of a play? I do not think my company will disappoint you. If you are so inclined—so kind, certainly—to consider this request tolerantly, I will be obliged if you place a note to that effect in my mailbox. I am respectfully yours, Simon Morris, M.D."

He did not go down to mail his letter. He thought he would keep it to the last moment. Then he had a fright about it that woke him out of momentary sleep. He dreamed he had written and sealed the letter and then remembered he had appended another sentence: "Be wearing your white panties." When he woke he wanted to tear open the envelope to see whether he had included Bradley's remark. But when he was thoroughly waked up, he knew he had not. He bathed and shaved early and for a while observed the cloud formations out the window. At close to nine Dr. Morris descended to the lobby. He would wait till Flaherty answered a buzz, and when he was gone, drop his letter into her box; but Flaherty that morning seemed to have no calls to answer. The doctor had forgotten it was Saturday. He did not know it was till he got his *Times* and sat with it in the lobby, pretending to be waiting for the mail delivery. The mail sack arrived late on Saturdays. At last he heard a prolonged buzz, and Flaherty, who had been on his knees polishing the brass door knob, got up on one foot, then rose on both legs and walked slowly to the elevator. His asymmetric face was gray. Shortly before ten o'clock the doctor slipped his letter into Evelyn Gordon's mailbox. He decided to withdraw to his apartment, then thought he would rather wait where he usually waited while she collected her mail. She had never noticed him there.

The mail sack was dropped in the vestibule at ten-after, and Flaherty alphabetized the first bundle before he responded to another call. The doctor read his paper in the dark rear of the lobby, because he was really not reading it. He was anticipating Evelyn's coming. He had on a new green suit, blue striped shirt, and a pink tie. He wore a new hat. He waited with anticipation and love.

When the elevator door opened, Evelyn walked out in an elegant slit black skirt, pretty sandals, her hair tied with a red scarf. A sharp-featured man with puffed sideburns and carefully combed medium-long hair, in a turn-of-the-century haircut, followed her out of the elevator. He was shorter than she by half a head. Flaherty handed her two letters, which she dropped into the black patent-leather pouch she was carrying. The doctor thought—hoped—she would walk past the mailboxes without stopping; but she saw the white of his letter through the slot and stopped to remove it. She tore open the envelope, pulled out the single sheet of handwritten paper, read it with immediate intense concentration. The doctor raised his newspaper to his eyes, although he could still watch over the top of it. He watched in fear.

How mad I was not to anticipate she might come down with a man.

When she had finished reading the letter, she handed it to her companion—possibly Bradley—who read it, grinned broadly, and said something inaudible as he handed it back to her.

Evelyn Gordon quietly ripped the letter into small bits, and turning, flung the pieces in the doctor's direction. The fragments came at him like a blast of wind-driven snow. He thought he would sit forever on his wooden throne in the swirling snowstorm.

The old doctor sat in his chair, the floor around him littered with his torn-up letter.

Flaherty swept it up with his little broom into a metal container. He handed the doctor a thin envelope stamped with foreign stamps.

"Here's a letter from your daughter that's just come."

The doctor pressed the bridge of his nose. He wiped his eyes with his fingers.

"There's no setting aside old age," he remarked after a while.

"No, sir," said Flaherty.

"Or death."

"They move up on you."

The doctor tried to say something splendidly kind, but could not say it.

Flaherty took him up to the fifteenth floor in his elevator.

Rembrandt's Hat

RUBIN, in careless white cloth hat, or visorless soft round cap, however one described it, wandered with unexpressed or inexpressive thoughts up the stairs from his studio in the basement of the New York art school where he made his sculpture, to a workshop on the second floor, where he taught. Arkin, the art historian, a hypertensive bachelor of thirty-four—a man often swept by strong feeling, he thought—about a dozen years younger than the sculptor, observed him through his open office door, wearing his cap amid a crowd of art students and teachers in the hall during a change of classes. In his white hat he stands out and apart, the art historian thought. It illumines a lonely inexpressiveness arrived at after years of experience. Though it was not entirely apt he imagined a lean white animal—hind, stag, goat?—staring steadfastly but despondently through trees of a dense wood. Their gazes momentarily interlocked and parted. Rubin hurried to his workshop class.

Arkin was friendly with Rubin though they were not really friends. Not his fault, he felt; the sculptor was a very private person. When they talked, he listened, looking away, as though guarding his impressions. Attentive, apparently, he seemed to be thinking of something else—his sad life no doubt, if saddened eyes, a faded green mistakable for gray, necessarily denote sad life. Sometimes he uttered an opinion, usually a flat statement about the nature of life, or art, never much about himself; and he said absolutely nothing about his work.

"Are you working, Rubin?" Arkin was reduced to.

"Of course I'm working."

"What are you doing if I may ask?"

"I have a thing going."

There Arkin let it lie.

Once, in the faculty cafeteria, listening to the art historian discourse on the work of Jackson Pollock, the sculptor's anger had flared.

"The world of art ain't necessarily in your eyes."

"I have to believe that what I see is there," Arkin had politely responded.

"Have you ever painted?"

"Painting is my life."

Rubin, with dignity, reverted to silence. That evening, leaving the building, they tipped hats to each other over small smiles.

In recent years, after his wife had left him and costume and headdress became a mode among students, Rubin had taken to wearing various odd hats from time to time, and this white one was the newest, resembling Nehru's Congress Party cap, but rounded—a cross between a cantor's hat and a bloated yarmulke; or perhaps like a French judge's in Rouault, or working doctor's in a Daumier print. Rubin wore it like a crown. Maybe it kept his head warm under the cold skylight of his large studio.

When the sculptor again passed along the crowded hall on his way down to his studio that day he had first appeared in his white cap, Arkin, who had been reading an article on Giacometti, put it down and went into the hall. He was in an ebullient mood he could not explain to himself, and told Rubin he very much admired his hat.

"I'll tell you why I like it so much. It looks like Rembrandt's hat that he wears in one of the middle-aged self-portraits, the really profound ones. May it bring you the best of luck."

Rubin, who had for a moment looked as though he was struggling to say something extraordinary, fixed Arkin in a strong stare and hurried downstairs. That ended the incident, though it did not diminish the art historian's pleasure in his observation.

Arkin later remembered that when he had come to the art school via an assistant curator's job in a museum in St. Louis, seven years ago, Rubin had been working in wood; he now welded triangular pieces of scrap iron to construct his sculptures. Working at one time with a hatchet, later a modified small meat cleaver, he had reshaped driftwood pieces, out of which he had created some arresting forms. Dr. Levis, the director of the art school, had talked the sculptor into giving an exhibition of his altered driftwood objects in one of the downtown galleries. Arkin, in his first term at the school, had gone on the subway to see the show one winter's day. This man is an original, he thought, maybe his work will be, too. Rubin had refused a gallery vernissage, and on the opening day the place was nearly deserted. The sculptor, as though escaping his hacked forms, had retreated into a storage room at the rear of the gallery and stayed there looking at pictures. Arkin, after reflecting whether he ought to, sought him out to say hello, but seeing Rubin seated on a crate with his back to him, examining a folio of somebody's prints, silently shut the door and departed. Although in time two notices of the show appeared, one bad, the other mildly favorable, the sculptor seemed unhappy about having exhibited his work, and after that didn't for years. Nor had there been any sales. Recently, when Arkin had suggested it might be a good idea to show what he was doing with his welded iron triangles, Rubin, after a wildly inexpressive moment, had answered, "Don't bother playing around with that idea."

The day after the art historian's remarks in the hall about Rubin's white cap, it disappeared from sight—gone totally; for a while he wore on his head nothing but his heavy reddish hair. And a week or two later, though he could momentarily not believe it, it seemed to Arkin that the sculptor was avoiding him. He guessed the man was no longer using the staircase to the right of his office, but was coming up from the basement on the other side of the building, where his corner workshop room was anyway, so he wouldn't have to pass Arkin's open door. When he was certain of this Arkin felt uneasy, then experienced moments of anger.

Have I offended him in some way? he asked himself. If so, what did I say that's so offensive? All I did was remark on the hat in one of Rembrandt's self-portraits and say it looked like the cap he was wearing. How can that be offensive?

He then thought: no offense where none's intended. All I have is good will to him. He's shy and may have been embarrassed in some way—maybe my exuberant voice in the presence of students—if that's so it's no fault of mine. And if that's not it, I don't know what's the matter except his own nature. Maybe he hasn't been feeling well, or it's some momentary mishigas—nowadays there are more ways of insults without meaning to than ever before—so why raise up a sweat over it? I'll wait it out.

But as weeks, then months went by and Rubin continued to shun the art historian—he saw the sculptor only at faculty meetings when Rubin attended them; and once in a while glimpsed him going up or down the left staircase; or sitting in the Fine Arts secretary's office poring over inventory lists of supplies for sculpture—Arkin thought maybe the man is having a breakdown. He did not believe it. One day they met in the men's room and Rubin strode out without a word. Arkin felt for the sculptor surges of hatred. He didn't like people who didn't like him. Here I make a sociable, innocent remark to the son of a bitch—at worst it might be called innocuous—and to him it's an insult. I'll give him tit for tat. Two can play.

But when he had calmed down, Arkin continued to wonder and worry over what might have gone wrong. I've always thought I was fairly good in human relationships. Yet he had a worrisome nature and wore a thought ragged if in it lurked a fear the fault was his own. Arkin searched the past. He had always liked the sculptor, even though Rubin offered only his fingertip in friendship; yet Arkin had been friendly, courteous, interested in his work, and respectful of his dignity, almost visibly weighted with unspoken thoughts. Had it, he often wondered, something to do with his mentioning—suggesting—not long ago, the possibility of a new exhibition of his sculpture, to which Rubin had reacted as though his life was threatened?

It was then he recalled he had never told Rubin how he had felt about his hacked-driftwood show—never once commented on it, although he had signed the guest book. Arkin hadn't liked the show, yet he wanted to seek Rubin out to name one or two interesting pieces. But when he had located him in the storage room, intently involved with a folio of prints, lost in hangdog introspection so deeply he had been unwilling, or unable, to greet whoever was standing at his back—Arkin had said to himself, better let it be. He had ducked out of the gallery. Nor had he mentioned the driftwood exhibition thereafter. Was this kindness cruel?

Still it's not very likely he's been avoiding me so long for that alone, Arkin reflected. If he was disappointed, or irritated, by my not mentioning his driftwood show, he would then and there have stopped talking to me, if he was going to stop. But he didn't. He seemed as friendly as ever, according to his measure, and he isn't a dissembler. And when I afterwards suggested the possibility of a new show he obviously wasn't eager to have—which touched him to torment on the spot—he wasn't at all impatient with me but only started staying out of my sight after the business of his white cap, whatever that meant to him. Maybe it wasn't my mention of the cap itself that's annoyed him. Maybe it's a cumulative thing—three minuses for me? Arkin felt it was probably cumulative; still it seemed that the cap remark had mysteriously wounded Rubin most, because nothing that had happened before had threatened their relationship, such as it was, and it was then at least amicable. Having thought it through to this point, Arkin had to admit he did not know why Rubin acted as strangely as he was now acting.

Off and on, the art historian considered going down to the sculptor's studio and there apologizing to him if he had said something inept, which he certainly hadn't meant to do. He would ask Rubin if he'd mind telling him what bothered him; if it was something *else* he had inadvertently said or done, he would apologize and clear things up. It would be mutually beneficial.

One early spring day he made up his mind to visit Rubin after his seminar that afternoon, but one of his students, a bearded printmaker, had found out it was Arkin's thirty-fifth birthday and presented the art historian with a white ten-gallon Stetson that the student's father, a traveling salesman, had brought back from Waco, Texas.

"Wear it in good health, Mr. Arkin," said the student. "Now you're one of the good guys."

Arkin was wearing the hat, going up the stairs to his office accompanied by the student who had given it to him, when they encountered the sculptor, who grimaced in disgust.

Arkin was upset, though he felt at once that the force of this uncalled-for reaction indicated that, indeed, the hat remark had been taken by Rubin as an insult. After the bearded student left Arkin he placed the Stetson on his worktable—it had seemed to him—before going to the men's room; and when he returned the cowboy hat was gone. The art historian searched for it in his office and even hurried back to his seminar room to see whether it could possibly have landed up there, someone having snatched it as a joke. It was not in the seminar room. Arkin thought of rushing down and confronting Rubin nose to nose in his studio, but could not bear the thought. What if he hadn't taken it?

Now both evaded each other. But after a period of rarely meeting they began, ironically, Arkin thought, to encounter one another everywhere—even in the streets, especially near galleries on Madison, or Fifty-seventh, or in SoHo; or on entering or leaving movie houses. Each then hastily crossed the street to skirt the other. In the art school both refused to serve together on committees. One, if he entered the lavatory and saw the other, stepped outside and remained a distance away till he had left. Each hurried to be first into the basement cafeteria at lunchtime because when one followed the other in and observed him standing on line, or already eating at a table, alone or in the company of colleagues, invariably he left and had his meal elsewhere.

Once, when they came in together they hurriedly departed together. After often losing out to Rubin, who could get to the cafeteria easily from his studio, Arkin began to eat sandwiches in his office. Each had become a greater burden to the other, Arkin felt, than he would have been if only one was doing the shunning. Each was in the other's mind to a degree and extent that bored him. When they met unexpectedly in the building after turning a corner or opening a door, or had come face-to-face on the stairs, one glanced at the other's head to see what, if anything, adorned it; they then hurried away in opposite directions. Arkin as a rule wore no hat unless he had a cold; and Rubin lately affected a railroad engineer's cap. The art historian hated Rubin for hating him and beheld repugnance in Rubin's eyes.

"It's your doing," he heard himself mutter. "You brought me to this, it's on your head."

After that came coldness. Each froze the other out of his life; or froze him in.

One early morning, neither looking where he was going as he rushed into the building to his first class, they bumped into each other in front of the arched art school entrance. Both started shouting. Rubin, his face flushed, called Arkin "murderer," and the art historian retaliated by calling the sculptor "hat thief." Rubin smiled in scorn, Arkin in pity; they then fled.

Afterwards Arkin felt faint and had to cancel his class. His weakness became nausea, so he went home and lay in bed, nursing a severe occipital headache. For a week he slept badly, felt tremors in his sleep, ate next to nothing. "What has this bastard done to me?" Later he asked, "What have I done to myself?" I'm in this against my will, he thought. It had occurred to him that he found it easier to judge paintings than to judge people. A woman had said this to him once but he denied it indignantly. Arkin answered neither question and fought off remorse. Then it went through him again that he ought to apologize, if only because if the other couldn't he could. Yet he feared an apology would cripple his craw.

Half a year later, on his thirty-sixth birthday, Arkin, thinking of his lost cowboy hat and having heard from the Fine Arts secretary that Rubin was home sitting shiva for his dead mother, was drawn to the sculptor's studio—a jungle of stone and iron figures—to look around for the hat. He found a discarded welder's helmet but nothing he could call a cowboy hat. Arkin spent hours in the large skylighted studio, minutely inspecting the sculptor's work in welded triangular iron pieces, set amid broken stone statuary he had been collecting for years—decorative garden figures placed charmingly among iron flowers seeking daylight. Flowers were what Rubin was mostly into now, on long stalks with small corollas, on short stalks with petaled blooms. Some of the flowers were mosaics of triangles fixing white stones and broken pieces of thick colored glass in jeweled forms. Rubin had in the last several years come from abstract driftwood sculptures to figurative objects—the flowers, and some uncompleted, possibly abandoned, busts of men and women colleagues, including one that vaguely resembled Rubin in a cowboy hat. He had also done a lovely sculpture of a dwarf tree. In the far corner of the studio was a place for his welding torch and gas tanks as well as arc-welding apparatus, crowded by open heavy wooden boxes of iron triangles of assorted size and thickness. The art historian studied each sculpture and after a while thought he understood why talk of a new exhibition had threatened Rubin.

There was perhaps one fine piece, the dwarf tree, in the iron jungle. Was this what he was afraid he might confess if he fully expressed himself?

Several days later, while preparing a lecture on Rembrandt's self-portraits, Arkin, examining the slides, observed that the portrait of the painter which he had remembered as the one he had seen in the Rijksmuseum in Amsterdam was probably hanging in Kenwood House in London. And neither hat the painter wore in either gallery, though both were white, was that much like Rubin's cap. The observation startled Arkin. The Amsterdam portrait was of Rembrandt in a white turban he had wound around his head; the London portrait was him in a studio cap or beret worn slightly cocked. Rubin's white thing, on the other hand, looked more like an assistant cook's cap in Sam's Diner than like either of Rembrandt's hats in the large oils, or in the other self-portraits Arkin was showing himself on slides. What those had in common was the unillusioned honesty of his gaze. In his self-created mirror the painter beheld distance, objectivity painted to stare out of his right eye; but the left looked out of bedrock, beyond quality. Yet the expression of each of the portraits seemed magisterially sad; or was this what life was if when Rembrandt painted he did not paint the sadness?

After studying the pictures projected on the small screen in his dark office, Arkin felt he had, in truth, made a referential error, confusing the two hats. Even so, what had Rubin, who no doubt was acquainted with the self-portraits, or may have had a recent look at them—at *what* had he taken offense?

Whether I was right or wrong, so what if his white cap made me think of Rembrandt's hat and I told him so? That's not throwing rocks at his head, so what bothered him? Arkin felt he ought to be able to figure it out. Therefore suppose Rubin was Arkin and Arkin Rubin— Suppose it was me in his hat: "Here I am, an aging sculptor with only one show, which I never had confidence in and nobody saw. And standing close by, making critical pronouncements one way or another, is this art historian Arkin, a big-nosed, gawky, overcurious gent, friendly but no friend of mine because he doesn't know how to be. That's not his talent. An interest in art we have in common, but not much more. Anyway, Arkin, maybe not because it means anything in particular—who says he knows what he means?—mentions Rembrandt's hat on my head and wishes me good luck in my work. So say he meant well—but it's still more than I can take. In plain words it irritates me. The mention of Rembrandt, considering the quality of my own work, and what I am generally feeling about life, is a fat burden on my soul because it makes me ask myself once too often—why am I going on if this is the kind of sculptor I am going to be for the rest of my life? And since Arkin makes me think the same unhappy thing no matter what he says—or even what he doesn't say, as for instance about my driftwood show—who wants to hear more? From then on I avoid the guy—like forever."

After staring in the mirror in the men's room, Arkin wandered on every floor of the building, and then wandered down to Rubin's studio. He knocked on the door. No one answered. When he tested the knob it gave, and he thrust his head into the room and called Rubin's name.

Night lay on the skylight. The studio was lit with many dusty bulbs but Rubin was not present. The forest of sculptures was. Arkin went among the iron flowers and broken stone garden pieces to see if he had been wrong in his judgment. After a while he felt he hadn't been.

He was staring at the dwarf tree when the door opened and Rubin, wearing his railroad engineer's cap, in astonishment entered.

"It's a beautiful sculpture," Arkin got out, "the best in the room I'd say."

Rubin stared at him in flushed anger, his face lean; he had grown reddish sideburns. His eyes were for once green rather than gray. His mouth worked nervously, but he said nothing.

"Excuse me, Rubin, I came in to tell you I got those hats I mentioned to you some time ago mixed up."

"Damn right you did."

"Sorry it happened. Also for letting things get out of hand for a while."

"Damn right."

Rubin, though he tried not to, then began to cry. He wept silently, his shoulders shaking, tears seeping through his coarse fingers on his face.

Arkin had taken off.

They stopped avoiding each other and spoke pleasantly when they met, which wasn't often. One day Arkin, when he went into the men's room, saw Rubin regarding himself in the mirror in his white cap, the one that seemed to resemble Rembrandt's hat. He wore it like a crown of failure and hope.

A Wig

IDA WAS an energetic, competent woman of fifty, healthy, still attractive. Thinking of herself, she touched her short hair. What's fifty? One more than forty-nine. She had been married at twenty and had a daughter, Amy, who was twenty-eight and not a satisfied person. Of satisfying, Ida thought: she has no serious commitment. She wanders in her life. From childhood she has wandered off the track, where I can't begin to predict. Amy had recently left the man she was living with, in his apartment, and was again back at home. "He doesn't connect," Amy said. "Why should it take you two years to learn such a basic thing?" Ida asked. "I'm a slow learner," Amy said. "I learn slowly." She worked for an importer who thought highly of her though she wouldn't sleep with him.

As Amy walked out of the room where she had stood talking with her mother, she stopped to arrange some flowers in a vase, six tight roses a woman friend had sent her on her birthday, a week ago. Amy deeply breathed in the decaying fragrance, then shut her door. Ida was a widow who worked three days a week in a sweater boutique. While talking to Amy she had been thinking about her hair. She doubted that Amy noticed how seriously she was worried; or if she did, that it moved her.

When she was a young woman, Ida, for many years, had worn a tight bun held together by three celluloid hairpins. Martin, her husband, who was later to fall dead of a heart attack, liked buns and topknots. "They are sane yet sexy," he said. Ida wore her bun until she began to lose hair in her mid-forties. She noticed the hair coming loose when she brushed it with her ivory-topped brush. One day the increasing number of long hairs left in the comb frightened her. And when she examined her hairline in the mirror, it seemed to Ida that her temples were practically bare.

"I think the tight bun contributes to my loss of hair," she told Martin. "Maybe I ought to get rid of it?"

"Nonsense," he had said. "If anything, the cause would be hormonal."

"So what would you advise me to do?" Ida looked up at him uneasily. He was a wiry man with wavy, graying hair and a strong neck.

"In the first place, don't wash it so often. You wash it too often."

"My hair has always been oily. I have to shampoo it at least twice a week."

"Less often," Martin advised, "take my tip."

"Martin, I am very afraid."

"You don't have to be," he said, "it's a common occurrence."

One day, while walking on Third Avenue, Ida had passed a wigmaker's shop and peered into the window. There were men's and women's wigs on abstract, elegant wooden heads. One or two were reasonably attractive; most were not.

How artificial they are, Ida thought. I could never wear such a thing.

She felt for the wigs a mild hatred she tied up with the fear of losing her hair. If I buy a wig, people will know why. It's none of their business.

Ida continued her brisk walk on Third Avenue. Although it was midsummer, she stepped into a hat shop and bought herself a fall hat, a wide-brimmed felt with a narrow, bright green ribbon. Amy had green eyes.

One morning after Ida had washed her hair in the bathroom sink, and a wet, coiled mass of it slid down the drain, she was shocked and felt faint. After she had dried her hair, as she gently combed it, close to the mirror, she was greatly concerned by the sight of her pink scalp more than ever visible on top of her head. But Martin, after inspecting it, had doubted it was all that noticeable. Of course her hair was thinner than it had been—whose wasn't?—but he said he noticed nothing unusual, especially now that she had cut her hair and was wearing bangs. Ida wore a short, swirled haircut. She shampooed her hair less frequently.

And she went to a dermatologist, who prescribed an emulsion he had concocted, with alcohol, distilled water, and some drops of castor oil, which she was to shake well before applying. He instructed her to rub the mixture into her scalp with a piece of cotton. "That'll stir it up." The dermatologist had first suggested an estrogen salve applied topically, but Ida said she didn't care for estrogen.

"This salve does no harm to women," the doctor said, "although I understand it might shrink a man's testicles."

"If it can shrink a man's testicles, I'd rather not try it," she said. He gave her the emulsion.

Ida would part a strand of hair and gently brush her scalp with the emulsion-soaked cotton; then she would part another strand and gently brush there. Whatever she tried didn't do much good, and her scalp shone through her thinning hair like a dim moon in a stringy dark cloud. She hated to look at herself, she hated to think.

"Martin, if I lose my hair I will lose my femininity."

"Since when?"

"What shall I do?" she begged.

Martin thought. "Why don't you consider another doctor? This guy is too much a salesman. I still think it could be caused by a scalp ailment or some such condition. Cure the scalp and it slows down the loss of hair."

"No matter how I treat the scalp, with or without medication, nothing gets better."

"What do you think caused it?" Martin said. "Some kind of trauma either psychic or physical?"

"It could be hereditary," Ida answered. "I might have my father's scalp."

"Your father had a full head of hair when I first met him—a shock of hair, I would call it."

"Not when he was my age, he was already losing it."

"He was catting around at that age," Martin said. "He was some boy. Nothing could stop him, hair or no hair."

"I'll bet you envy him," Ida said, "or you wouldn't bring that up at this particular time."

"Who I envy or don't envy let's not talk about," he replied. "Let's not get into that realm of experience, or it becomes a different card game."

"I bet you wish you were in that realm of experience. I sometimes feel you envy Amy her odd life."

"Let's not get into that either," Martin insisted. "It doesn't pay."

"What *can* we talk about?" Ida complained.

"We talk about your hair, don't we?"

"I would rather not," she said.

The next day she visited another skin man, who advised her to give up brushing her hair or rubbing anything into her scalp. "Don't stress your hair," he advised. "At the most, you could have it puffed up once in a while, or maybe take a permanent to give it body, but don't as a rule stress it. Also put away your brush and use only a wide-toothed comb, and I will prescribe some moderate doses of vitamins that might help. I can't guarantee it."

"I doubt if that's going to do much good," Ida said when she arrived home.

"How would you know until you've tried it?" Amy asked.

"Nobody has to try everything," Ida said. "Some things you know about without having to try them. You have common sense."

"Look," said Martin, "let's not kid ourselves. If the vitamins don't do anything for you, then you ought to have yourself fitted for a wig or wiglet. It's no sin. They're popular with a lot of people nowadays. If I can wear false teeth, you can wear a wig."

"I hate to," she confessed. "I've tried some on and they burden my head."

"You burden your head," Amy said.

"Amy," said her mother, "if nothing else, then at least mercy."

Amy wandered out of the room, stopping first at the mirror to look at herself.

Martin, that evening, fell dead of a heart attack. He died on the kitchen floor. Ida wailed. Amy made choked noises of grief. Both women mourned him deeply.

For weeks after the funeral, Ida thought of herself vaguely. Her mind was befogged. Alternatively, she reflected intensely on her life, her eyes stinging, thinking of herself as a widow of fifty. "I am terribly worried about my life," she said aloud. Amy was not present. Ida knew she was staying in her room. "What have I done to that child?"

One morning, after studying herself in the full-length looking glass, she hurried to the wigmaker's on Third Avenue. Ida walked with dignity along the busy, sunlit street. The wig shop was called Norman: Perukier. She examined the window, wig by wig, then went determinedly inside. The wigmaker had seen her before and greeted her casually.

"Might I try on a wig or two?"

"Suit yourself."

Ida pointed to a blond wig in the window and to another, chestnut brown, on a dummy's head on a shelf, and Norman brought both to her as she sat at a three-paneled mirror.

Ida's breathing was audible. She tried on the first wig, a light, frizzy, young one. Norman fitted it on her head as if he were drawing on a cloche hat. "There," he said, stepping back. He drew a light blue comb out of his inside pocket and touched the wig here and there before stopping to admire it. "It's a charming wig."

"It feels like a tight hat," Ida said.

"It's not at all tight," Norman said. "But try this."

He handed her the other wig, a brown affair that looked like a haircut Amy used to wear before she had adopted a modified afro in college.

Norman flicked his comb at the wig, then stepped back. He too was breathing heavily, his eyes intent on hers, but Ida would not let his catch hers in the mirror; she kept her gaze on the wig.

"What is the material of this wig?" Ida asked. "It doesn't seem human hair."

"Not this particular one. It's made of Dynel fiber and doesn't frizz in heat or humidity."

"How does a person take care of it?"

"She can wash it with a mild soap in warm water and then either let it dry or blow it dry. Or if she prefers, she can give it to her hairdresser, who will wash, dry, and style it."

"Will my head perspire?"

"Not in this wig."

Ida removed the wig. "What about that black one?" she asked hesitantly. "I like the style of it."

"It's made of Korean hair."

"Real hair?"

"Yes."

"Oh," said Ida. "I don't think I'd care for Oriental hair."

"Why not, if I may ask?" Norman said.

"I can't really explain it, but I think I would feel like a stranger to myself."

"I think you are a stranger to yourself," said the wigmaker, as though he was determined to say it. "I also don't think you are interested in a wig at all. This is the third time you've come into this shop, and you make it an ordeal for all concerned. Buying a wig isn't exactly like shopping for a coffin, don't you know? Some people take a good deal of pleasure in selecting a wig, as if they were choosing a beautiful garment or a piece of jewelry."

"I am not a stranger to myself," Ida replied irritably. "All we're concerned about is a wig. I didn't come here for an amateur psychoanalysis of my personality." Her color had heightened.

"Frankly, I'd rather not do business with you," said the wigmaker. "I wouldn't care for you among my clientele."

"Tant pis pour vous," Ida said, walking out of Norman's shop.

In the street she was deeply angered. It took her five minutes to begin walking. Although the day was not cool she knotted a kerchief on her head. Ida entered a hat shop close by and bought a fuzzy purple hat.

That evening she and Amy quarreled. Amy said, as they were eating fish at supper, that she had met this guy and would be moving out in a week or two, when he returned from California.

"What guy?" snapped Ida. "Somebody that you picked up in a bar?"

"I happened to meet this man in the importing office where I work, if you must know."

Ida's voice grew softer. "Mustn't I know?"

Amy was staring above her mother's head, although there was nothing on the wall to stare at, the whites of her eyes intensely white. Ida knew this sign of Amy's disaffection but continued talking.

"Why don't you find an apartment of your own? You earn a good salary, and your father left you five thousand dollars."

"I want to save that in case of emergency."

"Tell me, Amy, what sort of future do you foresee for yourself?"

"The usual. Neither black nor white."

"How will you protect yourself alone?"

"Not necessarily by getting married. I will protect myself, myself."

"Do you ever expect to marry?"

"When it becomes a viable option."

"What do you mean option, don't you want to have children?"

"I may someday want to."

"You are now twenty-eight. How much longer have you got?"

"I'm twenty-eight and should have at least ten years. Some women bear children at forty."

"I hope," said Ida, "I hope you have ten years, Amy, I am afraid for you. My heart eats me up."

"After you it eats me up. It's an eating heart."

Ida called her daughter a nasty name, and Amy, rising, her face grim, quickly left the room. Ida felt like chasing after her with a stick, or fainting. She went to her room, her head aching, and lay on the double bed. For a while she wept.

She lay there, at length wanting to forget their quarrel. Ida rose and looked in an old photograph album to try to forget how bad she felt. Here was a picture of Martin as a young father, with a black mustache, tossing Amy as a baby in the air. Here she was as a pudgy girl of twelve, never out of jeans. Yet not till she was eighteen had she wanted her long hair cut.

Among these photographs Ida found a picture of her own mother, Mrs. Feitelson, surely no more than forty then, in her horsehair sheitel. The wig looked like a round loaf of dark bread lying on her head. Once a man had tried to mug her on the street. In the scuffle he had pulled her wig off and, when he saw her fuzzy skull, had run off without her purse. They wore those wigs, the Orthodox women, once they were married, not to attract, or distract, men other than their husbands. Sometimes they had trouble attracting their husbands.

Oh, Mama, Ida thought, did I know you? Did you know me?

What am I afraid of? she asked herself, and she thought, I am a widow and losing my looks. I am afraid of the future.

After a while she went barefoot to Amy's room and knocked

on her door. I will tell her that my hair has made me very nervous. When there was no answer she opened the door a crack and said she would like to apologize. Though Amy did not respond, the light was on and Ida entered the room.

Her daughter, a slender woman in long green pajamas, lay in bed reading in the light of the wall lamp. Ida wanted to sit on the bed but felt she had no right to.

"Good night, dear Amy."

Amy did not lower her book. Ida, standing by the bedside looking at Amy, saw something she long ago had put out of her mind: that the girl's hair on top of her head was thinning and a fairly large circle of cobwebbed scalp was visible.

Amy turned a page and went on reading.

Ida, although tormented by the sight of Amy's thinning hair, did not speak of it. In the morning she left the house early and bought herself an attractive wig.

The Model

EARLY ONE morning Ephraim Elihu rang up the Art Students League and asked them how he could locate an experienced female model he could paint nude. He told the woman speaking to him on the phone that he wanted someone of about thirty. "Could you possibly help me?"

"I don't recognize your name," said the woman on the telephone. "Have you ever dealt with us before? Some of our students will work as models but usually only for painters we know." Mr. Elihu said he hadn't. He wanted it understood he was an amateur painter who had once studied at the League.

"Do you have a studio?"

"It's a large living room with lots of light.

"I'm no youngster," he went on, "but after many years I've begun painting again and I'd like to do some nude studies to get back my feeling for form. I'm not a professional painter you understand but I'm serious about painting. If you want any references as to my character, I can supply them." He asked her what the going rate for models was, and the woman, after a pause, said, "Six-fifty the hour." Mr. Elihu said that was satisfactory. He seemed to want to talk longer but she did not encourage him. She wrote down his name and address and said she thought she could have someone for him the day after tomorrow. He thanked her for her consideration.

That was on Wednesday. The model appeared on Friday morning. She had telephoned the night before and they settled on a time for her to come. She rang his bell shortly after 9 A.M. and Mr. Elihu went at once to the door. He was a gray-haired man of seventy who lived in a brownstone house near Ninth Avenue, and he was excited by the prospect of painting this young woman.

The model was a plain-looking woman of twenty-seven or so, and the old painter decided her best feature was her eyes. She was wearing a blue raincoat on a clear spring day. The old painter liked her face but kept that to himself. She barely glanced at him as she walked firmly into the room.

"Good day," he said, and she answered, "Good day."

"It's like spring," said the old man. "The foliage is starting up again."

"Where do you want me to change?" asked the model.

Mr. Elihu asked her name and she responded, "Ms. Perry."

"You can change in the bathroom, I would say, Miss Perry, or if you like, my own room—down the hall—is empty and you can change there also. It's warmer than the bathroom."

The model said it made no difference to her but she thought she would rather change in the bathroom.

"That is as you wish," said the elderly man.

"Is your wife around?" she then asked, glancing into the room.

"I happen to be a widower."

He said he had had a daughter once but she had died in an accident.

The model said she was sorry. "I'll change and be out in a few fast minutes."

"No hurry at all," said Mr. Elihu, glad he was about to paint her.

Ms. Perry entered the bathroom, undressed there, and returned quickly. She slipped off her terry cloth robe. Her head and shoulders were slender and well formed. She asked the old man how he would like her to pose. He was standing by an enamel-top kitchen table in a living room with a large window. On the tabletop he had squeezed out, and was mixing together, the contents of two small tubes of paint. There were three other tubes he did not touch. The model, taking a last drag of a cigarette, pressed it out against a coffee can lid on the kitchen table.

"I hope you don't mind if I take a puff once in a while?"

"I don't mind, if you do it when we take a break."

"That's all I meant."

She was watching him as he slowly mixed his colors.

Mr. Elihu did not immediately look at her nude body but said he would like her to sit in the chair by the window. They were facing a back yard with an ailanthus tree whose leaves had just come out.

"How would you like me to sit, legs crossed or not crossed?"

"However you prefer that. Crossed or uncrossed doesn't

make much of a difference to me. Whatever makes you feel comfortable."

The model seemed surprised at that, but she sat down in the yellow chair by the window and crossed one leg over the other. Her figure was good.

"Is this O.K. for you?"

Mr. Elihu nodded. "Fine," he said. "Very fine."

He dipped the brush into the paint he had mixed on the tabletop, and after glancing at the model's nude body, began to paint. He would look at her, then look quickly away, as if he was afraid of affronting her. But his expression was objective. He painted apparently casually, from time to time gazing up at the model. He did not often look at her. She seemed not to be aware of him. Once, she turned to observe the ailanthus tree and he studied her momentarily to see what she might have seen in it.

Then she began to watch the painter with interest. She watched his eyes and she watched his hands. He wondered if he was doing something wrong. At the end of about an hour she rose impatiently from the yellow chair.

"Tired?" he asked.

"It isn't that," she said, "but I would like to know what in the name of Christ you think you are doing? I frankly don't think you know the first thing about painting."

She had astonished him. He quickly covered the canvas with a towel.

After a long moment, Mr. Elihu, breathing shallowly, wet his dry lips and said he was making no claims for himself as a painter. He said he had tried to make that absolutely clear to the woman he had talked to at the art school when he had called.

Then he said, "I might have made a mistake in asking you to come to this house today. I think I should have tested myself a while longer, just so I wouldn't be wasting anybody's time. I guess I am not ready to do what I would like to do."

"I don't care how long you have tested yourself," said Ms. Perry. "I honestly don't think you have painted me at all. In fact, I felt you weren't interested in painting me. I think you're interested in letting your eyes go over my naked body for certain reasons of your own. I don't know what your personal needs are but I'm damn well sure that most of them are not about painting."

"I guess I have made a mistake."

"I guess you have," said the model. She had her robe on now, the belt pulled tight.

"I'm a painter," she said, "and I model because I am broke but I know a fake when I see one."

"I wouldn't feel so bad," said Mr. Elihu, "if I hadn't gone out of my way to explain the situation to that lady at the Art Students League.

"I'm sorry this happened," Mr. Elihu said hoarsely. "I should have thought it through but didn't. I'm seventy years of age. I have always loved women and felt a sad loss that I have no particular women friends at this time of my life. That's one of the reasons I wanted to paint again, though I make no claims that I was ever greatly talented. Also, I guess I didn't realize how much about painting I have forgotten. Not only that, but about the female body. I didn't realize I would be so moved by yours, and, on reflection, about the way my life has gone. I hoped painting again would refresh my feeling for life. I regret that I have inconvenienced and disturbed you."

"I'll be paid for my inconvenience," Ms. Perry said, "but what you can't pay me for is the insult of coming here and submitting myself to your eyes crawling on my body."

"I didn't mean it as an insult."

"That's what it feels like to me."

She then asked Mr. Elihu to disrobe.

"I?" he said, surprised. "What for?"

"I want to sketch you. Take your pants and shirt off."

He said he had barely got rid of his winter underwear but she did not smile.

Mr. Elihu disrobed, ashamed of how he must look to her.

With quick strokes she sketched his form. He was not a bad-looking man but felt bad. When she had the sketch she dipped his brush into a blob of black pigment she had squeezed out of a tube and smeared his features, leaving a black mess.

He watched her hating him but said nothing.

Ms. Perry tossed the brush into a wastebasket and returned to the bathroom for her clothing.

The old man wrote out a check for her for the sum they had

agreed on. He was ashamed to sign his name but he signed it and handed it to her. Ms. Perry slipped the check into her large purse and left.

He thought that in her way she was not a bad-looking woman though she lacked grace. The old man then asked himself, "Is there nothing more to my life than it is now? Is this all that is left to me?"

The answer seemed yes and he wept at how old he had so quickly become.

Afterwards he removed the towel over his canvas and tried to fill in her face, but he had already forgotten it.

A Lost Grave

HECHT WAS a born late bloomer.

One night he woke hearing rain on his windows and thought of his young wife in her wet grave. This was something new, because he hadn't thought of her in too many years to be comfortable about. He saw her in her uncovered grave, rivulets of water streaming in every direction, and Celia, whom he had married when they were of unequal ages, lying alone in the deepening wet. Not so much as a flower grew on her grave, though he could have sworn he had arranged perpetual care.

He stepped into his thoughts perhaps to cover her with a plastic sheet, and though he searched in the cemetery under dripping trees and among many wet plots, he was unable to locate her. The dream he was into offered no tombstone name, row, or plot number, and though he searched for hours, he had nothing to show for it but his wet self. The grave had taken off. How can you cover a woman who isn't where she is supposed to be? That's Celia.

The next morning, Hecht eventually got himself out of bed and into a subway train to Jamaica to see where she was buried. He hadn't been to the cemetery in many years, no particular surprise to anybody considering past circumstances. Life with Celia wasn't exactly predictable. Yet things change in a lifetime, or seem to. Hecht had lately been remembering his life more vividly, for whatever reason. After you hit sixty-five, some things that have two distinguishable sides seem to pick up another that complicates the picture as you look or count. Hecht counted.

Now, though Hecht had been more or less in business all his life, he kept few personal papers, and though he had rifled through a small pile of them that morning, he had found nothing to help him establish Celia's present whereabouts; and after a random looking at gravestones for an hour he felt the need to call it off and spend another hour with a young secretary in the main office, who fruitlessly tapped his name and Celia's into a computer and came up with a scramble of interment dates, grave plots and counter plots, that exasperated him.

"Look, my dear," Hecht said to the flustered young secretary, "if that's how far you can go on this machine, we have to find another way to go further, or I will run out of patience. This grave is lost territory as far as I am concerned, and we have to do something practical to find it."

"What do you think I'm doing, if I might ask?"

"Whatever you are doing doesn't seem to be much help. This computer is supposed to have a good mechanical memory, but it's either out of order or rusty in its parts. I admit I didn't bring any papers with me, but so far the only thing your computer has informed us is that it has nothing much to inform us."

"It has informed us it is having trouble locating the information you want."

"Which adds up to zero minus zero," Hecht said. "I wish to remind you that a lost grave isn't a missing wedding ring we are talking about. It is a lost cemetery plot of the lady who was once my wife that I wish to recover."

The pretty young woman he was dealing with had a tight-lipped conversation with an unknown person, then the buzzer on her desk sounded and Hecht was given permission to go into the director's office.

"Mr. Goodman will now see you."

He resisted "Good for Mr. Goodman." Hecht only nodded, and followed the young woman to an inner office. She knocked once and disappeared, as a friendly voice talked through the door.

"Come in, come in."

"Why should I worry if it's not my fault?" Hecht told himself.

Mr. Goodman pointed to a chair in front of his desk and Hecht was soon seated, watching him pour orange juice from a quart container into a small green glass.

"Will you join me in a sweet mouthful?" he asked, nodding at the container. "I usually take refreshment this time of the morning. It keeps me balanced."

"Thanks," said Hecht, meaning he had more serious problems. "Why I am here is that I am looking for my wife's grave, so far with no success." He cleared his throat, surprised at the emotion that had gathered there.

Mr. Goodman observed Hecht with interest.

"Your outside secretary couldn't find it," Hecht went on, regretting he hadn't found the necessary documents that would identify the grave site. "Your young lady tried her computer in every combination but couldn't produce anything. What was lost is still lost, in other words, a woman's grave."

"*Lost* is premature," Goodman offered. "*Displaced* might be better. In my twenty-eight years in my present capacity, I don't believe we have lost a single grave."

The director tapped lightly on the keys of his desk computer, studied the screen with a squint, and shrugged. "I am afraid that we now draw a blank. The letter *H* volume of our ledgers that we used before we were computerized seems to be missing. I assure you this can't be more than a temporary condition."

"That's what your young lady already informed me."

"She's not my young lady, she's my secretarial assistant."

"I stand corrected," Hecht said. "This meant no offense."

"Likewise," said Goodman. "But we will go on looking. Could you kindly tell me, if you don't mind, what was the status of your relationship to your wife at the time of her death?" He peered over half-moon glasses to check the computer reading.

"There was no status. We were separated. What has that got to do with her burial plot?"

"The reason I inquire is, I thought it might refresh your memory. For example, is this the correct cemetery, the one you are looking in—Mount Jereboam? Some people confuse us with Mount Hebron."

"I guarantee you it was Mount Jereboam."

Hecht, after a hesitant moment, gave these facts: "My wife wasn't the most stable woman. She left me twice and disappeared for months. Although I took her back twice, we weren't together at the time of her death. Once she threatened to take her life, though eventually she didn't. In the end she died of a normal sickness, not cancer. This was years later, when we weren't living together anymore, but I carried out her burial, to the best of my knowledge, in this exact cemetery. I also heard she had lived for a short time with some guy she met somewhere, but when she died, I was the one who buried her. Now I am sixty-five and lately I have had this urge to visit the grave of someone who lived with me when I was a young man. This is a grave which everybody now tells me they can't locate."

Goodman rose at his desk, a short man, five feet tall. "I will institute a careful research."

"The quicker, the better," Hecht replied. "I am still curious what happened to her grave."

Goodman almost guffawed, but caught himself and thrust out his hand. "I will keep you well informed, don't worry."

Hecht left, irritated. On the train back to the city he thought of Celia and her various unhappinesses. He wished he had told Goodman she had spoiled his life.

That night it rained. To his surprise he found a wet spot on his pillow.

The next day Hecht again went to the graveyard. "What did I forget that I ought to remember?" he asked himself. Obviously the grave plot, row, and number. Though he sought it diligently he could not find it. Who can remember something he has once and for all put out of his mind? It's like trying to grow beans out of a bag of birdseed.

"But I must be patient and I will find out. As time goes by I am bound to recall. When my memory says yes I won't argue no."

But weeks passed and Hecht still could not remember what he was trying to. "Maybe I have reached a dead end?"

Another month went by and at last the cemetery called him. It was Mr. Goodman, clearing his throat. Hecht pictured him at his desk sipping orange juice.

"Mr. Hecht?"

"The same."

"This is Mr. Goodman. A happy Rosh Hashanah."

"A happy Rosh Hashanah to you."

"Mr. Hecht, I wish to report progress. Are you prepared for an insight?"

"You name it," Hecht said.

"So let me use a better word. We have tracked your wife and it turns out she isn't in the grave there where the computer couldn't find her. To be frank, we found her in a grave with another gentleman."

"What kind of gentleman? Who in God's name is he? I am her legal husband."

"This one, if you will pardon me, is the man who lived with your wife after she left you. They lived together on and off, so don't blame yourself too much. After she died he got a court order, and they removed her to a different grave, where we also laid him after his death. The judge gave him the court order because he convinced him that he had loved her for many years."

Hecht was embarrassed. "What are you talking about? How could he transfer her grave anywhere if it wasn't his legal property? Her grave belonged to me. I paid cash for it."

"That grave is still there," Goodman explained, "but the names were mixed up. His name was Kaplan but the workmen buried her under Caplan. Your grave is still in the cemetery, though we had it under Kaplan and not Hecht. I apologize to you for this inconvenience but I think we now have got the mystery cleared up."

"So thanks," said Hecht. He felt he had lost a wife but was no longer a widower.

"Also," Goodman reminded him, "don't forget you gained an empty grave for future use. Nobody is there and you own the plot."

Hecht said that was obviously true.

The story had astounded him. Yet whenever he thought of telling it to someone he knew, or had just met, he wasn't sure he wanted to.

Zora's Noise

HERE'S THIS unhappy noise that upsets Zora.

She had once been Sarah. Dworkin, when he married her not long after the death of Ella, his first wife, had talked her into changing her name. She eventually forgave him. Now she felt she had always been Zora.

"Zora, we have to hurry."

"I'm coming, for godsake. I am looking for my brown gloves."

He was fifty-one, she ten years younger, an energetic, plump person with an engaging laugh and a tendency to diet unsuccessfully. She called him Dworky: an animated, reflective man, impassioned cellist—and, on inspiration, composer—with an arthritic left shoulder. He referred to it as "the shoulder I hurt when I fell in the cellar." When she was angry with him, or feeling insecure, she called him Zworkin.

I hear something, whatever do I hear? Zora blew her nose and listened to her ear. Is my bad ear worse? If it isn't, what are those nagging noises I've been hearing all spring? Because I listen, I hear. But what makes me listen?

The really bothersome noise had begun in April when the storm windows came off and the screens went up; yet it seemed to Zora she hadn't become conscious of its relentless quality until June, after being two months on a diet that didn't work. She was heavier than she cared to be. She had never had children and held that against herself too.

Zora settled on the day after her forty-first birthday, at the end of June, as the time when the noise began seriously to affect her. Maybe I wasn't listening with both my ears up to then. I had my mind elsewhere. They say the universe exploded and we still hear the roar and hiss of all that gas. She asked Dworky about that, forgetting to notice—Oh, my God—that he was practicing his cello, a darkly varnished, mellow Montagnana, "the best thing that ever happened to me," he had once said.

No response from him but an expression of despair: as though he had said, "I practice in the living room to keep you company, and the next thing I know you're interfering with my music." "Please pardon me," Zora said.

"The cello," he had defined it shortly after they met, "is an independent small Jewish animal." And Zora had laughed as though her heart were broken. There were two streams to her laughter—a full-blown humorous response, plus something reserved. You expected one and maybe got the other. Sometimes you weren't sure what she was laughing at, if laughing. Dworkin, as he seesawed his rosin-scented bow across the four steel strings, sometimes sang to his cello, and the cello throatily responded. Zora and Dworkin had met many years ago after a concert in L.A., the night he was the guest of the Los Angeles Philharmonic.

"My cello deepens me," he had told her.

"In that case I'll marry you both."

That was how she had proposed, he told friends at their dinner table, and everyone laughed.

"Do you hear that grating, sickening sound?" she had asked as they were undressing late one summer's night in their high-ceilinged bedroom. The wallpaper was Zora's, spread through with white cosmos pasted over the thickly woven cerise paper selected by Ella many years ago when she and Dworkin had first moved into this spacious, comfortable house. "Do you like it?" he had asked Zora. "Love it." She immediately had the upstairs sun deck built, and the French doors leading to it, giving her, she said, "access to the sky."

"What sickening sound?" he asked.

"You don't hear it?"

"Not as of right now."

"Well, it isn't exactly the music of the spheres," Zora responded. She had in her twenties worked in a chemistry laboratory, though her other interests tended to be artistic.

Zora was plump, in high heels about Dworkin's height; she had firm features and almost a contralto speaking voice. She had once, at his suggestion, taken singing lessons that hadn't come to much. She was not very musical, though she loved to listen and had her own record collection. When they were first married she had worked in an art gallery in Stockbridge. They lived in Elmsville, a nearby town, in a clapboard house painted iron-gray, with marine-blue shutters. The colors were Zora's own good colors. For Ella it had been a white house with black shutters. They were both effective with their colors.

Dworkin taught the cello to students in the vicinity and at a master class in the New England Conservatory of Music at Lenox. He had stopped concertizing a year after his fall in the cellar. Zora, who was not much tempted by travel, liked to have him home regularly. "It's better for your arthritis. It's better for me."

She said, referring to the noise, "I would describe it as absolutely ongoing, with a wobbly, enervating, stinky kind of whine."

That was in July. He honestly couldn't hear it.

At night she woke in slow fear, intently listening.

"Suppose it goes on forever?" She felt herself shudder. It was an ugly thrumming sound shot through with a sickly whine. She listened into the distance, where it seemed to begin, and then slowly drew in her listening as though it were a line she had cast out; and now she listened closer to shore. Far or near, it amounted to the same thing. The invasive noise seemed to enter the house by way of their bedroom, even when the windows were tightly shut, as if it had seeped through the clapboard and the walls, and once or twice frighteningly seemed to metamorphose into a stranger sitting in the dark, breathing audibly and evenly, pausing between breaths.

In the near distance there was a rumble of light traffic, though she knew no traffic was going through town at this time of night. Maybe an occasional truck, changing gears. The nearer sound was Dworkin sleeping, breathing heavily, sometimes shifting into a snore.

"Dworky," she said patiently, "snoring." And Dworkin, with a rasping sigh of contrition, subsided. When she had first taken to waking him out of a sound sleep to break his snoring, he had resented it. "But your snore woke *me* out of sound sleep," Zora said. "It isn't as though I had *planned* to wake you up." He saw the justice of her remark and permitted her to wake him if he was snoring. He would stir for a minute, break his galloping rumble, then more quietly slumber.

Anyway, if someone sat there, it wasn't Dworkin making dream noises. This was a quiet presence, perhaps somebody in the Queen Anne chair by the long stained-glass window in their bedroom, Ella's invention. Someone contemplating them as they slept? Zora rose on her elbow and peered in the dark. Nothing glowed or stank, laughed madly or assaulted her. And she was once more conscious of the unhappy sound she was contending with, a vibrato hum touched with a complaining, drawn-out wail that frightened her because it made her think of the past, perhaps her childhood oozing out of the dark. Zora felt she had had such a childhood.

"Zworkin," she said in a tense whisper, "do you hear this wretched noise I've been referring to?"

"Is that a reason to wake me again, Zora, to ask such a goddamn question? Is that what we've come to at this time in our lives? Let me sleep, I beg you. I have my arthritis to think of."

"You're my husband—who else will I ask? I've already spoken to the people next door. Mrs. Duvivier says the noise originates in a paint factory across town, but of that I'm not so sure."

She spoke in hesitation and doubt. She had been an uncertain young woman when he met her. She wasn't heavy then but had always been solid, she called it, yet with a figure and a lovely face, not fat. Ella, on the other hand, who could be a restless type, was always on the slim side of slender. Both had been good wives, yet neither would have guessed the other as his wife. As Zora gained weight her uneasiness seemed to grow. Sometimes she aroused in Dworkin an anguished affection.

He leaned on his arm and strained to listen, wanting to hear what she heard. The Milky Way crackling? A great wash of cosmic static filled his ears and diminished to a hush of silence. As he listened the hum renewed itself, seeming to become an earthly buzz—a bouquet of mosquitoes and grasshoppers on the lawn, rasping away. Occasionally he heard the call of a night bird. Then the insects vanished, and he heard nothing: no more than the sound of both ears listening.

That was all, though Dworkin sometimes heard music when he woke at night—the music woke him. Lately he had heard Rostropovich, as though he were a living element of a ghostly constellation in the sky, sawing away on the D-major Haydn cello concerto. His rich cello sound might be conceived of as a pineapple, if fruit was your metaphor. Dworkin lived on fruit, but his own playing sounded more like small bittersweet apples. Listening now, he only heard the town asleep.

"I don't hear anything that could be characterized as the whining or wailing you mention," he said. "Nothing of that particular quality."

"No steady, prolonged, hateful, complaining noise?"

He listened until his ears ached. "Nothing that I hear or have heard," he confessed.

"Thank you, and good night, my dear."

"Good night," Dworkin said. "I hope we both sleep now."

"I hope so." She was still assiduously listening.

One night she rose out of dizzying sleep, seemed to contemplate her blanket in the dark, and then hopped out of bed and ran to the bathroom, where she threw up. Dworkin heard her crying as she stepped into the shower.

"Anything wrong?" he asked, popping his head into the steaming room.

"I'll be all right."

"Something I can do for you?"

"Not just now."

He returned to bed and after a few troubled minutes drew on his trousers and a shirt, and in sneakers descended into the street. Except for a barking dog at the end of the block he heard only summer night sounds, and in the distance a rumble that sounded like traffic and might be. But if he concentrated, he could make out the whomp-whomp of machinery, indeed from the direction of the paint factory on the eastern edge of town. Zora and Dworkin hadn't been inconvenienced by the factory or its legendary smells until she began to hear her noise. Still, what she said she heard she no doubt heard, though it was hard to explain anything like a whine.

He circled the house to hear if one or another noise, by some freak of acoustics, was louder on the back lawn, but it wasn't. In the rear he saw Zora on the upstairs deck, pudgy in her short nightdress, staring into the moonlit distance.

"What are you doing outside in a nightgown at this time of night, Zora?" Dworkin asked in a loud whisper.

"Listening," she said vaguely.

"At least why don't you put on a robe after your hot shower? The night air is chilly."

"Dworkin, do you hear the awful whining that I do? That's what made me puke."

"It's not whining I hear, Zora. What I hear is more like a rumble that could be originating in the paint factory. Sometimes it throbs, or whomps, or clanks a little. Maybe there's a kind of a hum, but I can't make out anything else or anything more unusual."

"No, I'm talking about a different sound than you mention. How I hate factories in neighborhoods that should be residential."

Dworkin trotted up the stairs to bed. "It would be interesting to know what some of the other people on this street besides the Duviviers have to say about the sounds you are hearing."

"I've talked to them all," said Zora, "and also to the Cunliffes and the Spinkers."

Dworkin hadn't known. "What did they say?"

"Some hear something"—she hesitated—"but different things than I do. Mrs. Spinker hears a sort of drone. Mrs. Cunliffe hears something else, but not what I hear."

"I wish I did."

"I wouldn't want to afflict you."

"Just to hear it," he said.

"Don't you believe me, Dworky?"

He nodded seriously.

"It might have to come to our moving someday," Zora reflected. "Not only is there that zonky noise I have to contend with, which made me throw up, but the price of heating oil is way up. On the other hand, the real estate market is good, and maybe we ought to put the house up for sale."

"To live where?" Dworkin asked.

She said she might like to get back to city life sometime.

"That's news to me. I assumed you didn't care for city life anymore."

"I do and I don't. I'm forty-one and have been thinking I ought to be making changes. I think I'd like to get back into the art world. I'd like to be near a neighborhood of museums and galleries. That appalling noise all summer has made me honestly wonder if we shouldn't seriously be looking into the possibility of selling this house."

"Over my dead body. I love this house," Dworkin shouted.

As she was preparing a salmon soufflé for supper, the newsboy came to collect for the paper. After she had glanced at the first page, Zora uttered a short cry of surprise and sat down. Dworkin, who had been practicing in the living room, quickly laid down his cello and went to her.

"Here it is in cold print," Zora, her hand on her bosom, said. "Now I know I'm not going crazy."

Dworkin took the newspaper. An article described a class-action suit organized by several citizens in the eastern part of town against the D-R Paints Company "for pollution of the atmosphere." They cited "a persistent harrowing noise," and one of the women interviewed complained of "a sneaky sound that goes up and down like a broken boat whistle. I hear it at night, but I sometimes hear it during the day."

"I feel as though I have been reprieved from being thought mad," Zora said bitterly.

"Not by me," Dworkin insisted.

"But you never seemed to hear the whine I've been hearing."

"In good faith."

Zora began slowly to waltz on the rug in the living room. Dworkin's cello was resting on the floor, and he sat down and plucked strings to her dancing.

One rainy night, Dworkin in pajamas, vigorously brushing his teeth, heard an insistent, weird, thrumming whistle. "What have we here?" he asked himself uneasily. He had been attempting to develop a melody that eluded him, when a keen breeze blowing from afar seemed to invade his ears. It was as though he were lying in bed and someone had poured a pitcher full of whistling wind into both ears. Dworkin forcefully shook his head to dispel the uncomfortable sound, but it refused to disappear.

As Zora lay in bed perusing the paper—she complained she couldn't concentrate well enough to read a book—Dworkin went downstairs for a coat and rain hat and stepped out-of-doors. Facing toward the D-R Paints Company, he listened intently. Though he could not see the factory in the rainy dark, a few foggy, bluish lights were visible in the east, and he felt certain the plant was in operation. The low, thrumming wind in his ears persisted. It was possible that a machine had gone haywire in the factory and was squealing like a dying animal. Possible, but not highly likely—they surely would have found some means to shut it off, he thought irritably. Could it be that the experience was, on his part, a form of autosuggestion out of empathy for Zora? He waited for the droning whine to thin out and crawl off, but nothing happened. Dworkin shook his fist at the foggy blue lights and hurried inside.

"Zora, has your noise been sounding different lately?"

"It isn't only mine," she responded. "It's other people's too. You read that yourself in the *Courier*."

"Granted, but would you say it has increased in volume lately—or otherwise changed?"

"It stays more or less the same but is still with me. I hear it plainly enough. I hear it this very minute."

"In this room, or throughout the house?"

"There's no one place. I used to feel snug here and enjoyed reading in bed. Now I'm afraid to come up at night."

Listening affirmed it overwhelmingly—the ongoing intrusive sound—her keen wail, his thrumming whine.

Dworkin then told his wife about his own unsettling experience. He described what he was presently hearing in both ears. "It's an insult, to say the least."

But Zora responded jubilantly. "At least you've heard it. Thank God."

He was about to ask why that should make her so gay but didn't.

As if he had asked, she said, "If I seem relieved, it's simply because I feel that you can now confirm that what I heard, and was trying to get you to hear, last summer, was substantial and real."

"Whoever said it wasn't?"

Her lips trembled. Dworkin observed her watching him. When he coughed she cleared her throat.

In the morning he went to the music room and got his cello out of its case. It was like lifting a girl gently out of bed. The music room—Ella's name for it; she had named all the rooms in the house—was a large, white-walled room with a mellow pine floor. The eastern wall was rounded, containing four windows through which the morning sun shone warmly. It was a cold room in winter, but Dworkin had installed a wood stove. Here he practiced, composed, sometimes taught. After nervously tuning up he began the first bars of the Prelude to the Bach Unaccompanied D-minor Suite. He had played it in his sleep last night.

Dworkin crouched over the cello, playing somberly, slowly, drawing the sensuous melody out of his instrument. He played the Bach as though pleading with God. He speaks as a man stating his fate. He says it quietly and, as he plays, deepens the argument. He sings now, almost basso, as though he were someone imprisoned in a well singing to a circle of blue sky.

The music ceased. Dworkin, with bowed head, listened. He had been struggling to obliterate the whirling whistle in his head but it had effectively dirtied every note. He could not keep the Bach pure. He could not, past the opening measures, hear himself play. Gripping the cello by its neck, he rose from the chair with a cry.

"Zora," he called.

She arrived at once.

"What's happening?"

He said he could not go on with the suite. It was curdled by the disgusting whine in his ears.

"Something drastic has to be done."

She said they had already joined the class-action suit.

He threatened to abandon the accursed town if there was no quick improvement in the situation; and Zora, observing him, said that was entirely on his own head.

Away from home there was some measure of relief. Driving to Lenox for a class, he escaped the sound in his ears—certainly it diminished outside of Elmsville, but it worried him that he seemed still to be listening for its return. He couldn't be sure he was entirely rid of it. Yet just as he thought he had begun taking the noise with him wherever he went, the situation seemed to change.

One night in winter the *Courier* announced that the

malfunctioning ventilation system at the plant had been replaced by a noiseless apparatus. Zora and Dworkin, as they lay in bed bundled in blankets, listened with two of the three windows wide open. She heard the same unhappy sound, he only the delicious country silence. But the noise had diminished a little, Zora admitted, and possibly she could stand it now.

In the spring, as she approached her forty-second birthday, she was restless again. She had gone back to the gallery where she had formerly worked and was in the process of arranging a show of two women painters and a male sculptor. During the day Zora wasn't home; Dworkin was—practicing and teaching. He was at work on a sonata for four cellos that was developing well. Four cellos gave it an organlike choral quality.

But Zora, after the gallery day, was impatient with herself, self-critical, "not with it."

"Why don't you tell me what's on your mind," Dworkin said one evening after they had had dinner out.

"Nothing much."

"Or is it the usual thing?"

"I can't burden you with my every worry."

She wiped her eyes but was not crying.

That night she woke Dworkin and, in a hushed, hesitant voice, begged him to listen. "I mean, just listen to what you hear in this room. What do you hear?"

He listened until he heard the cosmos, the rush of stars; otherwise he heard nothing.

"Not much, I'm afraid. Nothing I can lay a finger on."

On earth he heard nothing.

"Don't you hear," she asked, slowly sitting up, "a sort of eerie whine? This is drawn out as though at the far end of someone crying. I would call it a ghostly sound."

She held Dworkin tightly.

"Ghostly?" he said, trying to see her in the dark.

She listened keenly. "It has that quality."

"No," Dworkin replied after a good two minutes. "I don't hear any wail, whine, or whatever. I emphatically don't."

In the morning she firmly asked, "Would you move out of this house if it came to that, Dworkin? I mean if I asked you to?"

He said he would once he felt certain he heard the noise she was hearing. She seemed to accept that as fair.

Dworkin waited by the D-R factory fence in every wind and weather. He had talked to the owner, who promised him the problem was already solved. Zora said she didn't think so. They listened together on the bedroom deck, and Zora, pale-faced, raised a pale finger when she heard the noise especially clearly. "As though it were directly in front of our faces."

He wondered whether what she was hearing might be psychologically inspired. Zora had wanted a child but had never had one. Might she who can't conceive begin to hear a ghostly wailing?

Too simple, thought Dworkin.

Ella had taken her troubles in stride. Their baby was born dead, and she had not wanted another. But Zora could never conceive, though she had wanted to very much.

She agreed to have her ears tested when Dworkin suggested it. He reminded her that years ago she had had a disease of the middle ear, and she consented to see her former ear doctor.

Then Dworkin privately telephoned two of his neighbors and confirmed they no longer heard the noise Zora said she still heard.

"It's been solved for my husband and me with the new ventilation system they put in," Mrs. Spinker explained. "So we dropped the suit because nobody hears those noises anymore."

"Or echo thereof?"

"Not anymore."

Dworkin said he too would drop it.

Zora said she would try a new diet before visiting the ear doctor; but she promised to go.

The diet, after several weeks, appeared not to be working, and she was still hearing the quavering, eerie noise. "It comes up like a flute that hangs still in the air and then flows back to its source. Then it begins to take on the quality of a moaning or mystical sound, if that's what you can call it. Suppose it's some distant civilization calling in, trying to get in touch with us, and for some reason I am the one person who can hear this signal, yet I can't translate the message?"

"We all get signals we don't necessarily pick up," Dworkin said.

She woke him that night and said in a hushed voice, "There it goes again, a steady, clear sound, ending in a rising wail. Don't you hear it now?"

"I tell you I don't. Why do you still wake me?"

"I can't help wishing you would hear it too."

"I don't want to. Leave me the hell out of it."

"I hate you, Zworkin. You are a selfish beast."

"You want to poison my ears."

"I want you to confirm whether something I hear is real or unreal. Is that so much to ask somebody you are married to?"

"It's your noise, Zora—don't bang it on my head. How am I going to support us if I can't play my cello?"

"Suppose I go deaf," she said, but Dworkin was snoring.

"La la, la la," she sang to herself in the looking glass. She had been gaining weight and resembled, she said, an ascending balloon.

Dworkin, returning from Lenox that evening, complained he'd had trouble in his master class because the arthritis in his shoulder was taking a harder bite.

When he came upstairs before midnight, she was reading a magazine in bed, both ears plugged with wads of cotton. Her legs snapped together when he entered the room.

"The bedroom is virtually a sound box," Zora said. "It captures every earthly sound, not to speak of the unearthly."

I'd better stop listening, he thought. If I hear what she does, that is the end of my music.

Zora drove off in a station wagon for three days, traveling into Vermont and New Hampshire. She had not asked Dworkin to come along. Each night she called from a different motel or country inn and sounded fine.

"How's it coming?" he asked.

"Just fine, I suppose. I confess I haven't heard anything greatly unusual in my ears."

"No noises from outer space?"

"Nor from inner."

He said that was a good sign.

"What do you think we ought to do?" she asked.

"Concerning what?"

"About the house. About our lives. If I go on hearing noises when I get back."

He said after a minute, "Zora, I would like to help you extricate yourself from this misery. I speak with love."

"Don't make me feel like a crippled pigeon," she said. "I know I hear a real enough noise when I am in that house."

"I warn you, I love this house," he said.

On the night after her return from her trip alone, Dworkin, awakened by a burst of cello music in the sky, stood in yellow pajamas and woolen navy robe on the deck, staring at the clustered stars.

Spanning the knotted strings of glowing small fires across the night sky, he beheld, after its slow coming into sight, like a lighted ship out of fog, his personal constellation: the Cellist. Dworkin had observed it in childhood, and often since then, a seated figure playing his cello—somewhere between Cassiopeia and Lyra. Tonight he beheld Casals sitting in a chair constructed of six jeweled stars, playing gorgeously as he hoarsely sang. Dworkin watched engrossed, trying to identify the music; like Bach but not Bach. He was not able to. Casals was playing a prelude lamenting his fate. Apparently he had—for him—died young. It was hours past midnight and Zora slumbered heavily, exhausted by her lonely journey. After the stars had dimmed and the celestial cellist and his music all but vanished, Dworkin drew on a pair of knee socks under his pajamas, and in tennis shoes he went quietly downstairs to the music room, where he lifted the dark cello out of its hand-carved casket and for a moment held it in his arms.

He dug the end pin into the pockmarked floor—he would not use a puck, he had informed both his wives. Dworkin wanted the floor to move if the cello caused it to. Embracing the instrument between his knees, the delicate curved shell against his breast, he drew his bow across the bridge, his left fingers fluttering as though they were singing. Dworkin felt the vibrations of the cello rise in his flesh to his head. He tried to clear his throat. Despite the time of night and the live pain in his shoulder, he played from the andante of Schubert's

B-flat major trio, imagining the music of the piano and violin. Schubert breaks the heart and calls it *un poco mosso.* That is the art of it. The longing heart forever breaks yet is gravely contained. The cello Dworkin passionately played played him.

He played for the space and solidity and shape of his house, the way it fitted together. He played for the long years of music here, and for the room in which he had practiced and composed for a quarter of a century, often looking up from his score to glance at the elms through the window of the arched wall. Here were his scores, records, books. Above his head hung portraits of Piatigorsky and Boccherini, who seemed to watch him when he entered the room.

Dworkin played for his gabled dark-gray, blue-shuttered house, built early in the century, where he had lived with both of his wives. Ella had a warm singing voice excellently placed and supported. Had she been braver she would have been a professional singer. "Ah," she said, "if I were a brave person." "Try," Dworkin urged. "But I'm not," said Ella. She had never dared. In the house she sang wherever she happened to be. She was the one who had thought of putting in the stained-glass windows of beasts and flowers. Dworkin played the allegro, and once more the andante of the heart-laden Schubert. He sang to Ella. In her house.

As he played, Zora, in a black nightgown, stood at the closed door of the music room.

After listening a moment she returned quickly to the bedroom. When he left the music room, Dworkin detected his wife's perfume and knew she had been standing at the door.

He searched his heart and thought he understood what she had expected to hear.

As he went along the hallway, he caught a glimpse of a fleeting figure.

"Zora," he called.

She paused, but it was not Zora.

"Ella," Dworkin sobbed. "My dearest wife, I have loved you always."

She was not there to assent or ask why.

When Dworkin got back to bed, Zora was awake. "Why should I diet? It's an unnatural act."

"Have you been lying there thinking of dieting?"

"I've been listening to myself."

"You hear something again, after being absolved in your travels?"

"I believe I am slowly going deaf," Zora said.

"Are you still hearing the whine or wail?"

"Oho, do I hear it."

"Is it like the sound of someone singing?"

"I would call it the sound of my utter misery."

Dworkin then told her he was ready to move.

"I guess we ought to sell the house."

"Why ought we?"

"It comes to me at this late date that it's never been yours."

"Better late than later." Zora laughed. "It is true, I have never loved this house."

"Because it was Ella's?"

"Because I never loved it."

"Is that what caused your noises, do you think?"

"The noises cause the noises," Zora said.

Dworkin, the next day, telephoned the real estate agents, who came that night, a man and his amiable wife in their sixties.

They inspected the house from basement to attic. The man offered to buy a child's fiddle he had seen in the attic, but Dworkin wouldn't sell.

"You'll get a good price for this place," the woman said to Zora. "It's been kept in first-rate shape."

When they were moving out in the early spring, Dworkin said he had always loved this house, and Zora said she had never really cared for it.

In Kew Gardens

Once, as they walked in the gardens, Virginia felt her knickers come loose and slip down her ankles. She grabbed at her maidenhair as the garment eluded her frantic grasp and formed a puddle of cloth at her feet. Swooping up her underpants, with a cry of dismay she plunged into the bushes, shrilly singing "The Last Rose of Summer." As she stood up, the elastic knot she had tied snapped, and the knickers again lay limp at her feet.

"Christ, goddamn!"

Vanessa listened at the bushes.

"Don't be hysterical. No one will see through your dress."

"How can you be certain?"

"No one would want to."

She shrieked slowly.

"Forgive me, dear goat," Vanessa told her. "I meant no harm."

"Oh, never, no, never."

Insofar as I was ever in love I loved Vanessa.

George Duckworth, affectionate stepbrother, carried his tormented amours from the parlor to the night nursery. He nuzzled, he fondled, he fiddled with his finger. To his sisters he was obscenity incarnate. He touched without looking.

"I meant no harm. I meant to comfort you."

Virginia lost her underpants and wondered where she had been.

Her erotic life rarely interested her. It seemed unimportant compared with what went on in the world.

I was born in 1882 with rosy cheeks and green eyes. Not enough was made of my coloring.

When her mother died she tore the pillow with her teeth. She spat bleeding feathers.

Her father cried and raged. He beat his chest and groaned aloud, "I am ruined."

The mother had said, "Everyone needed me but he needed me most."

"Unquenchable seems to me such presence": H. James.

The father moaned, "Why won't my whiskers grow?"

As Virginia lay mourning her mother, dreadful voices cried in the night. They whispered, they clucked, they howled. She suffered piercing occipital headaches.

King Edward cursed her foully in the azalea garden. He called her filthy names, reading aloud dreadful reviews of books she had yet to write.

The king sang of madness, rage, incest.

Years later she agreed to marry Mr. Leonard Woolf, who had offered to be her Jewish mother.

"I am mad," she confessed to him.

"I am marrying a penniless Jew," Virginia wrote Violet Dickinson. She wondered who had possessed her.

"He thinks my writing the best part of me."

"His Jewishness is qualified."

His mother disgusted her.

She grew darkly enraged.

In fact, I dislike the quality of masculinity. I always have.

Lytton said he had no use for it whatever. "Semen?" he asked when he saw a stain on Vanessa's dress.

Vanessa loved a man who found it difficult to love a woman.

She loved Duncan Grant until he loved her.

She had loved Clive Bell, who loved Virginia, who would not love him. Virginia loved Leonard, who loved her. She swore she loved him.

When Julia, the mother, died, the goat threw herself out of a first-story window and lay on the ground with Warren Septimus Smith. "He did not want to die till the very last minute." Neither had she.

The old king emerged from the wood, strumming a lyre. A silver bird flew over his head, screeching in Greek.

A dead woman stalked her.

Janet Case, her teacher of Greek, loved her. She loved her teacher of Greek.

She loved Violet Dickinson.

She loved Vita Nicolson.

Leonard and she had no children. They lay in bed and had no children. She would have liked a little girl.

"Possibly my great age makes it less a catastrophe but certainly I find the climax greatly exaggerated."

Vanessa wrote Clive: "Apparently she gets no pleasure from the act, which I think is curious. She and Leonard were anxious to know when I had had an orgasm. I couldn't remember, do you?"

"Yet I dare say we are the happiest couple in England. Aren't we, Leonard?"

"My dear."

Leonard and Virginia set up the Hogarth Press but they would not print Mr. James Joyce's *Ulysses*. "He is impudent and coarse."

Mrs. Dalloway loved Warren Septimus Smith though she never met him.

"He had committed an appalling crime and had been condemned by human nature."

"The whole world was clamoring, Kill yourself, kill yourself for our sakes."

(He sat on the windowsill.)

He jumped. Virginia fell from the window.

As for *To the Lighthouse*, I have no idea what it means, if it has a meaning. That's no business of mine.

"[Lily Briscoe] could have wept. It was bad, it was bad, it was infinitely bad! She could have done it differently of course; the colour could have been thinned and faded; the shapes etherealised; that was how Paunceforte would have seen it. But then she did not see it like that. She saw the colour burning on a framework of steel; the light of a butterfly's wing lying upon the arches of a cathedral. Of all that only a few random marks scrawled upon the canvas remained. And it would never be seen; never be hung even, and there was Mr. Tansley whispering in her ear, 'Women can't paint, women can't write . . .'

". . . She looked at the steps; they were empty; she looked at her canvas; it was blurred. With a sudden intensity, as if she saw it clear for a second, she drew a line there, in the centre. It was done; it was finished. Yes, she thought, laying down her brush in extreme fatigue, I have had my vision."

All I need is a room of my own.

"I hate to see so many women's lives wasted simply because they have not been trained well enough to take an independent interest in any study or to be able to work efficiently in any profession": Leslie Stephen to Julia Duckworth.

"There has fallen a splendid tear/From the passion-flower at the gate."—Alfred, Lord Tennyson

"There was something so ludicrous in thinking of people singing such things under their breath that I burst out laughing."

The Waves.

The Years. The bloody years.

The acts among *Between the Acts.*

No one she knew inspired her to more than momentary erotic excitement throughout her life. She loved Shakespeare's sister.

Leonard gave up that ghost.

"They also serve."

She felt a daily numbness, nervous tension. "What a born melancholic I am."

They had called her the goat in the nursery, against which she tore at their faces with her tiny nails.

They had never found Thoby her dead brother's lost portrait. Vanessa had painted and forever lost it.

Her mother died.

My father is not my mother. Leonard is my mother. We shall never conceive a living child.

"I shall never grow my whiskers again."

She heard voices, or words to that effect.

"Maiden, there's turd in your blood," King Edward chanted in ancient Greece.

Her scream blew the bird off its one-legged perch and it flapped into the burning wood.

An old king strode among the orange azaleas.

For years she simply went mad.

She spoke in soft shrieks.

She wrote twenty-one books whose reviews frightened her.

"That was not my doing," said Leonard Woolf.

"Nor mine," sobbed her Greek tutor.

Perhaps it was mine, Vita Nicolson said. "She was so frail a creature. One had to be most careful not to shock her."

I loved Vita. She loved *Orlando.*

Virginia wrote a biography of Roger Fry. She did not want to write a biography of Roger Fry.

Leonard served her a single soft-boiled egg when she was

ill. "Now, Virginia, open your mouth and swallow your egg. Only if you eat will you regain the strength to write your novels and essays."

She sucked the tip of his spoon.

"Though you give much I give so little."

"The little you give is a king's domain."

At that time the writing went well and she artfully completed *Between the Acts*, yet felt no joy.

Virginia relapsed into depression and denied herself food.

"Virginia, you must eat to sustain yourself."

"My reviews are dreadful," Virginia said.

"I am afraid of this war," Virginia said.

"I hear clamorous noises in my head," Virginia said.

One morning, to escape the noises of war, she dragged herself to the river Ouse, there removed shoes, stockings, underpants, and waded slowly into the muddy water. The large rock she had forced into her coat pocket pulled her down till she could see the earth in her green eyes.

"I don't think two people could have been happier than we have been."

Alma Redeemed

GUSTAV MAHLER'S ghost.

Bruno Walter had seen it as Mahler conducted one of his last concerts. It waxed in music as the conductor waned. The ghost appeared, more or less, to Alma Mahler one or two years after her husband was dead. Alma did not believe in ghosts, but this one troubled her. It had got into her bedsheets but hadn't stayed long.

Can Jews haunt people?

Gustav was a rationalist nonbeliever. "In that clear mind I never detected any trace of superstition," Bruno Walter said. He spoke of Mahler—as Alma clearly remembered—as a "God-struck man," whose religious self flowered in his music, viz., "*Veni, creator spiritus*," as it flashed in eternity in the Eighth Symphony. Alma felt that Mahler was too subtle a man to have believed simply in God, but that wouldn't mean he might not attempt to disturb her, although she was aware that some of her thoughts of Mahler had caused her more than ordinary fright. Might the fright have produced the ghost? Such things are possible.

In my mind, more than once I betrayed him.

Yet Mahler was a kind man, although an egotist who defined his egotism as a necessity of his genius.

"Gott, how he loved his genius!"

Now, all of Alma's husbands, a collection of a long lifetime including Mahler, Walter Gropius, Franz Werfel—and Oskar Kokoschka, the painter, made it a fourth if you counted in the man she hadn't married, whom Alma conceived to be her most astonishing (if most difficult) lover—they were all artists of unusual merit and accomplishment; yet Alma seemed to favor Mahler, even if she had trouble during her lifetime caring deeply for his music.

When she met Gustav Mahler, Alma stood five feet three inches tall and weighed 144 pounds. She loved her figure. Her deep blue eyes were her best feature. She drew men with half a glance. Alma never wore underpants and thought she knew who might know she wasn't wearing them. When she met him she felt that Mahler didn't know though he may have wanted to.

Alma, a lovely, much-sought-after young woman, one of the prettiest in Vienna in those days, felt Mahler was magnetic, but she wasn't sure she ought to marry him. "He is frightening, nervous, and bounds across the room like an animal. I fear his energy."

She wrote in her diary in purple ink: "At the opera he loves to conduct *Faust*."

She wanted Gustav. She felt she had snared him in her unconscious.

Yet his demands frightened her. "Is it too late, my dearest Almchi, to ask you to make my music yours? Play as you please but don't attempt to compose. Composition is for heroes."

"How can I make his music mine if I have loved Wagner throughout my life? What passion can I possibly feel for Mahler's music or even for Mahler?" These thoughts concerned her.

"You must understand, my tender girl, that my harmony and polyphony, for all their vivid modernity, which seems to distress you, remain in the realm of pure tonality. Someday your dear ears will open to the glories of my sound."

"Yes, Gustav," said Alma.

"Let us be lovers in a true marriage. I am the composer and you are, in truth, my beloved bride."

Mahler urged her to consult her stepfather and mother. "You must lay to rest your doubts, whatever they are. The matter must be settled before we can contemplate a union for life."

"Say nothing," Carl Moll, her stepfather, advised Alma. "Best get rid of the Jew."

"*Perhaps* get rid of him," said her mother. "I never trusted his conversion to Catholicism though he pleads sincerity. He became Catholic because Cosima Wagner insisted that no Jew be allowed to replace Richard Wagner at the Vienna Opera."

But Alma said she had thought about it and decided she loved Mahler.

She did not say she was already pregnant by him.

Mahler walked in his floppy galoshes to the church on their wedding day.

At breakfast the guests were spirited, although in memoirs

she wrote many years later Alma wasn't sure of that. She had trouble defining her mood.

She was twenty-two, Mahler was forty-one.

"If only I could find my own inner balance."

Mahler whispered into her good ear that he loved her more than he had loved anyone except his dear mother, who had died insane.

Alma said she was glad he respected his mother.

"You must give yourself to me unconditionally and desire nothing except my love."

He sounded more like a teacher than a lover.

"Yes, Gustav."

"He is continually talking about preserving his art but that is not allowed to me."

Nothing has come to fruition for me, Alma thought. Neither my beauty, nor my spirit, nor my talent.

Does his genius, by definition, submerge my talent? My ship is in the harbor but has sprung a leak.

He did not lie in bed and make love to her. He preferred to mount her when she was deeply asleep.

His odor was repulsive. "Probably from your cigars," she had informed Mahler. He was a stranger to her, she wrote in her diary, "and much about him will remain strange forever."

She tripped over a paraffin lamp and set the carpet afire.

Mahler dreamed Alma was wearing her hair as she used to in her girlhood. He did not like her to pile her tresses on the top of her head. Gustav said her hairdo was Semitic-looking and he wished to avoid that impression. He assured his friends he was not a practicing Jew. Alma wore her hair long most of the time.

When their daughter, Maria, caught diphtheria and died, Mahler could not stand being alone. Memories of his daughter seared his life. He went from person to person with a new message: "Alma has sacrificed her youth for me. With absolute selflessness she has subordinated her life to my work."

Alma let Ossip Gabrilowitsch hold her hand in a dark room.

"To gain a spiritual center, my Alma, that's the important thing. Then everything takes on another aspect."

Alma found his impersonal preaching repellent and frightening.

Since her youth she had been nervous among strangers and very sensitive about her impaired hearing.

Mahler became frightened at the thought of losing his wife.

Mahler and Freud met in Leiden and walked for four hours along the tree-lined canals. Freud told him a good deal about the life of the psyche and Mahler was astonished though he had guessed much that Freud had told him.

"My darling, my lyre," he wrote his wife, "come exorcise the ghosts of darkness. They claw me, they throw me to the ground. I ask in silence whether I am damned. Rescue me, my dearest."

Mahler suspected that he loved Alma more than she loved him.

He was as strict now about her going back to her music as he had been nine years ago in insisting she give up composing.

One night she woke up and saw him standing by her bed like a ghost.

He dedicated his Eighth Symphony to her.

He feared his Ninth.

"Ah, how lovely it is to love, my dearest Almscherl. And it is only now that I know what love is. Believe me, Tristan sings the truth."

"Alma blossoms, on a splendid diet, and she has given up tippling Benedictine. She looks younger day by day."

One day she had a cold; Mahler invited the doctor who had examined Alma to look him over too.

"Well, you have no cause to be proud of that heart," the doctor said after listening for a minute.

The bacterial tests sealed his doom. Mahler insisted he be told the truth, and he said he wanted to die in Vienna.

He talked to Alma about his grave and tombstone. She listened gravely. He did not want to be cremated. He wanted to be there if people came to the graveyard to see him.

"Mozart," said Mahler, before he died during a thunderstorm.

"Boom!"

Alma met the man who later became her second husband in a sanitarium, in Tobelbad when, exhausted by Gustav's pace and striving, she was advised by a country doctor to take the cure.

Gustav displayed an unyielding energy she couldn't keep up with. She was the young one but he made her feel old. That's the trick, she thought. He wants me to match him in age.

At Tobelbad she met a handsome architect, Walter Gropius, age twenty-seven, who lived down the hall and stared at her in astonishment as she walked by. He gazed at Alma with architectural eyes and she was aware she had form.

They began to go for long walks. Gustav usually gave her short lectures in philosophy as they walked together, but this one talked on about nature and architectural masses; he seemed surprised that she did not throw herself into his arms.

Gustav, promoting his conducting career, hurried from city to city, writing to her from where he happened to be, one opera house or philharmonic society after another; but she was in no mood to respond. In his letters to his tender Almscherl he wrote, "I could not bear this depleting routine if it did not end with delicious thoughts of you. Regain your health, my precious dear girl, so that we may again renew our affectionate embraces."

In his letters Mahler tickled her chin and ladled out bits of gossip laced with pious observations. His pace was again frantic; yet wherever he went, he worried about her, though for reasons of scheduling, etc., he found it difficult to visit her at Tobelbad, yet surely she knew the direction of his heart?

He had asked his mother-in-law, Anna Moll, to write Alma a letter requesting news; and soon thereafter she paid her daughter a visit, but there was no news to speak of. "She is responding to her cure, not much more." Gropius was invisible.

Alma had put him out of her mind and returned home. No one knew whether they had become or had been lovers.

"When shall we meet again?" the handsome Gropius had asked.

She wasn't sure.

"Seriously, my dearest—"

"Please do not call me 'my dearest,' I am simply Alma."

"Seriously, simply Alma."

"I am a married person, Herr Gropius. Mahler is my legal husband."

"A terrible answer," Gropius replied.

" 'None but the brave deserves the fair.' " He quoted Dryden in English.

When he translated the line, Alma said nothing.

"Mahler met me at the Toblach station and was suddenly more in love with me than ever before."

One night when Mahler and Alma were in Vienna, before returning to their farmhouse in Toblach, Mahler, looking around nervously, whispered, "Alma, I have the feeling that we are being followed."

"Nonsense," said Alma. "Don't be so superstitious." He laughed but it did not sound like a laugh. He did not practice sufficiently, Alma thought.

Gropius then sent Mahler a letter asking his permission to marry his wife. Alma placed her husband's mail on the piano and shivered at lunch as Mahler slowly read the letter, whose writing she had recognized. She had wanted to tear it up but was afraid to.

Mahler read the letter and let out a gasp, then a deep cry.

"Who is this crazy man who asks permission to marry my wife? Am I, then, your father?"

Alma laughed a little hysterically, yet managed to answer calmly.

"This is a foolish young man I met at the sanitarium. I do not love him."

"Who said love?" Mahler shouted.

Alma eventually calmed him, but he felt as though he had been shipwrecked and didn't know why.

That afternoon Alma saw Gropius from her car window as she drove past the village bridge. Gropius didn't see her.

She returned from her errand feeling ill and breathlessly told Mahler whom she had seen walking near the bridge: "That was the young man who was interested in me in Tobelbad although I did nothing to encourage him."

"We shall see." Mahler took along a kerosene lamp and went out searching for Gropius. He found him not far from their farmhouse. "I am Mahler," the composer said. "Perhaps you wish to speak to my wife?"

Gropius, scratching under his arm, confessed that intent. "I am Gropius."

Mahler lit the lamp. It was dark.

He called up the stairs and Alma came down.

"I come," she said.

"You two ought to talk," said Mahler. He withdrew to his study, where he read to himself in the Old Testament.

When Alma, white-faced, came to him in the study, Mahler told her calmly that she was free to decide in whatever way she wanted. "You can do as you feel you must." If he was conducting, no stick was visible.

"Thanks," said Alma. "I want him to go. Please let him stay until morning and then he shall go. I have spoken to him and explained that I will not tolerate bad manners."

Mahler went back to reading the Old Testament. He was thinking of *Das Lied von der Erde* though he had not yet written it.

Gropius stayed overnight and Alma drove him to his train to Berlin in the morning.

Gropius, holding his hat, said he was sorry for the trouble he had caused. Then he said, "When shall we meet again?"

"Never," said Alma. "I am a happy woman. Please stay away from my life."

"Never is *never*."

Gropius said none but the brave deserves the fair.

He got into the train and sent her a worshipful telegram from every station it stopped at.

Gustav, that night, collapsed outside Alma's bedroom. The candle he was holding fell to the floor and the house almost went up in flames.

Alma got him to bed; she put Gropius out of her mind, where he remained until years later, long after Mahler's death, when she felt she could no longer stand Oskar Kokoschka's wild fantasies and burning desires.

Mahler, leaning out of his window at the Hotel Majestic above Central Park, in New York City, heard "boom" in the street below. The boom was for a dead fireman in a horse-drawn funeral cortege.

Mahler wrote the muffled drumbeat into his Tenth Symphony: BOOM!

"I know I am lost if I go any further with the present confusion in my life."—Kokoschka

"May I see you?" he asked.

Alma loved men of genius.

He was worldly, sensuous. He needed love and money.

He came to visit and they went to bed. She woke him and said it was time to go home. When he left her he walked till dawn.

He signed her into his name: Alma Oskar Kokoschka.

"Read this letter in the evening."

He bought the Paris newspapers to check on the weather when she was there.

"Alma, I passed your house at one o'clock and could have cried out in anger because you see the others and leave me in the dirty street."

The women in his paintings resemble Alma.

Remembering Gustav and fearing that she was pregnant by Oskar, Alma worried about any Jew who might see her pregnant.

In view of the Jungfrau he painted her on a balcony.

Oskar's mother railed against his obsession. "She is like a high-society mistress, a whore without garters."

"Shut your black mouth," he told her.

Alma feared pregnancy. It was wrong to have had a child out of wedlock. Maria had died because Alma had become pregnant before her marriage to Mahler.

Oskar's mother threatened to shoot her.

Kokoschka went to Alma's house and found his mother walking around with a gun in her purse.

"Give it here."

She crooked her finger and said, "Boom."

"Those who sin will be punished," Alma said one night to Mahler's ghost.

Oskar: "I am not allowed to see you every day because you want to keep alive the memory of this Jew who is so foreign to me."

"I must have you for my wife or else my talent will perish miserably."

She said she would marry him only after he had created a masterwork.

"Alma, please don't send me any money. I don't want it."

Die Windsbraut is Oskar's painting of Alma and him. She sleeps with her head on his shoulder. He gazes into the distance.

"I dreamed that Gustav was conducting. I was sitting near him and heard the music but it clearly displeased me."

"How far behind me my life with Mahler seems."

"I need my crazy mystique of the artist and from this I always manage to fill my head. The whole world is ultimately a dream that turns bad."

In Kokoschka's painting at Semmering, Alma ascends to heaven in fiery immolation. Oskar is in hell, surrounded by sexy fat serpents.

Alma was pregnant. "She will marry me now": Kokoschka.

Gustav's death mask arrived in the mail. Alma unpacked it and hung it on the wall. She entered the clinic for an abortion.

Austria declared war on Serbia. Alma wrote in her diary: "I imagine I have caused the whole upheaval."

"I would like to break free from Oskar."

"God punished me by sending this man into my life."

"I would give up every man on earth for music."

"Wagner means more to me than anyone. His time will come again."

Mrs. Kokoschka picked up her clay pot and dropped it on the floor. She withdrew a blood-red string of beads she was holding for Kokoschka. Alma had given them to him as a memento of his love for her.

"Yesterday evening I ran away from Oskar."

"What of the Jewish question *now*? They need help and direction—brains and feeling from those of us who are Christians."

She wrote to Gropius.

"I will get him quickly. I feel this is, or will become, something important to me."

Walter's birthday fell on the day Mahler had died.

Alma went to see him. "Finally in the course of an hour he fell in love with me. We were where the wine and good food raised our spirits. I went to the train with him where love overpowered him so that he dragged me onto the moving train, and come what might I had no choice but to travel to Hanover with him."

Walter had the manners of a husband. He was talented, handsome, an Aryan. He was crazily jealous of Kokoschka. Alma married him.

"So married, so free, and yet so bound."

"I wanted to make my own music, or music about which I felt deeply, because Gustav's was foreign to me."

"Jews have given us spirit but have eaten our hearts."

"My husband means nothing to me anymore. Walter has come too late."

She had met Franz Werfel. "Werfel is a rather fat Jew with full lips and watery almond eyes. He says: 'How can I be happy when there is someone who is suffering?' which I have heard verbatim from another egocentric, Gustav Mahler."

Alma married Werfel. He was a Jew who looked like a Jew, yet passable. She had had half a Jew in Mahler, and Werfel made the other half. They had a lot to learn, these Jews. They needed a Christian quality. Gropius was a true Aryan, a fine gentleman, passionate in his way, though she had never loved him. She had given him up for Werfel. She often thought of Kokoschka but hated him. "He wants to annihilate me."

Werfel needed her. He lived in dirty rooms, his clothes uncared for, cigarette butts on the floor. He needed a wife. He already had fathered a son Gropius thought was his child. Walter guessed that out and departed. He had tried to keep their daughter, Manon, but Alma had fought him for her. Gropius retreated like a gentleman. Manon died and was buried next to her half sister, Maria Mahler.

Alma lived with Franz Werfel through her best days. He wrote *Verdi*, *The Song of Bernadette*, and *The Star of the Unborn*. He made money and they spent it freely. The only really bad time was when they were trying to find their way out of Europe as the Nazis sought them in Spain. Then an American diplomat assisted them and they got out of Portugal on a Portuguese ship and afterward lived in Beverly Hills, U.S.A. Alma was feeling happy again.

But there is no beating out illness and bad health. Werfel died in his sixties. Alma did not attend his funeral though the guests had assembled and were awaiting her. Bruno Walter thrice played a Schubert impromptu as they waited for Alma to appear, but she had had it with funerals of three husbands. She was drinking Benedictine and never got to Werfel's funeral. She often felt that Kokoschka had been her best lover.

"Mahler had a long white face. He sat with his coat buttoned up to his ears. He looked like death masquerading as a monk. I told him this, hoping to exorcise my ghostly pangs of dread."

"Why do I fancy I am free when my character contracts me like a prison?": Mahler.

"Where is *my* truth?": Alma.

"He was always stopping on a walk to feel his pulse. I had always known his heart was diseased."

"The Jews are at once an unprecedented danger and the greatest good luck to humanity."

"I see Hitler as a genuine German idealist, something that is unthinkable to Jews."

"But fortunately he was stupid."

"Oh, my God, my God, why do you *so* love evil?"

"Werfel believed in the world revolution through Bolshevism. I believed that Fascism would solve the problems of the world."

Alma wore long necklaces with earrings and used dark lipstick. She drank Benedictine and ate little.

"Death is a contagious disease. That is the reason," Alma wrote in her diary, "why I will not place a photograph of a living person next to someone who is dead."

She thought she had met Crown Prince Rudolf of Austria on a mountaintop and he asked Alma to bear his child.

One night Mahler's ghost appeared, momentarily freezing her fingers.

"Alma, aren't you yet moved by my classically beautiful music? One can hear eternity in it."

"How can one love Mahler if she best loves Wagner?"

"My time will come."

Mahler diminished as he faded.

Alma felt he had handled her badly in her youth.

Yet there were moments she thought she still loved Mahler. She pictured him in a cemetery surrounded by his grave.

Alma favored cremation.

She was eighty-five when she died in 1964, older than King Lear.

Alma redeemed.

OTHER WRITINGS

Introduction to
The Stories of Bernard Malamud

ONE DAY I began to write seriously: my writing had begun to impress me. Years of all sorts had gone by. The annunciation had long since tolled and the response was slow awakening. Much remained to do and become, if there was time. Some are born whole; others must seek this blessed state in a struggle to achieve order. That is no loss to speak of; ultimately such seeking becomes the subject matter of fiction. Observing, reading, thinking, one invents himself. A familiar voice asks: Who am I, and how can I say what I have to? He reads his sentences to see if the words answer the question. Thus the writer may tell his fortune. His imagination impels him to speak in several tongues though one is sufficient. At this point he, or she, may begin to write a story, a daring endeavor.

My early stories appeared in the nineteen-forties in non-commercial magazines, meaning I didn't get paid for them but was happy to have them published. "The Cost of Living" was the first story I sold. Diarmuid Russell, my agent, sent it to Pearl Kazin at *Harper's Bazaar*, in 1949, the year my wife and I left New York City for Oregon. About three years later and a few stories in print, to my surprise, Catharine Carver, of *Partisan Review*, wanted "The Magic Barrel," a story I had asked her to read. I had written it in a carrel in the basement of the library at Oregon State, where I was allowed to teach freshman composition but not literature because I was nakedly without a Ph.D. Later, they permitted me to offer a night workshop in the short story to townspeople who, for one reason or another, wanted to take a writing class; I earned about a hundred dollars a term and got more pleasure than I had expected.

New York had lost much of its charm during World War II, and my wife and I and our infant son took off for the Pacific Northwest when I was offered a job in Corvallis, Oregon. Once there, it was a while before I had my bearings. I was overwhelmed by the beauty of Oregon, its vast skies, forests, coastal beaches; and the new life it offered, which I lived as best I could as I reflected on the old. My almost daily writing—I taught three days a week and wrote the other four—helped me make reasonable choices: what to zero in on and what to omit. On the whole I was learning much about America and holding fast to the discipline of the writing life.

Yet, almost without understanding why, I was thinking about my father's immigrant life—how he earned his meager living and what he paid for it, and about my mother's, diminished by fear and suffering—as perhaps matter for my fiction. In other words, I had them in mind as I invented the characters who became their fictional counterparts. I didn't much worry about what I was asked to teach at the college so long as I had plenty of time to work. My wife, wheeling a stroller, handed me sandwiches at lunchtime through the window of the Quonset hut I wrote and taught in, until I gave up writing on Sundays.

It was a while before I was at ease in the new culture—longer for my New Rochelle–born wife. At first I felt displaced—one foot in a bucket—though unafraid of—certainly enjoying—new experience. Yet too much was tiresome. Oregon State, a former land-grant college, had barely covered its cow tracks: Liberal Arts was called the "Lower Division," to no one's embarrassment. But the writing held me steady as I reacted to a more surprising world than the one I had left in Brooklyn when my wife enticed me across the bridge into Manhattan. I was enjoying our young family—my son was four when my Western daughter was born. We were making friends, some of whom became lifelong friends, and were happy we had adventured forth.

At this time I was sharing an office with a colleague who often wished aloud that he were a Jew. I understood the sentiment. I was glad I was, although my father had his doubts about that. He had sat in mourning when I married my gentile wife, but I had thought it through and felt I knew what I was doing. After the birth of our son my father came gently to greet my wife and touch his grandchild. I thought of him as I began *The Assistant* and felt I would often be writing about Jews, in celebration and expiation, though perhaps that was having it both ways. I wanted it both ways. I conceived of myself as a cosmopolitan man enjoying his freedom.

Before we expected it we were on our way abroad with the happy prospect of a year in Rome. *Partisan Review* had recommended me for a Rockefeller Grant; and the college, somewhat reluctantly, kicked in with my first sabbatical leave. Back in New York City, in 1956, I said hello to Philip Rahv, who gazed at my innocence and thought it was a good idea that I go abroad. We looked up Edna and William Phillips in Paris and afterwards moved into their hotel, the Lutèce, in Montparnasse. In Rome we met Ralph and Fanny Ellison, who were at the American Academy.

Before meeting Ralph I had talked to Saul Bellow one night in Eugene, Oregon, at a lecture he gave. In 1952, after *The Natural* had appeared in a burst of imagination, I called on him at his apartment in Queens. He was about to publish *Augie March.*

That was in 1952. In 1956, after I had written *The Assistant*, Diarmuid Russell submitted it to Robert Giroux, who had bought *The Natural* for Harcourt, Brace. *The Assistant* had been to Harcourt before Giroux read it for Farrar, Straus, where he was now editor in chief. He cabled his acceptance as I sailed the high seas.

Almost from the beginning of my career as a writer I have more or less alternated writing novels with periods of work on short stories. I like the change of pace and form. I've enjoyed working in both forms—prose makes specific demands—although I confess having been longer in love with short fiction. If one begins early in life to make up and tell stories he has a better chance to be heard out if he keeps them short. "Vus hoks du mir a chinik?" (What tune are you banging on your pot?) my father once asked me when I went into a long tale about my mother's cousin.

Writing the short story, if one has that gift, is a good way to begin writing seriously. It demands form as it teaches it, although I've met some who would rather not be taught. They say that the demands of form interfere with their freedom to express themselves. But no good writer writes only as he pleases. He writes for a purpose, an idea, an effect; he writes to make himself understood and felt. I'm for freedom of thought, but one must recognize that it doesn't necessarily lead to art. Free thought may come close to self-deceit. One pays for free thought in the wrong cause if it intrudes, interferes with the logic of language and construction—if it falls like a hammer blow on the head as one is attempting to work out his fiction. Standards diluted at the start may exact a mean toll. Not many "make it" as serious writers of fiction, especially those who think of form as a catchword. Elitism in a just cause has its merits. Some in art have, by definition, to be best. There are standards in literature that a would-be writer must become familiar with—must uphold: as in the work of the finest writers of the past. The best endures in the accomplishment of the masters. One will be convinced, if he or she reads conscientiously and widely, that form as ultimate necessity is the basis of literature.

Soon I began to teach what Randall Jarrell called "imaginative writing," and most college catalogues—when these courses became popular after World War II—list as Creative Writing and teach too much of. I had gone into teaching with certain doubts—although I felt I could teach effectively—in order to support my family and get on with my writing. But being a teacher never interfered with my best concerns as a writer. I wrote steadily and happily, although it took Diarmuid Russell at least three years to sell a story. I had come to him via Maxim Lieber, who had never succeeded in selling any of my early work. "Here are some of your chickens coming home to roost" was his cheery word when he returned two or three stories. Afterwards, for one reason or another, he disappeared into Mexico, and when I last heard of him, was alive in Poland.

The doubts I speak of went with the job, for not everybody who joined my classes was a talented writer. Too many were in who should have been out. I had to teach anybody who wanted to be in my classes, though that changed when I began to teach at Bennington, where nobody frowned if I taught only six or eight people. Talent is always in short supply, although I had a handful of good writing students whom I enjoyed teaching and learning from. In essence one doesn't teach writing; he encourages talented people whom he may be able to do something for. I feel that writing courses are of limited value although they do induce some students to read fiction with care. On the whole I think such courses are overdone and overvalued. A year of them, at the most, can be helpful. After that, "creative writing" must yield to independent work with serious self-exploration going on, or the young writer will never come up with a meaningful subject matter and theme to organize his thinking around, and thus begin to provide himself with material for the long pull of a serious career. The more a writer does for himself, the better off he is. He mustn't be satisfied merely with learning tricks of the trade. Writing teaches the writer. Learning the art of the (human) sentence can keep him gainfully employed most, if not all, of his writing life.

Some writers don't need the short story to launch them into fiction, but I think it is a loss not to attempt to find out whether one can write them. I love the pleasures of the short story. One of them is the fast payoff. Whatever happens happens quickly. The writer mounts his personal Pegasus, even if it is an absent-minded nag who never made it on the race track; an ascension occurs and the ride begins. The scenery often surprises, and so do some of the people one meets. Somewhere I've said that a short story packs a self in a few pages predicating a lifetime. The drama is tense, happens fast, and is more often than not outlandish. In a few pages a good story portrays the complexity of a life while producing the surprise and effect of knowledge—not a bad payoff.

Then the writer is into the story for more than the ride. He stays with it as the terrain opens and events occur; he takes pleasure in the evolving fiction and tries to foresee its just resolution. As soon as his characters sense his confidence they show him their tricks. Before he knows it he becomes a figure in a circus with a boom-boom band. This puts him in high spirits and good form. If he's lucky, serious things may seem funny.

Much occurs in the writing that isn't expected, including some types you meet and become attached to. Before you know it you've collected two or three strangers swearing eternal love and friendship before they begin to make demands that divide and multiply. García Márquez will start a fiction with someone pushing a dream around, or running from one, and before you know it he has peopled a small country. Working alone to create stories, despite serious inconveniences, is not a bad way to live our human loneliness.

And let me say this: Literature, since it values man by describing him, tends toward morality in the same way that Robert Frost's poem is "a momentary stay against confusion." Art celebrates life and gives us our measure.

I've lived long among those I've invented.

"Good morning, professor. Are you by any chance looking for a bride, I offer only the best quality."

"I've got one, Salzman, but if she should come up with other plans I'll let you know. In the meantime, I'm hard at work on a new story."

"So enjoy," said Salzman.

Long Work, Short Life

I INTEND to say something about my life as a writer. Since I shan't go into a formal replay of the life, this will read more like a selective short memoir.

The beginning was slow, and perhaps not quite a beginning. Some beginnings promise a start that may take years to induce a commencement. Before the first word strikes the page, or the first decent idea occurs, there is the complicated matter of breaking the silence. Some throw up before they can breathe. Not all can run to the door at the knock of announcement—granted one hears it. Not all know what it means. Simply, not always is the gift of talent given free and clear. Some who are marvelously passionate to write may have to spend half their lives learning what their proper subject matter may be.

Not even geniuses know themselves in their youth. For years Emily Dickinson was diverted from her poetry by men she felt she loved, until one day she drew the shutters in her sunlit room and sat in loneliness at her table. She had at last unearthed a way of beginning. Those who loved her appeared in her home from time to time, perhaps less to love than to cause her to write her wondrous poems of intricate feeling and intricate love.

I began to write at an early age, yet it took me years actually to begin writing. Much diverted me. As a child I told stories for praise. I went for inspiration to the movies. I remember my mother delivering me, against her will, on a wet Sunday, to a movie house to see Charlie Chaplin, whose comedy haunted my soul. After being at the pictures I recounted their plots to school friends who would listen at dreadfully long length as I retold them. The pleasure, in the beginning, was in retelling the impossible tale.

When I over-contrived or otherwise spoiled a plot, I would substitute another of my own. I could on occasion be a good little liar who sometimes found it a burden to tell the truth. Once my father called me a "bluffer," enraging me because I had meant to tell him a simple story, not one that had elaborated itself into a lie.

In grammar school, where I lived in a state of self-enhancing discovery, I turned school assignments into stories. Once I married off Roger Williams of Rhode Island to an Indian maiden, mainly because I had worked up an early feeling for the romantic. When I was ten, I wrote a story about a ship lost in the Sargasso Sea. The vessel appeared in dreams, about to undertake a long voyage in stagnant seas. This sort of thing, to begin with, was the nature of my "gift" as a child, that I had awakened to one day, and it remained with me many years before I began to use it well. Throughout my life I struggled to define it, and to write with originality. However, once it had pointed at me and signaled the way, it kept me going even when I wasn't writing. For years it was a blessing that could bleed as a wound.

Thus began an era of long waiting.

I had hoped to start writing short stories after graduation from City College during the Depression, but they were long in coming. I had ideas and felt I was on the verge of sustained work. But at that time I had no regular means of earning a living; and as the son of a poor man, a poor grocer, I could not stand the thought of living off him, a generous and self-denying person. However, I thought the writing would take care of itself once I found steady work. I needed decent clothes; I would dream of new suits. Any work I found would make life different, I thought, and I could begin writing day or night. Yet I adamantly would not consider applying, in excess of pride, to the WPA. Years later, I judged that to have been a foolish act, or non-act.

I considered various things I might do to have time for writing, like getting up at five A.M. to work for an hour or two each morning before hitting the dreadful Sixth Avenue agencies in Manhattan to scrounge around for jobs. More often than not there were none, especially for someone with no work experience. And where there was no work there were no words.

The Second World War had begun in 1939. I was born at the beginning of the First World War, in 1914. The Second was being called "The Phony War." The French and German armies sat solemnly eyeing each other over the Maginot Line, yet almost not moving except for night forays. No one seemed about to launch a major attack. Neville Chamberlain, after Munich, was on his way out. He had rolled up his umbrella and was hastening away from the frightful future; Churchill came to power and was eloquently growling that Britain would never be conquered. Possibly diplomacy was in progress. Perhaps there would be no renewed conflict. Many Americans seemed to think the threat of war might expire. Many of us hoped so, though hoping was hard work; nor did it make too much sense, given the aberrations of Adolf Hitler. We worried about the inevitable world war but tried not to think of it.

Often young writers do not truly know what is happening in their lives and world. They know and they don't know. They are not sure what, in essence, is going on and are years in learning. Recently I was reading Ernst Pawel's book of the life of Kafka, and the author speaks of Kafka's "all-encompassing goal in which the writer searches for his own truth." Truth or no truth, I felt the years go by without accomplishment. Occasionally I wrote a short story that no one bought. I called myself a writer though I had no true subject matter. Yet from time to time I sat at a table and wrote, although it took years for my work to impress me.

By now I had registered at Columbia University for an M.A. in English, on a government loan. The work was not demanding. I told myself what I was doing was worthwhile; for no one who spends his nights and days devoted to great works of literature will be wasting his time as a writer, if he is passionate to write.

But when did I expect to begin writing?

My answer was unchanged: when I found a job that would support my habit: the self's enduring needs. I registered for a teachers examination and afterwards worked a year at $4.50 a day as a teacher-in-training in a high school in Brooklyn. I was also applying for, and took, several civil service examinations, including those leading to jobs of postal clerk and letter carrier. This is mad, I thought, or I am. Yet I told myself the kind of work I might get didn't matter so long as I was working for time to write. Throughout these unsatisfying years, writing was still my gift and persuasion.

It was now four years after my graduation from college, but the four felt like fifty when I was counting. However, in the spring of 1940 I was offered work in Washington, D.C., as a clerk in the Census Bureau. I accepted at once though I soon realized the "work" was a laugh. All morning I conscientiously checked estimates of drainage ditch statistics, as they appeared in various counties of the United States. Although the job hardly thrilled me, I worked diligently and was promoted, at the end of three months, to receive a salary of $1,800 per annum. That, in those times, was "good money." What was better was that I had begun to write seriously on company time. No one seemed to care what I was doing so long as the record showed I had finished a full day's work; therefore after lunch time I kept my head bent low while I was writing short stories at my desk.

At about this time I wrote a piece for *The Washington Post*, mourning the fall of France after the German Army had broken through the Maginot Line and was obscenely jubilant in conquered Paris. I felt unhappy, as though mourning the death of a civilization I loved; yet somehow I managed to celebrate on-going life and related acts.

Although my writing seemed less than inspiring to me, I stayed with it and tried to breathe into it fresh life and beauty, hoping that the gift was still in my possession, if by some magic act I could see life whole. And though I was often lonely, I stayed in the rooming house night after night trying to invent stories I needn't be ashamed of.

One night, after laboring in vain for hours attempting to bring a short story to life, I sat up in bed at an open window looking at the stars after a rainfall. Then I experienced a wave of feeling, of heartfelt emotion bespeaking commitment to life and art, so deeply it brought tears to my eyes. For the hundredth time I promised myself that I would someday be a very good writer. This renewal, and others like it, kept me alive in art years from fulfillment. I must have been about twenty-five then, and was still waiting, in my fashion, for the true writing life to begin. I'm reminded of Kafka's remark in his mid-twenties: "God doesn't want me to write, but I must write."

There were other matters to consider. What about marriage—should I, shouldn't I? I sometimes felt that the young writers I knew were too much concerned with staying out of marriage, whereas they might have used it, among other things, to order their lives and get on with their work. I wondered whether I could make it a necessary adjunct of my writing. But marriage was not easy: wouldn't it hurt my career if I urged on myself a way of life I could hardly be sure of? One has his gift—the donnée—therefore he'd better protect it from those who seem to be without a compelling purpose in life. Many young women I met had no clear idea what they wanted to do with their lives. If such a woman became a writer's wife, would she, for instance, know what was going on in his thoughts as he worked in his sleep? Would she do her part in keeping the family going? I was often asking myself these and related questions—though not necessarily of someone who might answer them. And I was spending too much time being in love, as an uneasy way of feeling good when I wasn't writing. I needed someone to love and live with, but I wasn't going out of my way to find her.

Meanwhile, I had nailed down an evening school job in September of 1940; I then completed an M.A. thesis and began to think of writing a novel. By now I had finished about a dozen stories, a few of which began to appear in university quarterlies. One of these, "The Place is Different Now," was the forerunner of *The Assistant.* And a novel I had started while I was teaching in Erasmus Hall Evening High School, in Brooklyn, was called *The Light Sleeper.* It was completed but not sold. Later, I burned it one night in Oregon because I felt I could do better. My son, who was about four at that time, watched me burning the book. As we looked at the sparks fly upward I was telling him about death; but he denied the concept.

Several years before that, not long after Pearl Harbor, while I was teaching at night and writing this novel, I met a warm, pretty young woman at a party. I was told she was of Italian descent and lived in a hotel with her mother and step-father, who was a musician. I observed my future wife for a while before we talked.

Soon we began to meet. Some nights she would come to Flatbush to watch me teach. We ate at Sears, or Oetgen's, and sometimes walked across the Parade Grounds to my room. We wrote each other during the week. Her letters were intense and witty, revealing an informed interest in politics and literature; in love and marriage. After the death of my own mother, I had had a step-mother and a thin family life; my wife, the child of a woman divorced young, had experienced a richer cultural life than I. And since we both wanted children we wondered how we would fare in a mixed marriage. She had been Catholic. I defined myself as Jewish.

Life in New York City was not easy or pleasant during the Second World War. Our friends Rose and James Lechay, the painter, had rented a small walk-up flat on King Street, in the Village, which we took over when they went off to live in Iowa, Jim to take Grant Wood's place as Professor of Painting at the university. After we were married we both continued working until my wife was pregnant. I taught day and evening classes, with practically no time to write. A few years later I left the evening high school and spent a year teaching in Harlem, incidentally picking up ideas for short stories like "Black Is My Favorite Color," before we decided to go west. I had now received an offer to teach at Oregon State College though I had no Ph.D. degree. In 1949, when my son was two, we moved to Corvallis, Oregon, where I taught three days a week and wrote four. In my own eyes I had become seriously a writer earning his living, though certainly not from his writing.

I think I discovered the Far West and some subject matter of my earlier fiction at almost the same time, an interesting conjunction, in imagination, of Oregon and the streets of New York. One's fantasy goes for a walk and returns with a bride.

During my first year at Oregon State I wrote *The Natural*, begun before leaving New York City. Baseball had interested me, especially its comic aspects, but I wasn't able to write about the game until I transformed game into myth, via Jessie Weston's Percival legend with an assist by T. S. Eliot's "The Waste Land" plus the lives of several ballplayers I had read, in particular Babe Ruth's and Bobby Feller's. The myth enriched the baseball lore as feats of magic transformed the game.

Soon we were making plans to go abroad. We had wanted to go earlier, but could not afford it until we experienced the fortunate coincidence of a sabbatical leave from Oregon State with a *Partisan Review*–Rockefeller Foundation grant.

We left in late August, 1956, for Italy. On board the S.S. *Constitution* I spent hours studying the horizon, enjoying the sight of ocean as the beginning of more profound adventure, amid thoughts of new writing. One night we passed our sister ship, the S.S. *America*, steaming along in the mid-Atlantic, all decks alight. I felt I was on the verge of a long celebration.

Previously, my wife had been abroad twice, once at age eight, for a year in Italy, and at another time for her college junior year, in France.

I was ready for a broader kind of living with as much range in writing as I could manage. Before leaving Oregon to go abroad, I had completed *The Assistant*, and had begun to develop several of the stories that became *The Magic Barrel*, some of which I wrote in Rome.

Italy unrolled like a foreign film; what was going on before my eyes seemed close to unreality. An ancient city seemed to be alive in present time. It was larger than life, yet defined itself as our new life. I felt the need to live in a world that was more than my world to live in. I walked all over the city. I walked in the ghetto. I met Italian Jews who had been tortured by the Nazis; one man held up his hand to show his finger-shorn fist. I felt I was too much an innocent American. I wandered along Roman streets and studied Roman faces, hoping to see what they saw when they looked; I wanted to know more of what they seemed to know. On All Soul's, I walked in the Campo Verano cemetery. I visited the Ardeatine Caves where the Nazis had slaughtered Italians and Jews. Rome had its own sad way of sharing Jewish experience.

Mornings I walked my eight-year-old son to Piazza Bologna where he took his bus to the American school. At noon, after finishing my morning's work, I picked up my four-year-old daughter at her kindergarten. She would hand me her drawings as we walked home. Home was 88 Via Michelo Di Lando, not far from where Mussolini had lived with Clara Petacci, his mistress. We had made friends of our landlords. Mr. Gianolla was an old Socialist who had been forced to swallow castor oil by Mussolini's Fascist thugs. His wife, thin and energetic, talkative, courteous, was one of the rare women university graduates of her time.

I returned to Oregon to an improved situation after our year abroad. From a teacher of freshman grammar and technical report writing, I was transformed into a teacher of English literature, as though a new talent had been discovered in a surprised self. What had happened was that the two gentlemen who administered the English department had heard I was acquiring a small reputation as a serious writer of fiction, and therefore I was no longer required to teach composition only, but might be allowed, even without a doctoral degree, to teach unsuspecting sophomores a little poetry, with even a touch of Shakespeare in the night. For this relief I gave happy thanks.

Let me, at this point, say a short word about the yeas and nays of a writer teaching what is called Creative Writing. I have done it because I teach decently well, but I wouldn't recommend that anyone devote his life to teaching writing if he takes little pleasure in informing others. Elsewhere I've said about teaching creative writing, that one ought to keep in mind he is not so much teaching the art of imaginative writing as he is encouraging people with talent how to work as writers. Writing courses are of limited value although in certain cases they may encourage young writers to read good fiction with the care it deserves. However, I think about a year of these courses should be enough for any serious student. Thereafter writing must become a way of life.

When my Western-born daughter appeared, my father sent us $350 for a washing machine. Once when I was twenty, he trudged up the hall stairs from his grocery store one morning. I had a summer cold and was stretched out in bed. I had been looking for a job without success. My father reached for my foot and grasped it with his hand.

"I wish it was me with that cold instead of you."

What does a writer need most? When I ask the question, I think of my father.

I had already begun to receive literary awards. It seemed to me that I did nothing to get them other than stay at the writing table, and the prizes would mysteriously appear. One day I had a phone call from New York. My publisher, Roger Straus, asked me whether I was sitting down. I said I was. He told me I had just won the National Book Award for *The Magic Barrel.*

I must know how to write, I told myself, almost surprised.

I was in a happy mood when I began to work on *A New Life*, my fourth book. Once, at Yaddo, while I was writing it, a visitor knocked at my door. I had just written something that moved me. He saw my wet eyes. I told him I was enjoying writing my book. Later the legend grew that I had wept my way through it.

During my early years at Oregon State I had gone nowhere, with the exception of our trip abroad, and a six-week visit to Montana, when Leslie Fiedler was there in the 1950s. He had sent me a copy of an article he had published in *Folio*, in Indiana. His was the first appreciation of *The Natural* that I had read by someone who knew how to read. Fiedler was always sui generis, but on the whole generous in his judgment of my work. I shan't forget that he appreciated the quality of my imaginative writing before anyone else wrote about it. That was long before Robert Redford, in his sad hat of failure, appeared on the scene, socking away at a ball that went up in the lights.

Not long after our return to Corvallis from Italy, I had a telephone call from Howard Nemerov, at Bennington College, where I was invited to teach for a year. I was glad to go. After our year abroad, stimulated by the life and art I had seen, I wasn't very patient with my experience in a small town, though my wife, after a difficult start, now enjoyed her Western life. I seized the opportunity to return to the East. She would have liked living in San Francisco, but there were no job offers. So we traveled to Vermont by way of Harvard Summer School, where I substituted for Albert Guérard. When the class filled quickly, someone at Harvard asked John Hawkes, the novelist at Brown University, to teach a second section of the course. Before long we were walking together in Cambridge streets, talking about fiction. Hawkes is a gallant man and imaginative writer. His work should be better known than it is.

In September, 1961, my wife and I arrived with our kids in Bennington, Vermont. The college, an unusual place to work and learn, soon became a continuing source of education for me. My teachers were my new colleagues: Howard Nemerov, poet and faithful friend; Stanley Edgar Hyman, a unique scholar and fine critic; and Ben Belitt, a daring, original poet and excellent teacher—from all of whom I learned. My other teachers were my students, whom I taught to teach me.

Stanley Hyman reminded me of Leslie Fiedler in more ways than one. They both knew a great deal about literature, and neither found it difficult to say what. Hyman was an excellent theoretician of myth and literature. His humor kept him young and so did his appetite. Once my wife and I invited him and his wife, the writer Shirley Jackson, to a restaurant, to help us celebrate one wedding anniversary. Stanley ordered the champagne. He and Shirley lived hard, and—I think they thought—well; and almost did not regret dying young. Flannery O'Connor once described them as two large people in a small car, when they came to call on her in Milledgeville, Georgia. She showed them her peacocks.

When I think of Hyman as a critic of literature, what stands out was his honesty of self and standards. One of his favorite words was "standards," and you weren't in his league if you didn't know what he meant. He defined and explicated. He was proud of what he knew, though I remember his saying, speaking of himself, "knowledge is not wisdom." He enjoyed the fun of wit, merriment, poker, horseplay, continuous laughter. He died young.

Before I come to the end of this casual memoir, perhaps I ought to say that I served as president of American PEN (Poets, Editors, and Novelists) from 1979 to 1981. PEN had come to life in 1921 as an international organization founded in London by John Galsworthy, the British novelist and dramatist. Basically, PEN brings together writers from all over the world to meet as a fraternity, to foster literature, and to defend the written word wherever threatened.

When I was president, I began to deal more frequently with publishers after the difficult period that followed a time of consolidation in the book industry. The consolidation I refer to was not always helpful to those who wrote, and much remains to be done to improve the situation of writers, dealing in whatever way with their own publishers.

Though my publisher is a good one, I fear that too many of them are much more concerned with making money than with publishing good books that will seriously influence generations of writers in the future. Stanley Hyman had preached standards, but one tendency in publishing today is that standards are forgotten. I can't tell you how badly some books are edited these days; one excuse given is "We can't afford too much time on one book. We've got to make our profit." I'm all for profit from the work of writers, but the simple fact is that we have begun to pay more in a loss of quality in publishing than our culture can afford. Happily, many people of good will, dissatisfied with present day publishing, are trying to find new ways to improve the industry. And some of the new presses that have begun to publish are quite good, a few even daring.

If I may, I would at this point urge young writers not to be too much concerned with the vagaries of the market place. Not everyone can make a first-rate living as a writer, but a writer who is serious and responsible about his work, and life, will probably find a way to earn a decent living, if he or she writes well. And there's great pleasure in writing, if one writes well. A good writer will be strengthened by his good writing at a time, let us say, of the resurgence of ignorance in our culture. I think I have been saying that the writer must never compromise with what is best in him in a world defined as free.

I have written almost all my life. My writing has drawn, out of a reluctant soul, a measure of astonishment at the nature of life. And the more I wrote well, the better I felt I had to write.

In writing I had to say what had happened to me, yet present it as though it had been magically revealed. I began to write seriously when I had taught myself the discipline necessary to achieve what I wanted. When I touched that time, my words announced themselves to me. I have given my life to writing without regret, except when I consider what in my work I might have done better. I wanted my writing to be as good as it must be, and on the whole I think it is. I would write a book, or a short story, at least three times—once to understand it, the second time to improve the prose, and a third to compel it to say what it still must say.

Somewhere I put it this way: first drafts are for learning what one's fiction wants him to say. Revision works with that knowledge to enlarge and enhance an idea, to re-form it. Revision is one of the exquisite pleasures of writing: "The men and things of today are wont to lie fairer and truer in tomorrow's meadow," Henry Thoreau said.

I don't regret the years I put into my work. Perhaps I regret the fact that I was not two men, one who could live a full life apart from writing; and one who lived in art, exploring all he had to experience and know how to make his work right; yet not regretting that he had put his life into the art of perfecting the work.

A Lost Bar-Mitzvah

WHEN I WAS TWELVE, one day I awoke frightened by the thought that I was doing absolutely nothing about my bar-mitzvah. Here I was, approaching thirteen, and not being prepared to participate in the bar-mitzvah ceremony. Other boys I knew were either in synagogue classes or had tutors. I had neither and was beginning to feel ashamed. My father, Max Malamud, who owned a delicatessen store in a gentile neighborhood in Flatbush, had a sick wife, and my younger brother, who seemed to enjoy life as a child, was involved in his own concerns. I looked after him when I thought of it, but was short of patience and used to sock him in the back when he didn't do what I wanted. He cried. No one told me to cut it out. My mother somehow managed to keep us clean—Eugene's shirts and short pants and my new knickers were almost daily washed and ironed although she was by now seriously oppressed by life. She had lost her first child, a boy, at birth, and suffered a depression thereafter. I was the second, privileged after the death of the first. My brother was the youngest child and, as it turned out, the least privileged.

My father was too much worried about her, and his meager place of business, to notice how badly I was treating my brother, or the troubles he was having in school. He got along but didn't like what he was doing, and though I inspected his homework at night, it wasn't one of his favorite activities. I, on the other hand, enjoyed privileges of status because I was in an "opportunity class" with a roomful of bright kids, in P.S. 181 in Brooklyn, on New York Avenue between Snyder and Tilden. My parents approved of me because I had wit and loved school. Eugene played happily with the neighborhood kids his age. He liked Mikey Pugliesi, who ate mustard sandwiches on Wonder bread, which his mother provided. Mikey's father was a laborer who hauled loads of rocks and dirt in his one-horse dump truck which he kept stabled nearby. On days I had nothing else to do, I played in the stable with the younger kids; I liked the sound of horses' hooves booming on the hard wooden floor.

I reminded my father of my impending bar-mitzvah. "Next year I'm going to be thirteen. The Jewish kids I know are getting Hebrew lessons, but not me. Do you want me to be bar-mitzvahed?" My father looked at me as if he was wondering why I was upset. He then said he wanted me to be, and promised to do something about it. I said I hoped it would be done right. My mother upbraided him for neglecting my religious education. He said he would take care of it. "Times are bad," he said, "but I'll take care of it." Yet as the months went by, he did nothing. He sat in the back of the store waiting for customers to enter—not many did. My father called himself a socialist and sat in the back with his knee resting on a chair seat as he read the "Daily Forward." I remember having heard him say that he was a free thinker, but even though he didn't believe in God, he wanted me to make up my own mind. He praised Eugene V. Debs, the American Socialist. He would light a large match and watch it burn as he extolled the merits of this good man "who liked to do something for somebody else besides himself, especially the poor workers." When the flame was almost spent, he would hastily light his cigarette and shake out the smoking matchstick. Sometimes, with match lit he would recite verses he had learned in night school, when he had come to America, in or around 1905.

My mother helped him in the store as best she could; she found it difficult to deal with customers. Lately she had been severely unwell, though she continued to look after us, and to relieve my father so he could go upstairs for his afternoon nap—to break the long monotony of his days of watching for the miraculous appearance of a customer. She was having a bad time but was continuing to cook and clean. For supper she made chicken soup, plain or with kasha, and served the chicken from the soup pot in large plates. Sometimes she broiled kosher steak, dished out with mashed potatoes. Or she fried meat patties until they were crisp, served with quartered tomatoes and an occasional leaf of lettuce. Lettuce was not popular. For dessert we ate rhubarb or rice pudding, and, if we asked for it, an occasional slice of apple pie from the store. That is to say nobody starved, but my hungers were already deep and endless. My father, at meals, drank a bottle of Jacob Ruppert's dark beer.

We ate in the back of the store under a bright electric bulb, and when, years later, my father had bought one, we listened afterwards to a large Kolster radio. My mother was uneasy with the radio, and went upstairs after she had slowly washed and dried the supper dishes. We were not asked to help and no one seemed to think of helping her.

On Sundays I listened to the symphony. Before the second World War began, when I came downstairs for breakfast, my father, with drawn face, was sometimes tuned in and listening closely to Adolf Hitler, crackling across the ocean, threatening, taunting, berating the Jews.

My mother was now showing serious signs of mental illness. She had two girlhood friends—Jennie Katz, married to Fred, and a friend whose name was Golda, whose married name I have forgotten. They came to see and plead with her, but she would not immediately talk to them and stayed in her room while they were begging her through the locked door to come out. At last they enticed her down to the store for a cup of tea, and everyone pretended to talk amiably, but my mother still said nothing. She sat silent, with eyes downcast, as her old friends talked. Golda had brewed the tea. "Brucha," pleaded Jennie Katz, "You were so smart in school, why don't you say something to your old friends who come to say hello?" She made no reply. When she tried to, she silently wept. My father begged her to say something to her dear friends who had traveled all the way from the Bronx, but she would not respond to him either.

At length she got up and left the room. She went upstairs and again entered the bedroom. I went up, too, and she smiled at my presence, and wept because she hadn't talked to her dear friends whom she had known ever since they were girls. They had all come to America from a small town in the Pale near Kiev. (I have no idea whether she had known my father in Russia, who had also lived in a small town near Kiev.) In America the women had got jobs and after a while had all married and borne children. Golda had a daughter, and Jennie a good-looking bright boy named Sid, who I think I saw once or twice at City College, many years later.

I imagine they came more than once and talked quietly to

my mother. Maybe she spoke to them? In those days little was known about mental illness, generally, and when they came to see her they begged her to get well because my brother and I needed her.

My father earnestly pleaded with her to get well. He woke every morning at 5 A.M., and though business was poor, he needed her to spell him in the afternoon so he could go up and rest. He used to say he wanted to go up for a "driml," a little dream. By afternoon he had been on his feet many hours, after waiting on the very early customers who had come in to buy rolls and lunch meat for sandwiches. When my mother could not come down my father stretched out on a cot in the back and lay there half asleep, not a refreshing rest because he slept with one eye open while waiting for a banging door to wake him up. Awake, he would slap water on his face and quickly go into the store. Sometimes no one was present when he entered. It seemed as if someone had been there and gone elsewhere—my father could not say. He hoped that whoever had been there hadn't walked out with an armful of groceries.

Since my father wasn't helping me prepare for my bar-mitzvah, I thought I ought to do something about it. I had been to the synagogue on Snyder Avenue with my friends Leon and Sam Snider, whose father, a slight man with a high voice, sold suits and rented tuxedos in his store on Rogers Avenue in Brooklyn. I. Snider had once been a tailor and was now a clothier. My father's store was up the block, on the corner of Albemarle Road. Nearby lived a girl I liked, an attractive Italian girl named Katie, whose mother one day jumped from a first floor window, but was not killed.

Leon was a grade ahead of me in school, and not as easy to get along with as his brother Sam, who was about a year younger than I. Once Leon wrote me a note calling me his brother's "erstwhile friend." I attempted to mock him by repeating the expression, but he laughed at me because I had mispronounced it "erstwise." I often went along with Sam and him when they had to deliver tuxedos in the neighborhood. We divided the tips. We walked when we had to, lugging the bulky tuxedo boxes, but usually Mr. Snider's salesman got into the car and drove us from one house to another. Sam and Leon also attended P.S. 181, where Dr. Nathan Peyser was principal. The school was about a mile from where I lived, at 2700 Albemarle Road, at that time a street of private houses. Diagonally across from us was the clothing store, with a large outside sign: "I. Snider, Clothier."

The Snider brothers attended the synagogue for their Cheder lessons. I had no formal connection with the shul because my father was not a member of the congregation. He was not concerned with matters of religion. I, however, had been in shul with Leon and Sam on Friday nights, when we scrambled along the aisles, competing with one another to see who could touch the Torah first. I tried to touch it before they did. My father knew I visited the synagogue, but had nothing to say about it; neither had my mother. She was, however, concerned about my bar-mitzvah. They spoke Russian to each other when they didn't want Eugene or me to know what they were saying.

I can still understand Yiddish though I rarely speak it; still, I can understand a Yiddish play when I see one, and I can give simple directions to people who hand me a slip of paper in the street and ask where that address is. At any rate, my father made no effort to join the synagogue although he tended not to work on Jewish holidays—"the goyim should see we are Jews"—and at times we went to shul on the High Holidays if someone had given him free tickets. However, I don't remember his being in the synagogue with my mother. She would have had to sit with the women, apart from the men. Though her father had been a shochet, a ritual slaughterer, she had no religious interests that I was aware of. When I was fourteen she attempted suicide, and died in a hospital about a year later from causes unknown to me. Eugene was twelve and still in grammar school. I was then a student at Erasmus Hall High School. My father got up frantically early one morning, and said I could not go to school that day because Mama was very sick. He said my brother could go to school. I stayed in the store, and in the afternoon a telegram came from my father to say that my mother had died. That was when I was fifteen.

But the situation concerning my bar-mitzvah as I approached thirteen was not being resolved. I decided to talk to a white-bearded old man whom I had seen praying at sundown, one Friday evening at the synagogue. I told him I was behind in my preparation for my bar-mitzvah and needed help. He asked me who would pay for the lessons and I hesitantly said my father would. The old man was a melamed, a Hebrew teacher, and he would teach me if my father promised to pay him his usual fee for the lessons. When he heard my last name he said he would come to my house on Monday after school. I told my father about the arrangement I had made with the rebbe. With some hesitation he agreed to pay the old man.

Soon the lessons began. Unfortunately the rebbe was not satisfied with me as a student. I knew less than he had thought, not even the Hebrew alphabet, and he had to start from scratch. We spent a long time over the alphabet. I wore a yarmulke as I learned by rote, saying aloud each sound as he had pronounced it. When I made a mistake the old man reached for his ruler on the table and struck the back of my hand. I was astounded, outraged. I did not cry but I cried out. I hated that ruler because the rebbe had meant it to hurt and it had. He grew exasperated by my errors of mispronunciation and shouted at me. I lived in fear of those lessons.

When the rebbe gave me a lesson after school, sometimes my mother would come out of her bedroom and sit on the bench along the wall, watching and listening. His ruler moved more carefully, but not his complaints about the inefficient student I was. She listened and said nothing.

At the end of one lesson, as he collected his books and papers and was ready to leave, he paused before the old ice box and asked if she could spare a red tomato. My mother opened the ice box door and took out a beefsteak tomato which she gave him. The rebbe thanked her. He said that his teeth were bad, but he could still bite into a tomato.

"Don't hurt his hand," she said to the old man.

"You can't learn by dreaming," he replied. "When he doesn't learn I have to wake him."

"Don't hurt his hand," she said fearfully.

When the old man was gone I told my mother I did not want to see him again.

I told my father the same thing and he made light of it.

"Don't worry, I will bar-mitzvah you myself."

"Without lessons?"

"I know this stuff."

"But I don't."

"I will tell you what to say."

I had my doubts. I wasn't sure what he knew about the bar-mitzvah ceremony, or didn't know.

And I was filled with rage for all I wanted and couldn't have.

I liked going to school, being out of the house. I liked to be reading books. My parents had several books in Yiddish around but no one read them to me and I never knew what they said. I used to thumb through them and wonder what they said. On Sundays I read the "funny papers," Jiggs and Maggie, Captain Katzenjammer and the Kids, Harold Teen, and Winnie Winkle. As I read I was listening to piano music coming across the back yard through the open window. I was moved by the music being played by someone in one of the houses nearby, perhaps a girl my age, and was hungry to hear more of it. But there was no other music, except what I heard when I listened to the symphony on Sundays, or heard in school during music appreciation classes, or perhaps when I went to visit one of my friends in the class. I used to visit Gene Lewis, whose father was a night school principal. He would sit in his arm chair by the window in his long bathrobe and read the *Brooklyn Daily Eagle* as he pulled on his cigar. His wife, Caroline, was hospitable and lovely. When I mispronounced a word she would smile and correct it. I said bandeet for bandit and for some reason called Africa Awfrica. Theirs was the first American home I had entered. I played with Gene and another friend, Richie Goldberger, without mentioning my father or mother until much later on.

The year moved slowly but had moved.

On the morning of the day I was thirteen years old, my father trudged up the stairs from the store with a pair of phylacteries in a blue cloth bag—I assume he had borrowed them from someone because I had never seen them before, and never saw them again. "Today you are thirteen years. It's time for your bar-mitzvah." He chanted the prayer in a sing-song. "Blessed art thou Master of the Universe, who has made us holy by

Thy Commandments, and has commanded us to wear the Tefillin."

He wound the Tefillin around my right arm and entwined them around my head and spoke the prayer again.

"Say the prayer like I do," he said, and he recited it slowly as I spoke it after him, as accurately as I could until we both had said the prayers he had asked me to say.

Then he kissed me and said I was bar-mitzvahed, and he went downstairs into the store, to wait on any customer who may have appeared.

But I felt a great rage against him because there had been no ceremony as I had seen it at Leon Snider's bar-mitzvah, one Saturday morning a year before, in the synagogue auditorium. Afterwards there were raisins and nuts, and cakes and wine to eat and drink, and a spirit of joyous festivity. There had been no celebration for me, and here I was set adrift in the world to become a man and a human being on my own.

I could not forgive my father.

Years later, long after he was dead, I realized he had kept his promise to bar-mitzvah me. The ceremony was my own seeking—I like ceremonies. I sought it because I hadn't been satisfied that weekday morning before school when he took the phylacteries out of the cloth bag and uttered the words of prayer without song or dance.

He had kept his promise but I found that hard to believe until I was a grown man and one day realized that he had given me what I had asked for, and I had not believed he had.

CHRONOLOGY

NOTE ON THE TEXTS

NOTES

Chronology

1914 Bernard Malamud born April 26 in Brooklyn, New York, the first child of Max (Mendel) Malamud and Bertha (Brucha) Fidelman. (Max, born 1885, a poor, uneducated grocer, had come to America in 1905 from a Jewish shtetl near Kamianets-Podilskyi in Ukraine, then part of the Russian Empire, fleeing from pogroms and the threat of conscription to join two of his brothers who had established themselves in Brooklyn. Born to a somewhat better-off family, the daughter of a *shochet* [a ritual slaughterer of meat], Bertha, born 1888, left Kamianets-Podilskyi in 1909 to join her brother in America, and married Max the following year. They lived first on Flushing Avenue, then above and behind a series of unsuccessful grocery stores in the Brooklyn neighborhoods of Williamsburg and Flatbush. A son had been delivered stillborn in 1912.)

1917 Brother Eugene born in May. Family believes that damage to mother's left leg was due to the birth of one of her sons; during his boyhood Malamud would feel guilty about causing the injury. Mother is increasingly depressed, reclusive, and overweight, and probably suffers from schizophrenia. Yiddish is the primary language spoken at home, with occasional Russian.

1919 With a partner, father buys grocery on 15th Avenue in the Borough Park section of Brooklyn, the largest and fanciest of his stores, but is forced to sell within a year after partner takes off with the money that had been invested. Malamud enters kindergarten and his English rapidly improves.

1920–23 Attends elementary school on Cortelyou Road in Brooklyn where he first finds access to books; reads *Robinson Crusoe*, *A Tale of Two Cities*, and *Treasure Island*, as well as dime novels and Horatio Alger's boys' adventure books. At home, would listen through living room window to piano-playing across the street: "I was moved by the music being played by someone in one of the houses nearby, perhaps a girl my age, and was hungry to hear more of it." Enrolls in the third grade at P.S. 181, an outstanding new school with a middle-class and largely Jewish student body, to which Malamud travels via trolley five miles every day on his own. Thrives and is challenged at the school, which he will recall as being "the most important school in my life," and displays a talent for telling and writing stories. Avidly goes to the movies and is enchanted by silent films. Catches pneumonia at age nine and is close to being pronounced dead when an injection of digitalis restores his heartbeat; in celebration of his recovery, father buys him *The Book of Knowledge*, a twenty-volume children's encyclopedia.

1924–26 After several of his grocery ventures have failed, father settles in to operating a German-style delicatessen at 1111 Gravesend Avenue (now McDonald Avenue), so called for its proximity to Washington Cemetery. Brother Eugene shows early signs of lifelong mental illness, and Malamud, sometimes reluctantly, takes a parental role toward him, especially during Eugene's unhappy experience at school, where he is mocked and bullied.

1927 Turns thirteen but is not given a bar mitzvah ceremony. Returns from school one afternoon to find his mother on the kitchen floor after she had swallowed a can of disinfectant in a suicide attempt. She is committed to Kings County Hospital; father manages to pay for her to be sent to a private mental hospital in Queens. Malamud works part-time in father's store.

1928 Enters Erasmus Hall High School in Flatbush, where he will edit the school magazine and act in the school's theater group.

1929 Mother dies in May in mental hospital; Malamud is not told the cause of death but in later years he will suspect suicide. His last view of mother is her waving through the window of the institution.

1931 Father marries Liza (Elizabeth) Merov. "Neither of the boys had any affection for their step-mother," Malamud would recall in 1951. The grocery store remains barely profitable: "It was not very good anywhere until the Depression, then it was bad."

1932–35 Wins Richard Young prize in 1932 for autobiographical essay "Life—From Behind a Counter," finishing second in the national Scholastic Awards. After graduating from Erasmus Hall, enters City College in Manhattan. Is praised by his professor Theodore Goodman for his stories, including an early version of "The Bill," which is later included in *The Magic Barrel*. Works part-time, including summers, at hotels in the Catskills.

1936–37 Graduates from City College with a B.A. in 1936. Works for $4.50 a day as teacher-in-training in New York public schools, but over the next two years twice fails teaching exams to become a permanent substitute teacher, first because of oversimplifying his writing style, then apparently because of his slight lisp. Takes out government loan to pay for graduate study in English at Columbia University.

1938–39 Works sporadically, taking odd jobs in factories and department stores and tutoring German-Jewish refugees in English (which will provide subject matter for story "The German Refugee," first published in 1963). Passes civil service examinations that lead to work as postal clerk and letter carrier. Receives first temporary teaching position as a substitute at Lafayette High School in Brooklyn in 1939.

1940 Accepts job as a clerk for U.S. Census Bureau in Washington, D.C., and is soon promoted; writes at his office in afternoons after his work is finished. Begins to submit short sketches of real life to *The Washington Post*, and for the first time is paid for his writing when several are published in column "The Post Impressionist" (including "The Refugee," "Sunday in the Park," "The People's Gallery," "Vacancy"). Writes story "Armistice." Returns to Brooklyn to teach at his former school, Erasmus Hall High, at evening classes there and at other New York City schools, while writing short stories during the day.

1942 Works on long autobiographical novel, "The Light Sleeper," about a young man's loneliness and despair. At a party in February, meets Ann deChiara (b. 1917), from New Rochelle, New York, of Italian immigrant parentage, who had graduated from Cornell University three years earlier with a degree in French; they soon become romantically involved, though during their long courtship Malamud worries about how he can combine marriage with a writer's life. Is exempted from military service as a result of stomach condition and teaching profession, though Eugene was called up for active service over four years, mainly in the Pacific, until discharged as a result of battle fatigue. Malamud moves out of family home to lodgings in Flatbush. Receives M.A. from Columbia after submitting thesis, "Thomas Hardy's Reputation as Poet in American Periodicals." Writes story "Spring Rain." Continues teaching in the evening, though he also works for a short time in a war materials factory. Briefly consults a psychiatrist.

1943–44 Writes posthumously published story "The Grocery Store" in 1943, the year his short stories are first published: "Benefit Performance" in *Threshold* (February); "The Place is Different Now," a forerunner of *The Assistant*, in *American Prefaces* (Spring); "Steady Customer" in *New Threshold* (August); and "The Literary Life of Laban Goldman" in *Assembly* (November).

1945 Marries Ann on November 6 in a civil ceremony at the New York Society for Ethical Culture. Is estranged from father because he has married a Gentile woman; Ann's father also refuses to receive them in his house for more than two years. Moves from Brooklyn to 1 King Street in Greenwich Village.

1947 On the basis of his published work, receives invitation to spend summer working on his novel at Yaddo artists' colony at Saratoga Springs, New York, but is unable to accept for family and economic reasons; Ann, who had worked for the advertising agency Young & Rubicam, is now pregnant with their first child, and will no longer be contributing to the family finances. Birth of son, Paul Francis, in October, which brings about reconciliation with father.

1948 At Malamud's urging, Eugene undergoes psychoanalytic treatment for anxiety, depression, and paranoia and visits the Malamuds weekly, struggling with employment while still living with father and stepmother. Malamud completes "The Light Sleeper" and his agent, Diarmuid Russell of Russell & Volkening, begins sending it to prospective publishers. Teaches evening classes at Harlem Evening High School, but to support his family must now also teach during the day at Chelsea Vocational High School.

1949 In response to the opportunities offered by the G.I. Bill, Ann types more than two hundred standard letters for Malamud in application for posts in the teaching of literature. One of the few replies is from Oregon State College in Corvallis, Oregon, a state-endowed institution of six thousand students providing practical education in agriculture in particular, with the liberal arts constituting merely "the Lower Division." Appointed in July, he is allowed to teach freshman composition but not literature because he lacks a Ph.D. Moves family to Oregon, where the landscape is a revelation to him. Teaches three days a week for an initial annual salary of $3,600; spends the other four days writing.

1950 Works on a novel combining baseball and myth that will become *The Natural.* Publishes "The Cost of Living," story about a struggling grocery store in Brooklyn, in *Harper's Bazaar* in March and sends copy to his father. Publishes "The Prison" in *Commentary* (September) and "The First Seven Years" in *Partisan Review* (September–October); these stories are admired by Harcourt, Brace and Company editor Robert Giroux, who writes Malamud to show interest in publishing a novel and a collection of short stories.

1951 Publishes "The Death of Me" in *World Review* (April), and "The Bill" and "An Apology" in *Commentary* (April and November). Burns manuscript of "A Light Sleeper" after it has been rejected by numerous publishers: "My only triumph was in completing it after so many years of toil." Completes *The Natural* in October, having worked through only two main drafts, fewer than those of his later, more continuously laborious process of revision. Writes on October 15 to brother Eugene, who is increasingly delusional, paranoid, and suicidal, that he felt he had to leave New York "to be an effective man, to provide for my family and do my work—the writing I had to do. . . . That this should hurt you was, as you describe it, a bad break." Eugene is committed in early November to Kings County Hospital, the facility where their mother had been taken after her suicide attempt in 1927; he is transferred to Kings Park State Hospital and then to Kings Park Veterans' Memorial Hospital on Long Island, where he is diagnosed as schizophrenic.

1952 Malamud receives telegram from Giroux on January 7 that *The Natural* has been accepted by Harcourt, Brace and Company. Daughter Janna Ellen born January 19.

To congratulate the family father sends $350 toward the purchase of a washing machine; not long afterward, in March, he suffers a heart attack, though at first he tells Malamud that he is taking bed rest merely because of a cold. Eugene is declared an incompetent person by order of the New York Supreme Court in May. Malamud takes train cross-country to see his father and visit Eugene in hospital in June. Publishes "The Loan" in July in *Commentary*. Eugene is allowed home in July; hereafter he writes to his brother weekly or fortnightly for twenty years and just as regularly Malamud replies. Under the editorship of Giroux, *The Natural*, dedicated to Malamud's father, is published in July to mixed reviews. In the summer, Malamud begins novel "The Broken Snow," later "The Man Nobody Could Lift," about a schizophrenic. Earns $1,225 in income from royalties, rising to $2,700 the following year.

1953 Publishes "The Girl of My Dreams" in *American Mercury* in January. Submits draft of "The Man Nobody Could Lift" to Giroux, who in November advises against publication on grounds of overall quality (the first chapter will be published posthumously in 1997 as "A Confession of Murder" in *The Complete Stories of Bernard Malamud*, edited by Giroux).

1954 Father dies of a heart attack in March. In April, Malamud begins a novel about a Brooklyn grocery store, with working title "The Apprentice," that will become *The Assistant*. Receives promotion to assistant professor at Oregon State and is allowed to teach literature. Publishes "The Magic Barrel" in *Partisan Review* in November.

1955 Continues working steadily on *The Assistant*; as with all of his subsequent novels, the manuscript goes through multiple drafts and repetitions since revision was for Malamud the essential life of a writer: "I have succeeded in afterthought. I connect revisions with reformation." Thinks of himself as one of what William James called "twice-born souls" who struggle to establish themselves from a poor start through second chances: "Some are born whole; others must seek this blessed state in a struggle to achieve order. That is no loss to speak of; ultimately such seeking becomes the subject matter of fiction." Publishes under pen name Peter Lumm a children's novel, *Kim of Korea*, coauthored with Faith Norris, a colleague at Oregon State who wrote the first, main version that was then revised by Malamud. Publishes "The Mourners" in *Discovery* (January) and "The Angel Levine" in *Commentary* (December). Having lived in rented houses since arriving in Oregon, buys house at 445 North 31st Street in Corvallis. Critic Leslie Fiedler publishes a brief appreciative essay on *The Natural* in *Folio*, which he sends to Malamud: "I shan't forget," Malamud would later write, "that he appreciated the quality of my imaginative writing before anyone else wrote about it."

1956 Under contract to Harcourt, Brace, submits *The Assistant* in spring but it is rejected, as it would be by Viking. Sends manuscript to Robert Giroux (now at Farrar, Straus & Cudahy), who is shocked by Harcourt's rejection. Receives $4,000 *Partisan Review*–Rockefeller Foundation fellowship in fiction and obtains sabbatical from Oregon State; takes family to live and write in Rome from autumn until the following summer. Departs by ship from New York in late August, and receives word on transatlantic crossing from Giroux that Farrar, Straus & Cudahy will publish *The Assistant.* Arrives in Rome, and the family settles into a two-bedroom apartment near Piazza Bologna: "Italy unrolled like a foreign film; what was going on before my eyes seemed close to unreality." Publishes "A Summer's Reading" in *The New Yorker* (September 22) and "Take Pity" in *America* (September 25).

1957 Travels throughout Italy and visits Austria and France. Makes final revisions to page proofs of *The Assistant*, which is published in April by Farrar, Straus & Cudahy to favorable reviews. Writes posthumously published story "The Elevator." Returns with family to the United States in the summer. In December, begins writing *A New Life*, novel loosely based on his experience at Oregon State. Earns $6,500 this year, including $2,800 in royalties.

1958 Publishes "The Last Mohican" in *Partisan Review* (Spring) and "Behold the Key" in *Commentary* (May), both included in *The Magic Barrel*, collection of thirteen short stories dedicated to Eugene and published by Farrar, Straus & Cudahy in May. Receives Rosenthal Foundation Award from the National Institute of Arts and Letters and the Daroff Memorial Fiction Award of the Jewish Book

Council of America for *The Assistant.* Spends two months at Yaddo on a summer fellowship, working on *A New Life.* Promoted to associate professor at Oregon State "through his distinction as a writer," he no longer has to teach freshman composition and can focus his teaching on literature and creative writing instead.

1959 Publishes "The Maid's Shoes" in *Partisan Review* (Winter). Wins National Book Award for *The Magic Barrel.* Receives Ford Foundation grant of $15,000 providing two years' time to devote himself to his writing; refuses invitation to teach at Harvard because it would violate the terms of the award.

1960–61 Works steadily on *A New Life* throughout 1960 and completes the novel early the following year. Eugene is again hospitalized, as suicidal, in Brooklyn State Hospital, from early 1961 to August. Malamud teaches creative writing in summer school at Harvard. Largely through the initiative of the poet Howard Nemerov, obtains teaching post in Division of Language and Literature at Bennington College in Bennington, Vermont, a progressive liberal arts college for women (until 1969, when it becomes coeducational), at a salary of around $8,000. Arrives with family in Bennington in September. Publishes *A New Life* with Farrar, Straus & Cudahy in October. Publishes "Idiots First" in *Commentary* in December.

1962 Publishes "Still Life" in *Partisan Review* (Winter). Searching for the subject of his next novel, spends several months reading about social injustice in the United States.

1963 Publishes "Suppose a Wedding" in *New Statesman* (February 8), "The Jewbird" and "Black Is My Favorite Color" in *Reporter* (April 11 and July 18), "Life Is Better Than Death" in *Esquire* (May), "Naked Nude" in *Playboy* (August), "The German Refugee" in *The Saturday Evening Post* (September 14), and "A Choice of Profession" in *Commentary* (September); these are among the twelve stories he collects in *Idiots First*, published by Farrar, Straus & Company in the fall. Travels to England and Italy. In the fall, begins *The Fixer*, novel about anti-Semitism drawing on the Dreyfus affair and the case of Mendel Beilis, a Jew arrested in Kiev in 1911 on false charges of having committed a ritual murder of a Christian boy.

1964 Is elected in February as a member of the National Institute of Arts and Letters.

1965 Completes first draft of *The Fixer*. In summer, travels in Spain, France, and, to research *The Fixer*, the Soviet Union.

1966 Completes *The Fixer* in early spring after more laborious revising than ever before: "The book nearly killed me." Moves to Cambridge, Massachusetts, for two years after being named visiting lecturer in the English Department at Harvard.

1967 Wins both National Book Award and Pulitzer Prize for *The Fixer*. Is elected member of American Academy of Arts and Sciences. *A Malamud Reader*, anthology with an introduction by Philip Rahv, is published by Farrar, Straus & Giroux. Malamud makes $230,000 in gross income, compared to $20,000 per year in the early 1960s.

1968 Visits Israel in March. Returns to Bennington after Harvard position ends. Buys 1930s colonial-style house on two-and-a-half acres at 11 Catamount Lane, Old Bennington, at cost of $35,000. Publishes "A Pimp's Revenge" in *Playboy* (September), "My Son the Murderer" in *Esquire* (November), "An Exorcism" in *Harper's* (December), and both "Man in the Drawer" and "Pictures of the Artist" (later "Pictures of Fidelman") in *The Atlantic* (April and December). Refuses offer to travel to the set of the film adaptation of *The Fixer* in Hungary, partly because the filmmakers tell him they do not wish to make the movie too Jewish; released in December, the film (directed by John Frankenheimer and starring Alan Bates) makes him more financially secure, earning him around $200,000.

1969 Begins novel *The Tenants*, set against the background of race relations in the 1960s. Publishes with Farrar, Straus & Giroux *Pictures of Fidelman: An Exhibition*. Inspired by his stay in Italy, it is a picaresque novel in six linked stories, including one previously published in *The Magic Barrel* and two in *Idiots First*. Receives O. Henry Prize for "Man in the Drawer," story inspired by his trip to the Soviet Union. Writes screenplay for *The Assistant* but option not taken up. Rents apartment in Manhattan; the Malamuds will increasingly spend the fall and winter in New York City. Begins giving his papers to the Library of Congress.

1970 Begins writing in notebooks labeled "The Juggler," working title for the novel that will become *Dubin's Lives*. Film adaptation *The Angel Levine*, directed by Ján Kadár and starring Zero Mostel and Harry Belafonte, is released in July.

1971 *The Tenants* is published in the fall by Farrar, Straus & Giroux. Malamud travels with Ann in the fall to London, where they live for five months.

1972 Purchases two-bedroom apartment in Lincoln Towers complex on Manhattan's Upper West Side. Publishes "God's Wrath" and "Talking Horse" in *The Atlantic* (February and April), "The Letter" in *Esquire* (August), and "The Silver Crown" in *Playboy* (December).

1973 Begins writing "The Juggler" in February: the first draft, instead of taking the usual one year, takes three. Settles for $39,000 in reluctant lawsuit with Elliott Gould and associates over bankruptcy in relation to proposed filming of *A New Life*. Publishes "Notes from a Lady at a Dinner Party" in *Harper's* (February), "In Retirement" in *The Atlantic* (March), and "Rembrandt's Hat" in *The New Yorker* (March), all of which are collected in a volume of eight short stories, *Rembrandt's Hat*, published by Farrar, Straus & Giroux in March. Eugene Malamud dies of heart attack, October 30, aged fifty-five: he had carried on living above his father's old store, with stepmother Liza until her death in 1967, and thereafter alone. Malamud writes the funeral eulogy ("He was a wounded man trying to keep going") but does not deliver it in person because he is admitted to hospital on October 31, with suspected heart problems of his own.

1974 Is interviewed by his friend Daniel Stern for *The Paris Review*'s "Writers at Work" series.

1976 Marriage of daughter Janna to David Smith. Writes in notebook on October 21, "[Saul] Bellow gets Nobel Prize, I win $24.25 in poker."

1977 In February, receives annual B'nai B'rith Jewish Heritage Award. Publishes excerpts from forthcoming *Dubin's Lives* in *The New Yorker* (April 18 and 25) and *Playboy* (December).

1978 Publishes excerpt from *Dubin's Lives* in *The Atlantic* (January). Completes *Dubin's Lives* in August. Makes visit with Ann to Hungary, arranged by translator and scholar Tamas Ungvari. Signs five hundred copies of *The Fixer* for Hungarian admirers; the Hungarian reception of the novel now gives him back his belief in that book.

1979 Publishes *Dubin's Lives* with a first printing of fifty thousand copies by Farrar, Straus & Giroux, his largest ever, and an advance of $150,000. Begins two-year term as president of PEN American Center, concerning himself in particular with writers' freedom throughout the world, the state of the publishing industry, and the provision of books within prisons in the United States.

1980 Publishes "A Wig" in *The Atlantic* (January). Begins novel *God's Grace*. Receives the Governor's Award for Excellence in the Arts from the Vermont Council on the Arts.

1981 Receives Brandeis Creative Arts Award. Awarded one-year fellowship at the Center for Advanced Study in the Behavioral Sciences at Stanford University; arrives with Ann in California in September. Increasingly concerned about his history of angina, decides on three-vessel coronary bypass operation at Stanford, requiring two weeks' hospitalization and two months' convalescence, to be delayed until following year so he can finish *God's Grace*.

1982 Completes *God's Grace*, published in the summer by Farrar, Straus & Giroux. Undergoes bypass surgery on March 10 and suffers a stroke on the operating table. When coming around, he is asked his name and age, and replies "William Dubin, fifty-seven." He is sixty-eight and the name he gives is that of the biographer protagonist of *Dubin's Lives*. By December, though he has recovered many of his functions, including use of his right arm, he experiences difficulty in reading, handwriting, memory, and spatial awareness. He has to relearn much vocabulary and reports feeling "diminished," registering an increased inability in social life to get people involved with him. His ability to write creatively is thereafter impaired.

1983 In May, receives Gold Medal for Fiction from American Academy and Institute of Arts and Letters. Publishes "The Model" in *The Atlantic* (August), the only new story to be included in *The Stories of Bernard Malamud*, his selection of his shorter fiction, which is brought out by Farrar, Straus & Giroux in the fall.

1984 Publishes brief stories "Alma Redeemed" in *Commentary* (July), and "In Kew Gardens" in *Partisan Review* (Fall–Winter), on Alma Mahler and Virginia Woolf, respectively, written as if through the interests of Dubin, his fictional biographer. Film of *The Natural*, starring Robert Redford, earns him $125,000, but he does not admire the adaptation, particularly the changed, more optimistic ending. Determined to write a new novel, he struggles to begin draft of *The People*, about a Jewish peddler who becomes chief of an American Indian tribe in the Pacific Northwest. Concerned about future, has worth of his total estate estimated at about $1,200,000. Prepares memoir "Long Work, Short Life," delivered at Bennington College in the Ben Belitt memorial lectureship series, October 13.

1985 Publishes "Zora's Noise" in *GQ* (January) and "A Lost Grave" in *Esquire* (May). Wins Premio Mondello, Italian literary prize. Struggling still to write *The People* (which will be posthumously published in draft state by the estate with most of his uncollected stories in 1989), he reads opening chapters in July to Philip Roth, who later writes: "He wanted to be told that what he had painfully composed while enduring all his burdens was something more than he himself must have known it to be in his heart."

1986 Dies of heart attack, March 18, in apartment in Lincoln Towers. Last note to self, found by his son Paul on writing desk, repeats four times "Don't be fragile." Is cremated; ashes are buried in Mount Auburn Cemetery, Cambridge, Massachusetts.

Note on the Texts

This volume contains Bernard Malamud's novels *The Tenants* (1971), *Dubin's Lives* (1979), and *God's Grace* (1982), thirteen of his stories published from 1972 to 1985, the author's introduction to *The Stories of Bernard Malamud* (1983), and his short memoir "Long Work, Short Life" (1985) as well as a previously unpublished autobiographical story, "A Lost Bar-Mitzvah."

The Tenants, Malamud's sixth novel, was begun in 1969 and completed in 1971, during the time Malamud and his wife, Ann, had begun to split their time between their home in Bennington, Vermont, and New York City, where they had rented an apartment. When asked in an interview for *The Paris Review* what the impetus for his novel was, Malamud replied: "Jews and blacks, the period of the troubles in New York City; the teachers strike, the rise of black activism, the mix-up of cause and effect. I thought I'd say a word." The short novel gave him more than the usual anxieties. These anxieties were heightened considerably because the book revolved around two writers (one white, the other Black) who were themselves anxious about finishing their books. "The novel was tied up with this," Malamud admitted in one of his notebooks, "which did not help." He put the novel through three drafts before submitting it in 1971 to his editor, Robert Giroux, at Farrar, Straus & Giroux. *The Tenants* was published in September 1971 by Farrar, Straus & Giroux, to generally favorable reviews. Eyre Methuen published the novel in London the following year without authorial revision. The text printed here is taken from the 1971 Farrar, Straus & Giroux edition of *The Tenants.*

In *Dubin's Lives*, his seventh novel, Malamud returned to the fraught subject of the writing life. Eight years separated the publication of *The Tenants* and *Dubin's Lives.* In between came many of the stories that were collected in *Rembrandt's Hat* (1973). "After a novel," Malamud explained in an interview for *The Harvard Crimson*, "I write half a book of short stories, in which I explore new ideas, experience and subject-matter. Generally this leads to a new novel: I write short stories to see where a novel may lie. All together that adds up to four or five years of work." But *Dubin's Lives* took considerably longer, five and a half years just for the composition of the novel, from February 1973 to July 1978. In fact, Malamud had begun thinking about and planning the novel well before the publication of *The Tenants.* From April 1970 to October 1971, he kept two notebooks in preparation for writing *Dubin's Lives*, then called "The Juggler," a reference to his protagonist, William Dubin ("He is the juggler—he keeps several balls in the air at once"). On August 23, 1978, Malamud made this note to himself: "My book is done, five years . . . three drafts . . . I've begun to relax, and understand how massively I had set myself to work. It was a hard book to write but I think I've done well." *Dubin's Lives* was published in New York by Farrar, Straus & Giroux in January 1979—though books had shipped to booksellers in advance of the holiday season. It was published in London by Chatto and Windus in March 1979 without authorial revision. Reviews were generally favorable or respectful, but sales did not meet his publishers' high expectations. This volume prints the text of the 1979 Farrar, Straus & Giroux edition of *Dubin's Lives.*

Malamud's next and last completed novel, *God's Grace*, was shorter and strikingly different than *Dubin's Lives*—an animal fable set in a time after a nuclear holocaust. In one of his notebooks in June 1973, he recorded his interest in "a larger and deeper try at a talking animal story." He had already published "The Jew Bird" (1963) and "Talking Horse" (1972). The idea for the novel, however, dated back even earlier, to at least the time of the composition of *The Tenants.* Malamud embarked on an extensive reading course in preparation for writing the novel, which included the Bible, Wolfgang Kohler's *The Mentality of Apes*, Jane Goodall's books on chimpanzees, E. O. Wilson's *On Human Nature*, and George Orwell's *Animal Farm*, among many others. He began writing the novel in 1980 and progressed steadily over the next two years, choosing to delay heart surgery in 1981 in order to complete it. He submitted a final draft to Robert Giroux and then underwent bypass surgery on March 10, 1982. *God's Grace* was published by Farrar, Straus & Giroux in New York in September 1982. It was also published that year by Chatto and Windus in London without authorial revision. Reception of the novel was mixed, some reviewers complaining about the book's unrelieved pessimism. This volume prints the text of the 1982 Farrar, Straus & Giroux edition of *God's Grace.*

All the stories in the section of this volume titled "Thirteen Stories" were first published in periodicals, and six of these were collected in *Rembrandt's Hat* (1973) and—with the exception of "Notes from a Lady at Dinner"—later included in the career-spanning collection *The Stories of Bernard Malamud*, published in October 1983 by Farrar, Straus & Giroux and the following year in London by Chatto and Windus without authorial revision. The texts of the stories chosen for that retrospective collection contain light revisions by Malamud. These changes are almost always sentence-level revisions that correct errors, improve diction or phrasing, add or subtract a small detail, or eliminate verbal redundancy. Less frequently, Malamud chose to cut an unnecessary sentence. Two of the stories in the present volume—"God's Wrath" and "The Model"—were first collected in *The Stories of Bernard Malamud.* The other five stories appeared in the posthumous collection *The People and Uncollected Stories* (1989), edited by Malamud's longtime editor, Robert Giroux. Listed below are the sources of the texts used in this volume, followed by other information about the publication history of the stories, keyed to the following abbreviations:

RH *Rembrandt's Hat.* New York: Farrar, Straus & Giroux, 1973.

SBM *The Stories of Bernard Malamud.* New York: Farrar, Straus & Giroux, 1983.

TP *The People and Uncollected Stories.* Ed. Robert Giroux. New York: Farrar, Straus & Giroux, 1989.

God's Wrath. *SBM.* First published in *The Atlantic*, February 1972.

Talking Horse. *SBM.* First published in *The Atlantic*, August 1972. Included in *RH.*

The Letter. *SBM.* First published in *Esquire*, August 1972. Included in *RH.*

The Silver Crown. *SBM.* First published in *Playboy*, December 1972. Included in *RH.*

Notes from a Lady at a Dinner Party. *RH.* First published in *Harper's*, February 1973.
In Retirement. *SBM.* First published in *The Atlantic*, March 1973. Included in *RH.*
Rembrandt's Hat. *SBM.* First published in *The New Yorker*, March 17, 1973. Included in *RH.*
A Wig. *TP.* First published in *The Atlantic*, January 1980.
The Model. *SBM.* First published in *The Atlantic*, August 1983.
A Lost Grave. *TP.* First published in *Esquire*, May 1985.
Zora's Noise. *TP.* First published in *Gentlemen's Quarterly*, January 1985.
In Kew Gardens. *TP.* First published in *Partisan Review*, Double Anniversary Issue, 51 (1984) and 52 (1985).
Alma Redeemed. *TP.* First published in *Commentary*, July 1984.

The section of this volume titled "Other Writings" presents Malamud's introduction to *The Stories of Bernard Malamud*, the memoir "Long Work, Short Life," and the previously unpublished "A Lost Bar-Mitzvah." The text of the introduction is taken from the 1983 Farrar, Straus & Giroux edition. "Long Work, Short Life" was originally delivered as a lecture at Bennington College on October 30, 1984, as part of the Ben Belitt Lectureship Series, and printed in a limited edition in the *Bennington Chapbooks in Literature* (Bennington, Vt.: Bennington College, 1985). After Malamud's death, it was included in *Talking Horse: Bernard Malamud on Life and Work*, edited by Alan Cheuse and Nicholas Delbanco (New York: Columbia University Press, 1996). The text presented here is taken from the 1985 limited edition. "A Lost Bar-Mitzvah" was composed in the early 1980s and seems to have been intended as either part of a memoir or one in a series of new stories. There are two typescript drafts—and rougher manuscript versions—held at the Harry Random Humanities Research Center, University of Texas, Austin. The earlier of the typescripts contains handwritten emendations by the author that were incorporated into the later typescript, also emended, lightly, in the author's hand. The typescript bears the attribution "Bernard Malamud, 1982" on its final page. The text presented here follows a photocopy of the later typescript and incorporates the author's emendations. Only typographical errors have been corrected.

This volume presents the texts of the original printings chosen for inclusion here, but it does not attempt to reproduce nontextual features of their typographic design. The texts are presented without change, except for the correction of typographical errors. Spelling, punctuation, and capitalization are often expressive features and are not altered, even when inconsistent or irregular. The following is a list of typographical errors corrected, cited by page and line number: 93.9, Lesser.; 99.20, in in my; 161.33, droaning; 177.24, blutbrüdershaft; 183.35, along; 190.30, "That; 219.3, and retching; 339.9, Don't; 342.22, troilius; 436.4, "Why; 445.40, Zen:; 461.13, destestable; 467.22, urged, him; 486.4, *ich in*; 493.20, *kömmt*; 510.40, law then; 546.21, The; 619.28, Eventually; 643.10, escaped, into the; 666.23, put in; 750.27, months'; 844.9, said, but; 845.10, Adolph; 845.25, silenty.

Notes

In the notes below, the reference numbers denote page and line of this volume (the line count includes chapter headings). Biblical quotations are keyed to the King James Version. Quotations from Shakespeare are keyed to *The Riverside Shakespeare*, ed. G. Blakemore Evans (Boston: Houghton Mifflin, 1974). For more biographical information than is contained in the Chronology, see *Talking Horse: Bernard Malamud on Life and Work*, ed. Alan Cheuse and Nicholas Delbanco (New York: Columbia University Press, 1996); Philip Davis, *Bernard Malamud: A Writer's Life* (Oxford: Oxford University Press, 2007); *Conversations with Bernard Malamud*, ed. Lawrence Lasher (Jackson: University Press of Mississippi, 1991); and Janna Malamud Smith, *My Father Is a Book: A Memoir of Bernard Malamud* (Boston: Houghton Mifflin, 2006).

THE TENANTS

3.1–4 "Alive and . . . *Tetralogies*] From the third *Tetralogy* by Antiphon of Rhamnus (480–411 B.C.E.), classical Greek rhetorician and orator. The third *Tetralogy* concerns homicide in self-defense.

3.5–6 "I got to make it . . . BESSIE SMITH] From song "Long Old Road" (1931), composed and recorded by American blues singer Bessie Smith (1894–1927).

6.5–7 Ah, this live earth . . . Third Avenue.] Cf. *Richard II*, II.i.40–68.

7.10 Robinson Crusoe] Titular character in Daniel Defoe's *Robinson Crusoe* (1719).

11.35 Lesser and Clark] Cf. the Lewis and Clark Expedition, 1804–6, commissioned by President Thomas Jefferson and led by Captain Meriwether Clark and Second Lieutenant William Clark, to explore the Louisiana Purchase and the Pacific Northwest.

11.39–12.1 Lesser in short-masted bark . . . all about.] See John 21:1–13: While seven of Christ's disciples are fishing in a boat, the resurrected Christ appears on the shore of Lake Galilee.

12.1–3 seeking Hendrik . . . metaphysical hills] While searching for the Northwest Passage, English explorer Henry or Hendrik Hudson (d. 1611) was marooned by his mutinous crew in Hudson Bay (later named after him) and never seen again. In "Rip Van Winkle" (1819), Washington Irving describes how Hudson's crew created thunder by playing ninepins in the Catskill Mountains.

12.3 sweet-flowing Thames] Cf. the refrain in Edmund Spenser's *Prothalamion* (1596): "Sweet Thames, run softly, till I end my song."

12.10 "Whereof my bowels . . . Isaiah.] Isaiah 16.11.

13.3 Goatskin siren] In Greek mythology, the Sirens lured sailors to their watery death with their enchanting song, but here the enchanter is the piper Pan, god of herdsmen, goat-footed and two-horned.

13.36 Hab rachmones] Yiddish: Have pity or mercy.

15.22 feshtinkineh] Yiddish: stinking.

16.28–29 "I should not . . . Coleridge.] From a letter of April 1797 by English poet and critic Samuel Taylor Coleridge (1772–1834) to his publisher, Joseph Cottle.

16.34–35 mysterious stranger if not heart of darkness] Possible references to Joseph Conrad's *The Secret Sharer* (1910) and *Heart of Darkness* (1899). In *The Secret Sharer*, Leggatt, rescued at sea, is referred to as "the stranger" and "the secret stranger." *The Mysterious Stranger* is also the title of a posthumously published novel by Mark Twain.

18.23–24 Aeolus' bag] Aeolus, Greek god who ruled the winds.

19.5–6 Jacob meet Ishmael. . . . brother's brother."] Ishmael was Abraham's first son by Hagar, handmaiden to his wife, Sara, who had seemed barren. He was sent away with Hagar for mocking his half brother, Isaac, born later to Sara (Genesis 16,17, 21, 25). Jacob was the son of Isaac and Rebecca, and grandson of Abraham. He deceived his blind father into bestowing the firstborn birthright on him rather than Esau, his older twin, and was sent away by Rebecca in flight from Esau's anger (Genesis 27). "Am I my brother's keeper?" was the cry of Cain in denial of his murder of Abel (Genesis 4:9).

20.17 L. C. Smith] The Smith Premier Typewriter Company was established in Syracuse, New York, by four brothers, led by Lyman Cornelius Smith, in 1886, and became the L. C. Smith and Bros. Typewriter Company in 1903.

22.32 Fourteenth Amendment] The Fourteenth Amendment to the U.S. Constitution, ratified in 1868, granted citizenship to all persons born or naturalized in the United States (including former enslaved people) and guaranteed all citizens "equal protection of the laws."

32.16 ofays?] Derogatory term for white person.

33.2–4 King David . . . psalms fiction.] In 2 Samuel 5, David is appointed second king of Israel. A warrior and giant-slayer, he was also the psalmist of

Israel (2 Samuel 23:1) and a talented musician whose lyre could ward off evil spirits (1 Samuel 16:15–19).

33.20 shmuck] Yiddish: a contemptibly stupid or foolish person.

33.38–34.3 Nigger, nigger . . . the night.] Cf. "The Tyger" by William Blake, in *Songs of Experience* (1794).

36.24–25 Stepin Fetchit] Stage name of Lincoln Theodore Monroe Andrew Perry (1902–1985), American comedian and first Black film star. Perry's Stepin Fetchit was promoted as "The Laziest Man in the World."

39.36–37 Ford Company] Ford Motor Company, Detroit-based automobile manufacturer that was founded by Henry Ford in 1903.

41.3–7 written before . . . by Richard Wright, Claude Brown, Malcolm X, and . . . Eldridge Cleaver.] *Black Boy* (1945) by novelist Richard Wright (1908–1960); *Manchild in the Promised Land* (1965) by writer Claude Brown (1937–2002); *The Autobiography of Malcolm X* (1965) by civil rights activist Malcolm X (1925–1965) and journalist Alex Haley (1921–1992); and *Soul on Ice* (1968) by writer and political activist Eldridge Cleaver (1935–1998).

45.5–6 nobody . . . was his Pygmalion.] In Ovid's *Metamorphoses* the Cypriot sculptor Pygmalion falls in love with the statue he has sculpted.

49.5–7 "If she . . . WILLIE SHAKESPEAR] *Othello*, II.i.131–33.

55.27–28 Lotte Lehmann singing Schubert lieder] Lotte Lehmann (1888–1976) was a German soprano associated with the German operatic repertory. Austrian composer Franz Schubert (1797–1828) wrote six hundred lieder (songs), including *Winterreise*, beloved of Malamud's Dubin in *Dubin's Lives.*

57.19–20 Mephistophelean . . . yellow dashiki] Mephistopheles is the devil of the Faust legend—most famously in Christopher Marlowe's 1604 play *Doctor Faustus.* Mephistopheles takes the soul of the scholar in exchange for limitless knowledge and earthly pleasure. "Yarmulke" is the Yiddish word for the skullcap worn by Jewish men. A dashiki is a colorful West African garment for men that covers the top half of the body.

58.32 yoishe] Hebrew word for justice or uprightness, used as an exclamatory demand in Yiddish.

63.14 Blind Lemon Jefferson] Lemon Henry "Blind Lemon" Jefferson, American blues and gospel singer (1893–1929). The son of African American sharecroppers in Freestone County, Texas, he was born blind.

65.16 Lucky Strikes] Brand of cigarettes introduced in 1871 and a top seller in the States in the 1930s and '40s.

66.35–37 "I am convinced . . . the world."] From a letter of August 24, 1819, by John Keats to his friend and fellow English poet J. H. Reynolds.

67.2–4 Coleridge: 'Nothing can . . . not otherwise.'"] From Coleridge's *Biographia Literaria* (1817), chapter 14.

68.23 mezuzah] A parchment inscribed with Hebrew verses from the Torah and enclosed in a case that is affixed to the doorposts of a Jewish home, in accordance with religious law.

69.18–21 green-and-orange picture . . . binding brush strokes.] See the "Woman" series of paintings by Willem de Kooning (1904–1997), Dutch American abstract painter, celebrated in Malamud's *Pictures of Fidelman* ("Portraits of the Artist").

70.13–15 complete by abandoning . . . Peace to Valéry.] French poet Paul Valéry (1871–1945) held the position that—in W. H. Auden's often quoted paraphrase—"a poem is never finished, only abandoned."

76.15 Hellespont] Ancient name for the narrow strait between the peninsula of Gallipoli and Turkey. Of great military and economic importance, the Hellespont (present-day Dardanelles) is the gateway from the Black Sea to Istanbul and the Mediterranean.

80.34 "A Salaam Aleikum,"] Arabic (Islamic greeting): Peace Be Upon You.

87.34 Rap Brown] Jamil Abdullah Al-Amin (b. 1943), 1960s civil rights activist and Black separatist who said "violence is as American as cherry pie."

90.8 Mr. Bones?] In *Mammy* (1930), a black-faced Al Jolson plays "Mr. Bones," a comic end man in a traditional minstrel show.

97.38 LBJ] Lyndon Baines Johnson (1908–1973), thirty-sixth president of the United States, but here "LBJ" signifies "Johnson" (penis).

98.5 "'None but . . . the fair,'"] The concluding line of the first stanza in "Alexander's Feast; or: the Power of Music" (1697) by English poet John Dryden (1631–1700).

100.28 my dybbuk?] In Jewish folklore, the soul of a dead person who enters the mind of a living one.

108.26–27 Bessie Smith, a Leadbelly . . . Charlie Parker] Bessie Smith, see note 3.4–5. Lead Belly, stage name of American folk and blues musician Huddie William Ledbetter (1888–1949). Charlie Parker, American jazz saxophonist and composer (1920–55).

117.36 *The Promised End* . . . from *Lear*] *King Lear*, V.iii.264.

118.27–28 from *Lear* . . . I am?"] *King Lear* I.iv.230.

127.6 "Feh,"] Yiddish: Yuck.

127.7 "Sha,"] Yiddish: Quiet.

130.30 shvartzer] Derogatory Yiddish term for a Black person.

131.7 Mogen David] Six-pointed star of David, symbol of Judaism and, later, Zionism; here, a New York wine company of that name, known for its kosher wines.

132.1 the seven benedictions] At traditional Jewish weddings, the seven blessings traditionally chanted over a cup of wine, which the couple drink from afterward.

134.33 Uncle Toms] Derogatory term for Black persons considered excessively servile to whites, referring to the saintly title character in Harriet Beecher Stowe's *Uncle Tom's Cabin* (1852).

135.35 Elijah?] Hebrew prophet and miracle worker in the book of Kings. In the Seder service, the door is opened in invitation to Elijah, a seat is left vacant for him, and a full glass of wine called the Cup of Elijah is placed in waiting on the table.

135.39 Ecce Homo!] Latin: Behold the Man! Words used by Pontius Pilate on presenting a scourged Christ. See John 19:5.

DUBIN'S LIVES

143.1–2 "*What demon* . . . THOREAU] Henry David Thoreau, *Walden; or, Life in the Woods* (1854), "Economy."

143.3–4 "*Give me* . . . AUGUSTINE] Augustine, *Confessions* (c. 400 C.E.), book 8.17.

146.24–25 "Now I . . . am sorrel."] Thoreau's *Journal*, June 6, 1857.

147.7 Capri in search of D. H. Lawrence] English novelist D. H. Lawrence (1885–1930) stayed in Capri for two months with his wife Frieda in late 1919 and early 1920.

147.14–17 Montaigne . . . a matter."] From Michel de Montaigne's prefatory note "To the Reader" in his *Essays* (1580–1595).

150.1–3 Mahler . . . Freud in Leiden—] In summer 1910, Austrian composer Gustav Mahler (1860–1911), suffering from deep depression, met with Sigmund Freud in Leyden, Holland. Mahler's crisis was at least partly precipitated by his young wife, Anna's, affair with architect Walter Gropius.

151.18–19 Thoreau . . . moral test."] Thoreau's *Journal*, June 21, 1852.

152.17 "All nature is my bride."] Thoreau's *Journal*, April 23, 1857.

152.19–20 trip to the Adirondacks . . . sixteen.] In a letter of May 12, 1963, to Sidney Richman, Malamud described a similarly transformative excursion to the Adirondack Mountains in New York: "When I was sixteen, at the invitation of a school friend, I made my first trip out of the city (except for an excursion to Bear Mt. or a flight when I was two or three and there was a polio epidemic) to the Adirondacks, and the effect of nature was overwhelming."

154.15–16 "Elinor has never . . . to me."] From a letter of November 7, 1917, by Robert Frost to his friend Louis Untermeyer.

154.19–21 "She was not . . . and nature."] From a letter of March 1, 1939, by Robert Frost to his daughter Lesley Frost Francis.

154.25–26 "There's only one subject for a poem,"] Cf. Frost's letter of January 1, 1916, to Louis Untermeyer: a poem "begins as a lump in the throat, a sense of wrong, a homesickness, a lovesickness."

154.36 Quentin Bell . . . biography of her.] Quentin Bell, *Virginia Woolf: A Biography* (London: Hogarth Press, 1972).

155.12–13 Prufrock had . . . measuring spoons] See T.S. Eliot's "Love Song of J. Alfred Prufrock" (1915), line 51.

155.37–38 "Why, then . . . least deed?"] Thoreau's *Journal*, September 17, 1839.

156.7–8 "Ach, ich flöte."] German: I play the flute; I float. Cf. "Ach, ich fühls," Pamina's aria in Mozart's *Magic Flute*.

157.28 Montaigne . . . "Confounded fool"] See Montaigne, *Essays*, book 1:38.

157.29–30 Dr. Samuel Johnson . . . crackpot mannerisms.] Dr. Johnson (1709–1784), English man of letters, may have suffered from Tourette's syndrome. See especially Boswell's description of his friend and mentor's peculiarities in *The Life of Samuel Johnson* (1791).

157.32 "Montaigne's motto . . . 'What do I know?'] See Montaigne, *Essays*, book 2:12.

157.33–34 Johnson—'winking and blinking,' Blake described him—] In William Blake, "An Island in the Moon" (1784).

163.10 vagina dentata] Vagina with teeth, a folk legend later identified with Freud on male fears.

163.14–15 J. Middleton Murry . . . Katherine Mansfield] John Middleton Murry and New Zealand writer Katherine Mansfield met D. H. Lawrence and Frieda von Richthofen in the London office of the small literary magazine *Blue Review* (edited by Mansfield and Murry), after Mansfield had solicited work from Lawrence the prior year—the same year Frieda had left her husband and three children to elope to Germany with Lawrence. Lawrence and Frieda married in 1914, and Mansfield and Murry in 1918.

163.34–35 "thoughtful centrality"—Samuel Johnson's expression.] The phrase comes not from Johnson but from Walter Jackson Bate's Pulitzer Prize–winning biography of Johnson, *Samuel Johnson* (New York: Harcourt Brace Jovanovich, 1975). See the conclusion of chapter 14.

166.39–167.2 "William James . . . saw one."] See William James, "Address Delivered at a Meeting of the Association of American Alumnae at Radcliffe College" (1907).

167.24 dybbuk] See note 100.28.

171.17 no wolf to her harried Pamela.] Allusion to English novelist Samuel Richardson's *Pamela; or, Virtue Rewarded* (1740), about a young maidservant harassed by her employer.

171.29–30 Susanna . . . leering elder—] See Daniel 13: the beautiful Susanna, wife of Joakim, is spied on by two lecherous elders who attempt to coerce her into sleeping with them.

173.7–8 Lidian . . . no impressive evidence.] Lidian Jackson Emerson (1802–1892) was the second wife of essayist Ralph Waldo Emerson. Thoreau served as a live-in handyman in the Emerson house from 1841 to 1843 and again four years later when Emerson made his second European trip.

173.32–37 In winter . . . the ice.] Hawthorne's wife, Sophia, described this particular winter outing on the frozen Concord in a letter of December 30, 1842, to Mrs. Caleb Foote: "One afternoon, Mr. Emerson and Mr. Thoreau went with him [Hawthorne] down the river. Henry Thoreau is an experienced skater, and was figuring dithyrambic dances and Bacchic leaps on the ice—very remarkable, but very ugly methought. Next him followed Mr. Hawthorne who, wrapped in his cloak, moved like a self-impelled Greek statue, stately and grave. Mr. Emerson closed the line, evidently too weary to hold himself erect, pitching headforemost, half lying on the air."

174.11 Perry Miller] Perry Gilbert Eddy Miller (1905–1963), American intellectual historian, Harvard professor, and author of numerous books, including *The New England Mind* (1953). He edited *Consciousness in Concord: The Text of Thoreau's Hitherto "Lost Journal"* (1958) and the highly influential anthology *The American Transcendentalists: Their Prose and Poetry* (1957).

174.16 'One doesn't . . . trade of life,'] Thoreau's *Journal*, December 29, 1841.

174.18–19 He said . . . hadn't lived."] See *Walden*, "Where I Lived and What I Lived For": "I went to the woods because I wished to live deliberately, to front only the essential facts of life, and see if I could not learn what it had to teach, and not, when I came to die, discover that I had not lived."

175.4–5 "One of his best friends . . . unfinished life.'] William Ellery Channing (1818–1901) makes this remark about Thoreau in his biography of his friend, *Thoreau: The Poet-Naturalist* (1873).

175.31 Lady Bird] Lady Bird Johnson (1912–2006), wife of President Lyndon B. Johnson.

177.24 blutsbrüderschaft] German: blood brotherhood.

178.35–37 A true marriage . . . throbbing blood-circuit'] See D. H. Lawrence, *Kangaroo* (1923), chapter 8.

178.37–40 once wrote . . . body and spirit.'] In D. H. Lawrence letter to Thomas Dunlop, July 7, 1914.

182.29–30 The sad thing . . . lacked refinement.] Fanny knight wrote of her aunt, Jane Austen's, commonness in a letter of 1869 after she herself had become Lady Knatchbull.

189.34–35 "Lawrence called it . . . meaningful stars.'"] In Lawrence's "Introduction to *The Dragon of the Apocalypse* by Frederick Carter," reprinted in *Phoenix: The Posthumous Papers of D. H. Lawrence* (1936).

191.11–12 "Why should I . . . the Milky Way?"] Thoreau, *Walden*, "Solitude."

192.1–2 practiced law . . . like Carlyle] Thomas Carlyle (1795–1881), Scottish historian and man of letters, spent three miserable years studying law at the University of Edinburgh.

192.15–16 Plato in *The Republic* . . . by lot.] See Plato's *Republic*, book 5.

195.3–4 nobody's done very much past Ernest Jones] Reference to Ernest Jones, *Sigmund Freud: Life and Works* (London: Hogarth Press, 1953–57).

195.6–10 daughter Anna. . . . Minna . . . Fleiss—] Anna Freud (1895–1982), psychoanalyst and daughter of Sigmund Freud. Minna Bernays (1865–1941), younger sister to Freud's wife Martha. Wilhelm Fleiss (1858–1928), a German otolaryngologist and close friend of Freud.

195.40–196.1 "Being married doesn't . . . simile was Montaigne's] In *Essays*, book 3:5, Montaigne likens marriage to a tether and a bird's cage.

196.37–38 "I could never love you . . . his wife,"] Attributed to Lawrence by Jessie Chambers in her memoir *D.H. Lawrence: A Personal Record* (1931).

197.30–31 "Un bel di vedremo," the Puccini went] Italian: One beautiful day. An aria from Pucccini's *Madame Butterfly* (1904).

198.5 Nixon] Richard Milhous Nixon (1913–1994), thirty-seventh president of the United States who resigned the presidency over Watergate on August 9, 1974.

198.15–17 "Mark Twain . . . that is all.'"] From Twain's *Autobiography*, first published in book form in 1924.

202.35 "'Had we but world enough and time,'] The first line of Andrew Marvell's "To his Coy Mistress" (1681).

205.15 Queen of Sheba?] See 1 Kings 10.

210.40 'Seize the day,'] *Carpe diem.* Adage of Latin poet Horace (65–8 B.C.E.)

211.35 La Fenice] Teatro La Fenice, renowned opera house in Venice.

214.30 Pat Rooney or Smith and Dale.] Pat Rooney (1844–1892), vaudeville singer and dancer known for his soft-shoe tap dancing. Joe Smith (1884–1981) and Charlie Dale (1885–1971), comic vaudeville duo with heavy Jewish accents.

214.31 RKO] RKO Radio Pictures, Inc., American film production company celebrated especially for its musicals in Hollywood's Golden Age of the 1930s. RKO ceased production in 1957.

216.36–37 J. S. Bach . . . twenty children] German composer Johann Sebastian Bach (1685–1750) married soprano Anna Magdalena Wilcke, sixteen years his junior, in 1721 after the death of his first wife, Maria Barbara, bearing him thirteen more children.

221.12–14 In a letter . . . in a poem . . . city of Venice.'"] See, respectively, Lawrence's letter of October 7, 1920, to Catherine Carswell and his poem "Pomegranate" (1923).

223.14 Pippa passes.] Title of an 1841 verse drama by Robert Browning set in Asolo, a hill town in the Veneto region of Italy, that concerns a day in the life of an innocent silk-winding girl.

224.6 motoscafo] Italian: speedboat.

224.17 "Va fan'gulo,"] Italian: Fuck you, go fuck yourself.

226.15–18 Rousseau said . . . heard more.] Jean-Jacques Rousseau's visit to the Ospedale dei Mendicanti is described in his *Confessions* (1782).

226.18 'il prete roso'] Italian: the red priest.

228.4–5 Venus bathing, Venus revived.] Allusion to the François Boucher painting *The Bath of Venus* (1751), after earlier classical sculptures of the goddess surprised in her toilette, re-created in the Renaissance by Giambologna.

228.29 "Al sinistro."] Italian: To the left.

237.23 a birthmark, not the Scarlet Letter.] Playful allusion to two works by Nathaniel Hawthorne: the short story "The Birth-mark" (1843) and the novel *The Scarlet Letter* (1850).

259.34 "Ett nyp?"] Swedish: Do you want to get laid?

265.35–36 Emerson's remark . . . not to lie."] In Emerson's lecture "The Transcendentalist" (1842).

268.7–10 D. H. Lawrence had said . . . can marry."] Attributed to Lawrence by Jessie Chambers in her memoir *D.H. Lawrence: A Personal Record* (1931).

270.27–29 Montaigne had believed . . . physical health.] See Montaigne, *Essays*, book 1:14.

271.5 exercised daily—shades of Gatsby—] See F. Scott Fitzgerald's *The Great Gatsby* (1925), chapter IX. The youthful Jay Gatsby kept a strict schedule for exercise and self-improvement.

272.31–32 "The safe . . . Johnson said.] In Samuel Johnson, *The Rambler* 47.

274.21 Nothing like . . . Johnson had said.] *The Rambler* 85.

275.23–24 Nietzsche had said . . . needs a mask.] In Friedrich Nietzsche, *Beyond Good and Evil* (1886), section 40.

276.2 dyer's bloodless hand] See Shakespeare, sonnet 111, line 7.

281.32–33 Thoreau had called . . . own music.] Thoreau, *Journal*, February 12, 1854.

287.13 Rampal] Jean-Pierre Rampal (1922–2000), French flautist.

288.9–11 *in diesem Hause . . . demselben Platz.*] From "Der Doppelgänger," one of six songs comprising Schubert's *Schwanengesang* (1828), written in the last year of the Austrian composer and in which he set to music poems by Heinrich Heine. Here, the text reads: "In this House my beloved once Lived: / She has long since left the Town, / But the House still stands, here in the same Place."

288.20–21 not the Eve of St. Agnes, nor was Dubin Porphyrio] John Keats's poem "The Eve of St. Agnes" (1818) is set in a medieval castle—Madeleine's family's ancestral home—on the bitterly cold night of the Eve of St. Agnes (January 20). As Madeleine pines for the love of Porphrio, sworn enemy to her kin, he gains entry into the castle.

289.24–25 "Death and the Maiden."] Schubert's String Quartet no. 14 in D Minor (1824), composed after Schubert first understood he was dying. The slow movement of Schubert's Quintet in C Major was played at Malamud's own funeral.

290.30–31 Irma went crazy that year."] In 1947 Robert Frost's daughter Irma was committed to the state hospital in Concord, New Hampshire.

291.33–34 "*In diesem Wetter . . . Kinder hinaus!*"] From the song cycle *Kindertotenlieder* ("Songs on the death of children") by Mahler, who set to music five poems by German poet Friedrich Rückert. Here, the quoted lines read: "In this Weather, in this windy Storm, / I would never have sent the Children out."

291.35–37 As Samuel Johnson . . . call, "Sam!"] Boswell describes the incident in his *Life of Johnson* (1791) in the entry for April 15, 1871.

297.5–6 Thoreau was wrong . . . with sorrow.] Thoreau, *Journal*, July 27, 1840.

297.20–21 "Be silent . . . not mad."] Thomas Carlyle's journal for December 23, 1835, quoted in J. A. Froude's 1884 biography of Carlyle, *History of His Life in London 1834–81.*

297.23–24 "Love," Lawrence wrote . . . patient effort."] In D. H. Lawrence, *Psychoanalysis and the Unconscious* (1921), chapter 6.

307.31–38 She was not content . . . die alte Marschallin?"] Allusion to Richard Strauss's comic opera *Der Rosenkavalier* (1911). See the conclusion of Act I: the Marschallin looks in the mirror and, seeing how much older she is than her young lover, Octavian, tells him that he will soon leave her. The German text reads: "You are still the old Marschallin?"

309.28–29 Hadn't Thoreau said . . . anticipate spring.] See Perry Miller's introduction to *Consciousness in Concord* (1958): "If you read the *Journal* consecutively you see that every winter is a retirement to prepared positions. At last there is only one stronghold: the mind can *anticipate* spring."

317.1 "Maud, Maud . . . parodied Tennyson] Allusion to *Maud* (1855), Alfred, Lord Tennyson's poem of sad yearning.

317.22–23 "Someone once said . . . a life."] See Thoreau's *Journal*, April 11, 1852.

321.1–4 O Thou . . . harvest time.] Opening lines of John Keats's sonnet "What the Thrush Said," included in a letter of February 1818 to J. H. Reynolds.

321.9 'Bright Star'] Sonnet by John Keats, written in 1819.

321.22 "To Fanny."] Keats's sonnet of 1819 is addressed to his beloved, Fanny Brawne.

331.26–31 David Garnett . . . a lioness.] English novelist David "Bunny" Garnett's physical descriptions of Lawrence and Frieda, loosely quoted here, appear in the second volume of his autobiography, *The Flowers of the Forest* (1955).

332.4–5 "My detachment . . . only you."] Postcard from Lawrence to Frieda, May 11, 1912.

332.5–8 "Frieda and I . . . is love."] Cf. Lawrence's letter to Sallie Hopkin, August 19, 1912.

332.8 "Look, we have come through!"] See *Look! We Have Come Through* (1917), Lawrence's verse record of his relationship with Frieda in its initial stage of crisis and conflict, after Frieda left her husband and children.

332.8–9 "two stars in balanced conjunction."] Cf. D. H. Lawrence, *Women in Love* (1920), chapter 13: "two single equal stars balanced in conjunction."

344.9–11 H.D.T. had wanted . . . the snow . . ."] See Thoreau's *Journal*, December 1, 1856. Thoreau speaks not about the "scrub oak" but about the "shrub oak."

347.5 Caveat emptor] Latin: Let the buyer beware.

353.26–28 "About marriage . . . "'Bear and forbear,' Sam Johnson defined it."] Johnson, *The Rambler* 18.

353.37–38 "Thomas Carlyle . . . called it 'a discipline of character.'"] The words are not Carlyle's but J. A. Froude's in his *Life of Carlyle, The First Forty Years*, chapter 19.

357.34 Havelock Ellis] English social reformer (1859–1939) with progressive ideas on sexuality, whose *The Psychology of Sex* appeared in six volumes.

359.1 epileptic daughter] Jean Clemens (1880–1909), the youngest of Twain's four children, who was diagnosed with epilepsy at age fifteen. She drowned in a bathtub on Christmas Eve 1909.

364.23–25 D. H. Lawrence . . . allo stomacho"—] Lawrence, letter of Christmas Day 1926 to American psychoanalyst Dr. Trigant Burrow. The Italian text reads: "It makes me sick to my stomach."

370.30–32 *H. D. Thoreau* . . . of this."] Thoreau, *Journal*, April 24, 1859.

373.3–4 "the unknown God . . . consciousness"—] "The unknown God" is a formulation that appears in several works by D. H. Lawrence: his poem "Shadows" (1932); *Kangaroo* (1923), chapter 16; and *The Plumed Serpent* (1926), chapters 6 and 21.

373.4–5 "the slow invasion . . . the ether"—] See D. H. Lawrence's letter to Mabel Dodge Luhan, October 17, 1923.

373.5–6 "the old Pagan vision."] D. H. Lawrence, letter to Bertrand Russell, December 8, 1915.

378.4 Jamaica] Neighborhood in the New York City borough of Queens.

378.12 Kaddish] Jewish prayer for the dead.

381.15–16 Mother Juana Inés de la Cruz] Nun and self-taught poet (1651–1695), living in Mexican part of Spanish Empire.

383.1 President Ford offers the deserters] In 1974 Gerald R. Ford (1913–2006), thirty-eighth president of the United States, offered a conditional amnesty for Vietnam draft dodgers.

386.27–29 "And at last . . . of this!] D. H. Lawrence, "Bei Heneef" (1913). Malamud misquotes the second line: "I can see it all, it is whole like the twilight."

387.18–20 Jonathan Swift . . . Vanessa . . . letters to him] Jonathan Swift (1667–1745), Anglo-Irish satirist, became secretly involved in an affair with his former pupil Esther Vanhomrigh, whom he nicknamed "Vanessa." Twenty-two years his junior, she followed Swift from London to Dublin before the relationship ended badly.

392.37–39 Freud had said . . . him away."] In Freud, *Fragment of an Analysis of a Case of Hysteria* (1905).

399.38 Queen of the Night] Villainous queen in Mozart's opera *The Magic Flute* (1791).

426.27–29 Chinese poem . . . color or sound."] In *Zen: The Path of Paradox*, by Indian mystic and guru Osho (1931–1990).

427.16–17 Lawrence had called Thomas Hardy "a bad artist,"] See D. H. Lawrence's essay "Study of Thomas Hardy" (1914).

427.31–33 Thomas Hardy fabricated a "biography" "by" . . . Florence.] Florence Emily Hardy, *The Life of Thomas Hardy* (1928).

427.33–34 "If I get . . . you tight."] See Thomas Hardy's letter of January 1913 to Florence Dugdale after the death of his first wife, Emma: "I am getting through E.'s papers. . . . It was, of course, sheer hallucination in her, poor thing, and not willfulness. . . . If once I get you here again, won't I clutch you tight?"

436.30 In Sicily] Frieda and Lawrence lived there for most of 1921.

439.5–9 he's talking about . . . alone understands.'] The poem is Lawrence's "Virgin Youth" (1916).

439.15–16 "Love means . . . Augustine had said.] Attributed to Augustine and admired by Martin Heidegger and Hannah Arendt, the statement does not appear in *Confessions.*

440.4–7 "Clouds arose . . . fog of lust."] Augustine's *Confessions*, book 2.2.

440.9–10 The expense of spirit] See Shakespeare, sonnet 129.

442.2 Faustus] See note 57.19–20.

443.22–23 Connie Chatterley] Protagonist in Lawrence's *Lady Chatterley's Lover* (1928).

448.5–6 in medias res?"] Latin: in the middle of things.

454.38–455.4 "I am not . . . or another."] From Lawrence's letter to S. S. Koteliansky, March 14, 1919.

456.18–20 On August 21, 1581, Montaigne . . . shape of a prick."] Recorded in Montaigne's *Journal du Voyage* for Switzerland, Germany, and Italy, 1580–81.

456.21–22 "My thoughts . . . overspread me."] Johnson, in his journal for *Prayers and Meditations*, Easter Eve, April 21, 1764.

456.22–24 "I wind round . . . Augustine.] *Confessions,* book 4.1.

456.29–33 Freud devastated . . . be useful."] From Freud's letter to Arnold Zweig, May 31, 1936.

456.33–34 "I shall be like . . . the top."] Attributed to Swift by Edward Young in his *Conjectures on Original Composition* (1759).

456.34–38 "But really . . . any minute."] From Lawrence's letter to English writer and editor Edward Garnett, July 3, 1912.

456.39–40 burning bushes on Sinai] Exodus 3:1–21. God speaks to Moses out of a burning bush, commanding him to lead the Israelites out of Egypt.

464.7–9 Lawrence . . . incarnate cosmos."] Lawrence, *Apocalypse* (1930).

468.21–22 Montaigne had complained . . . lack of memory] In *Essays*, 2.17.

468.23–26 Emerson . . . his thought.] Bronson Alcott on the subject of his friend's failing memory. See Alcott's *Journals*, September 13, 1874: "It must be mortifying to one of his accurate habits of thought and speech and his former tenacity of memory to find himself wanting in his once ready command of imagery to match his thought."

469.22 Trinitarian metaphysic] Lawrence wrote on the Father, Son, and Holy Spirit in his foreword to *Sons and Lovers*. He also wrote about the need to get beyond Law and Love to a third state in essays such as his "Study of Thomas Hardy" and "The Crown."

469.29–31 Augustine . . . my remembrance."] See *Confessions*, book 10.

470.33 "Don't go, Willie, out in the rain."] Adapted from a poem Malamud himself wrote to his mother forty-five years after her death, while making notes on Howard Nemerov's poetry collection *The Western Approaches* (1975). The poem concludes: "I walked in the rain." When a sixty-eight-year-old Malamud came around after heart surgery in 1982, he gave his name as "William"—Dubin's name—and his age as fifty-seven. He once told his friend Bert Pogrebin, "If you know *Dubin's Lives*, you know me."

476.26–27 "A grief . . . and drear."] Coleridge, "Dejection: An Ode" (1802), st. 2.

476.31–34 Samuel Johnson . . . over me."] See Johnson's journal for *Prayers and Meditations*, Good Friday, April 20, 1764.

477.13 St. Paul . . . on fornicators.] See 1 Corinthians 6:9–10.

478.14–15 Work which . . . human consciousness] See Lawrence's "Study of Thomas Hardy," chapter 4: "It seems as if the great aim and purpose in human life were to bring all life into human consciousness. And this is the final meaning of work: the extension of human consciousness."

483.15 Du bist Dubin] German: You are Dubin.

484.2–9 Dr Johnson . . . hadn't done.] An episode (November 1784) recounted in Boswell's *Life of Johnson*.

484.19 shammes] Sexton in a synagogue.

484.24–25 "Montaigne . . . premeditation of freedom.] See *Essays*, 1.20.

484.30–33 Montaigne . . . the whole."] See *Essays*, 3.12.

486.4 "*Denn ach, allein irre ich im Hain.*"] The concluding lines of Schubert's "Seufzer" D. 198 (composed 1815), with lyrics by Ludwig Hölty: "I, alas, wander in the Grove alone."

490.25 qui vive] French: literally "who lives"; on the alert, on the lookout.

493.1 Bach . . . *unser Gott* . . .] Johann Sebastian Bach, Cantata no. 80, based on Martin Luther's hymn "A Mighty Fortress Is Our God."

493.20 *Wohl auf, der Bräutigam kömmt* . . .] From Bach's Cantata no. 140, "Sleepers Awake": "Indeed, the Bridegroom is coming."

493.35–36 *So geh . . . Braut!*] From Cantata no. 140: "So come into me, You my chosen Bride!"

494.6 *Mit harfen . . . zimbeln schön.*] From Cantata no. 140: "With harps and even with cymbals." Malamud wrote thus to Arlene Heyman, the model for Fanny.

496.12 yarmulka] See note 57.19–20.

500.3 satori] Japanese Buddhist term for sudden enlightenment.

512.10–11 lives of Cromwell and Frederick the Great] Respectively, *The Letters and Speeches of Oliver Cromwell* (1845), with commentary by Carlyle, and Caryle's *History of Frederick II of Prussia* (1858).

516.2–7 letter to his sister-in-law . . . go away."] From Lawrence's letter to Else Jaffe, October 4, 1929.

516.12–13 soon thereafter . . . became lovers.] In the month after Lawrence's death. See F. A. Lea, *Life of Middleton Murry* (1959).

GOD'S GRACE

528.1–4 The Holy One . . . R. YITZHAQ NAPPAHA] Commentary by Rabbi Yitzhaq Nappaha, a second-generation Galiellean Amora, one of the Jewish scholars who spoke in interpretation of the Oral Torah (or Law), later codified as the Gemara (rabbinic commentary). Nappaha invokes Job 38:6.

528.5–7 I came upon . . . ROBINSON CRUSOE] Reference to rather than quotation from Daniel Defoe's *Robinson Crusoe* (1719). See Crusoe's discovery of the remnants of a cannibal feast in chapter 12.

528.8–10 Nobody seemed to know . . . JOHANSON, EDEY] From Donald C. Johanson and Maitland A. Edey, *Lucy, The Beginnings of Mankind* (1981), p. 99. The quotation concerns the finding of cranial fossils, which were given names.

531.9–10 Djanks and Druzhkies] Cf. Yanks and Ruskies.

532.3–5 "After Your first Holocaust . . . living creatures.] See Genesis 9:11.

533.10–11 "It says in Sanhedrin," . . . the world.'"] Jerusalem Talmud, *Sanhedrin* 4:1 (22a).

533.36–37 Einstein said . . . the universe] In a letter of December 12, 1926, to fellow physicist Max Born: "Quantum mechanics is certainly imposing.

But an inner voice tells me that it is not yet the real thing. The theory says a lot, but does not really bring us any closer to the secret of the 'old one.' I, at any rate, am convinced that *He* does not throw dice." See *The Born-Einstein Letters* (1971).

535.33–34 The rainbow . . . the earth.] See Genesis 9:13.

536.27 Only God and he "contending,"] See Job 9.3, 40:2.

536.36–537.2 Moses . . . endless back.] See Exodus 3:1–6, 33:9–23.

538.25–26 dove bearing . . . olive leaf?] See Genesis 8:11.

542.16 Konrad Lorenz] Konrad Zacharias Lorenz (1903–1989), Austrian zoologist and ethologist who specialized in instinctive behavior in animals.

543.34 Ameslan sign language for the deaf.] American Sign Language.

544.15 Pentateuch, his Torah] The first five books of the Old Testament and Hebrew Bible, comprising the Law of Moses: Genesis, Exodus, Leviticus, Numbers, and Deuteronomy.

544.20–22 Buz . . . the Patriarch] See Genesis 22:20–21.

547.22 cantor] Jewish prayer leader and singer, also known as a chazan.

548.14 baruch Ha-shem] Hebrew: Blessed is His name.

548.15–16 Yom Kippur] The Day of Atonement, the holiest day of the year in Judaism, reserved for repentance and fasting.

556.5 Kaddish] See note 378.12.

556.9 "Book of the Dead."] Ancient Egyptian funerary text, to assist the dead on their journey through the underworld.

560.16 Eohippus—] Extinct genus, resembling a small horse.

560.18–19 Pliocene . . . Jurassic . . . Miocene epoch] The Pliocene epoch in the geological timescale is from 5.3 million to 2.5 million years ago, preceded by the Miocene, from 23 to 5.3 million years ago. The Jurassic period extends from 200 to 145 million years ago.

562.32 matzo-like] Matzo is an unleavened bread, traditionally eaten during Passover in commemoration of the Israelites' deliverance from Egypt. In Deuteronomy 16:3, God instructed them to depart from Egypt in haste when they heard his voice, not waiting for the bread to rise.

563.34–35 aggie] Students and sports teams at Texas A&M (Agricultural and Mechanical) University.

567.9–10 yarmulke] See note 57.19–20.

567.22 Deo volente] Latin: God willing.

567.29–30 Bar Mitzvah] Initiation ceremony of Jewish males at age thirteen.

567.34–35 Aesop, La Fontaine, Dr. Dolittle, and *Tales of the Hasidim.*] Aesop (620–564 B.C.E.), ancient Greek author of *Aesop's Fables*, often concerning animals. Jean de la Fontaine (1621–1695), French author of *Fables*, who used animals to tell morals. Dr. Dolittle, central character in English author Hugh Lofting's *The Story of Doctor Dolittle* (1920), who spoke to animals in their own languages. *Tales of the Hasidim* (1947) by German Jewish philosopher Martin Buber (1878–1965).

568.14 alev hasholem—] Hebrew: peace be upon him (said of the deceased).

569.31 "'Sh'ma Yisroel . . . ad-nai echad—'"] Hebrew: Hear O Israel, the Lord our God, the Lord is One. The central prayer in Jewish morning and evening services.

571.11 "Ich tants far mayn tate."] Yiddish: I dance for my father.

572.16 sotto voce] Latin: in a quiet voice.

577.33–34 Walt Whitman . . . 'the handkerchief of the Lord'—] In Whitman's "Song of Myself," section 6, from *Leaves of Grass* (1855).

579.8–9 old snake . . . Adam and Eve."] See Genesis 2:14–3:24.

579.12 "Rashi—] Shlomo Yitzchaki (1040–1105), known today as Rashi, French rabbi who wrote the first extensive analytic commentary on the Talmud, the body of Jewish law.

579.24 Cain and Abel?"] See Genesis 4.

579.32 qui vive] See note 490.25.

580.3 story of Abraham and Isaac] Genesis 22.

581.33–35 Kierkegaard . . . murder Isaac.] Danish philosopher Søren Kierkegaard (1813–1855) considers the story of Abraham and Isaac in *Fear and Trembling* (1843).

581.36 Freud might have agreed—] Allusion to Sigmund Freud's emphasis in his writings on conflict between fathers and sons, and on the repressed murderous instincts in human beings.

585.25–26 escape of the Israelites . . . Red Sea] See Exodus 14:21–31.

589.24–26 Ortega y Gasset once said . . . before him.] In Ortega y Gasset, *Toward a Philosophy of History* (1941), quoting Wolfgang Kohler's *Mentality of the Apes* on the subject of memory.

601.33 Mary Modelyn."] Cf. Mary Magdalene, a follower of Jesus.

602.18–19 Esau . . . hairy ape.] Esau is a "hairy man," his brother, Jacob, smooth. See Genesis 27:11.

602.21 "Melchior] In the Gospel of St. Matthew, one of the magi who bring gifts to the newborn Jesus.

602.26 "Luke and Saul of Tarsus] Luke the Evangelist, the apostle traditionally ascribed authorship of the Gospel bearing his name and the Acts of the Apostles. He was a companion to Paul, the first-century apostle, also named Saul, who spread the teachings of Jesus after his conversion on the road to Damascus.

604.32 Nisan] In the Hebrew calendar, the first month of the ecclesiastical year (corresponding to March or April).

605.16–18 "May all the leaven . . . the earth."] Jewish prayer recited on the night before Passover, and again the next morning.

605.25 "Kol Nidre,"] Hebrew and Aramaic avowal chanted in the synagogue at the beginning of service on the eve of Yom Kippur (Day of Atonement).

606.1 Elijah's seat] See note 135.35.

606.19 Seder night] Ritual meal at commencement of the Jewish holiday of Passover.

606.20 white kitl] Traditional Jewish burial garment that is also worn by men during holiday services.

607.17 haroset] Paste made of nuts and fruit at the Passover Seder symbolizing the clay mixed by the Israelites when enslaved in Egypt.

607.30–31 Moshe Rebbenu] Hebrew: Moses, our rabbi.

608.20 kiddush] In Judaism, prayers said over wine, before the meal on the Shabbat or the eve of a holiday.

609.29–30 the Four Questions] Recited at the Passover Seder by the youngest person at the table: Why is this night different from all other nights? Why tonight do we only eat matzo (unleavened) bread? Why do we dip fingers in the wine, twice over? Why do we recline?

612.28–29 balcony scene from *Romeo and Juliet*] Act II, scene ii.

614.20 Bronx cheer] Flatulent-like noise made with the tongue between closed lips to express contempt or disapproval.

614.37–39 "A Kid for Two Farthings." . . . "Chad Gadye"] Carol Reed's *A Kid for Two Farthings* (1955)—whose title alludes to "Chad Gadya"—was adapted to the screen from the 1953 novel of the same title by Wolf Mankowitz about growing up in a Jewish neighborhood in London's East End. "Chad Gadya" is the last of the songs sung at the conclusion of the Passover seder. A chain song, it begins this way: "One little goat, one little goat / which my father bought for two zuzim."

616.25–26 "They that sow in tears . . . in joy."] Psalm 126:5.

620.4–6 God was . . . work on that day.] See Exodus 31:14.

620.27 Martin Buber . . . no Hasidim] German Jewish philosopher Martin Buber (1878–1965) was greatly interested in the Hasidim ("pious ones") and how they integrated religious practice in everyday life.

622.21–23 Darwin and Wallace . . . natural selection] English naturalist, geologist, and biologist Charles Darwin (1809–1882) and Welsh naturalist and explorer Alfred Russel Wallace (1823–1913) both advanced the theory of evolution through natural selection.

622.23 sociobiology] The study of the biological basis of social behavior. The term was popularized by American scientist Edward O. Wilson, on whose book *On Human Nature* (1978) Malamud made extensive notes in preparation for the writing of *God's Grace.*

622.32–33 Freud . . . pain Everywhere.] For Freud on God, trauma, neurosis, and religion, see *The Future of an Illusion* (1927), *Civilization and Its Discontents* (1930), and *Moses and Monotheism* (1939).

624.14 naarishkeit—] Yiddish: foolishness.

624.39–40 Pillar of Fire] See Exodus 13:21–22.

625.9–10 "'Why do you contend with Me] See Genesis 18:22–32, Exodus 17:2, Isaiah 50:8, Psalms 35:1, Jeremiah 2:29, as well as Job 9:3, 13:19, 23:6, and 40:2.

642.36–37 "It says in Leviticus . . . a diverse kind—'"] See Leviticus 19:19.

642.39–40 'If a man . . . kill the beast.'] Leviticus 20:15.

643.1–2 in Deuteronomy . . . kind of beast.'"] Deuteronomy 27:21.

644.7 Ramapithecus] Now known as Sivapithecus, a fossil primate from middle to late Miocene epoch; related to orangutans rather than *Homo sapiens.*

647.4–6 Lot's daughters . . . its successors] See Genesis 19:32–38.

648.3 chutzpah?] Yiddish: cheek, audacity.

665.12 sat shivah] Weeklong mourning period in Judaism.

670.11–12 the Second Law of Thermodynamics] The Second Law of Thermodynamics states that the total entropy of an isolated system always increases over time, dissipating energy.

670.20–21 "Each devours . . . from Isaiah] See Isaiah 9:20.

678.20 Et tu] Latin: You too. See *Julius Caesar*, III.i.77.

680.36–37 it had happened . . . Rashi had said . . . of creation."] In Rashi's commentary on Genesis, concerning the story of Adam's sin.

THIRTEEN STORIES

691.19 shul] Yiddish: synagogue.

691.21 kaddish] See note 378.12.

693.18 Yeshiva bocher] Young male student who attends an Orthodox Jewish religious school or college, especially for the study of the Talmud.

698.5–6 Jonah . . . in the whale—] See the book of Jonah 1:17–2:10.

712.37 "Gevalt!] Yiddish (interjection): Oh, violence; woe is me; Oh my God.

714.8 Kentucky Derby] Annual horse race held in Louisville, Kentucky, since 1875, typically on the first Saturday in May.

714.37 "Goldberg's Varieties."] Cf. J. S. Bach, Goldberg Variations for harpsichord, 1741.

715.32 ETV] Educational television.

716.5 pince-nez] Eyeglasses without temples that are held in place by gripping or pinching the nose, popular in the late nineteenth and early twentieth centuries.

716.15 centaur] In Greek mythology a creature with a human upper body and the lower body of a horse.

718.38 Guadalcanal."] In World War II, U.S. forces defeated the Japanese on the island of Guadalcanal in the Solomons after a land, sea, and air campaign that lasted from August 7, 1942, to February 9, 1943.

719.24 off your noodle."] Slang: crazy, lacking intelligence.

720.19 settles your pickle] Slang: settles the score, resolves the problem.

720.23 Iwo Jima] Battle of Iwo Jima (February 19–March 16, 1945), fought between U.S. Marines and Japanese in the Pacific for control of the island and its strategic airfields. After thirty-six days of intense fighting, the U.S. defeated the Japanese.

720.24–25 the Marne and the Argonne Forest] The battles of the Marne were two separate battles of World War I fought around the Marne River in northeast France, both repulsing German advances. The reference here is to the Second Battle of the Marne, July 15–August 6, 1918, in which American forces participated. The Allied victory was of decisive importance for the outcome of the war. The Argonne Forest in northeastern France, 135 miles east of Paris, was the location where American troops made the final offensive of World War I, known as the Meuse-Argonne Offensive, which lasted from September 26, 1918, until the Armistice on November 11, 1918. American troops sustained more than 110,000 casualties.

721.3 Bronx cheer] See note 614.20.

723.20 Theodor Herzl] Austro-Hungarian writer and political activist (1860–1904), one of the modern founders of Zionism. Herzl founded the Zionist Organization, now the World Zionist Organization.

726.13 terra incognita] Latin: unfamiliar, unmapped land.

726.20 Mishna, Proverbs, Kabbalah . . . the Torah] Mishna, the rabbinically edited compilation of Jewish oral traditions. Proverbs, wisdom writings that are part of the third division of the Hebrew Bible or Old Testament. Kabbalah, wisdom or esoteric knowledge concerned with the essence of God. The commentaries known as the *Zohar* are the foundations of Kabbalah. The Torah, or Pentateuch, the five books of Moses from Genesis to Deuteronomy—handwritten on scrolls, rolled around two wooden staffs, and treasured in the Ark of each synagogue.

736.19 dovening] Yiddish: prayer, recitation of prayer.

739.7 "Grubber yung!"] Yiddish: A coarse youth.

739.15 "Sha,"] See note 127.8.

741.1 qui vive] See note 490.25.

748.40 Mahler's "Songs of a Wayfarer."] Mahler composed the orchestral song cycle in 1884–85 after his unsuccessful love affair with soprano Johanna Richter. The first of the four songs in the cycle is entitled "When My Sweetheart Is Married."

752.3 Bulfinch] *Bulfinch's Mythology* (1867).

752.6 Gramercy Park] Private park in Manhattan, located off Park Avenue South between East 20th and East 21st Streets.

756.13–14 Sisyphus, Midas . . . eternally cursed.] In Greek mythology, the gods punished Sisyphus, King of ancient Corinth, for his deceitfulness by condemning him to an impossible task: to roll a boulder up a hill, only to watch it roll down again. Also in Greek mythology, Midas, a king of Phrygia, was granted his wish by Dionysus that everything he touched be turned to gold.

756.14–15 Tithonus . . . living forever.] In Greek mythology, Tithonus begged for immortality, but neglected to ask for eternal youth. As he grew older he prayed to be removed from the world; instead, he was transformed into a cicada.

763.11–12 Nehru's Congress Party cap] Jawaharlal Nehru (1889–1964), first prime minister of India, characteristically wore a white side cap, pointed in front and behind. The cantor in the synagogue wears a high mitre-like hat in black or white, in contrast to the usually flat yarmulke, a brimless skullcap.

763.13 like a French judge's in Rouault] Judges were a favorite subject of French expressionist painter Georges Rouault (1871–1958). See, for example, *The Three Judges* (c. 1938).

763.14 doctor's in a Daumier print.] See, for example, *The Clinic of Dr. Robert Macaire* (1837), in the Dr. Macaire series by French painter and caricaturist Honoré Daumier (1808–1879).

763.20 Giacometti] Alberto Giacometti (1901–1966), Swiss sculptor.

763.23–24 Rembrandt's hat . . . middle-aged self-portraits] Dutch painter Rembrandt Harmenszoon van Rijn (1606–1669) painted many self-portraits throughout his life; forty are known to survive.

764.3 vernissage] Private preview of an art exhibition.

764.38 mishigas—] Yiddish: craziness.

774.29 catting around] Slang: on the prowl sexually; sleeping around.

777.17 "Tant pis pour vous,"] French: Too bad for you.

785.20 Jamaica] See note 378.4.

790.33 Montagnana] Here, a cello made by Domenico Montagnana (1686–1750), Venetian maker of stringed instruments.

793.39 Rostropovich] Mstislav Rostropovich (1927–2007), Russian cellist.

802.19 Casals] Pablo Casals (1876–1973), Spanish cellist.

803.2 *un poco mosso.*] Italian: a little more. The second movement of Schubert's Trio no. 1 in B-Flat for Violin, Cello, and Piano is marked "Andante un poco mosso."

803.11 Piatigorsky and Boccherini] Gregor Piatigorsky (1903–1976), Russian-born American cellist. Luigi Boccherini (1743–1805), Italian composer and cellist.

805.1 *In Kew Gardens*] This story and the one that follows in this volume ("Alma Redeemed") are what Malamud called "biographed stories," undertaken during recuperation from open-heart surgery in 1982. He described his method in a note: "start with a scene in one life, explicate that as a fiction, then go into the biographical element and develop further. You come out, or should, *with an invention forward as a story*, limited but carrying the meaning of the life as a short story."

805.2 Virginia] Virginia Woolf (1882–1941), English novelist.

805.7 "The Last Rose of Summer."] Poem by Irish poet Thomas Moore (1779–1852) set to a traditional Irish song, in volume 5 (1813) of Moore's popular *Irish Melodies.*

805.11 Vanessa] Vanessa Bell (1879–1861), English painter and older sister of Virginia Woolf.

805.16 dear goat,"] Virginia's childhood nickname was "Billy Goat." In her correspondence with Vanessa, Virginia signed her letters as "Billy" or simply "B."

805.19–22 George Duckworth . . . without looking.] Vanessa and Virginia later accused their half brothers, George and Gerald Duckworth, of sexually abusing them when they were children.

805.36 "Unquenchable seems to me . . . H. James.] From the novelist Henry James's condolence letter of May 6, 1895, to Virginia Woolf's father, Leslie Stephen, on the death of his wife, Julia.

806.1 "Why won't my whiskers grow?"] The lament was reportedly made by the widower Leslie Stephen as he went upstairs to bed. See Quentin Bell's biography of his aunt, *Virginia Woolf: A Biography* (1972), chapter 4.

806.5–7 King Edward . . . to write] During her second mental breakdown in 1904, after the death of her father, Virginia Woolf lay in bed in the house of her friend Violet Dickinson, thinking that the birds were singing Greek choruses and that King Edward VII (1841–1910) was using foul language in the garden.

806.9–10 Leonard Woolf . . . Jewish mother.] The writer and publisher Leonard Woolf (1880–1969) came from a large Jewish family. Virginia and Leonard married in 1912.

806.12–13 Violet Dickinson] Longtime family friend who nursed Woolf back to health after her breakdown in 1904 and introduced her to the women's editor of *The Guardian.*

806.19–20 Lytton . . . "Semen?" he asked . . . Vanessa's dress.] Virginia recalled Lytton Strachey's bold remark in "Old Bloomsbury," published in the posthumous collection *Moments of Being.* Strachey (1880–1932) was the author of *Eminent Victorians* (1918) and a founding member of the Bloomsbury group with Virginia and Leonard Woolf, E. M. Forster, and Maynard Keynes.

806.21–22 Vanessa loved . . . Duncan Grant until he loved her.] Prior to his lifelong involvement with Vanessa Grant, British painter and designer Duncan Grant (1885–1978) had been engaged in strictly homosexual relationships. Vanessa Bell and Duncan Grant had a child together in 1918.

806.23–24 Clive Bell . . . not love him.] Art critic Clive Bell (1881–1964) and Vanessa Stephens married in 1907. The Bells had an open marriage, each taking lovers throughout their relationship, and remaining married long after they ceased to be a couple.

806.26–28 When Julia . . . Warren Septimus Smith.] Virginia Woolf's first suicide attempt by jumping from a window occurred after the death of her father. In *Mrs. Dalloway* (1925), the shell-shocked Warren Septimus Smith throws himself out a window.

806.33–34 Janet Case . . . teacher of Greek.] Janet Case (1863–1937) began tutoring Virginia Woolf in classics in 1902. Woolf wrote Case's obituary for *The Times* in 1937.

806.36 Vita Nicolson] Lady Victoria Mary Nicolson (1892–1962), better known as Vita Sackville-West, English writer and garden designer who became Woolf's lover in the late 1920s.

806.39–40 "Possibly my great age . . . greatly exaggerated.] See Virginia Woolf's letter of September 4, 1912, to Katherine Cox: "Why do you think people make such a fuss about marriage and copulation? Why do some of our friends change upon losing chastity? Possibly my great age makes it less of a catastrophe; but certainly I find the climax immensely exaggerated."

807.1–4 Vanessa wrote Clive . . . do you?"] Paraphrase of a letter of December 12, 1912, from Vanessa to Quentin Bell, four months after Virginia's marriage to Leonard Woolf.

807.13–14 "He had committed . . . human nature."] From *Mrs. Dalloway*, slightly misquoted: "He had committed an appalling crime and been condemned to death by human nature."

807.15–16 "The whole world . . . our sakes."] From *Mrs. Dalloway*. British spelling is Americanized here.

807.21–30 "[Lily Briscoe] could . . . can't write . . .'] *To The Lighthouse*, chapter 9.

807.31–35 ". . . She looked . . . my vision."] *To The Lighthouse*, chapter 14.

807.36 a room of my own] Cf. Woolf's *A Room of One's Own* (1928).

807.37–40 "I hate to see . . . Leslie Stephen to Julia Duckworth.] In a letter of July 18, 1877.

808.1–2 "There has fallen . . . Alfred, Lord Tennyson] From Tennyson's *Maud* (1855), 1.22.10.

808.3–5 "There was something . . . out laughing."] Cf. a passage from chapter 1 of *A Room of My Own*: "There was something so ludicrous in thinking of people humming such things even under their breath at luncheon parties before the war that I burst out laughing."

808.6–8 *The Waves. . . . The Years . . . Between the Acts*] Woolf's *The Waves* was published in 1931, *The Years* in 1937, and *Between the Acts* shortly after her death in 1941.

808.10–11 Shakespeare's sister] In *A Room of One's Own* Woolf considers the likely fate of a female writer in Shakespeare's day—Shakespeare's sister—had she shared his literary genius.

808.13 "They also serve."] From Milton's "When I consider how my light is spent" (1673), about the obstacles presented by his blindness to fulfilling the tasks God has set before him: "They also serve who only stand and wait."

808.14–15 "What a born melancholic I am."] From a diary entry by Woolf for June 23, 1929. See *A Writer's Diary* (1953), edited by Leonard Woolf.

808.18 Thoby] Thoby Stephen (1880–1906), eldest son of Leslie Stephen and Julia Duckworth, who died of typhoid at twenty-six.

808.38 Virginia wrote a biography of Roger Fry.] *Roger Fry: A Biography* (1940), a book that Woolf found difficult to write, feeling constrained by the form and the need for reticence, particularly concerning Fry's homosexuality. The book's poor reception may have contributed to her final depression.

809.19–20 "I don't think . . . have been."] From Woolf's handwritten suicide note left for her husband, Leonard. She took her life on March 28, 1941, drowning herself in the River Ouse near Lewes, England.

810.3 Bruno Walter] German-born American conductor, pianist, and composer (1876–1962) who was a champion of Mahler's music.

810.5–6 The ghost . . . husband was dead.] Alma Maria Mahler Gropius Werfel (1879–1964), herself a gifted composer, was nearly twenty years younger than her famous first husband, Austrian composer Gustav Mahler (1860–1911). She outlived him by more than fifty years.

810.9–10 Can Jews . . . rationalist nonbeliever.] Mahler was born a Jew, but in 1897 converted to Catholicism to become director of the Vienna Court Opera.

810.14 "*Veni, creator spiritus*,"] Latin: Come, Creator Spirit. An early church hymn used in Mahler's Eighth Symphony.

810.26–27 Walter Gropius, Franz Werfel . . . Oskar Kokoschka] Alma married German architect and founder of the Bauhaus School Walter Gropius (1883–1969) in 1915. She had an affair with him during Mahler's lifetime, after the death of their daughter Maria in 1907. She and Gropius divorced in 1920, by which time Alma was involved with the Jewish Austrian-Bohemian writer Franz Werfel (1890–1945), one of whose poems she had set to music. A son was born to them in 1918, but Anna refused to marry Werfel until 1929. From 1912 to 1914 as Mahler's widow, she had a passionate affair with the Austrian artist Oskar Kokoschka (1886–1980), who made her the subject of over four hundred of his works.

811.9 *Faust*."] Schumann's *Scenes from Goethe's Faust* (1853).

811.29 Carl Moll, her stepfather] Austrian painter Carl Moll (1861–1945) was a pupil of Alma's father, Emil Jacob Schindler. After Schindler's death, he married his former teacher's widow, Anna.

811.33 Cosima Wagner] German composer Richard Wagner's second wife (1837–1930). She helped found the Bayreuth Festival and dedicated her life to Wagner's music after Wagner's death in 1883.

812.5 good ear] A childhood illness left Alma Mahler deaf in one ear.

812.36 Ossip Gabrilowitsch] Russian-born American pianist (1878–1936).

813.4 Mahler and Freud met in Leiden] Freud advised him that his neglect of Alma's own music was a significant cause of the problem between them. See also note 150.1–3.

813.20 feared his Ninth] Mahler's last completed symphony, composed 1908–9.

813.22 Tristan sings the truth."] Allusion to Wagner's opera *Tristan and Isolde*, first performed in 1865. In Act II, Tristan sings of his undying love for Isolde.

813.35 "Mozart," said Mahler] As reported by Alma herself in *Gustav Mahler: Memories and Letters* (1940): "Mahler lay with dazed eyes; one finger was conducting on the quilt. There was a smile on his lips and twice he said: 'Mozart!'"

815.4 "'None but the brave . . . Dryden] From John Dryden's *Alexander's Feast; or The Power of Musique* (1697), stanza 1.

816.16 *Das Lied von der Erde*] Mahler's orchestral song cycle *Song of the Earth*, composed 1908–9.

817.22 Jungfrau] Summit in Bernese Alps.

818.6 *Die Windsbraut*] Kokoschka's *The Bride of the Wind* (1913–14).

818.15–17 painting at Semmering . . . fat serpents.] Fresco that Kokoschka painted in 1913 over the fireplace in Alma Mahler's villa in Breitenstein near Austria's Semmering Pass.

820.30 Crown prince Rudolph of Austria] Archduke of Austria (1858–1889), who died in a suicide pact with his mistress, Baroness Mary Vetsera.

821.4–5 older than King Lear] Shakespeare's Lear manages "fourscore and upward." See *King Lear*, IV.vi.60.

OTHER WRITINGS

825.19 Diarmuid Russell] Malamud's agent from 1948 to 1973, when Tim Seldes succeeded him after Russell's death.

825.19–20 Pearl Kazin at *Harper's Bazaar*] American journalist and critic (1922–2011), sister to literary critic Alfred Kazin.

825.22–23 Catharine Carver of the *Partisan Review*] American-British editor (1921–1997).

827.7–9 Philip Rahv . . . William Phillips] Philip Rahv (1908–1973), Russian-born American literary critic and editor; with American editor William Phillips (1907–2000), cofounder of influential *Partisan Review*.

827.11 Ralph and Fanny Ellison] American novelist Ralph Ellison (1913–1994), author of *Invisible Man* (1952), and his second wife, Fanny McConnell Ellison.

827.13 Saul Bellow] Malamud wrote in his notebook for October 21, 1976, about fellow Jewish American writer Saul Bellow: "Bellow gets Nobel Prize. I win $24.25 at poker."

827.19–22 Robert Giroux . . . editor in chief.] American book editor and publisher (1914–2008), who moved from Harcourt Brace to Farrar Straus, eventually becoming a partner in the latter in 1964, when the company name was changed to Farrar, Straus and Giroux.

828.16–17 Randall Jarrell . . . "imaginative writing,"] At the Woman's College of the University of North Carolina, American poet and critic Randall Jarrell (1914–1965) taught a course titled "Modern Poetry and Imaginative Writing," insisting on the formulation "imaginative writing" because "I can't stand the phrase 'creative writing.'"

828.25–29 Maxim Lieber . . . in Poland.] Maxim Lieber (1897–1993), Malamud's first agent in the 1940s, had a roster of clients that included Theodore Dreiser, Erskine Caldwell, Katherine Anne Porter, and Saul Bellow. After Soviet spy Whittaker Chambers named him as an accomplice in 1949, Lieber fled to Mexico and then to Poland.

829.17 Pegasus] Winged stallion tamed by Bellerophon in Greek mythology.

829.38 García Márquez] Gabriel García Márquez (1927–2014), Colombian novelist and short-story writer.

830.5 Robert Frost's poem is "a momentary stay against confusion."] See Frost's essay "The Figure a Poem Makes," published as the introduction to his *Collected Poems* (1939).

830.10 Salzman] Marriage broker in Malamud's short story "The Magic Barrel."

832.3–4 Roger Williams . . . an Indian maiden] Puritan dissident and founder of Rhode Island Roger Williams (1603–1683) had extensive contact with the Narragansett and Wampanoag Indians. He published *A Key into the Language of America: or, An help to the Language of the Natives in that part of America called New England* (1643).

832.27 the WPA] Works Progress Administration, an agency created by executive order in 1935 as part of President Franklin D. Roosevelt's New Deal. It employed millions to carry out public works projects.

832.38 the Maginot Line] Vast stretch of defensive fortifications built by France along its border with Germany, constructed in the 1930s.

833.1–2 Neville Chamberlain . . . on his way out.] Prime minister of the United Kingdom from 1937 to 1940, Chamberlain (1869–1940) initially followed an appeasement policy with Nazi Germany that culminated in the ill-fated Munich agreement of 1938, ceding portions of Czechoslovakia to Hitler. In his public remarks in September 1938, Chamberlain touted the

Munich agreement as "peace for our time." Later, after a disastrous campaign in Norway, Chamberlain resigned, being succeeded by Winston Churchill.

833.14–16 Ernst Pawel's book . . . own truth."] Ernst Pawel, *The Nightmare of Reason* (1984), p. 147.

834.35–36 Kafka's remark . . . must write."] In a letter of November 9, 1903, to his friend Oskar Pollak.

835.19 an M.A. thesis] "Thomas Hardy's Reputation as a Poet in American Periodicals," submitted to Columbia's Department of English and Comparative Literature in February 1942.

835.32–33 a warm, pretty young woman] Ann de Chiara (1917–2007), whom Malamud married four year later on November 6, 1945.

835.38–39 Flatbush . . . Sears, or Oetgen's . . . Parade Grounds] Flatbush is a neighborhood in central Brooklyn, defined by Prospect Park to the north, East Flatbush to the east, Midwood to the south, and Kensington and Parkville to the west. Sears occupied the Art Deco building along Bedford Avenue and Beverly Road in Flatbush from 1932 to 2021, when the department store chain shuttered its last New York City location. With a seating capacity of 1,500, Oetjen's Restaurant specialized in seafood, promoting itself with the slogan "From ocean to Oetjen's." Located at 2210 Church Avenue, the restaurant was sold in 1957 after thirty-five years at that location. The Parade Ground is a treeless park and recreational sports hub, adjacent to Brooklyn's Prospect Park.

836.10 James Lechay] Avant-garde American painter (1907–2001) who taught at the University of Iowa from 1945 to 1971.

836.32–34 Jessie Weston's Percival . . . T.S. Eliot's "The Waste Land"] See Weston's *The Legend of Sir Perceval* (1906–9), concerning the original hero in the quest for the Grail. In his notes to *The Waste Land* (1922) Eliot speaks of his indebtedness to *From Ritual to Romance* (1920)—a subsequent book by Weston that builds on her earlier work on the Arthurian legends.

836.35 Babe Ruth's and Bobby Feller's.] Baseball legends Babe Ruth (1895–1948) and Bobby Feller (1918–2010) never faced each other on the field, but an ailing Ruth used Feller's bat to lean on during his final public appearance, at Yankee Stadium on Babe Ruth Day, June 13, 1948.

837.3–4 S.S. *Constitution*] Passenger liner owned by American Export Lines, sister ship to the S.S. *Independence.* Both ships were commissioned in 1951.

837.28–29 Ardeatine Caves . . . Italians and Jews.] As a reprisal for an attack on SS police in Rome, German Occupation troops shot 335 Italian civilians and political prisoners in the Ardeatine Caves outside Rome.

839.1 Roger Straus] Straus (1917–2004) was publisher and cofounder of Farrar Straus in 1945. It was Straus who lured Malamud's former editor Robert Giroux from Harcourt Brace in 1955.

839.6 Yaddo] Artists' retreat in Saratoga Springs, New York, that opened its doors in 1926. Malamud was granted a residency for two months in 1958.

839.13–16 Leslie Fiedler . . . how to read.] Leslie A. Fiedler was an American literary critic (1917–2003). His appreciation of *The Natural*, "In the Interest of Surprise and Delight," appeared in *Folio* 20 (Summer 1955) and was reprinted in Fiedler's *No! In Thunder: Essays on Myth and Literature* (1960).

839.16 sui generis] Latin: of his own kind.

839.19–21 Robert Redford . . . in the lights] Redford (b. 1936) played Roy Hobbs in the 1984 film adaptation of *The Natural.*

839.23 Howard Nemerov] American poet (1920–1991) who twice served as U.S. poet laureate, from 1963 to 1964 and later from 1988 to 1990.

839.31 Albert Guérard] American literary critic and novelist (1914–2000).

839.32 John Hawkes] American novelist (1925–1998) whose many works include *The Lime Twig* (1961) and *Second Skin* (1964).

840.3 Stanley Edgar Hyman] American critic and theorist (1919–1970), best known for his book *The Tangled Bank* (1962), on Darwin, Marx, Frazer, and Freud as imaginative writers.

840.4 Ben Belitt] American poet (1911–2003) who translated many works by Pablo Neruda and Federico García Lorca.

840.15–16 He and Shirley . . . dying young.] American writer Shirley Jackson (1916–1965) died at forty-eight of a heart attack, Hyman several years later at fifty-one, also of a heart attack.

842.6–8 "The men . . . Henry Thoreau said.] Cf. a similar passage in Thoreau's *Journal*, March 27, 1857.

843.1 *Bar-Mitzvah*] See note 567.29–30.

843.8–9 Max Malamud . . . a sick wife] See p. 691 in this volume.

843.19–20 My brother . . . least privileged.] Like their mother, Eugene Malamud (1918–1973) was diagnosed as schizophrenic. He lived most of his life with Malamud's father's second wife, Liza.

844.11–13 My father called himself a socialist . . . "Daily Forward."] *The Jewish Daily Forward*—today known as *The Forward*—was originally a Yiddish-only socialist newspaper catering to Jewish immigrants.

844.16–19 Eugene V. Debs . . . poor workers."] Debs (1855–1926), a five-time candidate of the Socialist Party of America for president of the United States, was organizer of the American Railway Union in 1897, for unskilled workers.

844.39–40 Jacob Ruppert's dark beer.] Best-selling beer produced by Manhattan brewer and New York Yankees owner Jacob Ruppert (1869–1939). The Jacob Ruppert Brewing Co. operated from 1913 to 1965.

845.3 Kolster radio.] Founded as the Federal Telegraph Co., the electronics manufacturer began to make radios under the Kolster Radio brand in 1921 and operated until 1931, when it went bankrupt.

845.21 "Brucha,"] Hebrew name for Bertha ("blessing").

846.8 "driml,"] Yiddish: nap.

847.7 Cheder] Religious day school where Hebrew and Judaism are taught.

847.12 touch the Torah] The scroll of the Law is carried around the synagogue to be touched by the congregation, usually only by the fringes of the tallith (prayer shawl), which is then kissed.

847.23 the goyim] Hebrew: non-Jews, gentiles, Christians.

847.29–30 When I was fourteen she attempted suicide] Malamud found his mother on the kitchen floor, who had taken bleach in an attempt to kill herself. She was hospitalized, never to return home.

848.5–6 melamed, a Hebrew teacher] Malamud's own name derives from the Hebrew word "melamed"—a point of pride for the writer.

848.11 rebbe] Yiddish: rabbi, meaning master or teacher.

848.15 yarmulke] See note 57.19–20.

849.12–14 Jiggs and Maggie, Captain Katzenjammer and the Kids, Harold Teen, and Winnie Winkle.] Jiggs and Maggie, married couple—a former hod carrier and his social-climbing wife—featured in George McManus's long-running comic strip *Bringing Up Father* (1913–2000). Captain Katzenjammer and the Kids, the rebellious brothers and their surrogate father in long-running comic strip *The Katzenjammer Kids,* created in 1897 for the *New York Journal. Harold Teen*, popular comic strip (1919–1959) that featured Jazz Age adolescent Harold Teen. *Winnie Winkle*, comic strip (1920–1996) that featured a working woman of the same name who was supporting her parents.

849.21–22 Gene Lewis] One of the school friends to whom Malamud dedicated *Rembrandt's Hat* (1973).

849.24 *Brooklyn Daily Eagle*] Brooklyn daily newspaper, 1841–1955.

849.37–850.2 "Blessed art thou . . . the Tefillin."] Prayer for putting on the tefillin or phylacteries, two black leather boxes containing verses from the Torah attached to leather straps. The arm-tefillin is affixed to the upper arm by winding the leather strap down the arm; the head-tefillin is placed high on the forehead. On all days but the Sabbath and important holidays they are worn as an adult male recites his morning prayers.

This book is set in 10 point ITC Galliard, a face designed for digital composition by Matthew Carter and based on the sixteenth-century face Granjon. The paper is acid-free lightweight opaque that will not turn yellow or brittle with age. The binding is sewn, which allows the book to open easily and lie flat. The binding board is covered in Brillianta, a woven rayon cloth made by Van Heek–Scholco Textielfabrieken, Holland.

Composition by Jordan Koluch.

Printing by Sheridan Grand Rapids, Grand Rapids, MI.

Binding by BindTech, Inc, Nashville, TN.

Designed by Bruce Campbell.